**Praise for Harry Turtledove and
The Great War: American Front
Chosen by *Publishers Weekly* as one
of the Best Books of 1998**

"The definitive alternate history saga of its time."
—*Booklist* (starred review)

"[A] masterpiece . . . This is state-of-the-art alternate history, nothing less . . . With shocking vividness, Turtledove demonstrates the extreme fragility of our modern world, and how much of it has depended on a *United States* of America."
—*Publishers Weekly* (starred review)

"Turtledove again gives us rounded characters, honest extrapolations of historical branching, and a solid notion that all this could have happened."
—*The San Diego Union-Tribune*

"Turtledove has proved he can divert his readers to astonishing places. He's developed a cult following over the years; and if you already been there, done that with real-history novelists Patrick O'Brian, Dorothy Dunnett, or George MacDonald Fraser, for your Next Big Enthusiasm you might want to try Turtledove. I know I'd follow his imagination almost anywhere."
—*San Jose Mercury News*

The Great War: WALK IN HELL

Harry Turtledove

A Del Rey® Book

THE RANDOM HOUSE PUBLISHING GROUP • NEW YORK

A Del Rey® Book
Published by The Random House Publishing Group
Copyright © 1999 by Harry Turtledove
Excerpt from *The Great War: Breakthroughs*
Copyright © 2000 by Harry Turtledove
Excerpt from *Colonization: Down to Earth*
Copyright © 2000 by Harry Turtledove
Artwork copyright © 1998 by George Pratt

Published in the United States by Del Rey Books, an imprint of The Random House Publishing Group, a division of Random House, Inc., New York, and simultaneously in Canada by Random House of Canada Limited, Toronto.

Del Rey is a registered trademark and the Del Rey colophon is a trademark of Random House, Inc.

www.delreybooks.com

Library of Congress Catalog Card Number: 00-190354

ISBN 0-345-40562-5

Manufactured in the United States of America

First Hardcover Edition: August 1999
First Mass Market Paperback Edition: July 2000

OPM 9 8 7 6 5

"Who are these? Why sit they here in twilight?
Wherefore rock they, purgatorial shadows,
Drooping tongues from jaws that slob their relish,
Baring teeth that leer like skulls' teeth wicked?
Stroke on stroke of pain,—but what slow panic,
Gouged these chasms round their fretted sockets?
Ever from their hair and through their hands' palms
Misery swelters. Surely we have perished
Sleeping, and walk in hell; but who these hellish?"

—Wilfred Owens, "Mental Cases"

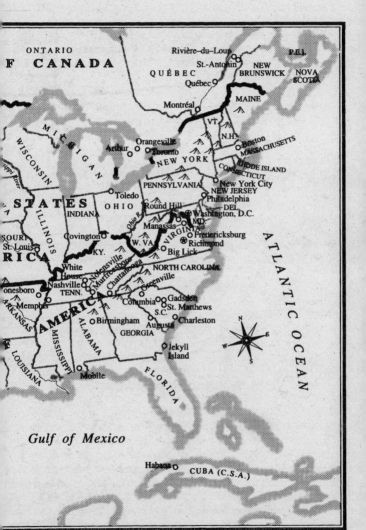

I

George Enos looked across the Mississippi toward Illinois. The river was wide, but not wide enough to let him forget it was only a river. Here in St. Louis, he was, beyond any possible doubt, in the middle of the continent.

That felt very strange to him. He'd lived his whole life, all twenty-nine years of it, in Boston, and gone out fishing on the Atlantic ever since he was old enough to run a razor over his cheeks. He'd kept right on going out to fish, even after the USA went to war with the Confederate States and Canada: all part of the worldwide war with Germany and Austria battling England, France, and Russia while pro-British Argentina fought U.S. allies Chile and Paraguay in South America and every ocean turned into a battle zone.

If a Confederate commerce raider hadn't intercepted the steam trawler *Ripple* and sunk it, George knew he'd still be a fisherman today. But he and the rest of the crew had been captured, and, being civilian detainees rather than prisoners of war, eventually exchanged for similar Confederates in U.S. hands. He had joined the Navy then, partly in hopes of revenge, partly to keep from being conscripted into the Army and sent off to fight in the trenches.

They'd even let him operate out of Boston for a while, on a trawler that had gone hunting for enemy vessels with a submarine pulled on a long tow. He'd helped sink a Confederate submersible, too, but the publicity that came from success made any future success unlikely. And so, instead of his being able to see his wife and children when he wasn't at sea and to work like a fisherman when he was, they'd put him on a train and sent him to St. Louis.

He called up to the deck officer aboard the river monitor USS *Punishment*: "Permission to come aboard, sir?"

"Granted," Lieutenant Michael Kelly said, and Enos hurried up the gangplank and onto his ship. He saluted the thirty-four-star flag rippling in the breeze at the stern of the *Punishment*. Kelly waited till he had performed the ritual, then said, "Take your station, Enos. We're going to steam south as soon as we have the full crew aboard."

"Aye aye, sir," Enos said. Because he was still new to the Navy and its ways, he hadn't lost the habit of asking questions of his superiors: "What's going on, sir? Seems like everybody's getting pulled on board at once."

From some officers, a query like that might have drawn a sharp reprimand. Kelly, though, understood that the expanded Navy of 1915 was not the tight-knit, professional force it had been before the war began. The formal mask of duty on his face cracked to reveal an exuberant grin that suddenly made him look much younger: like Enos, he was tanned and lined and chapped from endless exposure to sun and wind. He said, "What's up? I'll tell you what's up, sailor. The niggers down in the CSA have risen up against the government there, that's what. If the Rebs don't put 'em down, they're sunk. But while they're busy doing that, how much attention can they pay to us? You see what I'm saying?"

"Yes, sir, I sure do," Enos answered.

"Mind you," Kelly said, "I haven't got any great use for niggers myself—what white man does? And if the scuttlebutt is the straight goods, a lot of these niggers are Reds, too. And you know what? I don't care. They foul up the Rebels so we can lick 'em, they can fly all the red flags they want."

"Yes, sir," George said again. After the commerce raider snagged him, he'd been interned in North Carolina for several months. He'd seen the kind of treatment Negroes got in the CSA. Technically, they were free. They'd been free for more than thirty years. But—"If I was one of those Negroes, sir, and I saw a chance to take a shot at a Confederate—a white Confederate, I mean—I'd grab it in a second."

"So would I," Kelly said. "So would anybody with any balls. Who would have thought niggers had balls, though?" He turned away from Enos as a couple of other sailors reported back aboard the *Punishment*.

The river monitor was, in the immortal words that had described the first of her kind, a cheesebox on a raft. She carried a pair of six-inch guns in an armored turret mounted on a low, wide ironclad hull. She also had several machine guns mounted on deck for land targets not worth the fury of guns that could have gone to sea aboard a light cruiser.

Enos had been a fisherman, which meant he was adept at dealing with lines and nets and steam engines, even if the one the *Ripple* had carried was a toy beside the *Punishment*'s power plant. Having made use in his first assignment of the things he knew, the Navy plainly figured it had done its duty and could now return to its normal mode of operation: his station on the *Punishment* was at one of those deck machine guns.

He minded it less than he'd thought he would. Any New England fisherman worthy of the name was a born tinker and tinkerer. He'd learned to strip and clean and reassemble the machine gun till he could do it with his eyes closed. It was an elegantly simple means of killing large numbers of men in a hurry, assuming that was what you wanted to do.

At Kelly's shouted orders, sailors unfastened the ropes binding the *Punishment* to the pier. Black coal smoke pouring from her twin stacks, the monitor edged out into the Mississippi. The first hundred miles or so of the journey down the river, as far as Cairo, Illinois, were a shakedown through country that had always belonged to the USA.

Nobody got to relax, though, shakedown or no. Kelly shouted, "Keep your eyes peeled, dammit! They say Rebs sneak up from Arkansas and dump mines in the river every so often. Usually *they're* full of malarkey when *they* say something, but we don't want to find out the hard way, now do we?"

Along with everyone else, George Enos peered out at the muddy water. He was used to the idea of mines; Boston harbor had been surrounded by ring upon ring of minefields, to make sure no Canucks or Rebs or limeys paid an unexpected and unwelcome visit. He didn't see any mines now, but he hadn't seen any then, either.

A little north of Cairo, they took a pilot on board. The *Spray*, the steam trawler that had acted as a decoy for Entente warships, had done the same thing coming back into Boston after a mission. Here as there, the pilot guided the vessel through a U.S. minefield. The Confederacy had gunboats of its own on the Mississippi (though it didn't call them monitors), which had to be kept from steaming upstream and bombarding U.S. positions and supply lines.

When sunset came, the *Punishment* anchored on the river, the Missouri Ozarks on one side, Kentucky on the other. Kentucky was a Confederate state, but most of it, including that part lying along the Mississippi, lay in U.S. hands.

Over fried catfish and beans belowdecks, Enos said, "When I got transferred here, I thought we'd be going down the river looking for Rebel ships heading up, and we'd have a hell of a fight. That's what you read about in the newspapers back in Boston, anyway."

"It happens," said Wayne Pitchess, the closest friend he'd made on the *Punishment*: a former fisherman from Connecticut, though he'd joined the Navy back in peacetime. Pitchess scratched at his mustache before going on. Like George, he wore it Kaiser Bill–style, with waxed points jutting upward, but his was blond rather than dark. "It does happen," he repeated. "It just doesn't happen very often."

"Good thing it doesn't happen very often, too," added Sherwood McKenna, who was the third man in the tier of bunks with George and Pitchess. "Monitors can sink each other in a godawful hurry."

George Enos took a swig of coffee. It was vile stuff, but that wasn't the cook's fault. The Empire of Brazil, which produced more coffee than the rest of the world put together, had remained neutral. That meant both the Entente and the Quadruple Alliance went after its shipping with great enthusiasm. Most of the other coffee-growing countries were in the Entente camp. Not even the finest cook in the world could have done much with the beans that had gone into this pot.

"Well, if we don't fight other monitors much," George said, setting down his mug, "what do we do?"

"Bombard enemy land positions, mostly," Pitchess answered. "Moving six-inch guns down a river is easy. Hauling them cross-country is anything but. And we're a harder target to hit back at than guns on land, too, because we can move around easier."

"And because we're armored," Enos added.

"That doesn't hurt," Sherwood McKenna agreed. "Another monitor can smash us up, but we just laugh at those little fast-firing three-inch field guns the Rebs use. Lots of difference between a three-inch shrapnel shell and a six- or eight-incher with an armor-piercing tip."

Lifting the coffee mug again, this time as if to make a toast with it, George said, "Here's hoping we never find out what the difference is." Both his bunkmates drank to that.

Sleeping belowdecks was stifling, especially in the top bunk, which Enos, as a newcomer aboard the *Punishment*, had inherited. Sometime in the middle of the night, though, a couple of the deck machine guns began to hammer, waking up everyone who was asleep. George didn't stay awake long. As soon as he figured out the shooting wasn't aimed directly at him, he rolled over—carefully, so as not to fall out of the narrow bunk—and started sawing wood again.

Next morning, he found out somebody on the Kentucky shore had fired a machine gun at the *Punishment*, hoping to pick off someone on deck or in the cabin. Wayne Pitchess took that in stride. "He didn't hurt us, and we probably didn't hurt him," he said around a mouthful of sausage. "That's the kind of war I like to fight."

Cautiously, the *Punishment* pushed farther down the river. Now Tennessee lay to port. They steamed past the ruins of a Confederate fort that had mounted guns able to sink a battleship, let alone a river monitor. More such forts, still untaken, lay farther south. On the stretches of the Mississippi it owned, the USA had its share of them, too. They were another reason combats between monitors were scarce.

Enos eyed the woods running down to the river. U.S. forces were supposed to have cleared away all the Rebs, but the exchange of fire the night before showed that wasn't so. He wondered how he would get any sign of the enemy, or, for that matter, of the Negroes who had rebelled against the Confederacy. All he saw were trees. He saw a hell of a lot of trees. He was used to the cramped confines of Massachusetts, where everything was jammed up against everything else. It wasn't like that here. The land was wide, and people thin on the ground.

With a low rumble, the turret of the *Punishment* began to re-volve. The guns rose slightly. George had never heard them fired before. He braced himself.

Bracing himself wasn't enough. The roar seemed like the end of the world. Sheets of golden flame spat from the guns' muzzles. One of them blew a perfect smoke ring, as he might have done with a cigar, only a hundred times bigger.

His ears still ringing, he watched the gun barrels rise again, an even smaller movement than they had made before. They salvoed once more. He couldn't tell where the shells were com-ing down. Someone evidently could, though, and was letting the *Punishment* know, perhaps by wireless. That repositioning must have been what was wanted, for the twin six-inchers fired again and again. Somewhere, miles inside Tennessee, the shells were creating a good approximation of hell. Here, they were just cre-ating an ungodly racket.

After a while, the bombardment stopped. The gunners came out on deck. It had probably been hell inside the turret, too. They stripped off their sweat-soaked uniforms and jumped naked into the river, where they proceeded to try to drown one another. It was, George Enos thought, a strange way to fight a war.

Anne Colleton gunned the Vauxhall Prince Henry up the Robert E. Lee Highway from Charleston, South Carolina, toward her plantation, Marshlands, outside the little town of St. Matthews. The motorcar hit a pothole. Her teeth came together in a sharp click. The so-called highway, like all roads outside the cities, was nothing but dirt. Even with a lap robe and a broad-brimmed hat with a veil, Anne was caked with red-brown dust. She supposed she should count herself lucky she hadn't had a puncture. She'd already repaired two since leaving Charleston.

"Punctures?" She shook her head. "Punctures are nothing." She counted herself lucky to be alive. With a dashing sub-mersible commander, she'd been at a rather seedy hotel near the edge of one of Charleston's Negro districts when the riot or up-rising or whatever it was broke out. They'd piled into the Vaux-hall and escaped just ahead of the baying mob. She'd delivered Roger Kimball back to the harbor and then, not bothering to get the bulk of her belongings out of the much finer hotel where she was registered, she'd headed for home.

Down the road toward her, filling up most of it, came a wagon pulled by a horse and a mule and filled to overflowing with white men, women, and children—several families packed together, unless she missed her guess. She stepped on the brake, hard as she could. The Vauxhall came to a shuddering stop. Its sixty-horsepower engine could hurl it forward at a mile a minute—though not on the Robert E. Lee Highway—but slowing down was another matter.

Some of the whites wore bandages, some of those rusty with old blood. Over the growl of the motorcar's engine, Anne called, "What's it like up ahead?"

"It's bad, ma'am," the graybeard at the reins answered, tipping his battered straw hat to her—he could see she was a person of consequence, even if he didn't know just who she was. "We're lucky we got out alive, and that's a fact."

The woman beside him nodded vehemently. "You ought to turn around your ownself," she added. "Niggers up further north, they gone crazy. They got guns some kind of crazy way and they got red flags flyin' and sure as Jesus they're gonna kill any whites they can catch."

"Red flags," Anne said, and heads bobbed up and down again in the wagon. Her lips moved in a silent curse. Her brother Tom, a Confederate major, had said earlier in the year there were Red revolutionaries among the Negro laborers in the Army. She'd scoffed at the idea that such radicals might also have gained a foothold at Marshlands. Now fear clawed her. Her other brother, Jacob, was back at the mansion, an invalid since the Yankees had gassed him within an inch of his life. She'd thought it surely safe to leave him for a few days.

The fellow in the straw hat tipped it again, then guided his mismatched team off the road so the wagon could get around the automobile. As soon as she had the room, she put the Vauxhall in gear and zoomed forward again. Along with other innovations, she'd had a rearview mirror installed on the motorcar. Looking into it, she saw faces staring after her from the wagon as she drove toward trouble rather than away from it.

Every so often, trees shaded the road. Something dangled from an overhanging branch of one of them. She slowed down again. It was the body of a lynched Negro. A placard tied round his neck said, THIS IS IF WE KETCH YOU. He wore only a pair of ragged drawers. What had been done to him before he was hanged wasn't pretty.

Anne bit her lip. She prided herself on being a modern woman, on being able to take on the world straight up and come out ahead, regardless of her sex. Outdealing men had made her rich—well, richer, since she was born far from poor. But business was one thing, this brutality something else again.

And what were the Negroes, the Reds, doing in whatever lands—not Marshlands, surely—they'd seized in their revolt? How many old scores, going back how many hundred years, were they repaying?

As much to escape questions like that as to get away from the tormented corpse (around which flies were already buzzing), Anne drove off fast enough to press herself back into the seat. Perhaps a mile farther up the road, she came to another tree with dreadful fruit. The first had shocked her because of its savagery. The second also shocked her, mostly by how little feeling it roused in her. *This is how men get used to war,* she thought, and shivered though the day was warm and muggy: more like August than late October.

She drove past a burnt-out farmhouse from which smoke was still rising. It hadn't been much of a place; she wondered whether blacks or poor whites had lived there. Nobody lived there now, or would any time soon.

More traffic coming south slowed her progress. The road wasn't wide; whenever her motorcar drew near someone coming in the opposite direction, somebody had to go off onto the shoulder to get around. Wagons, buggies, carts, occasional motorcars came past her, all of them loaded with women, children, and old men: most of the young men were at the front, fighting against the USA.

Anne needed a while to wonder how widespread in the Confederacy the uprising was, and what it would do to the fight against the United States. Confederate forces had been hardpressed to hold their ground before. Could they go on holding, with rebellion in their rear?

"We licked the damnyankees in the War of Secession," she said, as if someone had denied it. "We licked 'em again in the Second Mexican War, twenty years later. We can do it one more time."

She came up behind a truck rumbling along toward the north, its canvas-canopied bed packed with uniformed militiamen. Some wore butternut, some the old-fashioned gray that had been banished from front-line use because it was too much like Yankee green-gray. A lot of the militiamen wore beards or mustaches. All of those were gray—except the ones that were white. But the men carried bayoneted rifles, and looked to know what to do with them. Against a rabble of Negroes, what more would they need?

They waved to her when she drove past. She waved back, glad to do anything to cheer them. Then she had to slow almost to a crawl behind a battery of half a dozen horse-drawn cannons. Those couldn't have come close to matching her Vauxhall's speed under the best of circumstances, and circumstances were anything but the best: the guns had to fight their way forward against the stream of refugees fleeing the revolt.

Some of the southbound wagons and motorcars had Negroes in them: a scattering of black faces, among the white. Anne guessed they were servants and field hands who'd stayed loyal to their employers (*masters* wasn't the right word, though some people persisted in using it more than a generation after manumission). She was glad to see those few black faces—they gave her hope for Marshlands—but she wished she'd spotted more.

Truck farms abounded all around the little town of Holly Hill, about halfway between Charleston and St. Matthews. The farms seemed to have come through pretty well. Not much was left of the town. A lot of it had burned. Bullet holes pocked the surviving walls. Here and there, bodies white and black lay unburied. A faint stench of meat going bad hung in the air; buzzards wheeled optimistically, high overhead.

Anne wished she could have got out of Holly Hill in a hurry, but rubble in the road made traffic pack together. A gang of Negro laborers was clearing the debris. That was nothing out of the ordinary. The uniformed whites covering them with Tredegar rifles, though . . .

A couple of miles north of Holly Hill, a middle-aged white man whose belly was about to burst the bounds of his butternut uniform stepped out into the road, rifle in hand, and stopped her. "We ain't lettin' folks go any further north'n this, ma'am," he said. "Ain't safe. Ain't nowhere near safe."

"You don't understand. I'm Anne Colleton, of Marshlands," she said, confident he would know who she was and what that meant.

He did. Gulping a little, he said, "I'd like to help you, ma'am," by which he undoubtedly meant, *I don't want to get into trouble with you, ma'am.* But he went on, "I got my orders from Major Hotchkiss, though—no civilians goin' up this road. Them niggers, they got a regular front set up. They been plannin' this a long time, the sons of bitches. Uh, pardon my French."

She'd been saying a lot worse than that herself. "Where do I find this Major Hotchkiss, so I can talk some sense into him?" she demanded.

The Confederate militiaman pointed west down a rutted dirt track less than half as wide as the Robert E. Lee Highway. "There's a church up that way, maybe a quarter mile. Reckon he'll be up in the steeple, trying to spot what the damn niggers is doin'."

She drove the Vauxhall down the road he'd shown her. If she didn't find the church, she intended to try to make her way north by whatever back roads she could find. This Major Hotchkiss might have banned northbound civilian traffic from the highway, but maybe he hadn't said anything about other ways of getting where she still aimed to go.

But there stood the church, a white clapboard building with a tall steeple. White men in butternut uniforms and old gray ones milled around outside. They all looked her way as she drove up. "I'm looking for Major Hotchkiss," she called.

"I'm Jerome Hotchkiss," one of the men in butternut said; sure enough, he wore a single gold star on each collar tab. He didn't look too superannuated. Then Anne saw he had a hook in place of his left hand. That would have left him unfit for front-line duty, but not for an emergency like this. He nodded to her. "What is it you want?"

"I'm Anne Colleton," she said again, and caused another stir. She went on, "Your sentry back by the highway said you were the man who could give me permission to keep going north toward Marshlands, my plantation."

"If any man could do that, I would be the one," Major Hotchkiss agreed. "I have to tell you, though, it's impossible. You must understand, we are not trying to put down a riot up ahead. It is a war, nothing less. The enemy has rifles. He has machine guns. He has men who will use them. And he has a fanatical willingness to die for his cause, however vile it is."

"No, you don't understand," Anne said. "I have to get back to the plantation. My brother is an invalid: the damnyankees gassed him this past spring. Do you know if Marshlands is safe? I tried to telephone from Charleston, but—"

"Specifically, no," Hotchkiss answered. "And most telephone lines are down, as you will have found. I can tell you this, though: it's not safe to be white—unless you're also a Red, and there are a few like that, the swine—between here and Columbia. Like I say, ma'am, we have ourselves a war here. In fact—" He stopped looking at her and started looking at the Vauxhall. "I'm going to ask you to step out of that motorcar, if you don't mind."

"What? I certainly do mind."

"Ma'am, I am confiscating your motorcar in the name of the Confederate States of America," Hotchkiss said. "This is a military area; I have that right. The vehicle will be returned to you at the end of this emergency. If for any reason it cannot be returned, you will be compensated as required by law." When Anne, not believing what she was hearing, made no move to get out, the major snapped, "Potter! Harris!" Two of his men trained rifles on her.

"This is an outrage!" she exclaimed. The soldiers' faces were implacable. If she didn't get out, they would shoot her. That was quite plain. Quivering with fury, she descended to the ground.

Major Hotchkiss pointed farther up the road. "There's a crossroads general store up there. We've got a fair number of folks in tents already. It's about half a mile. You go on, Miss Colleton. They'll take care of you best they can. We smash this Colored Socialist Republic or whatever the niggers are calling it, then we can get on with the fight against the damnyankees."

"Give me a rifle," Anne said suddenly. "I'm a good shot, and I'm a lot less likely to fall over dead than half your so-called soldiers here."

But the Confederate major shook his head without a word. She knew she was right, but what good did that do her if he wouldn't listen? The answer tolled in her mind: none. Dully, she began walking up the road. When war reached out its hand, what did wealth and power matter? A fool with a gun could take them away. A fool with a gun had just taken them away.

Major Irving Morrell and Captain John Abell took off their caps when they went into Independence Hall to see the Liberty Bell. Philadelphia, being the headquarters of the War Department, was full of U.S. military men of all ranks and branches of service. Only someone very observant would have noted the twisted black-and-gold cords on the caps that marked these two as General Staff officers.

Abell, who had a bookish look to him, fit the common preconception for the appearance of a General Staff man. Morrell, though, was more weathered, his face lined and tanned, though he was only in his mid-twenties. He wore his sandy hair cropped close to his head, as field officers commonly did. He felt like a field officer. He'd been a field officer: he'd almost lost a leg in the U.S. invasion of Confederate Sonora, and then, after a long recuperation, he'd led a battalion in eastern Kentucky. What he'd done there had impressed his division commander enough to get him sent to Philadelphia.

Intellectually, he knew what a plum this was. It didn't altogether fill him with joy, though. He wanted to be out in the forest or the mountains or tramping through the desert—somewhere away from the city and close to the foe.

"Come on, let's get moving," he said now, and hurried ahead of Abell to get a good look at the Liberty Bell. His thigh pained him when he sped up like that, and would probably go on paining him the rest of his life. He ignored it. You could let something like that rule you, or you could rule it. Morrell did not aim to let anything keep him from doing what he wanted to do.

"It's been here a long time, Major," Abell said. "It's going to be here for a long time yet."

"Yes, but *I'm* not going to be here for a long time," Morrell answered. When he'd learned enough, or so the promise had gone, they'd promote him and send him back to the field to command a unit bigger than a battalion. "I want to fight with guns, not with maps and dividers and a telegraph clicker."

He looked back over his shoulder as he said that, just in time to catch the sidelong glance Abell gave him. The captain, like most General Staff officers, preferred fighting the war at a distance and in the abstract to the reality of mud and bad food and wounds and terror. Battle always seemed so much cleaner, so much neater, when it was red and blue lines on a chart.

Then such thoughts left Morrell's mind as, with a good many other soldiers, he crowded round the emblem of freedom for the United States. The surface of the bell was surprisingly rough, testimony to the imperfect skill of the founders who had cast it. Around the crown ran the words from Leviticus that had given the bell its name: *Proclaim liberty throughout the land unto all the inhabitants thereof.*

He wondered whether Robert E. Lee had seen the Liberty Bell when he occupied Philadelphia in 1862. Lee's victories had given the Confederate States a liberty the USA had not wanted to grant them, but he hadn't taken the bell back south with him. That was something, albeit not much.

Morrell reached out and touched the cool metal. "We're still free," he murmured. "Still free, by God."

"That's right," John Abell said beside him. "The freest nation on the face of the earth." Normally cold-blooded as a lizard in a blizzard, he sounded genuinely moved by the Liberty Bell. Then, almost gloating, he added, "And we're going to pay the Rebs back for all they've done to us these past fifty years, and the English, and the French, and the Canadians, too."

"You'd best believe it," Morrell said, and took his hand away. The metal of the bell had grown warm under his fingers. He smiled, enjoying the idea that he had had a connection with history. No sooner had he stepped back from the bell than a fresh-faced lieutenant came up and caressed its smooth curves with almost a lover's touch.

Independence Hall also boasted a facsimile of the Declaration of Independence. Facsimiles, though, meant little to Morrell. What was real counted. If you wanted to be theoretical . . . you belonged on the General Staff. He snorted, amused by the conceit.

"What's funny, sir?" Captain Abell asked. Morrell just smiled and shook his head, not wanting to insult his companion.

They walked up Chestnut, back toward the War Department offices that had swallowed so much of Franklin Square. Philadelphia buzzed with all sorts of Federal activity; especially after the Confederate bombardment of Washington during the Second

Mexican War, the Pennsylvania city had become the *de facto* capital of the USA. That was as well, for Washington now lay under the bootheels of the Rebels.

The opening Confederate attack in the war had been aimed at Philadelphia, too, but was stopped at the Susquehanna, one river short of the Delaware. Here and there, buildings bore scars from Confederate bombing raids. These days, with the Rebels pushed back into Maryland, bombing aeroplanes came over more rarely. Even so, antiaircraft cannon poked watchful snouts into the air in parks and at street corners.

Abell bought a couple of cinnamon rolls, a Philadelphia specialty, from a street vendor. He offered one to Morrell, who shook his head. "I don't want anything that sweet," he said. Half a block later, he came upon a Greek selling grape leaves stuffed with spicy meat and rice. To make them easier to handle, the fellow had skewered them on sticks. Morrell bought three. "Here's a proper lunch," he declared.

He and Abell both slowed down to eat as they walked. They hadn't gone far when someone behind them shouted, "Get the hell out of here, you stinking wog! This is a white man's town."

Morrell turned on his heel, Abell imitating him. A beefy, middle-aged civilian was shaking his finger in the Greek food-seller's face. Ignoring the twinge in his bad leg, Morrell walked rapidly back toward them. As he drew near, he saw the beefy man wore a pin in his lapel: a silver circle, with a sword set slantwise across it. Soldiers' Circle members made up a sort of informal militia of men who had served out their terms of conscription. They were perhaps the leading patriotic organization in the country, especially to hear them talk.

A lot of them, of course, the younger ones, had been reconscripted since the war broke out. Others had proved useful in other ways: serving as additions to the New York City police, for instance, after the Mormons and Socialists had touched off the Remembrance Day riots this past spring. And some of them, like this chap, liked to throw their weight around.

"Sir, why don't you just leave this man alone?" Morrell said. The words were polite. The tone was anything but. At his side, Captain Abell nodded.

"He's a damned foreigner," the Soldiers' Circle man exclaimed. "He's almost certainly not a citizen. He doesn't look like he *ought* to be a citizen, the stinking wog. *Are* you a citizen?" he demanded of the Greek.

"Not your *gamemeno* business what I am," the foodseller answered, bolder than he had been before he had anyone on his side.

"You see? He doesn't hardly speak English," the Soldiers' Circle man said. "Ought to put him in a leaky boat and ship him back to where he came from."

"I got son in Army." The Greek shook his finger at the fellow who was harassing him. "In Army to do fighting, not to play games like you was. Paul is sergeant—I bet you never got no stripes."

The Soldiers' Circle man went bright red. Morrell would have bet that meant the Greek had scored a bull's-eye. "Why don't you take yourself somewhere else?" Morrell told the dedicated patriot. Muttering under his breath, the corpulent fellow did depart, looking angrily back over his shoulder.

Morrell and Abell waved off the foodseller's thanks and headed up Chestnut again, toward the War Department. "Those Soldiers' Circle men can be arrogant bastards," Abell said. "He was treating that fellow like he was a nigger, not just a dago or whatever the hell he is."

"Yeah," Morrell said, "and a Confederate nigger at that." He checked himself. "The other side to that coin is, the niggers down in the CSA are giving the white folks there a surprise or two."

"You're right," Abell said. "Now what we have to do is see how we can best take advantage of it."

Morrell nodded. Taking advantage of the enemy didn't come easy, not when machine guns knocked down advances before they could get moving—assuming artillery hadn't already done that before soldiers ever came out of the trenches.

He sighed. An awful lot of U.S. officers—including, as far as he was concerned, too many on the General Staff—didn't, maybe couldn't, think past slamming straight at the Rebs and overwhelming them by sheer weight of numbers. The USA had the numbers. Using them effectively was proving to be a horse of another color.

You went into General Staff headquarters through what looked like, and once had been, a millionaire's mansion. Morrell had always doubted that that fooled the Confederate spies surely haunting Philadelphia, but nobody'd asked his opinion. Inside, a sober-faced sergeant checked his identification and Abell's with meticulous care, comparing photographs to faces. *Bureaucracy in action,* Morrell thought: the noncom saw them every day.

After gaining permission to enter the sanctum, they went into the map room. Abell pointed to the map of Utah, where U.S. forces had finally pushed the Mormon rebels out of Salt Lake City and back toward Ogden. "That was your doing, more than anyone else," he said to Morrell, half admiring, half suspicious.

"TR listened to me," Morrell said with a shrug. Instead of straight-ahead slugging, he urged attacks through the Wasatch Mountains and from the north, to make the Mormons have to do several things at the same time with inadequate resources. He'd proposed that to the brass on arriving here. They'd ignored him. A chanced meeting with the president had revived the plan. Unlike a lowly major, TR could make the General Staff listen instead of trying without any luck to persuade it.

Except for the soldiers actually fighting there (and perhaps except for the resentment higher-ups in the General Staff might show against him for being right), Utah was old news now, anyhow. Morrell looked at a new map, one that had gone up only a few days before. On it, the Confederacy, especially from South Carolina through Louisiana, seemed to have broken out in a bad case of the measles, or maybe even smallpox.

He pointed to the indications of insurrection. "The Rebs will have a jolly time fighting their own Negroes and us, too," he said.

"That's the idea," John Abell said. Both men smiled, well pleased with the world.

Scipio was not used to wearing the coarse, colorless homespun shirt and trousers of a Negro laborer. As butler at the Marshlands mansion, he'd put on formal wear suitable for a Confederate senator in Richmond, save only that his vest was striped and his buttons made of brass. He wasn't used to sleeping in a blanket on the ground, either, or to eating whatever happened to come into his hands, or to going hungry a lot of the time.

But he would never be butler at Marshlands again. The mansion had gone up in flames at the start of the Marxist revolt—the mostly black revolt—against the Confederate States. If the Congaree Socialist Republic failed, Scipio would never be anything again, except a stinking corpse and then whitening bones hanging from a tree branch.

The headquarters of the Congaree Socialist Republic kept moving, as the Confederates brought pressure to bear against now one, now another of its fluid borders. At the moment, the red flags with the broken chains in black flew over a nameless crossroads not far north of Holly Hill, South Carolina.

Cassius came up to Scipio. Cassius had worn homespun all his life, and a shapeless floppy hat to go with it. He had been the chief hunter at Marshlands, and also—though Scipio hadn't known of it till after the war with the USA began, and had learned only by accident then—the chief Red. Now he styled himself the chairman of the Republic.

"How you is, Kip?" he asked, the dialect of the Congaree thick as jambalaya in his mouth. But he did not think the way white folks thought their Negroes thought: "Got we anudder one fo' revolutionary justice. You is one o' de judges."

"Where he is?" Scipio asked. When talking with his fellows, he used the Congaree dialect, too. When talking with whites, he spoke standard English better than almost any of them. That had already proved useful to the Congaree Socialist Republic, and likely would again.

"Here he come," Cassius answered, and, sure enough, two young, stalwart black men were hustling along a short, plump white. His white linen suit was stained with smoke and grass; several days of stubble blurred the outlines of what had been a neat white goatee. In formal tones, Cassius declared, "De peasants an' workers o' de Congaree Socialist Republic charges Jubal Marberry here wid ownin' a plantation an' wid 'sploitin an' 'pressin' he workers on it—an' wid bein' a fat man livin' off what dey does."

Two others came up beside Scipio to hear the case, not that there was much case to hear at one of these revolutionary tribunals. One was a woman named Cherry, from Marshlands, whose screams had helped touch off the rebellion there. The other was a big man named Agamemnon, who had labored at Marberry's plantation.

He spoke to his former boss—probably his former owner, too,

since, like Scipio, he was past thirty: "You got anything to say befo' the co't pass sentence on you?"

Marberry was old and more than a little deaf; Agamemnon had to repeat the question. When he did, the white man showed he had spirit left: "Whatever you do to me, they'll hang you higher than Haman, and better than you deserve, too."

"What is de verdict?" Cassius asked.

No one bothered with witnesses for the defense, or for the prosecution, either. The three judges walked off a few feet and spoke in low voices. "Ain't no reason to waste no time on he," Agamemnon said. "He guilty, the old bastard."

"We give he what he deserve," Cherry said with venomous relish.

Scipio didn't say anything. He'd been in several of these trials, and hadn't said much at any of them. He'd never intended to be a revolutionary—it was either that, though, or die for knowing too much. He had no love for white folks, but he had no love for savagery, either.

His silence didn't matter. Had he voted for acquittal, the other two would have outvoted him—and odds were he soon would have faced revolutionary justice himself after such an unreliable act. He'd survived so far by keeping quiet. He hoped he could keep right on surviving.

Agamemnon and Cherry turned back toward Cassius. They both nodded. So did Scipio, a moment later. Cassius said, "Jubal Marberry, you is guilty of the crime of 'pression 'gainst the proletariat of the Congaree Socialist Republic. De punishment is death."

Marberry cursed at him and tried to kick one of the men who held him. They dragged the planter off behind some trees. A pistol shout sounded, and then a moment later another one. The two Negroes came out. Jubal Marberry didn't.

With considerable satisfaction, Cassius nodded to the impromptu court. "You done fine," he told them. Agamemnon and Cherry headed off, both of them obviously well-pleased with themselves. Scipio started to leave, too. One of these days, he was going to let his feelings show on his face despite the butler's mask of imperturbability he cultivated. That would be the end of him. Even as he turned, though, Cassius said, "You wait, Kip."

"What you want?" Scipio did his best to sound easy and re-

laxed. The Congaree Socialist Republic went after enemies of
the revolution within its own ranks as aggressively as it pursued
them among the whites who had for so long oppressed and bat-
tened on the Negro laborers of the area.

But Cassius said, "Gwine have we a parley wid de white folks
officer. We trade de wounded white folks sojers we catches fo' de
niggers dey gives we. You gwine talk wid de officer." His long,
weathered face stretched into lines of anticipatory glee.

Scipio didn't need long to figure out why. With a deliberate effort of will, he abandoned the Congaree dialect: "I suppose you
will expect me to speak in this fashion, thereby disconcerting
them."

Cassius laughed and slapped his knee. "Do Jesus, yes!" he exclaimed. "You set your mind to it, you talk fancier'n any o' they
white folks. An' you don' git angried up in a hurry, neither. We
wants a cool head, an' you got dat."

"When we do dis parley?" Scipio asked.

"Right now. I take you up to de front." Cassius reached into
his pocket, pulled out a red bandanna, and tied it around Scipio's
left upper arm. "Dere. Now you official." No doubt because
the Confederacy, if you looked at it from the right angle, was
nothing but an elaborate hierarchy of ranks and privileges, the
Congaree Socialist Republic acted as if such matters did not
exist. The revolution was about equality.

The front was just that, a series of trenches and firing pits.
Both the black soldiers of the Socialist Republic and their Confederate foes were in large measure amateurs, but both sides
were doing their best to imitate what the professionals from the
CSA and USA had been doing.

Cassius took Scipio to a tent where the white officer waited.
"Ain't gwine let you cross out of de country we holds," he said.
"Cain't trust white folks not to keep you an' give you a rope
necktie."

Considering what had just happened to Jubal Marberry and to
many others, Scipio reckoned the barbarism equally distributed.
Saying so, however, struck him as inexpedient. And he knew he
should have been grateful that Cassius worried about his safety
rather than planning to liquidate him.

The tent was butternut canvas, captured Confederate Army

issue. Scipio pulled the flap open, ducked his head, and went inside. A man in Confederate uniform sat behind a folding table. He did not stand up for Scipio, as he would have on meeting a U.S. officer during a parley.

"Good day," Scipio said, as if greeting a guest at Marshlands. "Shall we discuss this matter in a civilized fashion, as it involves the well-being of brave men from both sides?"

Sure enough, the Confederate major's eyebrows rose. He wasn't a gray-bearded relic like a lot of the men the CSA was using to try to suppress the revolution; Scipio judged he would have been fighting the Yankees if he hadn't lost a hand. "Don't you talk pretty?" he said, and then, as if making a great concession, "All right, I'm Jerome Hotchkiss. I can treat for Confederate forces along this front. You can do the same for your people?"

"That is correct, Major," Scipio answered. "For the purposes of this meeting, you may address me as Spartacus."

Hotchkiss let out a bark of laughter. "All you damn Red niggers use that for an alias. Best guess I can give about why is that maybe you reckon we won't know who to hang once we've put you down. If that's what you think, you're dreaming."

Scipio feared the major was right. Showing that fear, though, would put him in Cassius' bad graces. Cassius being more immediately dangerous to him than were the forces of the CSA, he said, "I suggest, Major, that it is wise to kill your bear before you speak of skinning him."

"You want to watch the way you talk to me," Hotchkiss said, as if rebuking a Negro waiter at a restaurant.

"Major, you would be well advised to remember that you are in the sovereign territory of the Congaree Socialist Republic," Scipio returned. Hotchkiss glared at him. He looked back steadily. The shoe was on the other foot now, and the white man didn't care for the fit. Scipio understood that. He'd spent his whole life not caring for the fit. He said, "Shall we agree to put other matters aside for the time being, in the hopes of coming to terms on this one specific issue?"

"Fair enough," Hotchkiss said, making a visible effort to control himself. "Some of our wounded who got left behind when we had to pull back . . . When we advanced again, we found 'em chopped to bits or burned alive or . . . Hell, I don't need to go on. You know what I'm talking about."

"I also know that your forces are seldom in the habit of taking prisoners of any kind, wounded or not," Scipio answered. "How many Negroes have been hanged, these past days?"

Plainly, the thought in Hotchkiss' mind was, *Not enough.* "Negroes caught in arms against the Confederate States of America—"

Scipio surprised him by interrupting: "Lackeys of the oppressors caught in arms resisting the proletarian revolution of the Congaree Socialist Republic . . ." The Marxist rhetoric he'd learned from Cassius came in handy here, no matter how low his opinion of it commonly was. He went on, "Our causes being as repugnant to each other as they are, is it not all the more important to observe the laws of war with especial care?"

"That'd mean admitting you have the right to rebel," Hotchkiss said.

But Scipio shook his head. "The USA did not admit the CSA had that right in the War of Secession, yet treated Confederate prisoners humanely."

He could see Hotchkiss thinking, *White men on both sides.* But the major didn't say that. What he did say was, "Maybe."

Taking that for assent, Scipio said, "Very well. We undertake to exchange under flag of truce men too badly wounded to go on fighting at a place and time you may choose, said men to have been treated as well as possible by the side capturing them. Is it agreed?"

"Agreed," Hotchkiss said, "but only as a war measure. It doesn't mean we say you have any right to do what you're doing. After we smash you, you'll still hang for rebellion and treason."

"First catch the bear, Major," Scipio answered. He'd done what Cassius wanted. He thought it would bring some good. How much? For how long? He wished he knew how the revolution fared across the rest of the Confederacy.

The adobe farmhouse outside Bountiful, Utah, sat on a low rise, so that it commanded the ground in front of it. The Mormon rebels against the authority of the United States had had months of hard fighting in which to learn their craft. They'd learned it all too well, as far as Paul Mantarakis was concerned. When they found a position like this, they fortified it for everything it was worth, then stayed in it and fought, sometimes men and women both, until U.S. forces finally overwhelmed them.

A machine gun inside the farmhouse opened up, spitting death down at the trenches Mantarakis and his comrades had dug. He ducked, making sure the top of his head was below the level of the parapet. The fancy new helmet he wore didn't keep out direct hits. People had found out about that the hard way.

He waited till the machine gun's fire was directed elsewhere along the trench, then stood up on the firing step and popped a couple of rounds from his Springfield at the adobe. He didn't think they were likely to accomplish much: the mud brick in a lot of these Utah farmhouses was thick enough to stop a bullet, though it had been intended to keep out heat and cold, not flying lead. And, for good measure, the Mormons had put up corrugated iron sheets over the windows, turning them into first-rate firing slits.

Ben Carlton came up to Mantarakis. "Hey, Sarge, you want to come check the stew pot?"

"Sure." Paul followed him down the line of trench. Carlton was the official company cook, and had a gift for scrounging from sources both official and unofficial. But Mantarakis really had been a cook back in Philadelphia, though getting stripes on his sleeve kept him from exercising his talents these days as often as he would have liked.

The pot smelled more savory than it often did. "Chickens and a couple rabbits," Carlton said, "and potatoes and beets and onions and—all kinds of things. It's downright—bountiful around here." He laughed at his own joke.

"Yeah." Mantarakis tasted the stew. "Not bad," he said. "Just kind of bland, you know what I'm saying? You need some garlic and some basil, maybe, or oregano, to perk it up. Not too much," he added hastily as Carlton started to pour most of a tin of garlic powder into the pot. "You want to make the stew taste better— you don't want to just taste the spice, either." Little by little, he was educating Carlton.

He suddenly stopped worrying about the stew, for U.S. artillery opened up on the adobe and the line it anchored. The noise was terrific, overpowering, enough to drive a man mad. To Mantarakis, it was also sweet as fine wine. Without artillery, his

guess was that U.S. forces would still be bogged down somewhere south of Provo. It was the one thing government troops
had in prodigal supply and the Mormon rebels largely lacked.

Captain Cecil Schneider hurried up into the frontmost trench.
Schneider still wore single silver bars, not double; he'd won
his promotion just after the ruins of the Mormon Temple in
Salt Lake City passed into government hands. With him came
Gordon McSweeney, who, like Mantarakis, had started the war a
private and who, also like Mantarakis, now sported sergeant's
stripes.

"When the barrage lets up, we go after that farmhouse,"
Schneider said. He didn't sound enthusiastic—no one who'd
been through the fall of Salt Lake City was apt to be enthusiastic
about fighting ever again—but he sounded determined. Casualties had made him a company commander the same way they'd
made Paul and McSweeney noncoms, but he'd turned out to be a
pretty good one.

Because of that, the first thing out of Paul's mouth was, "Yes,
sir." The second thing, though, was, "What the devil is he got up
as, sir?" He pointed to Gordon McSweeney, who instead of a
pack wore a big metal drum on his back and carried in his hands
a hose attached to it.

McSweeney spoke for himself: "This is a device for sending
the misbelievers into the fiery furnace." As far as he was concerned, anyone less grimly Presbyterian than himself was
heading straight for hell. That included papists and the Orthodox
Paul Mantarakis, but it also most especially included Mormons,
who, as far as he was concerned, were not Christians at all.

Captain Schneider amplified that, saying, "The gadget's supposed to be able to deal with strongpoints that laugh at rifles and
machine guns. If the artillery doesn't punch the ticket on that
farmhouse, we'll send Gordon up to see what he can do. Only
disadvantage is, it's a short-range weapon."

"I will bring it close enough to the farmhouse to be used,"
McSweeney promised. Whatever the thing was, he sounded
quiveringly eager to use it. Mantarakis had no idea what the
Mormons felt about Gordon McSweeney, or even whether they
knew he existed among the multitude of soldiers in the U.S.
force. He knew McSweeney scared him to death.

Ever so warily, he peered up over the parapet. The rebels' line was taking quite a pounding; through dust and smoke, it looked as if several large bites were gone from the farmhouse. Maybe it would be easy this time. It had been, once or twice. Some of the other times, though . . .

He would have liked to see the artillery go on for days, for weeks, killing all the Mormons without any need for the infantry to do their work. But, for one thing, there wasn't enough ammunition for a bombardment like that, not on a secondary front like Utah. And, for another, he'd seen fighting the Confederates that even the longest, most savage barrages didn't kill all or even most of the enemy soldiers at whom they were aimed.

After an hour or so, the guns fell silent. Captain Schneider blew a whistle. Up out of the trenches swarmed his company and several others. "Come on!" Mantarakis called to the men of his squad. "We don't want to spend a lot of time in between the lines where they can shoot us down. We want to get right in there with 'em."

The ground was chewed up from previous failed assaults on the Mormon position, and chewed worse by short rounds from the latest shelling. None, for once, seemed to have come down on the U.S. trenches, which Paul reckoned a small miracle. He dashed past stinking corpses and pieces of corpses, some still in green-gray often stained black with old blood. Flies rose in buzzing clouds.

Sure enough, some of the Mormon defenders remained alive and angry at the world, or at least at that portion of the United States Army attacking them. All along their line, flames showed riflemen shooting at the soldiers in green-gray heading their way. Somewhere not far from Paul, a man took a bullet and began shrieking for his mother.

And, sure enough, the machine gun in the adobe farmhouse started up, too. As he dove headlong into a shell crater, Mantarakis was convinced the racket a machine gun made was the most hateful noise in the world.

He looked toward the farmhouse. He and however many men still survived from his squad had come well past the high-water mark of earlier U.S. attacks. He was, he thought, within a hundred yards of that infernal device hammering out death up ahead. He was also damned if he knew how he was going to be able to get any nearer than that.

Somebody thudded down into the crater beside him: Gordon McSweeney. "I have to get closer," the dour Scotsman said. "Twenty yards is best, though thirty may do: one for each piece of silver Judas took."

Mantarakis sighed. He too knew they had to take out that machine gun. If McSweeney had a way—"I'll go left. You go right a few seconds later. We'll keep moving till you're close enough." *Or until you get killed—or until I do.* He wished he could take out his worry beads and work them.

They weren't the only soldiers pushing up toward the adobe. The Mormons in there had even less idea than Paul did of what the strange contraption on McSweeney's back was. Working his way to within twenty yards of the machine gun was slow and dangerous work, but he managed.

To Mantarakis' horror, McSweeney stood up in the hole where he'd sheltered. He aimed the nozzle end of the hose he carried at the machine gun's firing slit. Before the gun could cut him down, a spurt of flame burst from the nozzle, played over the front of the farmhouse, and went right through the narrow slit at the crew serving the machine gun.

Paul heard the lyingly cheerful sound of rounds cooking off inside the farmhouse. McSweeney dashed toward it. He stuck the nozzle right up against the slit and let loose another tongue of fire.

Along with the sound of cartridges prematurely ignited came another—the sound of screams. Gordon McSweeney's face was transfigured with joy, as if he'd just taken Jerusalem from the pagans. And then something happened that Paul had never before seen in Utah: three or four men came stumbling out through a hole in the side of the adobe, their hands lifted high in surrender.

Joyfully smiling still, McSweeney turned the nozzle of the flamethrower hose on them. "No, Gordon!" Paul yelled. "Let 'em give up. Maybe we can break this rebellion yet."

"I suppose it could be so," McSweeney admitted reluctantly. The Mormons shambled off into captivity. Out from the adobe floated the strong stench of burnt meat. Mantarakis didn't care. With its linchpin lost, this line wouldn't hold. One fight fewer, he thought, till Utah was done.

*   *   *

For this first time since the land was settled in the seventeenth century, a paved road ran between Lucien Galtier's farm and the town of Rivière-du-Loup on the St. Lawrence. If Lucien had had his way, the road would have disappeared, and with it the American soldiers and engineers who had built it. But, regardless of what he wanted, the Americans maintained their hold on Quebec south of the St. Lawrence, and had pushed across the mighty river at Rivière-du-Loup, intending, no doubt, to sweep southwest toward Quebec City, and then toward Montreal.

The push across the river and the newly paved road were anything but unrelated. As Lucien trudged in toward the white-painted wood farmhouse with the steep red roof after feeding the horse, he glanced at the much larger wooden building, painted what he thought a most unattractive shade of green-gray, that had gone up not far away, on what had been some of his best wheat land.

While he watched, a green-gray ambulance bearing on each side panel a large red cross inside a white circle pulled up to the building. The driver leaped out. He and an attendant who emerged from the rear of the vehicle carried a man on a stretcher into the U.S. military hospital. They hurried back and brought in another injured man. Then the ambulance, engine snarling, headed back toward Rivière-du-Loup to pick up more casualties.

Lucien wiped his feet before he went into the farmhouse. Though not a big man himself, he towered over his wife, Marie. That did not mean he could track muck inside without hearing about it in great detail.

"Warm in here," he said approvingly. "It is only October, but the wind outside is ready for January."

"May it freeze the Americans," Marie answered from the kitchen. Like her husband, she spoke in Quebecois French. It was the only language she knew. Lucien had picked up some English during his conscript time in the Canadian Army, just as English-speaking Canadians soaked up a little French there. He'd forgotten most of what he'd learned in the twenty-odd years since he'd served, though having to deal with the Americans had brought some of it back.

He walked toward the kitchen, drawn not only by the warmth

of the stove but also by the delicious smells floating out toward him. He sniffed. He prided himself on an educated nose. "Don't tell me," he said, pointing to the covered pot. "Ham baked with prunes. And are there potatoes in the oven, too?"

Marie Galtier regarded him with mixed affection and exasperation. "How am I supposed to surprise you, Lucien?"

He spread his hands and shrugged. "As long as we've been married, and you still expect to surprise me? You make me happy. That is enough, and more than enough. What do I need of surprises?"

Also in the kitchen, helping her mother, was their eldest daughter, Nicole. She was slight and dark like Marie, and put Lucien achingly in mind of what her mother had been like when he'd first started courting her. Now she said, "I can surprise you, Papa."

"Of this I have no doubt," Lucien said. "The question is, my little bird, do I want to be surprised?" He didn't remember only what Marie had been like when he was courting her. He also remembered, all too well, what he had been like. He did not think the young male of the species likely to have shown any dramatic improvement over the intervening generation.

And when Nicole answered, "Papa, I do not know," his heart sank. She took a long, deep breath before going on, and that heart, seemingly a relentless gymnast, leaped into his mouth. Then she said, "I have been thinking of doing nurse's work at the American hospital. It is very close, of course, and we could use the money the work would bring."

After all the dreadful possibilities he had imagined, that one seemed not so bad . . . at first. Then Lucien stared. "You would help the Americans, Nicole? The enemies of our country? The allies of the enemies of France?"

His daughter bit her lip and looked down at the apron she wore over her long wool dress. To Galtier's surprise, his wife spoke up for her: "If a man is hurt and in pain, does it matter what country he comes from?"

"Father Pascal would say the same thing," Lucien replied, which made Marie wince, because the priest at Rivière-du-Loup, whatever anyone's opinion of his piety might be, collaborated eagerly with the Americans.

"But, Papa," Nicole said, "they *are* hurt and in pain. You can hear them moaning in the night sometimes." Lucien had heard those moans, too. They had been sweet to his ears. He shook his head in dismay to discover his daughter did not feel the same. Nicole persisted, "You know what I think of Father Pascal. You know what I think of the Americans. None of that would change. How could it? And they would be giving money to people who despise them."

"You don't even speak any English," Galtier said. As soon as the words were out of his mouth, he knew he was in trouble. When you had to shift your reasons for saying no, you were liable to end up saying yes.

And Nicole pounced: "I can learn it, I know that. It might even be useful for me to know if, God forbid—" She didn't go on. She didn't need to go on. Lucien had no trouble completing the sentence for himself. *If, God forbid, the United States win the war and try to make us all use English afterwards.* That was what she'd meant, or something very much like it.

He didn't try to answer on the spur of the moment. Believing Canada and France and England and the Confederacy could be defeated went dead against all his hopes and dreams. What he did say was, "How Major Quigley will laugh when he learns you are working for the Americans."

He spoke with more than a little bitterness. Nicole bit her lip. The French-speaking U.S. major had placed the hospital on Galtier land not least because Lucien would not collaborate with the American occupying authorities.

Marie spoke up again: "Actually, that may be for the best. The major may believe we are coming round to his view of things after all, and so become less likely to trouble us from now on."

Lucien chewed on that. It did make a certain amount of sense. And so, instead of putting his foot down as he'd intended, he said, "We shall speak of this more later." His wife and eldest daughter nodded, outwardly obedient to his will as women were supposed to be. He knew they both had to be smiling inside, though. Sooner or later, they would get what they wanted. Talking about things later was but one short step from giving in.

At supper, he discovered he was the last one in the family to hear about what Nicole had in mind. That saddened him but didn't unduly surprise him. For one thing, he did more work away from the farmhouse than anyone else. For another, he was the one from whom permission would have to come. Nicole would have wanted to know she had support from the rest before bearding him.

"I wish I could go there, too, and make money of my own," his daughter Susanne said wistfully. Since she was only thirteen, they would not have to worry about that unless the war went on appallingly long. *Or, of course, unless there is another war after this one,* Lucien thought, and then shivered, as if someone had walked over his grave.

His older son, Charles, did not approve of Nicole's plan. "I say the Americans are just another pack of *Boches*, and we should have as little to do with them as we can." He spoke with the certainty of seventeen. In another year, he would have gone into the Canadian Army to serve his time. The only good thing about the war was that it had rolled over this part of Quebec before he could take part in it.

"Oh, I don't know," said Georges, who was a couple of years younger than his brother and almost the changeling of the family: not only was he larger and fairer than his parents and brother and sisters, but he also had a rollicking wit out of keeping with the pungent sarcasm Lucien brought to bear on life. Now he grinned at Nicole across the table. "Maybe you'll meet a handsome American doctor and he'll sweep you off your—Oww!"

By the dull thud from under the table, she'd kicked him in the shin. To underscore a point that needed no underscoring, his littlest sister, Jeanne, said, "That was mean." Eight-year-old certainty wasn't of the same kind as the seventeen-year-old variety, but it wasn't any less certain, either. Denise, who was a couple of years older than Jeanne, nodded to show her agreement. Jeanne turned to Nicole and said, "You'd never do anything like that, would you?"

"Certainly not," Nicole said, frost in her voice. The look she turned on Georges should have turned him into a block of ice, too. It didn't. He stayed impudent as ever, even if he did have to bend over to rub his injured leg.

"Now wait, all of you," Lucien said. "No one has said that Nicole will have any opportunity to meet American doctors, even if she wanted to do such a thing, which I already have no doubt she does not."

"But, Papa," Nicole said, "are you changing your mind?"

"No, for I never said yes," he answered. His eldest daughter looked stricken. He glanced down to Marie at the foot of the table. He knew what her expressions meant. This one meant she'd back him, but she thought he was wrong. He sighed. "Perhaps it might be possible to try . . . but only for a little while."

II

Lieutenant General George Armstrong Custer slammed his fist down on the table that held the maps of western Kentucky. "By heaven," he said, "the War Department's finally come out with an order that makes sense. General attack all along the line! Draft the orders to implement it here in First Army country, Major Dowling. I'll want to see them by two o' clock this afternoon."

"Yes, sir," Abner Dowling said, and then, because part of his job as adjutant was saving Custer from himself, he added, "Sir, I don't believe they mean all units are to move forward at the same moment, only that we are to take the best possible advantage of the Confederates' embarrassment by striking where they are weakest."

Saving Custer from himself was a full-time job. Dowling had broad shoulders—there wasn't much about Dowling that wasn't broad—and needed them to bear up under the weight of bad temper and worse judgment the general commanding First Army pressed down on him. Custer had always been sure of himself, even as a brash cavalry officer in the War of Secession. Now, at the age of seventy-five, he was downright autocratic . . . and no more right than he had ever been.

His pouchy, wrinkled, sagging face went from pasty white to dusky purple in the space of a couple of heartbeats. Neither color went well with his drooping mustache, which he peroxided to an approximation of the golden color it had once had naturally. The same applied to the locks of hair that flowed out from under his service cap. He wore the cap all the time, indoors and out, for it concealed the shiny expanse of the crown of his head.

"When I see the order 'general attack,' Major, I construe it to mean attack all along the line, and that is what I intend to do," he

31

snapped now. The only time his voice left the range from petulant to irritable was when he was talking to a war correspondent:
then he spoke gently as any sucking dove. "We shall go at the
enemy and smash him up."

"Wouldn't it be wise, sir, to concentrate our attacks where he
shows himself to be less strong, break through there, and then
use the advantages we've gained to make further advances?"
Dowling said, doing his best—as he'd done his best since the
outset of the war, with results decidedly mixed—to be the voice
of reason.

Defiantly, Custer shook his head. Those dyed locks flipped
back and forth. Not even the magic word *breakthrough* had
reached him. "Without their niggers to help 'em, the Rebs are
just a pack of weak sisters," he declared. "One good push and the
whole rotten structure they've built comes tumbling down."

"Sir, we've been pushing with all we have for the past year
and more, and it hasn't tumbled down yet," Dowling said. *If it
had, we'd be a lot deeper into the Confederacy than we are—and
even good generals have trouble against the Rebs.*

"We'll drive them out of Morehead's Horse Mill," Custer said,
"and that, thank God, will have the added benefit of getting us
out of Bremen here. You can tell why this town is so small: no
one in his right mind would want to live here. And once we have
the railroad junction at Morehead's Horse Mill, how in the name
of all that's holy can the Rebs hope to keep us out of Bowling
Green?"

Dowling suspected there would be a number of ways the Confederate forces could keep the U.S. Army out of Bowling Green,
even with Negroes in rebellion behind Rebel lines. He didn't say
that to Custer; a well-developed sense of self-preservation kept
his lips sealed however much his brain seethed.

What he did say, after some thought, was, "So you'll want me
to prepare the orders with the *Schwerpunkt* aimed toward Morehead's Horse Mill?" With the Confederates in disorder, they
might actually take that town. Then, after another buildup, they
could think about moving in the direction of—not yet *on*—
Bowling Green.

"Schwerpunkt." General Custer made it sound like a noise a
sick horse might make. "It's all very well to have the German
Empire for an ally—without them, we'd be helpless against the

Rebs and the limeys and the frogs and the Canucks. But we imitate them too much, if you ask me. A general in command of an army can't walk to the outhouse without the General Staff looking in the half-moon window to make sure he undoes his trouser buttons in the proper order. And all these damned foreign words fog up the simple art of war."

The United States had lost the War of Secession. Then, twenty years later, they'd lost the Second Mexican War. Germany or its Prussian core, in the meantime, had smashed the Danes, the Austrians, and the French, each in short order. As far as Dowling was concerned, the country that lost wars needed to do some learning from the side that won them.

That was something else he couldn't say. He tried guile: "If we do break through at Morehead's Horse Mill, sir, we'll be in a good position to roll up the Rebel line all the way back to the Ohio River, or else to push hard toward Bowling Green and make the enemy react to us."

All of that was true. All of it was reasonable. None of it was what Custer wanted to hear. Much of Dowling's job was telling Custer things he didn't want to hear and making him pay attention to them. What Dowling wanted was to get up to the front and command units for himself. The only reason he didn't apply for a transfer was his conviction that more men could handle a battalion in combat than could keep General Custer out of mischief.

Before Custer could go off like a Yellowstone geyser, a pretty young light-skinned colored woman poked her head into the room with the map table and said, "General, suh, I got your lunch ready in the kitchen. Mutton chops, mighty fine."

Custer's whole manner changed. "I'll be there directly, Olivia. Thank you, my dear," he said, courtly as you please. To Dowling, he added, "We'll resume this discussion after I've eaten. I do declare, Major, that young lady is the one redeeming feature I have yet found in western Kentucky."

"Er—yes, sir," Dowling said tonelessly. Custer took himself off with as much spry alacrity as a man carrying three quarters of a century could manage. He didn't bother hiding the way he pursued Olivia. Amused First Army rumor said she'd been caught, too, not just chaste. Dowling thought the rumor likely true: the general carried on like an assotted fool whenever he was around his cook and housekeeper. The adjutant was more inclined to fault Olivia's taste than Custer's. You'd think the old boy would have had his last stand years before.

An orderly came in with the day's mail. "Where shall I dump all this, sir?" he asked Dowling.

"Why don't you give it to me, Frazier? The general's eating his lunch." *Or possibly his serving wench.* Dowling shook his head to get the lewd images out of it. Coughing, he went on, "I'll sort through it for him so he can go through it quickly when he's finished."

"Yes, sir." Frazier handed him the bundle and departed. Dowling made three piles on the map table. One was for administrative matters pertaining to First Army, most of which he'd handle himself. One was for communications from the War Department. He'd end up handling most of those, too, but Custer would want to look at them first. And one was for personal letters. Custer would answer some of those—most likely, the ones full of adulation—himself. Dowling would get stuck with the rest, typing replies for the great man's signature. His lip curled.

And then, all at once, the sour expression vanished from his broad, plump, ruddy face. He arranged the piles and waited with perfect equanimity for General Custer to return. Meanwhile, he studied the map. If they could break through at Morehead's Horse Mill, they really might accomplish something.

Custer came back looking absurdly pleased with himself. Maybe he'd managed to get a hand under Olivia's long black dress. "The mail came in, sir," Dowling said, as if reporting the arrival of a new regiment.

"Ah, capital! Let's see what sort of big thing it brings us today," Custer said grandly, hauling out a piece of slang forgotten by almost everyone since the War of Secession. As Dowling had known he would, he picked up the stack of personal mail first. As Dowling had known he would, he went from grand to glum in a matter of moments. "Oh. A letter from my wife."

"Was there, sir? I didn't notice," Dowling lied. He twisted the knife a little: "I'm sure you must be glad to hear from her."

"Of course I am." Custer sounded like a liar himself. His letter opener was shaped like a cavalry saber. He used it to slit the envelope. Elizabeth Custer was in the habit of writing long, even voluminous, letters. So was the general, come to that, when he bothered to write her at all. Dowling would have bet he hadn't said anything about Olivia in any of them, though.

Custer fumbled for his reading glasses, perched them on his nose, and began to wade through the missive. Suddenly, he turned red, then white. His hand shook. He dropped one of the pages he hadn't yet read.

"Is something wrong, sir?" Dowling asked, wondering if God had chosen this moment to give First Army a new commander.

But Custer shook his head, sending his curls flying once more. "No," he said. "It's good news, as a matter of fact." If it was, no one had reacted so badly to good news since Pyrrhus of Epirus cried, *One more such victory and we are ruined!* Custer went on, "Libbie, it seems, has secured permission from the powers that be to enter into the war zone, and will soon be brightening my life here in Bremen for what she describes as an extended visit."

"How lucky you are, sir, that you'll have your own dear wife here to help you bear the heavy burden of command." Dowling brought that out with an absolutely straight face. He was proud of himself. None of the delight he felt showed in his voice, either. Having Elizabeth Custer come to Bremen for a visit was better, more delightful news than any for which he'd dared hope.

He wondered what sort of convenient illness Olivia would contract the day before Mrs. Custer arrived, and whether she'd recover the day after Mrs. Custer left or perhaps that very afternoon. By the thoughtful look in his eye, the distinguished general might have been wondering the same thing.

Whatever Custer came up with, that, by God, was not something he could pile onto the shoulders of his long-suffering adjutant. He'd have to take care of it all by his lonesome.

"I'll draft the orders for the push against Morehead's Horse Mill," Dowling said.

"Yes, go ahead," Custer agreed abstractedly. Dowling had been sure he would be abstracted at the moment. Custer had made it plain he had no use for German terminology. Dowling reminded himself not to call the concentration against Morehead's Horse Mill the *Schwerpunkt* of First Army action. But German was a useful language. English, for instance, had nothing close to *Schadenfreude* to describe the glee Dowling felt at his vain, pompous, foolish commander's discomfiture.

*   *   *

Despite the many things Lieutenant Commander Roger Kimball had thought he might do in a submarine—and his fantasies had considerable scope, ranging from laying a pretty girl in the captain's cramped cabin to sinking two Yankee battleships with the same spread of torpedoes—sailing up a South Carolina river on gunboat duty hadn't made the list. But here he was, heading up the Pee Dee to bombard the revolting Negroes—in both senses of the word—who called themselves the Congaree Socialist Republic.

Diesel smoke poured from the exhaust of the *Bonefish* at the back of the conning tower on which he stood. The submersible drew only eleven feet of water, which meant it could go farther up the river before grounding itself than most of the surface warships that had been in Charleston harbor when the rebellion broke out.

All the same, Kimball was proceeding at a quarter speed and had a man with a sounding line at the bow. The sailor turned and called, "Three fathoms twain, sir!" He cast the line again. The lead weight splashed down into the muddy water of the Pee Dee.

"Three fathoms twain," Kimball echoed to show he'd heard. Twenty feet—plenty of water under the *Bonefish*'s keel. He turned to the only other officer on the submersible, a junior lieutenant named Tom Brearley, who couldn't possibly have been as young as he looked. "What I wish we had here is a river gunboat," he said. "Then we could haul bigger guns further upstream than we'll manage with our boat."

"That's a fact, sir," Brearley agreed. He wasn't long out of the Confederate naval academy at Mobile, and agreed with just about everything his commander said. After a moment, though, he added, "We have to do the best we can with what we've got."

That was also a fact, as Kimball was glumly aware. His own features, blunter and harsher than Brearley's, assumed a bulldog cast as he surveyed the weaponry aboard the *Bonefish*. The three-inch deck gun had been designed to sink freighters, not to bombard land targets, but it would serve that purpose. For the mission, a machine gun had been hastily bolted to the top of the conning tower and another one to the deck behind it. Take all together, the three guns and the vital sounding line used up everyone in the eighteen-man crew who wasn't required to stay below and keep the diesel running.

The hatch behind Kimball was open. From it wafted the reek with which he had become intimately familiar in three years aboard submersibles, a reek made up of oil and sweat and heads that never quite worked in the manner in which they'd been designed. Here, at least, as opposed to out on the open sea, he didn't have to keep the hatch dogged if he didn't want to flood the narrow steel tube inside which he and his men did their job.

"Three fathoms twain!" the sailor with the lead sang out again.

"Three fathoms twain," Kimball repeated. His eyes flicked back and forth, back and forth, from one side of the Pee Dee to the other. Most places, forest—or maybe jungle was a better word—came right down to the riverbank. He didn't like that. Anything could be hiding in there. He felt eyes on him, though he couldn't see anyone. He didn't like that, either.

Here and there, plantations had been carved out of the forest. He didn't know what they grew in these parts—maybe rice, maybe indigo, maybe cotton. He was from the hills of northeastern Arkansas himself. The farm where he'd grown up turned out a little wheat, a little tobacco, a few hogs, and a lot of strapping sons. Some Confederate officers looked down their noses at him because of his back-country accent. If you were good enough at what you did, though, how you talked mattered less.

But that wasn't why he growled whenever they passed a plantation. The mansions in which the Low Country bluebloods had made their homes were one and all burnt-out shells of their former selves. "I wonder if that happened to Marshlands, too," he muttered.

"Sir?" Tom Brearley said.

"Never mind." Kimball knew how to keep his mouth shut. It was none of Brearley's business that he'd been in the sack with the mistress of Marshlands at a cheap hotel when the Negro uprising broke out. He hoped Anne Colleton was all right. Like him, she had a way of running straight toward trouble. That was probably a good part of what had attracted the two of them to each other. It made for a good submarine commander. In a civilian, though, in what might as well have been the middle of a war . . .

A rifle cracked in the thick undergrowth. A bullet ricocheted off the side of the conning tower, a yard from Kimball's feet. He felt the vibration through the soles of his shoes. The rifle cracked again—or maybe it was another one. The round slapped past his ear.

"Hose 'em down!" he shouted to the men at the machine guns. Both guns started hammering away in the general direction from which the shots had come. The greenery by the riverbank whipped back and forth, as if in a hailstorm rather than a hail of bullets. Whether that hail of bullets was doing anything about getting rid of the uprisen Negroes who'd fired on the *Bonefish* was another matter. Kimball didn't know enough about fighting on land to guess one way or the other. He suspected he would acquire more of an education in that regard than he really wanted.

"Wouldn't it be fine, Tom, if we could land a company of Marines and let them do the dirty work for us?" he said.

"It surely would, sir," Brearley answered. He looked up and down the length of the *Bonefish*. "It would be nice if this boat could hold a company of Marines. For that matter, it would be nice if this boat would hold all of us."

"Hey, don't talk like that. You're an officer, so you've got a bunk to call your own, and a good foot of room between the edge of it and the main corridor," Kimball said. "You sleep in a hammock or triple-decked in five and a half feet of space and you'll find out all about crowded."

"Yes, sir," Brearley said. "I know about that from training."

"You'd better remember it," Kimball told him. Another reason he'd joined the submersible service was that you couldn't be an aristocrat here—the boats weren't big enough to permit it.

He was about to say something more when the man at the bow cried out and tumbled into the Pee Dee. The fellow came up a moment later, splashing feebly. Around him, the muddy water took on a reddish cast.

Then one of the sailors working the conning-tower machine gun crumpled. He pounded at the roof of the conning tower in agony, but his legs didn't move—he'd been hit in the spine. Crimson spread from around a neat hole in the back of his tunic.

For a moment, that didn't mean anything to Kimball. Then another bullet cracked past his head, and he realized the fire was coming not from the northern bank of the Pee Dee, the one the machines guns were working over, but from the southern bank.

"Christ, we're caught in a crossfire!" he exclaimed. The Pee Dee was no more than a couple of hundred yards wide. The Negroes hiding in the bushes had only rifles (he devoutly hoped they had only rifles), but they didn't need to be the greatest shots in the world to start picking off his men. He thought about turning the deck gun on the southern riverbank, but that would have been like flailing around with a sledgehammer, trying to smash a cockroach you couldn't even see.

"What do we do, sir?" Brearley asked.

Without waiting for orders, one of the men from the deck gun crew had leaped into the river after the wounded leadsman. He hauled the fellow back up onto the deck. It might have been in the nick of time. Kimball thought he saw something sinuous moving through the water toward the submersible, then going away. Did alligators live in the Pee Dee? Nobody had briefed him, one way or the other.

He didn't have a doctor on board the *Bonefish*, or even a pharmacist's mate. He knew a little about first aid, and so did one of the petty officers who kept the diesels going. He wished again for a river gunboat, one with its guns housed in protective turrets against just this sort of nuisance fire. It would have been nuisance fire against such a gunboat, anyway. Against the vessel he commanded, it was a great deal worse.

"All hands below!" he shouted. The sailors on deck scrambled up the ladder to the top of the conning tower, then swarmed down into the *Bonefish*. The leadsman had a bullet through his upper left arm, a wound from which he'd recover if it didn't fester. He got up and down as fast as an uninjured sailor. The man who'd been hit in the spine presented a harder problem. Moving him at all would do his wound no good, but leaving him where he sprawled was asking for him to be hit again and killed.

Kimball waited until he and the wounded machine gunner were the only men left on top of the conning tower. Bullets kept whipping past them. At the top of the ladder, Tom Brearley waited. "Nichols, I'm going to get you below now," Kimball said.

"Don't worry about me, sir," the sailor answered. "What the hell good am I like this?"

"Lots of people in your shoes now," Kimball told him. "That's a fact—goddamn war. They'll figure out plenty of things for you to do. And the wheelchairs they have nowadays let you get around pretty well."

Nichols groaned, maybe in derision, maybe just in pain. Kimball ignored that. As carefully as he could, he slid the wounded sailor toward the hatch. When Brearley had secure hold of Nichols' feet, he guided the man's torso through the hatchway, then hung on to him as they descended.

The petty officer—his name was Ben Coulter—was already bandaging the leadsman's arm. His jowly, acne-scarred face twisted into a grimace when he saw how Nichols was dead from the waist down. "Nothing I can do about that, sir," he told Kimball. "Wish there was, but—" He spread his hands. He'd washed them before he got to work, but he still had dirt ground into the folds of his knuckles and grease under his nails.

"I know," Kimball said unhappily. Then he burst out, "God damn it to hell, we're not built to fight close-in actions. We have any sheet metal or anything we can use to shield our gunners' backs?" The deck gun had a shield for the front, good against shell splinters but maybe not against bullets. As things stood, the machine guns were altogether unprotected.

"Maybe we could do something like that, sir," Coulter said. He hesitated. "You mean to go on after this?"

"Hadn't thought of doing anything else," Kimball answered. He looked from the petty officer to Tom Brearley to the rest of the crew packed together in the cramped chamber under the conning tower. "Haven't had any orders to do anything else, either. Anybody who doesn't want to go on, I'll put him off the boat right now and he can take his chances!"

"You mean here, among the niggers?" somebody asked. Lucky for him, he was behind Kimball, who couldn't tell who he was.

"Hell, yes, I mean here among the niggers," the submersible commander said. "Anybody who thinks I'm going to back off and let those black bastards—those Red bastards—take my country away from me or help the damnyankees whip us had better think twice. Maybe three times." He looked around again. If anybody disagreed with him, it didn't show. That was the way things were supposed to work. He nodded once, brusquely. "All

right. Let's get to work and figure out how to do what needs
doing."

Tiny Yossel Reisen woke up and started to wail. When he
woke up, everyone in the crowded apartment woke up with him.
Flora Hamburger opened her eyes. It was dark. She groaned—
softly, so as not to disturb anyone who, by some miracle, might
still have been asleep. This was the third time her baby nephew
had awakened in the night. Her parents and siblings had to get up
too early to go to work as things were. When a howling baby cut
into what little sleep they got, life was hard.

"*Sha, sha*—hush, hush," Sophie Reisen murmured wearily as
she stumbled toward the baby's cradle. Flora's older sister
scooped Yossel out, sat down in a chair, and began to nurse him.
Little urgent sucking noises replaced his desperate cries.

Flora rolled over on the bed she shared with her younger sister
Esther and tried to go back to sleep. She'd just succeeded when
the alarm clock beside her head went off, clattering as if all the
fire alarms in New York City were boiled down into its malevo-
lent little case.

Blindly, almost drunk with weariness, she fumbled at the
clock till it shut up. Then she staggered out of bed and splashed
cold water on her face to bring back a semblance of life. She
stared at herself in the mirror above the sink. Her dark eyes, usually so lively, were dull, with purplish circles under them. Her
skin had a pallor that had nothing to do with fashion, but threw
her cheekbones and prominent nose and chin into sharp relief.
And he's not even my baby, she thought with tired resentment.

Esther pushed her away from the mirror. She dressed quickly.
By the time she got out to the kitchen, her mother had sweet rolls
and coffee pale with milk already on the table. Her younger
brothers, David and Isaac, were there eating and drinking.
They'd risen no earlier than she had, but they hadn't had to
struggle with a recalcitrant corset.

Her father came in a moment after she did. The biggest mug
of coffee was reserved for him. He already had his pipe going.
The tobacco was harsher than what he'd used before the war cut
off imports from the Confederacy, but the odor of smoke was
still part of breakfast as far as Flora was concerned. Benjamin

Hamburger bit into a roll, sipped his coffee, and nodded approvingly. "That's good, Sarah," he called to Flora's mother, as he did every morning.

Sophie sat down, too. "He's asleep again," she said, sounding half asleep herself. "How long it will last—*Gott vayss*." Her shrug was barely visible, as if she lacked the energy to raise her shoulders any higher. She probably did.

Flora Hamburger's eyes went to the framed photograph of Yossel Reisen—baby Yossel's father—near the divan in the living room. There he stood in his Army uniform, looking nothing like the *yeshiva-bucher* he'd been till he enlisted. Because he was going into the Army and might very well never come back, Sophie, who'd been his fiancée then, had given him a going-away present as old as history. He'd given her one as old as history, too, though it had taken nine months to find out whether that one was a boy or a girl.

He had married her when he came back to the Lower East Side on leave: the baby did bear his name. That was all of him it had, though; shortly before Sophie's time of confinement, he'd been killed in one of the meaningless battles down in Virginia.

Flora had hated the war long before it came home to her family. As a Socialist Party activist, she'd done everything she could to keep the Socialist delegation in Congress—the second-largest bloc, behind the dominant Democrats but far ahead of the Republicans—from voting for war credits. She'd failed. Now it was the Socialists' war, too. She and her party were to blame for that picture of a man who wasn't coming home, and for so many like it from the black-bordered casualty lists the papers printed every day.

Her father, her sisters, her brother hurried off to work in the sweatshops that, these days, turned endless bolts of green-gray cloth into tunics and trousers and caps and puttees for men to wear as they went out to get slaughtered. David had just turned eighteen. She wondered how long it would be before he got his conscription call. Not long, she thought worriedly, not at the rate the war was going through the young men of two continents.

Before long, it was time for Flora to go, too. She kissed her mother on the cheek, saying, "I'll see you tonight. I hope the baby isn't too much trouble."

Sarah Hamburger smiled. "I've had a lot of practice with babies by now, don't you think?" She turned a speculative eye on Flora. "One of these days, *alevai,* it would be nice to take care of one of yours."

That got Flora out of the apartment in a hurry. She didn't even wait to adjust her picture hat in front of the mirror, but put it on as she was walking downstairs. If it was crooked, too bad. Her mother didn't see, wouldn't see, that living a full life didn't have to include a life full of men (or full of one man) and full of babies.

Socialist Party headquarters for the Fourteenth Ward were in a crowded second-floor office above a butcher shop on Centre Market Court, across the street from the stalls and little shops in the Centre Market. Buyers already went from stall to store, looking for early morning bargains. Soldiers' Circle men prowled through the marketplace, some of them wearing armbands, others pins, all of them carrying truncheons or wearing pistols on their hips. They'd been suppressing dissent and resistance to the war in Socialist neighborhoods ever since the Remembrance Day riots.

As often happened, a couple of them were leaning up against the brick wall near the stairway up to Socialist Party headquarters. They'd eased off on that for a time, but had come back in greater force since the Socialist uprising in the Confederate States. If the oppressed Negroes could rise up in righteous revolutionary fury there, what about the oppressed proletariat of all colors in the USA?

Flora waved to Max Fleischmann, the butcher downstairs. He waved back, smiling; she helped keep the Soldiers' Circle goons from bothering him. Nothing could keep them from leering at her. Not by accident did the flowers in her hat conceal a couple of long, sharp hatpins.

Perhaps grouchy from lack of sleep, she glared back at the Soldiers' Circle men. "I don't know why you waste your time hanging around here," she said, exaggerating for effect. "Aren't you grateful that people who see the need for class struggle are helping the United States win the war?"

"Reds are Reds, whether they're black or white," one of the men answered. "We've got the answer for any what gets out o' line." He set his fist by the side of his neck, then jerked his arm sharply upward and let his head fall to one side, as if he'd been hanged. "Anybody tries a revolution *here*, that's what they get, and that's what they deserve."

"I'm sure you would have told George Washington the same thing," Flora said, and went upstairs. She felt the eyes of the Soldiers' Circle men like daggers in her back till she opened the door and walked inside.

Party headquarters, as usual, put her in mind of a three-ring circus crammed into about half a ring. Typewriters clattered. People shouted into telephones in Yiddish and English, often with scant regard for which language they were using at any given moment. Other people stood in the narrow spaces between desks or sat on the corners of the desks themselves and argued loudly and passionately about anything that happened to cross their minds. Flora looked on the chaos and smiled. It was, in an even larger, even more disorderly style, her family writ large.

"Good morning, Maria," she said to her secretary as she hung her hat on a tree near the desk.

"Good morning," Maria Tresca answered. She was one of the few gentiles at the Fourteenth Ward office, but was as enthusiastic for Socialism and its goals as anyone else; her sister, Angelina, had died in the Remembrance Day riots the year before. She studied Flora, then added, "You look pleased with yourself."

"Do I? Well, maybe I do," Flora said. "I gave the bully boys downstairs something to think about." She explained her crack about Washington. Maria grinned from ear to ear and clapped her hands together.

Over at the next desk, Herman Bruck hung up the telephone on which he'd been speaking and sent Flora a stern look. A stern look from Bruck was not something to bear lightly. He might have stepped out of the pages of a fashion catalogue, from perfectly trimmed hair and neat mustache to suits always of fine wool and most modish cut. He often made a spokesman for the Socialists, simply because he looked so elegant. Money had not done it for him; coming from a family of fancy tailors had.

"Washington was no revolutionary, not in the Marxist sense of the word," he said now. "He didn't transfer wealth or power from the aristocracy to the bourgeoisie, and certainly not to the peasants. All he did was replace British planters and landowners with their American counterparts."

Flora tapped a fingernail against the top of her desk in annoyance. Herman Bruck would probably have made an even better Talmudic scholar than poor Yossel Reisen; he delighted in hairsplitting and precision. Only in chosen ideology did he differ from Yossel.

"For one thing, Soldiers' Circle goons don't care about the Marxist sense of the word," Flora said, holding onto her patience with both hands. "For another, by their use of the term, Washington *was* a revolutionary, and I got them to think about the consequences of denying the right to revolution now. Either that or I got them angry at me, which will do as well."

"It's not proper," Bruck answered stiffly. "We should be accurate about these matters. Educating the nation must be undertaken in an exact and thoroughgoing fashion."

"Yes, Herman." Flora suppressed a sigh. The one thing Bruck lacked that would have made him a truly effective political operative was any trace of imagination. Before he could go on with what would, no doubt, have been a disputation to consume the entire morning, his telephone rang. He gave whoever was on the other end of the line the same sharply focused attention he had turned on Flora.

Her own phone jangled a moment later. "Socialist Party, Flora Hamburger," she said, and then, "Oh—Mr. Levitzsky. Yes, by all means we *will* support the garment workers' union there. That contract will be honored or the rank and file will strike, war or no war. Teddy Roosevelt makes a lot of noise about a square deal for the workers. We'll find out if he means it, and we'll let the people know if he doesn't."

"I'll take that word to the factory manager," Levitzsky said. "If he knows the union and the Party are in solidarity here, he won't have the nerve to go on calling the contract just a scrap of paper. Thank you, Miss Hamburger."

That was the sort of phone call that made Flora feel she'd earned her salary for the day. Workers were so vulnerable to pressure from employers, especially with the war making everything all the more urgent: or at least seem all the more urgent. The Party had the collective strength to help redress the balance.

Herman Bruck got off the phone himself a minute or so later.

In a new tone of voice—as if he hadn't been criticizing her ideological purity a moment before—he asked, "Would you like to go to the moving pictures with me tonight after work? Geraldine Farrar is supposed to be very fine in the new version of *Carmen*."

"I really don't think so, not tonight—" Flora began.

Bruck went on as if she hadn't spoken: "The bullfight scene, they say, is especially bully." He smiled at his pun. Flora didn't. "So many people wanted to sit in the amphitheater while it was being photographed, I've heard, that they didn't have to hire any extras."

"I'm sorry, Herman. Maybe when Yossel sleeps a little better, so I can be sure I'll sleep a little better. He kept everyone awake through a lot of last night."

Herman Bruck looked like a kicked puppy. He'd been trying to court Flora almost as long as they'd known each other. The next luck he had would be the first. That didn't stop him from going right on trying. Abstractly, Flora admired his persistence: the same persistence he showed in his Party work. She admired it even more there than when it was aimed at her.

Turning away from Bruck and toward Maria Tresca, she asked, "What's next?"

Jake Featherston stuck out his mess tin. The Negro cook for the First Richmond Howitzers gave him a tinful of stew. He carried it back among the ruins of Hampstead, Maryland, and sat down with his gun crew to eat.

Michael Scott, the three-inch howitzer's loader, said, "Stew tastes pretty good, Sarge. Now all we have to do is hope it ain't poisoned."

"Funny," Jake said. "Funny like a truss." He dug in with his spoon. Scott had been right; the stew was good. Trying to look on the bright side of things, he went on, "This Metellus, he seems like a good nigger. He knows his place, and he don't give anybody any trouble."

"Not that we know about, anyways." That was Will Cooper, one of the shell haulers for the three-inch gun. Like Scott, he was a kid; both of them had joined the regiment after heavy casualties along the Susquehanna thinned out most of the veterans who had started the war with Jake. But the kids had been around for a while now; their butternut uniforms were stained and weather-beaten, and the red facings on their collar tabs that showed them to be artillerymen had faded to a washed-out pink.

Featherston kept on eating, but scowled as he did so. The trouble was, Cooper was right, no two ways about it. "Be a long time before we can trust the niggers again," Jake said glumly.

Heads bobbed up and down in response to that. "At this here gun, we were lucky—this whole battery, we were lucky," Scott said. "Our laborers just ran off. They didn't try and turn our guns on us or on the infantrymen in front of us."

Now Jake spoke with fond reminiscence: "Yeah, and we gave the damnyankees a good warm welcome when they came up out of their trenches, too. They figured we couldn't do nothin' about 'em with all our niggers givin' us a hard time, but I reckon we showed 'em different."

When the wind blew out of the north, it wafted the stench of unburied Yankee bodies into the Confederate lines. It was a horrible stench, sweet and ripe and thick enough to slice. But it was also the stench of victory, or at least the stench of defeat avoided. U.S. forces had driven the Confederacy out of Pennsylvania, but the Stars and Bars still flew over most of Maryland and over Washington, D.C.

Occasional crackles of gunfire came from the front: scouts thinking they'd spotted Yankee raiders, snipers shooting at enemies in the trenches rash enough to expose any part of themselves even for a moment, and, on the other side of the line, Yankee riflemen ready to do unto the Confederates what was being done unto them.

Another rifle shot rang out, then two more. Featherston's head came up and his gaze sharpened, as if he were a coon dog taking a scent. Those shots hadn't come from the front, but from well behind the line. He scowled again. "That's likely to be some damn nigger trying to bushwhack our boys."

"Bastards," Cooper muttered. "We finish dealin' with them, they're gonna spend the next hundred years wishin' they didn't try raisin' their hands to us, and you can take that to church."

"I know," Featherston said. "Back in the old days, my old man was an overseer. Till they laid him in the ground, he said we never ought to have manumitted the niggers. I always thought, you got to change with the times. But with the kind of thanks we got, damned if I think that way any more."

The whole gun crew nodded in response to that. Jake finished his stew. Maybe Metellus really knew which side his bread was buttered on and did all the things he was supposed to do. But for all Jake knew, maybe he unbuttoned his fly and pissed in the stewpot when nobody was looking. How could you tell for sure? You couldn't, till maybe too late.

From what he'd heard, it had been like that up and down the CSA—worst in the cotton belt, where whites were thin on the ground in big stretches of the country, but bad everywhere. He didn't know how many of the ten million or so Negroes in the Confederacy had joined the rebellion, but enough had so that some troops had had to leave the fighting line against the USA to help put them down.

No wonder, then, that the damnyankees were pushing forward in western Virginia, in Kentucky, and in Sonora. The wonder was that the Confederate positions hadn't fallen apart altogether. He glanced over to his gun. The quick-firing three-incher, copied from the French 75, was one big reason they hadn't. The USA lacked a field piece that came close to matching it.

He heard footsteps coming up from the south. He wore a pistol on his hip, in case Yankee infantry somehow God forbid got close enough to his gun for him to need a personal weapon. He hadn't drawn it till trouble broke out among the Negroes. Now—Now he was a long way from the only artilleryman to have a weapon ready. "Who goes there?" he demanded.

"This Battery C, First Richmond Howitzers?" Whoever owned the voice, he sounded crisp and decisive. He also sounded white. Featherston knew that didn't necessarily mean anything, though. He'd known plenty of Negroes who could put on white accents. But this voice . . . He scratched his head. He thought he'd heard it before.

"You're in the right place," he answered. "Advance and be recognized." He didn't take his hand off the pistol.

Into the firelight came a small, spruce major and a bedraggled Negro. Jake and the rest of the men in the gun crew scrambled to their feet and stood at attention. The major's pale eyes flashed; a hawk might have wished for such a piercing gaze. Those pale eyes fixed on Jake. "I know you. You're Sergeant Featherston." The fellow spoke with assurance.

"Yes, sir," Featherston said. He *had* met this officer before. "Major Potter, isn't it, sir?"

"That's right. Clarence Potter, Intelligence, Army of Northern Virginia." None too gently, he shoved the Negro up close to the fire. "And since you were here when I last visited the battery, perhaps you will be good enough to confirm for me that this ragged scoundrel"—he shoved the Negro again—"is in fact Pompey, former body servant to your commander, Captain Stuart. Captain Jeb Stuart III, that is." He spoke the battery commander's full name with a certain savage relish.

Everybody in the gun crew stared at the Negro. Jake could make a pretty good guess as to what the men were thinking. He was thinking a lot of the same things himself. But Potter hadn't asked the question of anyone save him. He had to look closely to be certain, then said, "Yes, sir, that's Pompey. He's usually a lot neater and cleaner than he is now, that's all."

"He's been living a little harder lately than he's used to, poor darling." Potter spoke with flaying sarcasm. He pointed to Will Cooper. "You. Private. Go find Captain Stuart and bring him here, wherever he is and whatever he's doing. I don't care if he's got some woman in bed with him—tell him to take it out, get dressed, and get his ass down here."

"Yes, sir," Cooper said, and disappeared.

Pompey spoke up: "I never done nothin' bad to you, did I, Marse Jake?" His voice didn't have the mincing lilt it had carried when he served as Captain Stuart's man. He'd put on airs then, as if he were something special himself because of who his master was.

Before Featherston could answer, Potter's voice cracked like a whiplash: "You keep your mouth shut until I tell you to speak." Pompey nodded, which Jake thought wise. The major was not the sort of man to disobey, most especially not if you were in his power.

Will Cooper came back with Captain Stuart a few minutes later. The captain bore a strong resemblance to his famous father and even more famous grandfather, except that, instead of their full beards, he wore a mustache and a little tuft of hair under his lower lip, giving him the look of a seventeenth-century French soldier of fortune.

"Captain," Major Potter said, as he had to Jake Featherston, "is this nigger here your man Pompey?"

"Yes, he's my servant," Stuart replied after a moment; he'd needed a second look to be certain, too. "What is the meaning of—?"

"Shut up, Captain Stuart," Potter interrupted, as harshly as he had when Pompey spoke without his leave. Jake's eyes widened. Nobody had ever addressed Jeb Stuart III that way in his presence. Jeb Stuart, Jr., wore wreathed stars on his collar tabs and was a mighty power in the War Department down in Richmond. But Potter sounded utterly sure of himself: "I'll ask the questions around here."

"Now see here, Major," Stuart said. "I don't care for your tone."

"I don't give a damn, Stuart," Clarence Potter returned. "I was trying to sniff out Red subversion among the niggers attached to this army last year—*last year*, Stuart. And I got information that your nigger Pompey wasn't to be trusted, and I wanted to interrogate him properly. Do you remember that?"

"I did nothing wrong," Stuart said stiffly. But he looked like a man who had just taken a painful wound and was trying to see if he could still stand up.

"No, eh?" The major from Intelligence knocked him down with contemptuous ease. "You didn't talk to your daddy the general? You didn't have me overruled and the investigation quashed? You know better than that, I know better than that—and the War Department knows better than that, too."

Till now, Jake had never seen Captain Stuart at a loss. Whatever else you said about him, he fought his guns as aggressively as any man would like, and showed a contempt for the dangers of the battlefield any hero of the War of Secession would have envied. But he'd never been threatened with loss of status and influence, only death or mutilation. Those latter two might have been easier to face.

"Major, I think you misunderstood—" he began.

"I misunderstood nothing, Captain," Potter said coldly. "I was trying to do my duty, and you prevented that. If you'd been right, you'd have gotten away with it. But this nigger was taken in arms with a band of Red rebels, and every sign is that he wasn't just a fighter. He was a leader in this conspiracy, and had been for a long time. If I'd questioned him last year—but no, you wouldn't let that happen." Potter's headshake was a masterpiece of mockery.

"Pompey?" Stuart shook his head, too, but in amazement. "I can't believe it. I won't believe it."

"Frankly, Captain, I don't give a damn," Potter said. "If I had my way, I'd bust you down to private, give you a rifle, and let you die gloriously charging a Yankee machine gun. Can't have everything, I suppose, no matter how much damage your damn-fool know-it-all attitude cost your country. But your free ride to the top is gone, Stuart, and that's a fact. If you drop dead at ninety-nine and stay in the Army all that time, you'll be buried a captain."

Silence stretched. Into it, Pompey said, "Marse Jeb, I—"

"Shut up," Potter told him. "Get moving." He shoved the Negro on his way. Jeb Stuart III stared after them. Jake Feather-ston studied his battery commander. He didn't quite know what he thought. With Stuart under a cloud, life was liable to get harder for everybody: the captain's name had been one to con-jure with when it came to keeping shells in supply and such. On the other hand, as an overseer's son Jake wasn't sorry to watch an aristocrat taken down a peg. *More chances for me,* he thought, and vowed to make the most of them.

The USS *Dakota* steamed over the beautiful deep-blue waters of the Pacific, somewhere south and west of the Sandwich Is-lands. Sam Carsten was delighted to have the battleship back in fighting trim once more; she had been laid up in a Honolulu dry-dock for months, taking repairs after an unfortunate encounter with a Japanese torpedo.

Carsten admired the deep blue sea. He admired the even bluer sky. He heartily approved of the tropic breezes that kept it from seeming as hot as it really was. The sun that shone brightly down from that blue, blue sky . . .

Try as he would, he couldn't make himself admire the sun. He was very, very fair, with golden hair, blue eyes, and a pink skin that turned red in any weather and would not turn tan for love nor money. When he was serving in San Francisco, he'd thought himself one step this side of heaven, heaven being defined as

Seattle. Honolulu, however pretty it was, made a closer approximation to hell. He'd smeared every sort of lotion known to pharmacist's mate and Chinese apothecary on his hide. None had done the least bit of good.

"Far as I'm concerned, the damn limeys were welcome to keep the Sandwich Islands," he muttered under his breath as he swabbed a stretch of the *Dakota*'s deck. He chuckled wryly. "Somehow, though, folks who outrank me don't give a damn that I sunburn if you look at me cross-eyed. Wonder why that is?"

"Wonder why what is?" asked Vic Crosetti, who was sanitizing the deck not far away and who slept in the bunk above Carsten's. "Wonder why people who outrank a Seaman First don't give a damn about him, or wonder why you look like a piece of meat the galley didn't get done enough?"

"Ahh, shut up, you damn lucky dago," Sam said, more jealousy than rancor in his voice. Crosetti had been born swarthy. All the sun did to him was turn him a color just this side of Negro brown.

"Hey, bein' dark oughta do me *some* good," Crosetti said. No matter what color he was, nobody would ever mistake him for a Negro, not with his nose and thick beard and arms thatched with enough black hair to make him look like a monkey.

Sam dipped his mop in the galvanized bucket and got another stretch of deck clean. He'd been a sailor for six years now, and had mastered the skill of staying busy enough to satisfy officers and even more demanding chief petty officers without really doing anything too closely resembling work. Crosetti wasn't going at it any harder than he was; if the skinny little Italian hadn't been born knowing how to shirk, he'd sure picked up the fundamentals in a hurry after he joined the Navy.

Carsten stared off to port. The destroyer *Jarvis* was frisking through the light chop maybe half a mile away, quick and graceful as a dolphin. Its wake trailed creamy behind it. The *Jarvis* could steam rings around the big, stolid *Dakota*. That was the idea: the destroyer could keep torpedo boats and submersibles away from the battlewagon. That the idea still had some holes in it was attested by the repairs just completed on the *Dakota*.

Crosetti looked out over the water, too. "Might as well relax," he said to Carsten. "Nobody in the Navy's seen hide nor hair of the Japs or the limeys since we got bushwhacked the last time. Stands to reason they're mounting patrols to make sure we ain't goin' near the Philippines or Singapore, same as we're doing here."

"Stood to reason last time, too," Sam answered. "Only thing is, the Japs weren't being reasonable."

Crosetti cocked his head to one side. "Yeah, that's so," he said. "You got a cockeyed way of looking at things that makes a lot of sense sometimes, you know what I'm saying?"

"Maybe," Carsten said. "I've had one or two guys tell me that before, anyway. Now if there was some gal who'd tell me something like that, I'd have something. But hell, gals here, they ain't gonna look past the raw meat." He ran a sunburned hand down an equally sunburned arm.

"If that's the way you think, that's what'll happen to you, yeah," Crosetti said. "It's all in the way you go after 'em, you know what I'm saying? I mean, look at me. I ain't pretty, I ain't rich, but I ain't lonesome, neither, not when I'm on shore. You gotta show 'em they're what you're after, and you gotta make 'em think you're what they're after, too. All how you go about it, and that's a fact."

"Maybe," Sam said again. "But the ones you really want to hook onto, they're the ones who won't bite for a line like that, too."

"Who says?" Crosetti demanded indignantly. Then he paused. "Wait a minute. You're talkin' about gettin' married, for God's sake. What's the point to even worrying about that? You're in the Navy, Sam. No matter what kind of broad you marry, you ain't gonna be home often enough to enjoy it."

Carsten would have argued that, the only difficulty being that he couldn't. So he and Crosetti talked about women for a while instead, no subject being better calculated to help pass time of a morning. Sam didn't really know how much his bunkmate was making up and how much he'd really done, but he'd been blessed with either a hell of a good time or a hell of an imagination.

An aeroplane buzzed by. Sam looked at it anxiously: following a Japanese aeroplane had got the *Dakota* torpedoed. But this one bore the American eagle. It had been out looking for enemy ships. Carsten guessed it hadn't found any. Had it sent back a message by wireless telegraph, the fleet would have changed course toward any vessels presumptuous enough to challenge the USA in these waters.

"You really think the English and the Japanese are just sitting back, waiting for us to come to them?" Sam asked Crosetti. "They could cause a lot of trouble if they took the Sandwich Islands back from us."

"Yeah, they could, but they won't," Crosetti said. "When the president declared war on England, I don't figure he waited five minutes before he sent us sailing for Pearl Harbor. We caught the damn limeys with their drawers down. They hadn't reinforced the place yet, and they couldn't hold it against everything we threw at 'em. But we got more men, more ships there than you can shake a stick at. They want it back, they're gonna hafta pay one hell of a bill."

"That's all true," Carsten said. "But now that we've got all those men there and we've got all those ships there, what are the limeys and the Japs going to think we'll do with 'em? Sit there and hang on tight? Does that sound like Teddy Roosevelt to you? They're going to figure we're heading out toward Singapore and Manila sooner or later unless they do something about it. Even if they don't land on Oahu, they're going to do their damnedest to smash up the fleet, right?"

Vic Crosetti scratched at one cheek while he thought. If Sam had done anything like that, he probably would have drawn blood from his poor, sunbaked skin. After a bit, Crosetti gave him a thoughtful nod. "Makes pretty good sense, I guess. How come the only stripe you got on your sleeve is a service mark? Way you talk, you oughta be a captain, maybe an admiral in one of those damnfool hats they wear."

Carsten laughed out loud. "All I got to say is, if they're so hard up they make *me* an admiral, the USA is in a hell of a lot more trouble than the Japs are."

The grin that stretched across Crosetti's face was altogether impudent. "I ain't gonna argue with you about that," he said, whereupon Sam made as if to wallop him over the head with his mop. They both laughed. Crosetti grew serious, though, unwontedly fast. "You do talk like an officer a lot of the time, you know that?"

"Do I?" Carsten said. His fellow swabbie—at the moment, in

the most literal sense of the word—nodded. Sam thought about it. "Can't worry about chasing women all the damned time. You got to keep your eyes open. You look around, you start seeing things."

"I see a couple of lazy lugs, is what I see," a deep voice behind them said. Sam turned his head. There stood Hiram Kidde, gunner's mate on the five-inch cannon Carsten helped serve. He had plenty of service stripes on his sleeve, having been in the Navy for more than twenty years. He went on, "Go ahead, try and tell me you were workin' hard."

"Have a heart, 'Cap'n,' " Carsten said, using Kidde's universal nickname. "Can't expect us to be busy every second."

"Who says I can't?" Kidde retorted. He was broad-faced and stocky, thick through the middle but not soft. He looked like a man you wouldn't want to run into in a barroom brawl. From what Sam had seen of him in action, his looks weren't deceiving.

"Petty officers never remember what it was like when they were seamen," Crosetti said. He looked sly. " 'Course, it is kind of hard remembering back to when Buchanan was president."

Kidde glared at him. Then he shrugged. "Hell, I figured you were gonna say, when Jefferson was president." Shaking his head, he walked on.

"Got him good, Vic," Carsten said. Crosetti grinned and nodded. They went back to swabbing the deck—still not working too hard.

Jefferson Pinkard kissed his wife, Emily, as she headed out the door of their yellow-painted company house to go to the munitions plant where she'd been working the past year. "Be careful, honey," he said. He meant that a couple of ways. For one, her usually fair skin was still sallow from the jaundice working with some of the explosives caused. For another, riding the trolley in Birmingham, as in a lot of cities in the Confederacy these days, was something less than safe.

"I will," she promised, as she did whenever he warned her. She tossed her head. These days, she'd cut her strawberry-blond hair short, to keep it from getting caught in the machinery with which she worked. Jeff missed the braid she'd worn halfway down her back. She kissed him again, a quick peck on the lips. "I got to go."

"I know," he said. "You may get home a little before me tonight—I got to vote, remember."

"I know it's today," she agreed. She gave him a sidelong look. "One of these days, I reckon I'll be voting, too, so you won't have to remind me about it."

He sighed and shrugged. It wasn't worth an argument. She'd come up with more radical ideas since she started working than in all the time they'd been married up till then. She hurried off toward the trolley. He stood in the doorway for half a minute or so, watching her walk. He would have forgiven a lot of radical ideas from a woman who moved her hips like that. It gave him something to look forward to when he came home from work.

Because the company housing was only a few hundred yards away from the Sloss foundry, he didn't have to leave as soon as his wife did to get to work on time. He went back in, finished his coffee and ham and eggs, set the dishes to soak in soapy water in the sink, grabbed his dinner pail, and then headed out the door himself.

As he walked into the foundry, he waved to men he knew. There weren't that many, not any more: most of the whites in the Sloss labor force had already been conscripted. Every time he opened his own mailbox, Pinkard expected to find the buff-colored envelope summoning him to the colors, too. He sometimes wondered if they'd lost his file.

Along with the white men in overalls and caps came a stream of black men dressed the same way. Many of them, nowadays, were doing jobs to which they wouldn't have dared aspire when the war began, jobs that had been reserved for whites till the front drained off too many. They still weren't getting white men's pay, but they were making more than they had before.

Pinkard had been working alongside a Negro for a good long while now. Though he'd hated the notion at first, he'd since come to take it for granted—until the uprising had broken out the month before. Leonidas, the buck he was working with these days, had kept right on coming in, uprisings or no uprisings. That would have made Pinkard happier, though, had Leonidas shown the least trace of brains concealed anywhere about his person.

He went into the foundry and out onto the floor. The racket, as always, was appalling. You couldn't shout over it; you had to learn to talk—and to hear—under it. When it was cold outside, it was hot in there, hot with the heat of molten metal. When it was hot outside, the foundry floor made a pretty good foretaste of hell. It smelled of iron and coal smoke and sweat.

Two Negroes waited for him: night shift had started hiring blacks well before they got onto the day crew. One was Agrippa, the other a fellow named Sallust, who didn't have a permanent slot of his own but filled in when somebody else didn't show up.

Seeing Sallust made Jeff scratch his head. "Where's Vespasian at?" he asked Agrippa. "I don't ever remember him missin' a shift. He ain't shiftless, like that damn Leonidas." He laughed at his own wit. Then, after a moment, he stopped laughing. Leonidas *was* shiftless, and, at the moment, late, too.

Agrippa didn't laugh. He was in his thirties, older than Pinkard, and right now he looked older than that—he looked fifty if a day. His voice was heavy and slow and sober as he answered, "Reason he ain't here, Mistuh Pinkard, is on account of they done hanged Pericles yesterday. Pericles was his wife's kin, you know, an' he stayed home to help take care o'—things."

"Hanged him?" Pinkard said. "Lord!" Pericles had been in jail as an insurrectionist for months. Before that, he'd worked alongside the white man in the place Leonidas had now. He'd been a damn sight better at it than Leonidas, too. Pinkard shook his head. "That's too damn bad. Maybe he was a Red, but he was a damn fine steel man."

"I tell Vespasian you say dat," Agrippa said. "He be glad to hear it." Sallust sent him a hooded glance. Pinkard had seen its like before. It meant something on the order of, *Go on, tell the white man what he wants to hear.* Very slightly, as if to say he meant his words, Agrippa shook his head.

The two black men from the night shift left. Jeff got to work. He had to work harder without Leonidas around, but he worked better, too, because he didn't have to keep an eye on his inept partner. One of these days, Leonidas would be standing in the wrong place, and they'd pour a whole great crucible full of molten metal down on his empty head. The only things left would be a brief stink of burnt meat and a batch of steel that needed resmelting because it had picked up too much carbon.

Leonidas came strutting onto the floor twenty minutes late. "Lord, the girl I found me las' night!" he said, and ran his tongue across his lips like a cat after a visit to a bowl of cream. He rocked his hips forward and back. He was always talking about women or illegal whiskey. A lot of men did that, but most of them did their jobs better than Leonidas, which meant their talk about what they did when they weren't working was somehow less annoying.

Pinkard tossed him a rake. "Come on, let's straighten up the edges of that mold in the sand pit," he said. "We don't want the metal leaking out when they do the next pouring."

Leonidas rolled his eyes. He couldn't have cared less what the metal did in the next pouring, and didn't care who knew it. Without the war, he would have had trouble getting a janitor's job at the Sloss works; as things were, he'd been out here with Pinkard for months. *One more reason to hate the war,* Jeff thought.

He kept Leonidas from getting killed, and so wondered, as he often did, whether that made the day a success or a failure. Pericles, now, Pericles had been a good worker, and smart as a white man. But he'd also been a Red, and now he was a dead Red. A lot of the smart Negroes were Reds. Pinkard supposed that meant they weren't as smart as they thought they were.

When the quitting whistle blew, he headed out of the foundry with barely a good-bye to Leonidas. That was partly because he didn't have any use for Leonidas and partly because he was heading off to vote and Leonidas wasn't. Given what Leonidas used for brains, that didn't break Jeff's heart, but rubbing the black man's nose in it at a time like this seemed less than clever.

Sometimes a couple of weeks would go by between times when Jefferson Pinkard left company grounds. He spent a lot of time in the foundry, his friends—those who weren't in the Army—lived in company housing as he did, and the company store was conveniently close and gave credit, even if it did charge more than the shops closer to the center of town.

The polling place, though, was at a Veterans of the War of Secession hall a couple of blocks in from the edge of company land. He saw two or three burnt-out buildings as he went along. Emily had seen more damage from the uprising than he had, because she took the trolley every day. He shook his head. Steelworkers armed with clubs and a few guns had kept the rampaging Negroes off Sloss land; the black workers, or almost all of them, had stayed quiet. They knew which side their bread was buttered on.

A line of white men, a lot of them in dirty overalls like Pinkard's, snaked out of the veterans' hall, above which flapped the Stars and Bars. He took his place, dug a stogie out of his pocket, lighted it, and blew out a happy cloud of smoke. If he had to move slowly for a bit, he'd enjoy it.

By their white hair and beards, the officials at the polling place were War of Secession veterans themselves. "Pinkard, Jefferson Davis," Jeff said when he got to the head of the line. He took his ballot and went into a booth. Without hesitation, he voted for Gabriel Semmes over Doroteo Arango for president; as Woodrow Wilson's vice president, Semmes would keep the Confederacy on a steady course, while Arango was nothing but a wild-eyed, hot-blooded southerner. Jeff methodically went through the rest of the national, state, and local offices, then came out and pushed his ballot through the slot of the big wood ballot box.

"Mr. Pinkard has voted," one of the elderly precinct workers said, and Pinkard felt proud at having done his democratic duty.

He walked home still suffused with that warm sense of virtue. If you didn't vote, you had no one to blame but yourself for what happened to the country—unless, of course, you were black, or a woman. And one of these years, the way things looked, they'd probably let women have a go at the ballot box, no matter what he thought about it. He supposed the world wouldn't end.

Emily came out onto the porch as he hurried up the walk toward the house. "Hi, darlin'!" he called. Then he saw the buff-colored envelope she was holding.

III

Lieutenant Nicholas H. Kincaid raised a forefinger. "Another cup of coffee for me here, if you please," the Confederate cavalry officer said.

"I'll take care of it," Nellie Semphroch said quickly, before her daughter Edna could. Edna glared at her. Half the reason Kincaid came into the coffeehouse the two women ran in occupied Washington, D.C., was to moon over Edna, his eyes as big and glassy as those of a calf with the bloat.

That was also all the reason Nellie tried to keep Edna as far away from Kincaid as she could. She'd caught them kissing once, and who could say where that would have led if she hadn't put a stop to it in a hurry? She shook her head. She knew where it would have led. She'd been down that path herself, and didn't intend to let Edna take it.

Edna filled a cup with the blend from the Dutch East Indies that Kincaid liked, set the cup on a saucer, and handed it to Nellie. "Here you are, Ma," she said, her voice poisonously sweet. She knew better than to argue out loud with Nellie when the coffeehouse was full of customers, as it was this afternoon. That didn't mean she wasn't angry. Far from it.

Nellie Semphroch glared back at her, full of angry determination herself. Given a generation's difference in their ages—a short generation's difference—the two women looked very much alike. They shared light brown hair (though Nellie's had some streaks of gray in it), oval faces, fine, fair skin, and eyes somewhere between blue and green. If Nellie's expression was habitually worried, well, she'd earned that. In this day and age, if you were an adult and you didn't have plenty to worry about, something was wrong with you.

She carried the steaming cup over to Lieutenant Kincaid. "Obliged, ma'am," he said. He was polite, when he could easily have been anything but. And, when he dug in his pocket, he put a real silver quarter-dollar on the table, not the Confederate scrip that let Rebel officers live like lords in the conquered capital of the USA.

Outside in the middle distance, a sudden volley of rifle shots rang out. Nellie jumped. She'd been through worse when the Confederates shelled Washington and then fought their way into town, but she'd let herself relax since: that had been well over a year ago now.

"Nothin' to worry about, ma'am," Kincaid said after sipping at the coffee. "That's just the firing squad getting rid of a nigger. Waste of bullets, you ask me. Ought to string the bastards up. That'd be the end of that."

"Yes," Nellie said. She didn't really like talking with Kincaid. It encouraged him, and he didn't need encouragement to come around. But Confederate soldiers and military police were the only law and order Washington had these days. The Negro rebellion that had tried to catch fire here hadn't been against the CSA alone; a good part of the fury had been aimed at whites in general.

Kincaid said, "Those niggers were damn fools—beg your pardon, ma'am—to try givin' us trouble here. Places where they're still in arms against the CSA are places where there weren't any soldiers to speak of. They take a deal of rooting out from places like that, on account of we can't empty our lines against you Yankees to go back and get 'em. But here—we got plenty of soldiers here, coming and going and staying. Why, we got three regiments comin' in tonight, back from whipping the Reds in Mississippi and heading up to the Maryland front. And it's like that every day of the year. Sometimes I don't think niggers is anything but a pack of fools."

"Yes," Nellie said again. *Three regiments in from Mississippi, going up to Maryland.* Hal Jacobs, who had a little bootmaking and shoe-repair business across the street, had ways of getting such tidbits to people in the USA who could do something useful with them.

"Bring me another sandwich here, ma'am?" a Confederate

captain at a far table called. Nellie hurried over to serve him. Despite the rationing that made most of Washington a gray, joyless place, she never had trouble getting her hands on good food and good coffee. Of themselves, her eyes went across the street for a moment. She didn't know exactly what connections Mr. Jacobs had, but they were good ones. And he liked having the coffeehouse full of Confederates talking at the top of their lungs—or even quietly, so long as they talked freely.

"You had a ham and cheese there?" she asked. The captain nodded. She hurried back of the counter to fix it for him.

Nicholas H. Kincaid was not without resource. He gulped down the coffee Nellie had given him and asked for another refill while she was still making the sandwich. That meant Edna had to take care of him. Not only did she bring him the coffee, she sat down at the table with him and started an animated conversation. The person to whom she was really telling something was Nellie, and the message was simple: *I'll do whatever I please.*

Seething inside, Nellie sliced bread, ham, and cheese with mechanical competence. She wished she could haul off and give her daughter a good clout in the ear, but Edna was past twenty, so how much good could it do? *Why don't young folks listen to people who know better?* she mourned silently, forgetting how little she'd listened to anyone at the same age.

She took the sandwich over to the captain, accepted his scrip with an inward sigh, and was about to head back behind the counter when the door opened and a new customer came in. Unlike most of her clientele, he was neither a Confederate soldier nor one of the plump, clever businessmen who hadn't let a change of rulers in Washington keep them from turning a profit. He was about fifty, maybe a few years past, with a black overcoat that had seen better times, a derby about which the same could be said, and a couple of days' stubble on his chin and cheeks. He picked a table near the doorway, and sat with his back against the wall.

When Nellie came over to him, he breathed whiskey fumes up into her face. She ignored them. "I thought I told you never to show your face in here again," she said in a furious whisper.

"Oh, Little Nell, you don't have to be that way," he answered. His voice, unlike his appearance, was far from seedy: he sounded ready for anything. His eyes traveled the length of her, up and down. "You're still one fine-looking woman, you know that?" he said, as if he'd seen right through the respectable gray wool dress she wore.

Her face heated. Bill Reach knew what she looked like under that dress, sure enough, or he knew what she had looked like under her clothes, back when she'd been younger than Edna was now. She hadn't seen him since, or wanted to, till he'd shown up at the coffeehouse one day a few months before. Then she'd managed to frighten him off, and hoped he was gone for good. Now—

"If you don't get out of here right now," she said, "I'm going to let these officers here know you're bothering a lady. Confederates are gentlemen. They don't like that." *Except when they're trying to get you into bed themselves.*

Reach laughed, showing bad teeth. It looked like a good-natured laugh—unless you were on the receiving end of it. "I don't think you'll do that."

"Oh? And why don't you?" She might be betraying Rebel information to Hal Jacobs, but that didn't mean she'd be shy about using Confederate officers to protect herself from Bill Reach and whatever he wanted.

But then he said, "Why? Oh, I don't know. A little bird told me—a little homing pigeon, you might say."

For a couple of seconds, that meant nothing to Nellie. Then it did, and froze her with apprehension. One of Mr. Jacobs' friends was a fancier of homing pigeons. He used them to get information out of Washington and into the hands of U.S. authorities. If Bill Reach knew about that—"What do you want?" Nellie had to force the words out through stiff lips.

Now the smile was more like a leer. "For now, a cup of coffee and a chicken-salad sandwich," he answered. "Anything else I have in mind, you couldn't bring me to the table."

Men, Nellie thought, a one-word condemnation of half the human race. *All they want is that. Well, he's not going to get it.* "I'll bring you your food and the coffee," she said, and then, to show him—to try to show him—she wasn't intimidated, she added, "That will be a dollar fifteen."

Silver jingled in his pocket. He set a dollar and a quarter on the table—real money, no scrip. He'd looked seedy the last time she'd seen him, too, but he hadn't had any trouble paying her high prices then, either. She scooped up the coins and started back toward the counter.

She almost ran into Edna. "I'm sorry, Ma," her daughter said, continuing in a low voice, "I wondered if you were having trouble with that guy."

"It's all right," Nellie said. It wasn't all right, or even close to all right, but she didn't want Edna getting a look at the skeletons in her closet. Edna was hard enough to manage as things were. One of the things that helped keep her in line was the tone of moral superiority Nellie took. If she couldn't take that tone any more, she didn't know what she'd do.

And then, from behind her, Bill Reach said, "Sure is a pretty daughter you have there, Nell."

"Thank you," Nellie said tonelessly. Edna looked bemused, but Nellie hoped that was because Reach's appearance failed to match the other customers'. At least he hadn't called her *Little Nell* in front of Edna. The most unwanted pet name brought the days when he'd known her back to all too vivid life.

"I'd be proud if she was my daughter," Reach said.

That was too much to be borne. "Well, she isn't," Nellie answered, almost certain she was right.

The cold north wind whipped down across the Ohio River and through the Covington, Kentucky, wharves. Cincinnatus felt it in his ears and on his cheeks and in his hands. He wasn't wearing heavy clothes—overalls and a collarless cotton shirt under them—but he was sweating rather than shivering in spite of the nasty weather. Longshoreman's work was never easy. Longshoreman's work when Lieutenant Kennan was bossing your crew was ten times worse.

Kennan swaggered up and down the wharf as if the green-gray uniform he wore turned him into the Lord Jehovah. "Come on, you goddamn lazy niggers!" he shouted. "Got to move, by God you do. *Get* your black asses humping. You there!" The shout wasn't directed at Cincinnatus. "You don't do like you're told, you don't work here. Jesus Christ, them Rebs were fools for ever setting you dumb coons free. You don't deserve it."

Another laborer, an older Negro named Herodotus, said to Cincinnatus, "I'd like to pinch that little bastard's head right off, I would."

"You got a long line in front of you," Cincinnatus answered, both of them speaking too quietly for the U.S. lieutenant to hear. Herodotus chuckled under his breath. Cincinnatus went on, "Hell of it is, he'd get more work if he didn't treat us like we was out in the cotton fields in slavery days." Those days had ended a few years before he was born, but he had plenty of stories to give him a notion of what they'd been like.

"Probably the only way he knows to deal wid us," Herodotus said.

Cincinnatus sighed, picked up his end of a crate, and nodded. "Ain't that many black folks up in the USA," he said. "They mostly didn't want us before the War of Secession, an' they kep' us out afterwards, on account of we was from a different country then. Me, I keep wonderin' if Kennan ever set eyes on anybody who wasn't white 'fore he got this job."

Herodotus just shrugged. He did the work Kennan set him, he groused about it when it was too hard or when he was feeling ornery, and that was that. He didn't think any harder than he had to, he couldn't read or write, and he'd never shown any great desire to learn. Saying he was content as a beast of burden overstated the case, but not by too much.

Cincinnatus, now, Cincinnatus had ambition. An ambitious Negro in the CSA was asking for a broken heart, but he'd done everything he could to make life better for himself and his wife, Elizabeth. When the USA seized Covington, he'd hoped things would get better; U.S. law didn't come down on Negroes nearly so hard as Confederate law did. But he'd discovered Lieutenant Kennan was far from the only white man from the USA who had no more use for blacks than did the harshest Confederate.

Along with Herodotus, he hauled the crate from the barge to a waiting truck. He could have driven that truck, freeing a U.S. soldier to fight; he'd been a driver before the war started. But the Yankees wouldn't let him get behind the wheel of a truck, for no better reason he could see than that he had a black skin. That struck him as stupid and wasteful, but how was he supposed to convince the occupying authorities? The plain answer was, he couldn't.

And so he did what he had to do to get along. He and Elizabeth had a son now. Better yet, Achilles was sleeping through the night most of the time, so Cincinnatus didn't stagger into work feeling three-quarters dead most mornings. He thanked Jesus for that, because what he did was plenty to wear him out all by itself, without any help from a squalling infant.

He and Herodotus finally loaded the day's last crate of ammunition into the last truck and lined up for the paymaster. Along with the usual dollar, they both got the fifty-cent hard-work bonus. The gray-haired sergeant who paid them said, "You boys is taming that Kennan half a dollar at a time, ain't you?"

"Maybe," Herodotus said. Cincinnatus just shrugged. The paymaster wasn't a bad fellow, but he didn't feel easy about trusting any white man, even one who criticized a comrade.

Herodotus spent a nickel of his bonus on trolley fare and headed for home in a hurry. Cincinnatus had always saved money, even before he had a child, so he walked through Covington on his way to the colored district that lay alongside the Licking River.

Walking through Covington was walking through a minefield of resentments. The Stars and Stripes floated over the city hall and all the police stations. Troops in green-gray uniforms were not just visible; they were conspicuous. The Yankees had the town, and they aimed to keep it.

Some local whites did business with them, too. With Cincinnati right across the Ohio, Covington had been doing business with the USA for as long as Kentucky had been in Confederate hands. But more than once, Cincinnatus saw whites cross the street when U.S. soldiers came by, for no better reason he could find than that they didn't want to walk where the men they called damnyankees had set their feet.

Cincinnatus didn't worry about that. He walked past Joe Conroy's general store. The white storekeeper saw him, but pretended he didn't. Nor was there any advertising notice taped to the lower left-hand corner of Conroy's window. That meant neither Conroy nor Tom Kennedy, who had been Cincinnatus' boss before the war and was now a fugitive from the Yankees, wanted to talk with him tonight.

"And that's a damn good thing," he muttered under his breath, "on account of I don't want to talk with them, neither." If he hadn't hidden Tom Kennedy when a U.S. patrol was after him, he never would have been drawn into the Confederate underground that still functioned in Covington and, he supposed, in other Yankee-occupied parts of the CSA as well.

He shook his head. If the U.S. soldiers had just treated Negroes like ordinary human beings, they would have won them over in short order. It hadn't happened; it didn't seem to have occurred to anyone that it should happen. And so he found himself, though far from in love with the government that had been driven out of these parts, no less unhappy with the regime replacing it. *As if life wasn't hard enough,* he thought.

After a while, the big white clapboard houses and wide lawns of the white part of town gave way to smaller, dingier homes packed tightly together, the mark of a Negro district in any town in the Confederate States of America. The paving on a lot of the streets here was bad. The paving on the rest of the streets did not exist at all.

Boys in battered kneepants kicked a football up and down one dirt street. One of them threw it ahead to another, who caught it and ran a long way before he was dragged down. "Yankee rules!" the two of them shouted gleefully. As football had been played in the Confederacy, forward passes were illegal. North of the Ohio, things had been different. This wasn't the first such pass Cincinnatus had seen thrown. The U.S. game was catching on here.

He walked past a whitewashed picket fence. Like fresh blood, red paint had been daubed here and there on the whitewash. A couple of houses farther on, he came to another fence similarly defaced. On the side of a shack that nobody lived in, somebody had painted REVOLUTION in big, crimson letters, and a crude sketch of a broken chain beside the word.

"Ain't nobody happy," Cincinnatus muttered. Whites in Covington hated the U.S. occupiers who kept them apart from the Confederacy most of them held dear. Blacks in Covington hated the U.S. occupiers who kept them from joining the uprising against the Confederacy most of them despised.

He turned a corner. He was only a couple of blocks from home now. Being an up-and-coming man, he lived on a street that was paved and that boasted real concrete sidewalks. That meant horses and mules drawing wagons and buggies didn't step on the wreaths there, and meant that the blood on the sidewalk, though it had gone brown rather than crimson and looked gray, almost black, in the deepening twilight, had not been washed away by rain.

He kicked at the sidewalk with his shabby shoes. Yankee soldiers didn't hesitate to shoot down Negroes aflame with the beauty of the notion of the dictatorship of the proletariat. Maybe the revolution would succeed down in the Confederacy, with so many armed whites having to stay in place and fight the USA. It would not work here, not now, not yet.

A kerosene lamp burned in the front window of his house. The savory smell of chicken stew wafted out toward him. All at once, he could feel how tired—and how cold—he was. As he hurried up the walk toward the front door, it opened. His mother came out.

His wife was right behind, Achilles in her arms. "You sure you won't stay for supper, Mother Livia?" Elizabeth asked.

Cincinnatus' mother shook her graying head. "That's all right, child," she said. "I got my own man to take care of now—he be gettin' home about this time. Got some good pork sausages I can do up quick, and fry some potatoes in the grease. I see you in the mornin'." She paused to kiss her son on the cheek, then headed back to her own house a few blocks away.

Achilles smiled a large, one-tooth smile at his father. Cincinnatus smiled back, which made the baby's smile get larger. Elizabeth turned and went back into the house. Cincinnatus came with her. He shut the door, then gave her a quick kiss.

Standing in the short front hallway, they looked at each other. Elizabeth looked worn; she'd put in a full day as a domestic while her mother-in-law watched the baby. No sooner had that thought crossed his mind than she said, "You look beat, honey."

"Could be," he admitted. "That Kennan, he'd be happier if they gave him a bullwhip for us, but what can you do?" He pulled money out of his overalls. "Got me the bonus again, anyways."

"Good news," she said, and then, "Come on into the kitchen. Supper's just about ready."

Cincinnatus dug in with a will. The way he worked, he needed to eat hearty. "That's right good," he said, and without missing a beat added, "but it ain't a patch on yours." That made Elizabeth look happy. Cincinnatus had learned better than to praise his mother's cooking at the expense of his wife's.

He played with Achilles in the front room while Elizabeth washed supper dishes. The baby could roll over but couldn't crawl yet. He thought peekaboo was the funniest game in the world. Cincinnatus wondered what went on inside that little head. When he covered his face with his hands, did Achilles think he'd disappeared? By the way the baby laughed and laughed, maybe he did.

Elizabeth came out, sniffed, gave Cincinnatus a reproachful stare, and went off to change Achilles. When she came back she sat down in the rocking chair to nurse the baby. She didn't have a lot of milk left, but enough to feed him in the evening before he went to sleep and sometimes in the morning when they first got up, too.

He fell asleep now. The tip of her breast slid out of his mouth. Cincinnatus eyed it till she pulled her dress back up over her shoulder. He'd thought he was too beat to try to get her in the mood for making love tonight, but maybe he'd been wrong. When she carried Achilles off to his cradle, Cincinnatus' gaze followed her. She noticed, and smiled back over her shoulder. Maybe she wouldn't need too much persuading after all.

She'd just sat down again when somebody knocked on the door. Cincinnatus wondered who it was. Curfew would be coming soon, and U.S. soldiers were especially happy about proving their shoot-to-kill orders were no joke in the black part of town.

Sighing, Cincinnatus opened it, and there stood Lucullus. The young black man, the son of Apicius, the best barbecue chef in a goodly stretch of the Confederacy, had yet to develop his father's formidable bulk. "Here's the ribs you ordered this afternoon," he said, and handed Cincinnatus a package. Before Cincinnatus could say anything, Lucullus had hurried down the walk, climbed into the Kentucky Smoke House delivery wagon, and clucked the mule into motion.

The package was not ribs. Considering what Apicius did with ribs, that sent a pang of regret through Cincinnatus. "What you got?" Elizabeth called. "Who was that, here and gone so quick?"

"Lucullus," Cincinnatus answered. Elizabeth caught her breath. Cincinnatus hefted the package. Though wrapped in old newspaper and twine like Apicius' barbecue, it made a precise rectangle in his hands, and was much heavier than he would have guessed from the size.

A note was attached. *Put in third trash can, Pier 5, before 7 tomorrow,* it said, very much to the point. After reading it, he tore it into small pieces and threw them away. Elizabeth asked no more questions. She took one look at the package, then refused to turn her eyes that way.

Cincinnatus wondered what was under the newspaper. Set type, by the size and startling heft: that was his best guess. Whoever picked it out of the trash can would print it, and the Reds would have themselves another poster or flyer or news sheet or whatever it was.

He shook his head. Being part of the Confederate underground was hard and dangerous. Being part of the Red underground was harder and more dangerous. Being part of both of them at once . . . at the time, all his other choices had looked worse. He wondered how long he could keep juggling, and how bad the smashup would be when he started dropping plates.

"Chow call!" the prison guard in the green-gray uniform shouted. Along with several thousand other captive Confederates, Reginald Bartlett lined up, tin mess kit and spoon in his hand. The guard, like all the guards, wore an overcoat. Reggie wore an ill-fitting butternut tunic and trousers, not really enough to keep him warm in a West Virginia autumn that had not a drop of Indian summer left to it.

Actually, the tunic fit better than it had when he'd got to the prison camp: he was skinnier than he had been. But he had to belt his pants with a piece of rope to keep them from sliding down over what was left of his backside. The boots they'd given him were too big, too; he'd stuffed them with crumpled paper to help keep his feet warm.

"This here prisoner business, it ain't no fun *a*-tall," Jasper Jenkins said. He and Reggie had been captured in the same raid on Confederate trenches east of Big Lick, Virginia. A lot of men from both sides had died in the struggle for the Roanoke valley between the Blue Ridge Mountains and the Alleghenies. A lot more from both sides had been captured. But—

"You never think it's going to happen to you," Reggie agreed. "Maybe if I think real hard, I'll find out it didn't." He gave a whimsical shrug to show he didn't intend that to be taken seriously. He'd always been cheerful, he'd always been good-natured, he'd always been able to make people like him . . . and what had it got him? A third-tier bunk in a damnyankee prison camp. *Maybe I should have been more of a bastard,* he thought. *Couldn't have turned out much worse, could it?*

Jasper Jenkins, on the other hand, *was* more of a bastard, a dark, lanky farmer who looked out for himself first and everybody else later. And here he was, too. So what did that prove?

Jenkins looked around at the prisoners, almost all of them as much alike as so many sheep. "This here war's too big for people, you ask me," he remarked.

"Now why the devil do you say that?" Bartlett asked, deadpan. He and Jenkins both laughed, neither of them happily. The line in which they stood made Reggie think of nothing so much as a trail of ants heading for a sandwich that had been dropped on the ground. Compared to the size of the war in which they'd been engaged, that was about what they were.

"And to think I went and volunteered for this." Jenkins shook his head. "I was a damn fool."

"Yeah, me, too," Reggie agreed. "I was there in Capitol Square in Richmond when President Wilson declared war on the damnyankees. I went and quit my job right on the spot and joined the Army—didn't wait for the regiment I'd been conscripted into to get called up. Figured we'd win the war in a couple of months and go on home. Shows how much I knew, doesn't it?"

"Nobody who didn't live by it knew about the Roanoke then," Jasper Jenkins said. "Wish I didn't know about it now. That damn valley is going to be sucking lives till the end of the war."

"I only wish you were wrong," Bartlett answered.

They snaked toward the front of the line, moving not quite fast enough to stay warm in the chilly breeze. As they drew near the kettles that would feed them, Reggie held his mess tin in front of him with both hands. That was how the rules said you did it. If you didn't follow the rules in every particular, you didn't get fed. The cooks enjoyed finding an excuse not to give a prisoner his rations.

"Miserable bastards," Jenkins muttered under his breath, glaring at the men who wore white aprons over their baggy butternut clothes. But he made sure he kept his voice low, so low that only

Bartlett could hear. If the cooks found out he was complaining about them, they'd find ways to make him sorry.

They were prisoners, too; the USA wasn't about to waste its own men to feed the Confederates it captured. But whoever had thought up the prison-camp system the United States used had been a devilishly sneaky fellow. What better way to remind soldiers in enemy hands what their status was than to make them dependent on the goodwill of the Negroes who had formerly been their laborers and servants?

White teeth shining in their dark faces as they grinned unpleasantly at the men they fed, the cooks ladled stew—heavy on potatoes and cabbage and bits of turnip, thin on meat that was probably horse, or maybe cat, anyhow—into the mess kits. If they liked you, you got yours from the bottom of the pot, where all the good stuff rested. If they didn't, you ate nothing but broth. Complaining did no good, either. The damnyankees backed up the Negroes all the time.

A few men in front of Reggie, a Confederate cursed when he saw what he'd been given. "You stinkin' niggers're tryin' to starve me to death," he snarled. "I'll git you for that if it's the last thing I ever do, so help me God I will."

"Shut up, Kirby," one of his friends told him. "You're just gonna make things worse, you keep going on like that."

That was good advice. The prisoner named Kirby didn't take it. "To hell with all of 'em," he shouted, and shook his fist at the Negro cooks. They didn't say anything. They just looked at him. *Memorizing his face,* Reggie thought. Mr. Kirby was going to be on short commons for a long, long time. He must have known that, too, but he didn't care. Maybe he was already too hungry to care. He went on, "You black sons of bitches think you're so great on account of the damnyankees let you lord it over us'ns. But it don't matter. You're still niggers to them, too."

His friend shoved him along to keep the line moving. If the line didn't move, the prisoners caught hell from the guards. Kirby started cussing all over again when the piece of hardtack he got was both small and full of weevils. *What do you expect, you damn fool?* Bartlett thought, hoping Kirby's outburst wouldn't make the cooks take out their anger on everybody anywhere near the loudmouthed prisoner.

His bowl of stew, when he got it, had a decent amount of real food in with the watery broth. He nodded to the Negro who'd dished it out. "Thanks, Tacitus," he said. The cook nodded back, soberly. Some of the prisoners tried sucking up to the cooks— *acting like niggers themselves,* Reggie thought with distaste—in the hopes of getting better rations. He couldn't make himself do that, and he hadn't seen that it helped, either. Treating them a little better than he would have before he got captured seemed like a good idea, though.

He took the square of hardtack another cook handed him. It wasn't too big, but it wasn't too small, either. He shrugged. It would do. He and Jenkins found a place where the wind wasn't blowing too hard, sat down there, and began to eat.

"Lettin' niggers lord it over white men just ain't right," Jenkins said. "That Kirby fellow knew what he was talkin' about. This here war's over and done with, it's time to pay back what we owe 'em."

"Wonder what it's going to be like when we get home again," Reggie said around a mouthful of potatoes. "Wonder what's going on with the Negro uprising down there."

He and Jasper Jenkins had argued about that for a while. Jenkins had refused to believe blacks could rise up against the whites who had dominated the Confederacy since its founding, and the South before that. But fresh-caught prisoners confirmed at least some of the stories the Yankee guards so gleefully told to the men who had been captured earlier.

Now Jenkins said, "We'll smash the bastards flat, and then we'll go on and smash the damnyankees, too, no matter how long it takes."

Reggie nodded. Inside, though, he wondered. He still wanted to believe everything would turn out all right, but it got harder every day. It had been getting harder since the first time he saw what machine guns did to charging men, no matter whose uniform those men wore. If the war went on long enough, he figured nobody on either side would be left alive.

When he'd finished eating, he took his mess tray over to a barrel of water, waited for his turn, and sluiced the tray around before drying it on his shirttail. He made sure he'd got all the gunk out of the corners. If you came down with food poisoning here . . . well, the prison camp was a bad place, but the hospital next door was worse.

"Work detail!" a Confederate officer bawled. Some men went off to chop firewood, others to clean the latrines, still others to police up the grounds of the camp.

Jasper Jenkins shook his head in bemusement. "Never thought I'd be glad of a chance to work," he said, "but it sure as hell beats standing around doing nothing like we been doin'."

"Yeah," Reggie agreed; like Jenkins, he had no duties today. And when there wasn't anything to do, you just waited for the minutes and the hours to crawl by, and every one of them moved on hands and knees. He'd never imagined the worst part of being a prisoner of war was boredom, but the damnyankees didn't care what their captives did in here, so long as they didn't try to escape and so long as they didn't try to get U.S. soldiers to do anything for them.

"Feel like some cards?" Jenkins asked.

"Not right now, no," Bartlett answered. "I think I'm going to stand here till the dust covers me up. Maybe the Yanks won't notice me any more after that." Jasper Jenkins laughed. He thought Reggie had made a joke. Reggie knew too well he hadn't.

Sergeant Chester Martin cowered in a bombproof shelter in a trench dug through the ruins of what had been Big Lick, Virginia, waiting for the Confederate artillery bombardment to end. The bombproof was thirty feet below ground level; even a shell from an eight-inch gun landing right on top probably wouldn't collapse it. And the Rebels didn't have many heavy artillery pieces, though their light field guns were better than anything the U.S. Army owned.

But a collapsed roof wasn't Martin's worst worry, although his lips skinned back from his teeth whenever a shellburst nearby made the candles jump. Nobody could see the expression on his face, though, not behind the soaked pad of cotton wadding he wore over his mouth and nose. The chemicals in the pad would—with luck—keep poison gas out of his lungs. Without luck . . .

He feared gas more than a direct hit. The dugout that sheltered him from explosives and splinters could be a death trap now, for gas, heavier than air, crept down and concentrated in such places. The USA had started using the deadly stuff several months before the Confederacy could answer in kind, but the Rebs had the knack now.

Sitting there beside him in the flickering near-dark, squeezed up tight against him as a lover, Corporal Paul Andersen muttered something over and over again. The mask he wore muffled the words, but Martin knew what he was saying: "Fucking bastards." He said it a lot. It was a sentiment with which few of the men in the company would have disagreed.

All at once, sudden as a kick in the teeth, the barrage stopped. Martin's stomach knotted in pain. He was senior man in the bombproof. He had to order the men to rush out to their posts—or to stay there. The Rebs were sneaky sons of bitches. Sometimes they'd stop shelling you long enough to draw you out from your cover, then pick up again with redoubled fury once you were more nearly out in the open.

But sometimes they'd send their men at your lines the minute after a barrage ended. If they reached the trenches before your troops got up to the firing steps and the machine guns, you were gone: captured if you got lucky, more likely dead. No wonder his guts knotted. He had to figure out which way to jump, his own life depending on the answer along with everyone else's.

He weighed his choices. *Better to guess wrong about more shelling than about a raid,* he decided. "Out! Out! Out!" The words were muffled and blurry, but nobody had any doubt about what he meant.

Men streamed out of the dugout and ran shouting up the steps cut into the earth. Those steps were full of dirt that had cascaded down from hits up above; enough hits like that and it wouldn't matter whether the bombproof caved in or not, because nobody could escape it anyway.

Clutching his rifle, Martin ran for a firing step, waving for his men to follow him. Sure as hell, here came the Rebels. They didn't move forward yowling like catamounts, not any more. They'd learned better than that. But come on they did.

Martin started shooting at the butternut-clad figures stumbling toward him through no-man's-land. The Rebs went down, not in death or injury so much as to take shelter in shell holes and what had been trenches and were now ruins. In their mud-caked boots, he would have done the same.

Not all of them took refuge. Some kept moving, no doubt thinking their best chance for survival lay in seizing a length of U.S. trench. They might have been right. But then a couple of machine guns added their din to the mix. At that, some of the Confederate soldiers did yell, in horrified dismay. Advancing against rifle fire was expensive, but might be possible. Advancing against machine-gun fire was suicide without the fancy label.

None of the Rebs made it into the trenches. The ones who hadn't fallen broke and made for their own lines. Some of the ones who had fallen lay still. Others twisted and writhed and moaned, out there in no-man's-land. Some U.S. soldiers took pleasure in shooting the Rebs who came out to try to recover their wounded. Some Confederates did the same thing to U.S. soldiers seeking to pick up their comrades.

Martin took off his gas mask. He breathed warily. The air still had a chlorine tang to it, but it didn't make him choke and turn blue. "We threw 'em back," he said. "Not too bad."

Maybe twenty feet down along the firing step, Joe Hammerschmitt suddenly cried out. He dropped his rifle and clutched a hand to his right shoulder. The Springfield fell in the mud. Red started oozing out between his fingers.

He opened his hand for a moment to examine the wound. Once he'd done that, pain warred with exultation on his long, thin face. Exultation won. "Got me a hometowner, looks like," he said happily.

Half the men up there with him made sympathetic noises; the other half looked frankly jealous. Hammerschmitt was going to be out of the firing line for weeks, maybe months, to come, and they still risked not just death but horrible mutilation every day.

"Get him back to the doctors," Martin called. A couple of Hammerschmitt's buddies roughly bandaged the wound and helped him out of the front line of trenches. They got envious looks, too. They weren't going on a long vacation like Joe's, but they were able to escape the worst of the firing till they'd turned him over to the quacks in the rear.

"You take care of yourself, Joe," Specs Peterson told his friend. "Don't let the bugs bite you back at the hospital." Everyone laughed at that. The bugs bit harder in the trenches than anyplace else. Peterson went on, "I'll see if I can't shoot the damn Reb who got you there." For that moment, he looked and sounded altogether serious. Birds who wore glasses were supposed to be peaceable types. Somehow Specs hadn't got the word.

Paul Andersen let out a long sigh. He sat down on the firing step, took off his iron helmet, and ran a dirty hand through his dirty-yellow hair. "Another one of the old boys down," he remarked.

Chester Martin sat down beside him and began to roll a cigarette. "Yeah," he said. "Time this war's finally done, ain't gonna be a lot of people left who went in at the start."

"Don't I wish you were wrong." Andersen touched the two stripes on his sleeve, then the three on Martin's. He didn't say anything. He didn't need to say anything. They'd both been promoted because men senior to them had gone down. One of these days, you had to figure they would go down, too, and fresh-faced kids would inherit their jobs.

Martin lighted the cigarette and sucked in smoke. It rasped his lungs raw. Maybe that was because the U.S. tobacco wasn't so good as the stuff from the CSA that you could get only from Rebel corpses nowadays. Or maybe the chlorine still mixed with the air had something to do with it. Martin didn't know. He didn't care, either. The cigarette eased his nerves.

Back of the line, U.S. artillery opened up on the Confederate forward positions. "Go ahead," Martin exclaimed with the bitterness any veteran comes to feel about the shortcomings of his own side. "Hit the sons of bitches *now*. That's bully, that's what that is. Doesn't do us a damn bit of good. Why didn't you shell them when they were coming up over the top at us?"

Andersen also got out makings for a cigarette. "Damn right," he said while rolling it. " 'Course, that would have done us some good, so we can't have it, now can we?" He leaned forward to get a light from Martin's smoke.

"They were probably getting shelled, too," Martin allowed, trying to be fair.

Paul Andersen wasted no time on such useless efforts. "Poor babies," he said. "Yeah, they get shelled every once in a while. So what? You bring those bastards up to the front line and they'd turn up their toes double quick. Tell me I'm lying—I dare you."

"Can't do it," Martin said. Infantrymen took as an article of faith the notion that nobody else in the Army had a nastier job

than theirs. It was, as far as Martin was concerned, a faith justified by works. He laughed. "At least the artillery fights. You ever
seen a dead cavalryman?"

"Not likely," Andersen exclaimed. "Hey, they're all sitting
back there, living soft and sharpening up their sabers for the
breakthrough."

"The breakthrough we're going to give them," Martin said. He
and his friend laughed. That they would see a breakthrough in
their lifetimes struck both of them as unlikely. That the cavalry
would be able to exploit it if it ever came was even more absurd.
Meditatively, Martin observed, "A horse makes a hell of a target
for a machine gun, you know that?"

"It's a fact, sure enough," Andersen said. They both smoked
on till their cigarette butts were too tiny to hold. Then they tossed
them into the mud at the bottom of the trench.

Rain began pattering down a few minutes later. "Always
comes right after a bombardment," Martin said. That wasn't
strictly true, but shelling and rain did seem to go together. At
first, he welcomed the rain, which washed the last remnants of
poison gas from the air. But it did not let up. It kept raining and
raining and raining, till the trenches went from mud to muck.

Martin ordered men to start laying down boards, so they could
keep moving up and down the trench in spite of the rain. That
would work—for a while. Eventually, if the rain kept up, the
muck would start swallowing the boards. Martin had seen that
the winter before. He'd never expected to spend two winters in
the trenches. But then, when the war started, he hadn't figured on
spending one winter in the trenches.

"Only goes to show," he muttered, and began to fix himself another cigarette. He hadn't known how to keep one going in miserable weather till the war started. He did now. *The sort of talent
I could live without,* he thought as he struck a match and lighted
the cigarette, shielding it from the wet with his cupped hands as
he did so. He sucked in more smoke. As long as he had the talent,
he saw no reason not to use it.

"Come on," Sylvia Enos said to George, Jr., and Mary Jane.
"We're going to be late to the Coal Board if you two don't stop
fooling around."

Her son was five, her daughter two. They didn't understand

why being late for a Coal Board appointment—as with any government appointment in the USA—was a catastrophe, but they did understand *that* it was a catastrophe. They also understood Sylvia would warm their backsides hotter than any coal fire if they made her late. She'd made that very plain.

Taking one of them in each hand, she started to head away from Brigid Coneval's flat, which lay down the hall with the one she and her children had shared with George, Sr., till the Navy sent him off to the Mississippi.

George, Jr., said, "Why can't we stay with Mrs. Coneval? We like staying with Mrs. Coneval." Mary Jane nodded emphatically. She couldn't have said anything so complex, but she agreed with it.

"You can't stay with Mrs. Coneval because she has an appointment with the Coal Board this afternoon, too," Sylvia answered. Had George meant, *We like staying with her better than staying with you*? Sylvia tried not to think about that. She worked all day five days a week and a half-day Saturday like everyone else. That meant her children spent more time awake with Brigid Coneval, who hadn't taken a factory job when her husband was conscripted but made ends meet by caring for the children of women who had, than with their own mother. No wonder they thought the world of her these days.

"Don't wanna go Coal Board," Mary Jane said.

Sylvia Enos sighed. She didn't want to go to the Coal Board, either. "We have to," she said, and let it go at that. The Coal Board, the Meat Board (not that she couldn't evade that one, with her connections to the fishing boats that came into T Wharf), the Flour Board . . . all the bureaucracies that kept life in the United States efficient and organized—if you listened to the people who ran them. If you listened to anyone else, you got another story, but no one in power seemed interested in that tale.

Mary Jane stuck out her plump lower lip, which had a smear of jam beneath it. "No," she said. Being two, she used the word in every possible intonation, with every possible variation on volume.

"Do you want to go to the Coal Board, or would you rather have a spanking?" Sylvia asked. As she'd known it would, that got Mary Jane's attention. Her daughter held still long enough so she could button the girl's coat all the way up to the neck. It was early December, still fall by the calendar, but it felt like winter outside, and a hard winter at that.

George, Jr., had buttoned his own buttons. He was proud of everything he could do on his own, in which he took after his father. He had, unfortunately, buttoned the buttons wrong. Sylvia fixed them quickly, and with as little fuss as she could, nodded to Mrs. Coneval, and took the children downstairs and down to the corner where the trolley stopped.

Had she imagined it, or did Brigid Coneval seem to be looking forward to a trip to the Coal Board offices? Putting up with a dozen or more little ones from before sunup to after sundown had to wear at her nerves; George, Jr., and Mary Jane were often plenty to make Sylvia wish she'd never met her husband, and they were her own flesh and blood. If you didn't sneak into the whiskey bottle while caring for your neighbors' brats, you were a woman of stern stuff.

Out on the street, newsboys wearing caps and wool mufflers against the chill hawked copies of the *Boston Globe* and other local papers. They were shouting about battles in west Texas and Sequoyah, and up in Manitoba, too. Sylvia thought about spending a couple of cents to get one, but decided not to. The black-bordered casualty lists that ran on every front page would only make her sad. So long as the newsboys weren't yelling about gunboat disasters on the Mississippi River, she knew everything about the war that mattered to her.

She clambered onto the trolley and put a nickel in the fare box. The driver cast a dubious eye at George, Jr. "He's only five," Sylvia said. The driver shrugged and waved her on. She was having to say that more and more. Next year, she'd have to pay her son's fare, too. When every five cents counted, that hurt.

"Coal Board!" the trolley man shouted, pulling up to the stop half a block away from the frowning gray-brown sandstone building. As if by magic, his car nearly emptied itself. It filled again a moment later, when people who had already arranged for their coming month's ration climbed aboard to go home.

"It didn't used to be this way," an old man complained to his wife as Sylvia shepherded the children past them. "Back before the Second Mexican War, we—"

Distance and the crowd kept Sylvia from hearing the rest of that. It mattered little. She knew how the old man would have gone on. Her own mother had always said the same sort of thing. Back in the 1870s, the USA hadn't been full of Boards watching every piece of everybody's life and making sure all the pieces fit together in a way that worked best for the government. Back then, the CSA, England, and France had humiliated the United States only once, in the War of Secession, and people figured it was a fluke. After the second time, though, it seemed pretty obvious that the only way to fight back was to organize to the hilt. Thus conscription, thus the Boards, thus endless lines and endless forms . . .

Coal Board forms were stacked in neat piles, a whole array of them, on a long table just inside the entrance. Sylvia started to reach for the one that said, ENTIRE FAMILY DWELLING IN SAME LIVING QUARTERS. She jerked her hand away. That hadn't been the right form for some months now. Instead, she grabbed the one reading, FAMILY MEMBER ON MILITARY SERVICE.

She sat down on one of the hard, uncomfortable chairs in the vast office. After fishing a cloth doll out of her handbag for Mary Jane and a couple of wooden soldiers painted green-gray for George, Jr., she guddled around in there till she found a pen and a bottle of ink. Normally, she would have contented herself with a pencil, if anything, but since the start of the war all the Boards had grown insistent on ink.

The form was long enough to have been folded over on itself four different times. As she did each month, she filled out the intimate details of her family's life: ages, address, square footage, location of absent member(s), and on and on and on. She wished the bureaucrats could remember from one month to the next what she'd put down the month before. That didn't seem to be in the cards, although, if you invented a palace for yourself so you could get a bigger coal ration, they generally did find out about that, whereupon you wished you hadn't.

"Come on," she said to the children. They got into the line appropriate to the form. It was, naturally, the longest line in the entire office: conscription had made sure of that. Up at the distant front, a clerk standing behind a tall marble counter like that of a bank examined each form in turn. When satisfied, he plied a rubber stamp with might and main: *thock! thock! thock!*

"Wonder what's keeping *him* out of the Army," the middle-aged woman in front of Sylvia muttered under her breath.

"When they start conscripting clerks, you'll know the war is as good as lost," Sylvia said with great conviction. The woman in front of her nodded, the ragged silk flowers on her battered old picture hat waving up and down.

The line inched forward. Sylvia supposed she should have been grateful the Coal Board offices stayed open all day Saturday. Without that, she would have had to leave work at the fish-canning plant in the middle of some weekday, which would not have made her bosses happy about her. Of course, she would have been far from the only one with such a need, so what could they have done? Without coal, how were you supposed to cook and to heat your house or flat?

When she was three people away from pushing her form over the high counter to the clerk behind it, paying her money, and collecting the ration tickets she'd need for the month ahead, the woman whose turn it was got into a disagreement with the clerk. "That's not right!" she shouted in an Italian accent. "You think you can cheat me on account of I don't know much English? I tell you this—" Whatever *this* was, it was in Italian, and Italian so electrifying that a couple of women who not only heard but also understood it crossed themselves.

It rolled off the clerk like seawater down an oilcloth. "I'm sorry, Mrs., uh, Vegetti, but I have applied the policy pertaining to unrelated boarders correctly, as warranted by the facts stated on your form there," he said.

"Lousy thief! Stinking liar!" The rest was more Italian, even more incandescent than what had gone before. People from all over the Coal Board offices were staring at anyone bold enough to vent her feelings in that way before the representative of such a powerful organ of government.

The clerk listened to the stream of abuse for perhaps a minute. So, wide-eyed, did George, Jr. "What's she saying, Mama?" he asked. "She sure sounds mad, whatever it is."

"I don't understand the words myself," Sylvia answered, relieved at being able to tell the literal truth.

Clang! Clang! The clerk had heard enough. When he rang the bell, a couple of policemen came up to the irate Italian woman. One of them put a hand on her shoulder. *Wham!* She hauled off and hit him with her handbag. The two cops grabbed her and hustled her out of the office. She screeched every inch of the way. "Shut up, you noisy hag!" one of the policemen shouted at her. "No coal for you this month!"

A sigh ran through the big room. The woman in front of Sylvia said, "It would almost be worth it to have the chance to tell the no-good rubber stampers what you really think of them."

"Almost," Sylvia agreed wistfully. But that was the operative word. The Italian woman was going to lose a month's fuel for the sake of a few minutes' pleasure. Like a foolish woman who fell into immorality, she wasn't thinking far enough ahead.

Sylvia smiled. There were temptations, and then there were temptations. . . .

At last, she reached the head of the line. The clerk took her form, studied it with methodical care, and spoke in a rapid drone: "Do you swear that the information contained herein is the truth, the whole truth, and nothing but the truth, knowing false statements are liable to the penalty for perjury?"

"I do," Sylvia said, just as she had when the preacher asked her if she took George as her lawful wedded husband.

Thock! Thock! Thock! The rubber stamp did its work, a consummation less enjoyable than the one that had followed the earlier *I do.* But then George had heated her only through the wedding night. The Coal Board clerk would let her keep herself and her children warm all month long.

She passed money over the counter, receiving in return a strip of ration tickets, each good for twenty pounds of coal. The clerk said, "Be ready for a ration decrease or a price increase, or maybe both, next month."

Nodding, she took George, Jr., and Mary Jane by the hand and headed out of the office. *Be ready,* the clerk had said. He made it sound easy. But where was the extra money supposed to come from? What was she supposed to do if they didn't—couldn't— give her enough coal for both cooking and heating?

The clerk didn't care. It wasn't his problem. "Come on," she told her children. Like all the others the war caused, the problem was hers. One way or another, she would have to deal with it.

Outside the farmhouse, the wind howled like a wild thing. Here on the Manitoban prairie, it had a long running start. Arthur McGregor was glad he wouldn't have to go out in it any time soon. He had plenty of food; the locusts in green-gray hadn't been so thorough in their plundering as they had the winter before.

He even had plenty of kerosene for his lamps. Henry Gibbon, the storekeeper over in Rosenfeld, had discovered a surefire way to cheat the Yankees' rationing system. McGregor didn't know what it was, but he was willing to take advantage of it. Cheating the Americans was almost like soldiers making a successful raid on their lines, up farther north.

As if picking that thought right out of his head, his son Alexander said, "The Yanks still don't have Winnipeg, Pa." At fifteen, Alexander looked old enough to be conscripted. He was leaner than his father, and fairer, too, with brown hair that partly recalled his mother Maude's auburn curls. Arthur McGregor might have been taken for a black Irishman had his craggy features not been so emphatically Scots.

"Not after a year and a half of trying," he agreed now. "The troops from the mother country helped us hold 'em back. And as long as we have Winnipeg—"

"We have Canada," Alexander finished for him. Arthur McGregor's big head went up and down. His son was right. As long as grain could go east and manufactured goods west, the dominion was still a working concern. The USA had almost cut the prairie off from the more heavily settled eastern provinces, but hadn't quite managed it.

"The real question is," Arthur rumbled, "can we go through another year like this one and the last half of the one before?"

"Of course we can!" Alexander sounded indignant that his father should presume to doubt Canada could hold on.

Arthur McGregor studied his son with a mixture of fondness and exasperation. The lad was at an age where he was inclined to believe things would turn out as he wanted for no better reason than that he wanted them to turn out so. "The United States are a big country," he said, that being another oblique way to say he wasn't so optimistic as he had been.

"We're a big country, too—bigger than the USA," Alexander said, "and the Confederacy is on our side, and England, and France, and Russia, and Japan. We'll lick the Yanks yet, you wait and see."

"We're a big country without enough people in it, and our friends are a long way away," McGregor answered. Always dark and cold, December was a good time of year in which to be gloomy. "If the Yankees had chosen to stand on the defensive against the CSA and throw everything they had at us, they would have smashed us in a hurry and then gone on to other things."

"Nahh!" Alexander rejected the idea out of hand.

But Arthur McGregor nodded. "They would have, son. They could have. They're just too big for us. But one thing about Americans is, they always think they can do more than they really can. They tried to smash us and the Confederates and England on the high seas, all at the same time. And I don't care how big they are, I don't care how much they love the Kaiser and the Huns, no country on the face of the earth is big enough and strong enough to do all that at once."

At last, he'd succeeded in troubling his son. "*Do* you think they're going to win the war, Pa?"

McGregor had lain awake at night from that very fear. "I hope not," he said at last. "It's just that there are so blasted *many* of them."

That put a sour twist on Alexander's mouth; it was inarguably true. In Arthur McGregor's mind's eye, he saw endless columns of men in green-gray tramping north, endless queues of snarling canvas-topped trucks painted the same shade, endless teams of horses hauling wagons and artillery pieces, endless trains also bringing men and supplies up toward the front. True, there were also endless ambulances and trains marked with the Red Cross, taking wounded Yankees away for treatment, and, no doubt, endless corpses at the front. But somehow the U.S. military machine kept grinding on despite the wastage.

Alexander said, "What can we do?"

"Hope," McGregor answered. "Pray, though God will do as He likes, not as we like." He was as stern a Presbyterian as he looked. "Cooperate with the Americans as little as we can— though if they hadn't bought our grain, however little they paid for it, I can't imagine what we'd do for money."

He scowled. A farm didn't need much in the way of cash, especially when a war knocked deeds and land taxes all topsy-turvy. You could live off your crops and your livestock and you might even make your own cloth from wool and from flax if you'd planted any, but you couldn't make your own coal or your own kerosene or your own glass or books or . . . a lot of things that made life come close to being worth living.

"It's not enough," Alexander said. "Not going along with the Yanks, I mean—it's not enough. We shouldn't be talking about not doing things with them—that's why you don't send my sister to the school they set up. Like I say, it's good, but it's not enough. We've got to figure out ways to do things *to* the Americans."

"Like that bomb in Rosenfeld?" Arthur McGregor asked. His son nodded, gray eyes fierce. But McGregor sighed. "It's possible, I suppose, but it's not easy. They almost made me one of the hostages they took after that bomb went off, remember. They would have given me a blindfold, lined me up against a wall, and shot me. This is a war, son, and you can't back out and say you didn't mean it if something goes wrong."

"I know *that*!" Alexander exclaimed. But the jaunty tone with which he'd replied gave him away. He didn't believe for a moment that anything could go wrong in a scheme to tweak the Yankees' tails. When you were fifteen, you knew everything always turned out fine in the end. Arthur McGregor was a good deal past twice fifteen. He knew how foolish you were at that age.

He addressed his son with great seriousness: "I want you to promise me you won't go off on your own to try to do anything to the Americans. And once you make that promise, I expect you to keep it."

Now Alexander McGregor looked most unhappy. "Aw, Pa, I don't want to have to lie to you."

"I don't want you to have to lie to me, either," his father said. McGregor was at the same time proud of his son for not taking a lie for granted and alarmed at how serious he was in wanting to do something to strike at the American soldiers holding—and holding down—Manitoba.

"Believe me, Pa," Alexander went on, "I'm not the only fellow who wants to—" He stopped. Kerosene light was on the ruddy side, anyhow, but McGregor thought he turned red. "I don't think I should have said that."

"I wish you hadn't, I'll tell you that." McGregor studied Alexander, who did his inadequate best to show nothing on his face. How many boys were there on the scattered farms of Manitoba—and boys they would have to be, for everyone of conscription age before the land was overrun had already been called to the colors—plotting heaven only knew what against the USA?

"Whatever these fellows have in their minds, you will not be a part of it. Do you understand me?" Arthur McGregor knew he sounded like a prophet laying down the Law. He hadn't taken that tone with Alexander for years; he'd had no need. Now he wondered whether his son, who was nearly a man and who thought himself more nearly a man than he was, would still respond to it as he had when he was smaller. And, sure enough, defiance kindled in Alexander's eyes. "I understand you, Pa," he said, but that was a long way from pledging his obedience.

McGregor exhaled heavily. "I'm not just saying this for myself, you know. What do you suppose your mother would do if the Yanks caught you at whatever mischief you have in mind?" He knew that was a low blow, and used it without compunction or hesitation.

It went home, too. Alexander winced. "It wouldn't be like that, Pa," he protested.

"No? Why wouldn't it?" McGregor pressed the advantage: "And how would you keep Julia out of it, once you got in? Or even Mary?"

"Julia's just a girl, and she's only twelve," Alexander said, as if that settled that.

"And she hates the Americans worse than you do, and she's stubborner than you ever dreamt of being," McGregor said. Before Alexander could respond, he went on, "And one of these days you and your pals would decide that the Yanks couldn't think she was dangerous because she's a girl and she's only twelve. And you'd send her out to do something, and she'd be proud to go. *And what if she got caught, son?* The Yanks are nasty devils, but Lord help you if you think they're stupid."

"We'd never—" Alexander began, but he didn't finish the sentence. When you were in a war, who could say what you might be driven to do?

Neither of them spoke of Mary. That was not because she had but seven years. It had more to do with a certainty father and son shared that the littlest girl in the house would take any chance offered her to hurt the U.S. cause, and an equally shared determination not to offer her any such chance. Mary was very bright for her age, but unacquainted with anything at all related to restraint.

"I asked you once for your promise, and you would not give it," McGregor said. "I'm going to ask you again." He folded his arms across his chest and waited to hear what his son would say. If Alexander said no . . . He didn't know what he would do if Alexander said no.

His son let out a long, deep sigh, the sigh not of a boy but of a man facing up to the fact that the world doesn't work the way he wished it would. It was the most grown-up noise McGregor had ever heard from him. At last, voice full of regret, he said, "All right, Pa. I promise."

"Promise what, Alexander?" That was Mary, coming out of the kitchen, where she'd been putting away the plates her mother had washed and her big sister dried.

"Promise to tickle you till you scream like there's American soldiers coming down the chimney instead of Santa Claus," Alexander said, and made as if to grab her. That could be dangerous; she fought as ferociously as a half-tame farm cat.

But now she hopped back, laughing. She turned to Arthur McGregor. "What did he promise, Pa?"

"To be a good boy," McGregor said. Mary snorted. That sort of promise meant nothing to her. McGregor had to hope it meant something to her brother.

IV

Jonathan Moss peered down at his whiskey, then up toward the ceiling of the officers' club; the rafters were blurry not from the effects of drink—though he'd had a good deal—but because of the haze of tobacco smoke. He knocked back the whiskey, then signaled the colored steward behind the bar for another one.

"Yes, sir," the fellow said, and passed him a fresh glass full of the magical amber fluid that inflamed and numbed at the same time.

His tentmates sat around the table: Daniel Dudley, who usually went by "Dud," the flight leader; Tom Innis, fierce as a wolf; and Zach Whitby, new in the tent, replacing a casualty, and still a little hesitant on the ground because of that. None of the four lieutenants was far past twenty. All of them wore twin-winged pilot's badges on the left breast pockets of their uniform tunics.

Tom Innis got a villainous pipe going. Its fumes added to those already crowding the air. Moss flapped a hand in his direction. "Here," he said, "don't start shooting poison gas at us."

"You should talk, those cheroots you smoke," Innis retorted, running a hand over his brown, peltlike Kaiser Bill mustache. "They smell like burning canvas painted with aeroplane dope."

Since that was at least half true, Moss didn't argue with it. He leaned back in his chair, almost overbalancing. Dud Dudley spotted that, as he might have spotted a Canuck aeroplane with engine trouble trying to limp back toward Toronto. "How are you supposed to handle a fighting scout when you can't even fly a chair?" he demanded.

"Well, hell." Moss landed awkwardly. "When I'm up in a fighting scout, I'll be sober. It does make a difference."

That struck all four men as very funny, probably because none of them was sober. The weather had been too thick to fly for several days now, leaving the pilots with nothing to do but fiddle with their aeroplanes and gather in the officers' club to drink. As Moss had found the year before, winter in Ontario sometimes shut down operations for weeks at a time.

He sipped his fresh whiskey and looked around the club. Other groups of pilots and observers had their own circles, most of them raucous enough that they paid little attention to the racket he and his friends were making. On the walls were pictures of the fliers who had served at the aerodrome: some posed portraits, some snapshots of groups of them or of them sitting jauntily in the cockpits of their aeroplanes, a few with their arms around pretty girls. Moss hadn't had much luck along those lines; most Canadian girls wanted little to do with the Americans who occupied their country.

A lot of the pilots in the photographs were men he'd never known, men killed before he'd joined the squadron as a replacement, new as Zach Whitby. Others had died after Moss came here: Luther Carlsen, for instance, whose place Whitby was taking. The rest were survivors . . . up till now. *The quick and the dead,* he thought.

Also on the walls were souvenirs of the aerial action that had accompanied the grinding, slogging American advance through southern Ontario toward—but, all plans aside, not yet to— Toronto: blue, white, and red roundels cut from the canvas of destroyed enemy machines. Some were from British aeroplanes, with all three colors being circles, others from native Canadian aircraft, where the red in the center was painted in the shape of a maple leaf.

Along with the roundels were a couple of two-bladed wooden propellers, also spoils of war. Seeing the souvenirs—or rather, noticing them—made Jonathan Moss proud for a moment. But his mood swung with whiskey-driven speed. "I wonder how many canvas eagles the Canucks and the limeys have in their officers' clubs," he said.

"Too damn many," Zach Whitby said. "Even one would be too damn many."

"We might as well enjoy ourselves," Dud Dudley said, "because we aren't going to live through the damned war any which way."

"I'll drink to that," Innis said, and did.

The quick and the dead, Moss thought again. The hell of it was, Dudley was right, or the odds said he was, which amounted to the same thing. Moss looked again at those photographs of vanished fliers. Back in the observers' unit from which he'd transferred after his photographer was wounded, they'd had a similar display. One of these days, would Zach be explaining to some newcomer still wet behind the ears who he'd been and what he'd done? Contemplating things like that was plenty to make you want to crawl into a whiskey bottle and pull the cork in after you.

The door to the officers' club opened. Captain Shelby Pruitt, the squadron commander, walked in. With him came a blast of cold Ontario air. Some of the smoke in the big room escaped, though not enough to do much good.

"I want to tell you miserable drunks something," Pruitt said loudly, and waited till he got something approaching quiet before going on, "Word from the weathermen in Manitoba is that they've had a couple of days of clear weather, and it's heading our way. We may be flying tomorrow. You don't want to drink yourselves altogether blind."

"Who says we don't?" Tom Innis demanded.

"I say so," Pruitt answered mildly, and Innis nodded, all at once meek as a child. The squadron commander hadn't earned his nickname of "Hardshell" by breathing fire every chance he found, but he expected obedience—and got it. Like Moss' previous CO, he not only commanded the squadron but also flew with it, and he'd knocked down four enemy aeroplanes on his own, even if he was, by the standards of the men who flew fighting scouts, somewhere between middle-aged and downright doddering.

Zach Whitby waved to the bartender. "Coffee!" he called. "I got to sober me up. We run into any limeys up there, I don't want to do anything stupid."

"Hell with coffee," Innis said. "Hell with sobering up too much, too. I'd rather fly with a hangover—it makes me mean."

"I'll have my coffee in the morning, and some aspirin to go with it," Moss said. "If I load up on java now, I won't sleep for beans tonight. We go up there, we ought to be in the best shape we can." Dudley nodded. Moss had noticed that he and his flight leader often thought alike.

Under Hardshell Pruitt's inexorable stare, the officers' lounge emptied. Fliers scrawled their names on bar chits and strode, or sometimes lurched, off to their cots. Pruitt sped them to their rest with a suggestion that struck Moss as downright sadistic: "Here's hoping Canuck bombing planes don't come over tonight."

His was not the only groan rising into the chilly night. The thought of enduring a bombing raid while hung over was not one to inspire delight. As things were . . . "The groundcrew will be cleaning puke off somebody's control panel tomorrow," he predicted.

"Puke is one thing," Dudley answered. "Getting blood out of a cockpit is a whole different business. But you know about that, don't you?"

"Yeah, I know about that." Moss remembered Percy Stone, his observer. He remembered how much blood had splashed Stone's cockpit after he'd been wounded. He'd heard Stone had lived, but the photographer still hadn't returned to duty.

Enough thick wool blankets stood on Moss' cot to have denuded half the sheep in Canada. Living under canvas in Canada wasn't easy half the year. It was, however, a hell of a lot easier than living in the trenches. Aviators who groused too much about how tough they had it sometimes got handed a Springfield, which did wonders for shutting them up.

He took off his boots, burrowed under the blankets like a mole, and fell asleep. Waking up in gray twilight the next morning was something he would sooner have skipped. He gulped coffee and aspirin tablets and began to feel human, in a somber sort of way. Tom Innis' morning preparation consisted of brandy and a raw egg, then coffee. One way probably worked about as well as the other.

Sure enough, the day dawned clear. The pilots swaddled themselves in the leather and fur of their flying suits. It was cold at altitude even in scorching midsummer; during the worst of winter, the flying suits rarely came off. Moving slowly— bending your knees wasn't easy with all that padding around them—they went out to their aeroplanes.

Groundcrew men had already removed the canvas covers from the Martin one-deckers: U.S. copies of a German design. Also copied from the Fokker monoplane was the interrupter gear that let a forward-facing machine gun fire through the spinning propeller without shooting it off and sending the machine down in a long, helpless glide . . . or that let the machine gun shoot through the prop most of the time, anyhow.

Clumsily, Moss climbed into the cockpit. A couple of bullet holes in the side of the fuselage from his most recent encounter with an enemy aeroplane had been neatly patched. The machine could take punishment. Had the bullets torn through his soft, vulnerable flesh, he would have spent much longer in the shop.

He nodded to a mechanic standing by the propeller. The fellow, his breath smoking in the cold morning air, spun the two-bladed wooden prop. After a couple of tries, the engine caught. Moss studied his instruments. He had plenty of gas and oil, and the pumps for both seemed to be working well. He tapped his compass to make sure the needle hadn't frozen to its case.

When he was satisfied, he waved. The airstrip was full of the growl of motors turning over. Dud Dudley looked around to make sure everyone in his flight had a functioning machine, then taxied across the field—ruts through gray-brown dead grass. Moss followed, watching his ground speed. He pulled back on the joystick, lifting the fighting scout's nose. The aeroplane bounced a couple of more times. After the second bounce, it didn't come down.

He climbed as quickly as he could, going into formation behind his flight leader and to his left. Zach Whitby held the same place relative to him as he did to Dudley. On the right, Tom Innis flew alone.

Down in the trenches, men huddled against cold and mud and frost. The line ran from southeast to northwest between Lake Ontario and Lake Huron. Behind it, on land the United States had had to fight to win, everything had been wrecked by stubborn Canadian and British defense and equally stubborn American attacks. On the other side, the terrain still showed what a fine country this was.

Machine guns spat fire at the aeroplanes from the enemy's trenches. That was futile; machine-gun bullets reached only a

couple of thousand feet, and the Martin single-deckers flew a
good deal higher. But soon Canadian and British Archibald—or
Archie, as he was more familiarly known—would start putting
antiaircraft shells all around them. A lucky hit could bring down
an aeroplane. Moss knew that, as he knew of a thousand other
ways he could die up here. He did his best to forget what
he knew.

Dud Dudley wagged his wings to draw the flight's attention.
He pointed to the south. The enemy was in the air, too. There,
buzzing along contentedly, as if without a care in the world, was
a Canadian—or perhaps a British—two-seater, an old Avro no
longer fit for front-line combat but still good enough to take a
photographer over the American lines to see what he could see.

As Moss swung into a turn toward the enemy reconnaissance
aircraft, he glanced in the rearview mirror, then up and back over
his shoulder. Were scouts lurking up there, waiting to pounce
when the Americans attacked the Avro? Keeping an eye peeled
for such was really Zach Whitby's job, but you didn't get to go
back to the officers' lounge and have more drinks if you took too
seriously the notion that you didn't have to worry about something because someone else would.

On flew the Avro, straight as if on a string. That meant the observer was taking his pictures, and the pilot, a brave man,
wouldn't spoil them even if he was under attack. Moss knew
what that took, since he'd piloted observation aircraft himself.
He prepared to make the enemy pay for his courage.

He'd just fired his first burst when tracers streaked past him—
not from the Avro, but from behind. Zach Whitby's fighting
scout tumbled out of the sky, not in any controlled maneuver but
diving steeply, a dead man at the controls, flame licking back
from the engine. Sure as hell, the Canucks had had a surprise
waiting.

Moss threw his own aeroplane into a tight rolling turn to the
right. He was more maneuverable than the two-seater on his tail,
but the biplane kept after him, firing straight ahead. That wasn't
right—the enemy wasn't supposed to have an interrupter gear
yet. And they didn't, but this enterprising chap had mounted two
machine guns on his lower wing planes, outside the arc of the
propeller. He couldn't reload them in flight, but while they had
ammo he was dangerous any way you looked at him.

Then, all at once, he wasn't. Tom Innis knocked him down as neatly as he and his chums had ambushed Whitby. Then Innis and Dudley teamed up against one of the other aeroplanes, which caught fire and fell like a dead leaf.

Moss' own turn brought him close to the decoy observation aircraft. The observer, done with photos now, blazed away at him from a ring-mounted machine gun. He fired a burst that made the observer clutch at himself and slumped the pilot over his joystick, dead or unconscious. If he was unconscious, he would die soon; his weight on the stick sent the aeroplane nosing toward the ground.

Jonathan Moss looked around for more foes. He found none. The last enemy two-seater had streaked away, and had gained enough of a lead while the Americans were otherwise engaged to make sure it would not be caught.

Got no guts, Moss thought with weary anger. But for himself and Dudley and Innis, the sky was clear of aircraft. He turned the nose of his Martin toward the aerodrome. *Wonder what they'll find us to fill the fourth cot in the tent.* With Whitby dead, he knew he should have felt more, but for the life of him that was all his weary brain would muster.

Rain drummed down on the big canvas refugee tent. Here and there, it came through the canvas and made little puddles on the cold ground. One of the puddles was right in front of Anne Colleton's cot. Unless she thought about it, she stepped right into the puddle when she got down.

A couple of little wood-burning stoves in the open space in the middle of the tent glowed red, holding the worst of the chill at bay. One of the women who made the dreary place her home looked at a watch and said, "Five minutes to twelve."

A couple of women and girls murmured excitedly. Anne knew her own face remained stony. Who cared whether 1916 was only five minutes away? The one thing for which she could hope from the year to come was that it would be better than the one that was dying. She did not see how it could possibly be worse, but what did that prove? She was no longer so confident as she had been that she had such a good grasp on what might lie ahead.

"Come on," said the woman with the watch—her name was Melissa. "Let's sing 'Auld Lang Syne.' "

Some of the women did begin to sing: softly, so as not to disturb those who had gone to sleep instead of staying up to see in the new year. Off in the distance, artillery rumbled, throwing shells at the territory still proclaimed to be the Congaree Socialist Republic, the territory that, shrunken though it was in the fighting of late, still included Marshlands.

Before the Red revolt, Anne could not have told that distant artillery from distant thunder, nor the crack of a Springfield from that of a Tredegar. She'd learned a lot, these past few weeks, and would have given a lot to unlearn it.

Melissa looked across the tent at her. "You're not singing, Miss Colleton," she said, her voice full of shrill complaint. She was plump and homely, and her hair must have stolen its golden sheen from a bottle, because the part of it closest to her head had grown out mouse-brown.

"That's right. I'm not singing," Anne replied. *Take it or leave it,* her tone said. She did not feel like being sociable. Unlike most of the women in the tent, unlike their male kin in other tents, she could have escaped the refugee camp any time she chose. But she could not make herself move any farther from Marshlands than she had to. She had food of a sort, shelter of a sort, clothing of a sort. Yes, she'd been used to better, but she was discovering *better,* while pleasant, was less than necessary. Here she would stay, till the rebellion collapsed—or till she strangled Melissa, which might come first.

The pale, pudgy woman with the two-tone hair certainly seemed to be trying to promote her own untimely demise. Glaring at Anne, she remarked, "Some people don't seem to care about anyone but themselves."

"Some people," Anne said, relishing the chance to release the bile that had been gathering inside her ever since the Negro uprising began, "*some* people don't care about anything except stuffing their faces full of sowbelly till they turn the same color as the meat and the same size as the hog it came from."

She heard the sharp intakes of breath from all around the tent. "*Here* we go," one woman said in a low voice to another. So they'd been expecting a fight, had they? They'd been looking forward to one? Anne had thought only of entertaining herself. But if she entertained other people, too . . . She showed her teeth in what was more nearly snarl than smile. If she entertained other people, too . . . that was all right.

Melissa's mouth opened and closed several times, as if she were a fish out of water. "Weren't for you damn rich folks, the niggers never would have riz up," she said at last.

Two or three women nodded at that. Anne Colleton laughed out loud. Melissa couldn't have looked more astonished had Anne flung a pail of water in her face. For about two cents, Anne would have, and enjoyed it, too.

"It's the truth," Melissa insisted.

"In a pig's eye," Anne replied sweetly. "It's you who—"

"Liar!" Melissa squealed, her voice shrill. "If you'd have been born on a little farm like me, nobody would've ever heard of you."

"Maybe," Anne replied. "And if you'd been born at Marshlands, nobody would ever have heard of you, either." A classical education came in handy in all sorts of unexpected ways. The jibe was so subtle, the eager listeners needed a moment to take it in. When they did, though, their hum of appreciation made the wait worthwhile.

Melissa needed longer than most of the women around her to understand she'd been punctured. When she did, she sent Anne a look full of hate. That look also had fear in it, as if she'd only now realized she might have picked a dangerous target. *Proves you're a fool, for not seeing it sooner,* Anne thought, not that she'd been in any great doubt of that.

But Melissa did not back away from the argument. "Go ahead, make all the smart cracks you want," she said, "but you rich folks, you—"

"Stop that," Anne said coldly. "You talk like the Negroes with their red flags, pitting rich against poor. Are you a Red yourself?" Melissa didn't have the brains to be a Red, and Anne knew it full well. But she also calculated the other woman would need some little while to find a comeback.

That calculation proved accurate. Melissa looked around the tent for support. When she saw she wasn't getting any—no one there, for good and sufficient reasons, wanted anything to do with either Reds or even ideas possibly Red—she resumed her attack, though she had only one string on her fiddle: "Weren't for you rich folks, niggers'd just stay in their place and—"

"What a pile of horseshit," Anne said, drawing gasps on account of the language as she'd known she would. She'd also shocked Melissa into shutting up, as she'd hoped would happen. Into that sudden and welcome silence, she went on, "Yes, I'm rich. So what? If you ask me, it's the way the po' buckra"—she dropped into the Negro dialect of the Congaree for those two scornful words—"like you treat the Negroes that—"

Melissa surged to her feet. "Po' buckra? Who are you calling white trash?"

"You," Anne told her. "And I don't need to give you the name, because you give it to yourself by the way you act. You're the sort of person who treats a Negro like an animal, because if you treated him any different, he might think—and you might think—he was as good as you."

She rose, too, as she spoke, and just as well, for Melissa rushed over to her, aiming a roundhouse slap at her face. As her brothers had taught her in long-ago rough-and-tumble, Anne blocked the blow with her left hand while delivering one of her own with her right. She didn't slap, but landed a solid uppercut with a closed fist square on the point of Melissa's chin.

The other woman staggered back and sat down hard. She'd almost stumbled into one of the stoves, which would have given her even worse hurt than Anne had intended. Blood dribbled from the corner of her mouth. She stared up at Anne like a dog that rolls over onto its back to present its belly and throat to a stronger rival.

"Before they sent me to this camp," Anne said, "I asked them to give me a rifle and let me fight alongside our soldiers and militiamen. They wouldn't let me—*men*—but I could have done it. And anyone who thinks I can't take care of myself without a gun is making a mistake, too."

Nobody argued with her, not now. She'd not only flayed Melissa with words but also thrashed her. The plump woman slowly stood up and went back to her own cot, one hand clutched to her jaw. She sat down on the canvas and blankets and didn't say a thing.

Anne spoke into vast silence: "Happy New Year." Before the war, people had celebrated the hour by shooting guns in the air. These past two New Years, they'd shot with intent to kill, not only on the hour but all day long, all week long, all month . . .

Convinced the trouble in the tent was over for the time being, Anne sat down again. As she did so, the irony of one of the arguments she'd used to discomfit Melissa suddenly occurred to her. She hadn't been wrong when she'd said that poor whites in the Confederacy were more concerned about keeping blacks down than were the rich, who would stay on top no matter what the relationship between the races happened to be.

A few miles to the north, though, the agitators of the Congaree Socialist Republic were using similar arguments to spur their followers to fresh effort against their white foes. Did that mean the Negroes had been right to rebel?

She shook her head. That wasn't what she'd had in mind at all. They weren't building anything up there, just tearing down. She wondered if anything would be left of Marshlands by the time she was finally able to return to it. One way or another, though, she figured she would get along. She wasn't Melissa, to fall into obscurity. No. Melissa hadn't fallen into obscurity. She'd never been anything but obscure. Many fates might yet befall Anne Colleton, but not, she vowed, that one.

"Look at that bastard burn," Ben Carlton said, his voice as full of joy as if he'd never seen anything more beautiful than the flaming factory in Clearfield, Utah.

Watching the Utah Canning Plant go up in smoke felt pretty good to Paul Mantarakis, too. As they had a habit of doing, the Mormons had used the big, strongly built building to anchor their line. Now that it was a blazing wreck, they'd have to abandon it, which meant the United States Army could take one more grinding step on the road toward the last rebel stronghold in Ogden.

"Three quarters of the way there," Mantarakis muttered under his breath. They were only nine miles from Ogden now. He could see the town from here—or he could have seen it, had the smoke from the great burning here in Clearfield not obscured the northern horizon.

"Soon all the misbelievers shall be cast into the fiery furnace and receive the punishment they deserve," Gordon McSweeney said. He had the drum and hose of the flamethrower strapped onto his back. He hadn't been the one who'd set the canning plant on fire, though; artillery had managed that. Had the big guns failed, Paul could easily imagine the other sergeant going out there and starting the blaze.

Pop! Pop-pop! Short, sharp explosions began sounding, deep within the bowels of the Utah Canning Plant. "Some poor dead son of a bitch's ammo cooking off," Ben Carlton said.

Paul shook his head. "Doesn't sound quite right for that."

Thump! Something slammed into the ground, hard, not ten feet from where he stood. Almost a year and a half of war had honed his reflexes razor-sharp. He was flat on his belly before he had the slightest conscious notion of what that thump was. Better by far to duck and not need to than to need to and not duck. Another thump came, this one from farther away.

Thump! A foot soldier nearby started to laugh. "What the hell's so funny, Stonebreaker?" Paul demanded. "We're under bombardment."

"Yeah, I know, Sarge." But Dan Stonebreaker was still laughing. He went on, "I damn near got killed by a can of string beans."

"Huh?" Mantarakis looked at the missile that had landed close to him. Sure as hell, it was a tin can that must have exploded in the fire inside the plant. He examined the goop inside the can. "This one wasn't beans. Looks more like apricots, something like that."

In short order, the soldiers also identified beets and peas. Whenever some more cans exploded inside the factory, the men would sing out, "Vegetable attack!" and take cover more melodramatically than they did against artillery or machine-gun fire.

They took casualties from the superheated produce, too. One fellow who wasn't wearing his helmet got a fractured skull when a one-pound can of peas landed right on his luckless, foolish head. Hot bits of metal, almost as dangerous as shrapnel or shell fragments, burned several more.

Then the U.S. guns opened up with another barrage. When it eased, the soldiers went up and over the top and drove the Mormons out of Clearfield. The men—and women—who fought under the beehive banner and the motto DESERET fought as hard as ever, but there were fewer of them in these trenches than there had been farther south.

"I think we've finally got them on the run," Captain Schneider said. He looked like a Negro with a bad paint job—his face was black with soot, but smeared here and there just enough to suggest he might be a white man after all. Paul Mantarakis looked down at himself. He couldn't see his own face, but his hands and uniform were as filthy as those of the company commander.

"Come on!" Gordon McSweeney shouted, his voice ringing over the field like a trumpet. "We have the heretics on the run. The more we push them, the greater the punishment we give. Forward!"

Mantarakis' opinion was that McSweeney was a hell of a lot crazier than the Mormons. He didn't say so; McSweeney was, after all, on his side. And the shouts were doing some good, pulling U.S. soldiers after the Scotsman as he singlehandedly advanced against the enemy. He would have advanced, though, had not a single man followed.

Crazy, Mantarakis thought again, and tramped north himself.

For the next mile, maybe two, the going was easy. The Mormons had no real line of solid fortifications here. Men retreating before the American advance traded shots with their pursuers, but it was hardly counted as a rear-guard action. "Maybe we do have 'em on the run," Paul said to nobody in particular. Even the fanaticism of the Mormons had to have limits . . . didn't it?

Before long, he was doubting that again. U.S. troops ran up against yet another defensive line prepared in advance and manned by still more determined warriors. Such a line called for spadework in return, and the Americans began turning shell holes into a trench line of their own.

Captain Schneider pointed west, toward some ruins not far from the horizon. "We want to be careful the enemy doesn't pull a fast one on us. Those buildings, or what's left of them, are the Ogden Ordnance Depot. It'd be just like the Mormons to pack 'em full of powder and touch 'em off as our forces were moving up to 'em."

The buildings were not part of the Mormon defensive line, which only increased Mantarakis' suspicions: the rebels fought from built-up positions till forced out of them by artillery or, more often, by the bayonet. But, before long, U.S. troops had not only occupied the Ordnance Depot buildings, they were firing from them on the Mormon defenses farther north. When an American aeroplane dropped a couple of bombs nearby—whether because it thought the enemy still held the depot or because it simply couldn't aim worth a damn, Paul never knew—the soldiers shooting from it began waving a big Stars and Stripes to show under whose ownership it had passed.

Maybe the sight of the American flag in the ruins of the Ordnance Depot was some kind of signal. Paul never knew that, either. But, whether by plan or by coincidence, the ground rocked under his feet a couple of minutes later.

He staggered, stumbled, fell. "What the hell . . . ?" he shouted while clods of earth rained down on him from the wall of the trench in which he'd been standing—and from on high, too, or so it seemed. He was afraid the whole trench would collapse.

Through the shaking, through the hideous din, Captain Schneider shouted, "Earthquake! I was in the Presidio in San Francisco ten years ago, and it was almost like this." He managed to stay on his feet.

"Make it stop! Jesus, make it stop!" Ben Carlton howled. It would have taken Jesus to make it stop; that was surely beyond the power of an infantry captain, or even of Teddy Roosevelt himself.

Mantarakis succeeded in standing. The rumble had faded, leaving behind an awful silence. The sound that came through it was not one he had expected to hear in the wake of a natural catastrophe: it was cheering, and it was all coming from the Mormon lines.

Gordon McSweeney got up on the firing step, or on what was left of it after the ground had shaken. "The misbelievers are coming out of their trenches and moving forward in an attack," he reported. His head turned to the left, so that he was looking west. For once, not even his stern rectitude was proof against merely human astonishment. "They've blown a hole in our lines you could drive a freight train through," he burst out, his voice squeaking with surprise.

"What?" Paul got up there beside McSweeney. Sure enough, any resistance from the U.S. lines ended perhaps a quarter of a mile west of where he stood. A great haze of dust and smoke hung in the air west of that, but no U.S. gunfire was coming from the ground under the haze. And that ground, what little he could see of it, looked different: sagging, slumped.

Captain Schneider's mouth fell open when he saw that. "It *wasn't* an earthquake," he said accusingly, as if angry at having been mistaken. "The filthy, stinking Mormons mined the ground under us, and touched off their charge when we got on top of it."

He went on cursing in a harsh, steady monotone. Mantarakis didn't blame him. It looked as if a whole great chunk had disappeared from the U.S. line—the U.S. line in an advance that had been, up till then, finally turning into the rout it should have been from the beginning.

Then a bullet cracked past his head. The Mormons weren't trying to overwhelm only the part of the line they'd blown to kingdom come. They were aiming to take out all of it, to throw the Americans back as far as they could. Of itself, the Springfield jumped to Paul's shoulder. He aimed and fired. A man in overalls went down, whether hit or diving for cover he couldn't have said.

"Bad position to try to defend," Captain Schneider muttered. "We don't have a whole lot of wire in front of us." He grabbed Carlton by the arm and pointed him west. "Go on down as far as there are any live men in the trench and tell them to fall back at a right angle to our line—or what used to be our line. We don't want the Mormons to be able to roll us all up. They've got their breakthrough—we have to keep them from exploiting it too much."

Carlton went. Mantarakis admired the captain's presence of mind. In these circumstances, he himself was having enough trouble figuring out what he needed to do. Worrying about the bigger picture was altogether beyond him. Schneider was earning his pay today—assuming he lived to collect it. Right now, that didn't look like the best bet in the world.

More and more Americans were shooting back at the Mormons now, but the enemy kept coming, some of them singing hymns as they advanced. They'd learned how to move forward against heavy fire, some shooting from cover to make their foes duck while others advanced. And they used their machine guns aggressively, manhandling the heavy weapons forward so they too could make the Americans keep their heads down.

"Jesus, you'd think we'd have killed all the damned Mormons

in Utah by now," Captain Schneider said. He was blazing away with the pistol he wore on his belt, and the enemy was close enough to the trench line for it to be about as effective a weapon as a Springfield.

"I wish we had," Paul said with great sincerity. He was getting low on ammunition, and heaven only knew when more would come forward.

Three Mormons popped up out of a shell hole not fifty feet away. The winter sun pierced the haze rising from the exploded mine to glitter off the bayonets of the rifles they carried. Shouting the rebel battle cry—"Come, ye saints!"—they rushed for the trench.

Gordon McSweeney laughed the triumphant laugh of a man seeing the enemy delivered into his hands. He fired a single jet of flame that caught all three Mormons in it. Only one of them had even the chance to cry out. All three jerked and writhed and shrank, all in the blink of an eye, blackening into roasted husks like those of insects that littered the street below gas lamps of a summer's evening.

"Come on!" McSweeney shouted. "Who wants the next dose? You might as well come ahead—you're all going to hell, anyhow."

The Mormons kept coming, up and down the line. Machine-gun fire hammered many of them into the ground, and McSweeney got to use his infernal weapon several more times. After that, the rebels avoided the stretch of trench where he was stationed; even their spirit proved to have limits. Here and there, they did break into the trench line, but they did not force the Americans out—not, at least, in the stretch where the line hadn't been blown sky-high.

Farther west, Paul could trace the progress of the fighting only by where the gunfire was coming from. By the sound of it, the Mormons were pushing on south toward Clearfield through a gap that was bigger than he'd thought.

"How much dynamite did they pack underground, anyway?" he asked, as if anyone nearby had the slightest chance of knowing.

"Tons," Captain Schneider said—not an exact answer, but one with plenty of flavor to it. "Has to be tons." He shook his head in disbelief. "And if we'd been over there instead of over here—"

That thought had already gone through Paul's mind. If he'd been over there instead of over here, he'd have been blown up or buried or one of any number of other unpleasant possibilities. As things stood, all he had to worry about was getting shot. He hadn't imagined that that could seem an improvement, but suddenly it did.

"What do we do now, sir?" he asked.

"Form a perimeter, try to hold on, hope there are enough government soldiers in Utah to patch something together again here," the company commander answered.

Mantarakis nodded. Schneider gave straight answers, even if they weren't the sort you were delighted to hear. If he was still alive tomorrow, and if he still remembered (he wondered which of those competing unlikelihoods was less likely), he'd have to tell the captain that.

Roger Kimball looked out from the conning tower of the *Bonefish* toward the northern bank of the Pee Dee. He hadn't brought the submersible so far up the river this time as he had on his earlier run against the black rebels of the Congaree Socialist Republic, not yet, but he figured he'd end up going farther now than he'd managed then.

Tom Brearley stood up there with him. "What do you think of the new, improved model, Tom?" he asked his executive officer.

Brearley answered with the same serious consideration he usually showed: "You ask me, sir, the boat looked better before."

"Yeah, you're right about that," Kimball admitted. "But who the hell ever thought they'd have to modify a sub to do gunboat duty?"

The plain truth was, nobody had ever thought of that. Nobody had imagined the need. But need and the *Bonefish* had been in the same place at the same time, and so . . . In the Charleston shipyard, they'd put steel armor all around the three-inch deck gun's mount, so its crew could shelter against bullets from the riverbank. And they'd mounted the machine guns on circular slabs of iron with cutouts in them, so the gunners could revolve them with their feet to bear on any target. More steel armor coming up from the outer edges of the slabs gave the machine guns protection against rifle fire, too.

Kimball pointed toward the bank. "You ask me, that's where our real improvement is."

"Oh, the Marines? Yes, sir," Brearley said. "This whole operation really makes you understand what the Army is talking about when it comes to how important seizing and holding ground is, doesn't it?"

"Yeah," Kimball said, and then, under his breath, "To hell with the Army." As far as he was concerned—as far as almost any Confederate States Navy officer was concerned—the Army was a dismal swamp that sucked up enormous sums of money, most of which promptly vanished without trace: money that could have gone for more battleships, cruisers, destroyers, submarines . . .

Marines, of course, were the Navy's admission that some action on dry land did have to be contemplated every now and again, no matter how distasteful the notion might be. Somehow or other, somebody with pull had arranged to land a couple of companies of them at the mouth of the Pee Dee and have them work their way northwest along the river toward the black heart of the Congaree Socialist Republic.

Had Anne Colleton managed that? It was the sort of thing Kimball would have expected from her, but he didn't know for a fact that she was alive. Whoever had thought of it, it was a good idea. The insurgent Negroes couldn't ignore the Marines, and Kimball didn't think any irregular troops in the world could stand against them.

No sooner had that thought crossed his mind than a brisk *pop-pop* of small-arms fire broke out along the riverbank. He couldn't see where the Negroes were; they'd concealed themselves in amongst the heaviest undergrowth they could find. But he knew where the Marines were; they'd made a point of keeping in touch with the *Bonefish* and apprising him of their position. He didn't have to be a Jesuit to own enough logic to realize that the fellows who were shooting and weren't Marines had to be the enemy.

"All right, boys," he called to the gun crews. "Let's show the people why they brought us to the dance."

The machine gun on top of the conning tower opened up a split second before the one mounted on the rear deck. The racket was appalling. Kimball's head started to ache. He tried to imagine standing next to a machine gun after a good, friendly night in port. The mere thought was plenty to make his headache worse.

He got the response for which he'd been hoping: the Negroes turned a machine gun of their own, either captured from Confederate forces or donated by the damnyankees, on the *Bonefish*. As soon as it started firing, he and Brearley ducked down the hatch into the conning tower. Being in there under machine-gun fire was like standing in a tin-roofed shed during one hell of a hailstorm.

But, in firing, the Negroes' machine gun revealed its position. The *Bonefish*'s machine guns were not the only weapons that opened up on it: so did the deck gun, at what was point-blank range for a cannon. After six or eight shells went into the woods, bullets stopped clanging off the side of the conning tower.

Kimball, who was closer to the top than Brearley, grinned down at his exec. "With luck, we just wrecked their gun. Even without luck, we just put a crew who knew how to serve it out of action."

"Yes, sir," Brearley said. "The Negroes can't have a whole lot of trained fighting men. The more of those we eliminate, the faster the rebellion as a whole will fall apart."

"That's right," Kimball said. "Hell, these niggers haven't been through conscription. Where are they going to come by the discipline they need to stand up against some of the best fighting men in the Confederate States?"

"Don't know, sir," Brearley answered. Then he went on, perhaps unwisely, "I never thought they had the discipline to stand up against whites any kind of way. If I'd known they could fight the way they've already shown, I'd have been for conscripting them along with us and letting 'em kill some Yankees."

Kimball shook his head, so sharply that he almost smacked it against the inside of the conning tower. "Mr. Brearley, I have to tell you that's a mistake." He hadn't called his executive officer by his surname since the first couple of days they were working together. "Suppose niggers do make soldiers. I don't believe it for a minute, but suppose. Suppose we send 'em up into the trenches and they do help us lick the damnyankees and win the war. Then they come back home. Right? You with me so far?"

"Yes, sir," Brearley answered. He sounded like a puppy that doesn't understand why it's just been paddled.

Normally, Roger Kimball would have felt some sympathy for him. Not now. He continued, "All right, the war is over, we whipped the Yankees, and we got, say, five divisions of nigger soldiers coming on home. What the hell do we do with 'em, Mr. Brearley? They've been up at the front. They've been killing white men. Hell, we've been payin' 'em to kill white men. What are they gonna do when we tell 'em, 'Good boys. Now go on back to the cotton field and the pushbroom and forget all about that business of shooting people'? You reckon they're gonna pay much attention to us?"

The junior lieutenant didn't answer right away. When at last he did, he said, "Seems to me, sir, if they fight for us, it'd be mighty hard to make 'em go back to being what they were before the war started. Thing of it is, though, it's already gotten to be hard to put 'em back where they were. So many of 'em have gone to factories and such, making 'em into field hands again is going to be like putting Humpty-Dumpty back together again."

"Yeah, well, it'd be a lot worse if they were toting guns," Kimball insisted. The executive officer's response hadn't been what he'd expected or what he'd wanted. "Hell, one of the reasons we fought the War of Secession—not the only one, but one—was so we could do what we wanted with our niggers, not what anybody else wanted us to do."

"Yes, sir, that's true," Brearley said. "When we decided to manumit them twenty years later, after the Second Mexican War, we did it on our own. And if we wanted to reward them for fighting for us, would it be so bad, sir?"

Kimball stared down at the innocent-looking youngster perched on the steel ladder a few rungs below him. It was as if he'd never seen Brearley before—and, in some important ways, maybe he hadn't. "You'd let 'em all be citizens, wouldn't you, Mr. Brearley? You'd let niggers be citizens of the CSA."

He might have accused Brearley of eating with his fingers, or perhaps of practicing more exotic, less speakable perversions. The executive officer bit his lip, but answered, "Sir, if they fought for us, how could we keep from making them into citizens? And if it's a choice between having them fight for us or against us, which would you sooner see?"

That wasn't the way the argument was supposed to go. "They're niggers," Kimball said flatly. "They can't fight whites, not really."

"Yes, sir," Brearley said, and said no more. He needed to say no more. If Negroes couldn't fight, why was the *Bonefish* coming up the Pee Dee for a second run against them? Even more to the point, why hadn't the Congaree Socialist Republic and the other Red rebel outfits the blacks had set up collapsed weeks before?

Would all this have been prevented had the Confederacy let blacks join the Army and, strange as the notion felt, let them vote? Kimball shook his head. "The Army laborers are Reds, too. And if the black bastards voted, they'd have elected that damn lunatic Arango last year."

This time, Brearley didn't say anything at all. When your commanding officer had expressed his opinion and you didn't agree with it, nothing was the best thing you could say.

Clang! A bullet hit the outside of the conning tower. The deck machine guns opened up, blasting away at where they thought the fire had come from. And then, defiantly, a machine gun—maybe the same machine gun that had shot at the *Bonefish* before—began hosing the submersible down again.

Boom! Boom! Boom! The deck gun roared out its reply. Kimball looked down at Brearley again. The exec still didn't say anything. But a silent reproach was no less a reproach because it was silent.

A portly colonel sporting the little medal that said he'd fought in the Second Mexican War looked down his nose at Irving Morrell. "Not as smart as we thought we were, eh, Major?" he said. Instead of a Kaiser Bill mustache, he sported white wraparound whiskers that, with his bald head, gave him a striking resemblance to Franz Joseph, the elderly Austro-Hungarian Emperor.

"No, Colonel Gilbert," Morrell answered tonelessly. Longtime General Staff officers had been saying things like that to him ever since the Mormons exploded their mines south of Ogden. The only safe response he had was agreeing with them, and also the only truthful one. The Mormons had done a hell of a lot of damage with those mines, and he hadn't anticipated them.

He looked glumly at the situation map for Utah. The drive toward Ogden, the last major rebel stronghold, no longer proceeded nearly north, with east and west ends of the line parallel to each other. The eastern end of the line was still about where it had been, anchored against the Wasatch Mountains, but now the line ran back on a ragged slant, the western end touching the Great Salt Lake a good ten miles farther south than it had been. Only frantic reinforcement had kept the disaster from being even worse than it was.

Colonel Gilbert studied the map, too. "If we hadn't had to pull those troops out of Sequoyah and Kentucky, Major, our progress against the Confederates would have been a good deal greater than it is."

"Yes, sir," Morrell said. The USA should have been taking advantage of the uprising within the enemy's territory, not quelling an uprising of its own. He knew that as well as the white-whiskered colonel. Knowing it and being able to do anything about it, unfortunately, were two different things.

Captain John Abell came into the room, too. Seeing Morrell and Colonel Gilbert examining the Utah situation, he came over and looked at the map himself. He put his hands behind his back and interlaced his fingers; his face assumed an expression of thoughtful seriousness. What he looked like, Morrell thought, was a doctor hovering over the bed of a patient who had taken a turn for the worse. Morrell had seen plenty of doctors with that expression, when it had looked as if he would lose his leg.

"Unfortunate," Abell murmured. He couldn't very well say anything more; Morrell outranked him. But what he was thinking was plain enough.

And there was nothing Morrell could do about it. He'd gained the credit for his notion of hitting the Mormons from several directions at once to weaken their resistance to the main line of effort. Because the notion had worked, he'd come to be thought of as the expert on Utah. And when something happened there that he hadn't allowed for, he found blame accruing to him as readily as credit had before.

No, more readily than credit, for credit had come grudgingly even after his success was obvious. No one blamed him only grudgingly. Here he was, an outsider, a newcomer, who'd dared to presume himself more astute, more clever, than General Staff veterans. When he turned out not to have thought of everything, it was as if he hadn't thought of anything.

The door to the map room opened. The newcomer was a lieutenant so junior, he hardly seemed to have started shaving. He too made a beeline for the map of Utah. That didn't surprise Morrell, not any more; misery loved company.

But the lieutenant wasn't interested, or wasn't chiefly interested, in the strategic situation there. He was interested in Irving Morrell. Saluting, he said, "General Wood's compliments, sir, and he would like to see you at your earliest convenience."

"I'm coming," Morrell said; when the chief of the General Staff wanted you at your earliest convenience, he wanted you right now. The lieutenant nodded; he might have been even greener than his uniform, but he understood that bit of military formality.

Behind Morrell, Colonel Gilbert spoke to Captain Abell: "Maybe the general is trying to figure out how we can get blown up on the Ontario front, too." Maybe he hadn't intended Morrell to hear that. Maybe. But when Abell snickered, Morrell knew he was supposed to have heard that. The young captain was too smooth to offer insult by accident.

Escape, then, became something of a relief. The lieutenant led him through the maze of General Staff headquarters without offering a word of conversation, and responded only in monosyllables when Morrell spoke. That made Morrell fear he did not stand in General Wood's good graces.

He clicked his tongue between his teeth. He thought he should still have had credit in his account with the head of the General Staff. Utah wasn't the only matter concerning which he'd come to Wood's notice. Along with a doctor back in Tucson, New Mexico, he'd suggested the steel helmets that by now had been issued to just about every U.S. front-line soldier. That should have counted for something against the troubles in Utah.

Wood's adjutant sat at a desk in an outer office, pounding away at a typewriter hard and fast enough to make the rattle of the keys sound almost like machine-gun fire. Idly, Morrell wondered if the adjutant had ever heard real machine-gun fire. They led sheltered lives here.

"Major Morrell," the adjutant said, rising politely enough. "I'll tell the general you're here." He went into Wood's private office. When he returned a moment later, he nodded. "Go on, sir. He's expecting you." The staccato typing resumed as Morrell walked past him.

Morrell came to stiff attention before General Leonard Wood. "Reporting as ordered, sir," he said, saluting.

"At ease, Major," Wood answered easily. "Smoke if you care to. It's not the firing squad for you, or the guillotine, either." One of his hands went to the back of his neck. "That's what a Frenchman comes up with when he thinks about efficiency. Let it be a lesson to you."

"Yes, sir." Morrell wouldn't have minded a cigar, but didn't light up in spite of Wood's invitation.

The general sighed and studied Morrell with that same sick-room expression he'd come to loathe. From the chief of the General Staff, the look came naturally: he'd earned an M.D. before joining the military. He sighed again. "It didn't quite work out, did it, Major?"

"I beg your pardon, sir?" Morrell replied, though he'd long since reached the same conclusion.

"It's too bad," Wood said. "I honestly don't know if this place is good for you, but you've certainly been good for it. We get insulated against the soldier in the field and what he needs. You're a breath of fresh air here."

"Too fresh, I'd say by what's happened lately." Morrell spoke without rancor.

"Major, it's not your fault we did not anticipate the Mormons' mining us," Wood said. "No blame for that will go into your record, I assure you. But Utah had turned into your baby, and when the baby turned out to have warts—"

"More than warts, I'd say, sir," Morrell answered. "They wrecked most of a division there, and we only had two in the front line."

"That is very much in people's minds right now," Wood agreed. "I think it's unfortunate, but it's true. As a result, your usefulness here has been compromised through what is, I repeat, no fault of your own."

"Sir, if my usefulness here is compromised, could you please return me to the field?" Morrell could hear the eagerness in his own voice. A chance to get out of Philadelphia, to get back to real action—

And General Wood was nodding. "I'm going to do exactly that, Major. As you know, I would have liked you to stay around longer, to learn some more tricks of the trade, so to speak. But situations have a way of changing, like it or not. My eye is still on you, Major. Now, though, I think it best to have it on you at a distance for a while. I assure you once more, no imputation of blame will appear in your personnel file."

Morrell barely heard that. It mattered little to him. What did matter was that he would be able to fight his way now, out in the open, face to face with the foe. He had learned a few things here, and was eager to try them out along with everything he'd known before he came.

"Where do you plan on sending me, sir?" he asked. "Some-place where things are busy, I hope."

"You've given the Rebels a hard time through the first year of the war," Wood said, which was true only if you neglected the months during which Morrell had been flat on his back. Being the chief of the General Staff, Wood was allowed to neglect de-tails like that. He said, "You've shown a knack for mountain war-fare. What would you say if they sent you up to the Canadian Rockies and helped us cut the Pacific Coast off from the rest of the Canucks?"

"What would I say? Sir, I'd say, 'Yes, sir!' " Morrell knew he was all but quivering as he stood there. The mountains in eastern Kentucky had been little gentle knobby things. The Canadian Rockies were mountains with a capital M, full of ice and snow and jagged rocks. Nobody would figure you could accomplish much on that kind of terrain at this time of year. All the more reason to go out and prove people wrong.

"I'll make the arrangements, then," Wood said. "Good luck, Major."

"Thank you very much, sir," Morrell said, much more for the promised arrangements than the polite wishes. *The Canadian Rockies* . . . The prospect sang in him. John Abell would think him a fool. He didn't care what John Abell thought.

*   *   *

After not too hard a day doing not too much—although anyone who heard him talking about it might conclude he'd been at slave labor since he tumbled out of his bunk—Sam Carsten lined up for evening chow call.

"We been out here a long time, wherever the devil 'here' is," he said. "I want to get back to Honolulu, spend some of the money I've earned. I can feel it burnin' a hole in my pocket while I'm standing here."

"Yeah, well, if it gets loose, it can come to me," Vic Crosetti said. "I got one pocket in every set of dungarees lined with asbestos, just for money like that."

Carsten snorted. So did everybody else who heard Crosetti. The sailor in front of him, a big, rangy fellow named Tilden Winters, said, "Wish my stomach had a pocket like that. The slop they've been giving us the past few days, I wouldn't feed it to a rat crawling up the hawser."

"You tried feedin' it to a rat crawling up the hawser, he'd crawl back down—rats aren't stupid," Carsten said. That got a laugh, too, but it was kidding on the square. The *Dakota* had indeed been out on patrol a long time, and gone through just about all the fresh food with which she'd left port. Sam went on, "Some of the things the cooks come up with—"

"And some of the things the purchasing officers bought, figuring we'd be stupid enough to eat 'em," Winters added. "That salt beef yesterday tasted like it had been in the cask since the Second Mexican War, or maybe since the War of Secession."

Again, loud, profane agreement came from everybody in earshot. There were several conversations farther back in the chow line that Carsten couldn't make out, but their tone suggested other people were also imperfectly delighted with the bill of fare they'd been enjoying—or rather, not enjoying—lately.

Vic Crosetti's long, fleshy nose twitched; his nostrils dilated. "Whatever that is they're gonna do to us, it ain't salt beef." He made the pronouncement in a way that brooked no disagreement.

A moment later, Carsten caught the whiff, too. "You're right, Vic." He made a sour face. "That's fish, and it's been dead a long, long time."

Tilden Winters delivered his own verdict: "You ask me, one of the cooks got diarrhea again."

"If that joke ain't as old as the Navy, it's only on account of it's older," Sam said. The closer he got to the pots from which the horrible smell was coming, though, the more he wondered if it was a joke this time.

He took a tray with more reluctance than he'd ever known. As he came up to one of the cooks, the fellow ladled a dollop of stinking yellowish stuff onto the tray, then added some sauerkraut, a hard roll, and a cup of coffee. Sam pointed at the noxious puddle. "You got a sick cat, Johansen?"

"Funny man. Everybody thinks he's a cotton-picking funny man," the cook said. "It's herrings in mustard sauce, and I'll say 'I told you so' when you come back for seconds."

"Don't hold your breath," Sam told him, which, considering the stench, was a curse of no mean proportion. He took the tray over to a table, sat down, and looked dubious. "Hey, Vic, maybe the padre ought to give it the last rites."

Crosetti shook his head. "Way it smells up the galley, it's been dead a hell of a lot too long for that to do any good."

Ever so cautiously, Carsten scooped up a forkful and brought it to his mouth. "Jesus!" he exclaimed. "It tastes as lousy as it smells." He looked down at the tray with loathing that was almost admiration. "I didn't figure it could."

Tilden Winters made the taste test, too, then gulped down his coffee as if it were the only thing standing between him and an early grave. Seeing their reaction, Crosetti said, "I don't think I want any. Never was much for sauerkraut, but tonight—"

Most of the time, such grumbling would have got them in Dutch with the cooks. This evening, their complaints went unnoticed in the wider tide of revolted complaint echoing through the galley. "Do the officers eat this shit, too?" somebody shouted.

Carsten's eyes lit up. He knew he could trust Crosetti for what he had in mind, and Winters was a pretty square guy, too. "Listen," he said, "if they try and feed us this kind of slop, they oughta know what we think of it, right?"

"Sounds good to me," Winters said. "Sounds damn good to me." Crosetti nodded, too. Carsten gestured to both of them. They all put their heads together. After they were done laughing, they solemnly clasped hands to seal the bargain.

Tilden Winters got up first. He slammed his tray down on the

stack, then started saying to the cooks what everybody else had
been saying to one another. He had a talent for abuse, and certainly a fitting subject for it, too. A good many other sailors
joined in his vehement griping. That brought several cooks over,
both to defend their honor, such as it was, and to keep the men
from getting any creative ideas like flinging the herrings around
the galley.

Carsten, however, had already had a more creative idea than
that. He and Crosetti took advantage of the confusion to slip
behind the galley counter, grab one of the kettles full of the
herring-and-mustard mixture—fortunately, one with a lid—and
slip off before anyone noticed what they were doing. As soon as
they were away, they looked like a couple of sailors on some assignment or other; the kettle wasn't that different from any of a
number of containers aboard the *Dakota*.

No one paid them the least attention as they headed up into officer country. Again, looking as if you belonged was more important than actually belonging. In a prison-yard whisper,
Crosetti said, "Only slippery part is gonna be if he's in there."

"Hey, come on," Carsten said. "If he is, we go, 'Sorry, sir,
wrong cabin,' and we ditch the stuff instead of dumping it. Either
way, we're jake."

The cabin door bore a neatly stenciled inscription: LIEUT.-
CMDR. JONATHAN Y. HENRICKSON, CHIEF SHIP'S PURCHASING OF-
FICER. Sam knocked, his knuckles ringing off steel. Nobody
answered. He turned the latch. The cabin door opened easily. He
grinned again. He'd been wondering if Henrickson was the sort
who locked his door. But no.

Inside, the cabin was as neat as a CPO's dreams of heaven,
with everything in its place—*exactly* in its place—and a place
for everything. Somehow, that only made what they were about
to do the sweeter.

"Come on, let's get going," Crosetti said. "Our luck ain't
gonna hold forever." That might have been cold feet, but it didn't
sound as if it was—just a steady professional warning his comrade (*no, his accomplice,* Sam thought) of things that could go
wrong.

They took the lid off the kettle. Instantly, the stink of the herrings filled the cabin. They proceeded to make sure the stink

wasn't all that filled it: they methodically poured herrings and mustard sauce over everything they could, desk, bedding, clothes, deck, everything. As soon as they'd finished, they got the hell out of there.

An officer in the passage would have spelled disaster. Sam's shoulders sagged in relief when the long, gray-painted metal corridor proved bare. "Now all we got to do is look ordinary."

"You're too ugly to look ordinary," Crosetti retorted. But Carsten took not the slightest offense—they'd pulled it off. When they got back down to their proper part of the ship, Tilden Winters looked a question at them. They both nodded. So did he. That was all he did, too, before returning to the friendly argument about Honolulu whores in which he'd been involved before his partners in crime returned.

The hue and cry started about an hour later. Grim-faced petty officers started escorting cooks and galley helpers up to officer country near the bridge. When the first batch of them returned, rumor of what had happened started spreading through the sailors. The general reaction was delight.

"If I knew who done that," Hiram Kidde declared, although no one yet was quite sure of what *that* was, "the first thing I'd do is kick his ass." He was, after all, a CPO himself. But he'd suffered through the herrings in mustard sauce, too. "And after that, by Jesus, I'd pick him up and buy him a beer. Hell, I'd buy him all the beer he could drink." The gunner's mate roared laughter. "What I wouldn't give to see Henrickson's face."

None of the cooks knew anything. Carsten carefully didn't look at Crosetti. Somebody might have noticed them lifting the kettle. But it didn't seem as if anyone had. That didn't stop the officers from trying to get to the bottom of who had perpetrated the atrocity. They kept right on trying, all the way up until the *Dakota* docked in Honolulu.

Carsten went up before Lieutenant Commander Henrickson himself. "No, sir," he said. "I'm sorry, sir. All I know is ship's scuttlebutt."

"What did you think of the fish?" the purchasing officer demanded, his thin mouth set in a tight, bloodless line.

"Sir, beg your pardon, but I didn't like it worth a damn," Carsten told him.

He sighed. "I'm afraid everyone says that. I hoped the bastards who did this would sing songs about how good it was, to try to turn looks away from them. No such luck, though. Damn sailors are too damn sly." That last was an angry mutter. Carsten carefully did not smile.

Back when Scipio had been butler at Marshlands, he'd wondered how a man could ever get used to the racket of battle. Even single gunshots had been plenty to set his heart pounding. He was inclined to laugh at his former self nowadays. He hadn't known much back then.

He hadn't known much about a lot of things back then. As far as a lot of them went, he would gladly have remained ignorant, too. Much of what Cassius fondly thought of as revolutionary practice looked to Scipio an awful lot like what the whites of the Confederate States had been doing, only stood on its head.

Sometimes the strain of keeping his mouth shut was almost more than he could bear. But he'd turned his own experience in the days before the Congaree Socialist Republic to his advantage, too. Anne Colleton hadn't been able to see past the smooth butler's mask he wore, and neither could Cassius now.

Fortunately, Cassius hadn't noticed that he hadn't noticed Scipio's mask. The chairman of the Republic had plenty of other things on his mind. He somehow managed to make the undyed, unbleached cotton homespun of Negro field laborers into a good approximation of a uniform, and even to look smart in it, which was far beyond Scipio's ability. What he could not do, though, was lose the worried expression on his face.

"Ain't got enough white folks wid we, Kip," he said now. "De po' buckra, de gov'ment 'press them same as it done to we. Dey gots to see where dey class int'rest is at. Dey gots to see de revolution fo' dey, too, not jus' fo' we." He shook his head. "But dey don'. Dey is still de dogs o' de massers dat 'sploits dey. Cipher dat out fo' me, Kip. Don' make no sense."

Scipio still found revolutionary rhetoric and the Congaree

119

dialect an odd blend. No one cared about his opinion in such matters, though, and he was canny enough to keep it to himself. Cassius had asked his opinion about the other matter, though, and might even have been ready to hear it. Scipio decided to take a chance there.

He pointed to what had been the country courthouse of Kingstree, South Carolina. The two-story, buff-colored building with a fancy, fanlighted pediment, built in the style of the early years of the last century, no longer flew the Stars and Bars. Instead, the red revolutionary banner of the Congaree Socialist Republic fluttered above it. Red paint had been daubed over the name KINGSTREE, which was carved into the frieze above the pediment. In letters equally blood-colored, someone had given the town a substitute name: PEOPLE'S TREE.

"Dat kind o' thing, Cass—an' we done a lot of it—dat kind o' thing, like I say, dat skeers de white folks out o' dey shoes," he said.

Cassius looked back at the courthouse, then swung his gaze toward Scipio once more. As soon as Scipio saw the expression on the chairman's face, he knew he had failed. "Ain't gwine have no backslidin' in this here revolution," Cassius declared. "We is bringin' liberty to de people, an' if dey is too foolish to be grateful, dey pays de price."

He truly did not seem to realize that terrorizing everyone who was not ardently on his side to begin with would ensure that he drew few new supporters who didn't have great grievances against the Confederate States. Hardly any Negroes lacked such grievances. But, exactly because whites had been inflicting grief instead of taking it, the system that had been in place suited them well enough.

And now he went on, "De niggers here in People's Tree, dey live in the sections dey call Buzzard's Roost and Frog Level. You t'ink de white folks, dey want to live in sections wid they names?" He spat on the ground to show how likely he reckoned that was. Scipio didn't think it was very likely, either. But destroying white privilege only boosted white fear. And then Cassius wondered why whites fought against the Red revolution with everything they had.

Once more, Scipio tried to suggest that: "De more we puts they backs up, the harder they tries to put us down."

For a moment, he thought he'd got through to Cassius. The chairman of the Congaree Socialist Republic sighed and shook his head. He said, "We git a messenger under flag o' truce las' night."

"Dat a fact?" Scipio said. If it was a fact, it was news to him. That was worrisome in and of itself. Cassius had been in the habit of letting him know what happened as soon as it happened. A change in the pattern was liable to mean Scipio's status was slipping, which was liable to prove hazardous to his life expectancy. Warily, he asked, "Dis messenger, what he say?"

"He say dat, if we doesn't lay down we arms, de white folks liable to start killin' de niggers in de part o' de country we ain't managed to liberate. What you t'ink o' dat?"

Scipio's first reaction was horror. His second reaction was horror, too. The Confederates could do that, and who would be able to stop them? The answer to that question came all too clear: *nobody*. "What you say?" he asked Cassius.

"I say two things," the ex-hunter answered. "I say, if dat de game dey gwine play, we got plenty white folks to kill, too. Dey got mo' niggers'n we got white folks, but dey think one white folks worth a whole heap o' blacks. So dat make dis cocky 'ristocrat think some."

Scipio nodded. It was a brutal ploy, but one to match the threat from the CSA. He had no doubt Cassius would carry it out, either, and was sure the chairman had left no doubt in the Confederate envoy's mind. "Dat one," he said, his voice showing his approval. "What de other?"

Cassius startled him by laughing out loud, a deep, rich, nasty laugh, the kind of laugh you let out after you'd heard a really good, really ripe dirty story. A moment later, Scipio understood why, for the chairman said, "I tell he, we don't even got to do no killin' to git our own back, if de 'pressors start de persecution in de unliberated land. I tell he, dere plenty white folks wimmin in the Congaree Socialist Republic. I don' say no more. Ain't got no need to say no more."

"Do Jesus!" Scipio said. Confederate laws against miscegenation were harsh, and vigorously enforced. For some reason, Confederate white men seemed convinced that the first thing blacks would do, given any sort of chance, was make a beeline

for white women. Even after the uprisings in the Congaree Socialist Republic, it hadn't happened much. Scipio had heard of a
few cases, but the revolutionary government had more urgent
things—survival, for instance—with which to concern itself.
But now, to use the mere idea as a club with which to beat the
Confederates over the head . . . Scipio stared at Cassius in astonished admiration. "You is a devil, you is."

Cassius took that as the compliment it was intended to be.
"Wish you was there. This white folks captain, he got a *see*gar in
he mouth. When I say dat, he like to swallow it." He laughed
again.

So did Scipio. The story was worth laughing about—if it
turned out to have a happy ending. "Once he cough de *see*gar up,
what he say?"

"He say we never dare do no such thing." Cassius' eyes glittered. "I tell he we is a pack o' desp'rate niggers, an' who know
what we do? De white-folks gov'ment been sayin' dat so much
an' so loud, dey lackeys all believes it. So he say, de honor o' de
white folks wimmin matter to de gov'ment, an' dey don't do
nuffin to hurt it. You know what dat mean."

"Mean dey don't want white folks wimmin birthin' a pack o'
yaller babies," Scipio said.

Cassius nodded with yet another chuckle. "Marx, he know
'bout dis. If de peasant wench have de lord's baby, dey call dat de
droit de seigneur." What he did to the pronunciation of the
French words was a caution, but Scipio understood him. He
went on, "But de lord's lady, if she have a baby by de peasant,
everybody run around like chickens wid a fox in the henhouse.
An' if that baby *yaller*, like you say—"

"You reckon de white folks think twice, then?" Scipio asked.

"Dey think fo'-five times 'fore they want the likes o' me
humpin' dis fifteen-year-old buckra gal wid de hair in de yaller
braids," Cassius said positively, and Scipio thought he was right.
The chairman spat again. "Like I got me trouble findin' wimmin
wants to do it."

He wasn't boasting, just stating a fact. He'd boasted plenty,
back when he was chief hunter on the Marshlands plantation. As
chairman of the Congaree Socialist Republic, he seemed to find
it beneath his dignity. Scipio prodded him a little: "Drusilla," he
said slyly.

He won a chuckle from Cassius, which relieved him: when Cassius was thinking about Cassius, he wasn't thinking about Scipio. "Ain't looked fo' she since de revolution come," Cassius said. "Maybe I ought to." His hands described an hourglass in the air. He'd used the excuse of fooling around with Drusilla, who'd lived on the late, purged Jubal Marberry's plantation, to travel by routes only he knew and bring back weapons from the USA.

Scipio spoke another name: "Cherry."

He'd intended that to come out sly and man-to-man, too. Somehow it didn't, not quite. And Cassius stopped grinning. His answer, this time, was serious: "Dat gal, she do anything to help de revolution. If dat mean sleep wif you, she do it."

"That so," Scipio agreed. She'd slept with Jacob Colleton, to keep the mistress' gassed brother distracted from any of the revolutionary buildup on the plantation, and then she'd used his abuse of her—or what she claimed to be his abuse of her—to touch off the uprising at the right moment. She was, Scipio knew, sharing a bed with Cassius these days.

But the chairman, instead of leering and bragging—for Cherry was one fine-looking, strong-minded woman—held up a forefinger in warning. "She do *anything* to help the revolution," he said. "Anything at all. If dat mean cut yo' balls off while you sleep, she do dat, too, an' she don' think twice."

If he thought Scipio would argue with him, he was mistaken. The former butler was more afraid of Cherry than he was of Cassius, and that was saying something. Finding out that she also intimidated the chairman was interesting. He wondered if and how he'd be able to use that.

Before he had a chance to think about it, he heard a screaming whistle in the sky, coming out of the south. Several artillery shells burst with thunderous roars a few hundred yards outside of the renamed People's Tree. More explosions farther south meant the People's Revolutionary Army line was taking a pounding. Artillery was the one thing the Republic conspicuously lacked.

Cassius swore with bitter resignation. "I don' reckon we gwine hold they white folks out of this here town more'n another two-three days."

"What we do then?" Now Scipio sounded nervous, and knew

it. When Cassius was optimistic about the way the fighting was going, he was often wrong; when he was pessimistic, he was always right.

"Fall back. What else *kin* we do?" the chairman answered. "We maybe lose dis here stand-up war"—the first time he had admitted the possibility, which sent a chill up Scipio's spine— "but we go to de deep swamp, fight they white folks forever. An' some o' we, we jus' goes back to bein' ordinary niggers again, niggers what ain't never done nothin' de white folk get theyselves in a ruction about—till we sees de chance. We sees de chance, an' we *seize* de chance." He looked sharply at Scipio, to make sure he caught the wordplay.

Scipio did, and gave back a dutiful smile. He hoped that smile covered what was no longer a chill but a blizzard inside him. If Cassius admitted the revolution was starting to come unraveled, then it was. And, while Cassius and some of his followers could no doubt carry on a guerrilla campaign against the Confederacy from out of the swamps they knew better than any white man did, Scipio wasn't any of those followers. His skills at living under such conditions were nonexistent. He couldn't go back to being an ordinary Negro, either; the uprising had literally destroyed the place he'd had in the world.

What did that leave? He saw nothing. He'd always had trouble believing the revolution would succeed. Whenever he'd oh so cautiously raised doubts, no one paid him any mind. Now he saw himself vindicated. *Much good it does me,* he thought bitterly.

George Enos looked to his left. The woody shoreline of Tennessee lay to port of the monitor *Punishment.* George looked to his right. To starboard were the hills of northeastern Arkansas. U.S. land forces held the Tennessee side of the Mississippi. God only knew who could lay claim to the Arkansas side of the river. It wasn't trench warfare over there—more like large-scale bushwhacking.

Wayne Pitchess came up to Enos. He was looking toward the Arkansas bank of the Mississippi, too. "If we ever clear out those Rebs, we'll have a better chance of heading down the river and grabbing Memphis," he said.

"Thank you, Admiral," George said, which made Pitchess glare at him in mock anger. He went on, "We get Memphis, that's a long step toward cutting the CSA right in half. Sure would be fine."

"Now who's the admiral?" Pitchess retorted, and Enos spread his hands, admitting to attempted strategizing. His buddy's face took on a wistful expression. "Wonder if we'll ever see the day. If it takes us a year and a half to clear a quarter of the river, how long do we need to do all of it?"

"Reminds me of the kind of questions that ran me out of school and onto a fishing boat," George said, to which Pitchess nodded. George looked south now, toward the distant Tennessee city. "I feel like Moses looking toward the Promised Land, knowing I'm never going to get there."

"Sailor, you have the wrong attitude," Pitchess declared, sounding very much like the morale-building lectures that came out of the Navy Department and were read with straight faces by the officers of the *Punishment*. "If only we don't worry about the minefields in the Mississippi and the shore batteries that can blow us out of the water and the Confederate river monitors, we'll waltz into Memphis day after tomorrow."

"Now there's sugar for my morning coffee," Enos exclaimed, and Wayne Pitchess laughed out loud. "Now, Mr. Sugar, sir, what happens if I do worry about those things, or even about one of 'em?"

"Then it takes longer," Pitchess said, "and you get written up for malicious fretting and impeding the war effort. They issue you a ball and chain and a sledgehammer, and you start making boulders into sand. Sounds bully, don't it?"

The *Punishment* inched down the Mississippi. Everyone on deck kept an eye peeled for the round, spiked ugliness of mines. George methodically checked and cleaned the action of his machine gun. Lieutenant Kelly would have given him hell had he neglected it, but he didn't need the officer riding him to make sure he attended to what needed doing. Hosing bullets out at the Rebs was the likeliest way he'd stay alive in an action; if the gun jammed, that gave the enemy a free shot at him. Best, then, that it didn't jam.

Kelly came up behind him and watched in approval so silent that George jumped when he turned around and discovered him there. "You take care of the equipment," the Navy man said, as if surprised to discover that trait in someone so recently a civilian.

"Sir, I put in a lot of years on a fishing trawler," George answered. "We didn't spend so much time polishing things as we do here, but everything had to work." The Atlantic, he thought, was much less forgiving of mistakes than the Mississippi. It would, quite impersonally, kill you if you gave it even a quarter of a chance.

On the other hand, the Rebels would kill you most personally if they got their chance, or even a piece of their chance. He supposed that pretty much balanced things out. Kelly might have been thinking along those lines, too, for he said, "We have to be ready every second."

"Yes, sir," Enos agreed.

Kelly sighed. "I do wish we were something more than fire support for the Army. Out on the ocean, by all I hear, ships do what they need to do, not what some fool in green-gray thinks they need to do."

As far as George was concerned, a dark blue uniform could also cover up a fool. He carefully did not mention that to Kelly, who was liable to think Enos had him in mind with the comment. What he did say was, "Crazy kind of war we're fighting here."

"Sailor, if you think I'm going to argue with you, you're the one who's crazy," Kelly told him. "Snapping-turtle Navy is a strange sort of place."

Enos would have said more, but klaxons started shouting. He would have run to his battle station, but he was already there. What he did do was run a belt into his machine gun, then look around to see what he was supposed to use for a target. He didn't spot anything.

Word was not long in coming. Fingers began pointing south. Squinting, Enos spotted a tiny smudge of smoke on the horizon. It was what the smoke from the *Punishment*'s stacks might have looked like, if seen from a distance of several miles. Which meant—

"Well, well," Lieutenant Kelly said, whistling tunelessly between his teeth. "You don't see ship-to-ship actions very often in river warfare. Aren't you glad we've found an exception for you, Enos?"

"Sir, I'll fight," George said. "You know I'll fight. Expecting me to be glad about it is probably asking too much." He'd had revenge enough by now for what the Rebs had done to him while he was a fisherman. He wouldn't have minded spending the rest of the war somewhere far away from the roar of guns and close to Sylvia, George, Jr., and Mary Jane. He wondered if his little girl remembered him. Then he wondered if Sylvia remembered him—he hadn't had a letter for a while.

Kelly said, "The next interesting question is whether we saw the Rebs before they saw us." *Interesting* was such a nice, bland word to apply to a question that was liable to determine whether the *Punishment* remained a river monitor or turned into a flaming hulk in the next few minutes.

With a small noise, half whir, half grind, the turret of the *Punishment* began to revolve. The big guns elevated a few degrees. Before they could fire, though, a couple of great columns of water fountained up from the Mississippi, several hundred yards ahead of the monitor. Secondary splashes rose from shell fragments hitting the water.

"Well, well," Kelly said again, as calmly as if the toast were too dark to suit him. "That answers that, doesn't it?"

It did, and, as far as George was concerned, it was the wrong answer. He felt singularly useless. Whatever happened in the duel between the *Punishment* and the Confederate monitor, it wasn't going to happen at ranges where a machine gun would do any good. That meant he had to remain a spectator at what might be his own destruction. He'd had to do that before, aboard the submersible-hunting trawler *Spray*. He didn't think he'd get used to it if he had to do it a hundred times.

The *Punishment*'s guns bellowed. The deck quivered under Enos' feet. He hoped the fellow at the rangefinder knew his business. No way to be certain, not with land and the twists of the river hiding the enemy from sight. Only smoke by which to gauge positions—it was a particularly deadly version of blindman's buff.

Smoke spurted from the *Punishment*'s stacks. Now the monitor had to move quickly, either that or present a sitting target to its Confederate counterpart. Moving, though, was as likely to mean heading into the path of enemy fire as away from it. George wondered how Commander Heinrich, the skipper of the

Punishment, chose which way to go. However he did it, he earned his money.

More shells from the Confederate gunboat splashed into the Mississippi. These were closer, so that some of the water they kicked up came raining down onto the deck of the *Punishment*. Enos wished he had his slicker from the *Ripple*.

Lieutenant Kelly, though, was grinning. "They haven't straddled us," he said. "Their next salvo will be long, and the one after that, if we're lucky, longer yet. That gives us more time to find them and hit them." He spoke as if that were all in a day's work—and so, in fact, it was. George still hadn't got used to the notion that, wearing this uniform, his day's work involved killing people.

Boom! Boom! The guns in the *Punishment*'s turret replied to the Confederate fire. George hadn't watched to see whether their muzzles had moved up or down or whether they thought they had the range. How, firing with only smoke to go by, would they know if they'd made a hit? By seeing more smoke, he supposed, or by having the enemy gunboat quit shooting at them.

It hadn't quit shooting at the moment, worse luck. As Kelly had predicted, the next two shells were long. Enos waited anxiously for the salvo after that. How clever was the Rebel captain?

George had heard the Confederate shells roaring overhead before they splashed into the Mississippi. When the roar came again, he cringed at his machine gun: the shells screaming down sounded as if they were going to land on top of his head. "Brace yourselves, boys," Lieutenant Kelly shouted through the screech of their descent. "They're—"

One of them hit just to port of the *Punishment*, the other, half a second later, to starboard. The monitor staggered under Enos' feet, as if it had fallen into a hole. But there were no holes in the Mississippi—or rather, there hadn't been. That stagger was part of what knocked George off his feet. The rest was blast, which flung him against the side of the turret.

A fragment from the shell clanged off the turret about the same time as he hit it. A fresh, bright scar appeared on the metal, less than six inches above his head. He sucked in a breath, wondering if he'd feel the stab of a broken rib or two. To his relief, he didn't.

Dazedly, he sat up and looked around. Lieutenant Michael

Kelly hadn't been so lucky as he was. There Kelly sprawled, cut almost in half by a piece of flying steel. To his horror, he saw the lieutenant's eyes still had awareness in them. Kelly's mouth moved, but only blood came from it. Then, mercifully, he slumped down dead.

And then, quite as if nothing had happened, the *Punishment*'s guns bellowed out a reply to the Confederate salvo. The crew might have been damaged, but the warship lived on. It would keep doing its job, too. George had an uneasy vision of a stream of men entering its hatches like beeves being driven into a slaughterhouse, the cannon firing, and out the far hatches coming, not steaks and ground meat, but coffins. But that would not matter to the ship. There would always be more men to feed into it, as there were always more men to feed into the trenches.

Across the water came a deep, low rumble, like thunder far away. For a moment, Enos thought it was the sound of the Confederate gunboat firing. But he hadn't heard it when the other vessel's previous salvos reached for the *Punishment*. The distant plume of smoke suddenly swelled enormously at the base.

"Hit!" somebody shouted. Somebody else yelled, "Blew the bastards to kingdom come!" George Enos started yelling, too. It was victory. Then he looked at Mike Kelly, or what was left of him, and at the gouge on the metal of the turret so close to where his own head had been. As easily as not, Kelly could have been alive and himself dead and mutilated. He yelled louder than ever.

Jefferson Pinkard was one of the lucky ones: he had a real seat in a real passenger coach on the troop train rumbling through the night somewhere in southern Georgia. *If this is good luck,* he thought, *I don't want to know what bad luck is like*.

His backside and the base of his spine ached; the seat was bare wood. It might have been a car for whites too poor to afford even second-class fare, or it might have been reserved for Negroes. If Pinkard had had to ride in cars like this whenever he took the train, he might have risen up himself against the people who made him do it.

He couldn't stretch his legs out, either; the space between his seat and the one in front of it was too narrow. It would have been too narrow even if he hadn't been kitted out with a pack on his back and a rifle between his knees. As things were, he felt like a sardine jammed into its tin. His newly issued helmet, a low-crowned iron derby with a wide rim on the British model, added to that canned feeling.

What he didn't feel much like was a soldier. They'd given him his uniform, they'd given him his Tredegar, they'd given him a couple of weeks' screamed instruction at close-order drill and riflery, and then they'd hauled him and his training regiment out of the camp near Birmingham and put them on the train.

Even his drill instructors—ogres in human shape if ever there were any—hadn't been happy about that. "Weren't for them damn niggers, y'all'd be here another month, likely tell longer," one of them had said when the orders arrived. "Y'all was goin' up against the damnyankees, wouldn't be a man jack of you left breathing in two weeks' time. But they reckon y'all are good enough now to whip them Red niggers back into line."

Pinkard turned to the raw private on the hard, cramped seat next to his: a skinny little fellow with spectacles who'd been a clerk in Dothan till the Conscription Bureau finally swept him up. "Stinky," he said, "if them niggers was soldiers as lousy as they say, we'd have done licked 'em already, don't you reckon?"

"My name," Stinky Salley said in tones of relentless precision, "is Christopher." He'd said the same thing in the same tone to the drill sergeants who'd rechristened him after he'd evaded bath call one evening. He'd kept on saying it even after they knocked him down—he had spirit, maybe more than his scrawny body could safely contain. It did no good; the nickname had stuck.

"Listen, Stinky," Pinkard went on, "it stands to reason that—"

One of the soldiers who sprawled in the aisle between seats, somewhere between sitting and lying, spoke up: "Stands to reason somebody's gonna kick your ass, you don't shut the hell up and let him sleep if he's able."

Pinkard did shut up. He wished he could sleep. He was too uncomfortable. He wondered how he'd be when the train finally stopped. *Probably shuffle around like a ninety-year-old man with the rheumatism,* he thought.

The window three seats in front of his suddenly blew in, spraying glass around the car. He yelped when a piece stung his cheek. A warm trickle of blood began to flow. "What the hell—?" somebody yelled.

Another window blew out, this one behind him. He felt something—probably more glass—rebound from his helmet. Back there, a man started screaming: "Oh, Mother!" he wailed. "I'm hit! Oh, God! Oh, Mama!"

Realization smote. "They're shooting at us, the sons of bitches—niggers in the night, I mean."

He couldn't do anything about it, either. He had no target at which to shoot. All he could do was sit there and hope the Red revolutionaries would miss him. That might have been worse than anything else about it—or so he thought till his squad leader, a dour corporal named Peter Ploughman, said, "Thank God they ain't got but a rifle or two. You boys ain't never seen what comes out of a train that done got chewed up by a machine gun."

A couple of the men near the wounded soldier did what they could for him, which wasn't much. The car held neither a doctor nor a medical orderly. Jeff had no idea how anybody who knew anything could have come from another car to the hurt man, not with the way soldiers had been shoehorned into this train. The poor fellow would have to suffer till it stopped.

And it wasn't stopping. The reverse, in fact: it was speeding up, to escape the harassing fire from the brush by the tracks. In a speculative voice, Ploughman said, "How sneaky are them damn niggers, anyways? They tryin' to spook us into runnin' right over some explosives they planted?"

"Jesus!" Jefferson Pinkard said. He was glad he wasn't the only one who said it. He'd thought working at the Sloss foundry was such a dangerous job, war would hardly faze him afterwards. But in the Sloss works even Leonidas, appearances to the contrary notwithstanding, wasn't actively trying to kill him and devoting all his ingenuity toward that end. The idea that the Red Negroes might be using a small incident to give rise to a big one, as if they were throwing stones to flush game out of deep cover to where it could more readily be shot—that made the hair stand up at the back of his neck.

Acceleration pressed him against his seat. Things in his pack dug into his spine and his kidneys. He tried to brace himself against an explosion that would fling the car off the tracks like a toy kicked by a brat with a nasty temper. He didn't think anything he did would help much, but sitting there like a lump of coal wouldn't help at all.

Without warning, he wasn't being pressed back any more. He had everything he could do to keep from going facefirst into the back of the seat in front of him. Soldiers in the corridor, who could not steady themselves, tumbled over one another in a shouting, cursing heap.

Iron screamed on iron, rails and wheels locking in an embrace so hot, it sent orange-red sparks leaping up higher than the window through which Jefferson Pinkard stared. Absurdly, he wondered if he'd helped bring any of that iron into being.

Groaning and shuddering, the train staggered to a halt. Pinkard saw a couple of men with kerosene lanterns outside. Their voices came through the shattered windows of the car: "Out! Out! Everybody out!"

That wasn't easy or quick. It wouldn't have been easy or quick with veteran troops. With raw recruits, all the shouting of their officers and noncoms helped only so much. They got in one another's way, went in this direction when they should have gone in that, and generally blundered their way out of the coaches into the night.

Cold nipped at Pinkard as he stood in the darkness. A coal stove and a lot of bodies had kept the car warm. Now he got out the overcoat stowed in his pack. He wished he were home in bed with Emily, who would warm him better than any Army overcoat could. Most of the time, he'd been too busy to notice how much he missed her. Not now, standing here all confused, breathing in coal smoke from the engine, breathing out fog from the chill.

"Just in time—" The phrase started going through the raw soldiers, some of them plainly repeating it without any clear idea of why they were. Then somebody who sounded as if he did know what he was talking about spoke up: "We hadn't been able to flag the engineer down in time, reckon this here train would have blown sky high."

"What did I say?" Corporal Peter Ploughman sounded both vindicated and smug. Pinkard shrugged. If Ploughman didn't know more about the soldiering business than the men he led, he had no business wearing stripes on his sleeves. But Jeff supposed the noncom did need to impress them every now and again with how much he knew.

"Where are we?" someone asked.

"About twenty miles outside of Albany," the authoritative-sounding voice answered. Albany, or its outskirts, had been their destination. Jeff had a ghastly suspicion he knew how they were going to get there now.

A moment later, that suspicion was confirmed. Captain Connolly, the company commander, shouted, "Form column of fours!" Grumbling and cursing in low voices, the soldiers obeyed, again less efficiently than veterans might have done. And off they tramped, eastward along the line of the railroad toward Albany.

Pinkard promptly tripped over a rock, almost falling on his face. "They're going to pay for this," he muttered. He'd had to make only one night march during his abbreviated training. He hadn't liked it for beans. Now he discovered practice was a lot easier than the real thing.

After some endless time, dawn began to break. What had been dark punctuated by deeper black turned into trenches and shell crates and burned-out Negro shacks and also the occasional burned-out mansion. Fresh-turned red earth in the middle of winter meant new graves. There were a lot of them. A faint odor of corruption hung in the air.

"Niggers are playing for keeps," Stinky Salley remarked, in tones full of the same surprise and disbelief Pinkard felt. "Never would have reckoned they could do nothin' like this."

"Whole damn world's gone crazy since the war started," Jeff said. "Women workin' men's jobs, niggers workin' white men's jobs, and now, hell, niggers fightin' damn near like white men. Shitfire, I wish they were fightin' the damnyankees, not me."

That argument had raged on the train and in the training camp, as it had all over the Confederacy since the Negro uprising began. Stinky Salley was on the other side. He stared at Pinkard with withering scorn. "Yeah, and I bet you wish they was marrying your womenfolks, too," he said.

"Don't wish anything of the kind, goddammit," Pinkard said. "Just use your eyes instead of your mouth for a change, why don't you? If niggers was the happy-go-lucky stay-at-homes everybody been sayin' they are, you and me wouldn't be *here*.

We'd be fighting the USA instead." Salley's glare didn't get any friendlier, but he shut up. Not even he could argue that they were where they'd figured on being, or that Negroes in arms weren't opposing the Confederate government.

"Let's get moving," Captain Connolly shouted. "You don't want to fall out of line hereabouts—niggers'd sooner cut your throat than look at you. Sooner we put these stinking Reds down, sooner we can get back to whipping the damnyankees. Train can't do the work, so your legs got to. Keep movin'!"

Keep moving Pinkard did, though his feet began to ache. He wondered if the CSA really could recover from this rebellion as if nothing had happened. The captain certainly seemed to think so. Looking at the devastation through which they were marching, Pinkard wasn't so sure. Who would repair everything that had been damaged?

A couple of Negroes, a man and a woman, were working in a garden plot near the tracks. They looked up at the column of white men in butternut. Had they been rebels a few days before? Had they hidden their weapons when government forces washed over them? Would they cut his throat if they saw half a chance? Or were they as genuinely horrified by the uprising as a lot of blacks in Birmingham were?

How could you know? How were you supposed to tell? Pinkard pondered that as he tramped past them. Try as he would, he found no good answers.

Lucien Galtier spoke to his horse as the two of them rolled down the road from Rivière-du-Loup toward his home: "This paving, it is not such a bad thing, eh? Oh, I may have to put shoes on you more often now, but we can go out and about in weather that would have kept us home before, n'est-ce pas?"

The horse didn't answer. The horse never answered. That was one of the reasons Lucien enjoyed conversing with it. Back at the house, he had trouble getting a word in edgewise. He looked around. Snow lay everywhere. Even with overcoat, wool muffler, and wool cap pulled down over his ears, he was cold. The road, however, remained a black ribbon of asphalt through the white. The Americans kept it open even in the worst of blizzards.

They did not do it for him, of course. The racket of an engine behind him and the raucous squawk of a horn told him why they did do it. Moving as slowly as he could get away with, he pulled over to the edge of the road and let the U.S. ambulance roar past. It picked up speed, racing with its burden of wounded men toward the hospital the Americans had built on Galtier's land.

"On my patrimony," he told the horse. It snorted and flicked its ears, as if here, for once, it sympathized with him. His land had been in his family for more than two hundred years, since the days of Louis XIV. That anyone should simply appropriate a piece of it struck him as outrageous. Had the Americans no decency?

He knew the answer to that, only too well. Major Quigley, the occupier in charge of dealing with the Quebecois, had blandly assured him the benefits of the road would make up for having lost some of his land. Quigley hadn't believed it himself; he'd taken the land for no other reason than to punish Lucien. But it might even turn out to be so.

"And what if it is?" Lucien asked. Now, sensibly, the horse did not respond. How could anyone, even a horse, make a response? Thievery was thievery, and you could not compensate for it in such a way. Did they reckon him devoid of honor, devoid of pride? If they did, they would be sorry—and sooner than they thought. So he hoped, at any rate.

Another ambulance came up the road toward him. He took his time getting out of the way for this one, too. That was a tiny way to resist the American invaders, but even tiny ways were not to be despised. Perhaps a man who might have lived would die on account of the brief delay.

He glanced toward the west. Ugly clouds were massing there: another storm coming. Even on a paved road, Galtier did not care to be caught in it. He flicked the reins and told the horse to get moving. The horse, which had been listening to him for many years, snorted and increased its pace from a walk . . . to a walk.

Here came a buggy toward his wagon. He stiffened on the seat. The man in the seat did not wear American green-gray. American soldiers at least had the courage to fight their foes face to face, however reprehensible their other habits might be. The small, plump man in black there, far from fighting his foes, embraced them with a fervor Galtier found incomprehensible and infuriating.

The priest waved to him. *"Bonjour,* Lucien," he called.

"Bonjour, Father Pascal," Galtier called back, adding under his breath, *"Mauvais tabernac."* Even English-speaking Canadians thought the Quebecois way of cursing peculiar, but Lucien did not care. It satisfied him more than their talk of manure and fornication.

Father Pascal's cheeks were always pink, and doubly so with the chilly wind rising as it was now. "I have given those poor injured men a bit of spiritual solace," he said, smiling at Lucien. "Do you know, my son, a surprising number of them are communicants of our holy Catholic church?"

"No, Father, I did not know that." Galtier did not care, either. They might be Catholics, but they were unquestionably Americans. That more than made up for a common religion, as far as the farmer was concerned.

Father Pascal saw the world differently. *"C'est vrai*—it's true," he said. Father Pascal, Lucien thought, saw the world in terms of what was most advantageous for Father Pascal. The Americans were here, the Americans were strong, therefore he collaborated with the Americans. Nodding again to Lucien, he went on, "I had the honor also to see your lovely daughter Nicole at the hospital. In her whites, I did not recognize her for a moment. The doctors tell me she is doing work of an excellent sort. You must be very proud of her."

"I am always very proud of her," Lucien said. That had the virtue of being true and polite at the same time, something which could not be said about a good many other possible responses. Galtier glanced over toward the building clouds. "And now, Father, if you will pardon me—" The horse broke into a trot this time, as if it truly did understand how much he wanted to get away.

"Go with God, my son," Father Pascal called after him. He waved back toward the priest, hoping the snowstorm would catch him before he got back to Rivière-du-Loup.

If Lucien was to reach the farmhouse, he had to drive past the hospital. It was almost as if Major Quigley had set a small town on his property: the hospital certainly had more ambulances coming to it and leaving it than Rivière-du-Loup had had motorcars at the start of the war. It also had a large gasoline-powered generator that gave it electricity, while trucks and big wagons brought in coal to keep it warm against the worst a Quebec winter could do.

People bustled in and out the front door, those going in pausing to show their bona fides to armed guards at the doorway. A doctor stood outside the entrance, smoking a cigarette; red spattered his white jacket. Out came a U.S. officer in green-gray, a formidable row of ribbons and medals on his chest and an even more formidable scowl on his face. Lucien would have bet he hadn't got what he wanted, whatever that was. And here came a couple of women pulling overcoats on over their long white dresses to fight the chill outside.

Galtier steered the wagon toward them and reined to a halt. *"Bonsoir, mademoiselle,"* he said, formal as a butler. "May I offer you a ride to your home?"

Nicole Galtier smiled at him. "Oh, *bonsoir,* Papa," she said. "I didn't expect you here at just this time." She started to climb into the wagon, then turned back toward the other nurse. "See you tomorrow, Henrietta."

"See you tomorrow," Henrietta said. She went over to the doctor. He gave her a cigarette and lighted it with his own, leaning his face close to hers.

The horse had taken several strides before Lucien fully noticed what he'd heard. "You spoke to her in English," he said to Nicole.

"I am learning it, yes," she answered, and tossed her head so that the starched white cap she wore almost flew off. "If I am to do anything that is important and not just wash and carry, I have to learn it." She glanced at him to see how he was taking that. When he didn't say anything, she went on, "You have learned it, and use what you have learned, is that not so?"

"Yes, it is so," he told her, and wondered where to go from there. Discovering he had no idea, he kept quiet till he had driven the wagon into the barn. "Go on to the house," he said then. "I'll see to the horse and be in with you in a few minutes."

Brushing down the animal and making sure it had food and water—but not too much of either—was a routine he took for granted. He had heard that rich farmers had motorcars of their own, and tractors and threshers with motors, too. He wondered what they thought of doing without horses. He shrugged. He was not a rich farmer, nor likely to become one.

As he often did, he sighed with pleasure on walking into the farmhouse. Not only was it warm, it was also full of the good smells of cooking. "Is that chicken stew?" he called in the direction of the kitchen.

Marie's voice floated resignedly out: "Yes, Lucien—chicken stew. One day, I swear, I shall buy a zebra or a camel, so I can roast it in the oven and not have you know at first sniff what it is."

"Zebra would probably taste like horse," their son Georges said, and then, exercising his gift for the absurd, "although it could be the meat would have stripes."

"Thank God we have not been hungry enough to have to learn the taste of horse," Lucien said. "Thank Him twice, for the beast we have is so old, he would surely be tough."

Charles said, "I have read in a book on the French Foreign Legion that the roasted hump of a camel is supposed to be a great delicacy."

"Since a man has to be a fool—a brave fool, yes, but a fool—to join the Foreign Legion, I do not think he is to be trusted in matters of taste," Galtier said. "And I do not think a camel would do well in the snow."

"You do not have reason, Papa," Charles said, glad to show off knowledge at his father's expense. "Not only are there camels that live in the desert, there are also others—Bactrians, they are called—that live in cold countries."

"But not in Quebec," Lucien said firmly. He caught the evil gleam in Georges' eye and forestalled him: "Nor, for that matter, have we any great herds of zebras here." Georges pouted; he hated having his father anticipate a joke.

Over the supper table, they talked of camels and zebras and of more practical matters like the price chickens were bringing in Rivière-du-Loup, whether the kerosene ration was likely to be cut again, and what a good bunch of applejack this latest one from their neighbor was. "Warms you better than the fire does," Charles said, sipping the potent, illegal, popular stuff.

And Nicole, as had become her habit, talked about the work she did at the hospital. "The officer had a wounded leg full of pus, and I helped drain it," she said. "I did not do much, of course, as I am so new, but I watched with great care, and I think I will be able to do more next time." Her nose wrinkled. "The smell was bad, but not so bad that I could not stand it."

Susanne screwed up her face into a horrible grimace. "That's disgusting, Nicole," she exclaimed, freighting the word with all the emphasis she could give. The rest of her sisters, older and younger, nodded vehemently.

Gently, Marie said, "Perhaps not at supper, Nicole."

"It is my work," Nicole said, sounding as angry as Lucien had ever heard her. "We all talk about what we do in the day. Am I to wear a muzzle because I do not do what everyone else does?" She got up and hurried away from the table.

Lucien stared after her. When he had hesitated over letting her take the job at the hospital, it had been because he feared and disliked the company into which she would be thrown there. He had never thought that, simply by virtue of doing different things from the rest of the family, she might become sundered from it—and might want to become sundered from it.

He knocked back his little glass of applejack and poured it full again. The problems he had expected with Nicole's job had for the most part not arisen. The problems he had not expected . . . "Life is never simple," he declared. Maybe it was the applejack, but he had the feeling of having said something truly profound.

"Gas shells," Jake Featherston said enthusiastically. "Isn't that fine? The damnyankees have been doing it to our boys, and now we get to do it right back."

Michael Scott grinned at him. "Chokes me up just thinkin' about it, Sarge," he said, and did an alarmingly realistic impression of a man trying to cough chlorine-fried lungs right out of his chest. After the laughter at the gallows humor subsided, he went on, "When they going to have 'em for the big guns?"

"God knows," Jake said, rolling his eyes. "Best I can tell, we got our factories stretched like a rubber band that's about to break and hit you a lick between the eyes. There's a war on, case you haven't noticed, so they got to make more stuff than they ever reckoned they could. They got to do that with most of the men who were workin' in 'em before totin' guns now. And they got to do it with half the niggers, maybe, up in arms instead of doin' the jobs they're supposed to be doin'. Damn lucky the Yankees ain't ridden roughshod over us."

That produced a gloomy silence. It also produced several worried looks toward the north. The first U.S. attacks after the Red uprising had been beaten back, and the damnyankees, as if taken by surprise that they hadn't easily overwhelmed the Confederates, seemed to have paused to think things over. Signs were, though, that they were building up to try something new. Whenever the weather was decent, U.S. aeroplanes buzzed over the Confederate lines, spying out whatever they could. Confederate reconnaissance reported more activity than usual in the Yankee trenches.

Featherston added one thing more, the artilleryman's tipoff: "Their guns been firing a lot of registration shots lately." When a few shells came over, falling around important targets, you started worrying. That usually meant the other side's artillery was taking exact ranges. Before too long, a lot more than a few shells would be dropping thereabouts.

"Sarge, we got these gas shells to go with the rest of what we shoot," Michael Scott said. He glanced around. Nobody was in earshot of the gun crew. Even so, he lowered his voice: "With things like they are with Captain Stuart and all, we gonna be able to get enough of 'em to shoot to do any good?"

"That's a damn fine question," Jake told him. "Wish to Jesus I had me a damn fine answer for it. Way things used to be, we had shells the way a fellow been eatin' green apples gets the runs— they were just fallin' out of our ass, on account of Jeb Stuart III was Jeb Stuart III, and that was plenty to get him everything he wanted. Nowadays . . ." He sighed. "Nowadays I reckon I'd sooner have me Captain Joe Doakes in charge of the battery, or somebody else no one ever heard of. We might not get a whole raft o' shells, but we wouldn't get shortchanged, neither. And I got the bad feeling we're gonna be from here on out."

Everybody in the gun crew sighed. Jeb Stuart III wasn't Richmond's fair-haired boy any more. Now he was under a dark cloud, and that meant the whole battery had to go around carrying lanterns. Sooner or later, Stuart would pay the price for not having kept a better eye on Pompey. Trouble was, the rest of the battery would pay it along with him.

Featherston filled his coffee cup from the pot above the cookfire. The coffee was hot and strong. Once you'd said those two things, you'd said everything good about it you could. Nothing was as good as it had been before the Negroes rose up against their white superiors, not the chow, not the coffee, not anything.

"Damn niggers," Jake muttered. "If we lose this damn war, it's their fault, stabbing us in the back like they done. We could have licked the damnyankees easy, wasn't for that."

As if to contradict him, U.S. artillery opened up in earnest then. As soon as he saw the flashes to the north, as soon as he heard the roar of explosions and the scream of shells in the air, Jake knew the enemy guns weren't doing registration fire this time. They meant it.

The howitzer he commanded had a splendid view north. "Come on!" he shouted, pointing toward the gun. "Let's give it back to 'em!"

He didn't think any of his men could have heard him, not through the blasts of shells landing close by and the whine and hiss of shrapnel balls and flying fragments of shell casing. But they'd been bombarded before. They knew what to do. In less than a minute, they were flinging shells—gas and shrapnel both—back at the U.S. lines.

Those lines were working, vomiting out men the way an anthill vomited ants after you kicked it. Featherston whooped when shells burst among the damnyankees swarming toward the Confederate lines, whooped when men flew through the air or sprawled bonelessly on the ground or threw themselves flat and stopped moving forward.

But a godawful lot of damnyankees kept right on toward the Confederate trenches, which were taking a fearful pounding. The infantry in the trenches couldn't do any proper shooting at the advancing Yanks, not with tons of metal coming down on their heads. So much dust and dirt flew up from the Confederate lines, Jake had trouble spotting targets at which to aim his piece. "They're gonna get in!" he yelled. If the U.S. troops didn't just get into the Confederate lines but also through them—if that happened, the Confederate position in north-central Maryland was going to come unglued in a hurry.

Back in his training days, he'd learned that the three-inch howitzer, with its muzzle brake to keep recoil short and not fling the carriage backwards at every shot, could in an emergency fire twenty rounds a minute. Most of the time, that was only a number; the normal rate of fire was less than half as fast. No picky drillmaster was standing over the crew with a stopwatch

now, as had been so back on the firing range. But if Jake and
his men didn't smash every firing-range record ever set, he
would have eaten his hat—had he had any idea where the damn
thing was.

In spite of the shells falling on them, the other guns of the
battery matched his round for round, or came close enough as
to make no difference. And in spite of all they did, the damnyankees kept coming. Men started emerging from the Confederate trenches up ahead—men in butternut, at first. Some of
them looked for new firing positions from which to shoot back at
the U.S. soldiers who had forced them out of what had been the
safety of their lines. Others were running, nothing else but.

Then Featherston spotted men in green-gray. "Shrapnel!" he
shouted, and depressed the barrel of the howitzer till he was all
but firing over open sights. He yanked the lanyard. The shell
roared. Again, he watched men tumble. They were closer now,
and easier to see. He could even spy the difference in shape between their roundish helmets and the tin hats some of the Confederate troops were wearing.

A rifle bullet cracked past the gun's splinter shield, and then
another. He shook his head in dismay. He'd done a lot of
shooting at enemy infantry during the war—that was what the
three-incher was for. Up till now, though, he'd never been in a
spot where enemy infantry could shoot back at him.

"Running low on ammunition!" somebody shouted in the
chaos—he wasn't sure who. Shells from the guns of the battery
still in action tore great holes in the ranks of the oncoming U.S.
soldiers, but they kept coming nonetheless, on a wider front than
the field guns could sweep free.

"Bring the horses up to the gun and to the limber!" Jake
shouted. He looked around for the Negro laborers attached to
the gun. They were nowhere to be seen. He wasted a few seconds
cursing. Nero and Perseus, who had been with the battery from
the day the war started, would have done as he told them no
matter how dangerous the work was. He'd seen that. But Nero
and Perseus had been infected by the Red tide, too, and had de-
serted when the uprising broke out. God only knew where they
were now.

"If the niggers won't do it, reckon we got to take care of it
our own selves," Will Cooper said. Along with a couple of

other men, he went back to the barn nearby and brought out the horses. The animals were snorting and frightened. Jake Featherston didn't worry about that. He was plenty frightened himself, thank you very much. And if they didn't get the howitzer out of there in a hurry, he'd be worse than frightened, and he knew it. He'd be dead or captured, and the gun lost, a disgrace to any artilleryman.

"God damn it to hell, what the devil do you think you're doing?" It wasn't a shout—it was more like a scream. For a moment, Featherston didn't recognize the voice, though he'd heard it every day since before the war. His head snapped around. There stood Jeb Stuart III, head bare, pistol in his hand, eyes blazing with a fearful light.

"Sir—" Featherston pointed ahead, toward the advancing Yankees. "Sir, if we don't pull back—" He didn't think he needed to go on. The Confederate front was dissolving. A bullet ricocheted off the barrel of the cannon. If they didn't get out, they'd be picked off one by one, with no chance of doing anything to affect the rest of what was plainly a losing battle.

Jeb Stuart III leveled the pistol at his head. "Sergeant, you are not going anywhere. We are not going anywhere—except forward. There is the enemy. We shall fight him as long as we have breath in us. Is that clear?"

"Uh, yes, sir," Jake said. The barrel of the pistol looked as wide to him as that of his howitzer.

"Call me naive, will they? Call me stupid? Say my career is over?" Stuart muttered, not to Featherston, maybe not even to himself—more likely to some superior who wasn't there, perhaps to his father. He had, Jake realized, decided to die like a hero rather than living on in disgrace. If he took a gun crew to glory with him, so what?

They unhitched the horses and fired a couple of shells at the damnyankees. Stuart made no effort whatever to seek shelter. On the contrary—he stood in the open, defying the Yankees to hit him. In short order, he went down, blood spurting from a neck wound. The gun crew got the horses hitched again in moments. Under Featherston's bellowed orders, they got the howitzer out of there—and Captain Stuart, too. They saved the gun. Stuart died before a doctor saw him.

*   *   *

Chester Martin wished he'd had a bath any time recently. He wished the same thing about the squad he led. Of course, with so many unburied corpses in the neighborhood—so many corpses all up and down the Roanoke front—the reek of a few unwashed but live bodies would be a relatively small matter.

Turning to the distinguished visitor (without whose presence he wouldn't have cared nearly so much about the bath), he said, "You want to be careful, sir. We're right up at the front now. You give the Rebel snipers even the littlest piece of a target, and they'll drill it. They won't know you're a reporter, not a soldier— and the bastards probably wouldn't care much if they did know."

"Don't you worry about me, Sergeant," Richard Harding Davis answered easily. "I've been up to the front before."

"Yes, sir, I know that," Martin answered. Davis had been up to the front in a good many wars over the past twenty years or so. "I've read a lot of your stuff."

Davis preened. He wasn't a very big man, but extraordinarily handsome, and dressed in green-gray clothes that were the color of a U.S. uniform but much snappier in cut—especially when compared to the dirty, unpressed uniforms all around him. "I'm very glad to hear it," he said. "A writer who didn't have readers would be out of work in a hurry—and then I might have to find an honest job."

He laughed. So did Martin, who asked, "Are you all right, sir?" Handsome or not, Davis was an old geezer—well up into his fifties—and looked a little the worse for wear as he strode along the trench.

He was game enough, though. "I'm fine. Bit of a bellyache, maybe. I eat Army chow when I come up to the front. God knows how you poor souls survive on it." It probably wasn't anything like the fancy grub he ate back in New York City, Martin thought with a touch—more than a touch—of envy. Then Davis went on, "As a matter of fact, Sergeant, I know your work, too. That's why I chose this unit when I decided to visit the Roanoke front."

"Beg your pardon, sir?" For a second, Martin didn't get it.

Richard Harding Davis spelled it out for him: "Teddy Roosevelt recommended you to me, as a matter of fact. He said you knocked him flat and jumped on him when the Rebs started shelling your men while he was on an inspection. If you'd do it for him, he said, you might even do it for me." He flashed that formidable smile again.

"Do you want to know the truth, sir?" Martin said. "I'd almost forgotten about that. Been a lot of war since, if you know what I mean."

Davis produced a notebook from a coat that had as many pockets as Joseph's must have had colors and scribbled in it. "If you forget about the president of the United States, Sergeant, what do you remember?"

Martin chewed on that. When you thought about it, it was a damn good question. Most of what happened in the trenches wasn't worth remembering. Most of what happened in the trenches, you would have paid anybody anything to forget. Davis right behind him, he turned out of a traverse and into a long firebay, and there found his answer. "When you get down to it, sir," he said, "the only thing you want to remember is your buddies."

Here came Paul Andersen, who'd been with him from the start. After so many casualties, that alone was plenty to forge a bond between them. Here came Specs Peterson, who looked as if he ought to be a pharmacist and who was probably the meanest, roughest son of a gun in the whole battalion. Here came Willard Tarrant, Joe Hammerschmitt's replacement, who carried the name of Packer because he worked at the Armour plant in Chicago.

"Fellas, this here's Richard Harding Davis," Martin said, and let them tell the correspondent their own stories.

They had plenty of stories to tell him. If you stayed alive for a week at the front line, even a week where the official reports called the sector quiet, you'd have stories enough to last you the rest of your life—stories of courage and suffering and fear and endurance and everything else you could name. Experience was intense, concentrated, while it lasted . . . if it lasted.

Davis' hand raced over the pages of the little notebook, trying valiantly to keep up with the flood of words. At last, after what might have been an hour or so, the tales that came of themselves began to flag. To keep things going, the correspondent pointed east across the rusting barbed wire, across the cratered horror of no-man's-land, over toward the Confederate line, and asked, "What do you think of the enemy soldiers?"

Now Packer and Specs and the rest of the privates fell silent and looked to Martin and Andersen. It wasn't, Martin judged, so much because they were sergeant and corporal: more because they'd been there since the beginning, and had seen more of the Rebels than anybody else. Chester paused to gather his thoughts. At last, he said, "Far as I can see, Rebs in the trenches aren't a hell of a lot different than us. They're brave sons of bitches, I'll tell you that. We've got more big guns than they do, and there was a good long while there last summer when we had gas and they didn't, but if you wanted to move 'em back, you had to go in there with more men than they had and shift 'em. No way in hell they were going to run then, and they don't now, either."

Paul Andersen nodded. "That's how it is, all right. They're just a bunch of ordinary guys, same as we are. Too damn bad they didn't let us have a real Christmas truce last year, way there was in 1914. Nice to be able to stick your head out of the trench one day a year and know somebody's not going to try and blow it off. But what the hell can you do?"

"I'll tell you something, Corporal," Davis said. "The reason there wasn't a truce last year is that the powers that be—in Philadelphia and Richmond both, from what I hear—made certain there wouldn't be, because they watched the whole war almost fall to pieces on Christmas Day, 1914."

"What? They think we'd have quit fighting?" Packer Tarrant shook his head at the very idea. "Got to lick 'em. Taking longer than anybody figured, but we'll do it."

Several men nodded, most of them new to the front. Richard Harding Davis wrote some more, then asked, "If they're just like you are in the trenches, what keeps you going against them?"

In a different tone of voice, the question would have been subversive. As it was, it produced a few seconds of thoughtful silence. Then Specs Peterson said, "Hell and breakfast, Mr. Davis, we done too much by now to quit, ain't we? We got to beat those bastards, or all of that don't mean nothin'."

"That's about the size of it," Chester Martin agreed. "One of my grandfathers, he got shot in the War of Secession—and for what? The USA lost. Everything he did was wasted. Jesus, it'd be awful if that happened to us three times in fifty years."

Corporal Andersen pointed over to the enemy lines. "And the

Rebs, they don't want to find out what losing is all about, either. That's why they keep comin' at us, I guess. Been a lot of what the newspapers been calling Battles of the Roanoke, anyway." As if to underscore his words, a machine gun started rattling away, a couple of hundred yards to the north. Rifles joined in, and, for five or ten minutes, a lively little firefight raged. Gradually, the firing died away. Anything might have started it. Martin wondered if anyone had died in the meaningless exchange of bullets.

"Are the Rebels any different since their Negroes rose in revolt?" Davis asked.

The soldiers looked at one another. "Not when we're coming at them, that's for sure," Martin said, and everybody nodded. "You think about it, though, they haven't been coming at us as hard lately. 'Course, it's been winter, too, so I don't know just how much that means."

"Confederates more inclined to stand on the defensive." Richard Harding Davis said the words aloud, as if tasting them before setting them down on paper. Then he grunted. It sounded more like surprise than approval. He looked at Martin—no, through Martin. His mouth opened, as if he was about to say something else.

Instead, he swayed. The notebook and pencil dropped from his hands into the mud. His knees buckled. He collapsed.

"Jesus!" Martin and the other soldiers crowded round the fallen reporter. Martin grabbed for his wrist. He found no pulse. "He's dead," the sergeant said in blank amazement. Davis' body bore no wound he could see. He knew a shell fragment as tiny as a needle could kill, but no shells had landed anywhere close by.

His shouts and those of his squadmates brought a doctor into the front line within a couple of minutes. The soldiers wouldn't have rated such an honor, but Davis was important. The doctor stripped the correspondent out of his fancy not-quite-uniform. Try as he would, he couldn't find a wound, either. "His heart must have given out on him, poor fellow," he said, and shook his head. "He's not—he wasn't—that old, but he'd been working hard, and he wasn't that young, either."

"Isn't that a hell of a thing?" Martin said as a couple of soldiers carried the mortal remains of Richard Harding Davis to the rear.

"Terrible," Paul Andersen agreed. "You got a cigarette?"

"Makings," Martin answered, and passed him a tobacco pouch. "Hell of a thing. You ever expect to see man die of what do you call 'em—natural causes—up here? What a fucking waste." Andersen laughed at that as he rolled coarse tobacco into a scrap of newspaper. After a moment, Martin laughed, too. Yes, graveyard humor came easy at the front. It was the only kind that did.

VI

"There is, there is, there *is* a God in Israel!" George Armstrong Custer chortled, brandishing a newspaper at his adjutant.

"Sir?" Abner Dowling said. He'd already seen the Army newspaper. He hadn't noticed anything in it to make him want to do a buck-and-wing. He wondered what the devil General Custer had spotted to bring him out of the bad-tempered depression in which he'd been sunk ever since his wife got to Kentucky.

Custer wasn't just happy, he was gloating. "Look!" he said, pointing to a story on the second page of the paper. "Richard Harding Davis had the good grace to drop dead on a visit to the front. I wish he would have done it while he was on *this* front, but damn me to hell if I'll complain."

Davis had written about Custer in less than flattering terms: a capital crime if ever there was one, as far as the general commanding First Army was concerned. "Sir, his work is being judged by a more exacting Critic now than any editor he knew here," Dowling said, which not only smacked of truth (if you were a believing man, as Dowling was) but was noncommittal, letting Custer pick for himself the way in which the late correspondent was likely to be judged.

He picked the way Dowling had been sure he would: "How right you are, Major, which means they've got him on a frying pan hotter than the one that does my morning bacon—and he'll stay there a lot longer and get a lot more burnt, not that that's easy these days." He hadn't stopped complaining about the ways the meals that were cooked for him had gone downhill since Olivia left. He hadn't stopped complaining to Dowling, that is. He hadn't said one word where his wife was liable to hear it. To

149

Dowling's regret, the old boy had a keenly developed sense of self-preservation.

Still snorting with glee, the illustrious general waddled into the kitchen. Dowling suspected the corporal doing duty at the stove for the time being would hear fewer fulminations than usual. When Custer was in a good mood, everything looked rosy to him. Trouble was, he wasn't in a good mood very often.

Libbie Custer came downstairs a moment later. She was only a few years younger than her husband, and had the look of a schoolmarm who would sooner crack a ruler over her pupils' knuckles than teach them the multiplication table. Her eyes were the gray of the sky just before it settles down to rain for a week. When she fixed her gaze on Dowling, he automatically assumed he'd done something wrong. He didn't know what yet, but he figured Mrs. Custer would tell him.

She, however, chose an indirect approach: "Did I hear the general laughing just now?" She often spoke of her husband in that old-fashioned way.

"Uh, yes, ma'am," Dowling answered. He had not taken long to decide that at least two thirds of the brains in the Custer family resided in the female of the species.

Libbie Custer did her best to prove herself more deadly than the male, too. "Where is she?" she hissed. "I'll send her packing in a hurry, I promise you that, and afterwards I'll deal with the general, too." She sounded as if she looked forward to it. More—she sounded as if she'd had practice at it, too.

But Dowling said, truthfully if not completely, "There's no woman here, ma'am. It was only—"

"Don't give me that." Mrs. Custer cut him off so abruptly, he was glad she didn't have a knife in her hand. "He's been doing this for forty years, the philandering skunk, ever since he found that pretty little Cheyenne girl, Mo-nah-see-tah—did you ever think you'd learn how to say 'stinking whore' in Cheyenne, Major Dowling? When he laughs that way, he's done it again. I know him. I ought to, by now, don't you think?"

"Ma'am, you're wrong." That was truthful, too, if only technically. Dowling had enough troubles serving as intermediary between Custer and the rest of First Army; serving as intermediary between Custer and Mrs. Custer struck him as conduct above and beyond the call of duty—far above. Rather desperately, he explained.

For a wonder, Libbie Custer heard him out. For another wonder, she didn't call him a liar when he was done. Instead, she nodded and said, "Oh, that explains it. Mr. Richard Harding Davis." George Armstrong Custer had sworn at Davis. He'd said he would use Davis' reportage in the outhouse. Nothing he had said, though, packed the concentrated menace of those four words. Mrs. Custer went on, "Yes, that would explain it. Thank you, Major."

She swept into the kitchen, her long, gray dress almost brushing the ground as she walked. She clung to the bustle, which had gone out of style for younger women a few years before. As far as Dowling was concerned, it made her look more like a cruising man-of-war than a stately lady, but no one had sought his opinion. No one was much in the habit of seeking his opinion.

From inside the kitchen came the sounds of mirth and gaiety—Dowling couldn't hear the words, but the tone was unmistakable. The general and his wife were happy as a couple of larks. Dowling scratched his head. A moment before, Mrs. Custer had been ready to scalp her husband. Now the two of them seemed thick as thieves. It didn't figure.

And then, after a bit, it did. Libbie Custer would come down on George like a dynamited building for any of his personal shortcomings. Given the scope of those, she had plenty of room for action. But Mrs. General Custer protected General Custer's career like a tigress. Bad press jeopardized the general, not the man.

"I couldn't live like that," Dowling muttered. And yet the Custers had been wed since the War of Secession. Marital bliss? Dowling had his doubts. He shook his head. He didn't have doubts, he damn well knew better. Whether they were what any outsider would call happy or not, though, they'd grown together. He doubted one of them would live more than a year or two if the other died. Libbie Custer looked ready to last another twenty years. Dowling wasn't so sure about the general. But he'd have bet Custer would have keeled over from a heart attack or a stroke, not Richard Harding Davis. You never could tell.

The two Custers came out of the kitchen arm in arm. For the moment, they presented a united front against the world, and would probably go right on doing so till Libbie found out for sure about Olivia. To his wife, the general said, "I do have to fight the war now. I'll see you in a while." She nodded and went upstairs. Custer turned to Dowling. "Major, I'll want to consult with you about the artillery preparation for the attack on Bowling Green. Give me ten minutes to study the maps, then come into my office."

"Yes, sir," Dowling said. Custer was acting more like a proper general these days. That was likely to be Libbie's influence, too. *The brains of the outfit,* Dowling thought again.

While he was waiting for Custer to finish studying (an unlikely notion in and of itself), the kitchen door opened again. "Uh, sir?" It was the corporal who'd been frying everything in sight since Olivia made herself scarce.

"What is it, Renick?" Dowling asked.

The corporal, who looked more like a light-heavyweight prizefighter than a cook, opened his left hand to display a small gold coin. "Look, sir, the general gave me a quarter eagle. Said I was the best cook anybody could ask for. Said he'd write me a letter of commendation any time I wanted."

"Good for you, Renick," Dowling said. "I'll make sure he does that today." Davis' death was doing the cook some good, anyhow—but if Custer didn't sign that letter while still in the warm glow of euphoria, Renick didn't stand a Chinaman's chance of getting it added to his record, not on skill alone he didn't.

Dowling hurried to the tiny downstairs room he used as his own office, ran a sheet of Army stationery into his typewriter, and banged out the letter. Eventually, Mrs. Custer would go back to Michigan and Olivia would replace Corporal Renick. If he had that letter in his file, he might end up cooking for some other officer, not in the trenches. He seemed a good kid—why not give him a better chance to come out of the war in one piece?

And, sure enough, General Custer did sign the letter. "Fine lad," he said, "that young—whatever his name is."

"Renick, sir." Dowling put the letter back in the manila folder from which he'd produced it.

"Ah, yes, of course," Custer said, which meant he hadn't heard the answer but was too vain to ask his adjutant to say it over again louder. He picked up a pointer and aimed it at the situation map of Kentucky. "I am of the opinion, Major, that Bowling Green falls at the next onslaught."

"Seeing as we're approaching from the west and the north, the Confederates will have a hard time keeping us out, yes, sir," Dowling agreed. "But fighting in built-up country can be expensive as the devil. As you said before, we need to use our superiority in artillery to the best advantage."

Custer hadn't actually said anything quite like that, but had talked about the artillery preparation, which, as far as his adjutant was concerned, came close enough. He scratched at his mustache. "We'll give the Rebs enough artillery preparation to blow them right back to the War of Secession," he growled. "And then we'll follow it with infantry, and then with cavalry—"

"I think the ground troops may well be able to capture the city without the cavalry, sir," Dowling said. Custer would probably remain sure to his dying day that cavalry could exploit any breakthrough the infantry made. Try as Dowling would, he hadn't been able to convince the general otherwise. Breakthroughs of any sort looked to be illusory in this war, and, if they came, the cavalry wasn't going to exploit them, not till somebody bred an armor-plated horse it wasn't.

"Ground troops," Custer grumbled. "Artillery." He let out a long, wheezy sigh. "The spirit has gone out of warfare, Major. It's not as it was when I was a young man."

"No, sir." Dowling wondered if he would be saying the same thing if he lived till 1950 or so. Maybe he would, but Dowling hoped he wouldn't try to turn an entire army on its head because he didn't care to adjust to a new reality.

Custer whacked the map with the stick. "And after Bowling Green falls, Major, we advance on Nashville! We took it in the War of Secession, and we held it, too, till the stinking limeys and frogs made us give it back. When we take it this time, we'll keep it."

Ah, but a man's reach should exceed his grasp, or what's a heaven for? The words from Browning ran through Dowling's head. They'd needed a year and a half to get to—not yet into, but to—Bowling Green. At that rate, another year might, with luck, see them on the Cumberland. By the way Custer talked, he expected to be there week after next. As grand strategy, what he said made a certain amount of sense. Turning it from grand strategy to tactical maneuvering, though . . . was liable to fall squarely on Abner Dowling's broad shoulders.

"We'll need help from the Navy," he warned. "And up till now, their monitors haven't been able to get anywhere near Nashville."

"Well then, seems to me that they'll need help from us, too," Custer observed. The comment was so much to the point that Dowling frankly stared at the general commanding First Army. He'd been glad to have Libbie Custer come visit for no better reason than to see her husband dismayed. But if her presence meant Custer turned into something close to the general First Army needed, Dowling hoped she'd never leave.

And if that meant Custer didn't get to jump on Olivia's sleek brown body any more, everyone had to make sacrifices to win the war. *Hell,* Dowling thought, *I'll even put up with Renick's godawful cremated bacon.*

Cincinnatus pulled the wool sailor's cap down over his ears to keep them warm as he walked to the Covington wharves. The sun wasn't up yet, though the eastern sky glowed pink. Days were getting longer now, noticeably so, but it was still one snowstorm after another.

He walked past a gang of U.S. soldiers. They were busy tearing posters off walls and pasting up replacements. Some of the ones they were destroying had been smuggled up from the unoccupied CSA. Cincinnatus turned a chuckle into a cough so the soldiers wouldn't notice him. He knew about those.

The other posters going down were printed in red and black—images of broken chains, stalwart Negroes with rifles, and revolutionary slogans. Cincinnatus knew about those, too.

He paused for a moment to have a look at the posters the U.S. soldiers were putting up to replace the Confederate and Red propaganda. The art showed three eagles—the U.S. bald eagle, the German black one, and the two-headed bird symbolizing Austria-Hungary—with their talons piercing four red-white-and-blue flags: those of the CSA, England, France, and Russia. The message was one word: VICTORY.

"Not bad," he murmured, and disguised another chuckle behind a glove. He'd never expected to become a connoisseur of poster propaganda, not before the war started. A lot of things he'd never expected had happened since the war started.

He saw more of the three-eagle posters as he came closer to the riverfront, and nodded to himself: so the Yanks were going to be putting out a new type, were they? It had the look of the first in a series. He wouldn't have thought of that kind of thing back in 1913, either.

When he got to the wharves, he waved to the other Negro laborers coming in to help keep the U.S. war effort moving. Some of them, no doubt, also belonged to Red revolutionary cells. He didn't know which ones, though. He hadn't had the need to know. What you didn't know, you couldn't tell.

Here came Lieutenant Kennan. *Goddamn pipsqueak,* Cincinnatus thought. If he ever got the chance, he knew he could snap Kennan in two like a stale cracker. But Kennan had the weight of the U.S. Army behind him. Now he fixed Cincinnatus with his customary glare. "You, boy!" he snapped.

"Yes, suh?" Cincinnatus said warily. Kennan sounded more filled with bile than usual, which was saying something.

"Don't I remember you bragging once upon a time that you could drive a truck?"

"Don't know about braggin', suh, but I can drive a truck," Cincinnatus said. "Been doin' it for a while before the war started." *Before the war started.* Here it was barely sunup, and that phrase had already crossed his mind several times. It was going to be a dividing line for his life, for everybody's life, for a long time to come.

Lieutenant Kennan looked as if every word he was about to say tasted bad. "You see that line of trucks over yonder? You get your ass over there, ask for Lieutenant Straubing, and tell him you're the nigger I was talking about."

"Yes, suh," Cincinnatus said. Were the Yanks finally getting smart? If they were, they'd taken their own sweet time about it. Better late than never? Cincinnatus wouldn't have bet on that, not till he saw for certain. "If I'm drivin' a truck, suh, what do they pay me?"

"I don't know anything about that," Kennan said, as if washing his hands of Cincinnatus. "You take it up with Lieutenant Straubing. You're his baby now." No, he didn't want to have anything to do with Cincinnatus. He rounded on the rest of the men in the labor gang. "What are you coons doing, standing around gaping like a bunch of gorillas? *Get* your nigger asses moving!"

Cincinnatus had all he could do not to spring over to the trucks to which Kennan had directed him. Nobody, he told himself, could be a worse boss than the one he was escaping. But then, after a moment, he shook his head. Since the war began, he'd learned you couldn't tell about things like that.

A sentry near the trucks wore one of the helmets that made U.S. soldiers look as if they had kettles on their heads. He carried a Springfield with a long bayonet, which he pointed at Cincinnatus. "State your business," he snapped, with a clear undertone of *it had better be good*.

"Lieutenant Kennan back there, suh"—he pointed toward the wharf where his old gang, under Kennan's loud and profane direction, was beginning to unload a barge—"he tol' me to come see Lieutenant, uh, Straubing here."

For a moment, he wondered if there'd be no Lieutenant Straubing, and if Kennan, for reasons of his own (maybe connected with Cincinnatus' dealings with one underground or another, maybe only with Kennan's loathing for blacks) had sent him here to get in trouble, or perhaps to get shot.

But the sentry, though he didn't lower the rifle, did nod. "Stay right here," he said, as if Cincinnatus were likely to be going anywhere with that bayonet aimed at his brisket. Then he raised his voice: "Hey, Lieutenant! Colored fellow here to see you!"

Colored fellow. It was just a description. Cincinnatus, not used to being just described, heard it with some incredulity. Out from around the row of trucks came an ordinary-looking white man with silver first-lieutenant's bars on the shoulder straps of his U.S. uniform. "Hello," he said to Cincinnatus. "You the man Eddie was telling me about last night?" Seeing Cincinnatus' frown, he added, "Lieutenant Kennan, I mean?"

"Oh. Yes, suh." Cincinnatus had labored for Kennan for well over a year without learning, or wanting to learn, his Christian name.

"He says you can drive a truck," Straubing said. He waited for Cincinnatus to agree, then went on, "How long have you been doing that?"

"Couple-three years before the war started," Cincinnatus answered. "Haven't had the chance to do it since."

Lieutenant Straubing cocked his head to one side. "You don't hardly look old enough to have been driving that long." For a moment, Cincinnatus thought he was calling him a liar. Then he realized Straubing meant he had a young-looking face. "Come on," the lieutenant said, and walked him past the sentry. He halted in front of one of the big, green-gray White trucks. "Think you can drive this baby?"

"Reckon I can," Cincinnatus said. The White was a monster, a good deal larger than the delivery truck he'd driven for Tom Kennedy. But it was still a truck. A crank was still a crank, a gearshift still a gearshift.

"All right. Show me. The key's in it." Lieutenant Straubing scrambled up into the truck, sliding over to the passenger's half of the front seat.

Cincinnatus had no trouble starting the truck. It was a bare-bones military model, without even a windscreen, which surprised him when he climbed in behind the wheel, but he didn't let it worry him. He didn't ask Straubing about pay, either, not right then. That he wasn't hauling heavy crates was plenty to keep him happy for the moment.

"Pull out of the line and take me on a spin through town. Be back here in, oh, twenty minutes or so," Lieutenant Straubing told him over the growl of the motor.

"Yes, suh," Cincinnatus said. He put the truck in gear and got moving. Every once in a while, he sneaked a glance over at the soldier beside him. He wanted to scratch his head, but didn't. Something in the way Straubing dealt with him was peculiar, but he had trouble putting his finger on it.

They didn't get back to the parked trucks in twenty minutes. They had a blowout not five minutes after getting on the road. Cincinnatus fixed it. Straubing helped, not the least bit fussy about getting mud and grease on his hands or on his uniform. "All right, where were we?" he said when the two of them got back onto the rather hard seat.

Cincinnatus didn't answer. He didn't feel he had to answer, even though a white man had just spoken to him. When he realized that, he realized what was funny about how the U.S. soldier was treating him: as one man would treat another, regardless of whether he was white and Cincinnatus black. No wonder

Cincinnatus had taken so long to figure that out: as best he could remember, he'd never run into anything like it before.

Some white men hated Negroes, plain and simple. He'd met a good many of those before having the imperfect delight of busting his hump for Lieutenant Kennan for so long. But that kind of out-and-out hatred wasn't the most common response he'd had from whites over the years. More treated him as they would have treated a mule: they gave him orders when they needed him and made as if he were invisible when they didn't.

He'd even had white men grateful to him: Tom Kennedy's image rose up in his mind. After he'd hidden his former boss and kept U.S. soldiers from finding him, Kennedy had been nice as you please. But it had been a condescending sort of niceness, even then: a lord being kind to a serf who by some accident of fate had been in position to do him a good turn.

He didn't feel any of that from Lieutenant Straubing. The way Straubing was acting, they might both have been white—or, for that matter, they might both have been black. He'd never run into that from Confederate white men. He hadn't run into it from Yankees, either, not till now. He didn't know how to react to it.

Straubing suddenly spoke up: "You can go on back now, Cincinnatus. I'm sold—you can drive a truck. Better than I can, wouldn't be surprised." As Cincinnatus turned back toward the riverfront, the lieutenant went on, "Dollar and a half a day suit you?"

"It's what I'm makin' now, most days," Cincinnatus answered, "but yes, suh, it suits. Work'll be easier."

"I thought longshoreman's rate was a dollar a day," Straubing said with a small frown. Then he laughed—at himself. "And I'm a dimwit. I think half the reason Kennan sent you over to me is that you were ruining his accounts, getting the extra half-dollar so often. The other half, unless I'm wrong, is that you were getting the extra half-dollar so often, you were ruining his notions of what colored people are like. He probably hasn't figured that half out for himself yet. Tell you what—I won't tell him if you don't."

Now Cincinnatus did stare at him. He almost ran down a horse and buggy before he started paying attention to the road again. Never in all his born days had he heard—or expected to hear—one white man discussing another's attitude toward Negroes, and discussing it in tones that made it obvious he thought Lieutenant Kennan was a damn fool.

"You're changing jobs—you ought to do better for yourself," Straubing said. "Hmm. Can you read and write?"

Cincinnatus looked at Lieutenant Straubing. One rule of survival for blacks in the Confederacy had always been, *Never let the white man find out how much you know.* Without that rule, the Red underground would never have had the chance to pull off its rebellion—not that the rebellion looked as if it would succeed, worse luck. He clicked his tongue between his teeth. "Yes, suh."

"Good," the U.S. lieutenant said. "In that case, my accounts'll stand paying you a buck six bits. How does that sound?"

Before the war—that phrase again—$1.75 a day had been white man's wages, and not the worst white man's wages. It was a good deal more than Tom Kennedy had been paying him. "You got yourself a driver, Lieutenant," Cincinnatus said.

"Good," Lieutenant Straubing answered. "Glad to hear it. I can use people who know what they're doing."

Cincinnatus expected him to go on, *I don't care if they're white or black.* He'd heard that before, every now and then. Most of the time, it was a thumping lie: that you needed to say it proved it was a lie. But Straubing didn't say it. By everything Cincinnatus could see, he took it for granted.

After Cincinnatus had parked the truck, Straubing led him into a dockside building and spoke to a clerk there. The clerk took down Cincinnatus' name and where he lived and who his family were. Then he swore him to loyalty to the United States. Cincinnatus was already sworn to loyalty to the Confederate underground and to the Negro Marxist underground. He took the oath without hesitation—after so many, what was one more?

The clerk slid papers across the desk at him. "Make your mark here to show all this information is correct and complete. Lieutenant, you'll witness it for him."

Cincinnatus took the pen. He looked at the clerk. He signed his name in a fine, round hand. The clerk stared at him. "Good thing you know your letters," Lieutenant Straubing said. "It'll make you a hell of a lot more useful."

Tom Kennedy had known he could read and write, too.

Kennedy had also used that to his advantage. But with him, there had always been something of the flavor of a man using a high-school horse. It wasn't there with Straubing. Cincinnatus' ear for such things was keen. Had it been there, he would have heard it.

Before long, blacks from the wharves were loading crates into the back of Cincinnatus' truck. They weren't from his labor gang, but he knew several of them even so. They looked at him from the corners of their eyes. Nobody said anything, not with white men all around: most of the other truck drivers were white, for instance. Cincinnatus waited to see how that would go.

The trucks rumbled out of Covington before nine o'clock. The front was between Lexington and Richmond, Kentucky: about a four-hour trip. A little more than halfway there, they rolled past the Corinth Monument, which commemorated Braxton Bragg's victory in late 1862 that had brought Kentucky into the Confederacy. Bragg's statue was gone from its pedestal these days, and the pedestal itself plastered over with fresh, crisp three-eagles posters. The USA aimed to keep as much of Kentucky as it had seized.

Laborers, mostly black but some white, unloaded the trucks. Some of what those had brought would go to the front in small wagons, some on muleback or on man's back. Cincinnatus ate his dinner out of the dinner pail, then drove the truck back to Covington. Everyone took him for granted. He still had trouble knowing what to make of that.

He got back into Covington with his headlamps on. Straubing paid off the drivers himself. Some got $1.50, some $1.75, some two dollars even. One of the two-dollar men was black. Nobody raised a fuss.

Money jingling in his pocket, Cincinnatus headed for home with more news for Elizabeth than he could shake a stick at. He went past Conroy's general store, as he always did when coming home from the riverfront. Conroy had a paper stuck in the bottom left-hand corner of his window. That meant he and Tom Kennedy wanted to see Cincinnatus.

"Well, I'll be damned if I want to see them," Cincinnatus muttered. "Paper? What paper? I didn't see no paper." He walked right past the general store.

*   *   *

Three eagles glared out at Flora Hamburger from every other wall as she walked to the Socialist Party offices. She glared right back at them. She was sick to death of wartime propaganda. What worried her most was that the Democrats were getting better at what she'd thought of as a Socialist specialty.

Other posters (some with text in Yiddish as well as English; the government didn't miss a trick) exhorted people to buy the latest series of Victory Bonds, to use less coal than their legal ration (which was, most of the time, not big enough as it was), to take the train as little as they could (which also saved coal), to turn back glass bottles and tin cans, to give waste grease to the War Department through their local butcher shop, to . . . she lost track of everything. Anyone who tried to do all the things the posters urged him to do would go mad in short order.

But then, the world already seemed to have gone mad.

Here and there, among the eagles and the handsome men in green-gray and the women who had to be their wives or mothers, Socialist Party posters managed to find space. Keeping them up there wasn't easy. As fast as boys went round with pastepots and brushes, Soldiers' Circle men followed, tearing down anything that might contradict what TR wanted people to think today.

PEACE AND JUSTICE, one of the Socialist posters said. A SQUARE DEAL FOR THE WORKER, shouted another. A good many copies of that one stayed up; some of the Soldiers' Circle goons took it for a government-issued poster. Stealing the opposition's slogan was always a good idea.

Fewer Soldiers' Circle men prowled the Centre Market than was usually so. And, most uncommonly, none loitered in front of Max Fleischmann's butcher shop. Fleischmann was sweeping the sidewalk in front of the shop when Flora came up. "Good morning, my dear," he said with Old World courtliness. He was a Democrat himself, which didn't keep the government goons from giving him a hard time. With his shop right under Fourteenth Ward Socialist Party headquarters, it was guilt by association in the most literal sense of the words.

"Good morning, Mr. Fleischmann," Flora answered. "How are you today?"

"Today, not so bad," the butcher answered. "Last night—" He rolled his eyes. "You've seen the 'turn in old grease' posters?" After pausing to see if Flora would nod, he went on, "Last night, just as I was closing up shop, one of those Soldiers' Circle *mamzrim* brought in a gallon tin—of lard."

"*Oy!*" Flora exclaimed. That was more nastily clever than the Soldiers' Circle usually managed to be. A gallon of pig's fat in a kosher butcher shop . . .

"*Oy* is right," Fleischmann agreed mournfully. "Thank God I had no customers just then. I shut the shop and brought my rabbi over. The place is ritually clean again, but even so—"

"I can complain to the City Council about that kind of harassment, if you'd like me to," Flora said.

But the butcher shook his head. "Better not. If one of them does it one time, a *kholeriyeh* on him and life goes on. If you give the idea to a whole great lot of them, it will happen over and over for the next six months. No, better not."

"It shouldn't be like that," Flora said. But she'd spent enough time as an activist to know the difference between what should have been and what was. Shaking her head in sad sympathy with Max Fleischmann, she went upstairs.

People were still coming into the Socialist Party offices, which meant the chaos wasn't so bad as it would be later in the day. She had time to get a glass of tea, pour sugar into it, and catch up on a little paperwork before the telephones started going mad.

"How are you this morning?" Maria Tresca asked.

"I've been worse—little Yossel slept through the whole night," Flora answered. "But I've been better, too." She explained what the Soldiers' Circle man had done to Max Fleischmann.

Maria was Catholic, but she'd spent enough time among Jews to understand what lard in the butcher shop meant. "It's an outrage," she snapped. "And he probably went out to a saloon and got drunk afterwards, laughing about it."

"Probably just what he did," Flora agreed. "Anyone who could think of anything so vile, he should walk in front of a train."

Herman Bruck walked in just then. Flora wished fleetingly that he would walk in front of a train, too. But no, that wasn't fair. Yes, Herman was a nuisance and wouldn't leave her in peace. But he'd never yet made her snatch a hatpin out from among the artificial flowers where it lurked, and she didn't think he ever would. There were nuisances, but then there were nuisances.

"Good morning, Flora," he said, setting his homburg on the

hat tree. "You look pretty today—you must have had a good night's sleep."

"Yes, thanks," she answered shortly. She wasn't going to tell him about little Yossel. She didn't encourage him—but then, he needed no encouragement.

He'd got himself some tea and sat down at his desk when a Western Union messenger opened the door to the office. Flora thought about the messenger who'd brought word of little Yossel's father's death back to Sophie at the apartment the family shared. She shook her head, annoyed at herself. That wouldn't happen here. People didn't live here, however much it sometimes seemed they did.

She accepted the yellow envelope, gave the delivery boy a nickel, and watched him head back down to the street. "Who is it from?" Herman Bruck asked.

"It's from Philadelphia," she answered, and tore the envelope open. Her eyes slid rapidly over the words there. She had to read them twice before she believed them. *No one would bring bad news here.* The thought jeered in her mind. "It's Congressman Zuckerman," she said in a voice so empty, she hardly recognized it as her own. "He was walking downstairs with Congressman Potts from Brooklyn, and, and, he tripped and he fell and, he, he broke his neck. He died not quite three hours ago."

She had never heard the Socialist Party office go so quiet, not even in the aftermath of the Remembrance Day riots. Myron Zuckerman had been a Socialist stalwart in Congress since before the turn of the century. Come November, his reelection would have been as automatic as the movement of a three-day clock. The Democrats wouldn't have put up more than a token candidate against him, and the Republicans probably wouldn't have run anyone at all. All of a sudden, though, everything was different.

"There's no doubt?" Maria Tresca asked.

"Not unless the telegram is wrong," Flora answered. Her voice was gentle; she knew Maria hadn't been doubting so much as hoping. She looked down at the telegram. It blurred, not from changing words but from the tears that filled her eyes.

"That's—terrible." Herman Bruck's voice was shaken, as if he was holding back tears himself. "He was like a father to all of us."

"What are we going to do?" Three people spoke at the same time. Everyone in the office had to be thinking the same thing.

Maybe because Yossel Reisen's death had got her used to thinking clearly through shocks, Flora answered before anyone else: "The governor will appoint somebody to fill out the rest of his term." That brought dismayed exclamations from everyone; Governor MacFarlane was as thoroughgoing a Democrat as anyone this side of TR.

"Almost a year of being represented by someone who does not represent us," Maria Tresca said bitterly. The syntax might have been imperfect, but the meaning was clear.

"It's liable to be longer than that," Flora said. "Whoever he is, he'll have most of that time to establish himself, too. He may not be so easy to throw out when November comes, either."

"We'll have to pick the finest candidate we can to oppose him, whoever he turns out to be," Herman Bruck said. He stood up and struck a pose, as if to leave no doubt where he thought the finest candidate could be found.

Flora studied him. He was bright. He was earnest. He would campaign hard. If he was elected, he would serve well enough. He was also bloody dull. If Governor MacFarlane named someone with spirit, the Socialists were liable to lose this district. That would be . . . *humiliating* was the word that came to Flora's mind.

I'd make a better candidate than Herman Bruck, she thought. At first, that was nothing but scorn. But the words seemed to echo in her mind. She looked at Bruck. She looked down at her own hands. Women could vote and hold office in New York State. She was over twenty-five. She could run for Congress—if the Socialists would nominate her.

She looked at Herman Bruck again. No one had shouted his name to the rafters, but there he stood, confident as if he were already the candidate. Of one thing she was certain: anyone so confident with so little reason could be overhauled. She didn't know how it would happen, or even if she would be the one to do it, but it could be done. She was sure of that.

Arthur McGregor rode the farm wagon toward Rosenfeld, Manitoba. Days were almost as long as nights now, but snow still lingered. They could have more snow for another month, maybe six weeks—and for six weeks after the thaw finally began, the road to Rosenfeld would be hub-deep in mud.

Most years, McGregor cursed the spring thaw, which not only cut him off from the world but also made working the fields impossible or the next thing to it. Now he turned to Maude, who sat on the seat beside him, and said, "The road'll make it hard for the Yanks to move."

"That it will," she agreed. "Weather's never been easy here for anyone. I expect they've found that out for themselves by now."

Alexander McGregor sat up in the back of the wagon. "You know what they say about our seasons, Pa," he said, grinning. "We've only got two of 'em—August and winter."

"When I first came to this part of the country, the way I heard it was July and winter," McGregor said. "But it's not far wrong, however you say it. And when the weather's bad, they have the devil of a time getting from one place to another."

"Except for the trains," Alexander said, making no effort to conceal his anger at the railroads. "If it's not a really dreadful blizzard, the trains get through."

"I can't say you're wrong, son, because you're right," McGregor answered. The way he thought about trains was another measure of how the past year and a half had turned the world on its ear. Up till the day the war started, he'd blessed the railroads. They brought supplies into Rosenfeld in all but the worst of weather, as Alexander had said. They also carried his grain off to the east. Without them, he would have had no market for most of what he raised. Without them, the Canadian prairie could not have been settled, nor defended against the United States if somehow it was.

But now the USA held the tracks leading up toward Winnipeg, and used them to ship hordes of men and enormous amounts of matériel to the fighting front. In peace, he'd blessed the railroad and cursed the mud. In war, he did the exact opposite. He nodded to himself. Things were on their ear, all right.

Mary stuck her head up and looked around. With her eyes sparkling and her round cheeks all red with cold, she looked like a plump little chipmunk. "We ought to do something about the railroads," she said in a voice that did not sound at all childlike. What she sounded like was a hard-headed saboteur thinking out loud about ways and means.

"You hush, Mary," her mother said. "You're not a soldier."

"I wish I was," Mary said fiercely.

"Hush is right," Arthur McGregor said. He looked back over his shoulder at Alexander. So far as he knew, his son was keeping the promise he'd made and not trying to act the part of a *franc-tireur*. So far as he knew. Till the war, he hadn't savored the full import of that phrase, either. It was what he didn't know that worried him.

Half a mile outside of Rosenfeld, a squad of U.S. soldiers inspected the wagon. McGregor hated to admit it, but they did a good, professional job, one of them even getting down on his back on the dirt road to examine the axles and the underside of the frame. They were businesslike with him, reasonably polite to Maude, and smiled at his daughters, who were too young to be leered at. If they gave Alexander a sour look or two, those weren't a patch on the glares he sent them. After a couple of minutes, they nodded and waved the wagon forward. Fortunately, Alexander didn't curse them till it had gone far enough so they couldn't hear him.

Julia gasped. Mary giggled. Arthur McGregor said, "Don't use that sort of talk where your mother and sisters can hear you." He glanced over to Maude. She was keeping her face stiff—so stiff, he suspected a smile under there.

Rosenfeld, as it had since it was occupied, seemed a town of American soldiers, with the Canadians to whom it rightfully belonged thrown in as an afterthought. Soldiers crowded round the cobbler's shop, the tailor's, the little café that had been struggling before the war started (what ruined most folks made a few rich), and the saloon that had never struggled a bit. There were three or four rooms up above the saloon that must have had U.S. soldiers going in and out of them every ten or fifteen minutes. McGregor had never walked up to one of those rooms—he was happy with the lady he'd married—but he knew about them. He glanced over to Maude again. She probably knew about those rooms, too. Husband and wife had never mentioned them to each other. He didn't expect they ever would.

Henry Gibbon's general store was full of U.S. soldiers, too, buying everything from five-for-a-penny jawbreakers to housewives with which to repair tattered uniforms in the field to a horn with a big red rubber squeeze-bulb. "You don't mind my askin',"

Henry Gibbon said to the sergeant in green-gray who laid down a quarter for that item, "what the devil you going to do with that?"

"Next fellow in my squad I catch dozing when he ain't supposed to," the sergeant answered with an evil grin, "his hair's gonna stand on end for the next three days." A couple of privates who might have been in his squad sidled away from him.

A tiny smile made the corners of McGregor's mouth quirk upward. Back in his Army days, he'd had a sergeant much like that. When they were just being themselves, the Yanks were ordinary people. When they were being occupiers, though . . . The smile disappeared. If they had their way, they'd do whatever they could to turn all the Canadians in the land they'd occupied into Americans. That was why Julia and Mary didn't go to the school they'd reopened.

McGregor held onto Mary's hand; Maude had charge of Julia. They picked their way toward the counter. Some of the U.S. soldiers politely stepped aside. Others pretended they weren't there. That rude arrogance angered McGregor, but he couldn't do anything about it. He held his face still. So did Maude. Their children weren't so good at concealing what they felt. Once he had to give Mary's hand a warning squeeze to get rid of the ferocious grimace she gave an American who'd walked through the space where she had been standing as if she didn't exist.

"Good day to you, Arthur," Henry Gibbon said. Had a moving picture wanted to cast somebody as a storekeeper, he would have been the man, if only his apron had been cleaner: he was tubby and bald, with a gray soup-strainer of a mustache that whuffed out when he talked. "Brought the whole kit and kaboodle with you, I see. Well, what can I do for you this mornin'?"

"Need a couple of hacksaw blades, and a sack of beans if you've got some. We'll get our kerosene ration, too, I expect, and the missus is going to make a run at your yard goods. And tobacco—"

"Ain't got any." Gibbon moved his hand just enough to suggest that the Yanks had bought him out. McGregor looked glum. So did Alexander. Life was hard. Life without a pipe was harder.

"And we'll see what kind of candy you've got here, too," McGregor said. His eye went to the Minnesota and Dakota papers piled on the counter. He reached out and shoved one of them at the storekeeper, too. It would be full of Yankee lies, but new lies might be interesting.

He went over and stood by the pickle barrel, waiting while Maude told Gibbon what she needed and he compared that to what he happened to have, which was a good deal less. He wasn't quite emptied out, though, as McGregor had feared he would be. That was something, anyhow.

When McGregor took a look at the hacksaw blades while walking back to the wagon, he understood why. "These were made in the United States," he exclaimed, and then, a few steps later, "No wonder Henry's still got stuff on his shelves."

"Traitor," Alexander said, low enough so that none of the U.S. soldiers passing by could hear him.

But, after a moment, McGregor shook his head. "Everybody's got to eat," he said. "Storekeeper can't live selling dust and spiderwebs. I'm surprised he's able to get things from the USA, that's all." He rubbed his chin. "Maybe I'm not, not with all the soldiers he has in there. No, maybe I'm not. They're getting things from him they likely can't get straight from their own quartermasters."

"I don't like it," Alexander said as they got into the wagon.

"Everybody's got to eat," Arthur McGregor repeated. "Rokeby the postmaster sells those occupation stamps with ugly Americans on them, because those are the only stamps the Yankees let him sell. That doesn't make him bad; he's just doing his job. Weren't for the Yankees buying our crop last fall, I don't know what we'd be doing for cash money right now."

That produced an uncomfortable silence, which lasted for some time. None of the McGregors cared for the notion of the United States as an entity with which they and their countrymen did business, and upon which they depended. But whether you cared for the notion or not, it was true.

When they got back to the farmhouse, the front door was open. Maude spotted it first. "Arthur," she said reproachfully, "all the heat will have gone out of the house." McGregor started to deny having failed to shut it, but he'd ducked back inside for his mittens after everyone else was in the wagon, so it had to have been his fault.

So he thought, glumly, till a man in green-gray walked out onto the front porch and pointed at the wagon. Several more U.S.

soldiers, all of them armed, came running out of the house. "What are they *doing* here?" Alexander demanded, his voice quivering with indignation.

"I don't know," McGregor answered. Some of the Yankees were aiming rifles at him. He made very sure they could see both his hands on the reins.

The man who'd first spotted the wagon walked toward it. He wore a captain's bars on each shoulder strap. "You are Arthur McGregor," he said in a tone brooking no denial. He pointed. "That is your son, Alexander."

"And who the devil are you?" McGregor asked. "What are you doing in my house?"

"I don't have to tell you that," the captain said, "but I will. I am Captain Hannebrink, of Occupation Investigations. We have uncovered a bomb on the railroad tracks, and arrested some of the young hotheads responsible for it. Under thorough interrogation"—which probably meant torture—"more than one of them named Alexander McGregor as an accomplice in their vicious attempt."

"It's a lie!" Alexander said. "I never did anything like that!"

Captain Hannebrink pulled a scrap of paper from his breast pocket. "Are you acquainted with Terence McKiernan, Ihor Klimenko, and Jimmy Knight?"

"Yes, I know them, but so what?" Alexander said. Arthur McGregor knew them, too: boys his son's age, more or less, from nearby farms. He knew Jimmy and Ihor were hotheads; he hadn't been so sure about the McKiernan lad.

"Do you deny having joined with them in discussing subversion and sabotage?" Hannebrink went on, all the more frightening for being so matter-of-fact.

"No, I don't even deny that," Alexander said. "I'm a patriot, the same as any good Canadian. But I never knew anything about a bomb on the tracks, and that's the truth."

The American captain shrugged. "We'll find out what the truth is. For now, you're coming with us." A couple of his soldiers gestured with their rifles. Alexander had no choice. He scrambled out of the wagon and walked with them to a big motor truck they had waiting behind the barn. Its engine roared to life. It rolled away, back toward Rosenfeld.

Arthur McGregor stared after it till it was no more than a

black speck. Alexander had been talking about the railroad that very morning, but his father still thought he had kept the promise he'd made. That Alexander's keeping the promise might not matter hadn't occurred to him, not till now, not till too late.

Jonathan Moss looked down from several thousand feet on a yellow-green cloud of gas rolling from the American line toward the defensive positions the British and Canadians were holding. Chlorine was heavier than air. None of it, surely, had any way of reaching him here, more than a mile up in the sky. In any case, the goggles he was wearing against the wind would have given his eyes some protection against the poison gas. They stung in spite of that, and he felt like coughing.

He shook his head, annoyed at himself. "If the cook takes the head off a chicken, you don't get a pain in the neck," he said. The roar of the engine drowned the words, while the slipstream blew them away.

Artillery thundered down onto the Canucks and limeys in the wake of the gas. Some of the shells ripped through the air alarmingly close to his Martin single-decker. Those near misses made the aeroplane buck like a poorly broken horse. Accidental hit . . . You didn't want to think about an accidental hit. *Odds are against it,* Moss told himself very firmly.

Sure as sure, the Canucks and the English soldiers who helped fill their trenches were catching hell. Whenever their long, slow retreat moved them back into another town, they fought harder than ever. Now they were trying to hold on to Acton, a no-account little place a few miles east of Guelph. Acton had been no-account, anyhow. Now its name was going into the history books in letters of blood.

When the artillery let up, Americans swarmed out of their trenches and rushed across fields, some snow-covered, others brown-black with mud, toward the enemy line. Watched from high in the sky, it looked as if God's hand were moving pieces on an enormous board: more like chess than war.

One thing neither God nor gas nor shelling had managed was to sweep all the Canucks and limeys from that board. Machine guns began winking from redoubts of timber and sandbags. Between them came flashes of rifle fire. From his lofty perch, Moss saw the American advance falter.

He also saw Dud Dudley wagging his wings up ahead of him. The flight was supposed to support the infantry attack on Acton. Dudley put the nose of his fighting scout down and dove on the enemy trenches. Tom Innis followed. So did Moss, the wind howling past the wires supporting his wings. So did Phil Eaker, who had replaced Zach Whitby, who had replaced Luther Carlsen, who had probably replaced . . .

Moss didn't want to think about that, either. He was a replacement here, too, even if he'd been in the war from the beginning. Instead, he thought about the rapidly swelling scene below. Yes, the attack had bogged down, sure as the devil. The artillery hadn't cut enough wire in front of the enemy trenches to give the Americans decent avenues to close with their foes. The United States had come as far as they had in Canada on the strength of overwhelming numbers. If they kept throwing men away at this rate, their numbers wouldn't stay overwhelming forever.

"That's what I'm here for," Moss said. "To get rid of some numbers on the other side."

He squeezed the firing button for his machine gun. Tracers let him guide the stream of bullets down the trench ahead of him as he roared over it at treetop height. The way the khaki-clad soldiers scattered before him made him feel treetop tall himself, as firing at men on the ground always did. He felt like a boy in short pants, amusing himself by stepping on bugs.

If you fooled with the wrong bug, though, you were liable to get stung. And the soldiers in the traverses, which ran perpendicular to his line of fire, blazed away at him instead of scattering. He laughed, as he would have laughed stepping on a bee while wearing shoes. They'd have a hell of a time hurting him: how could they draw a bead on a target streaking past at almost a hundred miles an hour?

Thwump! A bullet passing through canvas made a noise like a drumstick tapping on a rather loose drumhead. A lot of bullets were in the air. Some, dammit, *would* touch the aeroplane. He'd found that out in scraps with the limeys and Canucks, right at the start of the war. It was unnerving *(thwump!)*, but you could put a lot of holes in an aeroplane's canvas and it would keep on flying. *Thwump!*

Clang! He swore. That wasn't canvas, that was the engine. His oil pressure began to drop. Maybe, he thought hopefully, the bullet had only damaged the pump mechanism. He had a hand squeeze-bulb to augment that; the pump was often balky. He couldn't shoot and work the squeeze-bulb at the same time. When he stopped shooting to work the bulb, the pressure kept dropping. It wasn't the pump mechanism. A fine mist of oil started coating his goggles. He could leave them on and not see well from oil . . . or take them off and not see well from the breeze.

Clang! "That's not fair!" he shouted angrily. Fair or not, the damage the second bullet had done was immediately obvious. A plume of hot water from the radiator rained back on him.

He turned back toward the U.S. lines and put the Martin into a steep climb, figuring he'd need all the altitude he could get before—No sooner had the thought crossed his mind than the engine started dying. He throttled back for a moment, to see whether it would run better at low revs.

When it didn't, he gave it all the power it had. "A short life but a merry one," he said, and wondered whether he was talking about the engine or himself. He'd find out, one way or the other.

Abruptly, the engine went from dying to dead. That left him in charge of a nose-heavy glider a couple of hundred feet above no-man's-land. He kept the nose up as best he could. The ground got closer with every beat of his heart.

He was over the American trench line—not very far over it, either. An idiot took a shot at him. *Thwump!* The bullet drilled through the fuselage, not far behind him. *Nice to know our boys on the ground are such good shots,* he thought, and then, *If I ever find out who that son of a bitch is, I'll kick his teeth in.*

Between trenches and shell holes, he couldn't have found a worse landscape in which to try to set down an aeroplane. If he'd had a choice, he wouldn't have tried it. He had no choice. There was a road of sorts, one on which fresh ammunition and supplies came to the front. And there was a little train of wagons on it, bringing forward whatever they were bringing.

Would he—could he—get over them and set the Martin down? "I'll do it or die trying," he said, and giggled. Never had a hackneyed phrase been more literally true.

With his engine fallen silent, he could hear the horses whinny in fright. He could hear their drivers cuss, too. He thought that, if he'd wanted to, he could have reached down and snatched the caps off those drivers' heads. He cleared their wagons that closely.

A moment later, his landing gear thudded down on rutted earth. The ruts, God be praised, ran in the direction he was going. The surface, he thought thankfully, wasn't that much worse than the usual landing strip.

Then one of the wheels went into a hole. His teeth slammed together on his tongue. Blood filled his mouth. The aeroplane tried to stand on its nose. If it had succeeded, it would have shoved the engine and machine gun back into his chest and squashed him into jelly. It didn't have quite enough momentum. The tail slammed back to earth. Moss bit his tongue again.

He unfastened his harness and scrambled out of the Martin. It hadn't caught fire, but that didn't mean it couldn't. He stood there on the muddy, half-frozen ground, looking for any sign of the rest of his flight. He saw no aeroplanes at all.

The driver of the rearmost wagon hopped down and ran toward him. "You all right, buddy?" he asked.

Moss spat a mouthful of red into the muck, but then he nodded. "Think so," he answered. Talking hurt, but other than that and what would probably be bruises where the harness had kept him from going facefirst into the instrument panel, he didn't seem damaged.

"Thought you was going to clip me there," the driver said. "Had time for one Hail Mary"—he crossed himself—"and then you was over me."

"Yeah." Moss' legs suddenly felt as if they were made of some cheap grade of modeling clay, not flesh and bone. Now that he was down, he could realize what a narrow escape he'd had. Before, up in the air, he'd been too busy trying to stretch every last inch from his bus.

Soldiers came out of the trenches to shake his hands and congratulate him on being in one piece. Among them was a captain who asked, "Where's your aerodrome, pal?"

"Back near Cambridge," he answered.

"We'll get you home," the captain told him. "Probably tomorrow, not today. You can enjoy the hospitality of the trenches tonight." He stuck out a hand. "I'm Clyde Landis."

"Jonathan Moss, sir." Just then, the Canucks started lobbing artillery at where they thought his aeroplane had gone down.

Diving into the trenches seemed the most hospitable thing in the world.

All the rest of that day, the soldiers made much of him. They gave him cigars and big bowls of horrible slumgullion and enough shots of the rotgut they weren't supposed to have to make his head swim. They all sounded convinced he was a hero, and made him tell story after story of what fighting in the air was like.

More shells rained down. He wouldn't have done an infantryman's job for a million dollars. If there were any heroes in the war, the foot sloggers were the ones. They laughed when he said so.

"This is a letter from your father," Sylvia Enos said to George, Jr., and Mary Jane. "See how it says NAVAL POST on the envelope by the stamp?" George, Jr., nodded impatiently. He knew his ABCs, and he could read a few words. To Mary Jane, the rubber-stamped phrase didn't mean anything.

Sylvia opened the envelope and took out the letter. She read aloud in a portentous tone: " 'Dear Sylvia'—that's me—'I hope you and the children are well. I am fine here. We have done some fighting on the river. I came through it fine and so did the ship. We hit the enemy and he did not hit us.' "

"Boom!" George, Jr., yelled, as if he were a shell going off. Then, as best he could on the floor of the front room, he imitated a stricken warship capsizing and sinking, finishing the performance with a loud, "Glub, glub, glub!"

Mary Jane thought that was very funny. So did Sylvia, till it crossed her mind that the *Punishment* could have been the vessel going to the bottom as easily as its foe. "Do you want to hear the rest of the letter?" she asked, more sharply than she'd intended. *She* wanted to finish it; George didn't write so often as she wished he would. With a touch of guilt, she realized her own letters were also fewer and further between than they should have been.

"Yes, Mama," George, Jr., said, Mary Jane chiming in with, "Rest of letter!"

" 'I miss all of you and I wish I could come back to Boston,' " she resumed. " 'Here in the middle of the country you cannot get any fish that is very good. The cooks do up catfish we catch in the river but no matter what you do to it it still tastes like mud.' "

"Yuck!" George, Jr., exclaimed. Mary Jane stuck out her tongue.

" 'I love all of you and hope I will get some leave one day before too long,' " Sylvia finished. " 'Tell the children to be good. I bet they are getting as big as can be. Your husband, George.' "

"George," Mary Jane said in tones of wonder. She pointed to her brother. "George."

"That's right," Sylvia said. "George, Jr., is named after his papa—your papa, too, you know."

"Papa." Mary Jane dutifully repeated the word and nodded, but she didn't sound convinced. She hadn't seen her father for months. Sylvia wondered if she remembered him. She said she did, but then she said all sorts of things that had only the vaguest connection with reality. Seeing her, remembering George, Jr., at the same age, Sylvia was convinced two-year-olds lived in a very strange world. She wondered if she'd been like that at the same age. She probably had.

George, Jr., asked, "Will Papa ever come home before the war ends and we've beaten the Rebs all up?"

Where does he hear such things? Sylvia wondered. At home, she didn't talk much about the war. That left Brigid Coneval and the other children she watched. Sylvia shrugged. She supposed war needed hate, but wished it didn't. The question deserved an answer, though, no matter how it was framed. She said, "When Papa talked about getting leave in his letter, that meant he hoped he could come for a visit before he had to go back to his ship."

"Oh," her son said seriously. "Well, I hope he can, too."

"I'll get supper going now, and then we'll wash you two and put you to bed," Sylvia said. That drew mixed responses. Her children were hungry, but unenthusiastic about baths and even more unenthusiastic about bedtime. She told them, "If you eat all your supper up and you're good in the bathtub, maybe you can play for a little while afterwards."

They wolfed down fried halibut and potatoes, they didn't do anything too outrageous when she took them out of the apartment and down the hall to the bathroom at the end (a good thing, too, with her carrying hot water to mix with the cold), and they didn't splash up the place too badly. She brought them back swaddled in towels, and changed George, Jr., into pajamas (which made him look very grown-up) and Mary Jane into her nightgown.

George, Jr., played with toy soldiers, the U.S. troops storming trench after Confederate trench. Sylvia wished it were really so easy. Mary Jane gave her doll a bottle, then climbed up into Sylvia's lap and fell asleep there. Not even the bloodcurdling explosions her brother kept producing did anything to stir her.

Maybe so much warmaking had worn out George, Jr., too, for he didn't put up his usual complaints about going to bed. That left Sylvia the only one awake in the apartment, which seemed, as it often did at such times, too big and too quiet.

"I should write to George," she said. She found paper and a pen soon enough, but the bottle of ink had escaped. She finally came upon it lurking in her sewing box. "*I* didn't put it there," she declared, and wondered which of her offspring had. Mary Jane would say no to everything on general principles, and George, Jr., knew better than to admit to anything that would get him spanked.

Dear George, Sylvia wrote, *I got your letter. It was good to hear from you. I am glad you are well and safe. I saw Charlie White's wife on T Wharf and she says he is out to sea on a cruiser. They will have good food on that ship.* Despite his name, Charlie was black, not white, and had been the cook on the *Ripple.* Reinking her pen, she went on, *I am well. The children are well. We all hope you do get leave so we can see you. We miss you. I love you. Sylvia.*

When she was done, she read the letter over. It seemed so flat and empty. She wished she were a better writer, to be able to say all the things she wanted to say, all the things that really mattered. Maybe she could have done that if she'd had more schooling. As things were . . . it would have to do. More searching scared an envelope out of cover. *Seaman George Enos,* she wrote on it. *U.S. Navy. Central River Command. St. Louis, Mo.* She went on one more scouting expedition, this time through her handbag in search of a stamp. She found one, stuck it on the envelope, and put the letter in the handbag so she could mail it in the morning.

In the chaos of getting the children ready and over to Mrs. Coneval's and then of getting herself off to work, she forgot about the letter. She remembered only when her machine stuck the first label on a can of mackerel. Can after can followed that first one. She had to pull three levers for each can, keep the machine full of labels and paste, and clear the feeding mechanism when it jammed, as it did every so often.

After a while, she noticed Isabella Antonelli wasn't at the machine next to hers. The foreman, Mr. Winter, was running it instead. Mr. Winter was fat and fifty-five and walked with a limp from a wound he'd got in the Second Mexican War. The Army didn't want him, which made him a godsend for the canning plant.

When she asked him where her friend was, she thought for a moment he hadn't heard her over the rattle of the lines that sent the cans moving from one station to the next. Then he said, "She called on the telephone this morning. Western Union visited her last night."

"Oh, God," Sylvia said. Isabella Antonelli's husband had been a fisherman on a little boat that operated out of T Wharf. Then the Army had taken him and sent him off to Quebec. The newspapers did their best to be optimistic about the fighting north of the St. Lawrence, but their best wasn't all that good. The going was hard up there, and bad weather liable to last till May.

Mr. Winter nodded. He was bald, with a fringe of gray hair above his ears; the lights shone off his smooth pate. "She'll be out a few days, I'm afraid," he said. "They'll put a temporary on the machine here tomorrow, I expect, till she can come back."

Sylvia nodded, too, hiding a flash of fury frightening in its fierceness. Yes, Mr. Winter was a godsend for the canning plant, all right. He thought of getting the mackerel out before he worried about the people who got it out. *Keep the machines running, no matter what,* she thought. Antonelli was one more line in the casualty lists? So what?

She filled the paste reservoir to her machine from one of the cans under it. The foreman at the paste plant probably had the exact same attitude. For that matter, the generals probably had the exact same attitude, too. What was Antonelli to them but one more line in the casualty lists?

All the canning machines, including Sylvia's, ran smoothly, unlike the war machine. She pulled her three levers, one after the other, then went back and did it again and again and again. If you didn't notice how your feet got sore from standing by the machine for hours at a time, you could get into a rhythm where you did your job almost without conscious thought, so that half the morning could go by before you noticed. Sylvia didn't know whether to like those days or be frightened of them.

Mr. Winter's voice startled her out of that half-mesmerized state: "*Your* husband well, Mrs. Enos?"

"What?" she said, and then, really hearing the words, "Oh. Yes. Thank you. I got a letter from him yesterday, as a matter of fact. I wrote an answer, too," she added virtuously, "but I forgot to mail it this morning. I'll do it on the way home."

"Good. That's good." The foreman's smile displayed large yellow teeth, a couple of them in the lower jaw missing. "Good-looking woman like you, though, I bet you get lonely anyhow, no man around. Being lonely's no fun. I know about that, since Priscilla died a few years ago."

Numbly, Sylvia nodded. The machine ran low on labels, which let her tend to it without having to say anything. Mr. Winter hadn't been crude, as men sometimes were. But she felt his eyes on her as she loaded in the labels. He was the foreman. If he pushed it and she said no, he could fire her. The line kept running smoothly, but she never got the easy rhythm back.

VII

Among the butternut uniforms in the West Virginia prisoner-of-war camp were a few dark gray ones: Navy men captured by the damnyankees. Reggie Bartlett found himself gravitating toward them. For a while, he wondered why; he'd never had any special interest in the Confederate States Navy before the war began. After a bit, he found an answer that, if it wasn't the whole picture, was at least a good part of it.

The trouble was, soldiers were boring. He'd done as much hard fighting as any of them, and more than most—war in the Roanoke valley was as nasty a business as war anywhere in the world. He'd seen almost all the horrors there were, and heard about the ones he hadn't seen. Soldiers told the same kinds of stories, over and over again. They got stale.

Navy men, now, Navy men were different, and so were their stories. They'd been in strange places and done strange things—or at least things Reggie Bartlett had never done. Those tales made the time between stretches of chopping wood and filling in slit trenches and the other exciting chores of camp life pass more quickly.

Even when things went wrong in the stories, they went wrong in ways that couldn't happen on dry land. A senior lieutenant who somehow managed to look clean and spruce and well-shaved in spite of the general camp squalor was saying, "Damnyankees suckered me in, neat as you please. There sat this fishing boat, out in the middle of the Atlantic, no ships around her, naked as a whore in her working clothes. So up came my boat to sink her with the deck gun—cheaper and surer than using one of my fish—"

"One of your what, Lieutenant Briggs?" Reggie asked, a beat ahead of a couple of other prisoners who had gathered around the Navy lieutenant for reasons probably similar to his own.

"Torpedoes," Briggs explained. Under his breath, he muttered, "Landlubbers." But he resumed after a moment, as glad to tell the story as the others were to hear it: "You can't always trust a whore, though, even when she's naked. And sure enough, this was the badger game. The fishing boat was towing a Yankee sub on a cable with a telephone line attached. I let the fishermen go over the side before I sank their boat, and what thanks did I get? Their damned submersible blew me out of the water." His face clouded. "Only a couple-three of us lived. The rest went right to the bottom, never had a chance."

"It's almost like what the Mormons done to the damnyankees, blowin' up all that powder right under 'em," somebody said.

"More like sniper's work," Reggie contradicted. "A lot of times, a sniper'll be hiding, and he'll try and make somebody on the other side look up to see what's going on further down the trench. And if you're dumb enough to do it, the bastard with the scope on his rifle, he'll put one right in your earhole for you."

"Good analogy," Briggs said, nodding. He wasn't a whole lot older than Bartlett, but better educated and also stiffer in manner; had he been a civilian, he would have been something like a junior loan officer at a bank. He was steady, he was sound, he was reliable—and Reggie would have loved to play poker against him, because if the Yankees could play him for a sucker that way, Reggie figured he could, too.

He'd just noticed that his analogy, whether Briggs approved of it or not, took things back to the trenches when the U.S. guards started shouting, "Prisoners form by barracks in parade ranks!"

Senior Lieutenant Briggs frowned. "This isn't right. It's not time to form parade ranks." The break in routine irked him.

"Probably got some kind of special announcement for us," Bartlett said. The guards had done that before, a time or two. The special announcements they handed out weren't good news, not if you backed the Entente.

He didn't get the chance to learn Briggs' opinion of his guess; he had to hurry off to form up outside his own harsh, chilly building, a good ways away from where the Navy man was holding forth. The uniforms he and his comrades in misery wore would have given a Confederate drill sergeant a fit, but the ranks the men formed were as neat and orderly as anything that sergeant could have wanted.

"What do you reckon this is?" Jasper Jenkins asked, taking his place beside Bartlett.

"Dunno," Reggie told his friend. "I hope it's that we've had a couple more escapes, and they're gonna make the rest of us work harder on account of that. I don't mind paying the price they put on it. Worth it, you ask me."

"Yeah, that'd be good," Jenkins agreed. "They haven't figured out that we're gonna keep on tryin' to break out o' here no matter what they do. Only a fool'd want to stay, and that's a fact."

A U.S. captain strode importantly to the front of the prisoners' formation. He unfolded a sheet of paper and read from it in a loud, harsh voice: "The Imperial German government, the loyal ally of the United States, has announced the capture of the city of Verdun, the French having evacuated the said city after being unable in six weeks of battle to withstand the might of German arms. Victory shall be ours! Dismissed!"

The neat ranks of prisoners broke up into pockets of chattering men. Jasper Jenkins tugged at Bartlett's sleeve. "Hey, Reggie, where's this Vair-done place at?" he asked. Before the war, he probably would have asked the same thing about Houston or Nashville or Charleston; his horizon had been limited to his farm and the small town where he sold his crops and bought what little he couldn't raise for himself.

Reggie could have done better at the geography of the Confederate States. When it came to foreign countries, even foreign countries to which the CSA was allied . . . "I dunno, not exactly," he admitted. "Somewhere in France, it has to be, and I reckon somewhere near Germany, or the Huns wouldn't have been fighting for it. Past that, though, I can't tell you."

"Damnyankees sound like losin' it's about two steps from the end o' the world for the Frenchies," Jenkins said.

"I know they do," Reggie answered, "but you've got to remember two things. First one is, for all you know, they're lying just to get us downhearted. Second one is, even if they're not, I expect they're making it out to be more important than it really is. What are we going to do, call 'em liars?"

"They're damnyankees—of course they're liars," Jenkins said, as if stating a law of nature. "You got a good way of lookin' at things, pal. Thanks." He went off, whistling a dirty song.

Having made his friend happy, Reggie discovered he was unhappy himself: Jenkins had made his bump of curiosity itch. He went off looking for Senior Lieutenant Briggs. The naval officer being an educated man, he would be the one to know where Verdun was and what its fall meant.

He found Briggs without much trouble, then wished he hadn't. The Navy man sat on the ground in front of his barracks, head in hands, the picture of misery. Bartlett didn't think the news the Yankees had announced could do that to a man, and wondered if Briggs had just got word his brother had been killed or his sweetheart had married somebody else.

But when he asked what the matter was, Briggs, like Poe's raven, spoke one word and nothing more: "Verdun."

"Sir?" Reggie said. Losing one town didn't sound like that big a catastrophe to him. The Confederacy had lost a good many towns, all along the border, but was still very much in the fight.

"Verdun," Briggs repeated, and climbed heavily to his feet. "From everything I heard, the French were swearing they'd defend the place to the last man. Now they've pulled back instead. The Germans have hit 'em such a lick, they couldn't afford to keep on fighting where they were, not if they wanted to hang on. Best they think they can do now, looks like, is make the Huns pay such a price for the land they get that they decide it's not worth the cost."

"That's not so bad," Reggie began, but then corrected himself: "It's not so good, either. The Germans, they're inside France, and the French, they don't have any soldiers inside Germany."

"Now you're getting the picture," Briggs agreed. "Same sort of picture we've got over here, too—a goddamn ugly one."

"Yes, sir." Reggie tried to look on the bright side: "We've still got us Washington."

"For now," the Navy man said—the report from France seemed to have taken all the wind from his sails. "I tell you this, though, Bartlett: our country is going to need every man it can lay its hands on if we're going to give the American Huns what they deserve." He paused to let that sink in, then added in a low voice, "It is the positive duty of every prisoner of war to try to escape."

Reggie felt a sudden hollow in the pit of his stomach having nothing to do with the hunger that never left. "The Yankees can shoot you if they catch you trying to escape," he remarked. "They catch you after you've got out, they can pretty much do what they want to you." Under the laws of war, Confederate guards had the same rights with U.S. prisoners, but he didn't dwell on that.

Briggs just nodded, as if he'd remarked on the weather. "If we once get out, we can get away. We wouldn't be like Frenchmen stuck in the middle of Germany. We speak the same language as the Yankees."

"Not just the same language," Reggie objected. "They talk ugly."

"I think so, too," Briggs said. "But I know how they talk and how it's different from the way we talk. I can teach you. Come with me." The last three words had the snap of an order. Bartlett followed him into the barracks. The senior lieutenant picked up an object made of galvanized sheet iron and walked across the room with it, asking, "What am I doing?" as he walked.

"Why, you're toting that pail, sir." Reggie stated the obvious.

But Briggs shook his head. "That's what I'd be doing in the CSA," he said. "If I'm doing it in the USA, I'm carrying this bucket. You see?"

"Yes, sir," Bartlett said, and he did see. For that last part of the sentence, Briggs hadn't sounded like a Confederate at all. He'd not only chosen different words, he'd sort of pinched his mouth up, so all the vowel sounds were somehow sharper. "How'd you do that?"

"Got started in theatricals at the Naval Academy down in Mobile," Briggs answered. "If we can get outside the wire, it'll come in handy. Like I say, I can teach you. Do you want to learn? Do you want to do the other things you'll have to do to get outside the wire?"

It was a good question. If he stayed here, Reggie could sit out the war, if not in comfort, at least in security. If he tried to escape, he guaranteed himself all the risks involved with Yankee guards and patrols. If he managed to evade them and got back to the CSA, what would happen next? He knew exactly what would happen: they'd pat him on the back, grant him a little leave, and then hand him a new uniform and a Tredegar and put him back in the line. Hadn't he had enough of that for a lifetime?

"I'm carrying the bucket," he said, trying to pronounce the words as Briggs had. He wasn't getting them right. He could hear that.

"Listen." Briggs repeated the phrase. Bartlett tried it again. "Better," the Navy man said. Reggie didn't know exactly how he'd agreed to try to escape from the prisoner-of-war camp, but, by the time he left Briggs' barracks, he had no doubt he'd done just that.

"Closing time, gentlemen," Nellie Semphroch said as the clock in the coffeehouse finished striking nine. When none of the Confederate officers—or the Washingtonians who'd grown rich dealing with them—showed any sign of being ready to leave, she added, "I'm following the regulations you people set down. You wouldn't want me to break your own rules, would you?"

A plump, gray-haired colonel who did not look to be the sort for late night adventures rose from his chair, saying, "We must set an example for the lovely ladies here." He tossed a half-dollar down on the table and walked out into the night.

With him taking the lead, the rest of the men and the handful of women—*loose women,* Nellie thought, for what other kind would consort with the occupiers?—drifted out of the coffeehouse. Last of all went Nicholas H. Kincaid, who paused outside the doorway to send a mooncalf look back at Edna till Nellie almost broke his nose by slamming the door in his face.

"Ma, you keep doin' things like that, he won't come back no more," Edna said, gathering up cups and saucers and plates and tips, some in scrip, some in good silver money.

"God, I hope he doesn't," Nellie said. "He's not here for the coffee and victuals. He's here because he's all soppy over you." The reverse, as she knew, also held; she'd caught them kissing and well on their way to worse a year before, and had watched Edna like a hawk ever since.

Her daughter just tossed her head. "He's all right," she said carelessly. "There are plenty of others, though." That was calculated to make Nellie steam, and achieved the desired effect. Nellie was bound and determined that her daughter should go to the altar a maiden—she knew too well how grim the alternative could be. But Edna, and Edna's hot young blood, weren't making things easy.

Work helped. Running the coffeehouse kept the two of them hopping from sunup till long past sundown. If you were busy, you didn't have time to get into trouble. Nellie said, "Start doing up the dishes. I'll help in a minute—I want to count up what's in the till first."

"All right, Ma," Edna said. She *would* work, Nellie admitted to herself, more than a little grudgingly. She wasn't a *bad* girl, not really, just a *wild* girl, wild for life, wild for anything she could get her hands on, wild to let life—and the men crawling through life—get their hands on her.

The cash box was nicely heavy. Nellie had thought it would be. If she could do any one thing, it was gauge how busy the place had been through the day. Most of the take was in silver, too; as her place had become a favorite stop for the occupiers, they became more likely to give her real money and fob off their nearly worthless scrip on merchants whose goodwill mattered less to them.

"A couple of dollars less than I thought there would be," she murmured, and then shrugged. She was doing well enough that a couple of dollars one way or the other mattered much less to her than they would have before the war started. She had no use for the Rebs, she spied on them whenever their loose talk gave her the chance, but she was getting, if not rich, at least well-to-do off them. *Serves them right,* she thought, and went to help her daughter clean up.

Artillery rumbled, off to the north and northeast, the noise clearly audible through splashing and the clank of china on china. "Louder these days," Edna remarked, glancing in the direction of that deep-throated roar.

"Were you listening to the Rebs tonight?" Nellie asked. Edna shook her head. That exasperated her mother; Edna saw the war only in terms of how it affected her—not least by supplying her with handsome young Confederate officers to meet. Nellie went on, "They say they think they can stop our attack out of Baltimore, but it didn't sound to me like they were real sure about it. If we're lucky, we may run the Rebs out of here this summer."

Edna kept right on drying saucers. She didn't say anything for a while. The way she stood, though, suggested she wasn't altogether sure it would be good luck. She liked the way things were going. Business wouldn't be the same with the USA holding Washington again.

That wasn't all that wouldn't be the same. Mother and daughter spoke together. Nellie said, "The Rebs won't want to give this town back," while Edna put it more gamely: "They'll fight like bastards to hold on to Washington."

They finished doing the dishes in gloomy silence. There wouldn't be much left of Washington after a big fight for it. The city had been badly damaged when the Rebels overran it in 1914, and they'd taken it pretty quickly. What would it look like if they chose to defend it street by street, house by house?

Nellie lighted a candle at one of the downstairs gas lamps, then turned them out. She and Edna went up the stairs to their bedrooms by the light of the candle. She used it to light the lamps in those rooms, then blew it out. "Good night, Ma," Edna said around a yawn.

"Good night," Nellie answered, hiding a smile. Keep Edna busy enough and she wouldn't have time for mischief, all right. Maybe she wouldn't. Nellie undid the hooks and eyes that held her skirt closed, then unbuttoned the long row of mother-of-pearl buttons on her shirtwaist. She tossed it into the wicker clothes hamper. The hamper was almost full; she'd have to go to the laundry soon. The corset came off next. She sighed with pleasure at being released from its steel-boned grip. She put on a long cotton nightdress, turned off the gas lamp, and climbed under the blankets.

Falling asleep seldom took her long. She'd almost done it when the Confederates sent a column marching up the street in front of the coffeehouse. The tramp of boots on pavement, the rattle of steel-tired wagon wheels, and the clop of horses' hooves made her sit up. It was a good-sized column; they hadn't sent so many men north in a while.

She tried to figure out what that meant. Was it good news or bad? Good, if the Rebs were moving because they needed men against the U.S. attacks. Not so good, if these were troops freed up because the Negro uprisings in the CSA were collapsing. She'd have to see if she could find out tomorrow.

When the column had passed, she settled back down again. She was drifting toward sleep when someone knocked on the door. The knock was soft but insistent, as if whoever was there wanted to make sure she and Edna heard but also wanted to be equally sure no one else did.

She got out of bed in the dark. Her first suspicious glance, when she reached the hall, was to Edna's bedroom. But Edna was in there snoring. She'd never been able to fool her mother about being asleep. Scratching her head, Nellie slowly and carefully went downstairs.

The knocking persisted. She wished she had a pistol down there by the cash box. She'd never thought she'd need one, though, not with so many Confederate soldiers always in the coffeehouse. And the Rebs had made it against their rules for locals to keep firearms, with penalties harsh enough to make her not want to take the chance of hiding one right under their noses.

They hadn't made any rules against keeping knives. She picked up the biggest carving knife she had, one that would have made a decent sword with a different handle, and walked to the door. "Who's there?" she asked, making no move to open it.

"It's me, Little Nell." Bill Reach didn't name himself, confident she could identify his voice. She didn't, but no one else these days—thank God!—used the name from her sordid past. When she neither said anything nor worked the latch, he hissed, "Let me in, darlin'. I got nowhere else to go, and it's late—way past curfew."

Nellie knew what time it was. "Go away," she said through the door, quietly, so as not to wake Edna. That he had the nerve to call her *darling* filled her with fury. "Don't you ever come here again. I mean it." Her hand closed on the handle of the knife, hard enough to hurt.

"Listen, Nell," Reach said, also quietly, "if you don't let me in, I'm a dead man. I can't stay on the dodge any more, and they—"

"If you don't get out of here this instant," Nellie told him in a deadly whisper, "I'll scream loud enough to bring every

Confederate patroller for a mile and a half around this place on the dead run."

"But—" Reach muttered something under his breath. Then he grunted, an involuntary, frightened sound. "Jesus, Nell, here they come—it's a whole goddamn Confederate column. They see me here, I'm dead and buried."

For a moment, Nell thought he was trying to trick her. Then she too heard the rhythmic thump of marching men and the jingle of harness. Another column—probably another regiment—heading up toward the fighting. Nellie bit her lip till she tasted blood. She didn't want the Rebs to lay their hands on . . . anyone. *Even Bill Reach?* she asked herself silently, and, with great reluctance, nodded. *Even Bill Reach.*

She opened the door. Reach scurried inside like a rat running into its hole. "God bless you, Nell," he said while she closed it as quietly as she could. "If they'd have caught me, they'd have squeezed everything out of me, about you and this place and the shoemaker and—*guk!*"

Nellie held the tip of the knife against his poorly shaved throat. "Don't you talk about such things, not to me, not to them, not to anybody," she said in a voice all the more frightening for being so cold. "I'm not the foolish girl I was, and you can't blackmail me. When that column marches past, you're going out the door again. If you come around here after that, I'll shove this in"—she did shove the knife in, perhaps a quarter of an inch; Reach moaned and tried to pull away, but she wouldn't let him—"and I'll laugh while I'm doing it. Do you hear me? You laughed when you shoved it into me, didn't you? My turn now."

He didn't say anything. That was the smartest thing he could have done. A little moonlight came through the plate-glass window from outside. His eyes glittered. The fear smell, sharp and acrid, came off him in waves.

The Confederates tramped past the coffeehouse. Maybe the noise of their passing woke Edna. Nellie would have sworn she hadn't been noisy enough to disturb her daughter. But, from the hall, Edna asked, "Ma, what's going on? Who's this bird? And—" Edna's breath caught sharply. "What are you doing with that knife?"

"He's trouble, nothing else but." Nellie's voice was grim. "But he's in trouble, too, so he can stay here till the Rebs have gone by outside. After that, he's gone forever."

"I knew your mother, before you were born," Bill Reach said to Edna, "back in the house at—" He drew a frightened breath of his own, for Nellie had stuck the knife in farther. *How deep do you have to stab to kill a man?* she wondered. A couple of more words out of Reach and she would have found out.

The sounds of marching feet, clattering wagons, and clopping hooves drowned out the drone of aeroplane engines high overhead. Maybe someone in the Confederate ranks was unwise enough to strike a match to light a cigar or pipe; maybe the moonlight let a U.S. pilot spot the column even without such help. However that was—Nellie had no way of knowing—a stick of bombs came falling out of the sky.

"Oh, Jesus!" Reach said when he heard the high-pitched shriek of air rushing past the bombs' fins. Nellie needed a split second longer to identify the noise; U.S. bombers hadn't come over Washington all that often.

A split second after that, sharp explosions left no possible doubt of what was going on. One bomb fell a little in front of the head of the Confederate column. Then two more in quick succession landed right in the middle of it. Either the U.S. bomb-aiming was extraordinarily good or the bombardier was trying for another target altogether and got lucky—again, Nellie never knew.

Glass sprayed inward. A sharp shard caught Nellie in the leg. She yelped. Edna screamed. Bill Reach let out a groan and clutched at his midsection. Nellie staggered back from him. He sank slowly to the floor.

A moment later, the front door opened, hitting him and knocking him sideways. It wasn't another bomb; it was Confederate soldiers, seeking shelter from the rain of destruction from the sky. Outside in the street, injured soldiers screamed and groaned. A horse screamed, too, on a higher note. Officers shouted for medical orderlies and Negro stretcher-bearers.

Seeing Nellie, one of the Rebs pointed to Reach and said, "This here your husband the damnyankees done hurt, ma'am?" Even at such a time, he worked to separate the people of Washington from the government of the USA.

"I should say not," she answered, and raised her voice, hoping Reach wasn't too far gone to pay attention: "He's a burglar. I caught him breaking in here. I was going to give him to you." If they thought him an ordinary criminal, they wouldn't ask him questions about anything but burglary. She didn't know how he knew what else he knew, or exactly how much that was. She did know it was too much.

One of the Confederate soldiers said, "All right, ma'am, we'll take charge of him—throw him in a wagon till we find somebody we can give him to. Don't want to leave him bleedin' all over your floor here. Come on, you." He and a buddy got Bill Reach to his feet and out the door.

The bombs had stopped falling. The rest of the Rebels who'd tumbled into the coffeehouse took their leave. Some of them even apologized for bothering Nellie.

"—And your pretty daughter," one of them added, which did him less good in her eyes than he would have guessed.

Nellie shut the door after the last departing Reb, a futile gesture with the window smashed. She looked around at glinting, drifted glass. "Go on upstairs and get me some slippers, Edna," she said. "I'll cut my feet to ribbons if I try to walk through this stuff." She sighed, but went on, "It's not near so bad as it was after the Rebs shelled us."

"No, I reckon not," Edna agreed. She started toward the stairway, then stopped and looked back at Nellie. "What was that crazy fellow talking about houses for? I ain't never lived in a house, and I didn't think you had, neither."

Not all houses are homes, ran through Nellie's mind. "I never did live in a house," she answered. "He's crazy like you said, that's all. Get me those slippers—and get me a blanket, too, will you? With the windows gone, I think I better stay down here till sunup."

"All right, Ma," Edna said. "But I still think that feller knows you a whole lot better than you let on. If he didn't, you wouldn't let him get you all upset like you do."

"Just get me my things," Nellie snapped. Shaking her head, Edna went upstairs. Nellie shook her head, too. Sooner or later, the tawdry tale *would* come out. She could feel it in her bones. And what would she do then? How would she keep Edna in line at all?

Out in the street, wounded Confederates kept on groaning. They did give her a sense of proportion. You didn't die of mortification, however much you wished you could. Bombs falling out of the sky were something else again.

Thunder filled the air. Artillery was pounding ever closer to St. Matthews, South Carolina, from the south and from the east. Negroes streamed back through the town. Some of them wore red armbands and carried the rifles with which they had fought their white, capitalist oppressors so long and so hard. One or two even wore helmets taken from Confederate corpses. They still had the look of soldiers to them. More, though, had thrown away armbands and weapons and were looking for escape, not more battle.

Scipio wished he could have fled, too. But he was too prominent, too recognizable to escape the square so easily. He'd been one of the leaders of the Congaree Socialist Republic from the beginning—*from the beginning till the end,* he thought. The end could not be delayed much longer.

I tried to tell them. He hadn't sought the revolution. He'd been drawn into it, that seeming a safer course than letting himself be eliminated for knowing too much. And it had been a safer course—for a little more than a year. Now, with everything ending in fire, he saw—as he'd seen from the beginning—that going along with the Reds had bought him only a little time.

The rest of the leaders of what had been the Congaree Socialist Republic and was falling to pieces still refused to admit the game was up. Cassius stood in the town square, shouting, "Rally! Rally, God damn de lot of you! Rally 'gainst de 'pressors! Don' let dey take yo' freedom!"

He had picked men with him, men who could have formed a line and stopped—or tried to stop—the collapse, but who stood with their rifle butts trailing in the dust and watched men who had been fighters but were now only fugitives running past.

Cherry's appeal to the faltering followers of the Republic was more fundamental: "Kill de white folks! Got to kill de white folks! Dey catches you, dey kills you sure!"

She was probably right. No—she was almost certainly right. But the men who had done so much had concluded they could do no more. Neither her fiery words nor her even more fiery beauty were enough to turn them back toward the trenches they could not hold.

She rushed over to Scipio and, to his startlement and no small alarm, threw herself into his arms. Her breasts were firm and soft against his chest. "Make dey stop, Kip," she said in a bedroom voice. "Make dey stop, make dey fight. You de best talkin' man we gots. Make dey go back an' fight and I is yours. I do whatever you wants, you make dey stop." She ran her tongue over her full lips, making them even moister and more delicious-looking than they had been. Every sort of promise smoldered in her eyes.

Scipio sighed and shook his head. "Cain't," he said regretfully—not so much regret that he would not have her, for she frightened him more than he wanted her, but regret that this collapse would get so many people killed, with him all too likely to be among them. "Cain't, Cherry. It over. Don't you see? It over."

"Bastard!" she screamed, and twisted away from him. "Liar! Quitter!" She slapped him, a roundhouse blow that snapped his head sideways on his neck and left the taste of blood in his mouth. *Blood on my hands, too*, he thought. *Blood on all our hands*. Cherry cared nothing about the blood on her hands. He counted himself lucky she hadn't pulled out a knife and gutted him with it.

In spite of haranguing the Negroes who didn't want to be soldiers any more, Cassius heard the exchange between Cherry and Scipio. Cassius, as best Scipio could tell, never missed anything. He came trotting over to the two of them. Scipio's guts knotted with fear all over again. Cherry was Cassius' woman. No—Cherry was her own woman, and had been giving herself to Cassius. That wasn't quite the same thing, even if, from Cassius' point of view, it probably looked as if it were.

But Cassius didn't want to quarrel. The ex-hunter, now chairman of what was left of the Congaree Socialist Republic, sadly studied Scipio. "It over now, Kip?" he asked. "You t'ink it over now fo' true?"

"Don't you?" Scipio waved his arms. As he did so, a shell landed only a couple of hundred yards away, black smoke with angry red fire at the core. Dirt leaped upward in graceful arcs, beauty in destruction. "We done everything we kin do. Dey gots too many buckra, too many rifles, too many cannons. Dey whip we, Cass."

"Too many buckra," Cassius said bitterly. "Dey don' rise fo' dey class int'rest, de fools. De 'ristocrats got dey all mystified up." He lifted a weary hand. "We been over this before. I know. We make de struggle go on." He pointed north, toward the swamps of the Congaree. "Gwine make de stand up there. De niggers in de 'pressed zones, dey always gwine know de struggle go on. De white folks, dey never takes we fo' granted again."

That, no doubt, was true. Scipio wished he thought it likelier to help than to hurt. It was liable to be another fifty years before the Negro cause revived in the CSA. He didn't say that. What point, now? What he did say was, "I cain't go to de swamp with you, Cass."

To his surprise, the ex-hunter burst out laughing. "I knows that—you was just a house nigger, and you don't know nothin' 'bout that kin' o' life. What you gots to do is, you gots to blend in. Don' let nobody know you got dat white folks' talk hidin' in your mouth. Git work in de field, in de factory, be a good nigger till de heat die down, then hurt they white folks however you kin." He slapped Scipio on the back. Then he and Cherry, hand in hand, headed north along with some of the other Negroes who still had fight in them.

Scipio stood in the St. Matthews square till shells started landing a good deal closer than a couple of hundred yards away. Then he turned on his heel and ran, along with so many other blacks, men and women both. From behind came shouts of, "De buckra! De buckra comin'!" He ran harder. The leaders of the Congaree Socialist Republic, unlike their Confederate counterparts, hadn't gone in for fancy uniforms. In his undyed cotton homespun, he could have been anybody at all.

And anybody at all was just who he aimed to pretend to be. Once white control washed over this part of what was again South Carolina, he'd lie low, find work, eventually find better work, and spend the rest of his life trying to pretend this whole unfortunate business had never happened.

He stopped running about half a mile outside St. Matthews. That was partly because his wind wasn't all it should have been; before the uprising, he *had* lived soft. It was also partly because he calculated that a Negro overrun while fleeing was more likely to be killed on sight than one who looked to have some business where he was. If he seemed a field hand or a farmer, maybe the white soldiers wouldn't figure he'd been in arms against them. And, as a matter of fact, he hadn't. He'd never once fired a weapon at the duly constituted forces of the Confederate States of America.

Not that that mattered. His laugh came bitter as Cassius'. If the white folks ever figured out who he was, he'd hang. He wouldn't simply hang, either. What they'd do to him first . . .

He moaned a little, down deep in his throat. He'd never been a physically brave man. The idea of being tortured made him want to piss himself with fright. He forced himself to something dimly resembling calm. *Your wits are all you've got now,* he thought. *If you don't use them,* that *will kill you.*

Gunfire and faint shouts rose behind him. That would be the white folks, entering St. Matthews. He nodded to himself. The Congaree Socialist Republic was dead, all right, even if Cassius could keep a nasty ghost of it going in the swamps.

When Scipio came to a patch of woods, he chose a winding path through them over going around. In the woods, he thought, he would be perceived as doing something in particular rather than simply trying to escape from the victorious whites. That again might help keep them from shooting him for the fun of it.

Maybe there was a farm on the far side of the woods. Maybe the world had just gone topsy-turvy. Whatever the reason, a fat hen walked out from among the pine trees and stood in the path, staring at him from beady black eyes. For a moment, that didn't mean much to him. Then it did. *Food,* he thought. No more communal kitchens, no more suppers arguing the workings of the dialectic. If he was going to eat, he'd have to feed himself.

Slowly, he bent and picked up a fist-sized stone. The chicken kept watching him from about ten feet away. He drew back his arm—and let fly, hard as he could. The bird had time for one startled squawk before the stone hit. Feathers exploded out from it. It tried to run away, but had trouble making its legs work. He sprang on it, snatched up the stone, and smashed in its little stupid head.

He wore a knife on his belt. He cut off the broken head and held the chicken by the feet, letting it bleed out. Then he gutted it. He worked slowly and carefully there; he'd seen the job done in the kitchens at Marshlands more times than he could count, but couldn't remember the last time he'd done it himself. He saved the liver and gizzard and heart, putting them back inside the body cavity.

He'd just tossed the rest of the offal into the bushes by the side of the path—a fox or a coon or a possum would find a treat—when a white man called, "You there, nigger! What are you doin'?"

"Got me a chicken, suh," Scipio said. He turned toward the white man—a Confederate major—and put on a wide, servile smile. "Be right glad to share, you leave me jus' a little bit." That was how sharing between blacks and whites worked (when it worked at all) in the CSA.

"Give it here," the major said: a lot of the time, sharing didn't work at all in the CSA. Scipio handed the bird over without a word. The officer took its feet in his right hand. His left hand wasn't a hand, but a hook.

Scipio stiffened in dismay. He'd dealt with this white man, arranging to exchange wounded prisoners. Maybe, though, the fellow wouldn't recognize him. One raggedy Negro looked a lot like another, especially when you hardly saw them as human beings at all.

But Major Hotchkiss, even if he was mutilated, wasn't stupid. His eyes narrowed. "I know your voice," he said, half to himself. "You're the nigger who—" From narrow, his eyes went wide. He didn't bother saying, *talks like a white man,* but dropped the chicken and grabbed for his pistol.

He was a split second too slow. Scipio hit him in the face with the rock he'd used to kill the hen. The Negro leaped on him as he had on the bird, pounding and pounding with the stone till Hotchkiss was as dead as a man ever would be.

Scipio reached for the major's pistol, then jerked his hand away. He didn't want to be caught with a firearm, not in these times. He didn't want to be caught with a blood-spattered shirt, either. He stripped it off and hid it in a hole in the ground. A shirtless Negro would draw no comment.

The chicken was another matter. It was *his.* "You damn thief," he muttered to the late Major Hotchkiss. He picked up the bird and got out of there as fast as he could, before any more white soldiers came along to connect him to the major's untimely demise.

Paul Mantarakis strode warily through the ruins of Ogden, Utah. "Boy, this place looks like hell," he said. "I can't tell whether what I'm walking on used to be houses or street."

"Hell was let loose on earth here," said Gordon McSweeney, who still wore on his back the flamethrower which had loosed a lot of that hell. But then he went on, "Hell let loose on earth, giving the misbelievers a foretaste of eternity."

Beside them, Ben Carlton said, "Feels damn strange, walking along where there's Mormons around and not diving for cover."

"They surrendered," Mantarakis said. But he was warily looking around, too. He carried his Springfield at the ready, and had a round in the chamber.

"For all we know, they ain't gonna go through with it," Carlton said. "Maybe they got more TNT under this here Tabernacle Park, and they'll blow us and them to kingdom come instead of giving up."

"Samson in the temple," McSweeney murmured. But the big Scotsman shook his head. "No, I cannot believe it. Samson worked with the Lord, not against Him. I do not think Satan could steel their souls to such vain sacrifice."

"The whole damn state of Utah is a sacrifice," Paul said. "I don't know what the hell made the Mormons fight like that, but they did more with less than the damn Rebs ever dreamt of doing. Only way we licked 'em is, we had more men and more guns."

Here and there, people who were not U.S. soldiers picked through the remains of Ogden. Women in bonnets and long skirts shoved aside wreckage, looking for precious possessions or food or perhaps the remains of loved ones. Children and a few old men helped them. The spoiled-meat smell of death hung everywhere.

A few men not old also went through the ruins. Most of them wore overalls, with poplin or flannel shirts underneath. Their clothes were as filthy and tattered as the soldiers' uniforms, and for the same reason: they'd spent too long in trenches.

"If looks could kill . . ." Paul said quietly. His companions nodded. The Mormon fighting men no longer carried weapons; that was one of the terms of the cease-fire to which their leaders had agreed. They stared at the American soldiers, and stared, and kept on staring. Their eyes were hot and empty at the same time. They'd fought, and they'd lost, and it was eating them inside.

"My granddads fought in the War of Secession," Carlton said. "I seen a photograph of one of 'em after we gave up. He looks just like the Mormons look now."

They tramped past a five-year-old boy, a little towhead cute enough to show up on a poster advertising shoes or candy. His eyes blazed with the same terrible despair that informed the faces of the beaten Mormon fighters.

The women were no different. They glowered at the victorious U.S. troopers. The prettier they were, the harder they glared. Some of them had carried rifles and fought in the trenches, too. Soldiers who won a war were supposed to have an easy time among the women of the people they'd defeated. That hadn't happened anywhere in Utah that Paul had seen. He didn't think it would start happening any time soon, either.

But the Mormon women didn't aim that look full of hatred and contempt at the Americans alone. They also sent it toward their own menfolk, as if to say, *How dare you have lost?* Even the Mormon fighters quailed under the gaze of their women.

Carlton pointed ahead. "Must be the park."

Most of Ogden was shell holes and rubble. Tabernacle Park was, for the most part, just shell holes. The only major exception was the burned-out building at the southeast corner. It had been the local Mormon temple, and then the last strongpoint in Ogden, holding out until surrounded and battered flat by U.S. artillery.

Captain Schneider was already in the park. He waved the men of his company over to him. Pulling out a pocket watch, he said, "Ceremony starts in fifteen minutes. General Kent could have got himself a fancy honor guard, but he chose us instead. He said he thought it would be better if soldiers who'd been through it from the start saw the end."

"That is a just deed," Gordon McSweeney rumbled—high approval from him.

"Congratulations again on your medal, sir," Mantarakis said.

Schneider looked down at the Remembrance Cross in gold on his left breast pocket, won for rallying the line south of Ogden after the Mormons exploded their mines. "Thank you, Sergeant," he said. "I shouldn't be the only one wearing it, though. We all earned them that day."

Under his breath, Ben Carlton muttered, "Damn fine officer." Paul Mantarakis nodded.

Here came Major General Alonzo Kent, tramping along through the rubble like a common soldier. He waved to the veterans gathering in front of the wrecked Mormon temple. "Well, boys, it was a hell of a fight, but we licked 'em," he said. He wasn't impressive to look at, not even in a general's fancy uniform, but he'd got the job done.

And here came the Mormon delegation, behind a standard-bearer carrying the beehive banner under which the Utah rebels had fought so long and hard and well. Most of the leaders of the defeated Mormons looked more like undertakers than politicians or soldiers: weary old men in black suits and wing-collared shirts.

One of them stepped past the standard-bearer. "General Kent? I am Heber Louis Jackson, now"—he looked extraordinarily bleak as he spoke that word—"president of the Church of Jesus Christ of Latter-Day Saints. I have treated with your representatives."

"Yes," Kent said: not agreement, only acknowledgment.

The Mormon leader went on, "With me here are my counselors, Joseph Shook and Orem Pendleton. We make up the first presidency of the church, and are the authority in ultimate charge of the forces that have been resisting those of the government of the United States. And here"—he pointed to the youngest and toughest-looking of the Mormons in his party—"is Wendell Schmitt, commander of the military forces of the Nation of Deseret."

"The Nation of Deseret does not exist," General Kent said in a flat voice. "President Roosevelt has, as you know, declared the entire state of Utah to fall under martial law and military district. He has also ordered the arrest of all officials of the rebel administration in the state of Utah on a charge of treason against the government of the United States of America. That specifically includes you gentlemen here."

"Pity they'll shoot them or hang them," Gordon McSweeney whispered to Mantarakis as Heber Jackson bowed his head. "They should be burned." He touched the nozzle to his flame-thrower. Mantarakis hissed at him to be quiet; he wanted to hear what the Mormons said.

Wendell Schmitt took an angry step forward. "The terms you set us were already hard enough without that, General. The Constitution—"

"Does not apply here, because of the president's declaration," General Kent interrupted. "You people put yourselves beyond the pale when you hopped into bed with the Confederates and the Canadians. Now that you have made that bed for yourselves, you shall be made to lie in it. You tried to destroy our government here. You failed. We *will* destroy your government here. This surrender will let the common people of the state survive. If you reject it, we will destroy them, too, and turn Utah back into the desert it was before they came."

"And call that peace," Joseph Shook murmured. It sounded like a quotation, but Paul didn't know what it was from.

General Kent evidently did: "If you like, Mr. Shook. But you Mormons *will* not joggle our elbows again while we are fighting this bigger war, and you *will* not disturb the peace in the USA once we have won the war." He opened an attaché case and took out a sheet of fancy paper. "Here is the formal instrument of surrender. Before we affix our signatures to it, I am going to summarize its provisions one last time, so that we have no unfortunate misunderstandings. Is that agreeable to you?"

"Hard terms," Heber Jackson said softly.

"Having fought us tooth and nail for a year, you cannot expect a kiss on the cheek now," Kent retorted. He fumbled in the case again, this time for a pair of reading glasses. " 'Item: all troops in resistance to the government of the United States' . . . Well, we've done that; they laid down their arms when you asked for the cease-fire.

" 'Item: all firearms in Utah to be surrendered within two weeks. Penalty for possession after that time is death.

" 'Item: any act of violence against soldiers of the United

States shall be punished by the taking and execution of hostages, not to exceed ten for each soldier wounded or fifty for each soldier killed.

" 'Item: all public gatherings of more than three persons are banned. This includes churches, vaudeville houses, picnics'— you name it. 'Violators will be fired upon without warning by soldiers of the United States.

" 'Item: all property of the Church of Jesus Christ of Latter-Day Saints is forfeit to the government of the United States in reparation for the cost of suppressing this rebellion.

" 'Item: gatherings in private homes to worship in the fashion of the Church of Jesus Christ of Latter-Days Saints shall be construed as public gatherings under the meaning of the previous item, and shall be dealt with like any other public gatherings under the terms of that item.

" 'Item . . .' " He droned on and on. After a while, Paul stopped paying close attention. The Mormons had tried to break away from the USA, and they were paying a heavy price for it. In effect, they *had* broken away, and were being treated not as a state returning to the Union but as a conquered province. As far as he was concerned, they'd earned it. He'd been in Utah most of a year, and nasty strangers had been trying to kill him the whole time.

One of General Kent's aides unfolded a portable table and produced a pen and bottle of ink with which to sign the instrument of surrender. "May I say something before I set my name there?" Wendell Schmitt asked.

"Go ahead," General Kent told him. "If you think anything you say will change matters, though—"

"Not likely," the Mormon military commander broke in. "No, what I want to tell you is that terms like these will come back to haunt you, years from now. You're sowing the seeds of hatred and bloodshed that will grow up in the days of our grandchildren, and of their grandchildren, too."

"Do you know what?" General Kent said. "I don't care. Teddy Roosevelt doesn't care, either. And if they have to, Mr. Schmitt, my grandchildren will come in here to Utah and blow your grandchildren sky-high all over again. If more damn fools like you come to power here, that's just what will happen. If you people are smart enough to realize you're fighting out of your weight, it won't." He folded his arms across his chest.

Biting his lip, Wendell Schmitt signed the surrender document. So did the three men who made up the first presidency of the Mormon Church. Last of all, so did General Kent. His aides took the Mormon leaders into custody. The Mormon standard-bearer handed the beehive banner to one of those U.S. aides. With deliberate contempt, the American soldier let it fall in the dirt.

"It's over," Ben Carlton said.

"Yeah," Paul agreed. "Now we either get to stay here for occupation duty, with everybody hating us like rat poison, or else they ship us back to fighting the Rebs or the Canucks." He laughed ruefully. "Sounds like a bully time either way, doesn't it?"

Anne Colleton cranked to life the engine of the battered Ford they'd given her. The motorcar shivered and shuddered like a man with the grippe. It sounded as if it would fall to pieces at any moment—it was about as far a cry from her Vauxhall roadster as an automobile could possibly be.

She didn't complain, not any more. She'd had to move heaven and earth to pry the Ford out of Confederate officialdom. It would, with luck, get her back to Marshlands, which was all she wanted for the time being. God only knew where the Vauxhall Major Hotchkiss had confiscated was now. That might well have been literally true; Hotchkiss himself, she was given to understand, was dead, killed along with so many others in the death throes of the Congaree Socialist Republic.

"Anyone want to ride with me?" Anne asked, not for the first time. None of the women with whom she'd shared a refugee tent for so many months made a move toward her. The bayoneted Tredegar with a full clip she'd laid in the middle of the seat probably had something to do with that.

"The officers say you're asking to get yourself killed—or else somethin' even worse—if y'all go into that country now," the fat woman named Melissa declared. By her tone, she looked forward to that prospect for Anne.

"I'll risk it," Anne answered. "I've always been able to take care of myself, unlike a lot of people I can think of." Being on the point of leaving gave her the last word. She hopped into the Ford, released the hand brake, put the motorcar in gear, and *put-putt*ed away.

Going was slow, as she'd known it would be. The Robert E. Lee Highway had been one of the main lines of Confederate advance, which meant the Red Negro rebels had defended it as well as they could, which in turn meant the artillery had gone to work, which meant what was called a road was in many places anything but. Anne was glad she'd managed to get her hands on several spare inner tubes and a pump and patches.

Not many trees along the road were standing; most had been blasted to tinder. Those that did stand often held ghastly fruit: rebels captured and then summarily hanged. Ravens and buzzards flew up from them as the noisy Ford rattled past. The stench of death was everywhere, and far stronger than the hanged bodies could have accounted for by themselves. Anne wondered if the fronts between the CSA and USA were full of this same dreadful reek. If they were, how did the soldiers endure it?

In a field by the side of the road, Negroes were digging trenches that would probably serve as mass graves. From a distance, the scene looked almost as it would have before the Red uprising began. Almost, for the couple of whites who supervised the laborers carried rifles: the spring sun glinted off the sharp edge of a bayonet.

Anne bit her lip. Putting Humpty-Dumpty back together again in the CSA wouldn't be easy. If whites had to get labor out of blacks at gunpoint, how were they supposed to fight the damnyankees at the same time? And if they offered concessions to make Negroes more willing to go along with them, wasn't that as much as saying the Reds had been right to rise against the government?

Reaching St. Matthews took her more than twice as long as she'd thought it would, and she hadn't been optimistic setting out from the refugee camp. By the time she got to the town nearest Marshlands, she found herself astonished she'd made it at all. She was also filthy from head to foot, having repaired three punctures along the way.

St. Matthews shocked her again. It wasn't so badly smashed up as some of the territory through which she'd driven; the rebellion had been dying on its feet by the time Confederate forces reached the town, and the Reds hadn't fought house to house here. But St. Matthews was the town she knew best: in the back of her mind, she expected to see it as it always had been, with whitewashed picket fences, neatly painted storefronts and even warehouses, and streets lined with live oaks shaggy with moss.

Most of the fences had been knocked flat. Two of the four big cotton warehouses were only burnt-out wreckage. Some of the live oaks still stood, but the artillery bombardment before the assault on the town had put paid to most of them. It would be a hundred years before saplings grew into trees that could match the ones now ruined.

Anne's eyes filled with tears. She'd kept trying to think of the rebellion as something that, once defeated, could in large measure be brushed aside. Negroes working under white men's guns had gone a fair way toward telling her how foolish that was. The blasted oaks, though, warned even more loudly that the uprising would echo for generations.

A gray-haired white man in an old-fashioned gray uniform shifted a plug of tobacco from one ill-shaven cheek to the other and held up a hand, ordering her to stop. "What the—blazes you doin' here, lady?" he demanded. "Don't you know there's still all kinds o' bandits and crazy niggers running around loose?"

"What am I doing here?" Anne replied crisply. "I am going home. Here is my authorization." She handed the militiaman a letter she had browbeaten out of the colonel in charge of the refugee camp.

By the way this fellow stared at the sheet of paper, he couldn't read. That she had it, though, impressed him into standing aside. "If'n they say it's all right, reckon it is," he said, touching the brim of his forage cap. "But you want to be careful out there."

"I intend to be careful," Anne said, a thumping lie if ever there was one. She put some snap in her voice: "Now kindly give that letter back, so I can use it again at need."

"Oh. Yes, ma'am. Sorry, ma'am." Where her grimy appearance and this beat-up motorcar hadn't convinced the militiaman she was a person of quality, her manner did. He handed the letter back to her.

The road from St. Matthews to Marshlands was not so heavily cratered as the highway up to town had been. By the time the rebels abandoned St. Matthews, they'd pretty much abandoned organized resistance against Confederate forces, too. But that thought had hardly crossed her mind before she heard a couple of brisk spatters of gunfire from the north, the direction of the Congaree swamps. Not all the Reds, it seemed, had given up.

Woods blocked any view of Marshlands from the road till not long before a traveler needed to turn onto the lane leading up to the mansion. *I am ready for anything,* Anne told herself, again and again. *Whatever I see, I will bear up under it.*

Coughing and wheezing, the Ford passed the last trees. There, familiar as the mole she carried on one wrist, was the opening into that winding lane. Just before you turned, you looked along the lane and you saw . . .

"Hell," she said quietly. She'd been hoping the place had survived, but it looked like a skeleton with most of the flesh rotted away. Altogether against her will, tears blurred her eyes. "Jacob," she whispered. If Marshlands had burned, her brother must have burned with it.

By contrast, the Negro cottages off to one side of the great house looked exactly as they had before the Red uprising began. A couple of men were out hoeing in their gardens; a couple of women were feeding chickens; a whole raft of pickaninnies were running around raising hell.

After a little while, her eyes left the vicinity of the mansion and traveled out to the cotton fields. Her teeth closed hard on the soft flesh inside her lower lip. If anyone had done anything with the cotton since she'd left for Charleston all those months before, she would have been astonished. Was that what the Red revolution had been about—the freedom not to work? Her face twisted into an expression half sneer, half snarl.

If the rest of the plantations in what had been the Congaree Socialist Republic looked the same way, a lot of planters were bankrupt, busted, flat. She wasn't; she'd invested wisely ever since Marshlands came into her hands. Most people, though, couldn't see past their noses. And, speaking of seeing . . .

One of the men in the garden plots had spotted her. He dropped his hoe and pointed, calling out to the rest. One after another, heads swung in her direction. Other than that, none of the Negroes moved. That in itself chilled her. Before the uprising, they would have come running up to her motorcar, calling greetings and hoping she had trinkets for them. *Telling lies,* she realized. *Hiding what they really thought.*

For a moment, she was especially glad of the Tredegar on the seat beside her. Then, all at once, she wasn't. How much good would it do her? What kind of arsenal did the Negroes have hidden in those cabins? She'd prided herself on knowing her laborers well. She hadn't known them at all. Maybe the Army men had been right when they thought her crazy to come here by herself.

A woman walked slowly toward her. It was, she realized after too long, Julia, who had been her body servant. The young woman, instead of a maid's shirtwaist and black dress, wore homespun made gaudy with bits of probably stolen finery. She was also several months pregnant.

The only reason Anne hadn't taken her to Charleston was that she'd gone there for an assignation, not legitimate business. Had it been otherwise, would Julia have turned on her? The thought was chilling, but could hardly be avoided.

"So you's come back, Miss Anne," Julia said. Her voice had something of the old servile tone left in it, but not much.

"Yes, I'm back." Anne looked over the neglected acres of what had been the finest plantation in South Carolina. "I don't know why the hell I bothered."

"Things, they ain't the same no mo'," Julia said. Had truer words ever been spoken, Anne hadn't heard them.

Almost as one equal to another, she asked, "And what did you do in the uprising, Julia? What did the niggers here do?"

"Nothin'," Julia said. "We stay here, we mind we bidness." But now she didn't meet Anne's eyes.

Anne nodded. This was a lie she recognized. "What happens when the soldiers start asking the same thing?" she said. Julia flinched. Anne smiled to herself. Yes, no matter what, she could manage. "Mind my business"—she pointed to the forgotten fields—"along with your own, and I'll keep the soldiers off your back. You know I can do things like that. Have we got a bargain?"

Julia thought for most of a minute, then nodded. "Miss Anne, I think we has."

George Enos had felt constricted on the Mississippi. He was used to the broad reaches of the Atlantic, to looking around from his perch on deck and seeing nothing but the endless ocean in all directions. Next to the Atlantic, any river, even the Father of Waters, seemed hardly more than an irrigation ditch.

And the Cumberland was considerably narrower than the Mississippi. These days, he and his fellow deck hands aboard the *Punishment* wore Army helmets painted Navy blue. This stretch of the river was supposed to be pretty clear of snipers, but nobody with the brains God gave a haddock felt like betting his life on it.

Before the *Punishment* headed up the Cumberland, Navy ironworkers had installed protection around the deck machine guns, too. Little by little, the war heading toward two years old, they were figuring out that this riverine fighting had rules of its own. George was glad of that, but wondered what the devil had taken them so long.

As far as he could tell, the Rebs had got the idea from the beginning. He pointed to the mine-sweeping boat moving slowly down the Cumberland ahead of the *Punishment* and said, "Anybody would think the damn Rebs did nothing but build mines in all the time between the Second Mexican War and now."

"Near as I can tell, that's right," Wayne Pitchess answered, his Connecticut accent not far removed from the flat vowels and swallowed r's of Enos' Boston intonation. Then he shook his head and pointed out to the battered farms out beyond the river. "I take it back. They raise tobacco, too."

"That's so," George agreed. Some of it got into Navy supply channels, too, probably by most unofficial means. He had a pouch of pipe tobacco in a trouser pocket. It wasn't as good as it might have been—which meant it had been cured, or half cured, after the war started—but it was a lot better than nothing.

Flags fluttered up the minesweeper's signal lines. The *Punishment*'s engine changed its rhythm. The monitor began crawling away from the sweeper as the screw reversed to give power astern rather than ahead. "I'd say they found one," Pitchess remarked.

George nodded. "I'd say you're right. Other thing I'd say is, I hope they haven't missed one."

"There is that," Pitchess agreed. You had to hope they hadn't missed one, as you had to hope a storm wouldn't sink you out on the Atlantic. You couldn't do much about it, either way.

The mine-sweeping boat cut the cable mooring the deadly device to the bottom of the Cumberland. When it bobbed to the surface, the sweeper cut loose with its machine guns. The explosion showered muddy water down onto Enos a quarter of a mile away; the *Punishment* rocked as waves spread from the blast.

"Lord!" George had known what mines could do, but he'd never been so close to one when it went off. "If it's all the same to everybody else, I'd just as soon not run over one of those."

"Now that you mention it, I think I'd rather be on top of my wife, too," Wayne Pitchess said with a veteran's studied dryness.

George laughed at the comparison, then walked over to his machine gun and got busy checking the mechanism he'd finished cleaning not five minutes before. Most of the time, he managed not to think about how much he missed Sylvia. He hadn't yet visited one of the whorehouses that sprouted alongside rivers like toadstools after rain. He had stained his underwear once or twice, waking up from dreams he didn't much remember, dreams of the sort he hadn't had since not long after he started going to the barbershop for a shave.

Engineers were busy at Clarksville, Tennessee. As U.S. monitors pushed up the Cumberland toward the town, the Confederates had dropped two railway bridges right into the water. Before the U.S. monitors advanced any farther, the steel and timber and the freight cars the Rebs had run out onto the bridge to complicate their enemies' lives all had to be cleared away.

It was slow work. It was dangerous work, too; every so often, Confederate batteries off to the south would lob some three-inch shells in the direction of the fallen bridges. The engineers didn't have a lot of heavy equipment with which to work. Once they'd cleared the river, the U.S. presence in this part of Tennessee would firm up. Then they could bring in the tools they really needed now. Of course, they wouldn't need them so much then.

"Yeah, that's a hell of a thing," Pitchess said when George remarked on the paradox. "But hell, if you wanted things simple, you never would have joined the Navy."

"I suppose you're right," Enos said. "I joined the Navy so I could give the Rebs a kick in the slats to pay them back for the one they gave me. I was already a sailor, so what the hell?—and I didn't want to get conscripted into the Army. But I never thought they'd stick me here in the middle of the country. You join the Navy, you think you'll be on the ocean, right?"

"Didn't matter to me one way or t'other," his friend answered. "I wasn't making enough to keep a roof on my head and food in my belly when I was fishing. I figured I wouldn't starve in the Navy, and I was right about that." A wry grin stretched across his lean, weathered face. "Maybe I didn't think about getting blown to smithereens as much as I should've."

Men and mules, straining mightily, hauled a freight car out onto the north bank of the river. Pointing, George said, "I expect that'll be the last train to Clarksville for a good long time."

"Yeah," Pitchess said. "Till we get our own rolling stock running through, anyways."

Confederate field guns opened up with another barrage just then. Shells screamed down on the engineers, who dove for cover. Mules weren't smart enough to do that (*or*, George thought, *stupid enough to start a war in the first place*). Thin across the water, the screams of wounded animals floated over to the *Punishment*.

The guns had the bridge zeroed to a fare-thee-well, and could strike at the wreckage or at either bank, as they chose. They didn't have the range for the *Punishment* down so precisely. That didn't keep them from trying to hit her, though. Shells splashed into the river and chewed up the bushes on the northern bank.

George dove into the shelter the ironwrights had built around his machine gun. A splinter hit the steel and clattered away. He hadn't thought enough about getting blown to smithereens, either.

Growling and grumbling on its bearings, the *Punishment*'s turret swung round so the six-inch guns it carried bore on the field pieces harassing them. On land, six-inch cannon were heavy guns, hard to move at any sort of speed except by rail. On the water, though, they were nothing out of the ordinary, and the *Punishment* gave them a fine, steady platform from which to work.

They roared. The monitor heeled ever so slightly in the water from the recoil, then recovered. Sprawled out as he was, George felt the motion more acutely than he might have on his feet. Up in the armored crow's nest atop the mast, an officer with field glasses would be watching the fall of the shells and comparing it to the location of the Rebel guns.

More grumbling noises—these smaller, to correct the error in the turret's previous position. The big guns boomed again. Wafting powder fumes made George cough and sent tears streaming from his eyes.

Confederate shells kept falling, too. One of them exploded against the turret. A whole shower of splinters rattled off Enos' protective cage. He'd wondered whether the ironworkers had made it thick enough. Nothing tore through it to pierce him. Evidently they had.

The turret carried more armor than any other part of the *Punishment*. It was made to withstand a shell from a gun of the same caliber as those it carried. It didn't laugh at a hit from a three-inch howitzer, but it turned the blow without trouble.

And it replied with shells far heavier than those the field pieces threw. "Hit!" shouted the spotter from the crow's nest. "That's a hit, by God!" He whooped with glee. The guns fired several more salvos. The spotter kept yelling encouragement. What encouraged George more than anything else was that, after a while, no new fire came toward either the *Punishment* or the Clarksville bridges.

He got to his feet, ready to hose down the riverbank with machine-gun fire in case the Rebs, having lost their guns, chose to bring riflemen forward to make the engineers' jobs harder—and perhaps to snipe at the men on the monitor's deck, too. They often tried that after big, waterborne guns smashed their artillery.

Not this time, though. All was calm as the *Punishment* floated on the Cumberland. The engineers got back to work. The mine-sweeping boat ran right up to the wreckage to pick up a couple of wounded men. On the shore, pistol shots rang out. Soldiers were shooting wounded mules.

Just another day's work, George thought. Noticing that thought brought him up sharply. It was the sort of thought a veteran might have. "Me?" he muttered. No one answered, naturally, but no one needed to, either.

VIII

Roger Kimball stood up on the conning tower of the *Bonefish*. He looked around. All he saw were the cool, gray waters of the North Atlantic. All he smelled was clean salt air—none of the rotting stinks of the South Carolina swamps. He sucked in a long, deep breath and let it out like a connoisseur savoring a fine wine.

His executive officer smiled. "Feels good to be back at sea, doesn't it, sir?" Junior Lieutenant Brearley said.

"Feels better than good, Tom," Kimball answered. "We're doing our proper job again, and about time, too. If I'd wanted to be a policeman and wear a funny hat, I'd have joined the police in the first place."

A wave crashed against the *Bonefish*'s bow. The conning tower and the hatch leading down into the submersible were protected by canvas shields—or so claimed the men who'd designed the shields. Kimball supposed they were better than nothing. They didn't keep him and Brearley from getting seawater in the face. They didn't keep more seawater from puddling under their feet or from dripping down the hatch.

Brearley used a sleeve to wipe himself more or less dry. His smile now was rueful. "Harder to keep the boat dry than it was on the river."

"Price you pay for doing the proper job," Kimball said airily. He could afford to be airy now, up here. When he went below, the diesel-oil and other stenches inside the *Bonefish*—all produced despite everything the crew could do—would easily surpass those of the swamps flanking the Pee Dee.

Since that couldn't be helped, he put it out of his mind. Wiping the lenses of his field glasses with a pocket handkerchief, he raised the glasses to his eyes and scanned the horizon for a telltale plume of smoke that would mark a ship. The wind quickly whipped away the exhaust from the *Bonefish*'s diesel. Bigger vessels, though, burned coal or fuel oil, and left more prominent signatures in the air.

He spied nothing. The *Bonefish* might have been alone in the Atlantic. He didn't like that. Letting the binoculars thump down against his chest on their leather strap, he pounded on the conning tower rail with his fist. "Damn it, Tom, they're supposed to be out here."

"Yes, sir," the exec said. That was all he could say. Intelligence had reported the U.S. Navy was gathering for a push against the British and French warships protecting their home countries' merchant vessels. Sending one or two of those Yankee ships to the bottom would make life easier for the Entente powers against the twin colossi of the USA and Germany.

As if picking the thought from his mind, Brearley said, "We have managed to keep the damnyankees and the Huns from joining hands."

"We'd better go right on keeping 'em from doing that, too, sonny, or you can kiss this war good-bye," Kimball answered dryly. "We've got to keep the trade route from Argentina to French West Africa open, too, or England starts starving even worse than she is already. And we've got to keep the route from England to Canada at least partway open, or else the USA sits on Canada like an elephant squashing a mouse. If we manage to do all of that, the soldiers can go on doing what they're supposed to do."

"Have we got enough ships?" Brearley asked. "Have all of us together—us and the British and the French and the Russians and whatever the Canadians have left—have we got enough ships to do everything we have to do?"

Kimball clapped him on the back. "We've done it so far—just barely. Reckon we can keep on doing it—just barely. And don't forget the Japanese. They're giving England and Canada quite a hand in the Pacific, by everything I hear."

"Don't know as how I really care for them fooling around in a white man's war," Brearley said, "but I suppose we have to grab the help now and be thankful for it, and then worry later about sorting out what it means."

"That's how it works," Kimball agreed. As soon as he'd spoken, though, he wished he'd kept his mouth shut. Brearley was all for cutting a deal with the Negroes, too, and then sorting out what that all meant later.

Had his exec set him up, so he would notice he was arguing one way on one of the questions and the other way on the other? He let his eyes slide toward Tom Brearley. Sure as hell, the young pup looked ever so slightly smug. But Brearley had too much sense to say anything, so Kimball couldn't gig him for it. This round went to the junior lieutenant.

So Kimball wouldn't have to admit as much, he raised the field glasses once more to scan the horizon. He did not do it expecting to spot anything: more to give him an excuse not to answer, and to change the subject when he did speak again. But there, off to the northeast, rose an unmistakable plume of smoke.

He stiffened and thrust out an index finger, as if he were a bird dog coming to the point. Tom Brearley didn't have field glasses of his own. Before the war, most of them had been made in Germany, and they remained in short supply throughout the Entente powers. But, after a minute or so, Brearley nodded. "Yes, sir. I see it, too."

Kimball called down to the petty officer at the wheel: "Change course to 045."

"Oh-four-five, aye aye, sir," Ben Coulter answered. His voice caught with excitement as he sent a question up the hatchway: "You spotted something, sir?"

"Something, yes," Kimball answered: submersible officers and crew paid less attention to the minutiae of military formality than any other part of the C.S. Navy. "Don't know what yet."

He peered through the field glasses again. A swell lifted the *Bonefish*, extending the horizon for him. He got a glimpse of the hull producing the smoke. "That's a Yankee destroyer, sure as hell it is. Now the fun begins." His lips curled back from his teeth in what was more nearly snarl than smile.

He started calculating at a furious clip. A destroyer could run away from his submersible even when he was surfaced, or could attack him with bigger guns than he carried. Submerged, the *Bonefish* made only nine knots going flat out—a pace that would quickly exhaust her batteries and force her to the surface again. He couldn't pursue the U.S. ship, then. He had to see if he could place the submarine in her path and lie in wait for her. If not, he'd have to let her escape. If so . . .

"Let's go below, Tom," Kimball said. His exec nodded and dove down the hatch. Kimball followed, dogging it shut after him. He bawled an order to the crew: "Prepare to dive—periscope depth!"

Klaxons hooted. Tanks made bubbling, popping noises as water flooded into them. The *Bonefish* slid under the water in—

"Thirty-eight seconds, I make it," Brearley said, an eye to his pocket watch. Kimball grunted. That was acceptable but something less than wonderful.

He raised the periscope. "Hope the damn thing isn't too misted up to see through," he muttered. The odds were about even. He grunted again, this time appreciatively. The view was, if not perfectly clear, clear enough.

He turned the periscope in the direction of the destroyer he'd spotted. The fellow hadn't altered course, which Kimball devoutly hoped meant he hadn't a clue the *Bonefish* was anywhere about. He was, unless Kimball had botched his solution, making about twenty knots, and about two miles away.

"Give me course 090," Kimball told the helmsman, and then spoke to the rest of the crew: "Ready the torpedoes in the two forward tubes."

The *Bonefish* crept east. The U.S. destroyer was doing most of the work, coming right across his bow, leaving itself wide open for a shot—if it didn't pick up speed and steam past the submersible before the latter was in position to launch its deadly fish.

"I want to get inside twelve hundred yards before I turn 'em loose," Kimball remarked, more as if thinking out loud than talking to Tom Brearley. "I'll shoot from a mile if I have to, though, and trust to luck that I'm not carrying any moldies."

"Yes, sir," Brearley agreed; duds were the bane—and often the end—of a submariner's existence. The executive officer went on, "Are you sure you want to shoot from such long range, sir? A miss will bring the U.S. fleet after us full bore."

"Just because they're after us doesn't mean they'll catch us," Kimball said smugly. "So yes, I'll take the chance, thanks." He grinned. "After all, if I sink that destroyer, that'll bring the U.S. fleet after us, too."

"Yes, sir." Brearley sounded as if he was smiling, too; Kimball didn't look away from the periscope to see. *A good kid,* he thought absently. *A little on the soft side, but a good kid.*

And here came the destroyer, fat and sassy. He'd have lookouts peering in all directions for periscopes, but some of those fools would have seen enough periscopes that weren't there to make officers leery of taking their reports too seriously. They wouldn't be expecting Confederate company quite so far out to sea, either; the *Bonefish* was well past her normal cruising radius. But she'd picked up fuel from a freighter not long before, and so . . . "We'll give you damnyankees a surprise," Kimball muttered.

He wasn't going to get a shot off at twelve hundred yards. The electric engines were too puny to get him close enough fast enough. But he would be inside a mile. Any time you could split the difference between what you really wanted and what you'd settle for, you weren't doing too bad.

"Depth?" he asked quietly.

"Thirty-five feet, sir," Brearley answered after checking the gauge.

"Give me a couple more degrees south, Coulter," Kimball said. "A little more . . . steady . . . Fire number one!" Fearsome clangs and hissings marked the launch of the first torpedo. A moment later, Kimball shouted, "Fire number two!"

He studied both tracks with grave intensity. They looked straight, they looked good. The destroyer had less than a minute to react, and momentum that kept her from reacting fast. She started to turn toward the *Bonefish,* presenting the smallest area for the fish to reach.

Kimball couldn't tell whether the first torpedo passed under her bow or hit and failed to explode. He hadn't snarled more than a couple of curses, though, when the second one caught her just aft of amidships. "Hit!" he screamed. "Hell of a hit! She'll go down from that, damn me to hell if she don't." The destroyer lay dead in the water, and bent at an unnatural angle. She was already starting to list. Some of the Yankees aboard would make her boats, Kimball thought, but some wouldn't, too.

Rebel yells ripped through the narrow steel tube in which the *Bonefish*'s crew lived and worked. The men pounded one another on the back. "Score one for the captain!" Ben Coulter whooped. Everybody pounded Kimball on the back, too, something unthinkable in the surface Navy.

"Give me course 315," Kimball told the helmsman. Heading obliquely away from the path of the torpedoes was a good way not to have your tracks followed. "Half speed." He'd have mercy on the batteries.

After an hour, he surfaced to recharge them. Foul, pressurized air rushed out of the *Bonefish* when he undogged the hatch. All the stinks seemed worse, somehow, right at that moment. He went up onto the conning tower. To his relief, now, he spied no smoke plumes on the horizon.

"Good shooting, sir," Tom Brearley said, coming up behind him.

"Thanks," Kimball said. "That's what they pay me for. And speaking of pay, we just made the damnyankees pay plenty. We done licked 'em twice. They're stupid enough to think we can't do it three times running, no matter what our niggers try doin', they can damn well think again."

"Yes, *sir!*" Brearley said.

"Snow in my face in April!" Major Irving Morrell said enthusiastically. "This, by God, this is the life."

"Yes, sir." Captain Charlie Hall had rather less joy in his voice. "Snow in your face about eight months a year hereabouts." The snow blowing in his face and Morrell's obscured the Canadian Rockies for the moment. Morrell didn't mind. He'd seen them when the weather was better. They were even grander than they were in the USA. They were even snowier than they were in the USA, too, and that was saying something.

"I hope you don't mind my telling you this," Morrell said to Hall, "but I think you've been going at this the wrong way. Charge straight at the damn Canucks, and they'll slaughter you. You've seen that."

Hall's face twisted. He was a big, bluff, blond man, bronzed by sun, chapped by wind, with a Kaiser Bill mustache he kept waxed and impeccable regardless of the weather. He said, "It's true, sir. I can't deny it. We sent divisions into Crow's Nest Pass and came out with regiments. The Canucks didn't want to give up for hell."

"And they were waiting for us to do what we did, too," Morrell said. "Give the enemy what he's waiting for and you'll be sorry a hundred times out of a hundred. The Canucks made us pay and pay, and what did we have when we were done paying? Less than we'd hoped. They just stopped running trains through Crow's Nest Pass and doubled up in Kicking Horse Pass."

He pointed ahead. U.S. forces had been slogging toward Kicking Horse Pass for the past year and a half. He didn't intend to slog any more. He was going to move, and to make the Canadians move, too.

"And when we finally take this one, they'll go on up to Yellow-head Pass," Hall said. "This war is a slower business than anyone dreamt when we first started fighting."

"If we drive enough nails into their coffin, eventually they won't be able to pull the lid up any more," Morrell said.

"I like that." Hall's face was better suited for the grin it wore now than for its earlier grimace. A couple of Morrell's other company commanders joined them then: Captain Karl Spadinger, who for looks could have been Charlie Hall's cousin; and First Lieutenant Jephtha Lewis, who would have seemed more at home behind a plow on the Great Plains than in the Rockies of Alberta. With them came Sergeant Saul Finkel, who had a dark, quiet face and the long, thin-fingered hands of a watchmaker—which he had been before joining the Army.

"Here's what we're going to do," Morrell said, pointing to the Canadian position ahead of them and then to the map he took from a pouch on his belt. The view was better on the map; the snow didn't obscure it. "We've got this fortified hill ahead of us. I will lead the detachment advancing to the west. Sergeant Finkel!"

"Sir!" the sergeant said.

"You and one machine-gun squad from Lieutenant Lewis' company will cover the ridge road up there"—he showed what he had in mind both through the blowing snow and on the map—"and block the Canadians from coming down and getting in our rear. I rely on you for this, Sergeant. If I had to make do with anyone else, I'd leave two guns behind. But your weapon always works."

"It will keep working, sir," Finkel said. Morrell looked at his hands again. Anyone who could handle the tiny, intricate gearing of watches was unlikely to have trouble keeping a machine gun operating, and Finkel, along with being mechanically ept, was also a brave, cool-headed soldier.

Morrell pointed to Captain Spadinger. "Karl, you'll take the rest of your company and open the hostile position on the eastern side of the slope. Hold your fire as long as you can."

"Yes, sir," Spadinger said. "As you ordered, we'll be carrying extra grenades for when actual combat breaks out."

"Good," Morrell said. Spadinger's efficiency pleased him, which was why he'd given him the secondary command for the attack. He went on, "Captain Hall, your rifle company and Lieutenant Lewis' machine-gun company, less that one squad I'm leaving with Sergeant Finkel, will accompany me on the main flanking thrust. If we can chase the Canucks off this hill, we've gone a long way toward clearing the path to Banff. Any questions, gentlemen?" Nobody said anything. Morrell nodded. "We'll try it, then. We advance as rapidly as possible. Keep speed in your minds above all else. We move at 0900."

In the fifteen minutes before they began to move, he checked his men, especially the teams manhandling the machine guns across country. They were good troops; in grim Darwinian fashion, most of the soldiers who didn't make good mountain troops were dead or wounded by now.

He felt the men's eyes on him, too. This would be the first real action they'd faced with him commanding them. He didn't suppose they knew about his having had to leave the General Staff—he hoped they didn't, anyhow—but they had to be wondering about what he and they would be able to do together. Well, they were finding out he didn't care to huddle in trenches.

"Let's go," he said.

Spruce and fir and swirling snow helped screen the men in green-gray from the Canadians above. No firing broke out off to the right, which relieved Morrell to no small degree. He grinned, imagining Spadinger's men rounding up sentries and poking bayoneted rifles into dugouts, catching the Canucks by surprise.

His own men scooped up a fair number of prisoners, too. One of them, brought back to Morrell, glared at him and said, "What the devil are you bastards doing so far from where the fighting is?"

"Why, moving it someplace else, of course," he answered cheerfully, which made the Canuck even less happy.

Morrell's leg tried to protest when he pushed up to the very head of his force, but he ignored it. *It's only pain,* he told himself, and, as he usually did, managed to make himself believe it. He reached the lead just in time to help capture a machine-gun position the Canadians had blasted out of the living rock of the hill, again without firing a shot.

"This is wonderful, sir!" Captain Hall exclaimed. "We've got the drop on the Canucks for sure this time."

"So far, so—" Morrell began. Before *good* got out of his mouth, a burst of fire made him whip his head back toward the direction which Captain Spadinger and his company had gone. It sounded as if they were heavily engaged. "We appear to have lost the advantage of—" Morrell didn't get to finish that sentence, either. Machine guns from atop the hill opened up on his detachment before he could say *surprise*. That was a surprise to him, and not a pleasant one.

"Dig in!" he shouted. "Do it now! Sweat saves blood!" As the riflemen began to obey, he turned to Lieutenant Lewis. "Get those machine guns set up. We've got to neutralize that fire."

The machine-gun crews mounted their heavy weapons on top of the even heavier tripods in time that would have kept a drill sergeant happy on the practice field. It wasn't for prestige here; it was for survival.

Morrell cursed as one of his men slumped over, briefly kicking in a way suggesting he'd never get up again. "Advance on them!" he yelled. "Shift to the northeast, so we can take that hilltop and support Captain Spadinger's company. Move, move, move!"

It wasn't the fight he'd wanted, but it was the fight he had. Now he had to make the best of it. Keeping everything as fluid as possible would also keep the Canucks confused about how many men he had and what he intended to do with them. Since he suspected he was outnumbered, that was all to the good.

Back where this movement had originated, Sergeant Finkel's machine gun started hammering. Morrell nodded to himself. The Canucks wouldn't be getting into his rear. Now he had to see if he could get into theirs. "Hold fire as much as you can as you advance," he called to the riflemen. "Let them think Spadinger has the main force. If they concentrate on him, we'll make them regret it."

"Aren't you telling the men more than they need to know?" Captain Hall shouted as the two of them ran to a boulder and flopped down behind it side by side. Bullets whined away from the other side of the stone, then went elsewhere in search of fresh targets.

"Just the opposite, Captain," Morrell answered. "This way, if I go down, the attack will go forward, because they'll know what I expect of them." Hall didn't look convinced, but he didn't argue with his commanding officer, either. If Morrell's methods didn't work, odds were he'd end up dead and so beyond criticism. Morrell raised his voice: "Keep the machine guns well forward, Lieutenant Lewis!"

Lewis and his machine gunners, bless their hearts, didn't need that order. They treated the machine guns almost like rifles, advancing at a stumbling run from one patch of cover to the next they saw—or hoped they saw.

Even so, Morrell was worried, and worse than worried. From the sound of the fighting off to the east, Spadinger's men weren't withholding fire. On the contrary; it sounded as if every man was in the line, fighting desperately to stay alive. If the forces they'd run into could crush them, those forces would swing back on him and smash him up, too. "Hold on, Karl!" he whispered fiercely. "Make them pay the price."

One of the Canuck machine guns up at the crest of the hill fell silent. Morrell whooped as he ran forward. The Canadians were used to facing slow, carefully set up attacks, not to this sort of lightning strike with things hitting them all at once from every which way.

And then he whooped again, for men in khaki scrambled out of their trenches and ran down—to the southeast, toward Captain Spadinger's embattled company. They gave Morrell's men the kind of target soldiers dreamt about. "Now!" he shouted. "Give 'em everything we've got."

Again, the men did not need the order. They loosed a storm of lead at the Canadians, who shouted in dismay at taking such fire from the right flank and rear. Yelling with glee, the U.S. soldiers dashed forward to take out the foes giving their comrades so much trouble.

Half an hour later, Morrell stood on the height he'd intended to bypass. A long file of dejected prisoners, many of them roughly bandaged, stumbled back toward what had been the U.S. line. "You don't fight fair," one of them shouted to Morrell.

"Good," Morrell answered. The Canuck scowled. His own men laughed. They felt like tigers now. For that matter, he felt on the tigerish side himself. Things hadn't gone exactly as he'd thought they would, but they seldom did. One thing both real war and the General Staff had taught him was that no plan long survived contact with the enemy.

He looked around. The view was terrific. He'd taken the objective. He hadn't taken crippling casualties doing it. *How* he'd taken it didn't matter. *That* he'd taken it did. He looked around again. A new question burned in his mind—what could he do next?

Jefferson Pinkard looked down at himself. His butternut uniform was so full of stains from the red dirt of southern Georgia, it might as well have started out mottled. He smelled. By the way his head itched, he probably had lice. Emily would have thrown him in a kettle, boiled him, and shampooed him with kerosene before she let him into the house, let alone into her bed.

He didn't care. He was alive. He'd seen too many different kinds of horrible death these past few weeks—he'd dealt out too many different kinds of horrible death these past few weeks—to worry about anything past that. The Black Belt Socialist Republic was dying. When he'd set out, he'd supposed that would make everything worthwhile. Did it? He didn't know. He didn't care much, either.

He detached the bayonet from his Tredegar and methodically cleaned it. It was clean already, but he wanted it cleaner. It had had blood on it, a couple of days before. He couldn't see that blood, not now, but he knew it was there.

"Damn niggers ought to give up," he muttered under his breath.

"What you say?" That was Hip Rodriguez, a recruit from down in Sonora. He didn't speak a whole lot of English. Most of what he did speak was vile. Up till the Conscription Bureau nabbed Jeff Pinkard, he'd thought of Sonorans and Chihuahuans as one step above Negroes, and a short step to boot. But Rodriguez had saved his life. If that didn't make him a good fellow, nothing ever would.

And so, instead of barking, Jeff repeated himself, adding, "They're licked. They damn well ought to know it."

Rodriguez shrugged. "We keep licking they, they quit—one way or t'odder." He carried a thoroughly nonregulation knife on his belt, and a whetstone to go with it. When he honed that blade, it made a vicious little grinding sound. He smiled, enjoying it.

"That's true," Pinkard admitted. "No two ways around it, I guess. Question that keeps comin' up in my mind, though, is what happens afterwards. They gonna be pullin' knives like yours out o' their hip pockets and stabbin' white men twenty years from now when they think they got the chance? That's a hell of a way to try and run a country, you know what I'm sayin'?"

Rodriguez shrugged again. "They try that, they get killed. Is no big never-mind to me." He flashed a big, shiny grin at Jeff. "In Sonora, we don't have no *mallates*—no niggers—till you Confederates, you buy us from Mexico. You bring in the problem. You should ought to fix it, too."

With some amusement, Pinkard noted that Rodriguez looked down his nose at Negroes, too. In a way, it made sense: if not for them, he would have been on the bottom himself. But the blacks *were* on the bottom. That made putting them down harder, because they had so little to lose from their rebellion.

Off to one side, a field piece began barking, throwing shells into Albany, Georgia. Captain Connolly looked up from his tin cup of coffee and said, "All right, boys, now we go and take their capital away from 'em. About time, I'd say. And doing that'll just about put the last nail in the coffin. Can't hardly claim they've got a country when they haven't got a capital any more, can they?"

"Damnyankees do," Stinky Salley said.

Connolly didn't catch him opening his mouth. He looked around. "All right, who's the smart bird?" he demanded. Nobody said anything. He gulped down the rest of the coffee—heavily laced with chicory and God only knew what all else, if it was anything like Jeff's. Pinkard didn't care. It was hot and strong and made his heart beat faster. The captain said, "Come on, boys. Time to do it."

He didn't tell them what to do and sit back on his duff. He went out with them and helped them do it. Pinkard had appreciated that in a foundry foreman. He appreciated it even more in an officer. After patting himself to make sure he had plenty of spare clips for the Tredegar, he scrambled to his feet and trudged on toward Albany.

The front hereabouts was too wide, with too few men covering too many miles, for proper entrenchment. You dug foxholes where you happened to be, fought out of them, and advanced some more. The survivors of the new regiment to which he belonged weren't advancing in neat files of men now. They'd learned better. They moved forward in open order, well spread out. *More space for the bullets to pass between,* Pinkard thought.

A shot rang out—behind him. One of his comrades went down, clutching at the back of his left thigh. Half a dozen men close by went down, too, hitting the dirt at the first sound of gunfire. Pinkard was one of them. He'd developed a tremendous respect for the horrid things flying lead could do to the human body.

Another shot kicked up red dirt and spat it in his face. "It's another one of those hideout sons of bitches," he said unhappily. As their strength faltered, the Reds had formed the nasty habit of digging in with concealed foxholes facing not toward their Confederate foes but away, and holding their fire till the soldiers had gone past them. They'd done considerable damage that way. This fellow looked to have added to it.

Stalking him through the pine woods was a deadly game of hide and seek. He wounded another man before Rodriguez flushed him out of his hole with a grenade and three other soldiers shot him from three different directions. He wasn't quite dead, even after that. Jeff put a round through his head at close range, which made him stop thrashing and moaning.

"What did you go and do that for?" one of the other Confederates asked. "Bastard deserved to suffer, I reckon."

"Yeah, but if we went and left him, he might have found a way to do more mischief, even shot up like he was," Pinkard answered.

"Oh, tactics. That's all right, then," said the other soldier, a hulking Tennessean named Finley. "You talk kind of soft on niggers sometimes, so I wondered if you was just doing him a kindness."

Pinkard bristled. He wasn't a hardliner, and nobody could make him one—he was a free white man, with a right to his opinion. "Listen," he said, "there's ten million of 'em in the CSA, or ten million take away however many got themselves killed in this stupid uprising of theirs. We got to figure out what to do with 'em after this part of the shooting's done."

"Put the slave chains back on 'em," Finley snapped. "Serve 'em right."

Not many Confederates wanted to go that far, for which Pinkard thanked God. "They done showed they can fight," he said. "You buy a big buck nigger now, Finley, you think you ever dare turn your back on him?" Finley scowled from under the brim of his helmet. He didn't say anything, which suited Jeff fine.

They emerged from the woods a few hundred yards outside of Albany. Field pieces were still pounding the town. Answering fire came mostly from the big houses on the north side of the main street: from what had been the white section of the city. Red flags still flew defiantly above several of those houses. "Bastards are doing it on purpose, hurting whites as much as they can," Finley said. Now Pinkard was the one who didn't answer.

One of those big houses with a two-story colonnaded porch held a machine gun. It spat death out toward the advancing soldiers in butternut. The fields had been plowed with shell holes. Pinkard jumped into one. Once he was in it, he discovered he shared it with the stinking corpse of a Negro. He stayed where he was, stench or no stench. With bullets whining past overhead, he figured he'd wind up a corpse himself if he moved too soon.

But, however much you might like the notion, you couldn't huddle in a hole forever. When the machine gun chose a different target, he got up and ran for another hole closer to Albany. He got fired on again, but made it safely.

The Confederates were moving on the city from the west and the north. The Red rebels holed up inside did not have the firepower to keep them out. But instead of fading back into the countryside, the Negroes fought house to house, making the government forces clear them out with grenades and, once or twice, with the bayonet.

At last, the Reds were pushed back to the last couple of houses where they still had machine guns up and firing. A flag still flew from one of them. Inside, the Negroes shouted the defiant cry they'd raised through the whole unpleasant engagement: "The people! Fo' the people!"

When gunfire eased for a moment, Pinkard shouted back: "Give up, you lying bastards! We *are* the people!"

"Liar your own self!" One of those machine guns lashed the rubble in which he lay. He'd expected that, and stayed very low behind the big pile of red bricks that had been a chimney before a shell knocked it down. But his words seemed to have angered the black rebels so much, they didn't just want to kill him. The same fellow who'd yelled before shouted out again: "You ain't the people. You is the dogs o' the aristocracy, is what you is!" He barked derisively.

"The hell you say!" Pinkard answered, a measure of how good his cover was. "Lot more white men than niggers in the CSA."

"Not in the Black Belt Socialist Republic," the Red retorted. "Not in the others, neither." He laughed. "We havin' our own War o' Secession, if'n you want to put it like that."

Jeff didn't want to put it like that, even to himself. It would have made the fight the Negroes were raising seem altogether too legitimate to him. And then another Red let out a dark, nasty laugh and added, "Sure as hell ain't mo' white folks than niggers in the Black Belt Socialist Republic nowadays. We done took care o' that."

From off to the side, a Confederate soldier started pitching grenades into the house where the Red revolutionaries were holed up. Pinkard had no idea whether they wounded any of the Negroes. They did set the house on fire.

That left the Reds a desperate choice. They could stay and burn or flee and get shot down. They fled, disciplined enough to carry the machine gun with them to set up again if they found fresh refuge. They didn't.

One more house and the fighting was done. Captain Connolly carried a red flag as he strode through the shattered wreckage of what had been a prosperous Georgia farming town. "It's over," he said. "Here, it's over."

Pinkard looked around. He felt giddy, half stunned, half drunk at being alive. Wearily, he shook his head. The fighting might have ended, but the revolt and its aftermath weren't over. He wondered how many years would pass before they were. He wondered if they ever would be.

Remembrance Day passed quietly in New York City. Soldiers' Circle men and military bands paraded, as did newly raised units going off to the front. Enough soldiers with glittering bayonets and full clips in their rifles stood along the parade route to have marched on Richmond and taken it in about ten days—that was Flora Hamburger's sardonic thought, at any rate. The soldiers had orders—highly publicized orders—to shoot to kill at the first sign of trouble and a look that said they would have enjoyed doing it. They seemed disappointed when the Socialists didn't give them the chance.

"Now it's our turn," Flora said back at the Fourteenth Ward Socialist Party offices after the sun set on a day without incident. "May Day next week, and then we show them what we really think of their government and their war."

"They still may try to find some way to keep us from holding our parade," Herman Bruck said nervously.

"There is such a thing as the Constitution of the United States," Flora said. "We have the right to petition for redress of grievances, unless they put New York under martial law the way they did to Utah, and we'll make absolutely certain we give them no excuse to do that."

"We don't necessarily have to give them any excuses." Maria Tresca's brown eyes flashed. "An *agent provocateur*—"

"I wouldn't put anything past Teddy Roosevelt," Bruck said darkly.

"As a matter of fact, I doubt TR would authorize anything like that," Flora said. "He's a class enemy, but he has the full set of upper-class notions about legitimate and illegitimate ways and means." As a storm of disagreement washed over her, she held up a warning hand. "That doesn't mean I don't think there will be any provocations. His henchmen don't worry about the niceties. But I don't think the order for provocations comes straight from the top. Give the devil his due. Better—give him a good kick in the *tukhus* and send him home in November."

That swung people back to her. Planning went on—the order of march for unions from all the different trades that would be joining up, and, as important, the order of the speakers. Bruck said, "Such a pity Myron won't be here to tell the people the truth."

Everyone sighed. For a moment, the mood in the offices went soft and sad. Congressman Zuckerman had been able to rouse a crowd almost the way a *goyishe* preacher could in a tent-show revival. Reverently, Flora said, "If you weren't a Socialist after you heard Myron Zuckerman, you'd never be a Socialist." She forced herself back to business, back to practicality: "But he's not here, and we have to go on without him."

Herman Bruck appointed himself to the podium. Flora bit down on her lower lip. Herman wouldn't come close to Zuckerman as an orator if he lived twenty years longer than Methuselah. As far as she was concerned, Zuckerman dead was a better orator than Herman Bruck alive.

She was about to add her own name to the list to counteract Bruck (not that she would have put it so crassly) when he said, "And of course, to keep the ladies happy, we'll have a woman speaker or two. Flora, why don't you take care of that for us?"

She'd never had to get out the hatpin to stop him from feeling her up. She felt like pulling it from her hat now, though, and sticking it into him about three inches deep. The way he casually dismissed the importance of half the human race was, in a way, a worse violation than if he'd tried to squeeze her bosom. Maybe worse still was that he hadn't the slightest idea of what he'd done.

"I'll speak to the women," she said through tight lips, "and to the men, too."

"That's fine," Bruck said, nodding genially—no, he hadn't a clue. She studied him—perfect coif, perfect clothes, perfect confidence. Inside, where it didn't show, she smiled a hunter's smile. Perfect target.

When she got home that evening, she found her mother and her younger sister, Esther, in tears. Little Yossel, her nephew, was in tears, too, but only in the ordinary, babyish way of things. "What's wrong?" Flora exclaimed in alarm.

With trembling finger, her mother pointed to the supper table.

There, among the advertising circulars, lay an envelope with a
formidable heading:

𝕲𝖔𝖛𝖊𝖗𝖓𝖒𝖊𝖓𝖙 𝖔𝖋 𝖙𝖍𝖊 𝖀𝖓𝖎𝖙𝖊𝖉 𝕾𝖙𝖆𝖙𝖊𝖘 𝖔𝖋 𝕬𝖒𝖊𝖗𝖎𝖈𝖆, 𝖂𝖆𝖗 𝕯𝖊𝖕𝖆𝖗𝖙𝖒𝖊𝖓𝖙

The next line, set in slightly smaller type in the same hard-to-
read font, said,

𝕭𝖚𝖗𝖊𝖆𝖚 𝖔𝖋 𝕾𝖊𝖑𝖊𝖈𝖙𝖎𝖔𝖓 𝖋𝖔𝖗 𝕾𝖊𝖗𝖛𝖎𝖈𝖊

The envelope was addressed to David Hamburger.

"Oh, no," Flora whispered. The older of her younger brothers
had turned eighteen a few months before, and had dutifully
enrolled himself at the local Selection for Service Bureau offices. The penalties for failing to enroll—and the rewards for
informants—were too high to make any other course possible.
Ever since then, the family had known this day might and
probably would come. That made it no easier to bear on its
arrival.

Benjamin Hamburger came in next. He spotted the envelope
without prompting. He said nothing, but walked into the kitchen,
filled a shot glass with whiskey, and knocked it back. He
breathed heavily. After a moment, he filled the glass again and
drained it as quickly as before. He often took one drink. Flora
could not remember the last time he'd taken two.

The apartment was eerily silent when David walked in. As
Flora had, he asked, "What's wrong?" No one spoke, just as no
one ever mentioned the Angel of Death. But the angel was there,
mentioned or not. So was the envelope. No one had opened it;
the Hamburgers never opened one another's mail, and when it
was likely to be a letter like this . . . David did the job himself.
"They want me to report for my physical examination next
Tuesday—the second," he said.

Sophie had come in while he was opening the envelope. She
still wore mourning for her husband. She began to wail as she
had when she'd learned Yossel was dead. Nothing could console
her. Her dismay set little Yossel, who had calmed down, to
wailing again. That was the scene on which Isaac Hamburger
walked in.

"It'll be all right," David said, over and over, perhaps trying to convince himself as well as his kin. "It can't be helped, anyhow." Where the other might well have been wrong, that, at least, was true.

Flora never remembered what she had for supper that night. While she was making final preparations for the May Day parade, her brother would be looking forward to getting poked and prodded by coldhearted men in white coats, intent on seeing how he would suit as cannon fodder. She found herself wishing he were pale and consumptive, not strong and ruddy and bursting with life. Life could burst, all right, so easily. The family had seen that.

She went into the office the next morning full of grim determination to keep countless other young men from having to face the danger her brother was all too likely to confront. That meant throwing all her energy into working with the groups taking part in the parade, and into working with the authorities to make sure it went off with as little interference as possible.

"We *will* be peaceable," she promised over and over again. "We won't provoke anything. Don't provoke us in return, and don't let the Soldiers' Circle goons provoke us. The United States still have a Constitution, don't they?" The authorities needed to be reminded of that even more than Herman Bruck did.

Some of the answers she got from police captains and city bureaucrats were conciliatory, some ambiguous at best, and more than a few downright hostile. She did what she could to defuse those. Sighing late in the afternoon on the Saturday before the parade, she said, "I've made more compromises the past week than in all the time I worked here up till then."

"It's good training for Congress," Maria Tresca answered. The look she sent toward Flora was speculative, to say the least. Flora didn't answer, not in words, but her smile was jauntier than she would have thought possible, considering how tired she was.

Herman Bruck never noticed the byplay. He was busy, too—impressively, ostentatiously busy—drafting his speech.

May Day dawned warm and muggy, a day right out of July. More than a few men in the crowds lining Broadway sported straw hats instead of homburgs or caps, as if it truly were summer. The band at the head of the parade—not so fancy as the military bands that strutted down the avenue on Remembrance Day—struck up the "Internationale," then the "Marseillaise," and last the "Star-Spangled Banner." Everyone cheered the national anthem; the other two brought mingled cheers and boos.

"The hell with the frogs, and the hell with their song!" somebody shouted.

"It's a song of revolution," Flora shouted back as she marched along. "It's a song against tyranny and oppression, and for freedom. Don't you think we need that?"

"They're the enemy!" the heckler yelled to her.

"They've forgotten freedom," she returned. Defiantly, she added, "And so have we."

A few eggs flew out of the crowd toward the parade. The cops didn't do anything about that. When somebody threw a bottle instead, though, they waded in, nightsticks swinging. Flora gave a judicious nod. Throwing eggs wasn't that far from heckling, and the Constitution protected heckling no matter who did it. A bottle, now, a bottle was liable to be lethal.

One of the red banners the Socialists carried showed a bare-chested Negro carrying a rifle. REVOLUTION OF THE CSA—1915. REVOLUTION IN THE USA—19??.

"The Rebs put the niggers down!" That cry came out of the crowd at least twice every city block.

The Socialists were ready for it: "Does that mean you want us to act just like the Confederates?" Identifying U.S. actions with those of the hated enemy reduced all but the most politically savvy hecklers to confusion—better yet, to speechless confusion.

Jews and Irishmen, Italians and a few Negroes, Anglo-Saxons and Germans, too, the marchers made their way up to Central Park, where they congregated for the speeches. Herman Bruck and Flora climbed up onto the platform packed with politicians and labor leaders. Bruck eyed her with complacent glee and introduced her to some of the Socialist bigwigs (something even an egalitarian party possessed) she hadn't yet met.

Big Bill Haywood eyed her, too, in a manner that tempted her to take out the hatpin. He had only one eye that tracked and he stank of whiskey, but the furious energy he brought to any cause—whether organizing or striking—made him a force for the money power to reckon with. "Give 'em hell, missy," he said in a gravelly bass. "They deserve it."

Senator Debs of Indiana was more urbane but no more ready

to back down. "TR wants to deal with us as the French dealt with the Paris Commune," he said. "We'll show him we are stronger, even in the midst of this foolish war we never should have agreed to help finance." He grimaced at the tactical blunder his party had made back in 1914. Flora wondered, though, whether he would say the same thing if, as seemed likely, he gained the Socialist nomination for president later in the year.

One speaker after another went up to the podium, blasted the Democrats, praised labor to the skies, and withdrew. "And now, from the Fourteenth Ward, home of the late, great Congressman Zuckerman, Mr. Herman Bruck!" yelled the fellow in charge of keeping the speeches in some kind of order.

He stepped back. Herman Bruck stepped forward. He delivered his speech. Flora stopped listening to it about a minute and a half in. It was everything she'd thought it would be, in its strengths and weaknesses, the latter summarized by the yawns she saw out in the crowd.

Bruck finished and stepped back to polite, tepid applause. "Also from the Fourteenth Ward, Miss Flora Hamburger!" the presenter shouted.

Trying to ignore the pounding of her heart, Flora looked out over the podium at the sea of faces out there. "Birds have nests!" she cried, and pounded a fist down on the polished wood. "Foxes have dens! What does the proletariat have? Nothing but the strength of its right arms, for the capitalists have stolen everything else! And now, not content with that, they send the workers of our country—the workers of the world—out to die by millions in a war that has nothing to do with them. Do we sit idly by and let that happen? Or do we take action, brothers and sisters?"

Maybe fear for David, who would go in for his examination tomorrow, lent her even more passion than she would have had otherwise. However that was, by the time she finished, the applause she got lifted her far higher above the crowd than could have been accounted for by the platform alone. She stepped back dazed, hardly knowing what she'd done.

Big Bill Haywood's hungry stare put her in mind of a wolf eyeing a slab of steak. Eugene Debs said, "Young lady, I think I shall tear up my own speech." Herman Bruck looked half astonished, half terrified. That, somehow, was sweetest of all.

*   *   *

Tom Kennedy put a friendly arm around Cincinnatus' shoulder. "Come on into the back room," he said. "Have a cigar with us." He laughed. So did Joe Conroy. The storekeeper waved Cincinnatus into that back room.

With no small reluctance, he followed the two white men in there. Inside, he was sighing—no, worse, he was sweating. He didn't want to have anything to do with the Confederate underground still operating in Covington, Kentucky, not any more he didn't. But, quite literally, they knew where he lived. If they wanted him to play along, he either had to do it or betray them to the U.S. occupying authorities and then live in fear for the rest of his life. For now, going along seemed less dangerous.

The back room smelled of tobacco and spices and sweets and leather, with a faint undertone of potatoes going bad. To his surprise, Conroy reached into a cigar box and handed him a plump panatella. "Thank you, suh," he said in some surprise. Kennedy was the one who'd always treated him pretty well. To Conroy, he'd been just another hired nigger.

"Hear tell you've been drivin' trucks all over creation for the damnyankees these past few weeks," Conroy said. "Reckon that's why you ain't been in to see us much, even when we put the signal up in the window for you."

"It's a fact, suh," Cincinnatus agreed, gratefully seizing on the excuse the storekeeper offered him. "Sometimes I'm gone fo' days at a time."

"That's fine," Tom Kennedy said. He was thin and dapper and clever; it wasn't by accident he'd been running the hauling firm for which Cincinnatus had worked before the war. "I always knew there was a lot to you, Cincinnatus. Once we win the war, smart black fellows like you will have a lot more chances in the CSA, I reckon. It's in the cards."

"You say that even after the Red uprisin'?" Cincinnatus asked. Kennedy and Conroy didn't know he was a part-time Red himself, but he was in no danger of blowing his cover with the question—the only people who didn't know about the Red Negro attempted revolution were dead.

Kennedy nodded, quite seriously. "Hell, yes, I say that. Richmond won't ever want that kind of thing to happen again, not ever, I tell you. Too many niggers to hold down all of you, so I figure they'll have to give you some of what you want. Don't you?"

Cincinnatus shrugged. He eyed Joe Conroy. The storekeeper nodded, however unenthusiastically. That made Cincinnatus think Kennedy might be right. The next question was, did he care? That was harder to answer. A few weeks before, he would have said a Confederacy with some rights for blacks didn't sound too bad. But now that he'd met Lieutenant Straubing, it didn't sound too good, either. He'd seen that men who didn't care about color were rare in the USA. In the CSA, they weren't rare—they simply didn't exist.

Taking his silence for consent, Kennedy picked up the box from which Conroy had drawn the panatella and the box under it. He opened the one under that. It held, not cigars, but thin-walled lead cylinders of about the same size. Cincinnatus didn't know what they were for, but he figured Kennedy would tell him.

He was right. Kennedy picked up one of the tubes and said, "Thanks to these little sugar plums, we can make the Yankees very unhappy. There's a copper disk edge-on right in the middle here"—he held the cylinder toward a kerosene lamp, so Cincinnatus could see it wasn't hollow quite all the way through—"that divides it into two compartments. You put sulfuric acid in one, picric acid in the other, cork both ends with wax plugs—and then all you have to do is wait."

"Wait for what?" Cincinnatus was starting to get an idea, but, again, he didn't know enough to be sure.

"When the sulfuric acid eats through the copper, it mixes with the picric acid, right?" Kennedy said with a grin that would have made him a hell of a snake-oil salesman. "And out both ends of the tube comes the nicest little spurt of flame you ever did see. Melts down the bomb so nothing's left and starts a hell of a fire, both at the same time. Set one in a crate of shells, say—"

"I see what you're talkin' about, Mr. Kennedy, I surely do," Cincinnatus said. The Confederates had indeed come up with a nasty little toy here. "How much time goes by 'fore the stuff in there eats through the copper and the fire starts?"

"Depends on how thick the copper disk is," Conroy answered. "Anywhere from an hour or so to a couple of weeks. We got all kinds. You don't need to worry about that."

"Good," Cincinnatus said. It wasn't good, but it was better than it might have been. If he started setting firebombs all over creation, the Yankees would take a while to associate the blazes with him. But, sooner or later, they would. He had no doubt of that. The Yankees weren't stupid. Even Lieutenant Kennan did his job well enough, no matter how wrongheaded his ideas about Negroes were.

Conroy and Kennedy probably didn't think the Yankees were stupid, either. What they did think was that Cincinnatus was stupid. With a big, false smile pasted across his face, the store-keeper said, "See how easy it'll be, boy? Not a chance in the world of getting caught."

Cincinnatus glanced over to Tom Kennedy. Kennedy treated him as well as any Confederate white had ever done, and some-times showed, or seemed to show, some understanding that dark skin didn't mean no brains. If Kennedy warned him to be careful now when he picked his spots, and to make sure he didn't bring suspicion down on himself . . . he wasn't sure what he'd do then, but at least he'd have proof in his former boss' actions that the CSA might see its way clear to looking at Negroes as human be-ings once the war was done.

Kennedy smiled, too. "Joe is right, Cincinnatus," he said. "You can see for yourself, they won't ever have a clue about how the fires start. You can do the cause a whole lot of good."

"I see that, Mistuh Kennedy, suh," Cincinnatus said slowly. The Confederate cause came first with Kennedy, too. "How do I tell the few-hour bombs from the ones that go for days 'fore they catch on fire?"

Tom Kennedy's smile got broader. He clapped Cincinnatus on the back. "You're a good fellow, you know that? Here, I'll show you." He held out one of the lead tubes. "The time it's set for is stamped right here, you see. This one's a six-hour delay." He held up a warning forefinger. "That's not perfect, mind you. It might be four hours, and it might be eight. But it won't be two hours, and it won't be two days, either."

"I got you," Cincinnatus said. It was a good system. It would do damage. It would also get traced back to him, sure as the sun would set tonight and come up again tomorrow.

Conroy and Kennedy had a rucksack ready for him to carry home. It contained lead tubes inset with copper disks of vary-ing thickness, a glass jar full of oily-looking sulfuric acid, and another jar that held a powdery, yellowish substance, presum-ably picric acid. It also had a couple of dozen wax stoppers, a spoon, and a couple of glass funnels. "You don't want to get this stuff, either kind, on your skin, or let the one go through the funnel that's held the other," Conroy said. If the storekeeper was warning him, Cincinnatus figured he was dealing with nasty stuff indeed.

The rucksack was small, but surprisingly heavy—lead was like that. Cincinnatus felt almost as if he'd lugged a crate of ammunition home with him. When he got back to the house, Elizabeth's eyebrows shot up at the burden he brought in. "You don't want to know," he told her, and she didn't ask any more questions. She'd learned you were liable to be better off without some answers than with them.

That evening, working in the sink after Elizabeth had gone to bed, Cincinnatus carefully made up three firebombs, one with a one-day disk, one with a two-day disk, and one with a fourteen-day disk, the longest in the whole set of tubes the men from the Confederate underground had given him. He accidentally spilled a drop of sulfuric acid on the galvanized iron. It steamed and bubbled and was doing its best to eat its way right through the sink till he poured lots of water on it. Afterwards, he eyed the discolored spot with considerable respect.

He didn't like having the bombs in his pocket when he went to work the next morning. If a stopper came loose, he figured he'd like it even less. Nodding in a friendly way to Lieutenant Straubing came hard.

Along with the other drivers, he rattled south, and stopped to drop his cargo—small-arms ammunition, from what was stenciled on the crates—a little past one in the afternoon. While laborers unloaded the trucks, he ate his lunch and wandered around. Planting a couple of bombs was as easy as Kennedy and Conroy had said it would be.

Night had fallen by the time he got back to Covington. "See you tomorrow, Cincinnatus," Lieutenant Straubing called, and waved.

"Yes, suh." Cincinnatus waved back. He walked home. No signal for him in Conroy's front window today—the Confederate underground had got what it wanted from him. The general store was quiet and dark, closed for the day. He ducked into the alley behind the place to make sure nothing was wrong, then went on home.

He made up a couple of more bombs that evening, and planted them the next day. That evening, Conroy waved to him as he walked past—word of the first fire he'd set must have already got back to the storekeeper. *Glad you're happy,* Cincinnatus thought, and returned the wave, as he had Lieutenant Straubing's.

Twelve days later, Conroy's store burned to the ground.

Jonathan Moss' thumb stabbed the firing button. The tracers his machine gun spat helped him guide the line of fire across the fuselage of the British biplane whose pilot hadn't spied him coming till too late. The flier slumped over his controls, dead or unconscious. His aeroplane spun down, down, down. Moss followed it down, on the off chance the limey was shamming. He wasn't. The aeroplane crashed into the battered ground of no-man's-land and began to burn.

Moss pulled up sharply. Down there in the trenches, men in khaki were blazing away at him. He didn't take them for granted, not any more. They'd brought him down once. He wanted to give them as little chance of doing it again as he could.

A couple of bullets punched through the fabric covering his single-decker's wings. The sound brought remembered fear, in a way it hadn't when the Englishman put some rounds through there. No aeroplane had ever knocked him out of the sky, which meant he could make himself believe no aeroplane *could* knock him out of the sky. He couldn't pretend, even to himself, that the infantry, which had got lucky once, might not get lucky again.

Small arms still aimed his way. Looking back in the rearview mirror mounted on the edge of the cockpit, he saw muzzle flashes bright as the sun. But his altimeter was winding steadily. By the time he passed twenty-five hundred feet, which didn't take long, he was pretty safe.

Up above him, Dud Dudley waggled his wings in a victory salute. Moss waved back to the flight leader. His buddies had covered for him while he flew down to confirm his kill of the British biplane. He waved again. *Good fellows,* he thought.

Looking around for more opponents, he found none. Dudley waggled his wings again, and pointed back toward the aerodrome. Moss checked his fuel gauge. He had less gas left than he'd thought. He didn't argue or try to pretend he hadn't seen, but took his place in the flight above, behind, and to the left of Dudley.

One after another, the four Martin single-deckers bounced to a stop on the rutted grass of the airstrip outside Cambridge, Ontario. Groundcrew men came trotting up, not only to see to the aeroplanes but also to pick up the word on what had happened in the war in the air. "Johnny got one," Tom Innis said, slapping Moss on the back hard enough to stagger him. Innis' grin was wide and fierce and full of sharp teeth, as if he were more wolf than man.

"That's bully, Lieutenant!" The groundcrew men crowded around him. One of them pressed a cigar into a pocket of his flying suit. "Knock 'em all down, sir." "The more you sting, the fewer they've got left."

Eventually, the fliers detached themselves and headed for Captain Pruitt's office to make their official report. "That was really fine shooting, sir," Phil Eaker said. He was skinny and blond and unlikely to be as young as he looked. Nobody, Moss thought from the height of his mid-twenties, was likely to be as young as Phil Eaker looked. He also hadn't had enough flying time to harden him yet. That would come—if he lived.

"I dove on him out of the sun," Moss said, shrugging. He could smell the leftover fear in his sweat now that the slipstream wasn't blowing it away. "If he doesn't know you're there, that's the easiest way to do the job. He only got off a few rounds at me."

When the war broke out, he'd thought of himself as a knight of the air. Nothing left him happier now than a kill where the foe didn't have much chance to kill him. He suspected knights in shining armor hadn't cried in their beer when they were able to bash out a Saracen's brains from behind, either.

Hardshell Pruitt looked up from the papers on his desk when Dudley and the men of his flight ducked into his tent. The squadron commander pulled out a binder, dipped his pen into a bottle of ink, and said, "Tell me, gentlemen. Try to give me the abridged version. I spend so much time filling out forms"—he waved at the documents over which he'd been laboring—"I haven't been getting the flight time I need."

"Yes, sir," Dudley said. Concisely and accurately, he reported on the flight. The most significant item was Moss' downing the British flying scout. Moss told a good deal of that tale himself.

"Well done," Captain Pruitt said when he'd finished. "Let me just see something here." He shuffled through some manila folders, opened one, read what was in it, and grunted. Then he said, "Very good, Moss. You're dismissed. I have some matters I need to take up with your pals here. You may see them again, or I may decide to ship them all out for courts-martial."

"I'm sure they all deserve it, sir," Moss said cheerfully, which got him ripe raspberries from the other men in the flight. He ignored them, making his way back to his own tent. When he peeled off his flight suit, he realized how grimy and sweaty he was. The aerodrome had rigged up a makeshift showerbath from an old fuel drum set on a wooden platform. The day held a promise of summer. He didn't even ask to have any hot water added to what was in there. He just grabbed some soap and scrubbed till he was clean.

Dudley, Innis, and Eaker still hadn't returned from Captain Pruitt's office by the time Moss got back to his tent. He scratched his freshly washed head. Maybe Hardshell hadn't been joking, and they really were in Dutch.

He smoked the cigar the groundcrew man had given him, stretched out on his cot, and dozed for half an hour. His tentmates weren't back when he woke up. He muttered under his breath. What the devil had they done? Why the devil hadn't they let him do some of it, too?

He got up, went outside, and looked around. No sign of them. Hardly any sign of anybody, when you got down to it. He ambled over to the officers' lounge. You could always find somebody there. It was nearly sunset, too, which meant the place ought to be filling up for some heavy-duty, professional drinking, the way it did every night.

Except tonight. Oh, a couple of pilots from another squadron were in there soaking up some whiskey, but the place was dead except for them. "Somebody get shot down?" Moss wondered out loud. It was the only thing he could think of, but it didn't strike him as very likely. When a fellow died up in the sky, his comrades usually drank themselves stupid to remember him and to forget they might be next.

Drinking alone wasn't Moss' idea of fun, and the other two pilots didn't seem interested in company. Having nothing better to do, he was about to wander off and sack out when a groundcrew corporal poked his head into the lounge, spotted him, and exclaimed, "Oh, there you are, sir! Jesus, I'm glad I found you. Hardshell—uh, Captain Pruitt—he wants to see you right away. I was you, sir, I wouldn't keep him waiting." He disappeared.

Moss hopped to his feet. Whatever trouble his flightmates were in, maybe he'd found a piece of it after all. He hurried over to the captain's tent, which was only a few feet away, wishing he hadn't been so blithely agreeable about Hardshell's court-martialing his friends. He was liable to be seeing a court himself.

Captain Pruitt stood outside the tent. Moss didn't think that was a good sign. Shadow shrouded the squadron commander's face. He grunted on seeing Jonathan approach. "Here at last, are you?" he growled. "Well, you'd better come in, then."

Rudely, he ducked through the tentflap by himself and didn't hold it for Moss. Shaking his head, Moss followed. He was going to get it, all right. Braced for the worst, he lifted the canvas and followed Captain Pruitt inside.

Light blazed at him. All the fliers he hadn't been able to find packed the inside of the tent. They lacked only a coating of olive oil to be sardines in a can. Tom Innis pressed a pint of whiskey into Moss' hand. "Congratulations!" everybody shouted.

Moss stared in astonishment. "What the devil—!" he blurted.

Laughter erupted and rolled over him in waves. "He doesn't even know!" Dud Dudley hooted.

"Clear a space and we'll show him, then," Captain Pruitt said.

Clearing a space wasn't easy. A few people, grumbling, had to go outside. When Moss finally saw Pruitt's desk, it was for once clear of papers. A cake sat on top of it instead, a rectangular cake with white frosting. A big chocolate ♠ symbol turned it into an enormous playing card, with chocolate A's at the appropriate corners.

"My God!" Moss said. "Was that my fifth?" He counted on his fingers. "Jesus, I guess it was."

"Here we have something new," Pruitt observed: "the unintentional ace."

More laughter rang out. Dud Dudley said, "It's a good thing you finally showed up. We were going to eat this beauty without you in a couple of minutes, and then spend the next five years gloating about it."

"Give me a piece," Moss said fiercely.

"You want a piece, go to the brothel," Innis told him. "You want some cake, stay here." A bayonet lay next to the cake. He picked it up and started slicing.

Cake and whiskey wasn't a combination Moss had had before. After he'd taken a couple of good swigs from the pint, he didn't much care. The hooch was good, the cake was good, the company was good, and he didn't think at all about the man he'd killed to earn the celebration.

IX

Jake Featherston went from gun to gun, making sure all six howitzers in the battery were well positioned, supplied with shells, and ready to open up if the Yankees decided to pay the trenches a call. He didn't think that would happen; the drive through Maryland had taken an even crueler toll on U.S. forces than on those of the Confederacy, and the latest Yankee push had drowned in an ocean of blood a couple of days before.

All the same, he made sure he hunted up Caleb Meadows, the next most senior sergeant in the battery, and said, "You know what to give the damnyankees if they hit us while I'm gone and you're in charge."

"Sure do." Meadows' Adam's apple bobbed up and down as he spoke. He was a scrawny, gangly man who spoke as if he thought somebody was counting how many words he said. "Two guns sighted on that ridge they got, two right in front of our line, and t'other two ready for whatever happens."

"That's it," Jake agreed. "I expect I'll be back by suppertime."

Meadows nodded. He didn't say anything. That was in character. He didn't salute, either. How could he, when he and Featherston were both sergeants? Jake had commanded the battery ever since Captain Stuart went out in a blaze of glory. He was still a sergeant. He didn't like still being a sergeant.

He went back through Ceresville, past a couple of mills that had stood, by the look of what was left of them, since the days of the Revolutionary War. They weren't standing any more. U.S. guns had seen to that.

The bridge over the Monocacy still did stand, though the ground all around both ends of it had been chewed up by searching guns. Military policemen stood on the northeastern bank, rifles at the ready, to keep unauthorized personnel from crossing. Jake dug in his pocket, produced his pass, and displayed it to one of the men with a shiny MP's gorget held on his neck by a length of chain. The fellow examined it, looked sour at being unable to find anything irregular, and waved him across.

He had to ask several times before he could find his way to the headquarters of the Army of Northern Virginia. They were farther back toward Frederick than he'd thought, probably to make sure no long-range U.S. shells came to pay them a call. Once he got into the tent city, he had to ask for more directions to get to Intelligence.

A corporal who looked more like a young college professor was clacking away on a typewriter inside the flap of the tent, which was big enough to be partitioned off into cubicles. He finished the sentence he was on before looking up and saying, "Yes, Sergeant?" His tone said he outranked Featherston regardless of how many stripes each of them wore on his sleeve.

"I have an appointment with Major Potter." Jake displayed his pass once more.

The corporal examined it more carefully than the military policeman had done. He nodded. "One moment." He vanished into the bowels of the tent. When he came back, he waved for Jake to accompany him.

Major Clarence Potter was typing, too. Unlike the corporal, he broke off as soon as he saw Featherston. "Sit down, Sergeant," he said, and then, to the noncom who'd escorted Jake back to him, "Fetch Sergeant Featherston a cup of coffee, why don't you, Harold? Thanks." It was an order, but a polite one.

"*Good* coffee," Jake said a minute or so later. You couldn't make coffee this tasty up near the front, not when you were brewing it in a hurry in a pot you hardly ever got the chance to wash. Jake realized he couldn't complain too much, not when the infantry hardly boasted a pot to their name, but made their joe in old tin cans.

"I'd say you've earned good coffee," Major Potter said equably. "Glad you like it. We get the beans shipped up from a coffeehouse in Washington. But enough of that." He glanced down to whatever paper he had in the typewriter. "I'd say you've earned any number of things, but my opinion is not always the one that counts. Which is, I suppose, why you asked to see me today."

"Yes, sir," Featherston said. And then, as he'd feared it would, all the frustration came boiling to the top: "Sir, who the devil do I have to kill to get myself promoted in this man's Army?"

Potter frowned at him. The major didn't look like much, not till you saw his eyes. *Sniper's eyes,* the soldiers called a glance like that: they didn't necessarily mean the fellow who had them was good with a rifle, only that you didn't want to get on his bad side or he'd make you pay. But Jake was also frowning, too purely ticked off at the world to give a damn about what happened next.

And Potter looked down first. He fiddled with some of the papers on his desk, then sighed. "I'm afraid killing Yankees doesn't do the job, Sergeant. I wish it did. It's the criterion I'd use. But, as I told you, my views, while they have some weight, are not the governing ones."

"I been running that battery every since Captain Stuart went down, sir," Jake said, and Clarence Potter nodded. "We've fought just as good with me in charge of things as we did with him, maybe better. Besides"—he had enough sense to hold his voice down, but he couldn't keep the fury out of it—"that damned fool would have got every man jack of us killed for nothin' better than him goin' out in a blaze of glory. We would have lost every man and every gun we had."

"I don't doubt it for a moment," Major Potter said. "But you asked whom you had to kill to get a promotion, Sergeant?" After waiting for Featherston to nod in turn, he went on, "The plain answer is, you will never be promoted in the First Richmond Howitzers, and you are most unlikely to win promotion anywhere in the Confederate States Army, for the simple reason that you killed Captain Jeb Stuart III."

Jake stared at him. Potter was dead serious. "I didn't, sir, and you know I didn't," Jake said, holding up one hand to deny the charge. "When I was starting to move the battery out, I did everything I could to get him to come along. He stopped me. He stopped the whole battery. If the damnyankees hadn't shot him, he would have kept us there till they overran us."

" 'If the damnyankees hadn't shot him,' " Potter repeated.

"And why, Sergeant, did he put himself in a position where the Yankees were able to shoot him so easily?"

"You ought to know, sir," Jake answered. "On account of the trouble he got into with you for keeping that snake-in-the-grass nigger Pompey around and not letting anybody find out the son of a bitch really was a Red."

"That's right," Major Potter said. "And, having fallen under a cloud, he did the noble thing and fell on his sword, too—or the modern equivalent, at any rate." His nostrils twitched; by the way he said *the noble thing*, he meant something more like *the boneheaded thing*. "But now we come down to it. Who was it, Sergeant Featherston, who first alerted Army of Northern Virginia Intelligence to the possibility that there might be something wrong with this Pompey?"

When a heavy shell landed close to the battery, it picked you up and slammed you down and did its level best to tear your insides out right through your nose and mouth and ears. That was how Jake Featherston felt now, sitting in a wood-and-canvas folding chair in a tent too far back of the line to have to worry about shellfire. "Christ," he said hoarsely. "They're blaming me."

"Of course they are." Major Potter's manner was as mild as his appearance; to look at him or listen to him, you'd peg him for a schoolteacher—until you noticed what he had to say. "You wouldn't expect them to blame Jeb Stuart III, would you? All he did, Sergeant, was cause the suppression of an investigation. If some low, crass individual hadn't mentioned this Pompey's name, no one would have needed an investigation in the first place, and Captain Stuart could have continued on his brave, empty-headed track toward a general's stars and wreath."

Featherston stared at the Intelligence officer again, this time for an altogether different reason. Once he'd drunk the stuff the Russians cooked up from potatoes. It didn't taste like anything, so he hadn't thought he was drunk—till he tried to stand up and fell over instead. Potter's words were like that. They unexpectedly turned the whole world sideways.

"That's not fair, sir," Jake said. "That's—"

"Shooting the messenger for bad news?" Potter suggested. "Of course it is. What do you expect? That they should blame their own? Not likely, Sergeant. You must know the First Richmond Howitzers are a blue-blood regiment if ever there was one. You must know Jeb Stuart, Jr., has a fancy office in the War Department down in Richmond, from which he sends eager young men out to die for their country. I've done everything I can for you, Sergeant. I know your record. I've urged your promotion. Set that against the traditions of the First Richmond Howitzers and the animus of Jeb Stuart, Jr., and it doesn't amount to a hill of beans. I'm sorry."

"If I transfer out, I'll be—"

"A sergeant, I'm afraid, till your dying day," Major Potter interrupted. "Jeb Stuart III blighted his career by being wrong. You've blighted yours by being right. Sergeant Featherston, I *am* sorry. I feel I ought to apologize for the entire Confederate States of America. But there's not one damned thing I can do about it. Have you got any more questions?"

"No, sir." Jake got to his feet. "If that's how it is, then that's how it is. But if that's how it is, then something stinks down in Richmond. Sir."

He figured he'd said too much there. But Clarence Potter slowly nodded. "Something does stink down in Richmond. If we try to root it out now, we're liable to lose the war in the confusion that would follow. But if we don't try to root it out, we're liable to lose the war from the confusion it causes. Again, I have no good answers for you. I wish I did."

Featherston saluted. "Thank you for trying, sir. I hope you don't end up hurt on account of that. All I've got to say is, sooner or later there has to be a reckoning. All these damn fools in fancy uniforms who let the niggers rise up without having a notion they were going to, all the damn fools who can't think of anything past promoting their friends and relations—they ought to pay the price. Yes, sir, they ought to pay the price."

"That's a political decision, not one for the military," Potter said.

"If that's what it is—" Jake broke off. He saluted again and left the tent, heading back to his battery. All right, he wasn't going to be a lieutenant. He had a goal even so.

Major Abner Dowling hurried into the fancy house on the outskirts of Bowling Green, Kentucky. "Here's the motorcar, sir, come to take you back toward Bremen," he called loudly—you had to call loudly, if you expected General Custer to hear you.

Libbie Custer heard him. She was sitting in the parlor, reading *Harper's*. Her expression became remarkably similar to that of a snapping turtle on the point of biting. Back in Bremen was Olivia. She didn't know—Dowling didn't think she knew—about Olivia, not in particular, but she knew there was someone like Olivia back there, and she didn't like it for beans. But the car had been laid on not at General Custer's instance, but at that of the Secretary of War, and she couldn't do anything about it. No wonder she looked ready to chomp down on a broom handle.

And here came Custer, looking no happier himself. "This is all a pack of nonsense and idiocy," he said loudly. "Why don't they leave a man alone so he can run a proper campaign? But no, that doesn't satisfy them. Nothing satisfies them. Pack of ghouls and vultures is what they are back in Philadelphia, crunching the bones of good men's reputations."

At first, Dowling thought that soliloquy was delivered for Libbie's benefit. But Custer kept on grumbling, louder than ever, after he went outside and waddled toward the green-gray-painted Ford waiting for him in front of his residence. The driver scrambled out and opened the door to the rear seat for him and Dowling. Neither of them was thin, which made that rear seat uncomfortably intimate.

As they rattled off toward the northwest, Custer leaned forward and asked the driver, "What is this stupid barrel thing you're taking me to see? Some newfangled invention, I don't doubt. Well, let me tell you, Lieutenant, I am of the opinion that the world has seen too many new inventions already. What do you think of that?"

"Sir," the driver said, a gloriously unresponsive but polite answer. Dowling didn't know whether to wish the First Army commander would shut up or to hope he'd go on blathering and at long last give the War Department enough rope to hang him.

A couple of miles later, Custer ordered the driver to stop so he could get out and stand behind a tree. Along with so much of the rest of him, his kidneys weren't what they had been forty years earlier. He came back looking even more dissatisfied with the world than he had when he'd scrambled up into the motorcar.

The road ran roughly parallel to the railroad line. Every so often, it would swing away, only to return. At one of the places where it came very close to the tracks, the driver stepped on the brake. "Here we are, sir," he said.

Here was a meadow that had been part of the Confederate line defending Bowling Green, about halfway between the tiny towns of Sugar Grove and Dimple. But for wrecked trenches and dozens of shell holes big enough to bury an elephant, the only thing to be seen was an enormous green-gray tent with a couple of squads' worth of soldiers around it. Why the driver had chosen to stop at this particular place was beyond Abner Dowling.

It was evidently beyond Custer, too. "We aren't even halfway back toward Bremen," he complained. Olivia *had* been on his beady little mind, then. Libbie Custer knew her husband well.

"If you'll just come with me, sir." The driver got out of the automobile and handed down Custer and Dowling as if they were a couple of fine ladies. He headed for the tent. The general and his adjutant perforce followed: it was either that or be left all alone by the motorcar. At every other step, Custer snarled about what the mud was doing to his boots.

A man came out of the tent. He was wearing ordinary Army trousers, but with a leather jacket and leather helmet that put Dowling in mind of flying gear. With a wave, he hurried toward Custer. As he got nearer, Dowling saw he wore a major's oak leaves on that jacket, and, a few steps later, that he had the eagle-on-star badge of a General Staff officer.

"General Custer?" he said, saluting. "I'm Ned Sherrard, one of the men from the Barrel Works." The way he said it, you could hear the capital letters thudding into place. The only trouble was, Dowling had no idea whether or not whatever he was describing deserved those capitals.

Custer had evidently formed his own opinion. "And when do you and the Barrel Works go over Niagara Falls?" he inquired with acid courtesy.

Major Sherrard's smile showed white, even teeth, as if Custer had made a good joke. "We can't quite manage that yet with our barrels, sir, but we're working on it." He stuck out his hand to Dowling, a greeting of equal to equal. "Major, I'm pleased to meet you."

"Pleased to meet you, too, Major," Dowling returned. "So what are these barrels, anyway? I've heard the name a few times the past couple of weeks, and I'm curious."

"I wish you hadn't heard it at all," Sherrard said. "Security, you know. But it can't be helped, I suppose. We've got one inside the tent, and you can see for yourself. We'll even put it through its paces for you. We want the commanding generals on all fronts familiar with these weapons, because they will play an increasing role on the battlefield as time goes by."

"Newfangled foolishness," Custer said, not bothering to keep his voice down. But Sherrard's cheerful smile didn't waver. He was made of stern stuff. Turning, he led Custer and Dowling toward the tent. Some of the soldiers outside came to attention and saluted. Others ducked into the tent ahead of the officers.

Sherrard held the flap open, but not wide open. "Go on in," he said invitingly. "You can see what barrels are like better than I could explain them to you in a month of Sundays."

Custer, of course, went first. He took one step into the enormous tent and then stopped in his tracks, so that Dowling almost ran into him. "Excuse me, sir, but I'd like to see, too," the adjutant said plaintively.

As usual, Dowling had to repeat himself before Custer took any notice of him. When the general commanding First Army finally did move out of the way, Dowling stared in wonder at the most astonishing piece of machinery he'd ever seen.

It impressed Custer, too, which wasn't easy. "Isn't that bully?" he said softly. "Isn't that just the bulliest thing in the whole wide world?"

"More like the ugliest thing in the whole wide world," Dowling said, too startled for once to watch his tongue as well as he should have.

He got lucky. Custer didn't hear him. Major Sherrard did, but didn't act insulted. Custer said, "So this is what a barrel looks like, eh? Bigger than I thought. Tougher than I thought, too."

Had Dowling named the beast, he would have called it a box, not a barrel. Big it was, twenty-five feet long if it was an inch, and better than ten feet high, too: an enormous box of steel plates riveted together, with a cannon sticking out from the slightly pointed front end, four machine guns—a pair on either flank—a driver's conning tower or whatever the proper name was sticking up from the middle of the top deck, and, as Dowling saw when he walked around to the rear of the thing, two more machine guns there.

"You've got it on tracks instead of wheels," he remarked.

"That's right," Sherrard said proudly. "It'll cross a trench seven feet wide, easy as you please—climb out of shell holes, too, and keep on going."

"How big a crew?" Custer asked.

"Eighteen," Major Sherrard answered. "Two on the cannon—it's a two-incher, in case you're wondering, sir—two on each machine gun, two mechanics on the engines, a driver, and a commander."

"Engines?" Dowling said. "Plural?"

"Well, yes." Now the major sounded a trifle embarrassed. "*Sarah Bernhardt* here does weigh something over thirty tons. It takes a pair of White truck engines to push her along. They're a handed pair, like gloves, one with normal rotation, one with reverse. That lets us put the exhausts, which are very hot, in the center of the hull, and the carburetors and manifolds toward the outside."

"Thirty—tons," Dowling murmured. "How fast will, uh, *Sarah* go?"

"Eight miles an hour, flat out on level ground," the barrel enthusiast told him. "You must remember, Major, she's carrying more than an inch of steel armor plate all around, to keep machine-gun fire from penetrating."

"Are these chaps gathered here and around the tent the crew?" Custer asked eagerly. "If they are, may I see the barrel in action?"

"They are, and you may," Sherrard said. "That's why I brought you here, sir." He clapped his hands and called out a couple of sharp orders. The crew scrambled into the barrel through hatches Dowling had hardly noticed till they swung wide. Major Sherrard opened the whole front of the tent, which was, Dowling realized with that, a special model itself, made to shelter barrels. The War Department was serious about barrels, all right, if it had had tents created with them in mind.

The driver and commander, up in that little box of a conning tower, opened their armored vision slits as wide as they could; no one would be shooting at them today. The engine—no, engines, Dowling reminded himself—must have had electric ignition, because they sprang to noisy, stinking life without anyone cranking them.

"Let's step outside," Major Sherrard said. "Even with the slits wide, the driver hasn't got the best view of the road. Wouldn't do to have us squashed flat because he didn't notice we were there, heh, heh."

Dowling's answering chuckle was distinctly dutiful. Custer, though, laughed almost as loud as he had on learning Richard Harding Davis had dropped dead. He was enjoying himself. Dowling wasn't. The day was hot and sticky, the worst kind of day for anyone with a corpulent frame like his. As the sun beat down on him, he wondered what it was like for the crew of the barrel inside that steel shell. He wondered what it would be like in combat, with the hatches and slits closed down tight. He decided he was glad to be on the outside looking in, not on the inside looking out.

The rumble changed note as the driver put *Sarah Bernhardt* into gear. Tracks clattering, the barrel slowly crawled out of the tent. Through the slit, Dowling heard the commander shouting at the driver. In spite of the shouting, he wondered if the driver could hear anything.

Down into a shell hole went the barrel. The engine note changed again as the driver shifted gears. Up out of the hole the barrel came, dirt clinging to its prow. Down into another hole it went. Up it came once more. It rolled over some old, rusty Confederate barbed wire as if the stuff hadn't been there. As Major Sherrard had said, it showed no trouble crossing a trench wider than a man was tall.

"Do you know what this is, Major?" Custer said to Dowling. "This"—he gave an utterly Custerian melodramatic pause—"is armored cavalry. This, for once, is no flapdoodle. This is a breakthrough machine."

"It may well prove useful in trench warfare, yes, sir," Dowling agreed—or half agreed. Custer had always wanted to use cavalry to force a breakthrough. Dowling remembered thinking about armored horses, but, to his mind, *Sarah Bernhardt* didn't measure up—the barrel struck him as more like an armored hippopotamus.

But Custer, as usual, was letting himself get carried away. "Give me a hundred of these machines on a two-mile front," he declared, "and I'll tear a hole in the Rebs' lines so big, even a troop of blind, three-legged dogs could go through it, let alone our brave American soldiers."

Major Sherrard coughed the polite cough of a junior-grade officer correcting his superior. Abner Dowling knew that cough well. "War Department tactical doctrine, sir," Sherrard said, "is to employ barrels widely along the front, to support as many different infantry units with them as possible."

"Poppycock!" Custer exclaimed. "Utter goo and drivel. A massed blow is what's required, Major—nothing less. Once we get into the Rebs' rear, they're ours."

"Sir," Major Sherrard said stiffly, "I have to tell you that one criterion in the allocation of barrels to the various fronts will be commanders' willingness to utilize them in the manner determined to be most efficacious by the War Department."

Custer looked like a cat choking on a hairball. Dowling turned to watch *Sarah Bernhardt* climb out of yet another shell hole so his commanding officer wouldn't see him laugh. Custer had gall, all right, if on three minutes' acquaintance with barrels he presumed to offer a doctrine for them wildly at odds with that of the people who'd invented them in the first place. Well, Custer's gall wasn't anything with which Dowling had been unacquainted already.

"Very well," the general commanding First Army said, his voice mild though his face was red. "I'll use them exactly the way the wise men in Philadelphia say I should."

"Good." Major Sherrard smiled now. Of course he smiled— he'd got his way. "Progress on this front, I am sure, will improve because of them."

"I'm sure of that myself," Custer said. Now Dowling did look at him, and sharply. He was sure of something, too—sure his boss was lying.

Reggie Bartlett glanced over at Senior Lieutenant Ralph Briggs. Briggs no longer looked like a recruiting poster for the Confederate States Navy, as he had all through his stay in the prisoner-of-war camp near Beckley, West Virginia. What he looked like now was a hayseed; he was wearing a collarless cotton shirt under faded denim overalls he'd hooked off a clothesline while a farm wife was busy in the kitchen. A disreputable straw hat perched on his head at an even more disreputable angle.

Reggie looked down at himself. By his clothes, he could have been Briggs' cousin. His shirt, instead of hiding under overalls, was tucked into a pair of dungarees out at the knee and held up by a rope belt in lieu of galluses. The straw hat keeping the sun out of his eyes was even more battered than the one Briggs wore.

Catching the glances, Briggs clicked his tongue between his teeth. "We've got to do something about our shoes," he said fretfully. "If anyone takes a good long look at them, we're ruined."

"Sure are, Ralph," Bartlett said in his not very good rendering of a West Virginia twang, an accent altogether different not only from his own soft Richmond intonations but also from the Yankee way of talking Briggs had tried to teach him. His brown, sturdy Confederate Army boots were at least well made for marching. Briggs' Navy shoes, both tighter and less strongly made, had given him trouble after he and Reggie and several others tunneled their way out of the prisoner-of-war camp. Reggie went on, "Hard to steal shoes, though, and no promise they'll fit once we've done it."

"I know," Briggs said, unhappy still. "Wish we could walk into a town and buy some, but—" He broke off. Reggie understood why, all too well. For one thing, they had no money. For another, in these little hill towns they were strangers with a capital S. And, for a third, showing himself in Confederate footgear was the fastest ticket back to camp Reggie could think of.

Way off in the distance behind them, hounds belled. The sound sent chills running down Reggie's spine. He didn't think the hounds were after Briggs and him; they'd been free for several days now, and had done everything they knew how to do to break their trail. But other pairs of Confederate prisoners were also on the loose. Every bunch the damnyankees recaptured hurt the cause of the CSA.

And besides—"Now I know what niggers must have felt like, running away from their masters with the hounds after them," Reggie said.

"Hadn't thought of that." Briggs paused for a moment to take off his hat and fan himself with it. He set the straw back on his head. His expression darkened. "I'd like to set the dogs on some niggers, too, the way they rose up against us. They ought to pay for that."

"Way they lorded it over us in camp, too," Reggie said, full of remembered anger at the insults he'd endured.

"Damnyankees set that up," Briggs said. "Wanted to turn us and them against each other." Reggie nodded; he'd seen the same thing himself. The Navy man went on, "I will say it did a better job than I ever thought it would. Those niggers had no loyalty to their country at all."

He would have said more, but a bend in the road brought a town into sight up ahead. "That'll be—Shady Spring?" Reggie asked doubtfully.

"That's right." Ralph Briggs sounded altogether sure of himself. It was as if he had a map of West Virginia stored inside his head. Every so often, when he needed to, he'd pull it down, take a look, and then roll it up again. Reggie wondered how and why he'd acquired that ability, which didn't seem a very useful one for a Navy man to have.

Whatever the name of the town was, though, they had to avoid it. They had to avoid people and towns as much as they could. U.S. forces paid a bounty on escaped prisoners the locals captured. Even had that not been so, West Virginians weren't to be trusted. When Virginia seceded from the USA, they'd seceded from Virginia, and made that secession stick. They had no love for the Confederate States of America.

The hillsides surrounding Shady Spring weren't too steep. Forests of oaks and poplars clothed them. So Ralph Briggs said, at any rate; Bartlett, who'd lived all his life in Richmond, couldn't have told one tree from another to escape the firing squad.

When he and Briggs came to a rill, they stopped and drank and washed their faces and hands, then splashed along in the water for a couple of hundred yards before returning to dry land. "No point making the dogs' lives any easier, in case they are on our trail," Reggie remarked.

"You're right about that," Briggs said, although hiking through the water soaked his feet and did his shoes more harm than it did to Bartlett's taller boots.

Here and there in the woods, sometimes by themselves, sometimes in small clusters, sometimes in whole groves, dead or dying trees stood bare-branched, as if in winter, under the warm spring sun. Reggie pointed. "What's wrong with them?" he asked, having developed considerable respect for how much Bartlett knew.

And the Navy man did not disappoint him. "Chestnut blight," he answered. "Started in New York City ten, maybe twelve years ago. Been spreading ever since. Way things are going, won't be a chestnut tree left in the USA or the CSA in a few years' time. Damnyankees let all sort of foreign things into their country." He spat in disgust.

"Chestnut blight," Reggie echoed. Now that Briggs mentioned it, he remembered reading something about it in the newspapers a couple of years before. "So these are chestnuts?" He wouldn't have known it unless Briggs had told him.

"These *were* chestnuts," Briggs corrected him now. "The Yankees got the blight, and now they're giving it to us." He scowled. "Chestnuts, the war—what's the difference?"

Reggie's stomach rumbled. It had been doing that right along, but this was a growl a bear would have been proud to claim. Reggie went through his trouser pockets. He came up with half a square of hardtack: the last of the painfully saved food he'd brought out of camp. Even more painful was breaking the fragment in two and offering Briggs a piece.

"We don't get our hand on some more grub, we're not going to make it out of West Virginia whether the damnyankees catch up with us or not," Reggie said.

"You're right." Briggs sounded as if he hated to admit it. "We're going to have to kill something or steal something, one or the other."

They tramped on through the woods. Bartlett's nostrils twitched. "That's smoke," he said. At first, he thought it came from Shady Spring, but they'd gone west to skirt the town, and the breeze was blowing into their faces, not from their backs. "That's a farm up ahead somewhere," he added.

Briggs was thinking along with him. "Lots of chances to get food from a farm." He sniffed. "That's not just smoke, either.

Smells like they're smoking meat—venison, or maybe ham.
Hell, in these back woods, maybe even bear, for all I know."

Reggie knew nothing about bears. The thought of there being
bears in these woods hadn't occurred to him till the Navy man
mentioned it. He looked around, as if expecting to see black,
shaggy shapes coming out from behind every tree. Then he
sniffed again. Smelling meat after months on camp rations made
him ready to fight every bear in the USA for a chance at some—
or to eat one if the farmer had done the fighting for him. "Let's
follow our noses," he said.

Carved out of the middle of the woods were some tiny fields
full of corn and tobacco. A couple of children fed chickens
near a barn. A woman bustled between that barn and the farmhouse. No man was visible. "He's probably in the Army," Briggs
whispered as he and Bartlett stared hungrily from the edge of
the forest at the hollow log mounted upright over smoldering
hickory chips. From the top of the log issued the wonderful
smell that had drawn them here.

"We'll wait till dark, till they've all gone to bed," Reggie said.
"Then we grab it and get the hell out."

"Liable to be a dog," Briggs said. "Meat's liable not to be
smoked all the way through, either."

"I don't see any dog. I don't hear any dog. Do you?" Bartlett
asked, and Ralph Briggs shook his head. Reggie went on, "And I
don't care about the meat, either. Hell, I don't care if it's raw. I'll
eat it. Won't you?" When Briggs didn't answer, he presumed
he'd won his point.

And the thievery went off better than he'd dared hope. A
couple of kerosene lanterns glowed inside the farmhouse for
half an hour or so after sundown, then went out. That left the
night to the moon and the stars and the lightning bugs. Reggie
and Briggs waited for an hour, then sauntered forward. No dog
went crazy. No rifle poked out of a window. They stole the
hollow log and carried it away with nobody inside the farmhouse
any the wiser.

It proved to be pork in there, ribs and chops and all sorts of
good things. "Don't eat too much," Briggs warned. "You'll make
yourself sick, you were empty so long."

He was an officer, so Reggie didn't scream *Shut up!* at him.

He ate till he was deliciously full, a feeling he hadn't known for a long time.

Carrying the smoked pork they couldn't finish, the two of them headed south again. They'd done a deal of traveling by night, when they could use the roads with less risk of being recognized for what they were. And every foot they gained was a foot their pursuers would have to make up in the morning.

Since the war started, the USA had punched a railroad south and east from Beckley through Shady Spring and Flat Rock to join the lines already going into eastern Virginia. "The damnyankees are throwing everything they've got into this war," Reggie said, pointing to the new bright rails gleaming in the moonlight close by the road.

"I know." Briggs' voice was bleak. "It worries me."

Half an hour later, a southbound train came by. Reggie and Briggs hid by the side of the road till it passed. To Bartlett's surprise, it had only a few passenger cars; behind them came a long stretch of flatcars carrying big shapes shrouded in canvas. Each flatcar also carried a couple of armed guards.

"They're singing something." Now Ralph Briggs sounded indignant, as if U.S. soldiers had no business enjoying themselves. "What in blazes are they singing?"

"I know that tune," Reggie told him. "It's 'Roll out the Barrel.'"

A couple of officers from the Corps of Engineers came up to the stretch of trench on the Roanoke front Chester Martin's squad called their own. "What are you up to?" Martin called to them, curious about the strips of white cloth they were tying to pegs.

"Setting up the approach," replied one of the engineers: a stocky, bald, bullet-headed fellow with a close-cropped fringe of gray hair above his ears and at the back of his neck. The answer didn't tell Chester anything much, but it didn't anger him, either; the engineer sounded like a man who knew his own business so well, he forgot other people didn't know it at all. Martin approved of people who knew what they were doing. He'd seen too many who hadn't the foggiest notion.

Sunshine glinted off the wire frames of Captain Orville Wyatt's glasses. Martin worried about his captain, another competent man he didn't want to lose: those spectacles might make him easier for a sniper to spot. Wyatt said, "Don't joggle Lieutenant Colonel Gross' elbow, Sergeant. This has to do with what was discussed in the briefing yesterday."

Martin shook his head, annoyed at himself. "I'm sorry, sir. I should have figured that out." He looked around to see how many of his men were paying attention. He hated looking dumb in front of them.

"Don't worry about it," Lieutenant Colonel Gross said. He seemed younger when he smiled. "This is new for everybody, and we have to work out what needs doing as we go along. The real point is, this'll be new for the Rebs, too." He pointed over past the U.S. barbed wire, past no-man's-land, past the C.S. wire, to the trenches beyond.

"If everything goes according to Hoyle," Captain Wyatt said, "we'll take a big bite out of the Rebs' real estate tomorrow morning."

Specs Peterson was standing not far from Martin. He pitched his voice so the sergeant could hear but the captain couldn't: "Yeah, and if it doesn't work, they're going to bury us in gunnysacks, on account of the Rebs'll blow us all over the landscape."

"I know," Martin said, also quietly. "You got any better ideas, though, Specs? This duking it out in the trenches is getting us nowhere fast."

"Hey, what are you talkin' about, Sarge?" Paul Andersen said. "We've moved this front forward a good ten miles, and it hasn't taken us two years to do it. At that rate, we ought to be in Richmond"—the corporal paused, calculating on his fingers—"oh, about twenty minutes before the Second Coming."

Everybody laughed. Everybody pretended what Andersen had said was only funny, not the gospel truth. Specs Peterson liked an argument as well as the next guy, and wasn't shy about arguing with his superiors, but he didn't say boo. He just made sure he had the full load of grenades everybody was supposed to carry over the top.

Darkness fell. This sector of the front had been pretty quiet lately. Every so often, a rifle shot would ring out or somebody on one side or the other would spray the foe's trenches with a couple of belts of machine-gun fire, but the artillery didn't add its thunder to the hailstorm effects from both sides' small arms. Martin knew that wouldn't last. He rolled himself in his blanket and got what sleep he could. He wouldn't be sleeping much tomorrow, not unless he slept forever.

At 0200, the barrage began. Martin didn't sleep any more after that; the noise, he thought, was plenty to wake half the smashed-up dead whose corpses manured the Roanoke River valley.

Some of his men, though, did their damnedest to sleep right through the bombardment. He made sure everybody was up and ready to move. "Listen, this is my neck we're talking about, Earnshaw," he growled to one yawning private. "If you're not there running alongside me, it's liable to mean some damn Reb gets a chance to draw a bead on me he wouldn't have had otherwise. You think I'm going to let that happen so you can sleep late, you're crazy."

Captain Wyatt was up and prowling the trench, too. "Where the hell are the barrels?" he said about half past three. "They were supposed to be here at 0300. Without them, we don't have a show."

That wasn't quite true. The infantry, no doubt, would assault the Confederate lines with or without barrels. Without them, the foot soldiers were sure to be slaughtered. With them, they were . . . less sure to be slaughtered.

Two barrels came rumbling up at 0410. "Where the devil have you been?" Wyatt demanded, his voice a whiplash of anger. Chester Martin didn't say anything. This was the first time he'd actually seen barrels. Their great slabs of steel, spied mostly in silhouette, put him in mind of a cross between a battleship and a prehistoric monster.

"Sorry, sir," one of the men riding atop a barrel said through the unending thunder of the barrage and the flatulent snarl of the machines' engines. "We got lost about six times in spite of the tape, and we broke down a couple times, too."

"That's where *Bessie McCoy* is now," somebody else added. "The engine men said they thought they could get her running again, though."

Martin approached the barrel. "You fellows better get inside, if that's what you do," he said. "You're at the front now. The Rebs figure out you're here, a few machine-gun bursts and you won't be any more."

With obvious reluctance, the soldiers climbed down off the roofs of the barrels and into their places inside the contraptions. It had to be hotter than hell in there, and stinking of gasoline fumes, too. Maybe the steel kept bullets out, but it kept other things in.

Bessie McCoy limped into place at 0445, fifteen minutes before the attack was due to start. As twilight brightened toward dawn, Martin made out the names painted on the other barrels: *Vengeance* and *Halfmoon*, the latter with an outhouse under the word. He still didn't know whether to be encouraged all three barrels had made it or dismayed they'd had so much trouble doing it. If *dismayed* turned out to be the right answer, he figured he'd end up dead.

At 0500 on the dot, the barrage moved deeper into the Confederate trench system, to keep the Rebels from bringing up reinforcements. Captain Wyatt blew his whistle. The barrels rumbled forward at about walking pace, treads grinding and clanking. The cannon each one of them carried at its prow sent shells into the Confederate trenches.

From across no-man's-land, Chester Martin heard the shouts of fear and alarm the Rebs let out. Rebel rifles and machine guns opened up on the barrels. They might as well have been shooting at so many ambulatory boulders. Sedate but deadly, the barrels kept coming. They rolled through the U.S. barbed wire. They went down into shell holes and craters and came up the other side, still pounding the Rebel trenches. They flattened the Confederate barbed wire.

"Let's go, boys!" Captain Wyatt shouted. "That Bessie, she *is* the McCoy!"

Chester Martin and his squad scrambled out of the trench and sprinted toward the Confederate lines. Only light fire came their way; most of what the Rebs had was focused on the barrels. It wasn't doing much good, either. All three machines kept moving forward, firing not just cannon now but the machine guns on their sides, too.

Bessie McCoy rumbled up to the foremost Rebel trench and poured enfilading fire down its length. *Vengeance* and *Halfmoon* were only a few yards behind. *Vengeance* went right over that first trench and positioned itself to enfilade the second. *Half-moon* blazed away at Confederate soldiers who were—Martin rubbed his eyes to make sure he saw straight—running for their lives.

Half a mile to the north, a couple of more barrels had forced their way into the Confederate position. Half a mile to the south, two others had done the same, though a third sat burning in the middle of no-man's-land.

Martin noticed the other barrels only peripherally. He scrambled over the parapet and leaped down into the Confederate trenches. A lot of men in butternut lay in them, some moving, some not. He threw a grenade over the top into a traverse and then dashed into it, ready to shoot or bayonet whomever he'd stunned.

"Don't kill us, Yank!" several men cried at once. They threw down their rifles and threw up their hands. "We give up!"

"Go on back there, then," Martin growled, pointing toward the U.S. position from which he'd come. The new-caught prisoners babbled thanks and obeyed.

"What are those horrible things?" one of them asked, pointing toward the barrels, which were systematically raking trench line after trench line, concentrating most of all on machine-gun nests.

"I think," Martin said, "I think they're called victory."

All along the line, Rebs were giving up in numbers greater than he ever remembered seeing, and they were running away, too, unwilling to die to no purpose trying to halt the invincible barrels. In all the time he'd spent at the front line, he'd never seen Confederate soldiers run like that. He'd dreamt of it, but he'd never seen it.

Paul Andersen shouted another word of which he'd dreamt: "Breakthrough!"

For much of the rest of that morning, Martin thought his buddy was right. They stormed through the Confederate trench system. Whenever a machine gun or some holdouts in a strong position gave them trouble, one barrel or another waddled over to it and poured bullets or shells into it until the diehards either surrendered or died.

"I don't believe it," Captain Wyatt said, over and over. "We've come a good mile since daybreak." No wonder he sounded disbelieving; on this front, mobility was more often measured in yards. "We keep it up, we'll be out of the trenches and into their rear by nightfall."

"Yes, sir," Martin said. He had trouble believing it, too. A deep-throated rumble behind him made him turn his head. "Here comes *Bessie McCoy*, over another trench."

The barrel, by then, had crossed so many of them that he'd come to take its ability for granted. The lip of this one, though, was soft and muddy, and gave way under the weight of the massive machine. It went into the trench at an awkward, nose-down angle. Martin saw at a glance that it couldn't move forward any more. Its engine roared as it tried reverse. That didn't help, either.

One of the side machine-gunners opened up a hatch and shouted, "We're stuck! You're going to have to dig us out if you want us to keep moving." More hatches opened, and barrel crewmen came out to help with the digging and to escape the heat and fumes in which they'd been trapped for hours. Some of them simply sprawled in the dirt and sucked in great long breaths of fresh air.

Now Captain Wyatt looked worried. "That's the second barrel we've lost. *Halfmoon* broke down back there, and they still haven't been able to get it going again. If anything happens to *Vengeance*—"

The barrel in question fired its cannon. The men who'd pushed farthest into the Confederate works started shooting, too, and kept it up even though not much answering fire came back. Martin stuck his head up to see why everybody was excited.

Here came a battery of those cursed Confederate quick-firing three-inch guns. They sensibly stopped outside of rifle range, in such cover as they could find, and started firing over open sights at *Vengeance*. The barrel returned fire, but it had only one cannon, and that far slower between rounds than the Rebel pieces. *Vengeance* was armored against rifle and machine-gun bullets, but not against shells. If you let a sledgehammer fall onto an iron floor from a building a hundred stories high, you might get a noise like the one the shells made slamming into armor plate.

Vengeance started burning. Hatches popped open. Crewmen dove out. The Confederate guns shelled them, too. Rebel yells announced the arrival of reinforcements for the enemy. Now U.S. troops, thin on the ground and without barrels to support them, were the ones who had to fall back. *Bessie McCoy*'s crew salvaged her guns and set her afire to deny her to the Confederates, then joined the retreat.

When night fell, Martin was still in what had been Confederate trenches, but not very far in; the Rebs had taken back about two-thirds of what they'd lost in the morning. He turned to Paul Andersen and let out a long, weary sigh. "Not quite a breakthrough."

"No, I guess not," Andersen allowed. "We got more work to do." He started rolling a cigarette. "Not quite a breakthrough, but goddamn—you could see one from where we were."

"Yeah." Martin sighed again. "And I wonder how long it'll be before we see another one."

Arthur McGregor rode his wagon toward Rosenfeld, Manitoba. Maude sat on the seat beside him, her back ramrod straight, hands clasped tightly in her lap. They both wore seldom-used Sunday best; the wing collar and cravat seemed to be trying to strangle McGregor, who couldn't remember the last time he'd put on a jacket with lapels.

"Maybe we should have brought the girls," Maude said, her voice under tight rein. Only her mouth moved; she did not turn her head to look at her husband.

He shook his head. "No—better we left them with the Langdons." His own harshly carved face got harsher yet. "The Yanks won't take pity on us because we've got 'em along, Maude. Next Yank officer who knows what pity's about will be the first. If we're going to persuade them to let Alexander go, we'll have to make a case, like we were in court."

She nodded once, jerkily, and then sat still again. The wagon jounced on toward Rosenfeld. The ruts in the road didn't fit the width of the wheels any more; U.S. trucks had cut their own ruts. Outside of town, U.S. soldiers inspected the wagon as carefully as they had when the whole McGregor clan came into Rosenfeld the day Alexander was seized. Finding nothing, the soldiers let the wagon go on.

As usual these days, Yankees far outnumbered Canadians on Rosenfeld's few streets. Their traffic—wagons, trucks, a swarm of honking Fords—took priority over civilian vehicles, too. McGregor hitched the wagon as soon as he could, put a feed bag on the horse's head, and walked toward what had been the sheriff's office and jail but now confined not drunks and burglars but men guilty of nothing worse than wanting to be free of the smothering embrace of the United States.

Outside the entrance stood two armed sentries in green-gray. One of them patted down McGregor. The other spoke to Maude: "Come with me, ma'am. We have a woman next door to search you." When she made as if to balk, the sentry said, "Ma'am, if you aren't searched, you don't go in. Those are the orders I have, and I can't change 'em." Back quivering with indignation, she followed him.

"You aren't trying very hard to make friends for yourselves, are you?" McGregor said to the remaining sentry.

The fellow shrugged. "Better safe than sorry."

Maude returned in a couple of minutes, looking even more furious coming than she had going. She must have satisfied the searcher, though, for the sentries opened the door and stood aside to let her and her husband make their petition to the occupying authorities.

Captain Hannebrink sat at a desk, filling out forms. But for his uniform, he might have been a postmaster like Wilfred Rokeby, or perhaps a bank teller. But he'd seemed soldierly enough and to spare out at McGregor's farm. He set down his pen now and got to his feet. "Mr. and Mrs. McGregor," he said, polite enough even if his minions weren't.

"Good morning, Captain," Arthur McGregor said. He hated having to crawl before any man. He'd worked like a plow horse—he'd worked harder than his plow horse—before the war, but he'd been free.

No. He'd thought he'd been free. It was just that the government—the government he'd frequently despised—had held trouble at arm's length from him. Then it couldn't do that any more, and the regime under which he now lived made trouble as close as a punch in the eye.

He might not have crawled for himself. For Alexander, for his only son, he would crawl. What was pride worth, set against your boy? He began again: "Captain Hannebrink, sir, by now you must know Alexander didn't have anything to do with that bomb on the train tracks."

"I *must* know it?" The American officer shook his head. "Here, sit down, both of you. I'll hear what you have to say." The chairs to which he pointed were hard, angular, and functional: U.S. Army issue, as out of place in the office as his sharp American accent. He let Arthur McGregor do the fussing for his wife, accurately surmising she would not want him pushing the chair about for her. When she was as comfortable as she could be, he sat back down himself. "All right, tell me why I must know that."

"Because of what you done to the other boys you caught," McGregor blurted. His lips skinned back from his teeth in a snarl of anger at himself: he hadn't meant to say it like that. Saying it like that made him think about how harsh the occupying authorities really were.

Captain Hannebrink steepled his fingers. "The penalty for sabotage against the United States Army is death, Mr. McGregor," he said. "We have made that very plain. It cannot come as a surprise to anyone, not now."

"Boys," McGregor said thickly. "You shot boys."

"They were playing a man's game, I'm sorry to say. If they'd succeeded, what they would have done to our train would have been no different because they were young," Hannebrink said. "This way, perhaps, other boys here in Manitoba will come to understand that this is not a bully, romantic lark. This is a war, and will be waged as such."

He didn't look particularly fearsome. He was on the lean side, with sandy hair, mild gray eyes, and a long, thoughtful face. Only his uniform and his waxed Kaiser Wilhelm mustache said he wasn't a Canadian. Somehow, that very plainness made him more frightening, not less.

Licking his lips, Arthur McGregor said, "But you didn't shoot Alexander. That must mean you know he didn't have anything to do with it, because—" *Because if you had even the slightest suspicion, you would have dragged him out against a wall, given him a blindfold, and sent him home to me in a pine box for burial.* But he couldn't say that to the American.

"Your son's case is not clearcut: I admit as much," Hannebrink said. "It is possible he did not know about this particular explosive device." He held up one finger, as if expecting McGregor to interrupt. "Possible, I say. By no means proven. There appears to be no doubt he associated with these subversives and saboteurs."

"They're his *friends*," Maude McGregor burst out. "Captain, they're boys he's known as long as he's been on this earth. And besides, where in Canada will you find any boys that age who don't—"

Conversations with Captain Hannebrink had a way of breaking down in midsentence. This one should have broken down a few words sooner. Hannebrink fiddled with one point of that absurd, upjutting mustache, then finished for Maude: "Where will I find Canadian boys that age who don't despise the United States and everything they stand for? There are some, Mrs. McGregor, I assure you of that."

His matter-of-fact confidence was more chilling than bluster would have been. And Arthur McGregor feared he was right. Some people had to be on the winning side, no matter what, and the USA looked like the winning side right now. *Bootlickers,* McGregor thought.

But that did not help Alexander. McGregor said, "You can't blame him for what these others tried to do."

"Why can't I?" Hannebrink returned. "Canadian law recognizes the concepts of an accessory before the fact and of concealment of knowledge of a crime to be committed."

"You've never claimed you had anyone who said Alexander knew about this, only that he knew some of the boys you say did it," Arthur McGregor said stubbornly. "Is that enough to go on holding him?"

"Of course it is," Captain Hannebrink answered. "I assume anyone who consorts with saboteurs and says nothing about it either is a saboteur himself or wants to be one."

"You don't want reasons to let my boy go." Maude's voice went shrill. "You just want an excuse to keep him in an iron cage when he hasn't done anything."

Arthur McGregor set a big-knuckled, blunt-fingered hand on his wife's arm. "That doesn't help," he said mildly. If Maude lost her temper here, it wouldn't just be unfortunate. It would be disastrous.

Captain Hannebrink said, "Mrs. McGregor, I can understand how you feel, but—"

"Can you?" she said. "If we'd invaded your country and dragged your son away to jail, how would you feel?"

"Wretched, I'm sure," he answered, though he didn't sound as if he meant it. He went on, "Please let me finish the point I was trying to make. You still do not seem to fully understand the situation. You are in occupied territory, Mrs. McGregor. The military administration of the United States does not need any excuses to confine individuals. We have the authority to do it, and we have the power to do it."

Maude stared at him, as if she'd never imagined he would put it so baldly. And McGregor stared, too, catching as his wife had not quite done what lay behind the American captain's words. Hoarsely, he said, "You don't care whether Alexander had anything to do with that bomb or not. You're going to keep him locked up anyhow."

"I did not say that, Mr. McGregor."

"No, you didn't, Captain, did you? But you meant it, and that's worse, if you ask me." McGregor got to his feet. Maude rose with him, uncertainty on her face. He took no notice of it. He took no notice of anything but his contempt, and that was big as the world. "But then, what do you care what Canuck trash thinks? I'm sorry we wasted your time—and ours. I had chores I could have done instead of coming here." He walked out onto the street, Maude following.

Maybe Captain Hannebrink stared at his back. He didn't turn to see.

Nellie Semphroch was about to cross the street to visit Mr. Jacobs, the cobbler, when the guns started roaring north of Washington, D.C. As if drawn by a lodestone, her head turned in that direction. She nodded in slow, cold satisfaction. For a while, Washington had been too far south of the front line to let her hear much artillery fire. Then the rumble had been distant, like bad weather far away. Now it was guns, unmistakably guns, and louder, it seemed, every day.

A Confederate dispatch rider trotted past her, mounted on a bay gelding whose coat gleamed in the hot June sun. He tipped his slouch hat to her. Taken all in all, the Rebs *were* a polite lot. That made her distrust them more, not like them better.

Flies buzzed in the street as she crossed. She flapped with a hand to drive them away. There were fewer than there had been ten years before. Say what you would about motorcars, they didn't attract flies.

She opened the door to Mr. Jacobs' shop. The bell above it chimed. Jacobs looked up from the buttery-soft black cavalry boot to which he was fitting a new heel. The wrinkles on his face, which had been set in lines of concentration, rearranged themselves into a smile. "Good morning, Nellie," he said, setting down his little hammer and taking from the corner of his mouth a couple of brads that hadn't interfered with his speech at all. "It's good to see you today. It's good to see you any day."

"It's good to see you, too, Hal," she answered. She didn't view him with the relentless suspicion she aimed at most of the male half of the human race. For one thing, he was at least fifteen years older than she. For another, he'd never tried to get out of line with her. Up till the year before, they hadn't even called each other by their Christian names.

"Would you like some lemonade?" he asked. "I made it myself." He sounded proud of that. He'd been a widower for a good many years, and took pride in everything he did for himself.

"I'd love some, thank you," Nellie said. He went into the back room and brought it out in a tumbler that didn't match the one sitting by his last. Nellie sipped. She raised an eyebrow. "It's very good lemonade." And it was—tart and sweet and cool and full of pulp.

"For which I thank you," he answered, dipping his head in what was almost a bow. His courtly, antique manners were another reason why he set off no fire bells of alarm in her mind. "I am going to fill my glass again. Would you like another?"

"Half a glass," she answered. "I had a cup of coffee a couple of minutes before I came over here."

"Did you?" He chuckled. "Drinking up your own profits, eh?" He went into the back room again, returning with his glass full and Nellie's, as she'd asked, something less than that. After giving it to her, he asked, "And what do you hear in the coffee-house these days?"

Before Nellie could reply, a young Confederate lieutenant came in, picked up his boots, and bustled out again without looking at her once. That suited her fine. Once he was gone, she answered the question that had sounded casual but wasn't: "They've been talking about strengthening the bridges over the Potomac. I don't know why. It can't be for anything really important: they keep going on about barrels and tanks, not guns or trucks or wagons. Maybe they're bringing beer up for their men."

"Maybe they are. It would be fine if they were." Jacobs muttered something his bushy gray mustache swallowed. Aloud, he said, "Anything you hear about tanks and barrels would be—interesting."

"All right." Nellie knew he wasn't going to tell her anything more than that. Ignorance was her best protection, though she already knew too many secrets, guilty and otherwise. But Jacobs had connections—about most of which she was also ignorant—back to the U.S. government, whereas she was no more than one of his sources of news. She assumed that meant he knew how to run his business.

Another Confederate officer came in: the owner of the boot on which the cobbler was working. The fellow glowered. "You said that was going to be ready today," he growled.

"So I did, sir," Jacobs answered. "And it will be. I didn't say it would be ready first thing in the morning, though."

"As soon as you can," the Reb said. "My unit is heading north this afternoon, and I want these boots."

"I'll do all I can," Jacobs said. "If you come back about half-past eleven, this one should be all fixed up." Shaking his head unhappily, the Confederate left. Nellie would have bet Hal Jacobs knew to which unit he belonged, and that the information about its movements would soon be in U.S. hands. And Jacobs had his own way of harassing the enemy: "Won't it be a shame when some of the nails I put in go through the sole and poke the bottom of his foot? What a pity—he's made me hurry the job."

The bell rang again. Nellie wondered if it was the Reb, too impatient to wait for eleven-thirty. It wasn't. It was Edna. That meant something was wrong. Except for a couple of times to get shoes fixed, Edna didn't come in here.

"Ma," Edna said without preamble, "there's a Rebel major over across the street, says he's got to talk to you right now."

"You go tell him I'll be right there," Nellie said. When Edna had gone, she gave Mr. Jacobs a stricken glance. "What do I do now?"

"It depends on what he wants," replied the cobbler who wasn't only a cobbler. "I know you will do your best, come what may. Whatever happens, remember that you have more friends than you know."

Cold comfort. Nellie nodded, composed herself, and went back across the street. The major was waiting for her outside the coffeehouse, which she did not take as a good sign. When she first came up to him, he said, "Mrs. Semphroch, you are acquainted with William Gustavus Reach." It was not a question. She wished it had been.

"Yes, I know him some," she said through ice in her belly so cold, she thought it would leave her too frozen to speak at all. Part of it was fear for herself, part fear for Mr. Jacobs, and part, maybe the biggest part, fear of what Edna, standing not five feet away, would hear and learn. "He came by this place every so often." She made her lip curl. "Last time he came by, he was trying to steal things when they dropped bombs on us that night."

"The acquaintance goes back no farther than that?" The Confederate major was one of those smart men who think themselves even smarter than they are. How much did he know? How much had Reach spilled? How much could she say without spilling more to Edna?

She picked her words with care, doing her best to sound careless: "I knew him a long time ago, a little, you might say, but I hadn't set eyes on him from before my daughter here was born till he showed up again." That was all true, every word of it; it helped steady her.

"Uh-*huh*." The Reb looked down at his notebook. "You are not, and never have been, his wife?"

Edna stared at Nellie. Nellie stared, too, in astonishment commingled with relief. Maybe she'd come out of this in one piece after all. "I hope to Jesus I'm not," she exclaimed—more truth. "I hope to Jesus I never was, and I surely hope to Jesus I never will be! If I never see him again in all my born days, it'll be too soon."

"Uh-*huh*," the Confederate major said again. "Well, if you had been his wife and weren't any more, you might say the same thing, but I reckon—" He didn't say exactly what he reckoned, but it didn't seem like anything bad for Nellie. "Maybe you can tell me what sort of friends he has, then."

"Next friend of his I know about will be the first," Nellie said.

Edna giggled. The major started to smile, then stopped, as if remembering he was on duty. He said, "This here Reach tells more stories than Uncle Romulus, and that's a fact. Some of them, ma'am, we have to check." He chuckled. "We're going to send him to a place where nobody listens to his stories for a long, long time."

"If you think I'm going to miss him, Major, you can think again." Nellie sounded as prim and righteous as she did when taking the high line with Edna. The Rebel tipped his hat to her and went on his way.

"That wasn't so bad, Ma," Edna said. "Way he was asking after you, though, heaven only knew what he wanted."

"You're right," Nellie said. *You don't know how right you are*.

She went back across the street to the shoe-repair shop. The bell jangled. Mr. Jacobs looked up—warily—from his work. Her enormous smile said everything that needed saying. He set down the little hammer, came around the counter, and took both her hands in his. To her astonishment, she leaned forward and kissed him full on the mouth. She hadn't done that with a man since well before her husband died. His arms went around her, and he kissed her, too. She enjoyed it. That hadn't happened since well before her husband died, either.

"Some good out of Bill Reach after all," she murmured to herself.

Hal Jacobs stiffened. "Out of who?" he barked, his voice too loud, his mouth too near her ear. She explained, sure he'd misheard. He sagged away from her, his face pale as whitewash. "I wondered what was wrong," he gasped. "Hadn't heard from him in too long. Bill runs—ran, maybe—our whole organization here. And he's caught? Good God!"

"Good God!" Nellie said, too, for very different reasons. All at once, she wondered if she was backing the wrong side.

X

"Not much further now," Lucien Galtier told his horse as he rode up the fine American-paved road toward Rivière-du-Loup. In the back of the wagon, several hens clucked, but they were not a true part of the conversation. He and the horse had been discussing things for years. The hens' role, though they did not realize it, was strictly temporary.

Off to the east, perhaps a quarter of a mile away, a steam whistle shouted as a train hurried up toward the town. *"Tabernac,"* Galtier muttered under his breath: a Quebecois curse. The soldiers on the train, no doubt, would cross the St. Lawrence and then try to push on toward Quebec City. The Americans, worse luck, were making progress, too, for the artillery from the north bank of the river sounded farther off than it had when the campaign was new. The newspapers extolled every skirmish as one Bonaparte would have admired (clumsy propaganda, in a province that had never reconciled itself to the French Revolution), but anyone who believed all the newspapers said deserved nothing better than he got.

The whistle screamed again. The horse twitched his ears in annoyance. The chickens squawked and fluttered in their cages. No, they were not suited for serious talk—too flighty.

Cannon by the riverbank started going off—*wham, wham, wham!* The horse snorted. The chickens went crazy. Lucien Galtier raised a dark eyebrow. "Those are quick-firing guns," he told the horse, "the kind they use when trying to shoot down an aeroplane. And so—"

Through the cannons' roar, he picked up a rapidly swelling buzz. Then he spotted the winged shapes. Before the war, he had never seen an aeroplane. Here, now, were two at once, flying hardly higher than the treetops. They both carried blue-white-red roundels on their wings and flanks. The red was in the shape of a maple leaf.

"There, what did I yell you?" Lucien said to the horse. "And not just any aeroplanes, but Canadian aeroplanes." He reined in to watch.

In front of the pilots, machine guns hammered. He wondered how the men managed to fire through the propellers without shooting themselves down. However they did it, they shot up the troop train, spun in the air like circus acrobats, and then shot it up again. Then, still low, they streaked back toward the free side of the St. Lawrence.

Galtier expected the train to streak toward Rivière-du-Loup. Instead, it came to a ragged halt. Maybe the aeroplanes had killed the engineer, and the brakeman was doing what he did best. Maybe they had filled the boiler with so many holes, it was either kill the pressure inside or explode.

"It could even be—both," Galtier said, not altogether unhappily.

Soldiers started spilling out of the train. Some of them came running his way. He scowled and thought himself a fool for having stopped to watch the spectacle. But if he tried to leave now, those soldiers would not be pleased with him. And they had rifles.

"Frenchie! Hey, Frenchie!" they shouted as they got closer. "Bring your wagon on over here. We got wounded."

"Mauvais tabernac," Lucien snarled. No help for it, though. As he pulled the wagon off the road and bounced toward the track, he felt a curious mixture of joy at having the enemies of his country wounded and sorrow at having young men who had never personally done him wrong wounded.

The chickens did not approve of the rough ride he was giving them. "Be still, you fools," he told them, for the first time including them in his . . . He groped for a word. *In my salon,* he thought, pleased with himself. "This will keep you alive a little longer."

Ahead, soldiers in green-gray were sometimes helping out of the train, sometimes carrying from it other soldiers in green-gray extravagantly splashed with red. "How many can you hold?" a captain called to Lucien as he drew near. "Four, maybe five?"

"Yes, it could be," the farmer had replied. Exposure had improved his English—to a point. When he turned to indicate the chickens and their cages in the wagon bed, he was reduced to a helpless wave and a single word: "But—"

"Here." The American captain dug in a trouser pocket and tossed something to Galtier, who automatically caught it. "That ought to cover them." He looked down to see what he had: a twenty-dollar U.S. goldpiece.

He took off his hat in salute. *"Oui, monsieur. Merci, monsieur."* The American could simply have had the chickens thrown out onto the ground. He'd expected the *Boche americain* to do just that. Instead, the fellow had given him more than a fair price for them. Lucien jumped down and piled the cages in a wobbly pyramid, then hurried to help the Americans land their comrades in the space thus vacated. *A service for a service,* he thought.

"Here, pal," an unwounded U.S. soldier said. "Careful with Herb here. He's a damn good fellow, Herb is." As gently as he could, Lucien arranged the damn good fellow so he could sit against the side of the wagon. Herb had a rough bandage, rapidly soaking through with blood, on his right leg. He also had a streak of blood running down his chin from one corner of his mouth; he must have bitten through his lip against the pain.

The horse snorted and tried to shy, uneasy at the stink of blood. One of the American soldiers caught his head and eased him back toward something approaching calm. There was no earthly reason Americans should not be good with horses. Nonetheless, Lucien felt almost as betrayed as if his wife had been unfaithful with a man who wore green-gray.

"We came past a hospital back there, didn't we?" the captain asked. "I thought I saw it through the window."

"Yes, sir," Galtier answered. "It is, in fact, on my land." The American didn't notice the resentment with which he said that. Well, the fellow had paid him. One surprise of a day was plenty; with two, nothing would have seemed certain any more. In the memory of the one surprise, Galtier added, "And my daughter works as a nurse's helper there."

"I'm afraid we've given her more work to do," the captain said, to which Lucien could only nod. The wagon was already packed tight with wounded, some moaning, some ominously still. More lay on the ground. Their unhurt comrades were doing what they could for them, but most, obviously, had little skill.

Lucien pointed to the road. "There is an ambulance from the hospital. It goes to Rivière-du-Loup to pick up the blessed." The captain looked confused. Lucien realized he'd made a mistake, using a French word for an English one with the same sound but a different meaning. He corrected himself: "The wounded."

"He doesn't need to go that far, not now he doesn't," the captain said. Soldiers were waving to the ambulance. As Galtier had done before, it pulled off the road and came jouncing over the rough ground toward the tracks. The driver and his attendant scrambled out of the machine. The attendant shook his head. "What a mess," he said.

"Yeah." The ambulance driver scowled. He couldn't have been more than seventeen or so, not with that unlined face, but was dark and handsome and looked strong as a bull. "This is what you do. You die." He sounded world-weary beyond his years. "You do not know what it is about. You never have time to learn."

"Let's get 'em on the stretcher and into the bus," the attendant said.

"Yeah," the driver said again. But then he recognized Galtier. He nodded. "You are Nicole's father, *n'est-ce pas?*" His French was bad, but few Americans spoke any.

"Yes," Lucien answered. In spite of himself, he'd come to know some of the people at the hospital. "*Bonjour,* Ernest."

"Not a *bon jour* for them," the ambulance driver said. His broad shoulders—almost the shoulders of a prizefighter—went up and down in a shrug. "We will take them back. We will do what we can for them."

Up in Rivière-du-Loup and elsewhere along the St. Lawrence, the antiaircraft guns started banging away again. Lucien noticed that only in the back part of his mind till he heard the buzz of aeroplane engines.

"Jesus fucking Christ!" an American screamed—doubly a blasphemy for Galtier. Then the man in green-gray said something even worse: "Here they come again!"

Whether they were the same two aeroplanes or two others, Lucien never knew. All around him, soldiers scattered, some diving for cover under the halted train, others running as far away from it as they could. Lucien stood there, foolishly, as the machine guns began chewing up the dirt close by.

The pilots did not try to shoot up either his wagon or the ambulance near it. He was and remained convinced of that. But they were flying fast, and didn't miss by much. The captain who'd given him the goldpiece spun and toppled like someone with no bones at all, the top of his head shot off. Fresh cries of pain rose from every direction.

Roaring just above his head, the aeroplanes streaked away. A couple of Americans fired their rifles at them. It did no good. They were gone. Galtier looked around at carnage compounded.

A moan that stood out for anguish even among all the others made him turn his head. The young, strong ambulance driver lay beside the soldier he had been about to help. Now he was wounded, too. His hands clutched at himself. Lucien shivered and made the sign of the cross. Maybe, if God was kind, he had been wounded near there, but not *there*.

The ambulance attendant, whose name Galtier did not know, came over to him and the injured driver. "We're going to have to bandage that and get him back to the hospital," he said, to which Lucien could only nod. The attendant stooped beside the driver. "Come on, kid, you got to let me see that."

In the end, Lucien had to hold the fellow's hands away from the wound while the attendant worked. The driver writhed and fought. He wasn't altogether conscious, but he was, as he looked, strong as the devil. Hanging onto his hands turned into something just short of a wrestling match.

Lucien hadn't intended to look as the attendant cleaned and bandaged the wound. But his eyes, drawn by some horrid fascination of their own, went to it. He winced and wanted to cross himself again. *There,* indeed.

He and the attendant got the driver into the back of the ambulance with another wounded man. "Thanks for the help," the attendant said.

"Not at all." Galtier hesitated. "With this bl—*wound*—do you think he can—? Will he be able to—?" He ran out of English and nerve at the same time.

"If he's lucky," the attendant said, understanding him anyhow, "if he's real lucky, mind, he'll be able to *just* do it." He climbed into the ambulance and drove it back toward the hospital. Galtier followed at his necessarily slower pace. He said nothing at all to the horse.

Klaxons hooted, everywhere on the *Dakota*. Sam Carsten threw his mop into a bucket and ran for his battle station. He'd expected the call even before the battleship fished its aeroplane out of the waters of the Pacific. Officers had been bustling around with the look that said they knew something he didn't. The aeroplane must have spotted something out there ahead of the fleet and sent word back by wireless.

And, out here south and west of the Sandwich Islands, the only thing to spot was the enemy. "The limeys!" Carsten gasped to Hiram Kidde when he ducked into the forwardmost starboard five-inch gun sponson.

"Them or the Japs," Kidde agreed. The gunner's mate rubbed his chin. "Taken 'em damn near two years, but they finally figured they could come out and play with the big boys. Now we got to show 'em they made a mistake, on account of if we don't, the Sandwich Islands are up for grabs again." He'd been in the Navy his whole adult life. He might not have been able to order units around like an admiral, but he had no trouble figuring out the way tactics led into strategy.

Lieutenant Commander Grady stuck his head into the sponson. "All present and accounted for?" asked the commander of the starboard-side secondary armament.

"Yes, sir," Kidde answered. "Loader"—he nodded at Carsten—"gun layers, shell jerkers, we're all here. Uh, sir, who are we fighting?"

Grady grinned. "Looks like one hellacious fleet of British battleships over the horizon," he answered, "along with all their smaller friends. I don't expect they sailed out of Singapore just to pay their respects." His face clouded. "By what the pilots say, they're at least as big a force as we are. They're playing for keeps, no doubt about it."

"So are we, sir," Kidde said. "We'll be ready." Grady nodded and hurried away, his shoes ringing off the steel of the deck.

"We don't have the whole Sandwich Islands fleet out here on

patrol with us," Carsten said unhappily. "If the limeys smash us up and push past us—"

Kidde shrugged. "Chance you take when you join the Navy. If they smash us up and push past us, thing we have to make sure of is that we do some smashing of our own."

The sponson had only small vision slits for laying the gun. Even those had armored visors to protect against shell splinters in action. The visors were up now. Carsten looked out through one of the slits as the *Dakota* swung into a long, sweeping turn. The patrolling fleet was going into battle formation, the line of half a dozen battleships anchoring it, with smaller, swifter cruisers and destroyers supporting and screening them.

He felt a rumble through the soles of his feet. "That's the big turrets moving," he said unnecessarily.

Luke Hoskins, one of the shell-jerkers, made an equally unnecessary comment: "They've spotted the limeys, then." He already had his shirt off against the exertions that were to come. Even now, with him doing nothing, sweat gleamed on his muscle-etched torso.

Carsten peered through the vision slit again, looking for smoke on the horizon. He saw none, but the fire director for the main armament, up in the armored crow's nest, enjoyed—if that was the word—a view far better than his.

All at once, a great column of water fountained up into the sky, about half a mile from the *Dakota*. Sam might not have been able to see the British ships, but the director surely could, because they could see him. "Hell of a big splash," he said. That wasn't surprising, either: at a range like this, only a battleship's big guns had a chance of hitting.

A moment later, the *Dakota*'s main armament salvoed in reply. The noise was like the end of the world. "Here we go," Hiram Kidde said. He sounded, if not happy, at peace with himself and with the world. He was getting ready to do the job he did better than anything else in the world.

"Odds are, we're gonna sit here with our thumbs up our asses all day long, too," Hoskins grumbled. "Anybody think we're gonna get close enough to the limeys to really use secondary guns?"

"Listen, if we could sink 'em from a hundred miles away and they never came close to hitting us, I'd be happy as a clam,"

Carsten said. Nobody in the hot, crowded sponson argued with him.

In a thoughtful voice, Kidde said, "That wasn't a broadside we fired at the limeys, just the forward turrets. We'd better swing"— and sure enough, the *Dakota* was again heeling through the water in another turn—"or they'll cross the T on us at a range short enough to hurt us bad."

Carsten grimaced, and he wasn't the only one. If the enemy crossed your path and fired broadsides at you while you could answer only with your forward guns, he was sending you twice the weight of metal you were giving back. Every admiral dreamt of crossing the T, and every one had nightmares about its being crossed on him.

More splashes rose, these closer to the *Dakota*. If somebody dropped an elephant into the Pacific from a mile up, it might make a splash like that. Shrapnel rattled off the armored sides of the battleship. Carsten whistled softly. "Wouldn't care to be up on deck right now," he said.

The rest of the gun crew made noises showing they agreed. "Cap'n" Kidde said, "It's going to get worse before it gets better, too."

Nobody argued with that, either. "Hard standing around here," Carsten said, "waiting for something to happen or for us to get close enough to the limeys to shoot at them. I feel like I'm along for the ride, but I'm not doing anything to earn my keep."

He looked out through the vision slit again. Some of the cruisers had started firing their main armament: guns of a range not that much longer than those he served. His turn would come before too long.

And then, as he watched, one of the cruisers, the *Missoula*, took a direct hit from what had to be a battleship shell. Its turrets went up one after the other, like the most spectacular Fourth of July fireworks display he'd ever imagined. When, bare seconds after the hit, flame reached the main magazine, the whole ship exploded in a spectacular fireball. One of the cruiser's big guns hung suspended on top of the flames for what had to be close to half a minute. But when the flames and smoke finally cleared, only roiled water remained. Nothing else was left to show where six or seven hundred men had been—no boats, no wreckage, nothing.

"Jesus," Sam said, and looked away. Imagining the same thing happening to the *Dakota* was all too easy.

Kidde kept peering out of his slit. "You can see the limeys, all right," he said. "Won't be long now"—the same thought Carsten had had a minute or so earlier.

As the main armament thundered again, Lieutenant Commander Grady stuck his head in to say, "Pick your own targets, boys. Ship's movements will be to give the main armament the best possible firing opportunities. Us small fry down here, we have to take whatever we can find." He hurried off again.

Not much later, Kidde whooped with glee. "Sure as hell, that's a British cruiser out there," he said, pointing. He stared into the rangefinder and twiddled with the controls. "I make it about twelve thousand yards," he said, and shouted orders to the gun layers, who swung their cranks to shift the five-inch gun to bear on the foe. "Fire for effect!" the gunner's mate yelled.

Grunting, Luke Hoskins grabbed a heavy shell and passed it to Carsten, who slammed it into the breech, dogged it shut, and nodded to Kidde. The chief of the gun crew yanked the lanyard. The cannon roared and jerked. Cordite fumes filled the sponson.

"Short," Kidde announced, watching the splash, as Sam, coughing, got the casing out of the breech and threw it down to the deck with a clang. Pete Jonas, the other shell-jerker, passed him a new round. Ten seconds after the first one, it was on its way. No more than half a dozen rounds had gone out before Kidde whooped to announce a hit, and then another one.

And then another hit announced itself. It felt as if God had booted the *Dakota* right in the tail. All at once, she swerved sharply, and missed colliding with the next battleship in line, the *Idaho*, by what seemed bare inches. "What the hell—?" Pete Jonas burst out.

"We just lost our steering," Hiram Kidde said matter-of-factly. "Goddamn limeys got lucky." He looked out to see where they were headed, and his next words were much less calm: "Lord have mercy, we're steaming straight for the British line of battle."

Straight was not the operative word; the *Dakota* was swinging through an enormous circle. "Rudder must be jammed hard to port," Carsten said. "We've got to keep moving best way we can, though. If we're dead in the water, we're dead."

They passed a burning U.S. cruiser. Afterwards, Sam figured that did more good than harm: the fire that had been directed against the less heavily armored vessel now fell on the obviously out of control *Dakota*. At the time, it was a distinction he could have done without.

"What do we do if we get right in among 'em?" he asked, that being the worst thing he could think of.

"Sink," Kidde answered, which was very much to the point but not what Carsten wanted to hear. The gunner's mate added, "Hurt as many of 'em as bad as we can before we go down."

With nothing better to do, they kept firing as they spun within eight or nine thousand yards of the British line of battle. Smoke enveloped the enemy battleships: some the smoke of damage, more from the big guns the ships carried. Shells from those big guns and from the enemies' secondary armament rained down on the *Dakota*.

Sam lost count of how many times the ship was bracketed. Seawater from near misses rained down on her, too, and fragments pattering like deadly hail. And, every so often, she would shake when another shell struck home. Damage-control parties— everyone not serving a gun or the engines—dashed along the corridors, fighting fire and flood.

"Thank God, we're turning away," Kidde said, peering out through the vision slit. That meant that, for the time being, his gun didn't bear on the British fleet. *A chance to take it easy,* Carsten thought. But then the gunner's mate let out a hoarse, vile exclamation. "We got more ships bearin' down on us from the north." He stared at them, out there in the distance. His voice cracked in anger: "Those aren't limeys—they're Japs!"

"I don't care who they are," Luke Hoskins said. "We'll smash 'em up."

Methodically, as if they were a pair of machines, he and Pete Jonas took turns passing shells to Carsten. "Cap'n" Kidde yelled like a wild man when they started scoring hits on the Japanese. "The limeys, now, they're good," he said. "Till the slant-eyed boys messed with us, the only fight they ever picked was with Spain. Hey, I can lick my grandmother easy enough, too, but that don't mean I'm a tough guy."

Carsten heard that, but paid it little mind. He was a machine himself, a sweating machine coughing in the fume-laden air but doing his job with unthinking accuracy and perfection. Load, close, wait for the round to go, get rid of the case, load, close . . .

Shells kept falling around and sometimes on the *Dakota*. Were they British or Japanese? They didn't leave calling cards—not calling cards of that sort, anyhow. From not far away, Lieutenant Commander Grady screamed for sand to douse a fire. Nothing exploded, so Sam supposed the fire got doused. The guns in the turrets kept thundering away. So did all the weapons of the secondary armament that would bear on the foe.

"Christ on His cross," Kidde said, "we're going around through our own fleet again."

He was right. Carsten got glimpses of other ships with spouts from near misses splashing up around them and still others aflame. But the U.S. ships were shooting back, too; smoke from the guns, smoke from the fires, and smoke from the stacks all dimmed the bright sunshine of the tropical Pacific. "Are we winning or losing?" Sam asked.

"Damned if I know," "Cap'n" Kidde answered. "If we live and we make it back to Honolulu, we can find out in the papers." He barked laughter, then coughed harshly. "And if we don't live, what the hell difference does it make, anyway?"

Luke Hoskins came up with another good question: "We ever going to get this beast under control again? We've done one whole circle, just about, and now . . ."

With the five-inch gun screened from the enemy by the bulk of the ship, Sam took his place at a vision slit beside Hiram Kidde. He saw they'd come round behind most of the American fleet, and . . . He grimaced in dismay. "Looks like we're going to swing toward them again," he said.

Kidde whistled between his teeth. "It does, don't it? Well, that means the gun'll bear again. Get your ass back there, Sam. If they take us out, it ain't gonna be like we didn't give 'em something to remember us by."

"Yeah," Carsten said, and then, "You know, I wouldn't mind that much if they remembered some other guys instead." Pete Jonas handed him a shell. He slammed it into the breech.

*   *   *

Newsboys shouted their papers as Sylvia Enos walked from her apartment building to the trolley stop: "Battle of the Three Navies! Read all about it!" "Extra! USS *Dakota* in circle of death!" "American fleet crushes the Japs and limeys off Sandwich Islands!"

Sylvia paid her two cents and bought a *Boston Globe*. She read it on the way to the canning plant. As often seemed true in the war, the headlines screamed of victory while the stories that followed showed the headlines didn't know what they were talking about.

The U.S. fleet hadn't crushed those of the two enemy empires, any more than the German High Seas Fleet had crushed the Royal Navy in the North Sea the month before. The papers had shouted hosannas about that, too, till it became obvious that, even after the fight, the bulk of the German Navy couldn't break out to help the U.S. Atlantic Fleet against the British and the French and the Rebs.

In the Pacific, though, what seemed to be a drawn battle worked for the United States, not against them as it had on the other side of the world. Where the Germans hadn't been able to break out into the Atlantic, the British and Japanese hadn't been able to break in toward the Sandwich Islands, which remained firmly in American hands.

Though the *Globe* hadn't been the paper whose headlines screeched loudest about the *Dakota*, its account of the fight did prominently mention the battleship's double circuit straight into the guns of the opposing fleets. "The valiant vessel sustained twenty-nine hits," the reporter said, "nine definitely from the enemy's large-caliber guns, eleven definitely from smaller shells, and nine that might have come from either. Although drawing thirty-six feet of water at the end of the battle, as opposed to thirty-one at the outset, the *Dakota* and the heroes aboard her also inflicted heavy damage on the ships of the foe and, miraculously, suffered only fourteen killed and seventeen wounded, a tribute to her design, to her metal, and to the mettle of her crew."

Sylvia left the newspaper on the trolley seat when she got out and hurried over to the plant: let someone else have a free look. She'd wondered why the Navy, in its wisdom, had sent George to the Mississippi rather than the open sea. Now she thanked God for it. The *Dakota* had got off lightly as far as casualties were concerned, but what about the cruisers and destroyers and battleships that had gone to the bottom with all hands, or near enough to make no difference?

Going down with all hands could happen to a monitor, too. Sylvia made herself not think about that. Coming up the street toward the factory was Isabella Antonelli. Sylvia waved to her friend. "Good morning," she called.

"Good morning," Mrs. Antonelli answered. Seeing her, though, did not take Sylvia's mind as far away from the war as she would have liked. Isabella Antonelli wore black from head to foot, with a black veil coming down from her hat over her face. In her imperfect English, she said, "All this talk of the big Navy fight, I think of you, I think of your husband, I pray he is all right—" She crossed herself.

"He's fine, yes. He wasn't anywhere near this fight out on the ocean, thank God," Sylvia said.

"Thank God, yes," Mrs. Antonelli said. They walked into the plant and punched their time cards together. As Sylvia did whenever she talked about the war with her friend, she felt faintly guilty that George still lived while Mr. Antonelli had met a bullet or a shell somewhere up in Quebec. The black-bordered casualty lists the papers printed every day showed how easily it could have been the other way round.

She welcomed the mesmerizing monotony of the line that sent cans into her labeling machine and then out again. If she concentrated on the work, she didn't have to think about the war—although she wouldn't have been here without the war. She would have been at home with George, Jr., and Mary Jane.

Was what she had now better or worse? Having George away—and in harm's way—tipped the balance, of course. Suppose George were home—or home as often as he was when he went out on his fishing runs. What then? The children sometimes drove her mad. Even so, she missed them fiercely every moment she was away from them.

Mr. Winter came limping down the line to see how things were going. He smiled at her. She nodded back.

"Good morning, Mrs. Enos," the foreman said, smiling to show off his bad teeth. "How are you this morning? Your husband wasn't in the big battle the papers are talking about, I hope?"

"I'm fine, thank you, Mr. Winter," she answered. "My husband, too, so far as I know. He's on the Mississippi, not in the Pacific."

"That's right, you told me. I just remembered he was in the Navy, is all." Winter shook his head in chagrin, whether real or put on she couldn't tell. Then he went back to business, which relieved her: "Machine behaving all right?"

"It seems to be, yes." With someone else, Sylvia might have joked that saying it was working well would make it break down. The thought was in her mind, but she kept it there. The less she had to do with Mr. Winter outside of things that were strictly business, the better she liked it.

He nodded to her. "That's fine, then." With another nod, he headed over to the machine Isabella Antonelli ran. "Hello, 'Bella. How are you this morning?"

The paste reservoir on Sylvia's machine ran low just then. She had to bend down, pick up the bucket of thick white paste, and refill the reservoir, all without missing a beat on the three levers she had to pull for every can of mackerel feeding through to be labeled. While she was doing that, she felt like a juggler with too many balls in the air.

It also distracted her from the conversation the foreman and Isabella Antonelli were having. She couldn't have heard all of it anyhow, not over the unending clatter and rumble of the line that moved the cans ahead and the racket of the machines along the way, but she might have heard some. She wanted to hear some. She'd never noticed Mr. Winter using a shortened version of Isabella's name before. Did that mean he hadn't done it before, or that she hadn't noticed?

Like everyone else at the canning plant, Isabella Antonelli had taken off her hat when she started work. That was all the more necessary for her, what with the veil depending from the hat. Before heading toward the next machine on the line, Mr. Winter chucked her under the chin, said something Sylvia didn't catch, and made as if to kiss her on the cheek but didn't. He was laughing when he left her station.

Sylvia concentrated on her own machine with a fury whose

intensity startled her and was only made worse because it was so futile. She jerked the levers so hard, she jammed the machine, which shut down the whole line till she could clear it.

Mr. Winter came over at a limping trot. "Thought you said it was going good," he said. "You shut us down, it costs the owners money. They don't like that, Mrs. Enos. They don't like that even a little bit."

"I'm sorry," she lied. "It was behaving fine till a minute ago." She used a screwdriver to lever a tin can out of the works. "Let me just check." She pulled the lever that had started the trouble. It functioned smoothly now. "You can start things up again."

"All right." He gave her a grudging nod. "You fixed it fast enough, I will say that." Cans started flowing once more.

Restraining the anger she'd taken out on the labeling machine made her stomach hurt. She was glad when the lunch whistle blew. Picking up her dinner pail, she fell into step beside Isabella Antonelli. It was hot and muggy outside the factory building, and the view was only of another canning plant across the street, but that still meant cooler weather and a prettier prospect than inside.

They sat down on a bench. Sylvia had a fish sandwich—leftovers from the night before—and Mrs. Antonelli some sort of funny-shaped noodles in tomato sauce. After they'd eaten for a while, Sylvia asked, "Is he bothering you?"

"Who?" Isabella was intent on her food. They had only half an hour before they went back to work.

"Him. Mr. Winter. The foreman. I saw him, what he did this morning. That's not right." Remembering, Sylvia got angry all over again.

To her own mortification, a certain amount of relief accompanied the anger. *He's not bothering* me, *thank God,* was the nasty little thought somewhere near the bottom of her mind. Recognizing it for what it was only made her more furious, both at the foreman and at herself.

"Mr. Winter?" Isabella's eyes grew wide for a moment. Then, to Sylvia's surprise, she laughed. "Oh, that. No, that is nothing much. I do not worry about it. He is a lonely man, Mr. Winter. And I, now I am lonely, too." She set down her fork and touched the sleeve of the black dress.

"But—" Sylvia began. She stopped, not knowing how to go on. If, God forbid, something had happened to George, she wouldn't have been able to look at a man for years. She was sure of it. She was so sure of it, she hadn't imagined anyone else could be different.

Isabella Antonelli said, "I do not think anything will come of it. If anything does come of it, that would not be so bad." For a moment, she looked altogether pragmatic. "He is a Catholic. I have found out."

"Is he? Have you?" Sylvia didn't scratch her head, but she felt like it. The more you looked at the world, the more complicated it got.

The white man in the munitions plant hiring office scribbled something on the form in front of him, then looked across the table at Scipio. "Well, boy, you sound like you'll do," he said in the sharp accent typical of Columbia, South Carolina. "Why don't you let me have your passbook so we can get this here all settled right and proper?"

Scipio's heart leaped up into his throat. He'd expected the demand. No Negro in the CSA could have failed to expect the demand. Since the start of the war, things were supposed to have loosened up. That was how it had looked when he was the butler back at Marshlands, anyhow. God only knew what the aftermath of the rebellion had done toward tightening things again, though.

God knew, and he was about to find out. Donning what he hoped was an ingratiating smile, he said, "Ain't got none, suh. I used to, yes suh, but I plumb lost it in the ruction."

"I bet you did," the clerk said with a thin smile. "You talk like a nigger from further down on the Congaree—that right, Nero?"

"Yes, suh," Scipio said. Nero was one of the commonest names Negro men bore. He wondered what the white man—whose desk bore a little placard proclaiming him to be Mr. Staunton—would have thought had he suddenly started his other way of speaking. He didn't intend doing anything so foolish. Talking like an educated white might give him away and would surely get him tagged as uppity. He couldn't afford that, not if he wanted work.

"Let's see your hands," Staunton said suddenly. Trying not to show any reluctance, Scipio displayed them. That unpleasant smile flashed across the clerk's face again. "Not a field nigger—a house nigger, I reckon. And you don't have a passbook? My, my. What *were* you doing, these past few months?"

That hit too close to the center of the target. Scipio said, "A minute ago, suh, you says you wants to hire me. Now you talkin' like I was one o' dey bad niggers raise all de ruction." He wanted to flee. Only a well-founded suspicion that he wouldn't make it outside the door kept him standing where he was.

"Oh, I'll hire you," Staunton said. He lowered his voice. "For niggers without passbooks, though, we got a special arrangement. Have to get you a new book, right? Lots of patrollers around these days, that's a fact."

"Yes, suh," Scipio said again. Now he stood at ease once more. Staunton wasn't going to betray him, just shake him down. "How much I gots to pay you, git de new book?" He also spoke quietly.

"Ain't you a smart nigger?" By the way the clerk's pale eyes sparked, that was more warning than compliment. "Half your pay the first month," Staunton said, greed evidently overcoming suspicion. "End of the month, you be a good boy, you get yourself a book. Understand?"

"Yes, suh." The repetition was getting monotonous. Scipio let out a mournful sigh. "Not much left fo' me." At the start of the war, a dollar and a quarter a day would have been good money for a Negro, and half that survivable for a month. Wages and prices had gone up a good deal the past two years, though.

"Nigger without a passbook ain't gonna get a better deal no place else," Staunton said, and that, odds on, was true.

Scipio sighed again. He'd be drinking water and eating cornmeal mush for the next month, no two ways about it—and that with sleeping in the cheapest flophouse he could find. After Marshlands, even after the hectic life as part of the ruling council of the Congaree Socialist Republic, it had all the earmarks of a thoroughly joyless existence.

"God damn the Reds," he muttered. Nobody had bothered to listen to him, though he'd warned again and again that the uprising would lead only to disaster. Having acquired a fair smattering of a classical education at Marshlands, he found himself wishing Cassandra were a masculine name. He would have used it for an alias instead of Nero.

Mr. Staunton heard what he said, and interpreted it his own way. "God damn the Reds is right, Nero," he said. "Weren't for them, wouldn't hardly have to worry about passbooks at all, not the way things were going. We wanted bodies so bad, we didn't care. But now it's gonna cost you money to get fixed up right, on account of what they did. Too bad, boy." He spoke with the soppy condescension that seemed to be as close as a Confederate white could come to showing sympathy for a black.

"When do I start?" Scipio asked.

"Tomorrow morning, seven o'clock," the clerk answered. He shoved the form across the desk at Scipio and handed him a pen. "Put your mark right on the line here. We'll get you a time card made. Foreman'll punch it for you—you don't need to worry about pickin' it out. Just so you know to tell him, you're Nero number three."

Scipio placed an X on the line the clerk indicated. By what he saw of the form, his spelling and handwriting were considerably better than Staunton's. He didn't aim to show that. The less the white man knew about him, the better he liked it.

But, even though he'd written an X, the way he'd taken the pen, as if his hand was accustomed to it, made the clerk's eyes narrow. "House nigger," Staunton said, half to himself. "You read and write some, don't you, boy?"

"Some, yes, suh," Scipio answered cautiously. Damn it, why couldn't he have dealt with a dull, bored white clerk rather than an alert, grasping one?

But Staunton visibly decided not to make an issue of it. "Go on, get out of here," he said. "You ain't here at seven sharp tomorrow, don't ever come round again, neither." He pushed his chair back from his desk and swiveled so he could put Scipio's paperwork in a file cabinet. That was the first time the Negro had the chance to see his right leg was missing from halfway down the thigh.

After that, Scipio got out of there in a hurry. He had a couple of dollars in his pocket, from odd jobs he'd done on farms and in little towns before he decided the big city was safer. As he walked along Columbia's busy streets, he wondered if he'd made a mistake.

Probably not, he decided. Negroes were on the streets, and a lot of them looked as ragged as he did. Soldiers tramped along the streets, too, some of them regulars in butternut, some re-called militia in old-fashioned gray that made them look like policemen. They didn't seem to be checking blacks' papers, just showing themselves to keep trouble from breaking out.

Columbia had seen trouble during the Red insurrections. It was a city of fine and stately homes and shops, many of them dating from before the War of Secession. Here and there, a block would have a house missing, like a man with a missing front tooth. A couple of places in town, whole blocks were missing, even the rubble cleared away. The Negroes might have lost, but they'd put up a fight.

Much good it did them, Scipio thought gloomily. He ducked into a store whose sign forthrightly proclaimed CHEAP CLOTHES and bought a pair of dungarees and a couple of collarless cotton shirts. He wouldn't be able to afford any new clothes for the next month, not on sixty-two and a half cents a day he wouldn't.

A bowl of thin stew cost him another fifteen cents, and a mat-tress in a tiny, airless cubicle a quarter on top of that. He was left with the munificent sum of half a dollar with which to face the world. It was Wednesday night. Payday would be Friday. He had enough for a bed tomorrow night, and for some bread or mush to keep the hole in his belly from getting any worse. Sighing, he tried to sleep.

On that uncomfortable bed, in that uncomfortable roomlet, waking up in time to be at the munitions plant was not the problem. Sleeping at all before then was. When dawn began showing through the small, rectangular window that wouldn't open, he gave up, put on the dungarees and one of the shirts he'd bought the evening before, and then discovered he had to pay the flophouse proprietor a dime to watch the clothes he had left so they'd be there when he got back. *Day-old bread,* he thought, and sighed again.

"Nero number three, eh? All right, you're on time, boy," the foreman said when he got to the factory: grudging approval, but approval. The white man punched his card into the clock, then took him back into the factory. "They stack the crates of empty shells *here*, at the end of this line," the fellow said, pointing. "You haul 'em over *there*, where they pick 'em up to be filled. You got that?"

"Yes, suh," Scipio said. Several crates already stood there. "I do 'em one at a time by hand, suh?"

" 'Less you got a servant to do 'em for you, that's what you do, by Jesus," the foreman said. "I wanted me a butler, I'd've hired a nigger wearin' different clothes." He laughed at his own joke.

Scipio, luckily, managed to keep his face straight. "Don't mind workin', suh," he said. "Ain't what I mean. Jus' thinkin' that, you give me a hand truck, I could do mo' work in de same time."

The foreman laughed again. "First time I ever heard of a nigger wanting to do *more* work, 'stead of less." He rubbed his chin. "It ain't the worst idea I ever heard, though. Tell you what—you do it this way for today. We'll see what happens tomorrow. I got to talk with a couple people first." ·

"Yes, suh," Scipio said again. *If they think it's a good idea, I'm going to take the credit for it,* was what the white man meant. Scipio couldn't do anything about that. He strode over to the crates, picked one up, and carried it to where the foreman had told him to put it.

It was heavy. The rough wood bit into his hands. The edge of the crate struck his thighs halfway between knee and hip. He'd be bruised there by evening—hell, he'd be bruised there by noon. He walked back and got another crate. The foreman nodded, satisfied, and went back to supervising check-in.

A Negro in good, well-made work clothes picked up the crate Scipio had set down. The two black man stared at each other. Scipio spoke first. He had to speak first, before the other man used his true name. "How you is, Jonah?" he said. "You 'member ol' Nero, eh?"

Jonah had been a field hand at Marshlands. He and his woman had gone into Columbia looking for factory work not long after the war started, and not even Anne Colleton had been able to get them back. "Nero," he said now, after a brief, thoughtful pause. "Yeah, I 'member you good, Nero. So now we is workin' together again, is we?"

"Dis world a small place," Scipio said solemnly. He wished it hadn't been quite so small. If Jonah felt like betraying him, he could. They'd got on well enough at the plantation, but there was always the distinction between house nigger and field nigger. And Jonah might well have heard of the role he'd played in the Congaree Socialist Republic. If, like a good many Negroes, he disapproved of the uprising . . .

Then Jonah smiled and said, "You come home fo' supper wid me tonight, Nero. Letitia, she glad to see an ol' friend."

"T'ank you," Scipio said. "I do dat." It would get him fed and let him save what little money he had left. And it meant—Lord, how he hoped it meant!—Jonah wasn't going to turn him in to the Confederate authorities. He picked up another clanking crate of shell casings. It hardly seemed to weigh a thing.

The hall was packed. The hot, muggy air would have been thick enough to slice even had it been empty. A small, forlorn electric fan did overmatched battle against the heat of too many bodies, against the fact that a lot of those bodies hadn't bathed quite so recently as they might have, and against enough cigar, cigarette, and pipe smoke to make Flora Hamburger think of poison gas.

Coughing a little, she turned to Maria Tresca. "They've come out, no two ways about it," she said.

Maria nodded. "That works for you, not against you," she said. "The regulars would sooner see Herman Bruck with the nomination, even after Remembrance Day." She sniffed; the smoky air turned the sniff into a cough louder than Flora's. "They're reactionaries, that's what they are. How can they be reactionaries and Socialists at the same time? My sister Angelina never was."

"When they think of it, they're progressive," Flora said with a shrug. "You have to think about your ideology; if you don't think about it, you haven't got one. But if you don't think about your social attitudes, it's not that you don't have any, it's just that yours are the same as your neighbor's." She sighed. "And if your neighbors are petty bourgeoisie and proletarians who aspire to the petty bourgeoisie—"

Maria Tresca's face darkened into a frown. "In that case, they might as well be Democrats."

"No." Flora shook her head. "That's not the problem. The problem is making them think about social issues. When they do think instead of feeling, they're sound enough. They have to stop taking those concerns for granted, that's all."

"Or else the revolution, when it comes, will sweep them away with it," Maria said. "Sometimes I think you're too gentle, Flora. My sister was the same way, and look what it got her." Angelina Tresca had died in the Remembrance Day riots the year before. "If they cannot adapt, they deserve to be swept away." Maria was as full of revolutionary consciousness as anyone Flora knew: frighteningly full sometimes.

"Sometimes the uprising comes too soon," Flora said. "Look at the Confederacy. The proletariat failed there—nothing but banditry left now."

"Race mystified the white proletarians, splitting the laboring class," Maria returned. "That won't happen here in the United States. When the workers rise up against the trusts and the capitalists, they'll all rise together and overthrow the rotten system." She sounded messianically certain.

Up on the platform at the front of the hall, the chairman rapped loudly for order. Slowly, Saul Masliansky got some small semblance of it. When it didn't come fast enough to suit him, he rapped again, this time as if firing a gun. "Be quiet, there!" he shouted, first in Yiddish, then in English. "Do you want to caucus, or do you just want to talk?"

"With this crowd, that's about even money," Flora said with a smile.

"You should have accepted somebody besides Masliansky," Maria Tresca said, not smiling back. "He favors Herman."

"I know. Everyone who could chair this caucus favors Herman, as far as I can tell," Flora answered. "But Saul is honest. When he sees what the people want, he won't thwart them."

"Ha!" Maria said darkly. "He's assistant editor for the *Daily Forward*. He's going to go right on favoring Bruck, because Herman got everything he knows about Socialism straight out of the newspaper."

That was so unfair, and at the same time so delicious, that Flora couldn't help giggling. She'd expected to be too nervous here to see straight, let alone to speak well, and now she wasn't any more. She hoped the delightful, flighty feeling would last. "He's honest," she said again. "I've seen him admit he's wrong.

How many others who might have done the job can you say that about?"

"We're not going to have a caucus if you people can't keep quiet," Saul Masliansky said, like a schoolteacher confronting a classroom full of hooligans. He didn't look like a teacher, or like an editor, either. With an embroidered vest and a high, pale forehead, what he looked like was a professional gambler. He played his trump card with the air of a gambler pulling an ace out of his sleeve, too: "Do you want to hear the candidates? We've agreed we're all going to support whichever one we choose, so picking the better one strikes me as a pretty good idea. Anybody who thinks different can go outside to talk."

"Anyone who thinks different can *geh in drerd*," Maria Tresca said. Flora laughed again. Maria had acquired an excellent, often scurrilous command of Yiddish.

"Mr. Chairman," somebody called, "I move that, when we pick, we pick by secret ballot."

"Second!" Herman Bruck shouted.

"You keep quiet," Masliansky barked at him. "Candidates aren't members of the caucus. You can't second. You talk to us, and that's all. Do I hear a *proper* second?" He did, a moment later. The motion passed on a voice vote.

Member or not, Flora shouted against it. "If you can't stand up and be counted at a caucus, when can you?" she demanded.

"You're right—and you're wrong," Maria said. "Herman thinks secrecy will work for him, but I think he's wrong. More people will go against the bigwigs if they aren't looking over their shoulders."

"Maybe," Flora said.

Saul Masliansky plied his gavel once more. "Will the contenders please come forward?" he said.

"There he goes, selling his paper again," some wit shouted, and got a laugh.

Flora made her way up to the platform. So did Herman Bruck, in a dark gray suit that shouted *respectability* at the world. Had Flora been respectable in the same sort of way, she wouldn't have presumed to seek the Congressional nomination in the first place.

Herman nodded to her. He took her more seriously than he had before her Remembrance Day speech, but not so seriously as he would have taken, say, Saul Masliansky. Masliansky, after all, was a man, not someone he'd pestered to go to the cinema with him.

The chairman said, "We tossed a coin to see who would talk to you when. Our esteemed comrade, Mr. Herman Bruck here, won the toss. He chose to speak first. Herman Bruck!"

"Friends, Myron Zuckerman gave our district the best years of his life," Bruck said, and won sympathetic applause from everyone who revered Zuckerman's memory—which meant from everyone in the hall. "I aim to go to Philadelphia to do my best to fill his shoes, to keep the Fourteenth Ward as it has been, at the forefront in the fight against the trusts, and, I hope—*alevai*—to work with the next president of the United States of America, Senator Eugene V. Debs of Indiana!"

The Socialists' national convention wouldn't come until next month, but Debs' nomination to face TR was a foregone conclusion. Again, Herman Bruck got loud cheers. Flora did her best not to let that worry her. He'd been applauded for invoking Zuckerman's name, and again for invoking that of Debs. She wondered when he'd say anything about himself that deserved cheers.

As far as she was concerned, he never did. That didn't mean he didn't get applause, only that he was breathtakingly conventional in every position he took. He might as well have said, *I agree with what all the other Socialists think,* half a dozen times and then sat down.

After a while—after what seemed to Flora a very long while—he did sit down. Saul Masliansky said, "And now, Miss Flora Hamburger will tell you why she thinks Herman Bruck has been talking nonsense for the past twenty minutes." He grinned at her.

It wasn't quite the introduction she'd expected, but it would serve. She could make it serve, though that meant junking the opening she'd worked out in advance. She decided to take the chance: "Herman Bruck doesn't talk nonsense. He's a good Socialist. If you choose him, I will support him—that's what the caucus is all about. But—"

She took a deep breath. "Herman Bruck is *safe*. Is being *safe* what the Socialist Party, the party of revolution, stands for? I don't think so. He tells you what we've done in the past. He tells you what he'll do in the future if you choose him as your candidate. The one is just the same as the other. If we elect people who will go on doing the same things, are we radicals or are we reactionaries?" The talk with Maria before she'd come up here was paying dividends—an alarmingly capitalistic thought for a would-be Socialist candidate.

"If you want life to go on as it always has, if you don't want to work for radical change in this country, if you don't want peace between us and our neighbors, you might as well vote for a Democrat. If you want to let Teddy Roosevelt know we don't intend to let war mean unending oppression of the proletariat, you'll choose me."

She embroidered on that theme for a while, then returned to the other: "As I say, Herman Bruck is a sound man. He is a safe man. I think he's sound and safe enough to lose this November. If you want someone to run hard and do everything she can to get this seat out of TR's clutches, you'll vote for me today and you'll vote for me again in the fall."

She stepped back. She thought she got as much applause as Herman Bruck had. More? She couldn't tell. Saul Masliansky said, "Now we fight it out. We have a waiting room for the two of you. We have two waiting rooms, in fact, if you'd rather—?"

"It's all right," Flora said. "We aren't enemies." Herman Bruck nodded.

They didn't say much to each other in the waiting room. Flora sat in a hard chair under one of the electric lamps hanging from the ceiling. Bruck smoked a cigarette, and another, and another. Through the closed door, Flora listened to the shouts from the caucus. She wished she were out there. She and Bruck weren't members, so she couldn't be.

After what seemed like forever, the door opened. She and Herman Bruck both sprang to their feet, facing Masliansky with the same eager anxiety fathers in a hospital maternity-ward waiting room showed when the doctor came in. But only one of them would get to keep this baby; like the one in the biblical story of Solomon, it was indivisible.

"*Mazeltov,* Flora," the caucus chairman said.

Bruck stubbed out his last cigarette under the heel of his gleaming shoe. "*Mazeltov,*" he echoed. "Anything I can do, you know I will." He managed a joke, something rare for him: "That's true, even though you won't go out with me."

"Thank you." Flora felt light-headed. "Talk like that more often, and I might. But now"—she could hardly believe it—"let's put this seat back where it belongs."

"I am godalmighty sick of troop trains," Jefferson Pinkard announced to anybody who would listen as the one on which he was riding rumbled west through Texas toward the front line, which lay somewhere east of Lubbock.

Nobody said anything. As best Jeff could tell, nobody had the energy to say anything. It was hot and muggy outside. That meant it was hotter and muggier on the train. Every window that would open was open. The breeze that came in was like the breath of hell, the occasional cinder or tiny bit of coal blowing in with the breeze only adding to the resemblance.

Pinkard looked outside. Texas, as far as he could see, was nothing but miles and miles of miles and miles. It had been green and lush when the troop train pounded out of Arkansas. Some of the men who sounded as if they knew what they were talking about said parts of it were as swampy and wet as Louisiana, full of alligators and who could say what all else.

This part of Texas wasn't like that. If God had taken an iron about the size of South Carolina and pressed everything here down flat, that might have given the countryside its look. It was as hot as if it had just been ironed, too. They called it prairie, but wasn't the prairie supposed to be green with grass? This was yellow at best, more often brown.

"I never left home till they conscripted me," Jeff went on after a while. "Way things look here, I ain't never going to leave again once the war's over, neither." He sighed. "Birmingham, now, Birmingham is green all the time. Even in winter, most of the grass stays green. Does it ever even get green here?"

"I don't know why you complain so much, *amigo*," Hip Rodriguez said from the seat behind him. "This land here, this is better than what I was farming."

"Better?" Pinkard awkwardly turned around to stare at the little Sonoran. "How in blazes could this be better than anything?"

"It is very easy." As Rodriguez made his points, he ticked

them off on his fingers. "It is good flat land, not mountains like where I come from. It has not so much *calor*—heat. It gets more water—you can see."

"Maybe *you* can see," Pinkard said stubbornly. "Looks dry as the desert the Israelites walked through to me."

Rodriguez laughed in his face. "You do not know what a desert is, if you call this a desert." Only two things kept Jeff from starting a fight then and there. One was that he was in the Army, so he'd get in trouble. The other was that he really didn't know what a desert was like. Next to Alabama land, what they had here was pretty appalling. He tried to picture in his mind the kind of land that would make west Texas look good.

Mountains he could imagine. But land that was hotter and drier than this? If this wasn't hell, that would have to be.

The train chugged to a stop outside a little town called Post. To Jeff Pinkard's jaundiced eye, the town, as they rolled through it, seemed as sunbaked and defeated as the country surrounding it. The wooden buildings hadn't been painted or whitewashed for years, and most of the timber was more nearly gray than brown or yellow. Even the bricks seemed faded from their proper, bright oranges.

When Pinkard, grunting and sweating under the weight of his kit, came out of the car in which he'd been ensconced so long and so uncomfortably, he heard artillery off in the distance. When he'd been fighting the Negroes of the Black Belt Socialist Republic, that had been an encouraging sound: his side had the guns, and the enemy didn't. It wasn't going to be like that here.

Captain Connolly addressed the formed-up company: "We are going to stop the damnyankees, men. Not only are we going to stop them, we are going to throw them back into New Mexico where they belong." That got a few yips and cheers from the men, but not many. It was too hot. They were too tired.

Connolly went on, "This isn't going to be the kind of fighting they have on the other side of the Mississippi. Too many miles for that, and not enough men filling them. If we dig trenches, they go around, and the same the other way. Not a lot of railroads around here, either. Nobody can keep big armies supplied away from the tracks. So we're going to drive the Yankees back toward Lubbock, and we are going to have detachments out to make sure they don't get around us while we're doing it. That last is what the particular task of this company will be. Any questions?"

Nobody said anything. The captain didn't even give the order to march. He just started marching, and the men followed: not only the company, but a couple of regiments' worth. Pinkard and his companions were somewhere in the middle of the column. The dust was of a slightly redder shade than the butternut of his uniform. It got in his nose. It got in his eyes. It got in his mouth, so his teeth crunched whenever they came together.

He wasn't sure whether this had been a road before the war started. It was a road now, a road defined by marching men and by the ruts of wagons and those of motor trucks. It led to a bridge over a river that didn't look wide or deep enough to need bridging.

"If that poor thing was in Alabama," he said to Stinky Salley, "they'd ship it back to its mama, on account of it's too little to show itself in public."

"We're not in Alabama any more," Salley replied with his usual annoying precision. "Or maybe you hadn't noticed."

"Oh, put a sock in it, Stinky," Pinkard answered, too weary even to threaten doing any of the drastic things Salley so richly deserved. The captain came by just then, making sure everybody in the company—less a couple of men who'd passed out, overcome by the heat—was in good shape. Jeff called to him: "Sir, what river is this?"

"Unless the map they gave me is a liar—and God knows it's possible, way the hell out here—this is the Double Mountain fork of the Brazos," Connolly answered. Answering the next question before Pinkard could ask it, he went on, "From what they say, it's supposed to have a lot more water in it in the wintertime."

"Couldn't hardly have much less," Pinkard said.

The bridge, when he got to it, looked to have been there a while; it wasn't a recent erection by the Confederate Army Engineering Corps. That argued the road had been there a while, too. He wondered where it ended up going. As far as he could tell, it was a road to nowhere.

They camped a little north of the Double Mountain fork. Try

300 THE GREAT WAR: WALK IN HELL

as he would, Jeff couldn't see the mountains that were supposed to have given the fork its name. The ground was a little higher up ahead, but so what? He supposed that, in these parts, anything high enough to serve as a watershed got reckoned a mountain.

Night fell. It didn't get any cooler, not so far as Pinkard could tell. He ambled over to a chow wagon. The Negro cook was serving up stale bread, tinned beef, and coffee. "Reckon I'd do just about anything for some of Emily's fried chicken right about now," he said mournfully, examining the unappetizing supper.

"Hey, soldier, you've got food," said Sergeant Albert Cross, a veteran with the ribbon for the Purple Heart above his left breast pocket. "Believe me, time'll come when you're glad you've got anything. Ever carve a steak off a mule three days gone?"

He didn't sound as if he was joking. He didn't look as if he was joking, either. Sergeants seemed to have had their sense of humor surgically removed when they were children. Pinkard ate what was set before him. He unrolled his blanket and lay down on top of it. The next thing he knew, the sun was shining in his face.

The force of which he was a part resumed their march not long after sunrise. "We'll take that high ground," Stinky Salley declared in his best impression of the Secretary of War, "and then we'll defend it from the damnyankees when they show up."

From ahead, tiny in the distance, came the crackle of rifle fire. "Deploy from column into line by the left flank—move!" Captain Connolly shouted. The soldiers moved: awkwardly, because they hadn't had enough training in such maneuvers before they got thrown into action against the Red rebels.

Out ahead, through the dust of the march, Pinkard saw men on horseback blazing away at the advancing Confederates. *Yankee cavalry,* he realized. As Connolly had said, the land was wide hereabouts. Cavalry had room to maneuver, as it didn't farther east.

He didn't see the field artillery with the horsemen, not even after it started shelling him. He heard a whistle in the air, and then a crash somewhere close by. A moment later, he heard screams. Another whistle, another crash. More screams.

"Get down!" Sergeant Cross screamed. Jeff was already on his belly, wondering how the Negroes in Georgia had fought on without guns to give as they received. At Cross' order, he and his comrades started shooting at the U.S. cavalrymen. "Nothing to worry about—just a skirmish," the sergeant said. Pinkard supposed he was right, and found the prospect of a big battle even less appealing than supper the night before.

XI

Paul Mantarakis looked around. Most of what he saw was mountains baking under a savage sun. The rest was waterless valley full of boulders and cactus and nothing any man in his right mind could possibly want to own, let alone want it badly enough to take it away from the poor fools unfortunate enough to be in possession of it at the moment.

When he said that out loud, Gordon McSweeney's big, fair head went up and down in agreement. "Amen," the Scotsman said. "The Empire of Mexico is welcome to it, for all of me."

"You ought to take another couple of salt tablets, Gordon," Paul said. "You look like a lobster that's been in the pot too long."

For once, he was thankful for his swarthiness. Even here in Baja, California, all he did was go from brown to browner. Back in the normal world of the USA he dimly remembered, the whiter you were, the more breaks you got. Here, all you got was sunburn and heatstroke.

Captain Wyatt tramped past them. He wasn't cooked quite so badly as McSweeney, but he was suffering, too. He said, "If we take this miserable stretch of land away from the Mexicans, we'll be able to keep an eye on the Confederate Pacific coast—if the Rebs have any Pacific coast left once the war is done."

"That'd be fine, sir," Mantarakis said. "But once we've got bases here, how do we keep them supplied? No railroads except the one we built ourself. No roads, either, not unless you call what we're on a road."

"This isn't just a road, Sergeant," Captain Wyatt said. "This is damn near *the* road." He paused to swig from his canteen. The water it held, if it was anything like what Paul had, was blood-

302

warm and stale. Wyatt went on, "We cut across the peninsula here to Santa Rosalía, and then we can look across the Gulf of California at the Rebs in Guaymas."

"A shame and a disgrace that the Rebs still *are* in Guaymas," Gordon McSweeney observed.

"Well, you're right about that, Lord knows," Captain Wyatt said. "But they are, and, from everything I've heard, it's not much easier fighting over in Sonora than it is here." He made a sour face. "And, of course, we're starved for everything here, because we're so far west. The war on the other side of the Mississippi is the big top; we're just the sideshow."

Something glinted for a moment, high on the side of the conical mountain ahead. Mantarakis pointed to it, saying, "Sir, I think the Mexicans—or maybe it's the Rebs; who knows?— have an observation post way the hell up there."

"Up on the slope of the Volcano of the Three Virgins, you mean?" Wyatt said. Paul nodded. The captain shrugged. "I would, sure as the devil, if I were in their shoes. I didn't see anything. Show me again where you think it's at." After Mantarakis pointed, the captain nodded. "A little bit above that crag there?" He shouted for a runner, gave the fellow the location Mantarakis had spotted, and told him, "Pass it on to the field artillery. Maybe a howitzer can reach him from here. If that's no good, we'll just have to get used to them keeping an eye on everything we're doing."

Mantarakis said, "Haven't seen much in the way of real fighting since we got down here. Not that I miss it," he added hastily, "but are these Mexicans any good?"

"They won't be as good as the Mormons were," Ben Carlton put in. "'Course, nobody's going to be as good as the Mormons were, unless I miss my guess. But if they were all that bad, we'd've already licked 'em."

"Something to that," Captain Wyatt agreed. "But we've been fighting the terrain as much as the Empire of Mexico, and there are some Rebs, too, helping their pals. But if you ask me—"

Paul didn't ask the company commander. He didn't have a chance to ask the company commander. A whistle in the air made him throw himself to the ground without consciously thinking he needed to do that. A shell burst, maybe fifty yards away.

He had his entrenching tool out and was busy digging himself a foxhole before the second shell came down. "Where are they coming from?" somebody shouted. "Don't see any flash or anything."

"Got to be a trench mortar," Paul yelled back. "They must have put a couple of them on these hills, figured they'd drop some bombs on us. Trouble is, we don't have any trenches." He felt naked trying to fight without one, too.

"I'll lay odds you're right, Sergeant," Captain Wyatt said. "The Mexicans don't have any money to speak of; they can't afford real artillery. In a place like this, though, what they've got is plenty good."

It was, in Paul Mantarakis' opinion, better than plenty good. Shells or bombs or whatever they were kept falling on the Americans. The ground, under a few inches of sandy dust, was hard as a sergeant's heart (that Paul thought such things proved he'd come up through the ranks). He couldn't get the foxhole deep enough to suit him.

And then somebody shouted, "Here come the bastards!" Resentfully, he threw down the entrenching tool and set his rifle against his shoulder. The enemy wasn't playing fair. How was he supposed to kill them without getting hurt himself if they wouldn't let him dig in properly?

Trench mortars up on the hilltops might have been Mexicans. Like any American, he thought of Mexico as backwards and corrupt and bankrupt; if the Emperor had been able to pay his bills, he wouldn't have had to sell Chihuahua and Sonora to the CSA. And when the United States had fought Mexico, back before the War of Secession, they'd actually won. So Paul, in spite of what Captain Wyatt had said, expected any soldiers bold enough to charge to be Confederates propping up their allies.

But he was wrong. These men wore a khaki lighter than Confederate issue, so light it was almost yellow. In this terrain, it gave better protection than green-gray. They wore wide-brimmed straw hats, too, not felts or steel derbies. And their shouts yipped like coyotes' howls; they weren't the cougar screams the Rebs used for battle cries.

Mantarakis fired, one of the first who did. Several Mexicans went down. He didn't think they were all hit; they were taking cover, too. A bullet kicked dust into his face. He shivered despite the heat. A miss was as good as a mile, or so they said, but what did they really know, whoever *they* were?

Fire was coming at the Americans from the front and from both flanks. That wasn't good. That was how you got shot to pieces. That was also probably why, after most of two years of war, the Americans hadn't got to Santa Rosalía yet.

"Let's get moving," Mantarakis shouted to his squad. "We stay here, they're going to chop us to bits." Not without a pang of regret, he quit the unsatisfactory foxhole he'd dug and headed off to the right to see if he couldn't do something about the flanking fire coming from that direction. His men followed him. He'd known of officers who found out too late they were moving all by themselves. Most of them hadn't come back from moves like that.

Rifle bullets buzzed past him, clipped branches from the chaparral through which he ran, and made dust spurt up again and again. He noted all that only peripherally. What he did note, with glad relief, was that the Mexicans hadn't brought any machine guns forward with them. Maybe machine guns were like proper artillery: too expensive for them to afford. He fervently hoped so.

He dove behind a sun-wizened bush, snapped off a couple of rounds to make the enemy keep their heads down, and then got moving again. He came cautiously around a yellow boulder that might have been there since the beginning of time—and almost ran into a Mexican soldier doing the same thing.

They stared at each other. The Mexican had two cartridge bandoliers crisscrossed over his chest, which made him look like a bandit. His bristly mustache and the black stubble on his chin only added to the impression.

Paul saw the Mexican very distinctly, as if a sculptor had carved him and the entire scene behind him into a sharp-edged simulation of reality. The man seemed to raise his rifle with dreamlike slowness, though Paul's swung to bear on him no more swiftly.

They both fired at essentially the same instant. Time speeded up then. The Mexican let out a startled grunt and reeled away, blood coming from a small hole in the front of his uniform and a huge gaping exit wound about where his left kidney was—or had been.

With that hole in him, he was surely a dead man. He didn't know it yet, though. He still held his rifle, and tried to aim it at Paul. Mantarakis discovered his left leg didn't want to hold him. *I can't have been shot,* he thought—*I don't feel anything.* Falling heavily onto his side kept him from getting shot again, for the Mexican's bullet cracked through the place where he'd been.

Then he fired once more, and the enemy soldier's head exploded in red ruin. Paul tried to get up and discovered he couldn't. He looked down at himself. Red was soaking through the dust on the inside of his trouser leg. Seeing his own blood flooding out of him made him understand he really had been hit. It also made the wound start to hurt. He clamped his teeth together hard against a scream.

"Sergeant's down!" somebody shouted, off to one side of him. He did an awkward, three-limbed crawl back behind the shelter of that boulder. Then he detached his bayonet and cut the trouser leg with it before fumbling for the wound dressing in a pouch on his belt.

His hands didn't want to do what he told them. He'd barely managed to shove the bandage against the hole in his leg when a couple of U.S. soldiers grabbed him. "Got to get you out of here, Sarge," one of them said.

"Got to get us all the hell out of here," the other added. "Damn Mexicans got us pinned down good."

"We'll lick 'em," Paul said vaguely. His voice sounded very far away, as if he were listening to himself along a tunnel. He wasn't hot any more, either. A long time ago, hadn't they bled people who had fevers? He tried to laugh, though no sound came out. Sure as sure, he wouldn't have any fever now.

One of the men supporting him grunted just as the Mexican had and crumpled to the ground. A few paces farther on, the other soldier said, "Can you help any, Sarge? We'd move faster if you could do something with your good leg." Getting no reply, he spoke again, louder: "Sarge?"

He stooped, letting his burden down behind another of the strangely shaped rocks that dotted the valley. When he got up again, he ran on alone.

Anne Colleton felt trapped. Living as the only white person at what had been—and what she was fiercely determined would again be—Marshlands plantation with the remnants of her field hands was only part of the problem, though she made a point of carrying a small revolver in her handbag and preferred not to go far from the Tredegar rifle when she could help it. You couldn't tell any more, not these days.

That was part of the problem. The Red uprising had shattered patterns of obedience two hundred years old. The field hands still did as she told them. The fields were beginning to look as if she might have some kind of crop this year, no matter how late it had been started. But she couldn't use the Negroes as she had before. She'd taken their compliance for granted. No more. Now they worked in exchange for her keeping the Confederate authorities from troubling them for whatever they might have done during the rebellion. It was far more nearly a bargain between equals than the previous arrangement had been.

But only part of her feeling of isolation was spiritual. The rest was physical, and perfectly real. She'd made trips into St. Matthews and into Columbia, trying to get the powers that be to repair the telephone and telegraph lines that connected her to the wider world. She'd had promises that they would be up two weeks after her return to the plantation. She'd had a lot more promises since. What she didn't have were telephone and telegraph lines.

"God damn those lying bastards to hell," she snarled, staring out along the path, out toward the road, out toward the whole wide world where anything at all might be happening—but if it was happening, how could she find out about it? She'd prided herself on her modernity, but the life she was living had more to do with the eighteenth century than the twentieth.

Beside her, Julia stirred. "Don' fret yourself none, Miss Anne," she said. Her hands rested on the broad shelf of her belly. Before long, she would have that baby. If she knew who the father was, she hadn't said so.

Anne ground her teeth. Julia would have been ideally suited to the eighteenth century, or to the fourteenth century, for that matter. She let things happen to her. When they did, she cast around for the easiest way to set them right and chose that.

"Better to be actor than acted upon," Anne said, more to herself than to her serving woman. She'd always believed that, though she'd had scant experience of being acted upon till the

Red revolution cast her into the hands of the military. Having gained the experience, she was convinced she'd been right to loathe it.

She looked over toward the ruins of the Marshlands mansion. The cottage in which she was living now had belonged to Cassius the hunter. From what she'd heard, he'd had a high place in the Negroes' Congaree Socialist Republic. He'd been a Red right under her nose, and she'd never suspected. That ate at her, too. She hated being wrong.

Even more galling was having been wrong about Scipio, who was also supposed to have been a revolutionary leader. *I gave him everything,* she thought: *education, fine clothes, the same food I ate—and this is the thanks he gave me in return?* He'd vanished when the revolt collapsed. Maybe he was dead. If he wasn't, and she found him, she swore she'd make him wish he were.

And the Ford she was driving these days made as unsatisfactory a replacement for her vanished Vauxhall as the nigger cottage did for her vanished mansion. She hated the balky, farting motorcar. The only thing she would have hated worse was being without one altogether.

An automobile rattled past on the road, kicking up a trail of red dust as it went. It was, she saw, an armored car, with a couple of machine guns mounted in a central turret. Resistance still sputtered in the swamps by the Congaree. Otherwise, that armored car would have been of far more value shooting down damnyankees, its proper task.

Julia's eyes followed the armored car till it disappeared behind a stand of trees. Despite her broad lips, her mouth made a thin, hard line. She swore up and down that she'd never been a rebel, that she hated everything the Reds stood for. Anne's opinion was that she protested too much. Wherever the truth lay there, Julia did not take kindly to seeing such deadly machines out hunting black men. That was also true even of the Negroes who had, Anne thought, genuinely disapproved of the Socialist uprising. Anne sighed. Life kept getting harder.

A couple of minutes later, a party of horsemen turned off the road and onto the path leading up to . . . the ruins of Marshlands. Two of the three riders had the look of superannuated soldiers, and carried carbines across their knees. The third, the postman, wore a Tredegar slung on his back.

Anne walked toward him, nodding as she did so. "Good morning, Mr. Palmer," she called. With the telephone and telegraph out of commission, the postman was her lifeline to the wider world.

He swung down off his horse and touched the brim of his hat with a forefinger. Producing a pencil and a printed form, he said, "Mornin' to you, Miss Colleton. Got a special delivery you got to sign for—and quite a special delivery it is, too. Ah, thank you, ma'am." He passed her the envelope, and then the rest of the day's mail. That done, he gave her another half-salute, remounted, and urged his horse up from walk to canter. The two armed guards rode off with him, their eyes hard and alert.

"Richmond," Anne said, noting the postmark on the envelope before she spotted the return address in the upper left-hand corner, in a typeface that might have come straight off a Roman monument:

RESIDENCE OF THE PRESIDENT OF THE
CONFEDERATE STATES OF AMERICA

Her head went up and down in a quick, decisive nod. "About time Gabriel Semmes got off his backside and wrote to me."

"Who it from, Miss Anne?" Julia asked.

"The president," Anne answered, and the Negro woman's eyes got big and round.

Anne tore the envelope open. The letter was in Semmes' own hand, which partly mollified her for not having heard from him sooner. *My dear Miss Colleton,* the president of the CSA wrote, *Let me extend to you my deepest personal sympathies on the loss of your brother and the damage to your property during the unfortunate events of the recent past.*

"Unfortunate events," Anne snorted, as if the two words added up to some horrible curse—and so, maybe, they did. Before he'd been elected, Gabriel Semmes had made a name for himself as a man who went out and did things, not a typical politician. Anne had thrown money into his campaign on that basis. But if he called an insurrection an unfortunate event, maybe she would have been better served spending it elsewhere.

She read on: *As you no doubt know, these unfortunate events have adversely affected our ability to resist the aggression of the United States of America, which seek to reduce us once more to the state of abject dependency existing before the War of Secession. To meet their challenge, we shall have to utilize every resource available to us.*

"I should hope so," Anne said, as if the president were standing there before her. She was sure she knew what would be coming next: some sort of higher taxes, which she would be asked to support in the name of continued Confederate strength and independence.

She looked around Marshlands. She didn't know how she could pay higher taxes. She didn't know how she could pay the taxes already due. One way or another, she would have to manage. She understood that. If the choice was between paying more and having the damnyankees win, she would—somehow—pay more. With the Yankees' having gassed Jacob, and with Tom still at the Roanoke front, how could she do anything less?

Her eyes returned to the letter: *For that reason, I have introduced into the Congress of the Confederate States of America . . .* She nodded and stopped reading for a moment. Yes, Gabriel Semmes was perfectly predictable. . . . *a bill authorizing the recruitment, training, and employment against the United States of America of bodies of Negro troops, these to serve under white officers and noncommissioned officers, the reward for their satisfactory completion of service, or for their inability to do so because of wounds, to be the franchise and all other rights and privileges pertaining to full citizenship in the Confederate States of America, intermarriage being the sole exception thereto.*

"Good God," Anne said. Taxes, she'd expected. This, no. She felt as if she'd been kicked in the belly. The Negroes rose up in bloody revolt, and Semmes proposed to reward them for it? He did indeed go forth and do things, and she wished to high heaven he'd been content to hold still.

He continued, *I am soliciting your support for this measure because I know that you judge the continued independence of the country we both love to be of primary importance, with all else subordinated to it. Now we are come to a crisis the likes of which we have never known, one that calls for a supreme effort from every man, woman, and child in the Confederate States, white and black alike. Anything less would be a dereliction of duty from all of us. I hope and trust you will use your not inconsiderable influence both within your circle of acquaintances and with your Congressional delegation to let us turn back the ravening hordes of American Huns. Your ob't servant*—and a florid signature.

"Good God," Anne said again. "I should have backed Doroteo Arango."

"Miss Anne?" Julia knew nothing of politics, unless perhaps Red politics, and cared less.

"Never mind." Anne carried the rest of the mail into the cottage. Julia followed her. She sorted through it, separating out bills; requests for money and time for charitable organizations that, these days, would have to go unanswered; advertising circulars that would make good kindling for the fireplace but were otherwise worthless; and, at the bottom of the stack, a letter from Tom.

She opened that one eagerly. She wondered what Tom would think of having nigger troops put on Confederate butternut. No, she didn't wonder. She was perfectly sure. She'd never credited her brother with a whole lot of sense, but how much sense did you need to see folly?

Dear Sis, Tom wrote, *Just a note to let you know I'm alive and well. Not a scratch on me—they do say that if you're born to hang, nothing else can hurt you.* Anne snorted again. Her brother was about the least likely man to go to the gallows she could imagine. She read on: *It has been lively, I will say. The damnyankees have come as far as*—a censor had cut out the name of the place—*which we never expected them to do.*

The trouble is, they're using these armor-plated traveling forts prisoners call—another censor's slice denied her the knowledge of what they were called, though she could not for the life of her see why—*and they've gained a lot of ground because of it. Artillery will take them out. So will brave soldiers, but it's hard being brave with one of those things bearing down on you.* This time, the censor, damn him, had cut out a whole sentence. When she was allowed to resume reading what her brother wrote, he said, *If they keep throwing more and more machines at us, I don't know where we'll come up with the men to hold them back.*

I hope to get leave before too long, and will come home to have a look at Marshlands. I am sure you are whipping the old place back into shape. Tom was always sure of that. Till now, his confidence had always been justified. Now—Anne didn't want to think about now. Her eyes went to the last couple of sentences: *Who would have dreamt the damned niggers could raise so much Cain? If I'd thought they could do half so much, I'd have sooner had them shooting at the damnyankees so we could get some use out of them. But even though everything else is turned upside down from before the war, I still love you, and I'll see you soon—Tom.*

"Miss Anne?" Julia said when Anne stood there motionless, reading the letter over several times.

"Hush," Anne Colleton replied absently. After a bit, she put the letter down and picked up the one from the president of the Confederacy. She read through that letter twice, too. Her breath whistled out in a long sigh.

"You all right, Miss Anne?" Julia asked, sounding for once very much like the concerned body servant she'd been till not long before.

"No," Anne said. "Not even close." She'd misjudged her brother—and if she couldn't tell what Tom was thinking these days, how could she trust her judgment on anything else? The short answer was, she couldn't. She sighed again, even louder this time. "Maybe Gabriel Semmes isn't a complete utter damn fool after all. Maybe." She tried to make herself sound as if she believed it. It wasn't easy.

George Armstrong Custer stood at the edge of the road, by a sign that had an arrow saying KENTUCKY pointing north and another saying TENNESSEE pointing south. A photographer snapped several pictures. "These'll make bully halftones, General," he said.

"Splendid, my good man, splendid," Custer replied grandly. Major Abner Dowling felt ready to retch. That road sign was as resurrected as Lazarus—everything hereabouts, like everything everywhere the rake of war passed, had been stomped flat. When it came to getting his name—and, better yet, his photograph—in the papers, Custer was not a man to let mere rude facts stand in his way. Dowling would have thought he'd had the sign made up special for the occasion, but that order would have gone through him, so Custer must have come up with a real one instead.

The photographer put down the camera and pulled out a notebook and pencil; he doubled as a reporter. "To what do you attribute your success in this spring's campaign, General?" he asked.

Before Custer could reply, a barrel came rumbling down the road, heading south into Tennessee. Another followed, then another. Everybody except the drivers rode on top of the machines, not inside them. Men had died from heat prostration inside barrels, trying to fight in this hideous summer weather. Kentucky had been bad. Tennessee promised to be worse.

Custer pointed to the machines. "There is your answer, sir. The barrels have filled Rebel hearts not only with fear but also with a good, healthy respect for the prowess of the American soldier and for the genius lying behind what I call with pardonable pride old-fashioned Yankee ingenuity. I have always insisted that machines as well as men will make the difference—are you all right, Major Dowling?"

"Yes, sir. Sorry, sir," Dowling said. "Must have been the dust the barrels kicked up, or maybe those stinking exhaust fumes. I couldn't breathe for a second or two there."

"I hope you're better now," Custer said doubtfully. "You sounded like a man choking to death. Where was I? Oh yes, barrels. I—"

Custer barreled on. Dowling took out a pocket handkerchief and daubed at his sweaty forehead and streaming eyes. Custer disapproved of the aeroplane. He disapproved of the machine gun, though he'd risen to prominence in the Second Mexican War because he'd had a few attached to his command. He disapproved of the telephone and the telegraph. He undoubtedly would have disapproved of the telescope had it not been invented before he was born.

But barrels—he approved of barrels. Barrels, to him, remained cavalry reborn, cavalry proof against everything machine guns could do. Since he'd grown up in the cavalry, he'd transferred his affection to these gasoline-burning successors. And Custer, being Custer, never did anything by halves. When he fell in love, he fell hard.

To prosaic Dowling, barrels were bully infantry support

weapons. Past that . . . he failed to share Custer's enthusiasm. Custer had any number of enthusiasms he did not share, that for Custer being perhaps the largest.

But even Dowling was prepared to admit the barrels had done some good. The first few times the Rebs saw them, they'd panicked. They were good soldiers; as one of their sincerest foes, Dowling admitted as much. Even the best soldiers, though, would run if the alternative was dying without having the chance to hit back at their enemies.

They weren't panicking quite so much now. They were starting to figure out ways to blow up barrels, too. The armored machines had proved vulnerable to artillery fire, though artillery had trouble hitting moving targets even if the movement was no swifter than the barrels' mechanized waddle. Still, Dowling had thought he'd grow old and die in Kentucky, and here he was in Tennessee, or at least on the border.

"Next stop—Nashville!" Custer declared, waving his staff as if he were a train conductor. Dowling wished he thought it would be so easy.

"General, what will your men do if they come up against black troops in Confederate uniform?" the reporter asked.

"I'll believe that when I see it," Custer answered. Here, for once, Dowling agreed with him completely. He went on, "If it does happen, it will be only one more sign that the Rebels are scraping the bottom of the barrel—heh, heh. The frogs are padding their lines with African savages these days, so I suppose the Rebs *might* give their home-grown niggers guns—not that they haven't grabbed guns of their own already, to use on the whites who now talk about using them against us."

"Er—yes." The fellow with the camera and notebook hadn't bargained for a speech. He came back to the question he'd really asked: "But how will your soldiers respond to them, if they are enlisted?"

Custer's drooping mustache and even more drooping jowls made his frown impressively ugly. "How will they respond to them?" he repeated, not caring for the fact that his earlier answer hadn't satisfied the man. "I expect they'll shoot them in great carload lots, that's how."

"Great—carload—lots." The reporter scribbled furiously. "Oh, that's good, sir, that's very good. They'll like that—it'll probably get a headline."

"Do you think so?" All of a sudden, the general commanding First Army was sweetness and light once more. Even Dowling thought it was a pretty good line, and he was not inclined to give his commander much credit for such things.

The reporter asked a couple of more questions. Custer, having succeeded with one joke, tried some others, all of which fell flat. They fell so flat, in fact, that the reporter put away his notebook, picked up his camera, and departed faster than he might otherwise have done.

Custer, as usual, was oblivious to such subtleties. Puffing out his flabby chest, he turned to Dowling and said, "I think that went very well."

Of course you do, his adjutant thought. *It was publicity.* It was, as usual, hard to go wrong with an answer of, "Yes, sir."

"And now back to headquarters. I want to prepare the orders for our next attack against the Rebs' positions."

"Yes, sir," Dowling said again. Custer was taking a more active interest in the campaign these days, partly, Dowling supposed, because Libbie was still with him and partly because, like a child with new Christmas toys, he was playing with the barrels to find out what all they could do.

When he got back to the building doing duty for headquarters these days—a whitewashed clapboard structure with the legend GENERAL STORE: CAMP HILL SIMES, PROP.—orders got delayed for a while. Someone had brought in a wicker basket full of ripe, red strawberries and a bowl of whipped cream. Custer dug in with gusto, pinkish juice dribbling down his chin and bits of clotted cream getting stuck in the peroxided splendor of his mustache. Since Major Dowling wasn't shy about enjoying the bounty either, he refrained from even mental criticism of the general.

"Where did we come by these?" Custer asked after he'd eaten his fill.

"Little town called Portland, sir," said Captain Theodore Heissig, one of the staff officers. "Just south of the Tennessee line. They grow 'em in bunches."

"No, no," Custer said. "Bananas grow in bunches." Unlike the man with the notebook and camera, the staff officers were obliged to find all his jokes funny, or to act as if they did.

Dowling bared his teeth in what bore at least some resemblance to a grin.

Once the strawberries were all disposed of, Custer walked over to the map and examined it with less satisfaction than he might have shown, considering the amount of progress First Army had made since the Confederate States were distracted by their own internal turmoil, and especially since barrels had begun to make trenches something less than impregnable. "We need more help from the Navy," he grumbled. "How long have they been stuck just past this miserable Clarksville place? Weeks, seems like."

"Sir, they're saying they need Army help to go farther," Captain Heissig said.

"Balderdash!" Custer boomed, a fine, bouncing exclamation that sprayed little bits of cream onto the map.

"Sir, I don't think it is," Abner Dowling said, gingerly trying, as he so often had to do, to lead Custer back toward some vague connection to military reality. "The Rebs have mined the Cumberland heavily, and they've got big artillery south of the river zeroed on the minefields. The Navy's lost too many monitors to be very eager to push hard any more."

"Then what the devil good are they?" Custer demanded. "If they can't get where we need them, they might as well not be there at all." That conveniently ignored several facts, some small, some immense, but Custer had always been good at ignoring facts he didn't like. He rounded on the luckless Captain Heissig. "I want you to arrange cooperation on our terms, Captain, and I want you to do it by this afternoon."

"I'll do my best, sir," the young captain said.

"You'll do it, Captain, or this time next week you'll be chasing redskins and bandits through the parts of the Sonoran desert we were supposed to have pacified a year and a half ago," Custer said. He meant it, too, as the luckless Captain Heissig had to know; his staff had the highest turnover of any commander of an army's.

There were times—a lot of times—when commanding a battalion in the Sonoran desert would have looked very good to Dowling. But Custer, worse luck, didn't threaten to ship him out. He just used him as a whipping boy. Dowling sent poor Captain Heissig a sympathetic glance. Misery loved company.

* * *

Cincinnatus' nostrils dilated as he approached the Kentucky Smoke House. When the wind was right, you could smell the barbecue all over Covington. Even when the wind was wrong, as if was tonight, the irresistibly savory smell made spit flood into people's mouths for miles around.

And when you walked into Apicius' barbecue place, you felt certain you were going to starve to death before you got your pork or your beef, smothered in the hot, spicy sauce that made the Smoke House famous and spun on a spit over a hickory fire. Even if you weren't coming in for the food, as Cincinnatus wasn't, you wanted some—you wanted that splendid sauce all down your shirtfront, was what you wanted.

Blacks ate at the Kentucky Smoke House. So did Covington's whites, unwilling to let their colored brethren have such a good thing to themselves. And so did Yankee soldiers and administrators. A man who kept his ears open there would surely learn a lot.

Lucullus, Apicius' son, was turning the spit in the main room. The carcass of a pig went round and round above the firepit. However much his mouth watered, Cincinnatus ignored the prospect of barbecued pork. That Lucullus was working the spit meant Apicius had to be in one of the back rooms, and Apicius was the man he'd come to see.

But when he headed for the back rooms, Felix, Apicius' other son, stood in front of him to bar the way. "Pa's already in there talkin' with somebody," he said. "Be a good idea if you see him later."

"Who's he talkin' to that I ain't supposed to know nothin' about?" Cincinnatus answered scornfully. "Be a good idea if I see him *now*. I been drivin' all over creation the whole day long. I don't got to do none o' this, you know. I could go home to my wife and my little boy. Don't get to see them often enough, way things are. I'm goin' in."

Felix was a couple of years younger than Lucullus. He hadn't quite got his full growth, and he hadn't quite acquired the arrogance that would have let him tell a grown man no and get away with it. He looked toward Lucullus for support, but Lucullus kept basting that pig with a long-handled brush. When Cincinnatus took a step forward, Felix scowled but moved aside.

Cincinnatus knew which back room Apicius was likely to use— why not? He'd been in there himself, often enough.

The fat Negro barbecue cook looked up in startlement when the door opened. So did the man with whom he'd been bent in intent conversation. All at once, Cincinnatus wished he'd paid attention to Felix. The man with whom Apicius had been talking was Tom Kennedy.

"I'm gonna have to give my boy a good kick in the slack o' his britches," Apicius said, and then, to Cincinnatus this time, "Well, come in and shut that thing behind you, 'fore people out front start payin' more heed to what's goin' on in here than they should ought to." To Kennedy, he said, "Sorry, Mister Tom. Didn't 'spect we'd get interrupted."

"Could be worse," Kennedy said. "Cincinnatus and me, we've known each other for a long time and we've done a deal of work together. You know about that, I suppose."

His tone was—*cautious* was the word on which Cincinnatus finally settled. Cincinnatus had put firebombs into U.S. supply dumps over much of central Kentucky. He'd gone right on doing that after Conroy's general store burned down. He didn't like doing it, but he thought it would be wise. The Confederate underground hadn't troubled him, so he supposed he'd made the right choice. Buildings did sometimes burn down without firebombs, after all, or seem as if they did. There had, in fact, been a fire in a livery stable down the block from the general store a couple of nights later.

"Well, all right, you're here," Apicius said roughly. He slid down on the bench he was occupying to give Cincinnatus room to sit beside him. "What you got to say that won't keep for nothin'?"

But Cincinnatus didn't say anything, not right away. He kept an eye on Tom Kennedy. Kennedy had used Apicius and his sons to help spread Confederate propaganda in occupied Kentucky. Cincinnatus didn't know whether Kennedy knew Apicius headed a Red cell in Covington. Till he found out, he wasn't going to say anything to let Kennedy in on the secret. The war between the Reds and the Confederate government was liable to continue, here in this land neither of those two sides controlled.

Kennedy said, "I was just telling Apicius here about what I told you months ago would come true—more rights for Negroes in the CSA on account of the war and on account of the goddamn uprising."

"You did tell me about that, Mr. Kennedy—that's a fact," Cincinnatus said. "I own I didn't reckon you knew what you was talking about, but it do look like you did."

"Got to get through the Congress before it's real, and the Congress don't move what anybody'd call real quick," Apicius observed.

"I think Congress will move quicker here than you figure," Kennedy said. "You read the papers—"

Apicius shook his head. "Felix does, and Lucullus. Not me. All I knows is how to cook meat till it fall off the bone into yo' mouth."

And how to sandbag, Cincinnatus thought. Maybe Apicius was illiterate. If he was, he had the remarkable memory people who couldn't read and write often developed; details never slipped his mind.

The display of ignorance didn't impress Kennedy, either. "You know what's going on," he corrected himself impatiently. "You know the Confederate States need all the help they can get against the USA, and you know that if that means giving Negroes more, they'll do it."

"Reckon I do know that," the cook said. "Question is, do I care? The CSA is a pack o' capitalists and oppressors, an' de USA is a pack o' capitalists and oppressors, too. Why the devil does we care what the devil happens to one pack o' capitalists and imperialists or the other?"

Cincinnatus knew he was staring. Apicius chuckled. Tom Kennedy chuckled, too, a little self-consciously. They both started to talk at the same time. With a wave of the sort he'd probably learned as a boy back in slavery days, the black man deferred to the white. Kennedy said, "When you're underground, things are different. Down in Mississippi, I'd hang Apicius from the first branch—well, the first really big branch—I could find . . . if he didn't bushwhack me first. Up here, we both worry about the USA more than we do about each other." He nodded to Cincinnatus. "I know who I'm working with. And I know who's working with me, too."

Was that a warning about Conroy's store? What else could it be? But if Kennedy had drawn his own conclusions about that . . . Cincinnatus wondered why he was still breathing, in that case.

Apicius said, "That don't mean what I said beforehand don't hold. You got to remember that, Mister Tom. Most of the black folks who think about politics at all, we is Marxists. We is oppressed so bad, what else can we be? The war you got, it's an imperialist war. Why shouldn't we sit by and let the capitalists shoot each other full of holes?" Cincinnatus wondered how long the cook had been a Red, to talk that way if he couldn't read the words.

Kennedy answered, "Because whoever's left on top is going to lick the tar out of you if you do. You aren't strong enough to go it alone. You've seen that. If you couldn't lick the CSA when we had one hand and half of the other one tied behind our backs, you'll never do it. You can't fight, not well enough. You have to deal."

"Who says we didn't lick the CSA?" Apicius asked quietly. "The U.S. soldiers, they down in Tennessee these days. You think you ever gonna see soldiers in butternut back on the Ohio? Don't hold your breath, Mister Tom."

"The Yankees can put soldiers on every railroad track and streetcorner in this state. That doesn't mean they can run it." Kennedy would have been more impressive if he hadn't sounded as if he were whistling in the dark.

"It don't matter nohow," Apicius said. "In the long run, Mister Tom, it don't matter *a*-tall. The revolution gonna come in the CSA, and the revolution gonna come in the USA. Not all the soldiers in the world can stop it, on account of it's the way things gonna work out everywhere in the world. You kin fight it an' go under, or you kin be progressive an' make yourself part of the risin' power o' the proletariat."

"If the Yankees weren't holding us both down——" Kennedy said. Apicius nodded, his heavy-jowled face calm and certain. Cincinnatus had seen that look before, most often on the faces of preachers convinced of their own righteousness than anywhere else.

He wondered if Apicius really knew what he was talking about. If the united workers of the world were so strong—"If the workers are so strong," he said, more thinking aloud than intending to criticize, "why didn't they all say two years ago they didn't want to go out and kill each other, instead of lining up and cheering and waving their flags?"

But disagreeing with both of them at the same time, he did the same thing the U.S. invasion of Kentucky had done: he got Apicius and Tom Kennedy to unite against him, though for divergent reasons. "Why? Because they're patriots, that's why," Kennedy said. "And they'll go on being patriots, too, even the colored ones, when they find out they have something worth fighting for."

Apicius shook his head. "They fight on account of they is mystified into thinking country and race count for more than class. The capitalists got them fooled, is why they go off cheerin'."

"Nothing counts for more than country and race," Kennedy said with conviction.

Although Cincinnatus had worked with the Confederate underground, he did not think of himself as Tom Kennedy's political ally. But he had the feeling Kennedy was right here. You could usually tell a man's race just by using your eyes. You could usually tell a man's country just by using your ears to hear how he talked. Set against those basics, the idea of class seemed as fragile as something made from spun sugar.

As if to cleanse himself of agreeing with a white man against a black (and if that wasn't race in action, what was it?), Cincinnatus said, "Some of the states in the USA, I hear tell, they already let their colored men vote."

Kennedy accepted the challenge without flinching; he had nerve, no doubt of that. "Sure they do, Cincinnatus. They don't have enough blacks to worry about. You think the white men of Kentucky are going to feel the same way?"

Apicius smiled a nasty smile. "Maybe that don't matter none. Maybe the Yankees, they only think about who wants to do things for them, and about who they reckon they can't noway trust. Maybe when the war is over, maybe *only* the black folks in Kentucky gets to vote. How you gonna like that there, Mister Tom?"

Kennedy's face showed how well he would like that. He said, "There'd be an uprising so fast, it'd make your head swim. And you know what, Apicius? A lot of the damnyankee soldiers would join it, too."

Cincinnatus thought about Lieutenant Kennan. Would he back whites against blacks and against his own government? He might. But Kennan wasn't the only kind of Yankee there was. "Not all of them would," he said with as much certainty as Kennedy had shown not long before. "Not all of them would, not by a long shot."

"What are you doing here, then?" Kennedy asked. "You like the Yankees so well, why aren't you with them?"

"Because I saved your neck, Mr. Kennedy, once upon a time," Cincinnatus answered. That made Kennedy shut up. It also made Cincinnatus wonder if he was on the right side—any of the right sides—after all, which surely was not what the white man had had in mind.

Lucien Galtier led his family into the biggest church in Rivière-du-Loup for Sunday morning mass. More often than not, he and they worshiped in St.-Modeste or St.-Antonin, both of which were closer to his farm and both of which had priests less inclined to fawn on the American occupiers than was Father Pascal.

"Every so often, it is interesting to hear what the good father has to say," he remarked to his wife as they and their children filed into a pew and took their seats. "He speaks very well, it is not to be doubted."

"You have reason," Marie agreed in fulsome tones. No informer could have taken their words in any way amiss. That was fortunate, since they were surely under suspicion for having failed to collaborate with Father Pascal and the Americans as fully as they might have done.

Even in the midst of war, peace filled the church—or did its best to do so. The buzzing roar of aeroplane motors pierced the roof. The aeroplanes were flying north, across the St. Lawrence, to drop bombs or shoot at the soldiers defending unconquered Quebec from the invaders. Lucien had neither seen nor heard aeroplanes flying south since the ones that had shot up the American troop train. More from that than from the improbabilities the newspapers published these days, he concluded that the defenders of the province were having a hard time.

You could not tell as much from Father Pascal's demeanor. Here he came up the aisle toward the altar, flanked by altar boys in robes of gleaming white. The procession was not so perfectly formal as it might have been, for the priest stopped every few rows to greet someone with a smile or a handshake. He beamed at Lucien and his family. "Good to see you here today, my friends," he said before passing on.

Lucien nodded back, not so coldly as he would have liked. Part of that was simple caution, part his reaction, however involuntary, to Father Pascal's genuine charm. He scowled down at his hands once the priest's back was to him. He would have respected Father Pascal as a foe more easily had the man not pretended an amity that had to be false.

The mass, however, was the mass, no matter who celebrated it. The sonorous Latin that Lucien understood only in small snatches bound him, understood or not, with worshipers all over the world and extending back in time to the days of Christ Himself. Even in Father Pascal's mouth, it made the farmer feel a part of something larger and older and grander than himself.

Once the prayers were over, Father Pascal returned to French to address the congregation. "My children," he said, adding with a roguish smile, "for you are the only children I shall ever have: my children, I know that many among you are upset and disturbed in your hearts at the travail France is suffering in this great war that covers the whole of the earth. I do not blame you for this feeling. On the contrary—I share it with you."

He set both plump, pink, well-manicured hands over his heart for a moment. The woman in the pew in front of Lucien sighed at the gesture. Galtier suppressed the urge to clout her in the head. It wouldn't knock sense into her, and would get him talked about.

Father Pascal went on, "But although France is the mother from which we have all sprung, I must remind you, painful duty though it is, that the France of today, the France of the Third Republic, has cut herself off from the ways and traditions we proudly maintain. You must understand, then, that her punishment is surely the will of God."

"He's right," that woman whispered loudly to her husband. "Every word he says is true, and you cannot deny a one of them." Her husband's head went up and down in an emphatic nod. Now Lucien wanted to clout both of them. He needed a distinct effort of will to hold still and listen as the priest kept spinning his seductive web.

"The France we know today is not the France that sent our ancestors forth to this new world." Father Pascal's voice dripped regret. "This is the France that murdered its king, that disestablished our true and holy Catholic Church, that made the blessed pope a spectator as Bonaparte set the crown on his own head, that has lost her moral compass. Such a country, I believe, needs to be reminded of where her true duties and obligations lie. Once she has been purged in the fire of repentance, then, perhaps—I pray it shall be so—she will deserve our respect once more."

A couple of women, including the one in front of Lucien, broke into sobs at the iniquities of modern France. He was more inclined to dwell on the iniquities of Father Pascal, and to wonder how much the American Major Quigley had bribed him, and in what coin.

"I also note for your edification, my children, that in the United States all religions truly are treated as being equal," Father Pascal said. "You have surely seen for yourselves that the occupying authorities have in no way interfered with our worship here in Rivière-du-Loup or in the other regions of *la belle province* that they have liberated from the English."

At that, Galtier sat up very straight. He made a point of glancing over to his two sons to make sure they did nothing foolish. Georges laughed silently, but not with the good-natured laughter that was his hallmark. Charles was tight-lipped with anger. Neither one, fortunately, seemed ready to raise an outburst. Nor did his wife or Nicole. His three younger daughters, though—He caught their eyes, one by one. His warning might have been silent, but it got through.

Father Pascal continued, "The Protestants, the Presbyterians"—he loaded the names with scorn—"in Ottawa and all through Ontario are surely just as glad to have you, to have us, gone from their midst, gone from their Protestant dominion. Well, God will have an answer for them, too, if not in this world then in the world to come."

Now Lucien was the one who had to struggle to keep silent. *It's not like that!* was the shout he wanted to raise. Looking around the church, he saw several men of roughly his own age also seeming discontented. They were the ones who had been conscripted into the Canadian Army, served their terms, and who had done so enough years before that they were not recalled to the colors when the war began, not until the Americans had overrun this part of Quebec.

No one who had served in it could doubt the Army ran more nearly according to the wishes of the English than those of the French. That was hard to resent, with more Canadians being of English blood than French. But any man of either stock who buckled down and obeyed his superiors would get on well, and veterans knew that, too, whether Father Pascal did or not.

The priest said, "We have survived more than a century and a half of rule by Protestants who despise and fear us. France has suffered for more than a hundred years under one godless regime after another. Accommodating ourselves to the freedom we shall have in the United States, and to the chastisement of the erring mother country, should not be difficult or unpleasant for us, my children. We shall do well, and France, if God is kind, will return to the ways of truth abandoned so long ago."

"He is a beautiful man," the woman in front of Lucien said to her husband, who nodded again. "He sees the truth and he sets it forth, as if he were writing a book for us to read."

And then, to Galtier's alarm, Marie said, "He is a very persuasive man, is he not?" Lucien had to study her face carefully before noticing one eyebrow a hair's breadth higher than the other. He sighed in relief. For a moment, he'd feared Father Pascal had seduced his wife—no other word seemed to fit.

"Very persuasive, yes," Lucien said. He did his best to sound fulsome, in case that idiot woman or anyone else within earshot proved a spy.

People filed up to receive communion from Father Pascal. As he bent to let the priest place the wafer in his mouth, Lucien had to remind himself that a cleric was not required to be in a state of grace for the sacrament he administered to be efficacious; to believe otherwise was to fall into the Donatist heresy. Galtier could not recall—if he had ever known—who the Donatists were, or where they had lived. Staring at sleek, prosperous Father Pascal, though, he wondered if they hadn't been better theologians than the Church proclaimed them. On his tongue, the Body of Christ tasted like ashes.

When the last communicant had taken part in the miracle, Father Pascal said, "The mass is over. Go in peace." He again abandoned the ritual Latin for French to add, "And pray there may be peace here in our province and all over the world."

As Galtier and his family were leaving, they passed Major Quigley, who stood waiting outside the church. Nodding to Lucien as if to a friend, he walked over to the rectory next door, no doubt to speak with the priest who was doing so much for his cause.

"Some of the Americans," Nicole said hesitantly as the wagon made its slow way back to the farm, "some of the Americans are very nice people."

"This is what you get for working in the hospital," Charles snapped at his sister.

Lucien had had similar fears, but held up a hand. "If we quarrel among ourselves, on whom can we rely?" he asked. Both his daughter and his son looked abashed. *I have raised them well,* he thought with no small pride. He went on, "I agree— some of the Americans *are* very nice people. My opinion, however, is that all of them, without exception, would be nicer still were they back in America."

"You have reason, Father," Nicole said. Lucien had to fight to keep from crowing all the way back to the farm.

Still commanding the battery that had been Jeb Stuart III's, still a sergeant, likely to be a sergeant till the day he died, Jake Featherston knew that day was liable to be close at hand. The Army of Northern Virginia maintained its presence on this side of the Monocacy, but that was for the most part because the Yankees had been pushing harder elsewhere in Maryland, not because Confederate defenses were strong here.

And now the United States were pounding in this sector, too. Shells burst all around the battery. A couple of men were down. The worst of it, though, wasn't explosions or flying splinters. The worst of it was that the Yankees were firing a lot of gas shells along with their high explosives.

"Come on!" Jake shouted to the men of his own gun. "Pound those Yankee trenches! They're gonna swarm like bees any minute."

Even when he did shout, his words sounded hollow and

muffled. The gas helmets Confederate soldiers were wearing these days did a better job of protecting lungs and especially eyes from poison gas than had the chemical-soaked gauze pads that had been the original line of defense against the new and horrid weapon. But wearing a helmet of rubberized burlap that covered your entire head and neck was a torment in its own right, the more so as days got ever hotter and muggier.

Jake rubbed at the glass portholes of the helmet with a scrap of rag. That didn't help; the round windows weren't so much dirty as they were steamy, and the steam was on the inside of the gas helmet. He could have taken off the helmet. Then the portholes would have been clean. Of course, then he would have been poisoned, but if you were going to worry about every little thing . . .

The Yankee barrage dropped back into the front-line trenches. "Be ready, y'all!" Featherston shouted. "They're going to be coming out any—"

He didn't even get the chance to finish the sentence. The U.S. soldiers swarmed out of their trenches and rushed toward the Confederate lines. The U.S. bombardment didn't ease off till they were within fifty yards of those lines; Jake gave the enemy reluctant credit for a very sharp piece of work there.

Even before the damnyankees' guns stopped pounding the Confederate trenches, though, men in butternut were pouring machine-gun fire into their foes. The barrage was liable to kill them, but, if they didn't keep the U.S. soldiers out of their trenches, they were surely dead.

The battery poured shrapnel into the Yankees advancing across no-man's-land, shortening the range as the soldiers in green-gray drew closer to the Confederate line. Shell casings lay by the breech of the gun in the same way that watermelon seeds were liable to lie by a Negro sleeping in the sun: signs of what had been consumed.

Dirt fountained up from every explosion. Men fountained up, too, or pieces of men. Others dove for the shelter of shell holes old and new. For a moment, the attack faltered. Jake had watched a lot of attacks, both Yankee and Confederate, falter: generals had a way of asking men to do more than flesh and blood could bear. "Be ready to lengthen range in a hurry," he called to his gun crews. "When they run, we want to hurt 'em as bad as we can so they don't try this shit again in a hurry."

But then a cry of alarm and despair rose, not from the ranks of the Yankees but from the Confederates' trenches. Men started running away from the front, straight toward Jake Featherston's guns.

"Barrels!" Michael Scott shouted. With the gas helmet he had on, Jake couldn't see his face, but he would have bet it was as pale as whey. "The damnyankees got barrels!"

There were only three of them, belching out gray-black clouds of exhaust as they lumbered forward with a clumsy deliberation that put Featherston in mind of fat men staggering out of a saloon. But, like fat men not so drunk as to fall down, they kept on coming no matter how clumsy they looked.

Machine-gun bullets struck sparks from their armored hides, but did not penetrate them. They had machine guns, too, and poured a hail of bullets of their own on Confederate positions that kept on resisting. Where those machine-gun bullets proved inadequate, they used their cannon to pound the foes into silence.

They were, Jake saw, deadly dangerous weapons of war. They were also even more deadly dangerous weapons of terror. Rumors about them had raced through the Confederate Army weeks before this, their first appearance on the front here. Seeing that they were nearly as invulnerable as rumor made them out to be, most of the men thought flight the best if not the only answer.

"That armor of theirs, it doesn't keep shells out," Jake said. "They're not going any faster than a man can walk, and every damn one of 'em's as big as a battleship. We don't fill 'em full of holes, we don't deserve to be in the First Richmond Howitzers."

He felt the sting of that himself. As far as the powers that be were concerned, he didn't deserve to be an officer in the First Richmond Howitzers. When his life lay on the line, though, pride took second place. At his shouted orders, all the guns in the battery took aim at the barrels.

Despite the encouraging words he'd used, he quickly discovered hitting a moving target with an artillery piece was anything but easy. Shell after shell exploded in front of the barrels or far beyond them. "If I was a nigger, I'd swear they were hexed," Michael Scott growled.

"If you were a nigger—" Featherston began, and then stopped. He didn't know how to finish the thought. He'd fought that very gun with two Negro laborers, up in Pennsylvania, after a Yankee bombardment had killed or wounded everyone in the crew but him. The fire he and Nero and Perseus delivered had helped drive back a U.S. assault on the trenches in front of the battery.

Yet the two blacks had sympathized with the Red revolt enough to desert the battery when it began, and he hadn't seen them since. He wondered if they'd managed to get their hands on any guns and turn them against their Confederate superiors. He doubted he'd ever know.

But he was sure that, if not for the Negro uprising, the war against the USA would be going better now. Blacks were mostly back to work yes, but you couldn't turn your back on them, not the way you had before. That made them only half as useful as they had been before the red flags started flying—and that meant the war against the United States was still feeling the effects of the uprising.

"We'll pay 'em back one of these days," Jake said. He had no more time in which to think about it. One of the barrels was clumsily turning so that its cannon bore on his gun. Barrels couldn't stand hits from artillery. He'd told his gun crew as much, and hoped for the sake of his own neck he was right. He didn't need anyone to tell him guns out in the open couldn't do that, either.

Flame spurted from the muzzle of the cannon inside the traveling fortress. The shell was short. Fragments clattered off the splinter shield that was all the protection his gun crew had. Nothing got through. Nobody got hurt. He knew perfectly well that that was luck.

"Left half a degree!" he shouted, and the muzzle of the howitzer swung ever so slightly. He yanked the lanyard. The gun roared. So did he: "Hit! We hit the son of a bitch!"

Smoke poured out of the barrel. Hatches popped open all over the ungainly machine. Men, some carrying machine guns and belts of ammunition, dove out of the hatches and into whatever cover they could find. The gun crew raked the area where they were cowering. "I hope we kill 'em all, and I hope they take a long time dying," Michael Scott said savagely.

At Featherston's orders, his gunners also sent several more rounds into the burning barrel, to make sure the damnyankees couldn't salvage it. Another barrel had stopped on the open ground between two trenches. Jake didn't know why it had stopped. He didn't care, either. What difference whether it had broken down or its commander was an idiot? It made an easy target. Nothing else mattered. Soon it was burning, too.

Seeing the seemingly invincible barrels going up in flames put fresh heart into the Confederate infantry that had been on the point of breaking. The men in butternut stopped running and started shooting back at the U.S. soldiers in their trenches. The last surviving barrel made a slow, awkward turn—the only kind it could make—and lumbered away from the battery of field guns that had treated its comrades so roughly.

Its tail carried a two-machine-gun sting, but Jake had never been so glad to see the back of anything. All the guns in the battery sent shells after the barrel. No one was lucky enough to score a hit on it.

"It's going," Featherston said. "That's good enough for now, far as I'm concerned. If it comes back tomorrow, we'll worry about it tomorrow. Meantime, let's see if we can make the damnyankees sorry they ever made it into our trenches."

Before long, the U.S. soldiers in the Confederate positions were very unhappy; the battery showered them with both gas and shrapnel. The troops they'd driven back counterattacked aided by reinforcements hurrying across the Monocacy on bridges the Yankees hadn't been able to knock down.

The U.S. soldiers did hold on to the first couple of lines of trenches, but that wasn't enough of an advance to make the battery change site. Glum-looking Yankee prisoners filed back toward the Monocacy bridges, their hands high in the air.

Once the fighting had eased, officers came out to examine the burned-out hulks of the barrels. One of them was Major Clarence Potter. On his way back to Army of Northern Virginia headquarters, he stopped for a couple of minutes at Jake Featherston's battery. "I'm given to understand we have your guns to thank for those two ruined behemoths," he said.

"Yes, sir, that's right." Featherston dropped his voice. "They won't promote me for it, but I did it."

"Any way you could have gotten us a barrel in working order, not one that's been through the fire?" Potter asked. He held up a hand. "That won't get you promoted, either, Sergeant, but it will help our cause."

"Sir, if those barrels had kept running, they'd be visiting you about now, not the other way round," Jake answered. "We got any more men back of the line, sir? One more attack and we can push the Yankees all the way back where they started from."

But the intelligence officer shook his head. "Lucky we were able to throw in as much as we did." Now he was the one who spoke quietly: "If we don't get more men in arms, be they white or black, we'll be reduced to standing on the defensive all along the line, and that's no way to win a war."

"Black soldiers." Featherston's lip curled.

"You know they can fight," Potter said. "You of all people should know that." He'd heard about the use to which Jake had put Perseus and Nero.

"Yes, sir, I do know that," Jake said. "But I'll be damned if I think they ought to get any kind of reward for trying to overthrow the government in the middle of the war. That's what giving 'em guns and giving 'em the vote would be. They stabbed us in the back. Somebody—anybody—does that to me, I'll make him pay." Some of the faces in his mind when he said that were black. Some were white and plump and prosperous, the faces of soldiers and bureaucrats in the War Department in Richmond.

XII

Jonathan Moss peered down at the battlefield in dismay. The advance through Ontario toward Toronto had been slow and brutally expensive, but it had been a continuous advance. One enemy defensive line after another had been stormed and overwhelmed. Now, for the first time, American troops were in headlong, desperate retreat. From the air, they looked like ants fleeing a small boy's shoe.

That was, in effect, what they were. A handful of bigger shapes moved on the ground, grinding through American barbed wire and into the U.S. trenches. "Son of a bitch," Moss said, and the wind blew his words away. "The limeys and Canucks have barrels of their own."

They looked different from American barrels, of which he'd seen one or two. He flew lower for a better look, figuring that the more he could put in his report, the better it would be. That battalions of American infantrymen were getting much more intimately acquainted with the barrels advancing on them than he could in an aeroplane never once crossed his mind.

The lower he flew, the stranger the enemy barrels looked. They were forward-leaning rhomboids, with tracks going all the way around the outside of their hulls. He wondered why the Canucks—or was it the limeys?—had settled on such a stupid design till he saw a barrel climb almost vertically out of a trench into which it had fallen. However odd the setup seemed, it had its merits.

Instead of mounting a cannon in the nose like U.S. barrels, the ones currently pushing back the American infantry carried two, one on each side, mounted in sponsons whose design— if not the actual pieces of forged iron themselves—had been taken from the secondary armament of warships. Some of the barrels mounted machine guns in one or both sponsons instead of cannon.

"I wonder whose are better, theirs or ours," Moss said. He had no way to tell at the moment. American barrels still being thin on the ground, and used mostly to spearhead long-planned attacks, none was anywhere nearby to challenge the machines the enemy was hurling at the poor bastards down in the trenches.

Moss dove on the barrels, machine gun blazing. He walked his tracers across one, another, a third. As far as he could tell, they did the massive machines no harm. He cursed himself for a fool. American barrels were armored to hold out enemy machine-gun fire. Whatever you could say about the Canadians and the British, they weren't stupid. They'd do unto the USA as they'd been done by themselves.

He cursed his stupidity for another reason as well. The advancing foe loosed a storm of lead at his Martin one-decker. Ground fire had shot him down once already. Now again he heard the thrumming pop of bullets tearing through canvas.

Clang! That bullet hadn't torn through canvas—it had hit something metal. His eyes flicked over the instrument panel. Everything looked all right. If he was lucky, the bullet had ricocheted off the side of the engine block without breaking anything. If he wasn't lucky, he'd find out soon enough—most likely at the moment he could least afford to.

That *clang*, though, was an urgent reminder that he couldn't afford to linger indefinitely down here. He pulled back on the stick. The nose of his fighting scout rose.

As Moss gained altitude, Tom Innis made his own firing run on the advancing enemy. Perhaps profiting from his flightmate's experience, he didn't try to shoot up the barrels. Men were always more vulnerable. Banking toward the American lines—or what had been the American lines before the attack—Moss watched men in khaki dive for cover. He whooped with glee and shook his fist in the slipstream.

But not all the British and Canadians tried to shelter themselves from Innis' gun. They shot back at him as ferociously as they had at Moss. And a streak of smoke began streaming back from Tom's engine cowling.

"Get out of there!" Moss shouted—uselessly, of course. "Get

out of there while you can!" He looked around for Dud Dudley and Phil Eaker—they'd have to shepherd Innis back toward the aerodrome. He'd be a sitting bird if the Canadians or British pounced on his crippled bus.

He swung the one-decker back toward the west. The smoke wasn't getting better. It was getting worse. "Climb, damn you!" Moss yelled to him, as if he could hear. The more altitude he gained, the farther he'd be able to glide when his engine quit. Moss knew all about that, the hard way.

Innis had to know it, too. But the Martin didn't get any higher off the deck. The only reason for that, Moss figured, was that it couldn't get any higher off the deck. And that meant his flight-mate was in trouble.

Moss bared his teeth in an anguished grimace—it wasn't just smoke streaming back from the engine now, it was flame, too. The slipstream blowing in Moss' face made it hard for him to close his mouth again. The slipstream also blew the flames back toward Tom Innis.

He beat at them with his fist and arm. They spread faster than he could knock them down. "Land it!" Moss screamed. "Land it, God damn you!" He wasn't cursing his friend. He was cursing fate, without a doubt the most dreadful fate any airman could face. Better to yank out your pistol and put one through your head than go down in a burning crate, as far as he was concerned.

That was especially true if you were going down in a burning crate from, say, fifteen thousand feet. If you were only a couple of hundred feet off the ground when your aeroplane caught fire, you had a chance to put it down and get the hell out before you roasted, too.

You had a chance. . . . The trouble was, every yard of territory hereabouts was as cratered as the surface of the moon: the USA had had to blast the Canucks off the land before advancing through it, and then, even after having had it taken from them, the Canadians and the limeys had shelled it to a faretheewell to make sure the Americans didn't enjoy owning it.

With a healthy aeroplane, Tom Innis would have had more choices. Of course, with a healthy aeroplane, he wouldn't have needed to land in the first place. He did the best he could, steering for a meadow that still had some green grass mingled with the brown of earth thrown up from shell blasts.

"Come on. Come on," Moss whispered, his hand trying to move on the joystick as if he were landing his own aeroplane. Despite smoke and flames and what had to be mortal fear, Innis got the Martin down. You didn't need much in the way of ground to kill all the speed and hop out. "Come on," Moss said again as he buzzed overhead. "Taxi, taxi . . ."

The Martin nosed down into a shell hole and flipped over. It kept right on burning. Nobody came out of it. Nobody was going to come out. Moss knew that. If the fire hadn't killed Tom, getting the engine and machine gun slammed back into his chest would have done the job.

Infantrymen in green-gray ran toward the crash. Moss and his flightmates kept circling above it. Some of the infantrymen, their faces small pale ovals, looked up at them and shook their heads. No luck. It was over.

Moss felt empty inside as he flew back toward the aerodrome. *It could have been me* echoed in his mind again and again. It nearly had been him, not so long before. What was the difference between the way he'd put his damaged aeroplane down and how Tom Innis had done it? Luck, nothing more. You didn't like to think you were alive for no better reason than dumb luck. Was he an ace by dumb luck, too?

When only three returned where four had set out, the mechanics on the ground didn't need a handbook to figure out what had happened. "What went wrong?" one of them asked quietly. Dud Dudley was the flight leader. That meant he had the delightful job of telling them.

The surviving fliers went into Shelby Pruitt's tent. The squadron commander looked up from his paperwork. His mouth twisted. "Dammit," he said, and then, mastering himself, "All right, give me the details."

Dudley did that, too. When he was through, Moss spoke of the enemy barrels spreading havoc through the U.S. lines. That had seemed the most important news in the world when he'd spotted them. Now he had to flog his memory to come up with details.

Hardshell Pruitt took notes. He had to be a professional about the business of slaughter, too. He asked his questions, both about Innis' demise and about the barrels. Then he said, "All right, boys. I don't expect the three of you will be doing any flying tomorrow. Don't worry about morning roll call, either, come to that. You'll be recorded as present. Dismissed."

If that wasn't an order to head for the officers' club and get smashed, it might as well have been. Moss would have headed there anyway. Dudley and Eaker matched him stride for stride.

News traveled fast through the aerodrome. When the Negro behind the bar saw them come in, he set a bottle of whiskey, a corkscrew, and three tumblers on the bar, nodded, and said not a word. It was almost as if he stood at the bedside of a patient whose chances weren't good.

As suited his station as flight leader, Dud Dudley carried the bottle. Moss picked up the glasses. That left the corkscrew for Eaker, who brought it over to the table as if glad to have something to do.

Dudley used the corkscrew, tilted the bottle, and poured all the glasses full. "Well, here's to Tom," he said, and drained his without taking it from his lips. When it was empty, he let out a long sigh. "I always thought the ornery son of a bitch would be doing this for me, not the other way round."

"Yeah." The whiskey burned in Moss' throat, and in his stomach. He could feel it climbing to his head. "He went out the way you'd figure, if he was ever going to go. He wanted to hit the Canucks and limeys one more lick."

"That's a fact." Dudley filled the tumblers again. "He was a wolf when he drove a bus, nothing else but. Never saw a man who just aimed himself at the enemy and fired himself off like that."

"Best straight-out aggressive pilot I ever saw," Moss agreed. "And Luther was the best technical flier I ever saw. And they're both dead and we're alive, and what the hell does that say about the way the world works?"

"It's a damn shame," Eaker said. The whiskey was already slurring his speech, but he attacked the second glass as single-mindedly as Tom had ever shot up a target. "Not fair. Not fair."

He'd joined the flight as Luther Carlsen's replacement. Now another set of personal goods would have to be cleared from the tent. Somebody else new would be sleeping on Innis' cot. They'd have to point Tom out in the pictures on the wall and explain what kind of a man he'd been. It wouldn't be easy, any of it.

"God damn the Canucks, anyhow," Moss said. "If they'd just

rolled over when the war started, we wouldn't be in this mess in the first place."

"That's right," Eaker said. "Then we could have thrown everything we've got at the goddamn Rebs, and that would be the war over and done with, right there."

"Yeah, and if the Russians hadn't invaded Germany when things got started, France would have gone down the drain and Kaiser Bill would have won his war, too," Moss said. "But instead, we've got—this."

He waved a hand to encompass *this*. It was the hand holding the glass of whiskey. Fortunately, he'd already drunk most of it. A little spilled on the table and on his trouser leg, but not much. He started to pick up the bottle to fill the tumbler once more. "It's empty," Dud Dudley said.

"You're right. It is." Moss stared at it. "How did it get empty so fast?" Before he could get up and do anything about that, the bartender brought over a fresh bottle. Moss nodded. His neck felt loose. "That's better."

"How did it get empty so fast?" Eaker echoed. He sounded even more surprised than Moss had, as if there weren't the slightest connection between his stumbling speech and that poor dead bottle.

"It got empty the same way we did," Moss said. "It got empty the same way the whole stupid world did." Rapidly getting drunk as he was, he couldn't tell whether that was foolish maundering or profound philosophy. The next day, hung over and wishing he was dead, he couldn't tell, either, and the day after that, climbing into his one-decker for another flight above the trenches, he still didn't know.

Night lay like a cloak over the *Bonefish*. "Ahead one quarter," Roger Kimball called from his perch atop the conning tower.

"Ahead one quarter—aye aye, sir," answered Ben Coulter, the helmsman, his voice floating up the hatchway to the skipper.

"If we bring this off, sir—" Tom Brearley breathed.

Kimball made a sharp chopping motion with his right hand, cutting off his exec. "We *are* going to bring this off," he said. "No ifs, ands, or buts. I don't care how many mines the damn-yankees have laid in Chesapeake Bay, I don't care how many shore guns they've got watching from Maryland. We are going to pay them a visit. If they aren't glad to see us, too damn bad."

"Yes, sir," Brearley said, the only thing he could say under the circumstances. After a few seconds, he went on, "It's a shame the USA pushed down so far toward Hampton Roads."

"You're right about that," Kimball said. "If we were holding onto both sides of the mouth of the Bay as tight as we ought to . . . Things'd look a lot better if that was so, I tell you."

There were, at the moment, any number of ways in which the war could have looked better from the Confederate point of view. Kimball wasted little time worrying about them. They'd given him the job of penetrating as far up the Chesapeake Bay as he could and doing as much damage as he could once he got there, and he aimed to follow his orders to the letter.

Softly, under his breath, he let out a snort. "As if they'd hand this assignment to Ralph Briggs."

"Sir?" his executive officer said.

"Never mind, Tom," Kimball answered. "Woolgathering, that's all. And maybe there's more to old Ralph than I give him credit for, anyway."

He'd never expected to see Briggs back in the CSA till the war ended, not when he'd had his submersible torpedoed out from under him and been fished out of the drink by the damnyankees who did him in. But Briggs had managed to break out of the prisoner-of-war camp where they'd stowed him and to make it through enemy lines (or rather, to make it through some country so broken, it had no real front line) and back into Confederate territory. If he could run a submarine as well as he'd run his own escape, he might yet make a captain to be reckoned with.

Tom Brearley coughed, calling Kimball's attention back to the here-and-now. "Sir, we're passing between Smith Island and Crisfield."

"Thank you, Tom," Kimball said. "I guess we'll have to start paying attention, then, won't we?" Even in the midnight darkness, his grin and Brearley's answering one were broad and white.

The USA had run steel-mesh nets from Point Lookout on the western shore of Chesapeake Bay over to Smith Island, and then again from the island to Crisfield on the Bay's eastern shore, precisely to keep Confederate raiders like the *Bonefish* from coming up and making nuisances of themselves in the Bay's upper reaches. They backed up the nets with minefields and patrol boats.

From everything the Confederacy had been able to learn, though, the damnyankees had concentrated their efforts on the wider stretch of water west of Smith Island. Their ruling assumption seemed to have been that nobody was crazy enough to try to run a boat through Tangier Sound. Up at the northern end of the sound, only a mile or two of water separated the mainland from Bloodsworth Island. The nets would tangle a submersible that dove, and the guns would put paid to one that didn't.

Kimball whistled tunelessly between his teeth. "Do I look like a crazy man to you, Tom?" he asked.

"No more so than usual—sir," Brearley answered, which made Kimball laugh out loud.

"Best way to run through the nets," he said, "is to take 'em on the surface and slide through halfway between two buoys." He peered through his clandestinely imported German binoculars, trying to spot the buoys to which the nets were attached, and laughed again. "This is a trick we've learned from the Huns, mind: it's how they slip through the English obstacles in the Channel."

Brearley didn't have binoculars, but he did have sharp eyes. "There, sir!" He pointed ahead and to starboard. Sure enough, a buoy bobbed there in the light chop.

Kimball swept the binoculars to port till he found the next buoy supporting the net. He grunted in satisfaction. "Won't even have to change course," he said, and then called down the hatch: "All ahead full!"

"All ahead full—aye aye, sir!" The diesels that powered the *Bonefish* roared as the submarine sped up. Kimball hoped they didn't roar so loud as to draw the attention of guns and searchlights on the shore or on Smith Island. His lips pulled back from his teeth. Maybe the Yanks weren't so far wrong when they figured only a crazy man would try Tangier Sound.

"Through!" Brearley said, his voice rising in triumph. Kimball felt triumphant himself, with one set of buoys behind him.

At his order, the diesels throttled back. Now that he was in the Sound, the trick, he figured, was to act as if he owned the place. "All right, we've got the minefield coming up next," he said. "We have to steer along the chain of islands here, right close to shore. We'll be in good shape then."

If the damnyankees hadn't done any minelaying since the CSA got their latest reports, and if no mines had come loose and drifted into her path, the *Bonefish* would be in good shape. Kimball had to take the channel slowly, though, to give himself the chance to stop and withdraw if he or a sailor at the bow spotted a spiked sphere bobbing in the sea. That meant the submersible hadn't passed the Bloodsworth Island gap by dawn.

"Shall we dive, sir, and spend the day on the bottom?" Brearley asked. "That won't be much fun, but—"

"We'll do nothing of the sort," Kimball declared. "I want you to take down the naval ensign, Mr. Brearley, and go to the flag locker for—"

"A U.S. flag, sir?" the exec said in some alarm. "Going under false colors is—"

"Technically legal, if we run up the true ones before we start to fight," Kimball said. "But that's not what I want, Mr. Brearley. I want you to replace the naval ensign with the national flag. And then I intend to go through the channel as if I had every right to do so. I'll bet you a Stonewall the damnyankees see what they expect to see, not one thing more."

He wasn't betting a five-dollar Confederate goldpiece. He was betting his life and the lives of the boat's complement. But Tom Brearley, once he got the idea, didn't argue any more. Down came the naval ensign, which, like the Confederate battle flag on land, displayed St. Andrew's cross in blue on red. Both looked as they did for the same reason: the CSA's Stars and Bars too closely resembled the USA's Stars and Stripes for them to be readily distinguished at any distance. Normally, that confusion was dangerous. Every once in a while, it could be exploited.

Flying the Stars and Bars, the *Bonefish* made for the narrow passage between Bloodsworth Island and Maryland's eastern mainland. Kimball made no effort to avoid being seen. On the contrary. He sailed along as if he had every right in the world to be where he was. Field glasses were surely trained on him from the land. Guns could have been, at a moment's notice.

No one fired. He crossed the net as he had the one before, but with even greater panache. "This is astonishing, sir," Tom Brearley breathed.

Kimball shrugged. "They see a submersible out in the open. They look at the flag. They see red, white, and blue. Nobody'd be stupid enough to do what we're doing. And so—"

He looked north, toward the mainland. He saw a few gun positions, close by the shore, and there were surely others he didn't see farther inland, ones mounting bigger guns. The horizon dipped and swooped as he swung the field glasses around to examine Bloodsworth Island. The day was rapidly lightening. He could see men in white U.S. uniforms close by the edge of the sea. He waved in their direction. One of them was peering at him with field glasses, too. The fellow waved back.

"You know what it's like?" Kimball said, chuckling. "It's like seducing a woman." He thought of Anne Colleton; for a moment, warmth tingled through his loins. Then he returned to the subject at hand: "You let her see that there's any doubt in your mind about what you're going to do, all that happens is, you get your face slapped for your trouble. But if she's sure you're sure, hell, her corset's off and her legs are open before she worries about whether it's right or wrong or purple."

"Yes, sir," Brearley said, nothing but reverence in his voice. They were past the nets now. The sun came up, red as fire in the east. All the guns that could have turned them to crumpled, smoking metal lay silent, silent.

"Go below, Tom," Kimball said, following his exec down into the *Bonefish* a moment later. He dogged the hatch after him. "Take us down to periscope depth," he ordered Ben Coulter, his voice relaxed and easy. To the rest of the crew, he went on, "We'll go down nice and slow. No rush about submerging now. It's going to be like we're putting on our show for the damnyankees out there—this is how a submersible dives, boys."

"Of course I'll always love you, darling," Tom Brearley said, sounding very much like a successful seducer sliding out the door.

Kimball laughed out loud and clapped him on the shoulder. "You're learning, Tom. You're learning." The sailors didn't quite know what their officers were talking about, but it sounded dirty. That was plenty to get them laughing, too.

The *Bonefish* slid away from the dangerous narrow waters of Tangier Sound, out into Chesapeake Bay. Here behind the nets and the minefields, everything was clear. Kimball saw plenty of fishing boats through the periscope, but didn't waste fish on them or rise to sink them with gunfire. He wanted bigger prey—he hadn't taken these risks for fishermen.

And he got his reward. Steaming along came an ocean monitor, a bigger version of the river craft the USA and CSA both used: basically, one battleship turret mounted on a raft. It couldn't get out of its own way, but in these confined waters was deadly dangerous to anything those big guns could reach. Sneaking up on it was hardly tougher than beating a two-year-old at football.

The first torpedo, perfectly placed just aft of amidships, would have been plenty to sink the monitor. The second, a couple of hundred feet farther up toward the bow, made matters quick and certain. "Too easy, sir," Brearley said as the long steel tube echoed with cheers.

"You gonna make us throw her back, then?" Kimball demanded.

"No, sir," the exec answered. "Hell no, sir." He didn't ask how Kimball planned to extricate the *Bonefish* from Chesapeake Bay now that, belatedly, the Yankees knew she was there. He might have done that before, but not now. He figured Kimball would find a way.

I figure I will, too, Kimball thought. *Getting it in is the tough part. Once you manage that, pulling out afterwards is easy.*

Major Irving Morrell wondered why he in particular had been saddled with two officers from America's allies. Maybe someone on the General Staff back in Philadelphia remembered his service there and reckoned he could show visiting firemen how the war was fought on this side of the Atlantic. And maybe, too, someone on the General Staff—Captain Abell came to mind, among other candidates—remembered his work there and hoped he would wreck his career once and for all by botching this assignment.

If Abell or someone like him had had that in mind, Morrell thought he would be disappointed. Though the German officer belonged to the Imperial General Staff, both he and his Austrian counterpart gave every sign of being good combat soldiers. They seemed very much at home squatting by a campfire, sketching lines in the dirt with a stick to improvise a map.

"I'm glad both of you understand my German," Morrell said

in that language. "We all study it at West Point, of course, but I've used it more for reading than speaking since."

"It is not so bad, not so bad at all," said Major Eduard Dietl, the Austrian of the duo: a dark man, thin to scrawniness, with an impressive beak of a nose. "Your teacher was a Bavarian, I would say."

"Yes, that's so," Morrell agreed. "Captain Steinhart was born in Munich."

"Here in the United States, I feel surrounded by Bavarians," said the German officer, Captain Heinz Guderian. He was shorter and squatter than Dietl, with a round, clever face. He went on, "The U.S. uniform is almost the exact color of those the Bavarians wear." His own tunic and trousers were standard German Imperial Army field-gray, a close match for Dietl's pike-gray Austrian uniform. Neither differed much in cut from that which Morrell wore; the German uniform had served as the model for those of the other two leading Alliance powers.

Dietl sipped coffee from a tin cup. "This is such a—spacious land," he said, waving his hand. "Oh, I know I think any land spacious after Heinz and I crossed the Atlantic by submersible, but the train ride across the USA and up into Canada to reach the front here . . . amazing."

"He is right," Guderian agreed. "West of Russia, Europe has no such vast, uncrowded sweeps of territory."

"And these mountains." Dietl waved again, now at the Canadian Rockies. "The Carpathians are as nothing beside them." He spoke with the air of a man accustomed to comparing peaks one to another: unsurprising, since he wore the *Edelweiss* badge of a mountain soldier himself. Sighing, he went on, "Almost I wish the Italians had thrown away their neutrality. They've always wanted to; everyone knows it. But they never have dared. No nerve, damn them. Fighting in the Alps would be like this, I think."

"Fighting is not a sport. Fighting is for a purpose," Guderian said seriously. "The idea would be to break out of the mountains and into Venetia and Lombardy below—if there were a war, of course."

Morrell thought that would be more than Austria-Hungary could manage, still fighting the Russians and the Serbs as she was. But he held his peace. Dietl struck him as a man like himself, happiest in the field. Maybe Guderian had worn red stripes on his trousers a little too long.

And then the German officer said, "Besides, you can't conduct a proper pursuit in the mountains. Get around the enemy and smash him up—that's what the whole business is about." Morrell revised his earlier assessment.

Dietl said, "The problem of pursuit is the basic problem of this entire war. The foe retreats through territory not yet devastated, and toward his own railheads, while you advance over country that has been fought in, and away from your own sources of supply. No wonder we measure most advances in meters, not kilometers."

"Barrels help this problem by making breakthroughs possible once more," Guderian said.

"Barrels help, but they're not enough, not by themselves," Morrell said. "They're too slow—how can you have a breakthrough at a slow walk? How can you outrun the retreating enemy when you're not running? Once the barrels force a hole in the enemy's defenses, we need something faster to go through the hole and create the confusion that really kills."

Guderian smiled. "Some people would say cavalry is the answer."

"Some people will say the earth is flat, too," Morrell said. He made a quick sketch of a sailing ship falling off the edge. The German and Austrian observers laughed. He went on, "With machine guns and rifles, cavalry's no answer at all. We need better machines, faster machines."

"I can see why they called you to Philadelphia, Major," Guderian said. "You have the mind of a General Staff officer. You impose yourself on the conditions around you; you do not let them impose themselves on you."

"Is that what I do?" Morrell said, faintly bemused. He was a man without strong philosophical bent; his chief concern was to hit the enemy as hard as he could and as often as he could, until he didn't need to hit him any more.

Someone on the Canuck side of the line had the same idea. Canadian artillery, which had been quiet for the previous several days, suddenly sprang to life. Morrell threw himself flat on the ground. So did Dietl. So did Guderian; he might have spent most of his time in amongst the maps, but he knew how to handle himself in the open air, too.

Along with the bombardment came a great crackle of rifle fire off to Morrell's right. Trained on the British model, the Canucks made formidable riflemen. They were quick and accurate, and every shot of theirs counted. And, by the sound of what was going on over there, they had found the weak spot in Morrell's line. He'd posted one company rather thinly over a long stretch of woods he'd reckoned almost impassable. The Canadians seemed intent on showing why *almost* was a word that didn't belong in war-planners' dictionaries.

Guderian and Dietl were both looking at him. *All right, we have come into the field to observe the American Army and to observe this man:* he could all but hear what they were thinking. *He now finds himself in difficulty. How does he respond?*

"Runners!" Morrell shouted, and the men came over to him: some running, some crawling along the ground, for shells were still dropping thick and fast. An American machine gun started banging away, there on the right, and he let out the briefest sigh of relief. That was where he'd posted Sergeant Finkel's squad, and the Canadians would have a devil of a time shifting him if he didn't feel like being shifted. And sure enough, shouts of dismay said the Canuck advance had suddenly run into a roadblock.

Morrell snapped orders: "Half of Captain Spadinger's company to pull out of line and contain the damage. The same for the machine-gun company from Captain Hall's company. The rest of the units not under immediate assault will counterattack, aiming to pinch off the neck of the Canadian advance. I will lead this counterattack personally." The runners hurried away. Morrell smiled gaily at the observers. "Will you join me, gentlemen?"

Neither of them hesitated. Running doubled-over, ignoring his bad leg, Morrell got to Hall's company bare moments after the runner he'd sent. The machine-gun men were already on their way off to the east, to shoot up any Canadians who burst out of those not quite impassable woods. Dietl and Guderian, both breathing hard, flopped into foxholes.

Captain Hall said, "I don't think we'll have any trouble holding them, sir. They can't come too far."

"Ich will nicht nur zu—" Morrell snarled in exasperation and

switched from German to English: "I don't want to hold them. I want to drive them back, to hurt them." He pointed northeast.

"If their artillery is alert, they'll slaughter us, sir," Hall said.

"I don't think they will be," Morrell answered. *They'd better not be.* "They've got this bombardment laid on to cover an attack. Who'd be cuckoo enough to move forward when they're putting pressure on us?" He didn't give the company commander any chance to argue. He also didn't give himself any chance to think twice. "Let's go!" He scrambled to his feet and ran for the Canadian lines, Springfield in his hands.

His men followed, whooping like Red Indians. He'd gained them a couple of major advances toward Banff by all-out audacity; they were willing to believe he could buy them one more. For close to thirty seconds, the Canucks left behind in their trenches were too intent on their comrades' push to pay much attention to what the Americans were doing off to the west. That was about fifteen seconds too long. Before a machine gun started mowing down the oncoming men in green-gray, they were within grenade range of its position. It fell silent. More grenades flew into the Canadian trenches. The Americans followed.

As Morrell leaped over the parapet, a Canadian aimed at him from point-blank range. He braced himself for another wound. *Christ, not that leg again,* he thought. *I don't want to be on crutches or in a wheelchair for the rest of my life. Blow my brains out and get it over with.*

The Canuck fired. The bullet went wild, for the fellow in khaki had taken a wound of his own in the instant that he pulled the trigger. Morrell finished him with the bayonet, then looked over his shoulder to find Major Dietl there with a pistol in his hand. *"Danke schön,"* he said.

"Bitte," the Austrian answered, with such Hapsburg formality that Morrell expected him to click his heels. He didn't. He leaped down into the trench instead. Cleaning it of Canadians was the ugly business it always seemed to be. Dietl held his own. At one point, though, he observed, "These foes of yours are in greater earnest than the Russians and have discipline of a sort the Serbs have never imagined."

"The Canadians are good soldiers," Morrell agreed. "The Confederates, too, come to that."

Having driven the Canucks back, his men turned their fire on the Canadian detachment that had gone ahead. Caught between two forces, some of the Canadians went down, some threw down their rifles and threw up their hands in surrender, and some, the hard cases, dug in among the pines and firs and spruces to make the Americans pay a high price for them.

Morrell paid the price, having made the cold-blooded judgment that he could afford it. When the fighting had died away to occasional rifle shots, the Americans were still holding the trenches from which the Canadian attacking party had jumped off. "Very nicely done," Captain Guderian said. "You used the enemy's aggressiveness against him most astutely."

"Coming from an officer of the Imperial General Staff, that's quite a compliment," Morrell said.

"You have earned it, Major. It will be reflected in my report."

"And mine," Dietl agreed. Morrell grinned, more pleased with the day's work itself than with the praise it had garnered, but not despising that, either. *I wonder if favorable action reports from German and Austro-Hungarian observers cancel out the Utah fiasco,* he thought, and looked forward to finding out.

Reggie Bartlett examined the trench line just outside of Duncan, Sequoyah, with something less than awe and enthusiasm. "Lord," he said feelingly, "don't they teach people around here anything about digging in?"

"You listen good, Bartlett," said Sergeant Pete Hairston, his new squad leader. "Just on account of they gave you a pretty stripe on your sleeve for bustin' out o' the damnyankees' prisoner camp, that don't mean you know everything there is to know. Where were you fighting before the Yankees nabbed you?"

"I was on the Roanoke front," Bartlett answered.

Hairston's lantern-jawed face, the face of a man who'd acquired three stripes on his own sleeve more by dint of toughness than any other military virtue, changed expression. More cautiously, he asked, "How long you put in there?"

"From a few weeks after the war started till the Yanks got me last fall," Bartlett said with no small pride. Anybody who'd spent almost a year and a half fighting between the Blue Ridge Mountains and the Alleghenies could hold his head high among soldiers the world over.

Hairston knew that, too. "Shitfire," he muttered, "all the fighting in Sequoyah's nothin' but a football game in the park, you put it next to the clangin' and bangin' back there." He hadn't bothered asking about Reggie's previous experience till now. After a moment's thought, he went on, "But I reckon that's why this here ain't like you expected it would be. We ain't got the niggers to dig all the fancy trenches like I hear tell they got back there, and even if we did, we ain't got the soldiers to put in 'em."

"I see that," Bartlett said. "I surely do."

It horrified him, too, though he saw no point in coming out and saying so. The sergeant was right—there weren't enough trenches, not by his standards. A lot of what they called trenches here were only waist-deep, too, so you might not get shot while you crawled from one foxhole to another. Then again, of course, you might. There wasn't that much barbed wire out in front of the lines to keep the U.S. troops away, either. And, as Hairston had said, there weren't that many Confederate soldiers holding the position, such as it was.

The sergeant might have picked that thought out of Reggie's mind. "Ain't that many damnyankees up here, neither," he said. "They put four or five divisions into a big push, reckon they'd be in Dallas week after next." He laughed to show that was a joke, or at least part of a joke. " 'Course, they ain't got four or five spare divisions layin' around with dust on 'em, any more'n we do. An' if they did, they'd use 'em in Kentucky or Virginia or Maryland, just like we would. This here's the ass end o' nowhere for them, same as it is for us."

"Not quite the ass end of nowhere," Reggie said, liking the sound of the phrase. "I saw those oil wells when I came up through Duncan."

"Yeah, they count for somethin', or the brass reckons they do, anyways," Hairston admitted. "You ask me, though, you could touch a match to this whole goddamn state of Sequoyah, blow it higher'n hell, an' I wouldn't miss it one goddamn bit."

On brief acquaintance with Sequoyah, Bartlett was inclined to agree with the profane sergeant. To a Virginian, these endless hot burning plains were a pretty fair approximation of hell, or at least of a greased griddle just before the flapjack batter came down. Somewhere high up in the sky, an aeroplane buzzed. Reggie's head whipped round in alarm. For the briefest moment, half of him believed he wouldn't see any man-made contraption, but the hand of God holding a pitcher of batter the size of Richmond.

Hairston said, "We'll take you out on patrol tonight, start gettin' you used to the way things are around here. It ain't like Virginia, I'll tell you that. Ain't nothin' like Georgia, neither."

His voice softened. Reggie hadn't been sure it could. He asked, "That where you're from?"

"Yeah, I'm off a little farm outside of Albany. Hell." The sergeant's face clouded over. "Probably nothin' left of that no more anyways. By what I hear tell, them niggers tore that part o' the state all to hell and gone when they rose up. Bastards. You think about things, it ain't so bad, not havin' that many of 'em around."

"Maybe not." Reggie had been in the Yankee camp all through the Red Negro uprising. The U.S. officers had played it up, and the new-caught men had gone on and on about it, but it didn't feel real to him. It was, he supposed, like the difference between reading about being in love and being in love yourself.

Hairston stuck his head out of the foxhole and looked around in a way that gave Bartlett the cold shivers. Do that on the Roanoke front and some damnyankee sniper would clean your ear out for you with a Springfield round. But nothing happened here. The sergeant finished checking the terrain, then squatted back down again. "Yanks are takin' it easy, same as us."

"All right, Sarge." Reggie shook his head. "I am going to have to get used to doing things different out here." He didn't think he'd ever get used to exposing any part of his precious body where a Yankee could see it when he wasn't actually attacking.

As promised, Hairston took him out into no-man's-land after the sun went down. No-man's-land hereabouts was better than half a mile wide; he'd counted on a couple of hundred yards of it back in Virginia, but seldom more than that.

Going on patrol did have some familiar elements to it; he and his companions crawled instead of walking, and nobody had a cigar or a pipe in his mouth. But it was also vastly different from what it had been back in the Roanoke valley. For one thing, some of the prairie and farmland north of Duncan hadn't been cratered to a faretheewell.

For another . . . "Doesn't stink so bad," Bartlett said in some surprise. "You haven't got fourteen dead bodies on every foot of ground. Back in Virginia, seemed like you couldn't set your hand down without sticking it into a piece of somebody and bringing it back all covered with maggots."

"I've done that," said Napoleon Dibble, one of the privates in the squad. "Puked my guts out, too, I tell you."

"I puked my guts out, too, the first time," Bartlett agreed. But it wasn't quite agreement, not down deep. By the way Nap Dibble talked, he'd done it once. Reggie had lost track of how many times he'd known that oozy, yielding sensation and the sudden, stinking rush of corruption that went with it. By the time the damnyankees captured him, having it happen again hadn't been worth anything more than a mild oath.

Something swooped out of the black sky and came down with a thump and a scrabble only a few yards away. Hissing an alarm, Reggie swung his rifle that way. To his amazement, Sergeant Hairston laughed at him. "Ain't nothin' but an owl droppin' on a mouse, Bartlett. Don't they got no owls up on the Roanoke front?"

"I don't hardly remember seeing any," Reggie answered. "They've got buzzards, and they've got crows, and they've got rats. Don't hardly remember seeing mice—rats ran 'em out, I guess. Hated those bastards. They'd sit up on their haunches and look at you with those beady little black eyes, and you'd know what they'd been eating, and you'd know they were figuring they'd eat you next." Napoleon Dibble made a disgusted noise. Ignoring him, Bartlett finished, "The one good thing about when the Yankees would throw gas at us was that it'd shift the rats—for a little while."

"Gas," Hairston said thoughtfully. "Haven't seen that more than a time or two out here. Haven't missed it any, neither, and that's a fact. You run up against any of those what-do-you-call-'ems—barrels?"

"No, I've just heard about those, and seen 'em on a train after I got out of the Yankee camp," Bartlett answered. "They hadn't started using them by the time I got captured. They have 'em out here?"

"Ain't seen any yet," the sergeant said. "Like I told you, this is the ass end of the war. Those armored cars, now, I've seen some of those, but a trench'll make an armored car say uncle."

"Don't like 'em anyways," Nap Dibble said, to which the other members of the squad added emphatic if low-voiced agreement.

Not too far away—farther than the owl that had frightened Reggie, but not all that much—something started screaming. He froze. Was it a wounded man? A crazy man? A woman having a baby right out in the middle of no-man's-land? "Coyote," Sergeant Hairston explained laconically. "Scares you out of a year's growth the first time you hear one, don't it?"

"Lord, yes." Reggie knew his voice was shaky. His heart pounded too fast for him to feel more than mildly embarrassed. Crazy coyotes were something he hadn't had to worry about back on the Roanoke front.

And then, from up ahead, he heard a noise he did recognize: the metallic click of a bayonet against a rock. He stiffened and stared around for the nearest shell hole into which to dive. The other members of the patrol looked around, too, but not with the tight-lipped intensity they would have shown back in Virginia. Softly, Pete Hairston called, "That you, Toohey?"

"Yeah, it's me. Who the hell else is it gonna be?" A Yankee voice came floating out of the night. The accent was different from the one Ralph Briggs had tried to get Reggie to learn, but it wasn't like anything that had ever been heard in the CSA. Toohey went on, "Your damn artillery don't ease up, you're gonna run into a patrol where the sergeant don't feel like doin' any business 'cept shootin' you Rebs."

"Chance we take in this here line o' work," Hairston answered. "You got what you said you was gonna have?"

"Sure as hell do." Something in a jug sloshed suggestively. Toohey went on, "What about youse guys?"

Several of the men in Hairston's squad passed the sergeant their tobacco pouches. He went forward by himself and exchanged a few low-voiced words with the U.S. soldiers. When he came back, he didn't have the tobacco any more, but he was carrying the jug.

The Yanks withdrew. They were pretty quiet, but not quiet enough to have kept star shells from going up on the Roanoke front and machine guns and mortars from chasing them back to their lines. Things *were* different out here. "Is that what I think it is, there in the jug?" Bartlett asked, pointing.

"Sure as hell is," Hairston answered. "Hard to get popskull around these parts. All sorts of Indians here in Sequoyah, and they all got chiefs that hate the stuff. So what we do is, we swap smokes for it with the damnyankees: tobacco they got is so bad, it's a cryin' shame."

Napoleon Dibble added, "We got to fight the sons of bitches, sure, but that don't mean we can't do a swap every now and then when we ain't fightin'. Won't change how the war turns out, one way or t'other." He laughed a loud, senseless laugh; Reggie didn't think he was very bright.

"I suppose you're right," Reggie said slowly. "But what does Lieutenant Nicoll—is that his name?—think about it?"

Hairston stared at him. The whites of the sergeant's eyes glittered in the starlight. "You out of your mind, Bartlett? Who the devil you think set this deal up in the first place?"

Reggie didn't say anything. He couldn't think of anything to say. All he could do was try to figure out exactly what they thought the war was all about out here in the west.

"Here they come!" Chester Martin threw himself into a shelter dug into the forward wall of the trench a split second before the Confederate shells started landing. The earth shook. Fragments hissed through the air. He sniffed anxiously, wondering whether the Rebs were throwing gas and he needed to pull his mask on over his head. He didn't think so.

He wasn't the only one in the shelter. He was lying on top of Specs Peterson in a position that would have been a hell of a lot more enjoyable had Specs been a perfumed whore instead of a bad-tempered private who hadn't been anywhere near soap and water any time lately.

"They've been shellin' us like bastards the past couple weeks," Peterson bawled in his ear—not much, as sweet nothings went.

"Yeah, they—oof!" Martin's rejoinder was rudely abridged when somebody dove in on top of him, making him the squashed meat in a three-man sandwich. Peterson, in the role of the lower piece of bread, didn't much care for it, either. Everybody thrashed around till nobody was kneeing anybody too badly, at which point two more soldiers came scrambling into the hole in the ground. It couldn't hold five men, but it did.

"Amazing how you can pack these shelters when it's a choice

between packing 'em and getting blown to cat's meat out there," said Corporal Paul Andersen, one of the latest arrivals.

"Yeah," Martin said again. "Now what we got to do is, we got to synchronize our breathing. You know how the officers are always synchronizing their watches when we go over the top. If we all breathe in and out at the same time, maybe we all really can squeeze in here."

"Hell, maybe the Rebs'll drop a big one right on top of us," Specs Peterson said. "Then we won't have to worry about breathing at all no more." Martin and Andersen stuck elbows in him, which had the twin virtues of giving them more room and making him shut up.

Martin took advantage of the extra room to draw a deep breath. "Like I was saying before half the division jumped on me, I figure the reason the Rebs are shelling us so hard is on account of they ain't got no barrels. They've moved a hell of a lot of artillery forward to shoot at the ones we got when they come up—and to make life miserable for us poor bastards in between times."

"Makes sense, Sarge," Andersen said. "Wish it didn't, but it does." A big shell, a six-incher or maybe even an eight-, did land almost on top of the shelter then. Dirt rained down between the boards holding up the roof; some of the boards themselves cracked, with noises like rifle shots. That sent more dirt spilling down on the soldiers.

Can I claw my way out if I get buried? Martin wondered. Even inside the shelter, shielded from the worst of the blast, he felt his lungs trying to crawl out through his nose. Get too close to a big one and the blast would kill you without leaving a mark on your body.

With commendable aplomb, Andersen picked up where he'd left off: "We came up with the barrels, I thought that first morning we were going to win the war then and there. But even if the Rebs don't have any, they've sure as hell figured out how to fight 'em. Same with gas earlier."

"You notice, though," Peterson said, "the Rebs ain't makin' many attacks these days, not like they were doin' before we made it over to this side o' the Roanoke. Costs us more when we got to go to them instead of the other way round."

"We got what we came for," Martin said. "We got the iron

mines. 'Course, we can't use 'em much, because their long-range guns still reach most of 'em. And we got the railroad, too. 'Course, they've already built new track further east and slid around the part of the valley we took away from 'em."

"Ain't it great when we're winnin' the damn war?" Andersen said.

That drew a profane chorus from the men stuffed into the shelter with him. A few minutes later, the Confederate barrage abruptly stopped. It didn't do anything to ease Chester Martin's mind. Sometimes the Rebs would really stop. Sometimes they'd stop long enough for people to come out of their shelters and then start up again to catch them in the open. And sometimes, no matter what Specs Peterson said, they'd send raiders over the top, hoping the U.S. soldiers would stay huddled in the bomb-proofs. What to do? For this shelter, it was his call. He was the sergeant here.

"Out!" he shouted. "They start shelling again, we jump back in."

People spilled out. By the way things worked, Martin was the next to last one to make it out into the trench. Every muscle in his body twanged with tension. If the Rebs were going to open up again, it would be right about . . . now. When the moment passed without fresh incoming shells, he breathed a little easier.

Back behind the U.S. lines, artillery came to life, answering the Confederate barrage. "Let the big guns shoot at the big guns," Paul Andersen said. "Long as they leave me alone, I don't care, and that's the God's truth."

"Amen." Chester looked around the trenches and sighed. "Got us some spadework to do, looks like to me." High explosive and steel and brass had had their way with the landscape, blowing big holes in the trenches, knocking down stretches of parapet and parados, and incidentally knocking a couple of vital machine-gun positions topsy-turvy.

Here and there, up and down the line, wounded men were shouting—some wounded men were screaming—for stretcher-bearers. Heading toward one of those shouting men, Martin rounded the corner of a firebay, stepped into a traverse, and was confronted by a man's leg, or that portion of it from about the middle of the shin downward, still standing erect, foot in shoe, the rest of the man nowhere to be seen. A little blood—only a little—ran down from the wound to streak the puttee.

He'd seen too much, these past nearly two years. Put a man in a place where he grew acquainted with horror every day, and it ceases to be horrible for him. It becomes part of the landscape, as unremarkable as a dandelion puffball. He reached out with his own foot and kicked the fragment of humanity against the traverse wall so no one would stumble over it.

"Poor bastard," Paul Andersen said from behind him. "Wonder who he was."

"Don't know," Martin answered. "Whoever he was, he never knew what hit him. Hell of a lot of worse ways to go than that, and Jesus, ain't we seen most of 'em?" About then, by the noise, a couple of other men came on the wounded soldier for whom they'd been heading. He'd found one of those worse ways.

Andersen sighed. "Yeah," he said, and stood against the wall, a few feet away from the severed foot, to relieve himself. "Sorry," he muttered as he buttoned his fly. "Didn't feel like holding it till I got to the latrine. Damn shelling probably blew shit all over the place, anyway."

"I didn't say anything," Chester Martin told him. "You got any makings, Paul? I'm plumb out."

"Yeah, I got some." The corporal passed him his tobacco pouch.

He rolled a cigarette in a scrap of newspaper, pulled out a brass lighter, flicked the wheel, and got the smoke going. "Ahh, thanks," he said after a long drag. "Hits the spot." He looked around. "Sort of feels the way it does after a big rainstorm, you know what I mean? Peaceful-like."

"Yeah," Andersen said again, quite unself-consciously. A couple of rifle shots rang out, but they were three, four hundred yards away: nothing to worry about. "Might as well finish taking stock of what they did to us this time."

All things considered, the company had got off lucky. Only a couple of men had died, and most of the wounds were hometowners, not the sort where the fellow who'd taken them begged you to shoot him and put him out of his anguish, and where, if you did, nobody ever said a word about it to you afterwards. Martin had seen his share of wounds like that; talking with the other soldiers in his squad, he said, "You see one like that, it's your share for a lifetime and then some."

"Yeah." Specs Peterson laughed. "You want to hear something stupid, Sarge? Back before the war started, I was thinkin' about lettin' my beard grow out, on account of I couldn't stand the sight of blood when I nicked myself with a razor."

"That's pretty stupid, all right," Martin agreed, which made Specs glare at him in what might have been mock anger and might have been real. He went on, "You too cheap to pay a barber to do it for you? Those boys, they make damn sure they don't cut you."

"Too cheap, hell," Peterson came back. "Where you from, Sarge?"

"Toledo," Martin answered. "You know that."

"Yeah, you're right. I forgot," Peterson said. "All right, Toledo, that's the big city. Me, I'm off a farm in the western part of Nebraska. The barber in the little country town, he was so drunk all the time, it's a wonder he never cut anybody's throat. And I was ten miles outside of town, and we ain't never gonna have the money for a flivver. So how the hell am I supposed to get a barber to shave me?"

"Damned if I know," Martin answered. "So blood doesn't bother you any more, that right?"

Specs Peterson snorted. "What do you think?"

Martin inspected him. He was even filthier than he had been before the dive into the shelter, and had unkempt stubble sprouting on cheeks and chin. Frowning sadly, Martin said, "So why the hell haven't you shaved any time lately?"

"I was going to this morning, Sarge, honest, but the Rebs started shelling us." Behind his steel-rimmed spectacles, Peterson raised an eyebrow. "You may have noticed."

"Oh, yeah." Martin snapped his fingers. "You know, I knew something was goin' on then, but I couldn't quite remember what." Paul Andersen threw a clod of dirt at him. In the trenches, though, it passed for wit.

The *Dakota* steamed out of Pearl Harbor. Standing on deck, Sam Carsten said, "You know somethin', Vic? This ship puts me in mind of the old joke about the three-legged dog. The wonder is, she goes at all."

"Yeah, well, I ain't gonna argue with you, you know what I'm saying?" Vic Crosetti answered, scratching his hairy arm. "I'll tell you something else, too. She's as ugly as a three-legged dog right now."

"Yeah," Sam agreed, mournful for a couple of reasons. For one thing, if he'd scratched himself half as hard as Crosetti was doing, he'd have drawn blood from his poor, sunburned hide. For another, the *Dakota* really *was* ugly these days. "What she's really like is a guy who took one in the trenches and he ends up with a steel plate in his head."

"Got enough steel plates to eat a whole steel dinner off of," Crosetti said, whereupon Carsten made as if to pick him up and fling him over the rail.

Bad pun aside, though, the description was accurate enough. Not all the damage the *Dakota* had taken in the Battle of the Three Navies was repaired; parties were still patching, strengthening, refurbishing. Some of the damage wouldn't be fixed, probably, till the war was over. But the battleship could make twenty knots and fight, and the Japanese and the British hadn't disappeared off the face of the earth. Ugly or not, jury-rigged or not, she was going back out on patrol.

"I just hope the steering holds us," Carsten said.

Vic Crosetti's bushy eyebrows went up and down. "Why the hell do you want that? Didn't you think it was fun, charging the whole damn British fleet all by ourselves? Nobody else had the balls to try anything like that. The other guys, they stayed in line like good little boys and girls. You want to stand out from the crowd, is what you want to do."

"When they shoot you if you stand out, it's not as bully as it would be otherwise," Carsten said. Crosetti laughed. Then he got busy in a hurry, swiping a rag against the nearest stretch of painted metal. Sam imitated him without conscious thought. If somebody near you started working for no obvious reason, he'd spotted an officer you hadn't.

Commander Grady—the fat stripe where a thin one had been before got sewn onto his cuff after the Battle of the Three Navies—said, "Never mind the playacting, Carsten." He sounded amused; as sailors knew the nasty ways in which officers' minds worked, so officers had some clues about how sailors operated.

Grady went on, "You come with me. I've got some real work for you."

"Aye aye, sir," Sam answered. As he followed the commander of the starboard secondary armament, he knew without turning his head when Vic Crosetti would put down the rag and light himself a smoke. He also knew the little dago would be grinning like a monkey, because Sam had had to go do something real while he got to stand around a little longer.

Grady said, "We're trying to get the number-four sponson into good enough shape so we can fire the gun if we have to."

"Yes, sir," Carsten said doubtfully. The number-four sponson had taken a hit from somebody's secondary armament, whether British or Japanese nobody knew—nobody had been taking notes, and the shell hadn't left a *carte de visite*: except for smashing the sponson to hell and gone, that is. Nobody had come out of there alive. Thinking about it gave Sam the horrors. It could have been the number-one sponson, easy as not.

"I think they can do it," Grady said. "In fact, they damn near *have* done it. But the gun mount still isn't quite right, and there's not a lot of room in there, what with all the other repairs they've had to make. I want somebody familiar with a sponson as it's supposed to be to pitch in with some good advice for them."

"Yes, sir," Sam said again. "Uh, sir, so you know, 'Cap'n' Kidde has forgotten more about sponsons than I'll ever know."

"He's still helping with the rebuilding of the number-two on the port side. That got it worse than this one. He suggested you for the duty."

"All right, sir," Carsten answered. He didn't know whether Kidde was mad at him and wanted to keep him hopping or whether the gunner's mate was putting him in a spot where he could shine for the higher-ups. A little of both, maybe: that was "Cap'n" Kidde's way. If he did this right, he'd look good where looking good could really help him. If he fouled up, he'd pay for it.

He ducked through the hatchway. Commander Grady didn't follow; he had other fish to fry. Even the bulkhead around the hatchway showed the damage the sponson had taken. It was a mass of patches and welds, none of them smoothed down or painted over. There might be time for that later. There hadn't been time for it yet.

Inside, the sponson was even more crowded than it had been when the gun crew filled it during the Battle of the Three Navies. A bunch of men in dungarees turned their heads to stare at Sam. One of them said, "You must be the guy Commander Grady was talking about."

"Yeah, I'm Sam Carsten, loader on the number-one gun, this side." Carsten pointed toward the bow.

"Good." The fellow in dungarees nodded. "Then you know how one of these damn things goes when it's working right." He jabbed a thumb at his own chest. "Pleased to meetcha, Sam, by the way. I'm Lou Stein. These here lugs are Dave and Mordecai and Bismarck and Steve and Cal and Frank and Herman."

Sam spent the next couple of minutes shaking hands and wondering how the hell he was going to keep the repair crew straight in his head. The only one he knew he wouldn't forget was Mordecai, who'd lost a couple of fingers in some kind of accident and whose handshake was strange because of it. He couldn't have had any trouble with tools, though, or they wouldn't have let him do his job.

At the same time as Sam was sizing up the repair crew, he was also sizing up the sponson. It was even more cramped than it would have been otherwise, because they'd welded steel plates inside the inner curve to cover up the damage the entering shell had done. They hadn't covered quite all of it. Above the new steel, a dark, reddish brown stain still marked the inside of the armor plate. Carsten tried not to look at it. It might easily have come from a loader.

He shook himself. *Got to get down to business,* he thought. "Commander Grady said you were having some kind of trouble in here—I mean, besides all this stuff." He waved at the roughly welded steel slabs. He wouldn't have wanted to serve this gun— might as well put toilet paper between him and enemy gunfire as that thin metal. But then again, the armor plate over it didn't look to have done the best job of protecting the sailors in here, either.

Mordecai said, "Damn gun won't traverse the way it's supposed to. It gets all herky-jerky about a third of the way through the arc. Here, I'll show you."

He demonstrated. Sure as hell, there was one point at which the five-inch gun would not hold a target steadily. "That's pretty peculiar, all right," Carsten agreed. "Acts like there's a kink in the hydraulic line some kind of way, don't it?"

"That's what we figured, too," Lou Stein said. "But if there is, we sure as hell ain't been able to find it. Those things are armored, after all; they shouldn't kink."

"If I hadn't done all the things I shouldn't do, my mama would be a happier lady today," Sam answered, which made the repair crew laugh. He went on, "Besides, in this mess, how the devil can you tell which way is up, anyhow?" He waved his hand. The plate on the inner curve of the armor wasn't the only new, raw repair, not by a long shot it wasn't. Other rectangular plates of metal covered damage to the roof and to the deck.

As soon as the words were out of his mouth, he wondered if this crew had done all that quick, rough work. If they had, he'd just stuck his foot in his face. But Mordecai said, "Tell me about it, why don't you?"

"Let me go under there and take a look," Carsten said. "Got a flashlight I can borrow?"

Stein wore one on his belt. Hiram Kidde would have wanted one like it; it had the size and heft to make a hell of a billy club. The door that let Sam down below into the mechanism that moved the gun worked stiffly; the metal in which it was set had been bent and imperfectly straightened.

With the door open so he could call to the repair crew above, he said, "Run it through there, would you?" They did. He shined the flashlight on as much of the hydraulic line as he could see. "Damn. Doesn't look like anything wrong here."

"That's what we thought," Mordecai answered. "You're doing everything exactly the way we did it."

"Am I? All right." Stubbornly, Carsten traced the hydraulic line from the gun back to where it ran behind the steel door through which he'd come. Behind the door . . . He whistled tunelessly between his teeth. Wondering if Lou or Bismarck or any of them had done it before him, he shut the door.

He whistled again, louder. A peeled-back strip of steel from the shell hit had been pushed between two links of the flexible armor the hydraulic line wore. You couldn't see that from above, because the hasty repairs to the deck hid it. And you might not be able to see it when you came down here, either, because you literally shut the door on it. But when the gun moved to that particular position, the line moved and the steel pinched off the flow of hydraulic fluid.

"Lucky it never pierced the hose in the armor," Sam muttered. He opened the door again. "Lou, you want to come down here and take a look at this?"

"I'll be a son of a bitch," Lou Stein said when Carsten showed him what he'd found. "Jeez, I wish it *had* pierced the line. Then we would have found out what the hell was wrong. Well, we can fix it, anyhow."

A cutting torch made short work of the offending metal. Mordecai used it with as much assurance as if he'd had ten fingers, not eight. He said, "Sam, we get back to Pearl, everybody on this-here repair crew will buy you a beer. This one's been makin' us crazy for a while, let me tell you. Look *behind* the goddamn door. What do they call it? Hiding in plain sight?"

"Yeah." Sam chuckled. "Hell, any sailor who doesn't want to work knows how to do that." He and Mordecai grinned at each other.

XIII

"What's the matter, Ma?" Edna Semphroch asked. "Lord, you ought to be dancing out in the street at how bully things are, but you've done nothing but mope the past month." She dried a last cup and set it in the cupboard. "We've got more money than I ever thought I'd see in all my born days, and we haven't seen hide nor hair of that awful Bill Reach since the Rebs hauled him off. I don't miss him, neither. He gave me the horrors." She shuddered.

"I don't miss him, either," Nellie Semphroch answered. She was drying silverware, and threw a fork into the drawer with unnecessary violence. "I wish to God I'd never set eyes on him."

She waited for Edna to start prying again about who Reach was, who he had been, and what he'd meant to her. She'd fended off those questions for months now. What Edna would learn if she got the true answer would not only make her wilder, it would also probably make her despise Nellie.

But, for once, Edna took a different tack tonight. She said, "Is Mr. Jacobs across the street all right? You ain't been over there for a while now, and you were going every few days for a long time."

If Edna had noticed that, had some alert Confederate intelligence officer noticed it, too? Nellie grimaced; she wondered if she even cared. She dried a teaspoon. "As far as I know, he's fine," she answered, doing her best to sound unconcerned, indifferent.

Edna looked at her out of the corner of her eye. "Were you sweet on him, Ma?" she asked in a tone that invited woman-to-woman confidences. "Is that what it is? Were you sweet on him and you had a quarrel?"

"We've never had a quarrel," Nellie snapped, all pretense of indifference vanishing before she could try to keep it. The irony was that she *had* discovered she was sweet on Hal Jacobs—and he on her—bare moments before she discovered he was working for Bill Reach, whom she still loathed with the deep and abiding loathing that clung to every part of her life before she'd met Edna's father.

Too clever for her own good, Edna noticed the hot denial at once, both for what it said and for what it didn't. "It's all right, Ma, it really is," she said tolerantly. "You know I wouldn't mind if you found somebody. Pa's been dead so long, I don't hardly remember him anyways. And Mr. Jacobs seems nice enough, even if—" She stopped. "He seems nice enough."

Even if he's old and not very handsome. Nellie could read between the lines, too. She sighed. Edna wanted license for herself, and was consistent enough, maybe even generous enough, to grant the same license to everyone else, even to her mother. That Nellie might not want it never occurred to her. But then, she didn't know Nellie had had far too much license far too young. Nellie hoped she would never find out.

"You really ought to make up with him, Ma," Edna said. "I mean—" She stopped again. This time, she didn't amend anything. She didn't need to amend anything. Nellie could figure out what she meant. *You're not getting any younger. You're not going to catch anything better.*

"Maybe I will," Nellie said with another sigh. She hadn't brought Hal Jacobs any information gleaned at the coffeehouse since she found out to whom he'd been giving it. One reason— one big reason—the place flourished as it did was that his connections helped it get food and drink hard to come by in hungry, Confederate-occupied Washington, D.C. If she didn't do anything for him, why should he do anything for her?

I'll do this for you, and you'll pay me off, Nellie thought. How was that different from the sweaty bargains she'd made in little, narrow rooms back when she was too much younger than Edna? "Damned if I know," she muttered.

"What did you say, Ma?" Edna asked.

"Nothing." The coffeehouse had become so popular with the Rebels, they'd probably help keep her in supplies if the shoemaker across the street didn't. But that felt like an illicit bargain, too. They hadn't been the kindest nor the gentlest occupiers, and a good many of them frequented her place for no better reason than the hope of seducing Edna. Nellie was sure of that, too.

And, to make matters worse, who could guess how long the Confederates were going to hold on to Washington? If she aligned herself with them now, what would the reckoning be when the United States reclaimed their capital? She thought that *was* going to happen, and perhaps not in the indefinite future. Oh, the Confederates bragged about and made much of what a submersible of theirs had done in the Chesapeake Bay, but was that anything more than a pinprick when you measured it against the hammering U.S. forces were giving the Rebs in Maryland? She didn't think so.

"You ought to go over there, Ma," Edna said. "He's a nice man."

"Tomorrow." Nellie didn't often yield an argument to her daughter, but most of their arguments were about what Edna was doing, not about what she was doing herself. She turned off the gaslight in the kitchen. "It's late. Let's go on up to bed."

The next morning, she did cross the street to Mr. Jacobs' shop. Dirt and gravel had been shoveled into the hole the U.S. bomb made in the street; the Rebs weren't going to be bothered with proper pavement. She kicked at the gravel. Watching the little stones spin away from her shoe, she wished she could kick a lot more things.

It was early. She tried the doorknob anyway. She wasn't surprised when it turned in her hand. Hal Jacobs didn't sleep late. The bell above the door chimed. The shoemaker stood behind the counter, a hammer in his hand. His eyes widened a little beneath bushy eyebrows. His smile showed teeth not too bad, not too good. "Hello," he said, and then, more warily, "Widow Semphroch."

That he didn't use her Christian name said he'd noticed how she'd not been in lately. "You can still call me Nellie, Hal," she said.

He nodded. "Good morning, Nellie," he said. He coughed a couple of times. "I was afraid I had offended you the last time you were here."

Afraid he'd offended her by kissing her, she meant. "No, that's all right," she answered. As she had with Edna, she spoke before she'd fully figured out what she should have said. Claiming offense would have given her the perfect excuse for having avoided him. Now she couldn't use it. She found a question of her own: "What have you heard about Bill Reach?"

He made a face. "In prison. In a Confederate prison as a burglar. This had to do with you, didn't it?" She found she didn't like him scowling at her. But after a moment, he went on, "But you knew him some time ago, is that not true?" He looked at her with mixed kindness and suspicion.

"I kind of knew him, yes, you might say so." Nellie bit her lip. She wouldn't have recognized Reach now, any more than she would have recognized any of the other men she'd kind of known. But he'd recognized her, and presumed on old . . . acquaintance. "I thought he was just a tramp. And I thought—" But she couldn't say that.

"You thought, perhaps, he did not want to treat you as a lady should be treated," Jacobs said. Nellie nodded, grateful for the graceful phrase. The cobbler sighed. "He did have an eye for pretty women. I sometimes worried it would get him in trouble. I did not think it would get him into this sort of trouble."

"I wish to heaven he'd left me alone," Nellie said, which was nothing but the truth. "Why he had to come around after all these years—"

"No one is perfect." Hal Jacobs tugged at a stray curl of gray hair that had slid over the top of one ear. "You really must dislike him very much."

"Why do you say that?" Nellie asked, in lieu of screaming, *I hated him. I still hate him the same way I hate all the other men who used me, and all the men who want to use Edna, too.*

"Because if you were not embarrassed to come here for what we did, the only other reason you would not come here—the only other reason I can think of, anyhow—is that you dislike Bill Reach."

"Well, yes, that probably had something to do with it," Nellie admitted. "If Bill Reach was an angel, I'd think hard about rooting for the devil."

Hal Jacobs looked distressed. "But you must not say this! Without him, the United States would not know half of what we've learned of the doings of the enemy from the Atlantic to the mountains."

"Without *me*, you wouldn't know half of that stuff," Nellie returned with no small pride.

"I admit it," Jacobs said. "I have been very worried here. I—"

He had to break off then, because a Confederate corporal brought in a marching boot with a broken heel. "Kin I have it this afternoon?" he drawled. "We-uns is a-movin' out of here tomorrow."

"I'll have it for you, sir, I promise. By two o'clock." Jacobs was, no doubt, noting the regimental number and state abbreviation the corporal wore on his collar. Word that that regiment was on the move might well head for Philadelphia before this afternoon. Confirming that, the shoemaker waited till the soldier was gone and then said, "As you see, Wid—Nellie, I have my own sources of information."

"Yes, I see that," she said. "And I see you're managing to use 'em without having anything to do with Bill Reach. As far as I'm concerned, you can go right on doing that. If he rots in jail, I won't shed a tear."

"What did he do to you, to make you hate him so?" Jacobs asked. Nellie set her jaw and said nothing. The shoemaker let out a long, sad sigh. "Whatever it was, he does not deserve these feelings you have about him. He kept track of everything, sorted it out, put pieces of the puzzle together . . . If any one man kept the Rebs from reaching the Delaware and bombarding Philadelphia, he is the one."

"A few hundred thousand soldiers had something to do with it, too, I think," Nellie answered tartly. She looked down at the dingy rug on the dingy floor of the shoemaker's shop. "Most important thing I've heard in the past week is that the Rebs think they're going to be getting barrels—or maybe plans for barrels, I'm not sure which—from England sometime soon. I think they're talking about barrels, anyway. Sometimes they call 'em tanks instead."

"That's what the English call them," Jacobs said. "Worth knowing. I suppose we should have expected as much." He did not sound very surprised or very interested. Maybe he wasn't. Maybe he just didn't want her to know how important her information was. Then he inclined his head in what was almost a bow, part of the old-time courtliness she enjoyed with him. "I hope you will come in again on such matters. And if you wish to come in for other reasons, I want you to know I am always glad to see you."

Nellie felt her cheeks grow hot. He meant he wanted to kiss her again. She'd liked it when he'd kissed her before. She wasn't used to being kissed any more, or to enjoying it when she was. He might even have meant he wanted to do more than kiss her. The idea didn't disgust her as much as she thought it should.

Flustered, she said, "We'll have to see," and hurried out of there as fast as she could go.

A Confederate major stood outside the door to the coffee-house. "Ah, here you are," he said, tipping his cap. "I looked inside, but I didn't see anyone."

"That's odd." Nellie opened the door for him. The bell jingled merrily. "Please, sir, come in. My daughter should be here." She raised her voice: "Edna!"

"Coming, Ma!" Edna called from upstairs, and came down as fast as anyone could have wanted.

"Get the major here his coffee and whatever else he wants," Nellie said severely. "If we're open for business, I want you down here ready to work. We lose customers if you aren't."

"Yes, Ma. I'm sorry, Ma." Edna hurried over to the Rebel. "What can I get for you today, sir?"

"Cup of coffee and a fried-egg sandwich," the major answered. To Nellie, he added, "It's all right, ma'am. Don't you worry about it."

"I do worry about it," Nellie said, "and it's not all right." But she let it drop; Edna had the coffee on the table for the major in jig time, and was frying eggs and slicing bread with practiced efficiency.

The bell jingled again. A couple of lieutenants came in. One of them leered disgracefully at Edna. Nellie made a point of serving that pair herself. Breakfast business was slower than usual, though. After an hour or so had gone by, the place was for the moment empty.

Nellie took advantage of that for a trip to the bathroom. When she came out, Edna was setting a cup of coffee in front of Lieutenant Nicholas H. Kincaid. The big lieutenant nodded to Nellie. "Morning, ma'am," he said, polite as usual.

"Good morning," she answered coolly. She wished he wouldn't come around here. He wanted to do more than leer at Edna; he'd made that plain. And she, young and foolish as she was, wanted to let him. Nellie shook her head. That wouldn't happen, not if she had anything to do with it.

Suddenly, she stiffened. She hadn't heard the doorbell ring. She should have heard it; the bathroom door was thin. She usually heard customers come in when she was in there. If she hadn't . . . if she hadn't, Edna had been upstairs before, and probably Kincaid had, too. Did Edna look smug?

She did. Without a doubt, she did. She looked like a cat that had fallen into a pitcher of cream. And Lieutenant Kincaid . . . As always, his eyes followed Edna. Still, that gaze was different now. He didn't look as if he wondered and dreamt of what she was like under her clothes. He looked as if he knew.

Nellie's hands balled into fists. Edna saw that, and laughed silently. Nellie wanted to throw a cup at her daughter. But what could she do? She couldn't prove a thing. Edna had made sure of that. All in a rush, for the first time in her life, Nellie felt old.

Arthur McGregor came in from the fields. The sun was at last dipping toward the northwestern horizon. He'd been up since it rose, or a little before. Manitoba summer days were long. He thanked God for that. Otherwise, he wouldn't even have come close to doing all the things he had to do if he wanted to bring in a crop. He couldn't do them all, not now. With the long days, he could come close.

As he walked in, Julia came out of the barn. "I've taken care of the livestock, Pa," she said. She was thirteen now, shooting up fast as a weed, tall as her mother or maybe even taller. He shook his head in bemusement. She wasn't a little girl any more. Where had the time gone?

"That's good," he told her. "That's very good. One more thing I don't have to worry about, and I've got plenty."

"I know," she answered seriously—she'd always been serious, no matter how little. McGregor sometimes thought she'd used up all the seriousness in the family, so that her sister Mary ended up with none. Julia went on, "I know I can't do as much as Alexander could, but I'm doing all I can."

"I know you are," her father told her. The whole family was doing all it could. In spite of themselves, his wide shoulders slumped. When the damned Americans had arrested Alexander, he'd known at once how big a hole it would leave in the family. What he'd realized only gradually was how big a hole not having his son left in the daily routine of the farm.

He made himself straighten. You did what you had to do, or as much of it as you could possibly do. His nostrils twitched. "Whatever Ma's cooking in there, it sure smells good."

"Chicken stew," Julia said.

McGregor's eyes went to the chopping block between the barn and the house. The stains on it were fresh, and the hatchet stood at an angle different from the way it had this morning. He smiled and nodded at his older daughter. "Good," he said. "Sticks to the ribs."

The inside of the farmhouse, as always, was spotless, immaculate. McGregor wondered how Maude managed to keep it that way. She'd taken on extra work, too, with Alexander gone. The weeding in the potato patch, for instance, was in her hands, because no one else had time for it.

And here came Mary, a rag in her hand, a look of fierce concentration on her face, the tip of her tongue peeking out of the corner of her mouth. Whenever she saw dust on anything, she pounced on it like a kitten pouncing on a cricket—and looked to be enjoying herself like a kitten, too.

"Pa!" she said indignantly. "You didn't wipe your feet very well."

"I'm sorry," he said, and meant it. Maude would have given him a hard time about that, too. He went back out and did it better. Seeing that he'd satisfied Mary—who would have let him know if he hadn't—he walked past her into the kitchen.

His wife looked up from the stew she was stirring. "You look worn to a nub," she said, worry in her voice.

"So do you," Arthur McGregor answered. They smiled at each other, wanly. He poured water from a pitcher over his hands and splashed some onto his face. Maude handed him a towel with which to dry himself. That was all the washing he did. Finding time for a bath even once a week wasn't easy.

"Supper soon," Maude said.

"Good." Walking in from the wheatfields, McGregor had thought he was too tired to be hungry. The first whiff of stew convinced him otherwise. He was ravenous as a wolf, and his stomach, empty since dinner long, long before, was growling like one, too.

He sat down in a chair in the front room to wait, and pulled out a copy of *Ivanhoe* with which to spend those few minutes: the first rest he'd had since dinner, too. The book was old, the binding starting to work loose from the pages. It had come out here with him from Ontario, and felt more like a companion than a novel. He sighed. He'd found himself in a world harsher and more merciless than the one Sir Walter Scott's hero knew.

Over the stew, Maude said, "Biddy Knight came by in the buggy this afternoon, while you were out working."

"Did she?" McGregor said. "I hope there weren't any Americans on the road to see her." Not least because he'd known Biddy's son, Alexander was in the Rosenfeld gaol now. But Biddy had a harder burden than that to bear: her boy was dead, executed by Yankee bullets. "What did she want?"

"Social call," his wife answered lightly—too lightly. "Her husband would take it kindly if you dropped in on him one of these days."

"Don't know that I want to." McGregor, as usual, was blunt. "If the Americans know we visit those people, it won't do Alexander any good." Maude nodded. Julia looked angry— she'd been angry at the Americans since the day they invaded. For once, something got past Mary, who was playing with the wishbone.

But McGregor hadn't been so blunt as he might have been. He feared Jimmy Knight's father was cooking up some kind of scheme to hurt the Americans, and wanted him to be a part of it. He didn't aim to join any plots. However much he despised the United States and everything they stood for, U.S. soldiers could kill his son any time they chose. That was a powerful argument in favor of prudence.

When Maude said, "Maybe you're right," he just nodded. Whenever his wife and he saw things the same way, they weren't likely to be on the wrong track.

While the womenfolk washed dishes, he indulged himself in the luxury of a pipe. It wasn't much of a luxury, not with the vile U.S. tobacco Henry Gibbon had to stock these days, but it was better than nothing. McGregor sighed for lost Virginia and North Carolina leaf as he paged through *Ivanhoe*. Scott made war feel glorious, nothing like the squalid reality that had roared past the farm.

The kitchen went dark. Kerosene was in short supply these days, too; no lamp ever burned in an unoccupied room. "Let's go outside, then upstairs to bed," Maude said. Mary's yawn was big as the world.

McGregor was the last to use the outhouse. By the time he got back in, his younger daughter was already snoring. "Saxons," he muttered as he pulled off his boots. "Saxons in a country the Normans stole from them."

"What are you talking about?" his wife said. But she was puzzled for only a moment. "Oh. That's right. You've been reading *Ivanhoe* again."

He nodded and undid his overalls. They were old, and hardly blue at all any more; the fabric, softened by many washings, conformed perfectly to the shape of his body. "Living in a land that had been theirs, and then somebody took it away. How did they stand it? How could they?"

Maude sighed. "You're going to break your heart, Arthur, if you dwell on things you can't do anything about. Getting Alexander home, we can do something about that. Maybe we can. I pray to God every night we can. But getting Canada back, that's too big for the likes of us."

"It shouldn't be," he declared. But half of that—more than half—was Sir Walter Scott speaking through him, and he was wise enough to understand as much.

If he hadn't been, Maude would have nailed it down tight: "If you don't think so, why didn't you want to go see poor Jimmy Knight's father? Sounds like he's going to try to do something—"

"Stupid," he finished for her. She nodded; he hadn't meant it for a joke, and she hadn't taken it for one. She blew out the lamp, plunging the bedroom into blackness. No moon, not tonight, and no town close by, either. Sometimes, when all the guns up at the front were going at once, that glow would flicker on the horizon: the Northern Lights of death. But the guns were quiet tonight, too, or as quiet as they ever got.

Still in his union suit, McGregor slid under the covers. Afterwards, he didn't know whether he first reached for Maude or she for him. After being married so long, after working so hard every day, desire was a flame that guttered, and sometimes guttered low. But it had never quite gone out, and, like any guttering flame, sometimes flared high, too.

Neither one of them undressed. They were almost as formal with each other as they would have been with strangers. He kissed her carefully, knowing he hadn't had time to shave in the past couple of days, knowing also he would rasp her face raw if he wasn't careful.

His hand closed on her breast through the cotton nightshirt she wore. She sighed. He squeezed her nipple. It stiffened against the soft fabric. He did the same with her other breast. They were still firm after nursing three children—and, in any case, in the darkness she was always a bride and he a bridegroom ever so glad to be out of his uncomfortable fancy suit and the top hat he'd never had on a day of his life before or since.

He reached under the hem of the long nightshirt. Her legs slid apart for him. His hands were hard with endless labor, and she—she was softer there than anywhere else. Of themselves, her legs drifted wider. When her breath began to come short and quick, he stopped what he was doing and unbuttoned the union suit with fingers clumsy not only from work but from desire. He poised himself above her. The mattress rocked, ever so slightly. She was nodding, urging him to hurry, something she would never have done with words.

She gasped when he entered her, and soon shuddered beneath him. He went on, intent on what he was doing—and also too tired to be able to do it quickly. She began to gasp again, her arms tightened around his back, her hips moving no matter how unladylike motion at such times was. She let out a small, involuntary moan at about the same time joyous fire poured through him.

He rolled off her almost at once, and set his underwear to rights. "Good night," she said, turning onto her side to get ready to sleep.

"Good night," he answered. They always said that. He kept wondering if there shouldn't be something more. But if there was more, their bodies had said it. For a little while, he hadn't thought about anything, not even Alexander. But making love didn't make trouble go away; it just shoved the trouble to one side. He brooded, but not for long. Sleep shoved trouble to one side, too.

In the morning, though, the sun would rise. The trouble would still be there.

George Enos slapped at a mosquito. He killed it—he squashed it flat, smearing red guts across his forearm. "That means it's bitten somebody," Wayne Pitchess said. "That's blood in there."

"Of course it's bitten somebody, for God's sake." Enos rolled his eyes. "You think I squashed it because it was throwing pillows at me?"

The *Punishment* lay at anchor a few miles beyond Clarksville, Tennessee. George didn't like lying at anchor. He looked to the south, to the hills below which the Cumberland flowed. Somewhere out there, the Rebs were liable to have a gun waiting to start throwing shells at the river monitor, and a moving target was harder to hit than a stationary one.

What worried him more than anything else was that monitors regularly tied up here: so regularly that the locals—the colored locals, anyhow—had run up a couple of shanties by the riverside to cater to Yankee sailors' needs—or their desires, anyhow. If you were off duty, and if your commanding officer was in a good mood, you could row over to the shanties, eat fried chicken or roast pork, drink some horrible homemade rotgut that tasted as if it should have gone into a kerosene lamp instead of a human being, or get your ashes hauled in the crib next door.

George had eaten the food, which was pretty good. He'd drunk the whiskey, and awakened the next morning with a head that felt like the *Punishment*'s boiler at forced draft. He hadn't laid his money down for any of the colored women, not yet. The sailors who had gone into the shabby little makeshift whorehouse came out with stories of how ugly the girls were. That hadn't stopped a lot of them from going back.

That was another reason he wished the *Punishment* would go upstream or down. He didn't want to be unfaithful to Sylvia, or the top part of his mind didn't. But he'd been away from her and without a woman for a long time now. If he went over to one of those shacks for some pork ribs and had himself a glass or two of that godawful bad whiskey, maybe he wouldn't care how ugly the whores were supposed to be or how much he missed Sylvia. Sometimes you just wanted to do it so badly, you . . .

He found himself fondling the curve of the water jacket on his machine gun as if it were Sylvia's breast—or, for that matter, the breast of one of the colored women in that shack. He jerked his hand away from the green-gray painted iron as if it had become red-hot, or as if everyone on the monitor could see what was on his mind.

He went back to work, stripping and cleaning the machine gun with the same dogged persistence he might have shown trawling for haddock in the North Atlantic. He wished he were trawling for haddock in the North Atlantic, or would have wished it had the ocean not been full of warships and commerce raiders and submarines, all of which looked on a fishing boat as a tasty snack.

And keeping the machine gun in perfect order didn't only distract him from thoughts of Sylvia (though, when he thought on how he'd rubbed the cooling jacket, it hadn't distracted him much, had it?); it also made his coming through a fight alive more likely. He approved of that.

But, as the sun began to slide down the sky in the afternoon, three men made for one of the *Punishment*'s boats to improve their outlook on life. One of them called to George: "Come on, have a few with us."

The deck officer was standing close by. Moltke Donovan was a fresh-faced lieutenant who took his duties very seriously. One of those duties was keeping his men in top fighting trim, and that meant, every now and then, letting them go off on a toot. Lieutenant Kelly would probably have said no. His replacement smiled and said, "Go ahead, Enos. That machine gun's in better shape than when they tore it out of its crate."

"Yes, sir," George said, if not happily, then without sackcloth and ashes, too. He set down the rag, stuck the little screwdriver into a loop on his belt, and hurried for the boat.

As he clambered in, one of the other sailors said, "I know you got money in your pocket, on account of you were lucky last night."

"Lucky, hell," Enos said indignantly. "That was skill, Grover, nothing else but."

"Skill, my foot," Grover retorted. "Anybody who draws three

cards and comes out holding a flush shouldn't play poker with honest people. You ought to go looking for wallets instead."

Said in a different tone of voice, that would have been an invitation to brawl. As things were, it was only rueful mourning over lost cash. George said, "Well, all right, maybe I was lucky." Laughing, they rowed across the Cumberland to the waiting shacks.

They tied up the boat at a bush by the edge of the river, there being no other wharf: till the war, this hadn't been a place where anyone stopped. But it was a place where people stopped now. George smelled ribs cooking in some kind of spicy sauce. He hadn't known he was hungry, but he knew it now. He scrambled out onto the mud of the riverbank and hurried toward the shack.

"Good day to you, gentlemens," said the colored fellow who ran the place. His name was Othello. He grinned, showing white teeth all the whiter for being set in a black, black face. "Got me some barbecue cookin', best you gwine find this side o' the Kentucky Smoke House."

He spoke as if that were some kind of touchstone. Maybe it was, but it didn't touch George. Still, he said, "All I know about Kentucky is that we're on this side of it. And all I know about that meat is that it smells better than anything that ever came out of the galley."

To that, Grover and the other two sailors—Albert and Stanley—added loud, profane agreement. Othello grinned again, and served up great slabs of sizzling-hot meat. Barbecue wasn't something Enos had known back in Boston, but, he thought, it was something he could get used to.

Othello had rags for napkins and sometimes eked out his mismatched, battered china with box lids. None of that mattered. "This pig died happy," George declared, and again no one argued with him.

"You boys want somethin' to wash that there down?" Othello asked, looking sly. Cumberland water wasn't so bad. Next to the water of the Mississippi, Cumberland water was pretty damn fine. But the jars the cook displayed, though they'd come out of the Cumberland and were dripping to prove it, hadn't been in there to fill with water, only to keep cool.

Grover shook his head. "God only knows why we drink that

panther sweat," he said. "I could get the same feeling hittin' my-self in the head with a hammer six or eight times, and it'd be cheaper."

"Taste better, too," Stanley said. But when Othello set a jar on the rickety table around which the sailors sat, nobody asked him to take it away. Nobody threw the cups and mugs he gave them at him, either. They paid him, poured the deadly-pale whiskey, and drank it down.

"Jesus," George wheezed when he could speak again. Another mug of that, he thought, and he was liable to know Jesus face to face—and, in the mood he'd be in, he'd probably want to wrestle. He drank the second mug. Jesus didn't appear, and he didn't die. Tomorrow morning, he might want to, but not now.

A colored woman walked into the shack. All she wore was a thin cotton shift. When she was standing between anybody looking at her and a source of light, the shape of her body was easy to make out.

"Boys," she said, "if you done spent *all* your money here, my friends and me, we is gonna be powerful disappointed in y'all."

Othello laughed. George didn't know whether he got a rakeoff from the whores who'd set up shop next door, but that laugh made him think so. "Mehitabel, I left 'em with somethin'," he said. "You kin git yo' share." He made no bones about being there for any other reason than skinning the men from the *Pun-ishment* or any other U.S. river monitors that came by. And if the Confederate Navy made it back to this stretch of the Cumber-land, he'd skin them, too.

Mehitabel placed herself so she was displayed to best advan-tage. George wished he hadn't let that second mug of whiskey char its way to his stomach. He wasn't thinking about Sylvia now, any more than a stallion thought of anything when you put him in with a mare in season.

He got up from the table. The other sailors shouted bawdy ad-vice. Rolling her big hips, the whore led him out of one shack toward the other. In broad daylight, she might as well not have been wearing that shift. She sure as hell wasn't wearing anything underneath it.

George's heart drummed in his chest. His breath whistled in his throat. That was what he thought at first, with rotgut half stunning his senses. But he knew the sound of incoming shells in his gut, not just in his head, which wasn't working very well right then.

He threw himself flat—not on top of the whore, but to the ground. The roar of the explosions stunned him. Mehitabel screamed like a cat with its tail in a door. Dirt flew as shells smashed into the soft ground south of the Cumberland. Great columns of water leaped from shells landing in the Cumberland. And, to George's horror, two enormous columns of smoke and flame sprang from the *Punishment* as one shell struck her near the stern, the other square amidships.

More shells walked across the Cumberland toward him. Some of the water they kicked up splashed down onto him and onto Mehitabel, plastering the thin shift to her rounded contours. Enos didn't care about that. He didn't care about anything except approaching death and the fate of his crewmates.

The shells stopped falling before they reached the north bank of the Cumberland. He looked out toward the *Punishment*. The river monitor was burning and sinking fast. A moment later, as flame reached the magazines, it stopped burning and exploded. Mehitabel's mouth was open as wide as it would go, which meant she had to be screaming, but George couldn't hear a thing.

The heat of the fireball scorched his face. When at last it faded, twenty feet or so of the bow of the *Punishment* stuck up out of the river like a tombstone. The rest of the monitor was gone. A couple of bodies and a few pieces of bodies floated in the water, food for the snappers.

Stanley and Albert and Grover came out of the shack where they'd been drinking. They looked as bad as Enos felt. He suddenly realized he wasn't drunk any more. Horror and terror had scorched the whiskey out of him.

He also realized, looking at his crewmates, that they were the only four Yankee sailors in hostile country, and that none of them carried anything more lethal than a belt knife. Absurdly, he wished he hadn't wasted so much time on that machine gun when all it turned out to be good for was getting blown up.

"Get into bed this minute, do you hear me?" Sylvia Enos snapped at George, Jr., punctuating her words with a whack on his fanny.

As nothing else would have, that convinced him she meant

what she said. "Good night, Mama!" he exclaimed, and planted a large, wet kiss on her cheek. He hurried off into the bedroom, humming an artillery march.

Sylvia looked down at the palm of her hand. It still stung, which meant his behind had to sting, too. He hadn't even noticed, except that the swat had reminded him of what he needed to do. She stared after him. Was she raising a little boy or training a horse?

Mary Jane had peacefully gone to bed an hour before. By the haggard look on Brigid Coneval's face when Sylvia had picked up her children, the reason Mary Jane was peaceful in the evening was that she'd raised hell all afternoon, and worn herself out doing it.

It wasn't even nine o'clock yet. *An hour to myself,* Sylvia thought. *I can read a book. I can write a letter. I can just sit here and think about how tired I am.* That last sounded particularly good to her.

She'd sat for about five minutes when someone knocked on the door. That should have been the signal for George, Jr., to come bounding out of the bedroom, demanding to know what was going on. But he didn't: only soft, steady breathing came from there, not a little boy. Well, he'd been raising hell all afternoon, too; he must have run down as soon as his head hit the pillow.

Sylvia laughed to herself as she walked to the door. Try as she would, she had the devil of a time getting any peace and quiet. Here was somebody wanting to borrow some molasses or salt, or to tell her the latest scandal of the apartment house, or to give her some cookies or . . . a little community in its own right, the building was a busy place.

She opened the door. Standing there was no one she knew, but a youngster a year too young to do a proper job of raising the downy, fuzzy excuse for a mustache he had on his upper lip. He wore a green uniform, darker than the Army green-gray, with brass buttons stamped "WU." "Mrs. Enos?" he said, and, at her automatic nod, went on, "Telegram for you, ma'am."

Numbly, she accepted the envelope. Numbly, she signed for it. Numbly, she closed the door as the delivery boy hurried away. And, numbly, she opened the envelope with shaking fingers. It was, as she'd feared, from the Navy Department. REGRET TO IN-

FORM YOU, she read, and a low moan came from her throat, THAT YOUR HUSBAND, ABLE SEAMAN GEORGE ENOS, IS LISTED AS MISSING IN EXPLOSION OF USS PUNISHMENT. NO FURTHER INFORMATION AVAILABLE AT THIS TIME. YOU WILL BE INFORMED DIRECTLY SHOULD HE BE FOUND OR CONFIRMED LOST. The printed signature was that of the Secretary of the Navy.

She stared at the telegram till the words were only shapes on paper, shapes without meaning, without sense. But it did not help. The meaning had already been imparted, and lay inside her mind like an icy spear, piercing and freezing everything it touched. She crumpled the flimsy yellow sheet of paper. She felt crumpled, used and used up and thrown away by something bigger than herself, something bigger than the whole country, something eating the world. It was blind and sloppy, and it would not stop until it had its fill.

Her body knew what to do. Her mind did not fight it when it set the alarm on the clock by the bed, undressed itself, and lay down. It tried to make itself go to sleep, too. It knew how tired it was. But her mind had something to say about that, and said it, loud and emphatically.

She lay and lay and lay, mind spinning useless like a trolley wheel on an icy track. Convinced she would not sleep at all, she closed her eyes to look at the darkness inside her eyelids instead of the different darkness of the ceiling. She tried to guess when it was four, when five, when six and time to rise.

She jerked in horror when the alarm went off. She had fallen asleep after all. She wished she'd had a moment's forgetfulness on first getting up, but no. She knew. As she had after the telegram arrived, she let her body do what needed doing, and roused her children, fed them breakfast, and took them over to Brigid Coneval's apartment almost without conscious thought.

"Are you all right, dearie?" Mrs. Coneval asked. Her husband was in the Army. "You look a bit peaked, you do."

"It's—nothing," Sylvia said. She kissed her children and left for work. Brigid Coneval stared after her, shaking her head.

Mechanically, Sylvia boarded the trolley. Mechanically, she rode to the right stop. Mechanically, she got off. Mechanically, she punched in. And, mechanically, she headed for her machine.

The mechanism broke when she saw Isabella Antonelli, or rather when her friend saw her. "Sylvia!" Isabella exclaimed, recognizing the dazed, haggard face staring at her for what it was. "Your husband, your Giorgio. Is he—?"

"Missing." Sylvia forced the word out through numb lips. "I got—the telegram—last night . . ." She started to cry. She should have been working already. "I'm sorry, but—" She dissolved again.

Isabella Antonelli came over and wrapped her arms around Sylvia, as Sylvia might have done for Mary Jane had her little daughter broken a favorite doll. "Oh, my friend," Isabella said. "I am so sorry he is gone."

"Missing," Sylvia said. "The telegram said missing."

"I will pray for you," Isabella answered. She said nothing more than that. *Missing* was a forlorn hope, and one all too likely to sink on the sea of truth. She knew that. Sylvia knew it, too. She would not have admitted knowing it, not if her own life depended on that admission.

Mr. Winter came limping along to see that the day shift's run was beginning as it should. When he saw the two women huddled together between their machines, he hurried over to them. "Here, what's this?" he asked, his voice not angry but not calm, either. For him, the line came first, everything else afterwards. "What's going on?"

Sylvia tried to answer and could not. Calmly—with the sort of calm that comes from having experienced too much rather than not enough—Isabella Antonelli spoke for her: "Her husband, he is missing, she hears last night from the Department of Wars." Sylvia didn't bother correcting her.

"Oh. I am sorry to hear that," the foreman said, and sounded as if he was telling, if not the whole truth, then at least most of it. He studied Sylvia. "Do you want to go home, Mrs. Enos?"

"No," Sylvia answered quickly. If she went home, they would find a substitute for her, and they might keep the substitute, too. But that was not the only reason she spoke as she did: "I'd rather be here, as a matter of fact. It will help me take my mind off, off—" She didn't go on. Going on would have meant thinking about what she most wanted not to think about.

Mr. Winter gnawed at his mustache. "I dunno," he said. But Isabella Antonelli gave him such a reproachful look that he softened. "All right, Mrs. Enos; we'll see how it goes." Had he not been interested in Sylvia's friend as something more than an employee, he might have decided differently. Sylvia noted that enough to be amused by it, and then got angry at herself for letting anything amuse her.

She went to her machine and began pulling levers. She hoped desperately to fall into the routine that sometimes overtook her, so that half the day would go by without her consciously noticing it. To her disappointment, it didn't happen. Her body did what it had to do, pulling her three levers, loading labels, filling the paste reservoir, and her mind ran round and round and round like a pet squirrel in a wheel.

When she went home, she said nothing to Brigid Coneval. The Irishwoman's green eyes glowed with curiosity, though; surely the whole floor and probably the whole apartment building knew by now that she'd got a telegram in the night. But explaining to Mrs. Coneval would have meant explaining to George, Jr., who, like any little pitcher, had enormous ears. She sometimes marveled that he could hear anything, what with all the noise he made, but here he did. *George is only missing,* Sylvia told herself fiercely. *I don't have to say anything till I know for certain. Time enough then.*

She did her best not to let her demeanor show either of her children anything was wrong. That she was even more tired than usual from having slept so badly the night before probably helped rather than hurt her cause. The evening passed quietly, not too far from normal.

Four days went by like that. Sympathy replaced curiosity in Brigid Coneval's face. "It's a brave front you put up, Mrs. Enos," she said, having drawn her own conclusions. When Sylvia only shrugged, Mrs. Coneval nodded, as if she'd received all the answer she needed.

Sylvia's mood veered from despair to fury, with many stops in between. She'd expected a second telegram hard on the heels of the first, either letting her know George was well or—more likely, she feared—very much the reverse. Either way, she would have known how to respond. She couldn't respond to nothing, though. It left her adrift on a chartless sea.

Her work was not all it might have been. Mr. Winter proved more forbearing than she'd expected. "You're doing the best you can, Mrs. Enos; I can see that," he told her. Was he saying that because he was a veteran himself, and a widower, too, and so knew what suffering was like, or because he had an ulterior motive if George really was lost? With no way to be sure, she cautiously gave him the benefit of the doubt.

Another four days went by. Sometimes life seemed almost normal. Sometimes Sylvia thought she was losing her mind. Sometimes she hoped she would.

Press, step, press, step, press, go back to the beginning and begin the cycle anew . . . She *had* succeeded in immersing herself in the rhythm of her machine when another Western Union delivery boy interrupted her. "Mrs. Enos?" he said, holding out a yellow envelope. "They told me at your apartment house where you was at, ma'am."

She signed the sheet he had on his clipboard. He got out of there in a hurry—telegraph delivery boys were not welcome visitors, not in wartime. Cans began to stack up as Sylvia pulled none of her three levers.

She opened the envelope. Yes, from the Navy Department—who else? Isabella Antonelli came hurrying over to her. She didn't notice. Again, she was reading: MY PLEASANT DUTY TO INFORM YOU YOUR HUSBAND, ABLE SEAMAN GEORGE ENOS, CONFIRMED AS UNINJURED SURVIVOR OF LOSS OF MONITOR USS PUNISHMENT. TO BE REASSIGNED, LEAVE POSSIBLE. She read but did not notice the Secretary of the Navy's name.

"God hears my prayers," said Isabella, who had been looking over her shoulder.

"Good heavens!" Sylvia exclaimed. "The line!" All at once, life stretched out ahead of her again. Small things mattered. Waving the telegram like a banner, she hurried back to deal with all the cans that had stacked up. Mr. Winter never said a thing.

"This west Texas country would be wonderful terrain for tanks," Stinky Salley said.

Several of the Confederate soldiers gathered around the campfire looked at him. "You mean barrels, don't you?" Jefferson Pinkard said at last.

"I prefer to use the name our allies have given them," Salley said loftily, with his usual fussy precision. "Let the damnyankees call them what they will."

"Oh, give it up, Stinky," Pinkard said. "Everybody's calling the damn things barrels, us and the Yanks both."

"That does not make it proper," Salley returned, "any more than it is proper to call me Stinky rather than my given name."

"Proves my point, doesn't it?" Jeff said, and got a laugh from his squadmates. Stinky Salley glared, but he spent a lot of time glaring.

"It would be good country for barrels, except only for one thing," Hip Rodriguez said, holding one finger up in the air.

"What the devil do you know about it, you damn greaser?" Salley said with a snort. "It's perfect country for tanks." He kept on using his word, regardless of what anyone else did. Waving a hand, he continued, "It's flat, it's wide open—it's ideal."

Rodriguez looked at him expressionlessly. "I gonna tell you two things," he said in his uncertain English. As he had before, he held up one finger. "It ain't no perfect country for barrels on account of ain't no train stations close to here nowhere. Barrel got to run by itself, barrel breaks down."

"Everything I've heard about them damn things, he's right," Sergeant Albert Cross said. "Bastards break down if you look at 'em sideways."

"Gracias." With considerable dignity, the Sonoran soldier inclined his head to the noncom. Then he undid his bayonet from his sheath and made as if to clean his nails with it. Looking straight into Salley's face, he went on, "I tell you the second thing now. You call me a damn greaser again, I cut your fucking throat." His voice was flat and emotionless—not so much a threat as a simple statement of how the world would be.

Salley's pale eyes went wide. His mouth formed a startled O. He turned to Cross. "Sergeant, did you hear that?"

"I heard it," the noncom answered. "I heard you, too. If I was you, I'd watch the way I ran my big mouth." He noisily sipped coffee from his tin cup.

Salley stared at Hip Rodriguez as if he'd never seen him before. Maybe he hadn't, not really. Sonorans and Chihuahuans and Cubans—Cubans without black blood in them, anyhow—had a curious place in the CSA: better off than Negroes, but not really part of the larger society, either, cut off from it by swarthiness, language, and religion. But a Sonoran with a weapon in his hand was not something to take lightly. Stinky Salley kept quiet after that—he made a point of keeping quiet after that.

Instead of making cornmeal into little loaves, Rodriguez wet his share and shaped it into patties he fried in lard and wrapped around his tinned rations. Pinkard and a couple of other soldiers in the squad were doing that, too; beans and beef went down easier and tastier. Pinkard took a bite out of his—*tortilla,* Hip called a cornmeal patty—then said in a low voice, "You shut him up sharp."

Rodriguez shrugged. "If you step on a scorpion when he is small, he don't get no bigger."

"Yeah." Jeff's eyes slid to Stinky Salley. The ex-clerk still didn't look as if he knew what had hit him. That, Pinkard thought, wasn't so good. Stinky'd done well enough against U.S. soldiers, out at a distance. But when Rodriguez delivered his warning, he'd folded up. In a way, it was just Stinky's problem. But in another way, it warned of a weakness in the squad, and that was everybody's problem.

Off in the distance, a rifle barked. Pinkard's head came up, as a watchdog's would do at the sound of someone walking past his house. Another shot followed, also a long way off. Then silence. He relaxed.

Rodriguez swigged from his canteen and wiped his mouth on his sleeve. He'd already put the bayonet away, having made his point with it. "You know what?" he said to Pinkard. "I miss my *esposa.* How you say *esposa,* Jeff? My woman, my—"

"Your wife?" Pinkard said.

"*Sí,* my wife." Rodriguez pronounced the word with care. "I go to sleep in the night, I see my wife in a *sueño.*" Not knowing or not caring that wasn't English, he went on, "When I wake up, all I see is *soldados feos*—ugly soldiers." *Sueño* was something like *dream,* Jeff realized. Hip Rodriguez sighed. "I do better, I stay to sleep." He glanced over toward Pinkard. "You got a wife, yes, Jeff?"

"Yeah. I wish I was home with her, too." Pinkard was amazed at how little he'd thought of Emily since he got his notice from the Conscription Bureau and reported for duty. Now that she flooded into his mind, he understood why he'd done his best to block the memories—they hurt too much, when set alongside the squalid reality of the life he was living.

Fleas and lice and fear and mutilation and stinks and—He turned away from the campfire, a scowl on his face. If he weren't here, if he hadn't got that damned buff-colored envelope, he could have been in Emily's arms right now, making the bed-springs creak, her breath warm and moist on the skin of his neck, her voice urging him on to things he hadn't imagined he could do or else rising to a cry of joy that must have made Bedford Cunningham and all his other neighbors jealous. Dear God, she loved to do it!

Courteous as a cat, more courteous than most curious Confederates would have been, Hip Rodriguez left him alone with his thoughts. For a few seconds, Jeff was glad of that. And then, all at once, he wasn't.

Back before the government put him in butternut and stuck a rifle in his hands, he'd matched Emily stroke for stroke, given her everything she'd wanted in the way of loving. Now he wasn't there any more. She'd grown used to making love all the time. Would she be looking for a substitute?

He shivered, regardless of how hot and muggy the evening was. In his imagination, he could see her thrashing on the bed with—whom? The face on the male form riding her didn't matter. It wasn't his own. That was enough, and bad enough.

His fists bunched. *This is all moonshine,* he told himself fiercely. He'd never had any reason to believe Emily would want to be unfaithful to him. If ever two people loved each other, Emily and he were those two. But he'd never been away from her before. And she didn't just love him. She loved love, and he knew it. *Moonshine, dammit, moonshine.*

When he hadn't said anything for some little while, Rodriguez quietly asked, "You are lonely, *amigo?*"

"You bet I am," Pinkard said. "Ain't you?"

"I am lonely for my *esposa,* my wife. I am lonely for my farm. I am lonely for my village, where I go to drink in the *cantina.* I am lonely for my proper food. I am lonely for my *lengua,* where I can talk and I don't got to think before I say every word. I am lonely for not being nowhere near these *yanquis* who try of killing me. *Sí,* I am lonely."

Jeff hadn't thought of it like that. Even though the filthy picture in his imagination wouldn't go away, he said, "Sounds like I got it easy next to you, maybe."

"Life is hard." Rodriguez shrugged. "And after life is done, then you die." He shrugged again. "What can anyone do?"

It was a good question. It was, when Pinkard thought about it, a very good question. If there were any better questions out there, he had no idea what they might be. "You do the best you can, is all," he answered slowly, and then looked around at the hole in the ground in the middle of nowhere he was currently inhabiting. "If this here is the best I can do, I been doin' somethin' wrong up till now."

"I also think this very thing," Rodriguez said with a smile. "Then I think what they do to my *compadres* who do not come into the Army when it is their time. Beside that, this is *muy bueno.*"

"Yeah, you try and dodge conscription, they land on you with both feet." Pinkard yawned. Exhaustion was landing on him with both feet. He spread his blanket under him—too hot to roll himself in it—and smeared his face and hands with camphor-smelling goo that was supposed to hold the mosquitoes and other bugs at bay. As far as he could see, it didn't do much good, but he was happier with it in his nostrils than with what he smelled like after God only knew how long since his last bath.

The next morning, Captain Connolly got the company moving before sunup. The promised drive on Lubbock hadn't happened. Nobody was saying much about that, but nobody was very happy with it, either. Trying to build a front to keep the damnyankees from moving deeper into Texas wasn't the same as throwing them out of the state when they had no business there.

What can anyone do? Hip Rodriguez's question echoed in Jeff's mind. So did his own answer. *You do the best you can, is all.* If the best the CSA could do was keep the USA from pushing deeper into Texas, the war wasn't going the way everybody'd figured it would when it started.

The Yankees were extending their line northward, too. Texas, Jeff thought wearily as he tramped through it, had nothing but room. The invaders kept hoping they could get around the Confederates' flank, and the job for the boys in butternut was convincing them they couldn't.

A brisk little fire fight developed, both sides banging away at each other from little foxholes they scraped into the hard earth as soon as the bullets started flying. Neither U.S. nor C.S. forces were there in any great numbers; it was almost like a game, though nobody wanted to be removed from the board.

"Hold 'em, boys," Captain Connolly yelled. "Help's on the way." Firing at a muzzle flash, Jeff figured the Yankees' commander was probably shouting the same thing. One of them would prove a liar. After a moment, Jeff realized they both might prove liars.

But Captain Connolly had the right of it. A battery of three-inch howitzers came galloping up behind the thin Confederate line and started hurling shrapnel shells at the equally thin Yankee line. The U.S. soldiers, without artillery of their own and not dug in to withstand a bombardment, sullenly drew back across the prairie. The Confederates advanced—not too far, not too fast, lest they run into more than they could handle.

"We licked 'em," Jeff said, and Hip Rodriguez nodded. Pinkard took off his helmet to scratch his head. Victory was supposed to be glorious. He didn't feel anything like glory. He was alive, and nobody'd shot him. He fumbled for tobacco and a scrap of paper in which to wrap it. Right now, alive and unshot would do.

Barracks swelled Tucson, New Mexico, far beyond its natural size. In one of those barracks, Sergeant Gordon McSweeney sat on a cot wishing he were someplace, anyplace, else. "I want to get back to the field," he murmured, more than half to himself.

Ben Carlton heard him. McSweeney outranked Carlton, but, as cook, the latter enjoyed a certain amount of license an ordinary private soldier, even a veteran, would not have had. "Rather be here than that damn Baja, California desert," he declared, "and you can take that to church."

McSweeney shook his head. He was big and tall and fair, with muscles like rocks, a chin and cheekbones that might have been hewn from granite, and pale eyes that looked through a man, not at him. He said, "A soldier's purpose is fighting. If I am not fighting, I am not fulfilling my appointed purpose in life." If he did not do that, his infinitely stern, infinitely just God would surely punish him for it in the days to come.

Carlton would not be silenced. "To hell with my appointed purpose, if the damn fool who appointed me to it gets his brains out o' the latrine bucket. Sendin' us down there with no support or nothin', that was murder, and that's all it was." He stuck out his own chin, which was nowhere near so granitic as McSweeney's. "Go ahead and tell me I'm wrong. I dare you."

From most men, to most men, that would have been an invitation to fight. Gordon McSweeney reserved his wrath for the men on the other side, a fact for which his mates had had a good many occasions to be thankful. "God predestined our failure, for reasons of His own," he said now.

Ben Carlton looked as if he had bitten into something that tasted bad—*something he cooked himself, then,* McSweeney thought. "Damn me to hell if I can see how God's will had anything to do with poor Paul bleedin' to death like a stuck pig way the devil out in the middle of the desert," Carlton said.

McSweeney's gaze fixed on him as if over the sights of a Springfield. "God will surely damn you to hell if you take His name in vain." His expression softened, ever so slightly. "Paul Mantarakis, as I saw, was a brave man, for all that he was a papist."

"He weren't no Cath-*o*-lic," Carlton said. "He was whatever Greeks are—orthosomething, he called it."

"He carried with him a rosary of beads, which condemns him of itself. A pity, I admit, for he was a man of spirit." McSweeney spoke with the assurance of one who knew himself to be a member of the elect and thus assured salvation.

Carlton gave it up. "There's worse men than Paul as are still breathing in and out," he said.

"Such is God's will," McSweeney answered. "Only a fool, and a blasphemous fool at that, would question it. Be assured: the unjust shall have their requital."

He got left alone after that, which suited him well enough. Even in the crowded trenches of western Kentucky, he had been left alone a good deal. He knew why: a man of fixed purpose naturally confounded the greater number who had none, but drifted through life like floating leaves, going wherever the current chanced to take them. God anchored him, and anchored him firm.

That he used the time to make sure his flamethrower was in good working order also helped ensure his privacy. Few in the company seemed eager to associate, either in the field or away from the fighting, with anyone who carried such horror on his back. In the field, the enemy made flamethrower operators special targets, so McSweeney could see the sense in staying away from him, even if it filled him with scorn. Back here? He shrugged. If the men gave in to superstition, how could he stop them?

After evening mess call, the soldiers gossiped and smoked and gambled till lights out. McSweeney read the Book of Kings, an island of rectitude in the sea of sin all around. Then one of the men in his squad shouted "Goddammit!" after losing a poker hand he thought he should have won.

"Thou shalt not take the name of the Lord in vain, Hansen," McSweeney said, glancing up from the small type of the Bible.

"Yes, Sergeant. Sorry, Sergeant," Private Ulysses Hansen said hastily. He was not the smallest nor the weakest nor the least spirited man in the regiment, but his sergeant not only outranked him but also intimidated him. He kept his language circumspect thereafter.

In the morning, McSweeney inspected the persons and kits of his squad with his usual meticulous care. When he'd reported to Captain Schneider the infractions he'd found, the company commander raised an eyebrow and said, "Sergeant, can't you learn to let some of that go? You gig men for things that aren't worth noticing."

"Sir, they are against regulations," McSweeney answered stiffly.

"I understand that, Sergeant, but—" Schneider looked exasperated. For the life of him, Gordon McSweeney could not understand why. He stood at stolid attention, not showing his perplexity. Schneider was a brave soldier, and not altogether ungodly; he might perhaps have been numbered among the elect. After a pause to marshal his thoughts, he went on, "A smudged button or a speck of dust on a collar won't cost us the war. These are real soldiers, remember, not West Point cadets."

"Sir, I did not invent the infractions," McSweeney said. "All I did was note them and report them to you."

"You'd need a magnifying glass to note some of them," Schneider said.

McSweeney shook his head. "No, sir, only my eyes."

Schneider looked unhappier still. "Could you stand the kind of inspection you're giving your men?"

"Sir, I hope so," McSweeney answered. "If I fail, I deserve whatever punishment you care to inflict on me."

Now the captain shook his head. "You don't get it, Sergeant. I don't want to punish you for small things. I don't want you making your men hate you so much they won't follow you, either."

"Sir, they will follow me." McSweeney spoke with a calm, absolute confidence. "Whatever else they may feel about me, they're afraid of me."

"I don't doubt that," Captain Schneider muttered, perhaps more to himself than to McSweeney. But he shook his head again. "That won't do, I'm afraid. A U.S. noncom or officer whose men hate him or fear him ends up with a wound from a Springfield, not a Tredegar."

Gordon McSweeney considered that. "Whoever would do such a thing would surely spend eternity in hell."

"As may be," Schneider said. "That's not the point. The point is to keep your men from wanting to shoot you in the first place."

"If they would only do that which is required of them, we would not have this problem," McSweeney said.

Captain Schneider sighed. "Sergeant, have you ever, even once in your life, considered the wisdom of tempering justice with mercy?"

"No, sir," McSweeney answered, honestly shocked.

"I believe you," Schneider said. "The one thing—the only thing—I'll give you is that you hold yourself to the same standards as everyone else. That time a couple of days ago when you reported yourself for not polishing the inside of your canteen cup—that was a first for me, I tell you. But what did I do about it?"

"Nothing, sir." McSweeney's voice reeked disapproval.

Captain Schneider either didn't notice or pretended not to. "That's right. That's what I'm going to keep on doing when you bother me with tiny things, too. Sergeant, I order you not to report trivial infractions to me until and unless they constitute a clear and obvious danger to the discipline or safety of your squad. Do you understand me?"

"No, sir," McSweeney said crisply.

"All right, then, Sergeant. I am going to leave you with two quotations from the Good Book, then. I want you to concentrate on the lessons in John 8:7 and Matthew 7:1." With an abrupt about-face, Schneider stalked off.

Gordon McSweeney knew the Scriptures well. But those were not verses he was in the habit of studying, so he had to go and look them up. *He that is without sin among you, let him first cast a stone at her,* he read in John. The verse in Matthew was even shorter and more to the point, saying, *Judge not, that ye be not judged.*

He stared out the door through which Captain Schneider had departed. The captain, as far as he was concerned, had the letter without the spirit. If God chose to urge mercy, that was His affair. Could a man not so urged by the Lord afford such a luxury? McSweeney didn't think so.

He was, in any case, by temperament more drawn to the Old Testament than to the New. The children of Israel, now, had been proper warriors. God had not urged them to mercy, but to glorify His name by smiting their foes. And their prophets and kings had obeyed, and had grown great by obeying. Against such a background, what did a couple of verses matter?

Jesus Christ hadn't always been meek and mild, either. Hadn't He driven the money-changers from the Temple? They hadn't been doing anything so very wrong. *Trivial infractions,* Captain Schneider would have called their business, and thought Jesus should have left it alone.

McSweeney flipped back a few pages in the Book of Matthew and grunted in satisfaction. "Chapter 5, verse 29," he murmured: *And if thy right eye offend thee, pluck it out, and cast it from thee: for it is profitable for thee that one of thy members should perish, and not that thy whole body should be cast into hell.*

He looked at the men in his squad. None of them dared meet his eye. Would any have the nerve to shoot him under cover of battle? He shook his head. He didn't believe it, not for a moment. Would they leave him in the lurch when he attacked? Maybe they would. His glance flicked to the flamethrower. Anyone who carried one of those infernal devices was on his own anyhow.

"Justice," McSweeney said, and gave a sharp nod. Only the wicked feared justice, and with reason, for they deserved chastisement. Thus the United States would chastise their seceded brethren, and chastise as well the wicked foreigners who had made secession possible.

God wills it, McSweeney thought, for all the world like a Crusader before the walls of Jerusalem. And Jerusalem would fall. He would make it fall, and break anyone and anything standing in the way.

XIV

Achilles smiled at Cincinnatus, a smile that showed one new tooth in a wide, wet mouth. The baby said something wordless but joyful. Cincinnatus smiled back. To Elizabeth, he said, "He's in a happy mood this mornin', ain't he?"

His wife smiled back, wanly. "Why shouldn't he be happy? He can sleep as long as he wants, an' he can wake up whenever he please. An' he's still too little to know his ma can't do likewise."

"I heard him there in the middle of the night," Cincinnatus said, digging into the ham and eggs Elizabeth had made. "He sounded happy then, too."

"He *was* happy," she said, rolling her eyes, which were still streaked with red. "He was so happy, he wanted to play. He didn't want to go back to bed, not for nothin' he didn't. Did you?" She poked Achilles in the ribs. He thought that was the funniest thing in the world, and squealed laughter. When he did, his mother visibly melted. All the same, she said, "What I wanted to do was give him some laudanum, so he'd go back to sleep and I could, too." She yawned. Achilles squealed again—everything was funny this morning.

No sooner had Cincinnatus shoveled the last fluffy scrambled egg into his mouth than someone knocked on the door. He grabbed for his mug of coffee and gulped it down while hurrying to let in his mother. "How's my little grandbaby?" she asked.

Cincinnatus was still swallowing. From the kitchen, Elizabeth answered, "Mother Livia, he must be sleepin' while you got him, on account of he sure don't do none o' that in the nighttime."

"He jus' like his father, then," Cincinnatus' mother said. She turned to him. "You was the wakinest child I ever did hear tell

393

of." Without taking a breath, she went on in a different tone of voice: "Looks like it's fixin' to storm out there, storm somethin' fierce."

"Does it?" Cincinnatus looked outside himself. His mother was right. Thick, dark clouds were boiling up in the northwest, over Ohio, and heading rapidly toward Covington. The air felt still and heavy and damp. He reached into the pocket of his dungarees and pulled out a nickel. "Gonna ride me the trolley down to the docks."

"Gettin' pretty la-de-da, ain't you?" his mother said. "Trolley here, trolley there, like you got all the money is to have. Pretty soon you gwine buy youself a motorcar, ain't that right?"

"Wish it was," Cincinnatus said, and gave her a kiss as he hurried out the door. When the CSA had ruled Covington, a motorcar for a black man would have been out of the question, unless he wanted to be branded as uppity—and, perhaps, literally branded as well. Under the USA . . . maybe such a thing would be possible, if he got the money together. Maybe it wouldn't, too.

The rain began just before he got to the trolley stop, which wasn't particularly close to his house. One stop served the entire Negro district near the Licking River. He remembered the complaints he'd heard about routing the track even so close to his part of town.

When the trolley car rattled up, he threw his nickel into the fare box and sat down in the back. The Yankees hadn't changed the rules about that sort of thing; they had rules of their own, not quite so strict as those of the Confederacy but not tempered by intimate acquaintance, either. He sighed. If your skin was dark, you had trouble finding a fair shake anywhere.

Lightning flashed. Thunder boomed. Rain started coming down in sheets. The trolley filled up in a hurry, as people who usually would have walked to work decided against it today. Whites started moving back into the Negro section. One by one, Cincinnatus and his fellow blacks gave up their seats and stood holding the overhead rail. None of them complained, not out loud. Men down from the USA ousted them as casually as did native Covingtonians.

Water sprayed up from the trolley's wheels as it slid to a stop near the wharves. Cincinnatus and several other Negro men

leaped down and ran for their places. The others were all
roustabouts; they'd be drenched by the time the day was through.
Cincinnatus didn't expect to be much better off. For one thing, it
was almost as wet inside the cab of a White truck as it was outside. For another, he'd be outside a good deal of the time, certainly while loading and unloading his snarling monster, and
probably while fixing punctures as well.

"Morning, Cincinnatus," Lieutenant Straubing said when he
splashed into the warehouse that served as headquarters for the
transportation unit. "Wet enough out there to suit you?"

"Sure enough is, suh," Cincinnatus answered. As usual, his
color seemed not to matter to Straubing. He still had trouble believing that could be true, but had seen no evidence to make him
suppose it was an act, either.

The lieutenant looked troubled. "Cincinnatus, we have a
problem, and I think we could use your help to solve it."

"What kind of problem you talking about, sir?" the Negro
asked, expecting it to be something to do with the bad weather
and what it was doing to the schedule and to Kentucky's miserable roads.

Lieutenant Straubing looked even less happy. "A sabotage
problem, I'm afraid," he answered. Just then, an enormous clap
of thunder gave Cincinnatus an excuse for jumping, which was
just as well, because he would have jumped with an excuse or
without one. Straubing went on, "An unhealthy number of fires
have broken out in areas we've served. Please be on the alert for
anything that seems suspicious."

"Yes, suh, I'll do that," Cincinnatus said, knowing everyone
would be on the alert for *him*, a distinctly alarming notion.

Straubing said, "Damned if I can figure out who's playing
games with us, either. Maybe it's the Reds"—he didn't say anything about niggers, as most whites, U.S. or C.S., would have
done—"or maybe it's Confederate diehards. Whoever it is, he'll
pay when he gets caught."

"Yes, suh," Cincinnatus said again. "He deserve it." He shut
up after that, not wanting to draw the U.S. lieutenant's attention
to himself. Part of that, of course, was simple self-preservation.
Part of it, too, was not wanting the one white man who'd ever
treated him like a human being to be disappointed in him. If

the United States had produced more men like Lieutenant Straubing, Cincinnatus never would have worked to harm them. As things were . . .

"I'm letting everyone know," Straubing said. "If you've seen anything, if you *do* see anything, don't be shy."

"I won't, suh." Cincinnatus wondered if he could buy his own safety by betraying the Confederate underground. The trouble was, the only man whose whereabouts he knew for certain was Conroy. No, that was one trouble. The other was that, here in Covington, Confederates and Reds worked hand in hand. He'd betray Apicius and his sons along with the men who waved the Stars and Bars. Some things cost more than they were worth.

More drivers, white and black, came dripping into the shed. Straubing spoke to them all. Cincinnatus wondered how good an idea that was. Everyone would be eyeing everyone else now. And anyone who had a grudge against anyone else would likely seize the chance to have the occupation authorities put the other fellow through the wringer.

"Let's move out," the lieutenant said at last. "We've got a cargo of shells the artillery is waiting for."

"Weather like this, they're going to be waiting a while longer," said one of the drivers, a white man Cincinnatus knew only as Herk.

Lieutenant Straubing was a born optimist. A man who treated blacks and whites the same way had to be a born optimist—*or a damn fool,* Cincinnatus thought darkly. Even the Yankee soldier did not contradict Herk. All he said was, "We've got to give it our best shot."

Out they went. Cincinnatus was glad he hadn't had to buck the heavy crates of shells into the bed of the White truck himself. He wondered when he'd get home again: not as in *at what time*, but as in *on what day*. The front kept moving south. That meant an ever-longer haul from Covington. If he was lucky, the roads would be terrible and not too crowded. If he wasn't lucky, they'd be terrible and packed, and he might not get home for a week.

Right from the start, he had the feeling he wouldn't be lucky. The truck's acetylene headlamps didn't want to light, and, once they finally did, hissed and sputtered as if about to explode. He had to crank the engine half a dozen times before it turned over. One of those fruitless tries, it jerked back on him, and he yanked his hand off the crank just in time to keep it from breaking his arm.

Unlike some, the truck had a windshield and a wiper for it. It thrashed over the glass like a spastic man's arm, now two or three times quickly, now all but motionless. The idea was good. As far as Cincinnatus was concerned, it needed more work.

Even on the paved streets of Covington, the White seemed to bang unerringly into every pothole. Nor was Cincinnatus the only one with that complaint: a couple of trucks limped toward the curb with punctures. Changing an inner tube in the rain was not something he looked forward to with delight.

So thick were the clouds, it seemed more like twilight than advancing morning. Cincinnatus stuck close to the rear of the truck in front of him, and saw in his mirror the headlamps of the next White to the rear just behind him. He thought of elephants in a circus parade, each grasping the tail of the one in front with its trunk.

Paved road ended about twenty-five miles south of Covington. Before the war, it had ended at the city limits: Yankee engineers were pushing it on toward the front for reasons of their own. The difference between pavement and dirt was immediate and appalling. Muck flew up from the back tires of the White in front of Cincinnatus, coating his truck's headlamps and splattering the windshield. The wiper blade smeared more than it removed.

Swearing, Cincinnatus slowed down. Spacing between trucks got wider as other drivers did the same thing. Then they came upon what had to be at least a division's worth of infantry heading south along the road. Drivers in the lead trucks squeezed the bulbs on their horns for all they were worth. That was supposed to be the signal for the infantrymen to get out of the way. Even in good weather, the soldiers in green-gray didn't take kindly to moving onto the shoulder. With the rain, they barely seemed to move at all. The Whites splattered them as readily as one another. Curses rang in Cincinnatus' ears as he crawled past and through the marching men.

The trucks sped up again once they finally got beyond the head of the infantry column. A little farther along, *they* had to go onto the shoulder: a pair of bogged barrels plugged the road tight as a cork in a bottle. Cincinnatus hoped he'd reach the next fuel depot before his truck ran out of gas.

A noise like a gunshot made him jump in his seat. The truck slewed sideways. It wasn't Confederates or Reds. "Puncture," he said resignedly, and pulled off the road to fix it.

By the time he scrambled back into the cab of the truck, he was soaked from head to foot and all over mud. He felt as if he'd been wrestling somebody three times his size. He'd put a board under the jack before he tried using it. It had done its level best to sink into the ooze board and all. The ordeal was almost enough to make him wish he were back at the docks.

He shook his head. "I ain't that stupid," he said, gunning the engine to try to catch up with the rest of the convoy.

He did, too, soon enough; no one could make any sort of time through the mud. He managed to get more gasoline before he stopped dead. Putting everything together, the trip wasn't so bad as he'd expected. *Only goes to show I don't expect much,* he thought.

The raiders hit the convoy a little south of Berea. One moment, Cincinnatus was contentedly chugging along not far from the rear—other fellows who'd had to stop for one breakdown or another had fallen in behind him. The next, an explosion up ahead made him stamp on the brake. As the truck skidded to a stop, rifle and machine-gun fire rang out from the side of the road, stitching down the convoy toward him.

He had no gun. He carried nothing more lethal than a clasp knife. Without a moment's hesitation, he dove out of the cab and away from the White as fast as he could go. That proved smart. Flames started licking up from under the hood in spite of the rain: a bullet or two must have smashed up the motor. Cincinnatus just watched those flames for a moment. Then, with a moan of fright, he crawled farther away from the truck, not to escape the bullets still flying, but to get away from the—

The flames spread rapidly. With a soft *whoomp,* the gas tank went up, setting the whole truck ablaze. A minute or so after that, the fire reached the artillery rounds in the bed. At first, a couple of them exploded individually. And then, with a great roar, the whole truckload went up.

Cincinnatus had been on his hands and knees. The blast

knocked him facedown into the mud. Shell fragments and shrapnel balls slashed the air around him. Some of them fell hissing into puddles of rainwater close by.

As other trucks began exploding, he tried desperately to put more distance between himself and them. He heard screams from drivers who hadn't been able to get away, and Rebel yells from the raiders still shooting up the convoy. The explosions, though, kept the raiders from coming after him.

Or so he thought, till a shape wallowed toward him. He grabbed for his little knife, knowing it would do no good against a rifle, but then stopped. "That you, Herk?" he asked, not sure he recognized the filthy, dripping driver.

But the white man nodded. "Yeah. How the hell do we get out of this?"

"Dunno," Cincinnatus answered. He started laughing. Herk stared at him, eyes wide and shining in his dirty face. Cincinnatus explained: "We got us the chance to find out, though." Very solemnly, Herk nodded again.

Very solemnly, Abner Dowling peered south through his field glasses, toward the wooded hills north of the little Tennessee town called White House. He stood under a green-gray canvas awning, so the hot August rain didn't splash down onto his lenses. But the rain cut down on visibility nonetheless, masking those hills from clear observation. What little he could see, he didn't like.

He turned to General Custer. "Sir, the Rebs have that line as fortified as all get-out. They're not going to be easy to shift, not even a little bit."

"Yet shift them we must, and shift them we shall," Custer said, as usual mixing desire and ability. He raised his field glasses to his face, holding them with one shaky, liver-spotted hand. "That line in front of White House is the last one they can hold to keep our artillery out of range of Nashville. Once it goes down, we commence bombarding the city." He let the binoculars fall down on the leather strap holding round his neck so he could rub his hands in anticipation.

"I understand that, sir," Dowling said. "The trouble is, I'm very much afraid the Confederates understand it, too. That is a formidable position they have there—not only high ground, but wooded high ground, so we have trouble pinpointing their dispositions."

He had no trouble pinpointing Custer's disposition: it was petulant. The general commanding First Army said, "I intend to bombard that area until every tree in it has been made into tooth-picks and matchsticks. Toothpicks and matchsticks," he repeated, relishing the rhyme.

"Yes, sir," Dowling said, working to remind Custer of reality. "We lost a good deal of ammunition when that convoy was ambushed last week."

"True," Custer said. "You will of course note that, although those munitions were intended for my force, that shocking breach of security occurred in an area under General Pershing's jurisdiction, not mine."

"Of course, sir," his adjutant agreed: where self-preservation was concerned, Custer had a keen enough grasp on reality. Dowling went on, "However that may be, though, the ammunition is not here. And"—he pointed toward the dark, tree-clad, rolling hills—"that's not good country for barrels. No country is good country for barrels in this rain."

"We'll send them in anyhow," Custer said, which was just like him: he'd found a weapon that worked once, so he'd keep right on using it, regardless of whether circumstances warranted such use. He continued, "And we have plenty of ammunition, even without that which was lost. And, no doubt, our soldiers will make up with their courage any minor deficiencies in the preliminaries."

Translated into English, that meant a hell of a lot of young Americans were about to get shot, a good many of them unnecessarily. Custer had already fought a lot of battles like that in western Kentucky, and advanced at a snail's pace: the pace of a snail whose trail was blood, not slime. Dowling said, "It might be wiser to hold off a bit, sir, until the weather's more favorable and we have better reconnaissance."

"Major, we have been fighting for two years and more now," Custer replied. "Would you not say we have already seen a sufficiency of delay?" Without giving Dowling a chance to answer, he said, "I expect the bombardment to commence tomorrow morning and to continue until the Rebel positions are pulverized, at which point we advance, barrels and infantry both."

What Custer expected, Custer got. That was the advantage of being a lieutenant general. The next day, the guns began to roar. Dowling didn't envy the artillerymen serving them in the mud. Again, no one asked his opinion. He watched explosions wrack the Confederate hilltop lines. First Army had a lot of guns and a lot of ammunition even without what the raiders had blown up. They pounded the positions north of White House with high explosive and shrapnel and gas.

Custer watched, too, with the delight of a small boy at a fireworks show. "Give it to 'em," he said hoarsely. "Give it to 'em, by jingo!"

As Dowling had foreseen, the Confederates understood perfectly well what the unending barrage implied. Their own guns pounded the U.S. trenches. In the wretched weather, accurate counterbattery fire was next to impossible, because the U.S. artillery had and could gain no exact notion of the Rebel guns' positions.

The U.S. artillery preparation went on for five days. By the end of that time, as Custer had desired, the hills were no longer tree-covered. Seen through Dowling's field glasses, they resembled a close-up photograph of an unshaven man who'd survived a bad case of smallpox: all over craters and old eruptions, with now and then, as if by afterthought, something straight sticking up from one of them. It was easy to imagine that every Confederate in those hills had been blown to kingdom come.

It was especially easy for Custer to imagine as much. "We've got 'em now," he told Dowling in the middle of it, preening like a cock pheasant. "The Lord has delivered them into our hands, and our soldiers have only to storm forward and capture whatever demoralized wretches chance to remain alive."

"I hope you're right, sir," Dowling said, "but in the big fights in Pennsylvania and Maryland, and even the ones First Army had in western Kentucky, the defenders ended up with an advantage all out of proportion to their numbers."

"That's why we're laying on the artillery preparation." Custer looked at his adjutant as if he'd just crawled out from under a flat rock. "Never in the history of the planet had any place on the face of the earth been bombarded like those hills there. Only a wet blanket would think otherwise."

Dowling sighed. Custer had reckoned him a wet blanket since the earliest days of their association. That he'd proved right more often than not had done nothing to endear him to the general commanding First Army—on the contrary. This was one of the times Dowling devoutly hoped he was wrong. Custer had laid on one hell of a bombardment, and maybe it would be good enough to wipe out the foe. Maybe.

It went on for two more days, till the artillerymen were as near deaf as made no difference. Even when the U.S. soldiers swarmed out of their trenches and rushed for the ruined woods, the barrage kept on, now dropping down on where Intelligence thought the Rebels had their front-line trenches. Some of the Americans unrolled telephone wire as they advanced. Others carried signal flags, in case the wires broke as they so often did.

From under that camouflaged awning, Custer and Dowling watched the troops. Dowling saw sparklike points of light begin to spurt here and there in the woods. "We didn't get quite everyone, sir," he said.

"Leftover dust to be swept away by the broom of the infantry," Custer said grandly. "A broom five miles wide, Major."

Confederate artillery started falling in no-man's-land. U.S. troops got hung up in the belts of barbed wire not even the titanic American barrage had been able to tear up. More and more Confederate machine guns, muzzle flashes winking like malign eyes filled with horrible amusement, opened up on the U.S. soldiers stuck out in the open.

Every so often, a runner or a staff officer would bring news of the progress the attack was making. By the time the news reached Custer and Dowling, it was old and stale. "What's the slowdown?" Dowling demanded.

"Too many phone lines broken by the Rebel artillery, sir," answered a lieutenant who didn't seem to realize he was bleeding from a wound in his upper arm. "Too many runners getting shot before they can make it back, too. And the goddamn Rebel snipers are concentrating on our signalers. It's worth your life to stick up a banner."

Custer moved blue counters on a map. "We *are* making

progress," he insisted. "We need to send in the reserves, to take advantage of the gains the first wave has carved out."

In went the reserves. For all they gained, the ground might as well have swallowed them up. The ground had swallowed too many of them up, and they would never rise from it again. Toward evening, Custer committed more reserves. "Once we break the hard crust and reach the softness it protects, they are ours," he said.

The third wave of reserves went in the next morning, a couple of hours slower than they might have. The Rebs had been dislodged from most of their forward trenches, and from some of the secondary trenches as well. The line, though, still held. And the cost! "Sir," Dowling said late that second afternoon, "we've lost almost a division's worth of dead, and twice that many wounded. How long can we go on like this?"

"As long as it takes," Custer replied. "All summer, if we need to."

By the end of summer, Dowling feared, First Army would be down to battalion size. The question, he supposed, was whether the Confederates opposing them would have any men left at all. Even if they didn't, was that a victory? Could the U.S. survivors go on and take Nashville, which was, after all, the point of this entire exercise?

Custer seemed to entertain no doubts. "If you hammer the anvil long enough, Major, it breaks."

Dowling didn't answer. He had blacksmiths in his family, and knew what Custer might not: if you hammered the anvil long enough, it broke, all right, but *it* was the hammer, not the anvil. He wondered if he should try explaining that to the general commanding First Army. After a moment, he shook his head. General Custer hadn't been in the habit of listening to him before. Why would he start now?

Major Irving Morrell said, "What we've got going now is the big push toward Banff. The last thing we want to do is go straight at the place. The Canucks are set up and waiting for us to try it. If we do, they'll slaughter us. We have to make them watch the cape, the way the bullfighters do in the Empire of Mexico. If they keep their eyes on the cape, they won't notice the sword."

Captain Heinz Guderian nodded. "This is sound doctrine, Major. Deception. Deception by all means." He spoke in German, which not only Morrell but also his officers understood.

"Thanks, Captain." Morrell turned an ironic eye on the German staff officer. "I thought you'd have headed back to Philadelphia along with Major Dietl."

Guderian shrugged. "Dietl goes back to a real war, so he has no compunctions about leaving this one. If I go back to Germany, I go back to fighting at a desk, with machine pencil and large-caliber typewriter." His eyes sparkled. "If I am to make my life as a soldier, I intend to *be* a soldier, not a clerk in a field-gray uniform."

"Fair enough." Morrell took a map from one of his pockets. "Let's have a look at exactly what we've got here."

Guderian and Morrell's own company-grade officers huddled close to him. Captain Karl Spadinger pointed to the map. "What do these 'I.T.' markings stand for?" he asked.

"The abbreviation means 'Indian trail,'" Morrell answered. "Shows what kind of country we're operating in. And we'll have the devil's own time doing anything with the Canadians watching us—they're bound to have observers here on this peak"—he pointed toward Pigeon Mountain—"and it's almost two miles high."

"How are we going to fool them, then?" Captain Charlie Hall asked. "If they know we're coming, they're going to bake us a cake."

He had a gift for the obvious; Morrell had long since seen that. But what was obvious to him would also be obvious to the Canadians. "What's obvious," Morrell observed, "isn't always true."

Guderian's head bobbed up and down. He got it. So did Captain Spadinger. So, for that matter, did Lieutenant Jephtha Lewis. Hall's tanned, handsome face was still blank. Rather sourly, Morrell decided that made him perfect for leading half the attack he had in mind: if its own commander didn't understand it, the Canadians were sure to be fooled.

But no, he decided after a brief hesitation. Sending Hall in blind would surely get him killed. He was liable to get killed anyway; his role would be expensive. And so Morrell condescended to explain: "You'll take your company and most of the machine guns around to the east of the mountain there. Don't do anything in particular to keep from drawing attention to yourself. As soon as you get opposition, I want you to plaster it with rifle fire and those machine guns—make it seem as if you're in charge of the whole battalion. While you're keeping the Canucks busy, the rest of us are going to be sneaking up one of these Indian trails to see if we can slide past the observer without getting observed."

Captain Hall's eyes widened. "What a good idea, sir!" he exclaimed.

"I'm glad you like it." Morrell knew his voice was dry, but he couldn't help it. It didn't matter. Hall no more noticed the tone than he had figured out what lay in Morrell's mind before the battalion commander put it in words of one syllable for him.

Morrell kept Sergeant Finkel's machine-gun squad; the rest went on the diversionary move. Since he was leaving himself with only one gun, he chose the best. Guderian had seen that, too. "The sergeant there should be an officer," he observed quietly. "Is he held back because he is a Jew?"

"Maybe a little," Morrell answered. "He holds himself back, too, though: he'd rather deal with the machine guns himself than with men who would be dealing with machine guns, if you know what I mean."

"I know exactly what you mean," Guderian said, nodding. "Those are indeed the ones who make the best noncommissioned officers."

Once he judged Captain Hall's force well begun on its diversionary move, Morrell led the rest of the battalion north and west on narrow trails through the thickest woods he could find. He strung the men out so that, even if the Canadians up on Pigeon Mountain should spot them, they would have a hard time judging how many U.S. soldiers were on the march.

He tramped along at the head of the column, map in one hand, compass in the other, hoping the two of them could guide him. His boots scuffed almost soundlessly through a carpet of needles fallen from the tall, dark conifers all around. Their resinous, aromatic scent filled his nostrils.

"You are a lucky man, Major," Captain Guderian said, "to have escaped being chained behind a desk."

"I think so, anyhow," Morrell said. "Some people *want* to coop themselves up with stoves and electric lamps and telephones and typewriters. You need those people, too, if you're going to win a war, but I am not any of them. This, for me, is better."

Guderian was on the point of replying when gunfire broke out, off to the east. It was a good deal of gunfire. The German's head went up, like a hound's on taking a scent. "The Canadians' attention has been drawn, I should say. Nothing like machine guns to do that, is there? Soon we see how much attention they are paying over on that side of the mountain."

"They can't have a whole great swarm of men themselves," Morrell said. "They're trying to hold off the USA all across their country, and we're bigger than they are, even if we're fighting the Confederacy, too."

"One hopes they can't," Guderian answered. Morrell grinned. The foreigner was as dry with him as he'd been with Captain Hall. Unlike Hall, though, he was alert enough to the world around him to realize as much.

He was sure the Canadians had pickets in the woods—he would have, in their shoes. He didn't run into any of them for quite a while, though. As the trees hid him from Pigeon Mountain, they also hid the mountain from him. That meant he had no choice but to navigate by the map, which he didn't fully trust. If it was even close to right, he was almost to decent terrain that would take him straight toward the railroad line—and toward the last line of Canadian defenders in front of it.

Just when he'd begun to think he'd used the Indian trails so cleverly as to evade every picket the Canucks had posted, a rifle shot rang out up ahead. The bullet zipped past his head before he heard the report from the rifle that had sent it on its way. He was burying his face in those fragrant needles before a second bullet drilled through the space where his body had been.

Map and compass went flying when he dove. As he grabbed for his Springfield, he shouted, "Get 'em fast. Don't let this look big." He fired in the direction from which the shots had come.

His men dashed into the woods on either side of the trail. The little battle that followed was a lot like fighting Indians—running from tree to tree, ambushes, small desperate stands of resistance. After ten or fifteen minutes, no one was shooting anymore. Morrell hoped the Canucks were dead and hadn't been able to send runners back to announce he and his soldiers were on the way.

The racket of the fight was liable to have done that for them. "Now we push it!" Morrell called as the Americans moved forward once more. "If the Canucks know we're here, we don't want them to have time to get ready for us."

He'd rescued the map—that was precious. God only knew where the compass had landed. He commandeered Captain Spadinger's. Twenty minutes later, the U.S. force burst out of the woods. There in the distance was the railroad running alongside the Ghost River. A train, tiny as a toy, chugged west. But between him and the object of his desire lay rifle pits and trenches with Canadians in them. He shouted for Sergeant Finkel.

Quiet and competent, the noncom and his crew had kept up with everyone else. Setting up the machine gun on its tripod was a matter of moments. One gun wasn't much to cover the advance of a battalion, but it was what Morrell had. If nothing else, it would make the Canucks, however many Canucks there were, keep their heads down some of the time.

"Fire and move!" Morrell yelled. "Fire and move!"

As they often had before, his men ran toward the Canadians in small groups, flopped down and fired so their comrades could sprint past them, then moved up again when those comrades took cover. The Canucks fought hard, but, as he'd hoped, their lines weren't so full as they might have been. Sergeant Finkel engaged at long range some men trying to rush back from the east.

When the first U.S. soldiers started jumping down into the Canadian trenches, Morrell refrained from following them long enough to shout for a runner. He told the men, "Get back to division HQ and tell 'em to send reinforcements after us. From where we are, all we have to do is hold and we can mortar that railroad line to hell and gone. Tell 'em to push it, too; the Canucks'll try and throw us out. We'll hold on here as long as we can."

Bent low at the waist to make himself a small target, the runner dashed back the way he'd come. Morrell figured his men would have to hold on by themselves for most of a day. He figured they could do it, too. And then—and then the Canadians would have only one pass left through the Rockies, and that one higher and farther north and less usable through the winter than either of the two that would be lost to them.

"One more nail in the coffin," he muttered. But that wasn't quite right—it was one more stroke of the saw that was cutting the country in half. He nodded, as pleased with his metaphor as he was with his victory.

Brakes squealing, the train pulled into the Richmond and Petersburg Railroad depot. "Richmond!" the conductors shouted, again and again. "All out for Richmond!"

Anne Colleton shook her head in mingled scorn and bemusement. After the train had rattled over the long bridge across the James River, people would have to be idiots not to know it was coming in to the capital of the Confederate States. But then, a lot of people were idiots. She'd seen that often enough. She'd grown rich, then richer, because of it. And she'd grown poorer because of it, too, since blacks proved no more immune to the disease than whites.

"Porter!" she called, stepping out of the compartment. A Negro with a hand truck came hurrying up. Despite the black uprising, that tone of imperious command got results. The colored fellow piled her trunks—not so fine as the ones she'd had before the Marshlands burned—onto the dolly and followed her out of the Pullman coach onto the smoky, noisy platform that served as gateway between train and world. Once out there, she stuck two fingers in her mouth and let out a piercing whistle she'd learned from her brothers. "Taxi!" she yelled, imperious as ever.

Others had got there before her, but her clothes, her manner, and the way the porter followed her all said she was a person of consequence. She forced her way through the milling crowd. The porter loaded her luggage into the automobile. She gave him a quarter. He grinned and tipped his cap and went off to help someone else, his brass buttons gleaming.

"Where to, ma'am?" the taxi driver asked after handing her into the car.

"Ford's Hotel," she answered. He had hardly put the cab into gear before she found a question of her own: "Why aren't you in uniform?"

"Ma'am, I got hit once in the shoulder and once here." He took his left hand off the wheel for a moment. It was encased in a leather glove, three of whose fingers were unnaturally full and stiff. "They decided they'd had as much of me as they could use, so they let me go."

"Very well," she answered. As he drove north toward Capitol Square, she saw plenty of other such expended men on the street: men on crutches with one trouser leg pinned up, men who had no legs in wheelchairs, men with an empty sleeve or a hook doing duty for one hand, men with a patch over one eye, and a couple of men with black silk masks who kept a hand on a companion's shoulder so they could find their way.

Traffic was appalling, with trucks and heavily laden horse-drawn wagons slowing things to a crawl for everyone else. The air tasted of exhaust fumes and coal smoke and horse manure and chemical stinks Anne could not name. The driver coughed a couple of times when it got particularly ripe, then spoke as if in apology: "Place stinks like one of those miserable U.S. cities, don't it, ma'am?"

"It had better," Anne said sharply. "We need weapons and men both, and we have to make the weapons, because the sea war won't let us import them."

"You know about these things," the cabbie said respectfully.

He'd turned left on Canal Street for a block, then gone up Seventh to Grace, where he turned right and went on till he came to Ninth, which abutted Capitol Square. There he waited and waited and waited till he finally found the chance to turn left and go on for half a block, and then to turn right onto Capitol Street. When he got to Eleventh, he—slowly—turned left again, and went past the bulk of Ford's Hotel to the entrance, which was at the corner of Eleventh and Broad.

A Negro in a uniform fancier than any a general wore took charge of Anne's luggage. She paid the fare, adding a tip of the same size. The taxi driver took off his cap with his good hand and bowed to her. "Stay well," she told him.

"Ma'am," he said, "I used to cuss about traffic till the first time I got shot. Now it don't worry me none—not even a little bit."

"No servants, ma'am?" the desk clerk asked.

"Do you see any?" Anne demanded. Julia was not long delivered of a baby girl. No one else who remained at Marshlands seemed suitable as a traveling companion, and she had not wanted to hire a servant. She had enough trouble trusting Negroes she knew—or thought she knew.

Flushing, the clerk gave her a big bronze key with the number 362 stamped onto it. An arthritic elevator took her, the bellman, and her cases upstairs. The room was large and fancy, with thick carpets, landscapes on the walls, elaborately carved tables, and a great profusion of lacework doilies and maroon plush upholstery. It was, no doubt, intended to impress the daylights out of the prosperous businessmen and lobbyists who usually stayed here, and no doubt succeeded. The exhibition of modern art Anne had put together just before the war broke out had been the antithesis of everything the room stood for. "Looks more like a whorehouse than a hotel room," she remarked as she tipped the bellhop. He let out a scandalized giggle and fled.

Anne unpacked—after living for months in a refugee camp, she could still see having a room to herself as a luxurious waste of space—and went downstairs for supper. The restaurant was as spectacularly overdecorated as the room. But they did a fine job on crab cakes—the boast of "Best in the CSA" on the menu didn't seem misplaced—so she had little cause for complaint.

The bed was comfortable enough, too. After a Pullman, any bed that didn't sway and rattle seemed splendid. The next morning, she looked at the gray linen dress she'd intended wearing and shook her head. She hadn't seen how wrinkled it was the night before, or she would have had it pressed. She chose a maroon silk instead.

After breakfast in the hotel, she hailed a cab. "The Executive Mansion," she said crisply. The driver, a sensible man, did not bother pointing out that the building was only two blocks north and one east from where she'd got in. What the damnyankees still disparagingly called the Confederate White House also stood near the top of Shockoe Hill; Anne had no intention of arriving there as draggled and sweaty as a housemaid. The cab labored up the hill to the corner of Clay and Twelfth, where the driver let her out. She reckoned the quarter fare and dime tip money well spent.

Armed guards patrolled the grounds of the mansion behind a wrought-iron fence whose points were not only decorative but looked very sharp. A white man who wore formal attire but carried himself with a military bearing examined her letter of invitation and checked her name off on a list before allowing her to proceed. "I am not an assassin," she remarked, half annoyed, half amused.

"I know that, ma'am—now," the fellow replied. Anne Colleton seldom yielded anyone else the last word, but made an exception here.

As she'd expected, she had to wait before being admitted to President Semmes' presence. A Negro servant offered her coffee and cakes dusted with powdered sugar. She ate one, then prudently checked her appearance in the mirror of her compact. *Wouldn't do to see the president with sugar on my chin,* she thought.

After most of an hour—half an hour past the nine-thirty for which her appointment was scheduled—another servant led her into Gabriel Semmes' office. Since the man who walked out past her was the secretary of war, she did not think the president had delayed meeting her to be inconvenient.

President Semmes certainly received her with every sign of pleasure. "So very good of you to come up from South Carolina," he said, and moved the chair across from his desk slightly to suggest that she sit in it. "Here, please—make yourself comfortable. Can I have the staff bring you anything?"

"No, thank you," she answered. "Let's get straight down to business, shall we?"

"However you like, of course," he answered. He looked like a Confederate politician, or rather the apotheosis of a Confederate politician: in his early fifties, handsome, ruddy, a little beefy, with a mane of gray hair combed straight back from his forehead, a mustache, and a little chin beard that was almost pure white. The absence of tobacco stains from that beard was enough almost by itself to place him outside the common herd. He went on, "I won't beat around the bush with you, Miss Colleton—I need your help on this bill to arm our Negroes and use them against the USA."

Any time a politician said he wouldn't beat around the bush, you were well advised to keep your hand on your wallet. "You'll have to show me things are as bad as you said in your letter inviting me here," she told him. "The press certainly does not make them out to be so desperate."

"Have you ever heard of any war in the history of the world where the press did not make things out to be better than they were?" Gabriel Semmes returned. "If you look at papers in the USA during the War of Secession and the Second Mexican War, you will see they thought they were winning each time until almost the moment of their overthrow."

"As may be," she said. "I am not yet convinced." She did not tell him what her brother Tom kept saying in his letters. Politicians were not the only ones who learned to hold their cards close—business taught the same lesson.

President Semmes said, "A glance at the map will show you much of the trouble. We have lost ground against the USA almost everywhere, and our remaining gains in Maryland are threatened. Our latest effort to reclaim western Texas failed—there is no other word. They hammer us on every front. We do have some counterstrokes in the offing, and we have thus far managed to avoid losing anything vital, but that cannot continue forever. We are under more pressure than our allies in Europe, and have little prospect of aid from them."

"We hurt the Yankees worse than they hurt us in every fight, is that not so?" Anne said. "That's one reason why we stand on the defensive so much."

"Yes, we do, by a ratio of close to three to two," Semmes answered. "Each U.S. conscription class, though, outnumbers our corresponding class of whites by about three to one. Add in the Negroes and the deficit shrinks to about two to one. Better, actually, for we would be calling up several conscription classes of blacks at once."

Anne pursed her lips thoughtfully. "But not all the U.S. soldiers are used against us," she pointed out. "Many of them go into the fight against Canada. That helps even the numbers somewhat."

"Somewhat, yes, for now," President Semmes agreed. "But, even with troops from Britain aiding them—they have the advantage of the northern route—the Canadians, I tell you in confidence, are in a bad way. How long we can rely on them to continue siphoning off Yankee resources, I cannot say."

Beyond what he asserted, beyond what the papers asserted (which, thanks to censorship, was liable to be the same thing), she didn't know how things stood with Canada. Would he lie for political advantage alone? Probably. But she could check what he said with her senators and the congressman from her district, the men he wanted her to influence. He would know that. Therefore, he was likely to be telling the truth, or most of it.

"The other question is," she said, as much to herself as to him, "what will the Confederate States be like with Negroes as citizens? Is that better, or is losing as we are?"

"Miss Colleton, I always thought you were on the side of modernity, of progress, of change," President Semmes said, a shrewd shot that proved he—or his advisors—knew her views well. "And if we lose, can we stay as we are? Or would we face another round of Red upheaval?"

That was another good question. The answer seemed only too obvious, too. Try to freeze in the mold of the past, or take a chance on the future? If you didn't gamble, how were you going to win? But when she thought about what blacks had done to Marshlands and to her brother—"I hate this," she said quietly.

"So do I," the president of the Confederate States replied.

"I'll do what I can," Anne said, trying not to see the disapproving look on dead Jacob's face. Well, better the damnyankees should have gassed a Negro than poor Jacob. If you looked at it the right way, they'd killed him before the Negro uprising could finish the job.

"From the bottom of my heart, I thank you, and your country thanks you as well," President Semmes said. He rose and bowed to her, then went on, "Now that we know ourselves to be in agreement, perhaps you will accompany me to a ceremony where your presence will surely serve as an inspiration to the brave men we honor."

Roger Kimball was bored. The ceremony should have started at half past ten. He drew out his pocket watch. It was closer to eleven. Almost imperceptibly, he shook his head. Civilians could get away with nonsense like that. For a naval officer, it would have meant trouble at least, maybe a court-martial.

Not only was he bored, he was hot, too. They'd run up an

awning so he didn't have to stand in direct sunshine, but it didn't cut the heat much or the humidity at all. He felt as if he were melting down into his socks. The only advantage he found to sweating so much was that he wouldn't have enough water left in him to need to take a leak—probably for the next three days.

Out on the lawn, old people sat in folding chairs and looked at him and the other hunks of uniformed beef on display under the awning. Ladies fanned themselves. Some of their male companions used straw hats to make the air move. By the way the old folks were turning red in the vicious sunshine, they needed the awning worse than he and his companions did.

Off to one side of the awning, a band struck up "Dixie." Kimball came to attention; maybe that meant things really would get rolling now. The Negro musicians were in black cutaway coats and black trousers. They didn't have an awning, either. He wondered how they could play without keeling over. He shrugged. They were just niggers, after all.

A woman walked quickly forward to take a seat near the front. Roger's eyebrows came to attention, as the rest of him had at the national anthem. Unlike most of the audience, she was anything but superannuated. Her maroon silk dress clung tightly to her rounded hips and, daringly short, revealed trim ankles. Under her hat, her hair shone in the sun, but it shone gold, not silver.

Next to Kimball, an Army sergeant murmured through unmoving lips, "The president ought to pin her on my chest instead of a medal."

"Yeah," he whispered back. Then he stiffened far beyond the requirements of attention. "Christ on a crutch, that's Anne Colleton!"

"You *know* her?" the sergeant said. Microscopically, Roger nodded. The Army man sighed. "Either you're a liar, Navy, or you're one lucky bastard, I'll tell you that." And then, recognizing him, too, Anne waved, not too obviously but unmistakably. The sergeant sighed again. "You *are* a lucky bastard."

Here came President Gabriel Semmes, all sleek and clever, to present their decorations. Kimball noticed him only peripherally. He'd had a note from Anne when she was stuck in that refugee camp, but nothing since. He hadn't been a hundred percent sure she was still alive, and found himself damn glad to discover she was.

President Semmes made a speech, of which he heard perhaps one word in three. The gist of it was, with bravery like that which these heroes had displayed, the Confederate States were surely invincible. Roger Kimball didn't believe that for a minute. Semmes didn't believe it, either, or why was he pushing that bill to put guns in the hands of black men?

A flunky brought the president a silver tray with dark blue velvet boxes stacked on it. Reporters scribbled as Semmes read out the deeds of the heroes he was honoring. One of the awards was posthumous: a Confederate Cross for a private who'd leaped on a grenade to save his pals.

Kimball wasn't up for a C.C. himself; Semmes would pin an Order of the *Virginia* on him, the next highest award a Navy man could get. To earn the Confederate Cross and live through it, you had to be brave, lucky, and crazy, all at the same time. Without false modesty, he knew he was brave and he'd been lucky, but he hadn't—quite—been crazy up there in Chesapeake Bay.

The sergeant standing there next to him *had* won a Confederate Cross. "P.G.T.B. Austin, without concern for his own safety, climbed onto the top of a U.S. traveling fort," President Semmes said, not calling it a barrel, "and threw grenades into the machine through its hatches until fire forced the crew to flee, whereupon he killed three with his rifle, wounded two more, and accepted the surrender of the rest. Sergeant Austin!" The audience applauded. Photographers snapped away as Austin went up to get his medal. Kimball nodded to himself. Brave, lucky, and crazy, sure enough.

His own turn came a moment later. After hearing what the Army man had done, he felt embarrassed to accept even a lesser decoration. The president shook his hand and told him what a splendid fellow he was. He already knew what a splendid fellow he was, so he didn't argue. The medal, a tiny gold replica of the Confederacy's first ironclad hanging from a red, white, and blue ribbon, did look impressive on his chest.

He went back to his place under the awning and waited for the rest of the medals to be awarded. Then, as he'd expected, the men who'd won them got the chance to mingle with guests and reporters.

He wondered if Anne Colleton would still give him the time of day. He wasn't a big fish, not in this pond. If she wanted heroes, she had her pick here. But she came straight up to him. *Maybe she wants an ornery so-and-so,* he thought. *Takes one to know one.*

"Congratulations," she said, and shook his hand man-fashion. "I'm glad to see you here and well."

"Same to you," he answered. The feel of her flesh against his sent a charge through him, as if he'd touched a bare wire. He watched her face. Her pupils got bigger; her nostrils flared, ever so slightly. She wanted to be alone with him, too. Heat different from that of Richmond August filled him. "Last I got a look at you, you were seeing how fast you could get away from the Charleston docks."

"I did fine, halfway to Marshlands." Her voice turned bitter. "Then my car got stolen."

"Rebels? Reds?" Kimball said. "You're lucky they didn't kill—"

"Not Reds," Anne broke in. "Soldiers. Our soldiers. Oh, I suppose they needed it against the uprising, but—" She didn't go on.

Out of the corner of his eye, he saw men gathering around them, drawn to Anne Colleton like moths to a flame. He knew how good a comparison that was, too. But he was no moth; he had fire of his own. So he told himself, anyhow. Quickly, while he still had the chance, he asked, "Where are you staying?"

"Ford's," she answered. "Would you like to celebrate your medal by having supper with me there tonight?"

"Can't think of anything I'd like better," he said. He could, in fact, think of several things, but those were things you did, not things you talked about. "Half past six?" he asked, and, when she nodded, he drifted away as if she were just someone in the crowd he happened to know.

He showed up at the hotel a couple of minutes early. She was waiting in the lobby and, again, had drawn a crowd. Some of the officers were of considerably higher rank than lieutenant commander; all the civilians looked more than prosperous. Everyone stared after Kimball and Anne when they went off to the dining room, her hand on his arm.

He grinned over at her. "I could get used to this," he said.

A tiny vertical crease appeared between her eyebrows. "Don't," she said, more seriously than he'd expected. "If people think of you because of whoever's with you—so what? Make them remember you for yourself."

He thought about that, then nodded. "I started on a little farm. I've come this far on my own. I'll go farther, if I can."

"That's the way to look at it," she agreed. "Any one of those fat lawyers back there would love to take care of my affairs—and you can take that any way you like. I won't let them. *I* run my life, no one else." That had the sound of hard experience behind it, and also, perhaps, a note of warning.

Ford's Hotel did right by its dinner spread. "Wouldn't hardly know there's a war on," Kimball said happily, digging into almost fork-tender leg of lamb.

Anne Colleton stayed serious. "What do you think of President Semmes' bill?" she asked. She didn't need to say which bill. Only one mattered now.

"I'm against it," he answered firmly. "As long as we're holding our own, or even anything close, we should go on doing what we've been doing. Far as I can see, we're giving the darkies a kiss on the cheek, right after they tried to up and knock our heads off."

She nodded, slowly. "Is that how most Navy men feel?"

Kimball knocked back the whiskey in his glass. "It's not even the way my exec feels. All you hear these days is arguments."

"What if we can't win the war, can't hope to win the war, if things keep on going as they have been?" Anne said. "Would you want to arm Negroes then?"

"Hung for a sheep or hung for a lamb, you mean?" He shrugged, unable to come up with a better answer. "If we're that bad off, putting rifles in niggers' hands won't help us, far as I can see. And if we do that, and we lose anyhow, what will the country look like afterwards? Be a hell of a mess, begging your pardon—not that it isn't already."

"A point," she said. "It may be the most serious point in opposition I've heard yet." A colored waiter came up and cleared away plates. After a tutti-frutti ice, brandy, a cigar for Kimball and a couple of cigarettes for Anne, the waiter came back.

"Charge this to my room," she told him, and he dipped his head with practiced obsequiousness.

Roger Kimball's hand had been going to his wallet. He scowled, angry that she'd accepted the bill before he had the chance. "I'm not broke——" he began.

"I know," she answered, "but, for one thing, I invited you to supper, not the other way round, and, for another, I promise I have more money than you do; I know what naval officers make. It's my pleasure, believe me."

"Weren't you the one talking about making your own way when we came in here?" he asked, unhappy still.

"I didn't suggest annoying your friends by being stubborn when that's plainly foolish," she said, a touch of sharpness in her voice.

He subsided, looking for a word he'd heard a few times but had had little occasion to use. *Gigolo,* he thought. *She's made me her gigolo tonight.* He seemed to have no choice but to accept that. Well, all right. Gigolos had privileges of their own. He remembered how she looked under that maroon silk, and how she felt, and how she tasted, too.

If the Ford Hotel boasted a house detective, he was good at making himself invisible. Kimball and Anne went up to her floor and walked down the richly carpeted hallway to her room without interference. She opened the door with her key, leaned forward to brush his lips with hers . . . and then said, "Good night, Roger. I hope you sleep well."

It was not an invitation to come in. "What the devil——?" he said roughly. "We've been——"

"I know what we've been," she answered. "We won't be, not tonight. The very first time we met, you did a splendid job of seducing me." Her eyes glinted, half amusement, half remembered anger of her own. "And so, tonight, no. Call it a lesson: never, ever take me for granted. Maybe another time, probably another time——but not tonight."

He wasn't that much bigger than she, but he knew he was stronger. With a lot of other women, he would have picked them up, thrown them on the bed, and taken what he wanted. If he tried that with her——even if he succeeded, because he knew she'd fight like a wildcat——he figured she was liable to stab him or shoot him as he left.

"You *are* a bitch," he said, reluctantly admiring.

"I know." She knew, all right, and she was proud of it.

He seized her, jerked her chin up, and kissed her, hard. He figured she'd fight that, too, but she didn't. Her body molded itself against him. When the kiss broke, though, she pushed him away. She was laughing—and panting a little. So was he. "Thanks for supper," he said, and tipped his hat. He strode down the hall toward the elevator without a backward glance.

Out on the sidewalk, a drunken artillery sergeant walked right into him. "Watch where you're going, you goddamn medal-wearing son of a bitch," the fellow snarled. By the way his mouth twisted, he was looking for a fight wherever he could find one.

Kimball didn't feel like fighting, which, since he hadn't got laid, surprised him. "I'm an officer," he warned, meaning the sergeant would catch special hell if he fought with him.

"Watch where you're going, you goddamn medal-wearing son of a bitch, *sir*," the sergeant said.

Laughing, Kimball peeled off a five-dollar note he hadn't spent at supper and pressed it into the noncom's hand before that hand could close into a fist. The sergeant stared. "Go on, get drunker on me," Kimball said. He slapped him on the back, then headed off to his barracks close by the James.

Jake Featherston gaped in owlish disbelief at the banknote that had magically appeared in his hand. Even if the fellow who'd given it to him was a Navy man, he had, until the grayback pressed it on him, wanted to smash his face: not only was he an officer, he was a decorated officer. Jake knew damn well he deserved to be an officer. He also knew he deserved several medals, not just one.

"And am I gonna get 'em?" he asked the empty air around him. "Sure I am—same time as I get promoted." He laughed a loud, raucous, bitter laugh. He wasn't holding his breath.

He ambled around Capitol Square, like a sailing ship tacking almost at random. That was how he felt, too. He wasn't going anywhere in particular, just letting his feet and the crowds in the streets take him wherever they would. Half seriously, he saluted the statues of Washington and Albert Sidney Johnston in the square.

"They'd know how to take care of a soldier," he muttered to himself. Muttering did no good. Complaining out loud did no good, either. He'd seen that when he went to Major Clarence Potter. Maybe if he walked into the Capitol itself and started screaming at congressmen and generals—

He shook his head, which made the world spin alarmingly. No good, no good. It was late. He didn't know how late it was, but it was late. No congressmen working in the Capitol now, by Jesus. They'd all be in bed with their mistresses. And the generals . . . the generals would be in bed with Jeb Stuart, Jr. He laughed. The truth in that hurt, though. If the powers that be in the Confederate War Department hadn't been sucking up to the father of his late, brave, stupid company commander, they would have given him his due. But they did suck up, they hadn't given it to him, and they damn well never would.

"Bastards," he said. "Sons of bitches." The words were hot and satisfying in his mouth, the way the whiskey had been at that saloon—those saloons—earlier. Pretty soon, he figured he'd go looking for another saloon. He was sure he'd have no trouble finding one.

Around him, Richmond didn't so much ignore the war as take it in stride. He wandered south and east, away from Capitol Square. Plenty of soldiers and sailors on leave clogged the sidewalks and the streets themselves, making people in buggies and motorcars yell at them to get out of the way. They didn't want to get out of the way, not with so many women to look for, so many stores open so late, so many saloons . . .

Most of the men in civilian clothes were Negroes. Featherston glowered at them. They were out celebrating as hard as the white people. They had their nerve, he thought. Here white men went out to fight and die, and all the blacks had to do was stay home and have a high old time. Stories of lazy niggers his overseer father had told him ran through his head. He had no doubt every goddamn one of them was true, too.

A big buck in a sharp suit—too sharp for any Negro to deserve to wear—bumped into him. "Watch it, you ugly black bastard," he snarled.

"Sorry, suh," the Negro said, but he wasn't sorry—Jake could see it in his eyes. If people had been paying better attention, the whole Red uprising would have been nipped in the bud. When the fellow didn't get out of the way fast enough, Featherston shoved him, hard. The black's hand closed into a fist as he staggered.

A fierce joy lit Jake. "So you want to play, do you?" he said genially, and gave the black buck a knee square in the balls. The fellow went down as if he'd been shot. Jake wished he had shot him. He wished he could shoot all of them. Brushing his hands together, he headed off down the street, leaving the Negro writhing on the pavement behind him. No one said boo.

He was about to cross Franklin Street, a good way down from Capitol Square, when military policemen blocked the way. He felt like cursing them, too, but that would land him in jail, and he still had a couple of days' leave before he had to go back to the Maryland front. So he stood and watched as a long column of soldiers tramped past.

Farther up the street, people were laughing and cheering. A hell of a racket was coming from somewhere up there, too. Jake craned his neck. A moment later, he laughed and cheered, too. Four barrels—nobody who'd faced the Yankee version said *tanks*—rumbled toward him, battle flags painted on the front and sides. They looked different from the ones the USA manufactured; Featherston wondered whether the CSA had built them or they'd somehow been imported from England.

However that was, he was damn glad to see them. "Give 'em hell!" he shouted, and a soldier riding on top of one of them waved his way. He yelled again: "Let the damnyankees know what it's like, by Jesus!" Had he been in the infantry, he probably would have shouted even louder.

The barrels were so heavy, their wraparound tracks tore up the concrete surface of the street. They'd probably come through town to build morale. *Sure built mine,* Jake thought. More soldiers followed, young, serious-looking men intent on keeping step. They'd learn what was important and what wasn't pretty damn quick. Jake knew that.

Having been born and raised in Richmond, he also knew which railroad station the men and barrels were heading for: the Richmond and Danville. He wished they'd been coming up to Maryland, but the Roanoke front was probably the next best place for them. Grudgingly, he admitted to himself that the Roanoke front might have been the best place to send them. The Yanks were in Virginia there, as opposed to fighting them on their own soil farther north and east.

To celebrate the chance of throwing the damnyankees out of his own state, Jake went into a saloon and poured down whiskey. To celebrate that whiskey, he had another one, and then another. When he came out of the saloon, he'd spent a good piece of the note that Navy man had given him. And, when he came out, he didn't need to turn his head sharply to make the world revolve.

Off in the distance, he heard, or thought he heard, a low-pitched, droning rumble. More barrels? He shook his head, and almost fell over. The troop trains pulling out? No, this wasn't a train noise. It was real, though. He hadn't been sure of that before, but he was now.

It sounded like . . . aeroplanes. His face twisted in slow-witted puzzlement. "If it is aeroplanes, it's a hell of a lot of 'em," he said, thinking out loud. He wondered why the Confederacy would put so many aeroplanes in the sky so late at night. "Damn foolishness," he mumbled.

The part of his mind that functioned at a level below conscious thought came up with the answer. "Sweet suffering Jesus, it's the Yankees!" he exclaimed, a moment before the first antiaircraft gun outside the Confederate capital began pounding away at the intruders.

He knew too well how futile antiaircraft fire often turned out to be. At night, hitting your target was even harder. And the United States had put a hell of a lot of aeroplanes in the air. They'd bombed the front. They'd bombed Confederate-occupied Washington. Till now, they hadn't done much to Richmond. All that, evidently, was about to change. Featherston dove under a bench at a trolley stop, the first shelter he spied.

With so many lights on in the Confederate capital, the bombers had targets to dream of. Most of the explosions sounded as if they were close to Capitol Square—most, but not all. The damnyankees seemed to have plenty of bombing aeroplanes to carpet the whole city.

From under the bench, Featherston watched a sea of feet and

legs, men's and women's both, running every which way. "Like chickens with their heads cut off," he said, and then raised his voice to a shout: "Take cover, dammit!"

They didn't listen to him. Nobody listened to him. Civilians paid him no more mind than soldiers ever had. And, when the bombs started falling all around, the civilians of Richmond found out that they should have paid attention, just as the Confederate brass should have listened when he tried to tell them Pompey was no damn good.

Crummp! Crummp! For him, the bombing of Richmond was like being under a medium-heavy artillery bombardment, except it didn't last so long. It wasn't that he had no fear—anybody who wasn't afraid when things were blowing up nearby was crazy, and Mrs. Featherston had raised no fool. But he, like most of the soldiers in town, had faced such horrors before. His chiefest wish was to be able to shoot back.

For civilians, though—for Negroes, for women, for the old and the young—the raid had to seem like the end of the world. Screams rose into the night, those of the panicked side by side with those of the injured. Then secondary screams went up as the panicked discovered the injured, and the dismembered, and the dead. Civilians had no notion of what high explosives and sharp-edged fragments of flying metal could do to the human body. Courtesy of the Yankees, they were learning.

Bombs or no bombs, somebody had to do something to help. Jake got out from under his bench as if he were leaving a dugout to serve his howitzer under fire. He passed by a groaning black man to bandage a cut on a white woman's head.

More bombers roared past up above. He could hear them, but couldn't see them. No—he could see one, for smoke and fire were trailing from it, getting brighter every second. The antiaircraft guns ringing Richmond weren't entirely useless, then: only pretty much so.

The stricken bomber nosed down and dove. It seemed to be coming right at him. He flattened himself out on the street, absentmindedly knocking down the woman he'd just bandaged, too. The bombs the aeroplane hadn't had the chance to drop exploded when it crashed a block away.

He got picked up and slammed down again, right on top of the woman. It wasn't anything erotic. He scrambled off her. The houses where the bomber had crashed were burning furiously.

Through the chaos, he heard the fire alarm bell from Capitol Square. It made him throw back his head and laugh. "Thanks for the news!" he shouted. "Thanks for the goddamn news! Never would have known it without you!"

XV

"I don't like it," Paul Andersen said, peering across no-man's-land toward the Confederate lines. "Those bastards are too damn quiet."

"Yeah." Chester Martin took out his entrenching tool and knocked some bricks that had probably been part of a chimney out of the way. If he had to flatten out in a hurry, he didn't want to land on them. "One thing about the Roanoke front is, they never give anything up cheap and they always hit back any way they can."

"You got that right." Andersen nodded emphatic agreement.

"This past while, though," Martin went on, "they haven't been counterattacking, they haven't been shelling us ... much—they've just been sitting there. Whenever they do things they haven't done before, I don't like it. It's liable to mean they'll do something else they haven't done before, and that's liable to mean yours truly gets his ticket punched."

Andersen nodded again. "Two years o' this shit and hardly a scratch on either one of us. Either I'm leading a charmed life and you're all right, too, on account of you hang around with me—or else it's the other way round. You know what? I don't want to find out which."

"Yeah, me neither," Martin said. "We've seen a hell of a lot of people come and go." He scowled. He didn't want to think about that. Too many men dead in too many horrible ways.

Somebody's observation aeroplane buzzed overhead. It was too high up for Martin or anyone else on the ground to tell whether it belonged to the USA or the Rebels. That didn't stop Specs Peterson from raising his Springfield to his shoulder and squeezing off a couple of rounds at it.

"What the hell you doing?" Martin demanded. "What if it's on our side?"

"Who gives a damn?" Peterson retorted. "I hate all those flyboy bastards. War'd be a lot cleaner if they weren't up there spying on us. If it's a Reb, good riddance. If it's one of our guys—good riddance, too."

Martin reminded himself the aeroplane was too high for rifle fire to have any chance of hitting it. If Specs wanted to work out some anger by blasting away at it, why not?

And, evidently, it belonged to the CSA anyhow. U.S. antiaircraft guns opened up on it. Puffs of black smoke filled the air all around the biplane. Like every other small boy ever made, Martin had tried catching butterflies in flight with his bare hands. The antiaircraft rounds had about as much luck with Confederate aeroplanes as he'd usually had going after butterflies.

Every once in a while, though, every once in a while he'd caught one. And, every once in a while, antiaircraft guns knocked down an aeroplane. He let out a yell, thinking this was one of those times—something red and burning came out of the aircraft and hung up there in the sky. Then he swore in disappointment.

So did Paul Andersen. "It's only a flare," the corporal said.

"Yeah," Martin said ruefully. "I really thought they'd nailed the son of a bitch." He eyed the observation aeroplane with sudden suspicion. "What the hell are they doing shooting off flares? They've never done anything like that before."

A moment later, the Confederates gave him the answer. The eastern horizon exploded with a roar that, he thought, would have made the famous Krakatoa volcano sound like a hiccup. One second, everything was quiet, as it had been for so long. The next, hell came down on earth.

Along with everybody else in the trenches, he scrambled for the nearest bombproof he could find. Some limey cartoonist had drawn one where a soldier was saying to his buddy, "Well, if you knows of a better 'ole, go to it." The Rebs had got the slogan from the limeys, and U.S. soldiers from the Rebs. For anybody on either side who'd ever been in a trench, it summed up what life under fire was like.

Men started banging on empty shell casings, which meant the Rebs were throwing gas along with all their other lovely presents. Trying to fumble a gas helmet out of its canvas case when he was jammed into a dugout with twice as many soldiers as it should have held was not one of the things Chester Martin enjoyed most, but he managed. Somebody who couldn't manage started coughing and choking and drowning for good air, but Martin couldn't do anything about that except curse the Confederates. He couldn't even tell who the poor bastard getting poisoned was.

The bombardment went on for what felt like forever. It covered miles of the front. The Rebs didn't stick to the trenches right up against the barbed wire, either. They gave it to the U.S. positions as far back as they could reach, and they had more heavy guns firing along with their damned three-inchers than had been so during the first year of the war.

During a lull—which is to say, when the Rebs were going after U.S. guns rather than front-line troops—Martin shouted to Paul Andersen, "Well, now we know why they were so goddamn quiet for so long."

Andersen nodded mournfully. "They were savin' it up to shoot off at us all at once." A couple of miles to the west, something blew up with a thunderous roar loud even through the surrounding din. "There went an ammo dump—stuff we ain't gonna be able to shoot back at 'em."

"Yeah, and it's a shame, too." Martin frowned. "Next question is, are they just shelling the hell out of us, or are they going to come over the top when all this lets up?"

"That's a good one," Andersen said. "No way to know till we find out."

Before long, Martin became sure in his own mind the Confederates were coming. They'd never laid on a bombardment like this one before. He heartily hoped they'd never lay on another one, either.

Andersen reached the same conclusion. "Get ready for the hundred and forty-first battle of the Roanoke, or whatever the hell this one is," he said. They both laughed. Back when the war was new, they'd joked about how many battles this valley had seen. They'd seen all of them, small and big alike. Martin had the feeling this was going to be one of the big ones.

Sneaky as usual, the Rebels halted their barrage several times, only to resume a few minutes later, catching U.S. defenders out of their shelters and slaughtering them. The real attack, though, was marked by long bursts of machine-gun fire from the Confederate trenches, supporting the soldiers who were moving on the U.S. lines.

"Up!" Martin screamed. "Up! Up! Let's get 'em!" He'd come up before, and counted himself lucky not to have been killed. Now he stood in the wreckage of the trench line, blinking like a mole or some other animal not used to the light of day. The barrage had blown most of the parapet to hell and gone, and a lot of the wire that had stood in front of it, too. He could look out across no-man's-land at the Confederate soldiers running toward him.

If he could see them, they could see him. He dropped to one knee and started shooting. Specs Peterson did the same thing beside him, but then pointed off to the left and hollered, "Barrel!"

A barrel it was, but not a U.S. barrel. Martin hadn't known the Rebs had any of their own. They were picking a good time to spring the surprise, too. He watched the ungainly contraption go into a trench and climb out the other side. It looked to climb even better than the ones made in the USA, though it seemed to carry fewer guns.

As far as he could tell, the one Specs had spotted was the only one close by. He wondered how many of the stinking machines the Confederates had altogether. Getting up and trying to find out didn't strike him as the best idea he'd ever had. He shoved a fresh clip into his Springfield, peered over the sights to find a Reb to shoot at, and—

The bullet caught him in the left arm, just below the shoulder. "Aww, shit!" he said loudly. Without that hand supporting it, the muzzle of the Springfield dropped; he fired a round into the dirt almost at his feet.

"Sarge is hit!" Specs Peterson shouted. He quickly wrapped a bandage around the wound, then tugged Martin's good arm over his shoulder. "Let's get you the hell out of here, Sarge."

"Yeah." Martin knew he sounded vague. Everybody said a wound didn't hurt when you first got it. As far as he was concerned, everybody lied. His arm felt as if he'd had molten metal poured on it. He knew too many people in Toledo to whom that had happened. He tried to wriggle the fingers of his left hand, but couldn't tell whether he succeeded or not.

Getting him the hell out of there turned out to be hell of its own kind. The Confederate bombardment had pasted the communications trenches along with everything else. Plenty of other wounded men were trying to get to the rear, too, and plenty of men who weren't wounded as well. "Jesus," Peterson said, struggling through the chaos all around. "The whole fucking line is coming to pieces."

Martin was less interested than he might have been. Putting one foot in front of the other so he wasn't a dead weight took all the concentration he had. The bandage Specs had slapped on him was red and dripping.

Somewhere back toward the rear, a couple of men with Red Cross armbands took charge of him. "Go back to your unit, Private," one of them said to Peterson.

"If I can find it," Specs answered. "If there's anything left of it. Good luck, Sarge." He turned around and trotted toward the sound of the fighting before Martin could answer.

He spoke to the stretcher-bearers—who bore no stretcher—instead: "How is it?"

He'd meant his wound, but they had other things on their mind. "It's a hell of a mess, Sergeant," one of them answered as they helped him stumble westward, away from the firing. "They drove a hell of a lot of barrels through up to the north and down south of us, too. With those bastards on their flanks, a lot of our infantry just caved in."

As if to demonstrate the truth of that, several unwounded soldiers trotted past them. A military policeman shouted a challenge. Several shots rang out. Martin didn't see the panicked soldiers coming back his way, which meant they'd shot first or best and were still running.

"It's a disaster, is what it is," the second stretcher-bearer said. "They're liable to push us all the way back to the river—maybe over it, for God's sake." Even through the blazing agony of his wound, that got through to Martin. The USA had spent two years and lives uncounted to drive the Confederates back to the Roanoke River and then over it. If they lost all that in one battle . . .

He stumbled just then, jarring his arm. He'd only thought he hurt before. The battered landscape turned gray before his eyes. He tasted blood, from where his teeth had bitten down too hard on a scream. Whatever he'd been about to say disappeared, burned away by shrieking nerves.

When they got him to the field hospital, the stretcher-bearers exclaimed in dismay, because it was dissolving like Lot's wife in the rain. "Evacuation!" somebody yelled. Somebody else added, "We're gettin' the hell out before the Rebs overrun us."

By luck—and maybe because, since he wasn't on a stretcher, he didn't take up much room—Martin got shoved aboard an ambulance. Jouncing west over the shell-pocked track toward the river was a special hell of its own. He couldn't look out, only at the other wounded men shoehorned in with him. Maybe that was a blessing of sorts. He couldn't see how many Confederate shells were falling on the road, how many others throwing up water from the Roanoke River as they searched for the bridge.

Engine roaring flat out, the ambulance sped across. The driver whooped triumphantly when he got to the other side: "Made it!" He, of course, was still in one undamaged piece. Martin couldn't decide whether he was glad he hadn't been blown up or sorry.

Flora Hamburger stood on a little portable stage in front of the Croton Brewery on Chrystie Street. The brewery was a block outside the Fourteenth Ward, but still in the Congressional district, whose boundaries didn't perfectly match those used for local administration. She thought she would have come here even had it been outside the district. The associations the brewery called up were too perfect to ignore.

"Two years ago," she called out to the crowd, "two years ago from this very spot, I called on President Roosevelt to keep us out of war. Did he listen? Did he hear me? Did he hear the will of the people, the farmers and laborers who *are* the United States of America?"

"No!" people shouted back to her, some in English, some in Yiddish. It was a proletarian crowd, women in cheap cotton shirtwaists, men in shirts without collars and wearing flat cloth caps on their heads, not bourgeois homburgs and fedoras or capitalist stovepipes.

"No!" Flora agreed. "Two years ago, the Socialist Party spoke out against the mad specter of war. Did Teddy Roosevelt and his plutocratic backers heed us? Did they pay the slightest attention to the call for peace?"

"No!" people yelled again. Too many of the women's shirt-waists were mourning black.

"No!" Flora agreed once more. "And what have they got with their war? How many young men killed?" She thought of Yossel Reisen, who hadn't had the slightest notion of the ideological implications of the war in which he'd joined—and who would never understand them now. "How many young men maimed or blinded or poisoned? How much labor expended on murder and the products of murder? Is that why troops paraded through the streets behind their marching bands?"

"They wanted victory!" someone shouted. The someone was Herman Bruck, strategically placed in the crowd. He'd borrowed clothes for the occasion, the fancy ones he usually wore being anything but suited for it.

"Victory!" Flora exclaimed. Bruck was doing everything he could to help her beat the appointed Democrat. That she had to give him. "Victory?" This time, it was a question, a mocking question. She looked around, as if she thought she would see it close by. "Where is it? Washington, D.C., has lain under the Confederates' heavy hands since the first days of the war. We have won a few battles, but how many soldiers has General Custer thrown away to get to Tennessee? And how many battles were shown to be wasted when the Confederates, only two weeks ago, drove our forces back to the Roanoke River? How can anyone in his right mind possibly claim this war is a success?"

Applause poured over her like rain. Two years ago, when she'd urged the people here not to throw the United States onto the fire of a capitalist, imperialist war, she'd been ignored or booed even in the Socialist strongholds of New York City. Now people had seen the result of what they'd cheered to the skies. Having seen it, they didn't like it so well.

She went on, "My distinguished opponent, Mr. Miller, will tell you this war is a success. Why shouldn't he tell you that? It's made *him* a success. He was a lawyer no one had ever heard of till Governor MacFarlane pulled his name out of a top hat after Congressman Zuckerman died, and sent him off to Philadelphia to pretend to represent this district.

"Friends, comrades, you know I wouldn't be standing here today if Myron Zuckerman were alive. No, I take that back: I might be standing here, but I'd be campaigning for him, not for myself. But I tell you this: if you remember what Congressman Zuckerman stood for, you'll send me to Philadelphia this November, not a fancy-pants lawyer who's made his money doing dirty work for the trusts."

More applause, loud and vigorous. In preparation for her speech, party workers had done a fine job of sticking up election posters printed in red and white on black all over the brewery, the synagogue across the street, and even the school at the corner of Chrystie and Hester. The Democrats had more money and more workers, which meant they usually put up more posters and hired people to tear down the ones the Socialists used to oppose them. Not this time, though.

And no hulking Soldiers' Circle goons lurked to break up the rally, either. As the fighting heated up, more and more of them—the younger ones—had been called into the Army they so loudly professed to love. And, as the Remembrance Day riots of 1915 slowly faded into the past, the lid on New York City politics slowly loosened. Socialists elsewhere in the country were using government repression in New York as a campaign issue, too. Embarrassment was often a good tool against the minions of the exploiting class.

A couple of caps went through the crowd. Before long, they jingled as they passed from hand to hand. Party workers talked that up: "Come on, folks, give what you can. This is how we keep the truth coming to the American people. This is how we beat the Democrats. This is how we end the war."

Flora descended from her platform. A couple of men—boys, rather—and a couple of solidly built women who looked like factory workers disassembled it and hauled it off to the wagon on which it had come from Socialist Party headquarters. Conscription had hit the party as hard as anyone else.

Herman Bruck made his way out of the crowd. Flora wondered how and why he'd been lucky enough to stay in gabardine and worsted and tweed and out of the green-gray serge most men his age wore. Her brother David was in green-gray, and, from his latest letter, about to be shipped off to one of the fighting fronts. If the war went on long enough, the same thing would happen to Isaac, who was two years younger.

So how *had* Herman escaped? It wasn't as if he had a job in an essential industry. On the contrary—a lot of Socialist activists had been conscripted in spite of employment in industries related to the war. Asking him would have been rude, but she almost asked anyhow. Before she could, he said, "That was a fine speech. Hearing you out in the crowd instead of being up on the platform with you, I see how you came to be our candidate. I think you'll win."

She knew he had an ulterior motive—several ulterior motives, some personal, some political—for speaking as he did. But she was no more immune to flattery than any other human being ever born. "Thank you," she said. "I think I will, too. The bad news in the war does nothing but help us. It reminds the people that we opposed the fighting from the start, and that we were right when we did."

Bruck's mouth twisted down. Her record on opposing the war was sounder than his. But then a sly glint came into his eye. "When they do elect you, you'll have the salary of a capitalist— $7,500 a year. What will you do with all that money?"

Any notion of asking him why he wasn't in the Army flew out of her head. She'd thought about winning the election and about taking her seat in the House of Representatives. Up till that moment, she hadn't thought about getting paid for her services. Herman Bruck was right—$7,500 was a lot of money. "I'll be able to make sure my family doesn't want for anything," she said at last.

He nodded. "That's a good answer. Wouldn't it be wonderful if all the families here"—his wave encompassed the entire district—"didn't want for anything? *Nu*, that's why you're running." The sly look returned to his face. "And now you'll have another reason to say no when I ask you out: what would a rich and important lady see in a tailor's son?"

Flora snorted. "One thing I see in a tailor's son is someone who nags like a grandmother."

"If I ask you out, maybe you'll say no, but maybe also you'll say yes," Herman answered. "If I don't ask you out, how can you possibly say yes?"

She had to laugh. As she did so, she was more tempted to let him persuade her than she had been for a long time. This didn't seem to be the right place, though, not with the crowd drifting away after the rally. And here came a couple of policemen, looking like old-time U.S. soldiers in their blue uniforms and forage caps. "All right, Miss Hamburger, you've had your speech," one of them said in brisk tones. "No one gave you a bit of trouble during it or before it, and I'll thank your people not to give me trouble now."

"No trouble because of what?" she asked warily.

The cop didn't answer. A couple of his friends came down Chrystie Street, one of them twirling a nightstick on the end of its leather strap. And then a shiny new White truck, the same sort the Army used, pulled to a stop in front of the Croton Brewery. Instead of being green-gray, it was painted red, white, and blue. DEMOCRATIC PARTY OF NEW YORK CITY, said the banner stretched across the canvas canopy. Another, smaller, banner below it read, *Daniel Miller for Congress.*

Out of the back of the truck jumped half a dozen men in overalls. A couple of others handed them big buckets of paste, long-handled brushes, and stacks of freshly printed posters. On the front of every one was Miller's smiling face, half again as big as life, and the slogan, HELP TR WIN THE WAR. VOTE MILLER—VOTE DEMOCRATIC.

Into the buckets went the brushes. Matter-of-factly, the work crew went about the business of smearing fresh paste over Flora's posters that had gone up only the day before. She stared in mute outrage that did not stay mute long. "They can't do that!" she snarled at the policeman.

"Oh, but they can, Miss Hamburger," he answered, respectful enough but not giving an inch. "They will. It's a free country, and we let you have your posters and your speech and all. But now it's our turn."

Up went Daniel Miller's posters, one after another. "Free country?" Flora said bitterly. Some of the last of the crowd she'd drawn were hanging about, watching with anything but delight as her message was effaced. If she shouted to them, they'd resist these paperhangers. New York City had seen political brawls and to spare since the rise of the Socialists. But, after Remembrance Day the year before, could she contemplate another round of riots, another round of repression?

"Don't even let it cross your mind," the cop said. He had no trouble thinking along with her. "We'll land on the lot of you like a ton of bricks, and hell will freeze over before you get yourself another peaceable rally, I promise you."

"Do you mean we, the police, or we, the Democratic Party?" she demanded. The policeman just stared at her, as if the two were too closely entwined to be worth separating. In fact, that wasn't *as if*. Coppers could harass the Socialists, and so could Democratic agitators and hooligans. Her party could return the favor, but only on a smaller scale.

She glanced at Herman Bruck. If he was ready to raise hell to keep the Democrats from silencing her posters, neither his face nor his body showed it. Maybe he'd avoided the Army by the simple expedient of being afraid to fight. Or maybe, she admitted to herself, he'd simply done a good job of figuring out how likely—or how unlikely—they were to succeed here.

"Democrats are free," she told the policeman. "Socialists and Republicans and other riffraff are as free as the Democrats let them be." He stared steadily back at her, a big, stolid man doing his job and doing it well and not worrying about the consequences of it, maybe in honest truth not even seeing that those consequences were bad.

Inside half an hour's time, Daniel Miller's posters had covered every one of hers.

Flying was beginning to feel like work again. Jonathan Moss' eyes went back and forth, up and down, flicking to the rearview mirror mounted on the side of the cockpit. He looked back over his shoulder, too, again and again. It was the one you didn't see who'd get you, sure as hell.

He still felt out of place, flying to the right of Dud Dudley. That was Tom Innis' slot in the flight, no one else's. Or it had been. But Tom was pushing up a lily now, with a rookie pilot named Orville Thornley sleeping on the cot that had been his. Thornley got endless ribbing because of his first name, but he didn't seem to be the worst flier who'd ever come down the pike.

"A good thing, too," Moss said, his eyes still on the move. The limeys had managed to sneak a few Sopwith Pups across the Atlantic, and, if you were unlucky enough to run up against one of them in a Martin one-decker, odds were the War Department would be sending your next of kin a telegram in short order. A Pup was faster, more maneuverable, and climbed better than the bus he was riding, and the British had finally figured out how to do a proper job with an interrupter gear.

Just thinking about the Pup was plenty to make him grimace. "Good thing they don't have very many of 'em here," he said. "It'd be a damn sight better if they didn't have any at all. Damn Navy, asleep at the switch again."

That was not fair. He knew it wasn't fair. He didn't care. The Atlantic Fleet had been built to close the gate between Britain and Canada, and to help the High Seas Fleet open the gate between Germany and the USA. It hadn't managed to do either of those things. Among them, the British, the French, and the Confederates made sure none of the Atlantic was safe for anyone at any time, and the Germans remained bottled up in the North Sea. *Too bad,* Moss thought. *Too damn bad.*

He looked down. The front over which he flew was quiet now, nobody doing much of anything. The Canucks and the limeys had run out of steam after pushing the U.S. line four or five miles farther from Toronto, and the Army hadn't yet tried pushing back. It was as if the mere idea of having had to fall back so startled the brass, they hadn't figured out what to try next.

Dud Dudley waggled his wings and pointed off toward the west. *Let's go home,* he meant, and swung his fighting scout into a turn. Moss wasn't sorry to get away from the line, not if that meant another run where he didn't meet any Pups. A year before, the enemy had been terrified of the Martins and their deadly synchronized guns. Now, for the first time, he understood how the fliers on the other side of the line had felt.

No sooner had the thought crossed his mind than a single aeroplane dove at his flight from the rear, machine gun spitting flame through the prop disk. He threw the joystick hard over and got the hell out of there. The flight exploded in all directions, like a flock of chickens with a fox in among them.

Tracers stitched their way across Orville Thornley's bus. It kept flying, he kept flying, and he was shooting back, too, but Jesus, Jesus, how could you keep your gun centered on the other guy's aeroplane when he was thirty miles an hour faster than you were? The short answer was, you couldn't. The longer—but only slightly longer—answer was, if you couldn't, you were dead.

Moss maneuvered now to help his flightmate, trying to put enough lead in the air to distract the limey bastard in the Pup from his chosen prey. He couldn't keep a bead on the enemy aeroplane. Everything they'd said about it looked to be true. If it wasn't doing 110, he'd eat his goggles. You couldn't make a Martin do 110 if you threw it off a cliff.

And climb—The enemy pilot came out of his dive and clawed his way up above the U.S. machines as if they'd been nailed into place. And here he came again. Yes, he still wanted Thornley. He'd probably picked him for easy meat: last man in a flight of four would be either the worst or the least experienced or both.

The kid was doing his best, but his best wasn't good enough. The Pup got on his tail and clung, chewing at him. Moss fired at the limey, but he was a few hundred yards off, unable to close farther, and he didn't think he scored any hits.

Thornley's single-decker went into a flat spin and plummeted toward the ground below, smoke trailing from the engine cowling. Moss didn't see Thornley doing anything to try, no matter how uselessly, to bring the aeroplane back under control.

No time to worry about that now anyway. The Pup was like a dragonfly, darting everywhere at once, spitting fire at the American aeroplanes from impossible angles. Bullets punched through the canvas of the fuselage. None of them punched through Moss. None of them started a fire, for which he would have got down on his knees and thanked God—but he had no time for that, either.

And then, as swiftly and unexpectedly as it had appeared, the terrible Pup was gone, darting back toward the enemy lines at a pace that would have made pursuit impossible, even had the shaken Americans dared to try. Maybe the bus had run low on fuel. That was the only thing Moss could think of that might have kept it from destroying the whole flight. What would have stopped it? It had the American aeroplanes outnumbered, one against four.

Landing was glum, as it always was after losing a flightmate. "What happened?" one of the mechanics asked.

"Pup," Moss said laconically.

The fellow in the greasy overalls bit his lip. "They really as bad as that?"

"Worse." One word at a time was hard enough. More would have been impossible.

Along with Dudley and Phil Eaker, Moss went into Shelby

Pruitt's office. The squadron leader looked up at them. He grimaced. As the mechanic had, he asked, "What happened to Thornley?"

Instead of answering directly, Dudley burst out, "God damn it to hell, when the devil are we going to be able to sit our asses down in an aeroplane that'll give us half a chance to go up there and come back alive, not one of these flying cart horses that isn't fast enough to go after the Canucks and isn't fast enough to run away from 'em, either?" All of that came out in one long, impassioned breath. On the inhale, Dudley added, "Sir."

Major Pruitt looked down at his desk. The flight leader had told him what he needed to know. "Pup," he said. It was not a question.

"Yes, sir." Moss spoke this time. "One Pup against the four of us. Those aeroplanes are very bad news, sir. How many do the Canucks have? Like Dud says, how long till we get something that can stand up to them?"

"They don't have many," Pruitt said. "We know that much. They aren't manufacturing them on this side of the water, either: not yet, anyhow. What do you suggest we do, gentlemen? Only go up in squadron strength so we can mob them when we come across them?"

Moss and his flightmates looked at one another. What that meant was, they weren't going to get an aeroplane that could stand up to the Pup, not tomorrow they weren't, and not the day after, either. Slowly, Dud Dudley said, "That might help some, sir. We'd pay a bundle for every one we brought down, but we might bring some down, sure enough. Once they ran out of 'em, things'd be like they were—except we'd be missing a hell of a lot of pilots."

"I wish I could tell you you were wrong, but I don't think you are," Pruitt said, shaking his head. "And it'll all be wasted effort, too, if the limeys get another shipload of 'em over here. The Germans, now, the Germans have aeroplanes that can match these Pups and whatever the froggies are throwing at 'em. We were supposed to get plans for some of 'em, I hear, but the submersible that set out with them didn't make it across the Atlantic. These things happen."

"And how many of us are going to end up dead because they

happen?" Moss burst out. The question had no exact answer. It didn't need one. The approximate answer was quite bad enough.

Eaker said, "What do we need the Germans for, anyway? Why can't we build our own aeroplanes, good as any in the world? We invented them."

"I know we did," Pruitt answered. "Up till the start of the war, ours were as good as anybody's, too. But the Germans and the French and the British, they've all been pushing each other hard as they could, ever since the guns started going off. The Rebs and the Canucks haven't done that to us, not to where we've needed to come up with a new kind of fighting scout every few months because the old ones would get shot down if we kept flying 'em. What do they call it? Survival of the fittest, that's right."

"We've got to worry about it now," Dud Dudley said.

"I know we do," Pruitt answered. "This time next year, if the war's still going, I expect we'll have aeroplanes to match anything the Kaiser's building. Once we know we need to do something, we generally manage."

"A lot of people are going to end up shot to pieces because Philadelphia was slow getting the message," Moss said. "Thornley was a good kid. He had the makings of a good pilot— if he'd had a decent bus to fly." *And if the fellow in the Pup had decided to go after me instead of him . . .*

"I don't even run this whole aerodrome, let alone the Bureau of Aeroplane Production." Hardshell Pruitt got up from his swivel chair, which squeaked. He led the three survivors of Dudley's flight to the officers' club, threw a quarter-eagle down on the bar, and carried a bottle of whiskey over to a table.

As Moss started to drink, he looked over at the photographs of fliers dead and gone. *One more to put up,* he thought, and then wondered whether Orville Thornley had had a photo taken since he joined the squadron. Moss didn't think so. Thornley hadn't been here very long. Moss gulped down his drink. If he tried hard enough, maybe he could stop thinking about things like that. Maybe he could stop thinking at all.

When Lucien Galtier came in from the fields, the sun was going down. As summer slid into fall, it set ever sooner, rose ever later. The air had—not quite a chill, but the premonition of a chill—it hadn't held even a couple of weeks earlier. Pretty soon, frost would fern across the windows when he got up in the morning.

Marie came bustling out of the farmhouse to meet him before he came inside. She didn't usually do that. Automatically, he began to worry. Any change in routine portended trouble. A lifetime's experience and a cultural inheritance of centuries warned him that was true.

So did his wife's face. "What is it now?" he asked her, and picked the two worst things he could think of: "Have we had a visit from Father Pascal while I was cultivating? Or is that the American, Major Quigley, was here?"

"No, neither of those, for which I thank *le bon Dieu*," Marie answered. "But it is, all the same, something of which I wish to speak to you without having any of the children hear." She looked down to make sure none of their numerous brood was in earshot.

Lucien did the same thing. "Of course, our trying to keep them from hearing but makes *them* try the more to hear," he said, again from long experience. "But what is it that you would keep a secret from them?"

"Not from all of them, not quite." Marie took a deep breath. When she spoke, the words tumbled out all in a rush: "Nicole just came home from the hospital"—she did not look at the big building the Americans had run up on Galtier land; she made a point of not looking at it—"and she, she, she asked permission of me to bring to supper tomorrow night one of the doctors who works there."

" 'Osti," Lucien said softly. Once, and once only, he stomped a booted foot on the ground. "I knew it would come to this. Did I not say it would come to this? When she went to work at that place"—he not only did not look at the hospital, he refused even to name it—"I knew it would come to this."

"His name is O'Doull," Marie said, pronouncing the un-Quebecois appellation with care. "He speaks French, Nicole says, and he is himself a member of the holy Catholic Church—so she assures me."

"He is himself a member of the United States Army," Lucien retorted. Since that was manifestly true, Marie could only nod. Her husband went on, "The people in Ottawa—the Protestants in Ottawa—had the courtesy, more or less, to leave us alone.

The Americans, merely by their coming, are taking from us our patrimony."

"I did not tell Nicole yes, and I did not tell her no, either," Marie answered. "I told her I would tell you, and that you would decide."

Galtier opened his mouth to declare that he had already decided, and that the answer was and would always be no. Before he did so, though, he cast a quizzical eye on Marie. She knew everything he'd said, and knew it at least as well as he did. More cautiously than he'd expected, he asked, "Why did you not say no on your own behalf?"

Marie let out a long sigh. "Because I fear the Americans will remain here in Quebec for a long time to come, and I do not believe we shall be able to make it as if they do not exist. And because I do not believe that Nicole would come to know any fondness for a man who is wicked, even if he is an American. And because one supper, here in front of the lot of us, is not the end of the world. And it could even be that, seeing this . . . man O'Doull here in our own place, not at the other one where she works, would be the best way to convince her he is not the proper one."

Yes, I had good reason to be cautious, Lucien thought. Aloud, he said, "And if I still believe this should not be?"

"Then it shall not be, of course," his wife replied at once. She was always properly submissive, and she usually got her way.

She would get her way this time, too. "It could even be," Galtier said in a speculative voice, "that seeing all of her family will have a chilling effect on this Dr. O'Doull." He smiled, remembering. "This is often true, when a man who is not serious meets a young lady's family."

"You have reason," Marie answered, smiling too. "Let us go in now, and tell Nicole she may bring him, then."

"Very well," Lucien said. It wasn't very well, or anywhere close to being very well, but he seemed to have no good choices whatever. In that, he thought of himself as a tiny version of the entire province of Quebec.

Nicole squealed when Marie told her (Lucien could not make himself do anything more than nod) she might invite the doctor for supper. Georges said, "Ah, so I am to have an American brother-in-law, *n'est-ce pas?*" Nicole's face turned the color of fire. She threw a potato at him. It thumped against his ribs. Grinning still, he said, "I am wounded! The doctor must cure me!" and thrashed about on the floor.

Charles, his older brother, said nothing, not with words, but the look he sent Lucien said, *Father, how could you?* Galtier's shrug showed how little true choice he had had. Nicole's three younger sisters couldn't seem to decide whether to be horrified or fascinated by the news.

Galtier went through the next day's work as if he were a machine wound up to perform its tasks without thought. His mind had already leapt to the evening, and to the meeting with the American, O'Doull. In his mind, he ran through a dozen, a score of conversations with the man. Whether any of them would have anything to do with reality he had no idea, but he played them out all the same.

He looked up in some surprise to see the sun near setting. *Time to go in,* he realized, on most days a welcome thought but today one so much the opposite that he looked around for more chores to do. Talking with the American in the privacy of his own mind was one thing. Talking with the man in the real world was a different, far more daunting prospect.

He wiped his boots with special care. Even so, he knew he brought the aromas of the farmyard into the house with him. How could he help it? Knowing he could not help it, knowing he was not the only one on the farm who did it, he thought nothing of it most of the time. Now—

Now, there in the parlor sat a tall, skinny stranger in town clothes; he was talking with Nicole and doing what looked to be his gallant best not to be upset at having her brothers and sisters stare at him. He sprang to his feet when Lucien came in. So did Nicole. "Father," she said formally, "I would like to introduce to you Dr. Leonard O'Doull. Leonard, this is my father, *Monsieur* Lucien Galtier."

"I am very pleased to meet you, sir," O'Doull said in good French, the Parisian accent with which he'd learned the tongue overlain by the rhythms of the Quebecois with whom he'd been working. Galtier took that as a good sign, a sign of accommodation. He could not imagine Major Quigley sounding like a Quebecois if he stayed in this country a hundred years.

O'Doull's hands were pale and soft, but not smooth. The skin on them was chafed and reddened and cracked in many places, some of those cracks looking angry and inflamed. Doctors had to wash often in corrosive chemicals to keep their hands free of germs.

As for the rest of the doctor, he looked like an Irishman: fair skin with freckles, sandy hair, almost cat-green eyes, a dimple in his chin so deep a plow might have dug it. He was unobtrusively sizing up Galtier as the farmer examined him. "I do thank you very much for letting me come into your home," he said. "I know it is an intrusion, and I know it is a"—he cast about for a word— "an awkwardness for you as well."

He was frank. Lucien liked him the better for that. "Well, we shall see how it goes," he said. "I can always throw you out, after all."

"Father!" Nicole exclaimed in horror. But one of O'Doull's gingery eyebrows lifted; he knew Galtier hadn't meant that seriously. Again, against his will, Galtier's opinion of the doctor went up.

Marie served up potatoes and greens and ham cooked with prunes and dried apples. Lucien got out a jug of applejack he'd bought from one of the farmers nearby. He hadn't expected he'd want to do that. O'Doull, though, even if he was an American, seemed a man of both sense and humor. He also made appreciative noises about Marie's cooking, which caused her to fill up his plate once more after he'd demolished his first helping. The second disappeared as quickly.

Georges made a show of looking under the table. "Where does such a scrawny fellow put it all?" he asked.

"I have a secret pocket, like a kangaroo," O'Doull answered gravely. Georges blinked, unused to getting as good as he gave.

When supper was done and the womenfolk went off to wash and dry, the American handed cigars to Lucien and Charles and Georges. Lucien poured more apple brandy for them all. *"Salut,"* he said, raising his glass, and then, experimentally, before drinking, *"Je me souviens."*

I will remember: the motto of Quebec in the face of many difficult times, this one more than most. He was not surprised to see that Leonard O'Doull understood not only the words but also the meaning behind them. The American doctor drank the toast, then said, "I understand how hard this is for you, and I thank you again for being so hospitable to an outsider."

Galtier had had enough applejack by then to loosen his tongue a little. He said, "How can you understand, down deep and truly? You are an American, an occupier, not one of the occupied."

"My homeland is also occupied," O'Doull answered. "England has done more and worse for longer to the Irish than she ever did to Quebec." He spoke now with absolute seriousness. "My grandfather was a starving boy when he came to the United States because all the potatoes died and the English landowners sold the wheat in the fields abroad instead of feeding the people with it. We are paying back the debt."

"The Irish rebellion has not thrown out the English," Galtier said.

"No, but it goes on, and ties down their men," O'Doull replied. "It would be better if the U.S. Navy could bring more arms to them, but boats do put in at little beaches every now and then, in spite of what the British fleet can do to stop them, and machine guns aren't so big and bulky."

"You say this here, to a country that might rise in revolt against the United States as Ireland has against England?" Even with applejack in him, Lucien would have spoken so openly to few men on such brief acquaintance: fewer still among the occupiers. But while the doctor might disagree, Lucien did not believe he would betray him to the authorities.

O'Doull said, "You will be freer with the United States than you ever were in Canada. It has proved true for the Irish; it will prove true for you as well. This I believe with all my heart."

Charles, who usually kept his own counsel, said, "Few countries invade their neighbors for the purpose of making them free."

"We came into Canada to beat the British Empire," O'Doull answered, blowing a smoke ring. "They and the Rebels stabbed us in the back twice. But I think, truly, you will be better off outside the Empire than you were in it."

"If we left Canada, if we left the British Empire, of our own will, then it could be you are right," Lucien said. "Anyone who forces something on someone and then says he will be better for it—you will, I hope, understand me when I say this is difficult to appreciate."

"It could be you said the same thing when your mother gave you medicine when you were small," O'Doull replied.

"Yes, it could be," Lucien said. With dignity, he continued, "But, *monsieur le docteur,* you are not my mother, and the United States are not Quebec's mother. If any country is, it is France."

"All right. I can see how you would feel that way, M. Galtier." O'Doull got to his feet. "I do thank you and your wife and your enchanting family for the fine supper, and for your company as well. Is it possible that I might come back again one day, drink some more of this excellent applejack, and talk about the world again? And we might even talk of other things as well. If you will pardon me one moment, I would like also to say good-bye to Nicole."

She was one of the other things the American would want to talk about, Galtier knew. He felt the pressure of his sons' eyes on him. Almost to his own surprise, he heard himself saying, "Yes, this could be. Next week, perhaps, or the week after that." Until the words were out of his mouth, he hadn't fully realized he approved of the doctor in spite of his country and his ideas. *Well,* he thought, *the arguments will be amusing.*

" 'Nother day done. Praise de lord," Jonah said when the shift-changing whistle blew. "I see you in de mornin', Nero."

"See you then," Scipio agreed. He was very used to his alias these days, sometimes even thinking of himself by it. He wiped his sweaty forehead on the coarse cotton canvas of his shirt. Another day done indeed, and a long one, too. The white foreman stuck his card in the time clock to punch him out of work. He trudged from the factory onto the streets of Columbia, a free man.

Even after three months or so at the munitions plant, he had trouble getting used to that idea. His time was his own till he had to get back to work in the morning. He'd never known such liberty, not in his entire life. As house servant and later as butler at Marshlands, he'd been at the white folks' beck and call every hour of the day or night. As a member of the governing council of the Congaree Socialist Republic, he'd been at Cassius' beck and call no less than at Miss Anne's before. Now . . .

Now he could do as he pleased. If he wanted to go to a saloon and get drunk, he could. If he wanted to chase women, he could do that. If he wanted to go to a park and watch the stars come out, he could do that, too—though Columbia still had a ten o'clock curfew for blacks. And if he wanted to go back to his apartment and read a book, he could also do that, and not have to worry about getting called away in the middle of a chapter.

He walked into a restaurant not far from the factory, ordered fried chicken and fried okra and cornbread, washed it down with chicory-laced coffee, and came out full and happy. Nobody knew who he was. Nobody cared who he was. Oh, every now and then he still saw wanted posters for the uncaptured leaders of the Congaree Socialist Republic, and his name—his true name—still appeared among them, but that hardly seemed to matter. It might have happened a lifetime before, to someone else altogether.

Had Cassius understood that desire to escape the revolutionary past, it probably would have been enough for him to want to liquidate Scipio. Out in the swamps by the Congaree, Cassius and his diehards kept up a guerrilla war against Confederate authority even yet. Every so often, the newspapers complained of some outrage or another the rebels—the papers commonly called them bandits—had perpetrated.

But the papers talked much more about the bill to arm Negroes under debate up in Richmond. People talked about it, too, both white and black. The talk had only intensified once it cleared the House and got into the Senate. More than half of the black men Scipio knew were for it. As best he could judge, fewer than half the whites in Columbia were. How much his judgment was worth, he had trouble gauging.

When he got back to his apartment building, he let out a heartfelt sigh of relief. Now that he no longer had to pay half his salary to the white clerk who'd hired him, he could afford something better than the dismal flophouse where he'd endured his first nights in Columbia. The place was shabby but clean, with gas lights and a bathroom at the end of the hall. It had cockroaches, but not too many, and his own astringently neat habits gave them little sustenance.

Coming up the corridor from the bathroom, the mulatto woman who had the apartment across the hall from his smiled. "Evenin', Nero," she said.

"Evenin', Miss Sempronia," he answered. He thought she was a widow, but he wasn't sure. He didn't pry into the business of others, not least because he couldn't afford to have anyone prying into his. That smile, though, and others he'd got from her, made him think he wouldn't have to run very fast if he decided to chase her.

He went into his own apartment and closed the door after him. It was getting dark early these days; though he'd left the drapes open, he had to fumble to find the matches he'd set on the shelf near the gaslight. He struck one and got the lamp there going. That gave him the light he needed to start the lamp above his favorite chair.

Since the apartment boasted only one chair, that made the choice easier than it would have been otherwise. But it *was* comfortable, so he didn't complain. If the upholstery was battered, well, so what? This wasn't Marshlands. "I am, however, not the tiniest bit dissatisfied with my present circumstances," he said softly, in the starchy white-folks' voice he hadn't used more than a couple of times since the Red uprising broke out. He smiled to hear himself. Now that he wasn't used to it any more, that accent struck him as ridiculous.

On the rickety pine table beside the chair lay a battered copy of Flaubert's *Salammbô* he'd picked up for a nickel. He opened it almost at random and plunged in. He wondered how many times he'd read it. More than he could count on his fingers, he was sure of that. Most literate Negroes in the CSA had read *Salammbô* a good many times. The story of the revolt of the army of dark-skinned mercenaries against Carthage after the First Punic War struck a chord in the heart of the most peaceable black man.

He grimaced and sighed. That revolt had failed, too. He kept reading anyhow.

When the cheap, loudly ticking alarm clock he'd bought said it was a little past nine, he carried a couple of towels and a bar of soap down to the bathroom. One thing years of being a butler had done: made him more fastidious than most factory hands, white or black, in the CSA. The weather was still warm enough for him to find a cold-water bath invigorating. How he'd feel about that when winter came around, he didn't want to think.

Next morning, the alarm clock's clatter got him hopping out

of bed, heart pounding as if Confederate soldiers were bombarding the apartment house. He dressed, made himself coffee, breakfasted on bread and jam, and made a sandwich of bread and tinned beef to throw in his dinner pail. Thus fortified, he walked the half a mile to work, the dinner pail brushing his left thigh with every step he took.

A lot of black men in overalls and collarless shirts and heavy shoes were on the street; he might have been invisible among them. Some, like him, went bareheaded; some wore homemade straw hats, as if they still labored in the fields; some wore cloth caps like most white factory hands. Not many white factory hands were left, though: supervisors, youngsters not yet ripe for conscription, wounded veterans no longer fit for the front, and a few others with skills or pull enough to keep them out of butternut.

Here and there, men who worked in his plant waved to him and called out his *nom de travaille*. "Mornin', Nero." "How you is, Nero?" The broader he made his Congaree patois in answer, the happier the other workers seemed. He'd seen that back at Marshlands, too. It saddened him—his fellows were locking themselves away from much that was worthwhile—but he also understood it.

Greetings flew thick and fast as he lined up to punch in. He'd made his own place here, and felt no small pride at having done so. "Mornin', Solon," he said with a wave. "How you is, Artaxerxes? A good mornin' to you, Hadrian."

The foreman said, "Apollonius already took off, Nero, so I reckon you got yourself a few crates to haul there."

"I'll do it," was all Scipio said, to which the white man nodded. The fellow who worked the night shift slid out of the factory as fast as he possibly could every morning. One day he'd slide out too fast, and have the door slammed in his face when he came back. It wasn't as if the bosses couldn't find anyone to replace him.

Sure enough, several crates of empty shell casings waited to be hauled to the belt that would take them to the white women who filled them and installed their fuses and noses. Scipio loaded two onto a dolly and pushed it over to Jonah, who stood waiting to receive it. When he hurried back to do more, Jonah shook his head. "Dat Apollonius, he one lazy nigger," he observed. "You, Nero, you does yo' work good."

"T'ank you," Scipio said. Jonah, as usual, sounded faintly surprised to admit that, no doubt because he remembered Scipio from his soft-handed days as a butler. None of the then-field hands had ever realized how much work Scipio actually did at Marshlands because so much of it was with his head rather than his hands or his back. He was ready to admit headwork was easier, but it was still work.

Back and forth, back and forth. He got no credit for the dolly, but it helped. Lift, carry, push, lift, carry, push. His hands and his muscles had hardened; he didn't go home every night shambling like a spavined horse any more. He knew a certain amount of pride in that. He was stronger than he had been, and sometimes tempted to get into fights to show off his new strength. He resisted that temptation, along with most others. Fighting might make him visible to the whites of Columbia, which was the last thing he wanted.

Working with his body left his mind curiously blank. He listened to what was going on around him, to the clatter of the lines, to the chatter of the people working them, and, after a while, to the foreman out front: "Are you sure you want to go back there? It's a dirty, smelly place, and parts of it are dangerous, too, what with the explosives and fuses and such-like."

The words weren't far out of the ordinary. The tone was. The foreman, normally master of all he surveyed here, sounded deferential, persuasive. That more than what he was saying made Scipio notice his voice in the first place. A moment later, he understood why the foreman sounded as he did. The reply came with the unquestioning, uncompromising arrogance of a Confederate aristocrat: "I am a stockholder, and not a small stockholder, in this corporation. I have the right to see how its operations function. You may guide me, or you may get out of the way and let me see for myself. The choice is yours."

Scipio dropped at Jonah's feet the crate he was hauling; the shell casings clanked in their plywood-partitioned pigeonholes. "Do Jesus!" Scipio exclaimed in a horrified whisper. "Dat are Miss Anne!"

"I knows it," Jonah answered, looking at least as discomfited as Scipio felt. Regardless of what his passbook had said he could do, Jonah had left Marshlands for his factory job two years earlier. His position was less desperate than Scipio's, but far from what he would have wanted.

Before Scipio could make up his mind whether to hope he wasn't recognized or to flee, Anne Colleton came in, the foreman trailing after her and still trying ineffectually to slow her down. As Scipio knew, anyone who tried to slow her down was bound to be ineffectual. "This area here, ma'am," the foreman said, still not grasping how outgunned he was, "is where the casings come off the line over yonder and go to get filled over here."

"Is it?" Anne said. She nodded to the Negro laborers. "Good day, Scipio, Jonah." Then, without another word, she headed off into the filling area. The two Negroes looked at each other. She knew who they were—she knew and she hadn't done a thing about it. That worried Scipio more than anything else he could think of.

Sylvia Enos knew how drunk she was. She rarely touched whiskey, but she'd made an exception tonight. She was ready to make exceptions about lots of things tonight. She giggled. "Good thing I'm not going anywhere," she said, and giggled again. "I couldn't get there."

"Not going anywhere at all," her husband agreed. George had drunk more than she had, but showed it less. The whiskey wasn't making him laugh, either. It was just making him very certain about things. His certainty had swept her along, too, so that she lay altogether naked beside him even though the children couldn't have been in bed more than fifteen minutes themselves.

If George, Jr., came in right now—well, that would be funny, too. Whiskey was amazing stuff, all right. Sylvia ran her hand over George's chest, the hair there so familiar and so long absent. From his chest, her hand wandered lower. Ladies didn't do such things. Ladies, in fact, endured it rather than enjoying it when their husbands touched them. *If George gets angry, I'll blame it on the whiskey,* she thought as her hand closed around him.

"Oh," he said, more an exhalation than a word. Nor was that the only way he responded to her touch.

"Is that what you learned in the Navy—how to come to attention, I mean?" she said. He laughed. Then, without even being asked, she slid down and took him in her mouth. Ladies not only didn't do such things, they didn't think of such things. A lot of ladies had never heard of or imagined such things. Since she had . . . His flesh was smooth and hot. *The whiskey,* she thought again. Being inexperienced in such things, she bore down more than she should have, and had to withdraw, choking a little.

If they hadn't been married, if she hadn't wanted him as much as he wanted her, what followed would have been a rape. As it was, she wrapped her arms and legs around him while he plunged above her, and whispered endearments and urged him on.

He shuddered and groaned sooner than she would have liked, which was, she supposed, a disadvantage of doing as she'd just done. Instead of pulling free, though, he stayed in her. In an amazingly short time, he was hard again. The second round was almost as frantic as the first, but, kindled by that first time, she felt all thought go away just as he spent, too.

"Always like a honeymoon, coming back to you after I've been away at sea," he said, a smile in his voice. "I've been at sea a long time this time—and I never even saw the ocean."

Sylvia didn't answer right away. She felt lazy and sated, at peace with the world even if the world held no peace. But the body had demands other than those of lust and love. "Let me up, dear," she said, and, regretfully, he rolled off her. She regretted it, too, when he came out. *Nothing good ever lasts,* that seemed to say.

She pulled the chamber pot out from under the bed and squatted to use it. Some of his seed ran out of her, too. That she did not mind; it made getting pregnant less likely. She got back into bed. George stood and used the chamber pot, too, then lay down beside her in the darkness once more.

"I got the telegram that said you were missing," she said, "and—" She didn't, couldn't, go on with words. Instead, she clutched him to her, even tighter than when his hips had pumped him in and out of her as if he were the piston of a steam engine and she the receiving cylinder.

He squeezed her, too. "I hid in the woods with my pals till another boat got down there to see if anybody had lived through the explosion. They were the brave ones, 'cause the Rebs had that spot zeroed. None of the shells hit, though, and we rowed out to them and they got us away from there."

"Four," she said wonderingly. "Four, out of the whole crew."

"Luck," George answered. "Fool luck. We were up at this colored fellow's shack on the riverbank. Charlie White would have killed anybody who kept a place that dirty, and they made the whiskey right around there. You drank it, you could run a gaslight on your breath. I had a glass, and some food—place was dirty, yeah, but they cooked better than anything our galley turned out—and I had some more whiskey, and then I went outside, and then . . . the Rebels dropped two, right on the *Punishment*." Remembering made him shiver.

"What did you go outside for?" Sylvia asked.

She meant the question casually. *To stand next to a tree* was the answer she'd expected, or something of that sort. George stiffened in her arms, and not in the way she'd found so enjoyable. "Oh, just to get a breath of air," he said, and she knew he was lying.

"What did you go outside for?" she repeated, and tried to see his face in the darkness. No good: he was only the vaguest blur.

He stayed unnaturally still a little too long. Was that the glitter of his eyes opening wide to try to see her expression, too? "It wasn't anything," he said at last.

Where the whiskey had made her giddy and then randy, now it made her angry. "What did you go outside for?" she said for the third time. "I want you to tell me the truth."

George sighed. When Sylvia breathed in as he breathed out, she could smell and taste that they'd been drinking together. Sober, he might have found a lie she would believe, or else might have been able to keep his mouth shut till she got sick of asking questions. He'd managed that, every now and then.

He sighed again. "There was another place, next to this saloon or tavern or whatever you call it. I was going over there, but I never made it. I hadn't taken more than a couple of steps that way when the shelling started."

"Another place?" she echoed. George nodded, a gesture she felt instead of seeing. "Well, why didn't you say so?" she demanded. "What kind of place was . . . ?" All at once, she wanted to push him away from her as hard as she could. "You were going to a—" Her hiss might have been more deadly than a shout.

"Yeah, I was." He sounded ashamed. That was something, a small something, but not nearly enough. He went on, "I didn't get there. Sylvia, I swear to you it's the only time I was gone that I was going that way. I'd been away so long, and I didn't know when I'd be back or if I'd ever be back." He laughed, which enraged her till he went on, "I guess God was telling me I shouldn't do things like that even once."

"And I let you—" Her voice was cold as the ice in the hold of a steam trawler. She hadn't just let him touch her, she'd wanted him to touch her, she'd wanted to touch him. She couldn't say that; her body had fewer inhibitions than her tongue did. Her tongue . . . She'd had that part of him in her mouth, and she thought she'd throw up. She gulped, as if fighting back seasickness.

"Nothing happened," George said.

She believed him. She wanted, or part of her wanted, to think he was lying; that would have given her all the more reason to force him away from her. Had he been telling the truth when he said that was the only time he'd gone to—or toward—such a place? Again, she thought so, but she wondered if it mattered when you got down to the bottom of things. Still in that frozen voice, she said, "Something would have happened, wouldn't it?"

"Yes, I guess it would," he answered dully.

He wasn't trying to pretend. That was something, too. Try as she would, she had trouble keeping the flame of her fury hot. Being apart from him had been hard on her, too, and she'd known he wasn't a saint before she married him. "You were pretty stupid, do you know that?" she said.

"I thought so myself," he answered, quickly, eagerly, a man splashing in the sea grabbing for a floating spar. "If I hadn't had that second glass of whiskey, I never would have done it."

"Whiskey gets you into all sorts of trouble, doesn't it?" she said, not quite so frosty now. "Makes you go after women you shouldn't, makes you talk too much when you're with the woman you should—"

He laughed in relief, feeling himself slide off the hook. His thumb and forefinger closed on her nipple; even in the dark, he found it unerringly. Sylvia twisted away: he wasn't *that* for-given yet.

"I was plenty stupid," he said, which not only agreed with what she'd just said but had the added virtue of likely being truer than *I'm sorry*.

"I hope to heaven this terrible war ends soon, so you can come home and spend the rest of your days with me," Sylvia said. *And,* she added to herself, *so I can keep an eye on you*. She'd never thought she'd need another reason for wishing the war over, but George had given her one.

He understood that, too. "I hope they'll really send me out to sea this time," he said. "Then I'll be away from everything"— *everything in a dress,* he meant—"for months at a time."

Sylvia nodded. George didn't mention what happened when sailors came into a port after months at a time at sea. Maybe he was trying not to think about it. Maybe he was hoping she wouldn't think about it. If so, it was a forlorn hope. Boston was a Navy town. More than one sailor had accosted Sylvia on the street. She did not imagine her husband was a great deal dif-ferent from the common lot of men. Had she so imagined, he would have taught her better.

He clutched her to him. "I don't want anybody but you," he said.

Now you don't, she thought. He gave proof with more than words that he did want her. With a small sigh, she let him take her. He was her husband, he had come home alive out of danger, he hadn't (quite) (she didn't think) been unfaithful to her. So she told herself. But, where only the speed of his explosion the first time had kept her from joining him in joy, where she had done just that the second time, and been as eager, even as wanton, then as ever in her life, now, though she tried, though she strained, though she concentrated, pleasure eluded her.

George didn't notice. Somehow that hurt almost worse than anything he'd told her. In a while, she supposed, he'd want a fourth round, too. "Have we got any more whiskey?" she asked.

XVI

Arthur McGregor tramped through the snow toward the barn. The harvest was in, and just in time; freezing weather had come early this year. But the livestock still needed tending. He shook his head. Alexander should have been out here helping him. But Alexander still languished in the Rosenfeld gaol. If he ever got out—

Sometimes, now, hours at a time would go by when McGregor didn't think of his son's being freed. Every fiber of him still hoped it would happen. (*How could it not happen?* he thought. *The only thing the boy did was hang about with a few of the wrong people and let his tongue flap loose. Not one in a hundred would be left free if you locked up everybody who did that.*) He didn't count on it or expect it as he had right after Alexander's arrest, though. Scar tissue was growing over the hole the extraction of his son from the family had left.

He fed the horses, the cows, the pigs, the chickens. He forked dung out of the stalls. He gathered eggs, storing them inside his hat. The hens pecked at his hands, the way they always did when he robbed their nests. The rooster couldn't have cared less. All he had eyes for was his harem, as splendid to him as the Ottoman sultan's bevy of veiled beauties.

McGregor's breath smoked as if he'd just lighted a cigarette when he left the barn. The first inhalation of cold outside air burned in his lungs like cigarette smoke, too. After a couple of breaths, though, he felt all right. Once winter really came down, he'd feel as if he were breathing razors whenever he stuck his head out of any door.

Off to the north, artillery coughed and grumbled. It was farther away than it had been halfway through the summer, when

Canadian troops and those from the mother country had pushed the Yankees south from Winnipeg. "But not south to Rosenfeld," McGregor said sadly. Winnipeg still held, though. So long as Winnipeg held, and Toronto, and Montreal, and Quebec City, Canada lived. The Americans had claimed Toronto's fall a good many times. Lies, all lies. "What they're good for," Mc-Gregor told the air, and started back toward the farmhouse with the eggs.

As usual, the north-south road that ran by the farm was full of soldiers and guns and horses and trucks on the move, most of the traffic heading north toward the front. What went south was what didn't work any more: ambulances full of broken men, trucks and horses glumly pulling broken machines. The more of those McGregor saw, the better he reckoned his country's chances.

And here came an automobile, jouncing along the path toward the farmhouse. The motorcar was painted green-gray. Even had it not been, he would have known it for an American vehicle. Who but the Americans had gasoline these days?

As if it had not been there, McGregor brought the eggs in to Maude. "Trouble coming," he said. His wife didn't need to ask him what he meant. Automobiles were noisy things, and you could hear their rattle and bang and pop a long way across the quiet prairie.

"Americans," Mary said fiercely, sticking her head into the kitchen. "Let's shoot them."

"You can't say that, little one, not where they can hear you," McGregor told his younger daughter. "You can't even think it, not where they can hear you." Mary's nod was full of avid comprehension. She had an instinctive gift for conspiracy the war had brought out young in her, as a hothouse could force a rose into early bloom.

The automobile sputtered to a stop. A door slammed, then another. Booted feet—several pairs of booted feet—came stomping toward the door. "Shall we open it?" Maude whispered.

McGregor shook his head. As quietly, he answered, "No. We'll make 'em knock. They have to know we're here—where else would we be? It'll annoy them." By such tiny campaigns was his war against the invaders fought. Mary's eyes glowed. She understood without being told the uses of harassment—but then, she had an older brother and sister.

"Damn Canucks," said one of the American soldiers outside. McGregor nodded, once. Mary giggled soundlessly.

"Quiet." That was a voice McGregor recognized: Captain Hannebrink. All the farmer's pleasure at annoying the occupiers changed to mingled alarm and hope. What was the man who had arrested Alexander doing here? He hadn't come out to the farm since the day of the arrest.

Maude knew his voice, too. "What does he—?" Her voice cut off in the middle of the question. Hannebrink was knocking at the door.

It was an utterly ordinary knock, not the savage pounding it should have been with a car full of American ruffians out there. Stories said they used rifle butts. Not here, not today.

McGregor went to the door and opened it. The captain nodded, politely enough. Behind him, the three private soldiers came to alertness. They had rifles, even if they hadn't used them as door knockers. Hannebrink didn't say anything, not right away. "What is it?" McGregor asked as silence stretched.

From behind him, Mary asked, "Are you going to let my brother go?"

"Hush," Maude said, and pushed Mary back to Julia, hissing, "Take care of her and keep her quiet"—not an easy order to follow.

Captain Hannebrink coughed. "Mr. McGregor, I have to tell you that over the past few days we obtained information confirming for us that your son, Alexander McGregor, was in fact an active participant in efforts to harm United States Army occupying forces in this military district, and that he should therefore be judged as a *franc-tireur*."

"Information?" McGregor said, not taking in all of the long, cold, dry sentence at once. "What kind of information?"

"I am not at liberty to discuss that with you, sir," Hannebrink said stiffly. He scratched at the edge of his Kaiser Bill mustache, careful not to disturb its waxed perfection.

"Means somebody's been filling your head up with lies, and you don't have to own up to that or say who it is," McGregor said.

The American shrugged. "As you know, sir, the penalty for civilians resisting in arms the occupying forces is death by firing squad."

Behind McGregor, Julia gasped. He heard Maude stop breathing. Through numb lips, he said, "And you're going to—shoot him? You can't do that, Captain. There has to be some kind of appeal, of—"

Hannebrink held up a hand. "Mr. McGregor, I regret to have to inform you that the sentence was carried out, in accordance with U.S. Army regulations, at 0600 hours this morning. Your son's body will be released to you for whatever burial arrangements you may care to make."

Mary didn't understand. "Father—?" Julia said in a halting voice; she wasn't sure she understood, and desperately hoped she didn't. Maude set her hand on McGregor's arm. She knew. So did he.

They shot him at sunrise, he thought dully. *Before sunrise.* It would have been dark and chilly, even before they wrapped a black rag over Alexander's bright, laughing eyes, tied him to a post or stood him up against a wall or did whatever they did, and fired a volley that made him one with the darkness and ice forever.

The American soldiers behind Captain Hannebrink were very alert. McGregor would have bet they'd had this duty before, and knew hell could break loose. "If it is any consolation to you, sir," the captain said, "he went bravely and it was over very fast. He did not suffer."

McGregor couldn't even scream at him to get out. They had Alexander's body, the body that, the Yank said, had not suffered, but was now dead. "Take it," McGregor said, stumbling over the words, "take it to the Presbyterian church. He'll go in, in the graveyard there."

Julia shrieked. So did Mary—she knew what the graveyard meant. She sprang for Captain Hannebrink as she had for the U.S. officer in Rosenfeld when he'd wanted to arrest her father. McGregor grabbed her and held her. He didn't know what those narrow-eyed soldiers behind Hannebrink might do to an attacker, even an attacker who was a little girl, and he didn't want to find out.

"I shall do as you request," Captain Hannebrink said. "As I told you, sir, I deeply regret the unfortunate necessity for this visit."

"Somebody went out and told you one more lie, Captain, and

you piled it on top of all the other lies you heard, and it finally gave you enough of a stack so you could shoot my boy, the way you've been looking to do all these months," McGregor said.

"We do not believe it was a lie," Hannebrink said.

"And I don't believe you," McGregor said. "Now get out of my sight. If I ever set eyes on you again—" Maude's hand tightened on his upper arm and brought him a little way back toward himself.

"Mr. McGregor, I understand that you are overwrought now," the U.S. officer said, trying to be kind, trying to be sympathetic, and only making McGregor hate him more on account of it. He turned to his soldiers. "Come on, boys. We've done what we had to do. Let's go."

All the men walked back to the Ford. Hannebrink got in. So did the private soldiers, one at a time, ever so warily. When one cranked the engine back to life, another covered him. McGregor wondered how often they'd been fired on after delivering that kind of news. Some people, after hearing it, wouldn't much care whether they lived or died.

He didn't much care whether he lived or died himself. But he did care about Maude and Julia and Mary. His family. All the family he had left.

He turned back to his wife. Tears were running down her face. He hadn't heard her start crying. He was crying, too, he suddenly realized. He hadn't noticed that start, either. They clung to each other and to their daughters—and to the memory of their son.

"Alexander," Maude whispered, her faced pressed against his shoulder.

"Alexander," he echoed slowly. His mind raced ahead. Look ahead, look behind, look around—if you didn't look at where you were, you wouldn't have to think about how bad things were here at the focused moment of *now*.

He saw Alexander laid to rest in the churchyard, the grass there already sere and brown. He saw past that. His son had said—had no doubt said up until the very moment the rifles fired—he'd had no part in the things he was accused of doing. McGregor believed him.

Someone had lied, then. Someone had lied to bring him to death before sunrise. Someone, probably, whose son really had done the things Alexander stood accused of doing, and wanted to see the McGregors suffer along with him, no matter how unjustly. Whoever it was, McGregor figured he could find him, sooner or later. *An eye for an eye. A tooth for a tooth.*

And the Americans had believed the lie. They must have known it was a lie. But they hadn't shot anybody lately, and maybe they needed examples to keep the Canadians quiet.

Whatever their reasons, he vowed they weren't going to keep him quiet. They'd shot Alexander for a *franc-tireur*. He hadn't been one. McGregor was sure of that, down to the marrow of his bones. But in shooting him, they'd made themselves a *franc-tireur*, all right.

"I'm twenty years out of the Army," he murmured. Maude stared at him. She would know what he was thinking. He didn't care, not now he didn't. He'd forgotten a lot of things over half a lifetime or so. If he had to use them again, though, he expected they'd come back soon enough.

Having wished that, after so long in river monitors, he might go back to sea, George Enos was repenting of his decision. He had gone to sea in fishing boats since before the time when he needed a razor. Going to sea in a destroyer was a altogether different business, as he was discovering day by day.

"It's like you've ridden horses all your life, and they were the horses the brewery uses to haul beer barrels to the saloon," he said to Andy Conkling, who had the bunk under his. "Then one day they put you on a thoroughbred and they tell you you'll do fine because what the hell, it's a horse."

Conkling laughed at him. He had a round red face and a big Kaiser Bill mustache, so that he put George in mind of a clock with its hands pointing at ten minutes to two. He said, "Yeah, she does go pretty good, don't she?"

"You might say so," Enos answered, a New England understatement that made his new friend laugh again. To back it up, he went on, "She cruises—just idles along, mind you—at fifteen knots. No boat I've ever been on could do fifteen knots if you tied down the safety valve and stoked the engine till it blew up."

"Not brewery horses," Conkling said. "Mules. Maybe donkeys."

"Yeah," George said. "And the *Ericsson* gives us what, going flat out? Thirty knots?"

"Just under, at the trials. Some other boats in the class made it. But she'll give twenty-eight easy," Conkling told him.

Fifteen felt plenty fast to Enos. He stared out at the Atlantic racing past under the destroyer's keel. The USS *Ericsson* was a bigger, more stable platform than any steam trawler he'd ever sailed, displacing over a thousand tons, but the waves hit her harder, too. And besides—"You've got to remember, I'm just off a river monitor. After that, any ocean sailing is rough business."

"Those things are snapping turtles," Andy Conkling said disdainfully. "This here is a shark."

From what Enos had seen and heard, deep-sea sailors had nothing but scorn for the river-monitor fleet. From what he'd seen aboard the *Punishment*, the monitors didn't deserve any such scorn. Trying to convince shipmates of that struck him as a good way to waste his breath. He kept quiet.

In a thoughtful tone of voice, Conkling went on, "Of course, this here is a *little* shark. That's why we need to be able to run so damn fast: to get away from the big sharks on the other side."

"Yeah," Enos said again. He looked out across the endless sweep of the Atlantic once more. That was no idle sightseeing—far from it. Spotting smoke on the horizon—or, worse, a periscope perilously close—might mean the difference between finishing the cruise and sliding under the waves as smoking refuse. "The limeys are out there looking for us, too."

"You bet your ass they are, chum," Conkling said. "They don't want us running guns to the micks. They don't want it in a really big way. If they can, they're gonna keep us from doing it."

"I know about micks," Enos said. "Coming out of Boston, I'd damn well better know about micks. If the ones on our side of the ocean can't stand England, what about all the poor bastards over there, living right next to it? No wonder they rose up."

"No wonder at all, at all," Conkling said, winking to make the brogue he'd put on seem funnier. He set a finger by the side of his nose. "And no wonder the good old Kaiser and us, we all got to give 'em as big a hand as we can."

"Hell of a mess over there, if half what you read in the papers is true," George said, though that was by no means guaranteed. "Shooting and sniping and bombs on the bridges and the Ulstermen massacring all the Catholics they can catch and the

Catholics giving it right back to 'em and more limeys tied down there every day, sounds like."

"England's got to do it." Now Andy Conkling made himself sound serious, as if he were a Navy Department bigwig back in Philadelphia. "They let the Irish go and we or the Germans put men in there, that's curtains for the King, and they know it damn well."

"*I* don't know it," Enos said. "The Kaiser can't supply soldiers in Ireland. When the Germans send guns to the Irishmen, they have to do it by submarine. And look at us, sneaking in like we're going to bed with somebody else's wife. Don't suppose we can go at it any other way, not in England's back yard."

"Say you're right," Conkling replied. "I don't think so, but say you are. How come England's making such a big to-do over something that can't happen?"

"A lot of times people make a big to-do over things that didn't happen." For about the hundredth time, George wished he hadn't had to tell Sylvia where he'd been going when the *Punishment* was wrecked. *I was drunk when I went and I was drunk when I told her,* he thought. *That tells me I shouldn't get drunk.* She still blamed him for what he hadn't done. She probably wouldn't have been much angrier if he had gone and done it, which made part of him wish he had. Only part, though: Mehitabel, looked back on in memory rather than at with desire, wasn't much.

Smoke poured from the *Ericsson*'s four stacks. George thought the design was ugly and clumsy, but nobody cared what a sailor thought. The destroyer picked up speed, fairly leaping over the ocean. "Getting close to wherever we're going," Conkling remarked.

"Yeah," George answered. Nobody bothered telling sailors much of anything, either. Ireland the crew knew, but only a handful knew where they'd stand off the coast of the Emerald Isle.

Officers and petty officers went up and down the deck. "Be alert," one of them said. "We need every pair of eyes we've got," another added. A third, a grizzled CPO, growled, "If we hit a mine on account of one of you didn't spot it, I'll throw the son of a bitch in the brig."

That drew a laugh from Conkling, and, a moment later, after he'd worked it through, one from Enos as well. He said, "If they've laid mines, how the devil *can* we spot 'em, going as fast as we are? The monitor I was on just crawled along the Mississippi, and we had a sweeper go in front of us when we thought the Rebs had mined the river."

"Turtles," Conkling said again. That didn't answer George's question. After a few seconds, he realized the question wasn't going to get answered. That probably meant you couldn't spot mines very well when you were going full speed ahead, an imperfectly reassuring idea.

"Land ho!" somebody shouted. George stared eastward. Sure enough, in a couple of minutes he saw a smudge on the horizon too big for a smoke plume and too steady to be a cloud. After a moment, he realized that, if he could see land, people on land could also see the *Ericsson*. Someone might be tapping on a wireless key or cranking a telephone even as he stood on the deck, in which case the boat would have visitors soon.

Moved by that same thought, Andy Conkling murmured, "The limeys on shore'll take us for one of their own. Always have before." Whether that was expectation or mere pious hope, George didn't know. He did know it was his hope, pious or not.

"Landing parties to the boats," a petty officer shouted. Enos hurried to the davits. He had more practice in small boats than most of the men aboard the *Ericsson*, and less experience on the destroyer herself. That made him a logical man for the landing party.

Each boat had a small gasoline engine in the stern, and each was packed with crates that bore no markings whatsoever. Enos scrambled up into a boat. "Steer between Loop Point and Kerry Head," the petty officer told him and his five comrades. "Ballybunion's where you're going, on the south side of Shannonmouth past the lighthouse. You'll know the place by the old castle—a big, square, gray, ugly thing, I'm told, not hardly what you think of when *castle* goes through your head. Your chums'll be waiting for you a little west of the castle. Good luck."

Hoists lowered Enos' boat and two more into the sea. They rode low in the water. Those crates weren't stuffed with feathers. George got the motor going and steered for the distant land. "Jesus," said one of the sailors in the boat with him, a big squarehead named Bjornsen, "I feel naked in something this small."

"Italians go fishing out of T Wharf back home every day in boats smaller than this," George said.

"Crazy damn dagos," Bjornsen muttered, and fell silent.

"Should have taken along a line and some hooks," Enos said. "Might have brought back something the cooks could have fried for our supper." He peered down into the green-gray sea. "Wonder what they have in the way of fish over here."

That sparked another couple of sentences from Bjornsen: "Fish is one thing. I just hope they haven't got any cooked goose."

Loop Point boasted a lighthouse. Enos hoped nobody was staring down from it with a pair of field glasses. If somebody was staring down from it with a pair of field glasses, he hoped his boat and the two chugging along behind it looked enough like little local fishing boats to draw no notice.

The land was low and muddy and not particularly green, in spite of Ireland's fabled reputation. Here and there, George spotted stone houses with turf roofs. They looked little and cramped and uncomfortable, a small step up from a sodbuster shack out on the prairie. He wouldn't have wanted to live in any of them.

A petty officer named Carl Sturtevant had a map. "There's the Cashen River inlet," he said, pointing to a stream that, as far as George was concerned, wasn't big enough to deserve to be a river. "A couple-three miles to Ballybunion."

Ballybunion Castle had, at some time in the distant past, had part of one wall blown out of it, making it worthless as a fortification. Enos saw it only in the distance. Closer, some men were waving cloth caps to signal to the boats. "There they are," he said happily.

"Yeah, those should be our boys," Sturtevant agreed. "If those ain't our boys, we're in a hell of a lot of trouble."

"Shit, if the limeys were wise to us, they wouldn't waste time with no ambush," said Bjornsen, a born optimist. "They'd haul a field piece out behind a haystack, wait till we got close, and blow us so high we'd never come down." He glanced at those anonymous crates. "One hit would do the job up brown, I calculate."

The men in baggy tweeds came trotting toward the boats. Out from behind a haystack came not a British field gun but several carts. "We've got more toys here than they can haul away in those," George said as his boat beached.

"That's their worry," Sturtevant said. He and the other sailors, Enos among them, started unloading the crates.

"God bless you," one of the Irishmen said. His comrades were lugging the Americans' presents to the carts. He had a present himself: a jar with a cork in it. "Have a nip o' this, lads."

Quickly, the jar went from sailor to sailor. The whiskey tasted different from what George was used to drinking, but it was pretty good. He took a long pull. When he swallowed, he felt as if he'd poured lava down his gullet. The Irishmen didn't water it to make it stretch further, as bartenders were in the habit of doing.

Wise in the ways of the sea, the Irishmen helped the sailors shove the boats back into the water, some calling thanks in brogues so thick, Enos could barely make them out. Free of the crates, the boats bobbed like corks. He headed out to sea once more, out toward the *Ericsson*.

"How about that?" Sturtevant said. "We just bit the King of England right in the ass."

"Now all we have to do is see whether we got away with it," George said. He wished the boat would go faster.

"Will you *look* at that crazy son of a bitch!" Vic Crosetti burst out.

Sam Carsten looked. The Sandwich Islander in question was indeed crazy, as far as he could tell. The fellow was skimming over the waves toward shore standing upright on a plank maybe nine or ten feet long and a foot and a half or two feet wide.

"Why the devil doesn't he fall off and break his fool neck?" Sam said. "You wouldn't even think a monkey could do that, let alone a man."

"Yeah, you're right," Crosetti said. "But I ain't gonna let him hear me call him a monkey. He'd break me in half." That was undoubtedly true. The surf-rider, who came up onto the beach with the plank on his head, was a couple of inches above six feet and muscled like a young god, which was all the more evident because he wore only a dripping cotton loincloth dyed in bright colors.

"Hey, pal," Carsten said, and tossed him a dime. "That's a hell of a ride you had there." Crosetti coughed up a dime, too.

"Thank you both very much, gentlemen," the fellow said. Like a fair number of his people, he talked like an educated

Englishman, which made it hard to treat him like a nigger. His skin was only a couple of shades darker than Crosetti's, anyhow.

"Where did you learn to do that, anyway?" Sam asked. The moment the words were out of his mouth, he realized he'd been stupid. Too late to do anything about it then, of course. That was the way the world worked.

The native laughed at him. It wasn't a snotty laugh, it was a friendly laugh: maybe because the surf-rider was a friendly guy, maybe because he knew better than to get himself in trouble squabbling with the U.S. Navy. Both, Sam judged. The fellow said, "Having grown up here in Honolulu with the sea as my neighbor, so to speak, it was a sport I acquired as a boy. I confess I can see how surprising it might appear to those born in other climes."

"Other climes, yeah," Carsten said, while Vic Crosetti did his best, which wasn't any too good, to keep from snickering. As always, every inch of Sam's flesh the sun touched was cooked red and juicy.

"How come you talk so damn fancy?" Crosetti asked.

"This is how English was taught to me," the Sandwich Islander said with another shrug. "Since you Americans came here, I have learned the language may be spoken with a number of different accents."

"Haven't heard anybody here who's got quite as much mush in his mouth as you do," Crosetti said. Was he looking for a fight in spite of denying it before? He hadn't had that much to drink yet; he and Sam had only just come on leave from the *Dakota*.

The surf-rider sighed. "You must understand, gentlemen, that under the previous administration my father was assistant minister for sugar production, thus enabling me to acquire rather better schooling than most of my contemporaries."

Sam needed a moment to realize that *under the previous administration* meant *when the British ran the show*. He needed another moment to realize something else. "Your father was assistant what-do-you-call-it, and you took our dimes? Christ on His cross, I bet you can buy and sell both of us and hardly even notice you've done it."

"It may be so, but, for one thing, we Hawaiians—we prefer that to Sandwich Islanders, if it matters to you—have discovered expediency to be the wiser course in dealing with the occupying authorities. Had I refused your money, you might have thought I was insulting you, with results unpleasant for me." The fellow's smile revealed large, gleaming white teeth. "And besides, you both chose to reward me for my skill out of what I know to be your small pay. Especially in wartime, acts of kindness and generosity should not be discouraged, lest they disappear altogether off the face of the earth."

"Whew!" Carsten couldn't remember the last time anybody had done that much explaining. "You ought to be a chaplain, uh—"

"John Liholiho, at your service." The surf-rider's bow could have been executed no more smartly had he been wearing top hat, cutaway, and patent-leather shoes rather than gaudy loincloth and bare feet. "And with whom have I had the pleasure of conversing?"

Carsten and Crosetti gave their names. Crosetti plucked at Sam's sleeve, whispering, "Listen, do you want to spend the time chewing the fat with this big galoot, or do you want to get drunk and get laid?"

"We got a forty-eight, Vic—don't have to be back on board ship till day after tomorrow," Sam answered, also in a low voice. "God knows it's easy to find a saloon and a piece of ass in this town, but when are you going to run across another real live aristocrat?"

"Ahh, you want to be a schoolteacher when you grow up," Crosetti snarled in deeply unhappy tones. But he didn't leave. He hooked his thumbs into the pockets of his tropical white bell-bottoms and waited to see whether Sam could make standing on the beach banging his gums with a native more interesting than a drunken debauch.

John Liholiho peered over toward the jutting prominence of Diamond Head while the two sailors talked with each other. The presumably British school he'd attended had trained him in more things than an upper-crust accent; he showed very plainly that he was not listening to a conversation not intended for him. Carsten wished most of the sailors he knew had a matching reserve instead of being snoops.

He didn't really know how he was going to make this more fun than getting lit up and having his ashes hauled, either. After a little thought, he asked, "So how do you like it, living under the Stars and Stripes?"

The Sandwich Islander—no matter how he thought of himself, that was how Carsten thought of him—frowned. "You do realize, of course, that this is a question on which circumspection might be the wisest course for me?" Seeing Sam hadn't the slightest idea what circumspection was, he translated his English into English: "I might be wiser to keep quiet or lie."

"What am I going to do, shoot you?" Sam said, laughing. Crosetti plucked at his sleeve again. He shook off his pal.

Liholiho gave him a serious look. "Two friends of my father's of whom I know for certain have suffered this fate. It does give one pause. On the other side of the coin, the protectorate the British exercised over these islands was also imperfectly humane. Mr. Carsten, would you prefer to be thought of as a bloody wog or a nigger?"

Since Sam had been thinking of John Liholiho as a nigger not ten minutes before, he had to work as hard at keeping his face straight as when he was raising on a pair of fives in a poker game. "Anybody called me either one of those things, I'd punch him in the teeth."

"Yeah." Now Vic Crosetti's attention was engaged. "I get called a fuckin' dago or a wop, that's bad enough."

"People seldom *call* me these things to my face, though I have heard *nigger* in a mouth or two since you Americans came." The surf-rider seemed to have a British sense of precision, too. He went on, "What one is *called*, however, sometimes matters less than how one is *seen*. If the powers that be reckon one a wog or a nigger, one is not apt to be taken seriously regardless of the potential value of one's contributions."

"That's too complicated for me," Carsten said, thinking he should have headed out and got drunk after all.

But Crosetti got it. "He's saying it's like he's an ordinary sailor, and he's trying to convince an admiral he knows what he's talking about."

John Liholiho beamed at him. "Mr. Crosetti, I am in your debt. You Americans and our former British overlords do tend to look at race as if it were rank, don't you?—yourselves being admirals, by the very nature of things. I shall have to use the analogy elsewhere."

A Sandwich Islander as near naked as made no difference . . . with whom would he use an analogy (whatever an analogy was; Sam gathered it meant something like *comparison*, but it was another word he didn't think he'd ever heard before)? Then Carsten remembered that, even though John looked like a savage, he was a local bigwig's son. That he had to think twice before the fellow's station came to mind went a long way toward making his point for him.

Dipping his head again, the brown-skinned man said, "And now, if you will excuse me—" He turned and, carrying his surf-riding board, trotted out into the Pacific. Once in the water, he climbed up onto the board, lay on his belly atop it, and used his arms to paddle farther from shore.

Sam turned to Vic Crosetti. "All right, *now* we can have all the fun we want to. That didn't take real long, and it was sort of interesting."

"Yeah, sort of." Crosetti stared out at John Liholiho's receding shape. "I bet he's a limey spy. He sure talks like a limey spy, don't he?"

"He talks like a limey, anyway," Carsten answered. "But so what? Even if he is a spy, how's he going to get word off the island? And if you're going to start seeing spies under every bed—"

"If I look under a bed," Crosetti said with great assurance, "it's to make sure I can hide there if her husband comes home before he's supposed to." Both men laughed, and headed into town to see what kind of damage they could do to the fleshpots there.

Reggie Bartlett trudged wearily into Wilson Town, Sequoyah. Seeing houses around him felt strange after so long on the prairie with no human-made artifacts close by but the occasional oil well . . . and the trenches, and the shells, and the other appurtenances of war.

Lieutenant Jerome Nicoll called, "We got to hold this town, boys. Ain't a whole hell of a lot of Sequoyah left to us, and we have to hang on to what there is, not let the damnyankees run us out of the whole state. Remember, the Germans don't hold all of Belgium even now."

"I ain't seen any Germans in Sequoyah," Nap Dibble said. Sweat cut ravines through the dust caking his face. "You see any o' them damn Huns, Reggie? Yankees is bad enough, but them folks—"

"Haven't seen any Germans, Nap," Bartlett answered. He'd long since figured out Nap, while a good fellow, wasn't what anybody would call sharp. When Dibble lined up in front of the paymaster, he signed his name with an X. No wonder he'd be on the lookout for Germans smack in the middle of Sequoyah.

"We have to save this town," Lieutenant Nicoll repeated. A shell crashed down a few hundred yards off to the left, arguing that the Confederate soldiers didn't have to do any such thing.

Bartlett would have been more impressed with the speech if the lieutenant hadn't said the same thing about Duncan, which had fallen several weeks before. He'd heard the same kind of speech on the Roanoke front, too. There it had sometimes presaged a retreat like this one, and sometimes a counterattack that left dead men piled high in exchange for retaking a couple of hundred yards of chewed-up, worthless ground.

Nicoll tried something new. Pointing south, he spoke in dramatic tones: "There are the people who depend on us to protect them."

As far as Reggie could see, the people of Wilson Town weren't depending on the Confederate Army for any such thing. A lot of houses already looked to have been abandoned. More folks—Indians, whites, a handful of Negro servants and laborers—were throwing whatever they could into buggies and wagons and high-tailing it south toward the Texas line.

Sergeant Pete Hairston spat in the dust of the road. "If the damnyankees want a pack of damn redskins, they're welcome to 'em, far as I can tell. Weren't for the oil round these parts, hell, I'd give Sequoyah to the USA and say, 'You're welcome to it.' "

"Will you look at that?" Bartlett pointed to a side-curtained grocery wagon and to the tall, gray-bearded man in a black suit and homburg who was, instead of loading things into it, selling things from it. "Crazy Jew peddler, doesn't he know he's liable to get blown to hell any minute?" He raised his voice to a shout: "Hey, you! Hymie!"

That got the peddler's attention. He wasn't just big; he looked strong and tough, too, in spite of those snowy whiskers. "Vot you vant?" he asked, his voice wary—no matter how tough he was, he had the brains not to argue with anybody toting a Tredegar.

"You'd better get out of here before you get killed," Bartlett told him.

"Oh. Dot vot you talk about." The peddler shrugged. "Soon I go."

Hairston made money-counting motions. "Business is good, huh?" He laughed. "Damn fool Jew. Money ain't worth your neck."

The Jew muttered something under his breath. Reggie didn't think it was a compliment. He didn't think it was English, either, which was likely to be just as well: if he didn't understand it, he didn't have to notice it. That made something else occur to him: "Hey, Hymie, you sell a lot to the Indians around here?"

"A lot, yes," the peddler answered. "Is most of folk."

"How do you talk to 'em?" Bartlett asked. The Jew stared at him, not following the question. He tried again: "What language do you use when you sell to them?"

"Oh." The Jew's face lit with intelligence. "They speak Henglish, same like me." Reggie burst out laughing; from what little he'd seen of them, most of the local Chickasaws and Kiowas spoke English better than the peddler.

"Go on, get the hell out of here," Hairston said, and the peddler, not without a sigh or two of regret for business lost, scrambled up into the wagon and rattled south out of Wilson Town, almost the last one to leave it.

Methodically, the troops of Lieutenant Nicoll's company began to dig in. Nap Dibble said, "Wish them niggers what was in this town would've stayed a bit. They could have done this here entrenching for us."

"Back on the Roanoke front, we had us lots of nigger labor battalions," Reggie said as he made the dirt fly. "Haven't seen so much of that here out west."

"*Ain't* that much of it," Sergeant Hairston said. "Like I been tellin' you since you got here, Bartlett, ain't that much of anything."

"Except Yankees," Reggie said.

"Yeah, except them," Hairston agreed. "But they ain't got any more'n—well, ain't got a whole lot more'n—what we do, 'cept maybe soldiers."

"Except," Reggie said again. He dug and dug, steady as a steam shovel. The ground was the perfect consistency: not so hard that he had to labor to force his entrenching tool into it, not so soft or muddy that the edges of the trench he was digging started falling down into what he'd already dug. He flipped the dirt up in front of his excavations to form a parapet. "Wish we had some more barbed wire." He scooped out another couple of shovelfuls. "Wish we had *any* barbed wire."

"Wish for sugarplums for Christmas while you're at it," Sergeant Hairston said. "Oh, we may get some wire—we had a good bit in front o' Duncan, once we'd stayed there a while. But this here ain't the Roanoke front—that kind of good stuff don't grow on trees here. I just told you that a couple seconds ago, dammit. Ain't you listenin' to me?"

"Yeah, Sarge. I always listen," Bartlett answered, so mildly that Hairston went back to digging for another stroke or two before giving him a dirty look. Reggie grinned back, a grin that had occasionally softened even the Yankee prison guards in West Virginia. He looked around, not to see if the Yankees were coming or the Chickasaws getting the hell out but to spot his company commander. "Now that the fighting's picked up again, what's the lieutenant going to do for his hooch?"

"Damned if I know." As if reminded of what he'd traded to the men in green-gray for Lieutenant Nicoll's supply of whiskey, Hairston rolled himself a cigarette. He sucked in smoke before going on, "Hope nothin' bad's happened to Toohey. He ain't a bad guy." After another drag, he chuckled. "Crazy sayin' that about one of those Yankee bastards, but it's so."

"I know what you mean, Sarge," Reggie replied. "Fellow who captured me, there in the Roanoke valley, he could have shot me and my pals easy as not. I ever run into him once this damn war is over, he can do all the boozing he wants. I'll buy till he can't even see, let alone walk."

The sporadic Yankee shelling had been falling short of Wilson Town, so much so that the Confederate soldiers had gone on about the business of digging in without pausing at the explosions a couple of furlongs to the north. Now, suddenly, the U.S. gunners began to find the range. Hearing the hideous whistle of a shell that might have his name on it, Reggie dove headlong into the stretch of trench he'd just dug. The round hit behind him. Fragments and shrapnel balls hissed through the air. One of the lead spheres with which the shell had been loaded drilled a neat hole in the dirt he'd heaped up in front of the trench. It would have drilled a neat hole in him, too.

He got back up and started digging again. A hoarse shout from the southern edge of town made him turn his head. The Jewish peddler didn't care for artillery close by. He was getting his horses up to a gallop so he could escape Wilson Town in jig time. Others who had lingered, the last few, now delayed their departure no more.

Reggie laughed. "Look at 'em go," he said, pointing. After a moment, though, it didn't seem funny. "If two guys are in a dangerous place, and one leaves while the other stays, which one of 'em is stupid?"

Hairston laughed, too, but singularly without humor. "That'd be funny, Bartlett, if only it was funny, you know what I mean?"

"Yeah, Sarge, I do. Wish to Jesus I didn't." Bartlett looked out across the broad Sequoyah prairie. "Here come the damn-yankees. I don't think they think we're ready for 'em yet."

"Yeah, well, if they don't, they're gonna be real sorry real fast," Hairston said.

The artillery fire supporting the men in green-gray who trotted forward got heavier, but it didn't turn into anything that would have been reckoned worse than harassment back in Virginia. Here and there, a Confederate soldier shrieked or abruptly fell silent, forever blasted from man to butcher-shop display in the blink of an eye.

But most of the C.S. troopers crouched down in the field fortifications they'd been digging and waited for the Yankees to get closer, so they could sting the enemy hard. Reggie wouldn't have wanted to be trudging through that yellowed autumn grass, waiting for the machine guns to open up on him. He wondered how much experience the damnyankees up there had. Were they brave men advancing into what they knew would be awful or raw fish too ignorant to tell they were heading for a fish fry? In the end, it didn't much matter. They'd kill him or he'd kill them. War reduced everything to a brutal simplicity.

Closer, closer . . . A couple of Confederate riflemen opened up on the Yankees. Men in green-gray started dropping, most not because they were hit but to keep from getting hit. Others kept coming forward, running now, not trotting, as if they knew they didn't have much time to do before they were done by. Raising his rifle to his shoulder, Bartlett picked one.

He pulled the trigger at the same time as the first machine gun began spraying precisely measured death at the U.S. soldiers. More and more of the men in green-gray were falling, and taking cover had little if anything to do with it. A couple of hundred yards off to the left, the second Confederate machine gun joined its satanic chattering to that of the first. More and more Yankees toppled.

None of the foe got within a hundred yards of the position the Confederates had chosen to defend. As the attack finally broke down, cold rain began falling on U.S. and C.S. troops alike. Looking west, Reggie saw more and more clouds rolling his way. He pointed in that direction and said, "Looks like we've got ourselves a new commanding officer."

"What are you talkin' about?" Pete Hairston asked.

"General Winter," Bartlett answered. Hairston did a double take, but then he nodded. If the rain kept coming, the way it looked as if it would, nobody on either side would go anywhere fast, not for a good long while.

"Ma'am?" Lieutenant Nicholas H. Kincaid loomed over Nellie Semphroch. "May I speak to you for just a minute, ma'am?"

"What do you want?" Nellie knew her voice was cold, and did nothing to warm it. Speaking with the Confederate officer who'd seduced her daughter (or so she'd thought of it, not that Edna would have needed much seducing) was the last thing she wanted. "Whatever it is, you'd better make it snappy. We're goin' to be busy very soon, I expect."

"Yes, ma'am. I know that, ma'am. That's why I came here so early, ma'am." Kincaid stood there, holding his butternut slouch hat in both hands. He kept twisting it every which way, though he didn't seem to notice. He took a deep breath, held it so long he began to turn red, and then blurted, "Ma'am, me and your daughter, we'd like to get married, ma'am."

Nellie's head whipped around. There stood Edna, stacking cups on the countertop by the coffeepots so she and Nellie could serve a lot of coffee in a hurry. Edna's face wore what Nellie could think of only as an idiot grin. "That's right, Ma," she said, and the grin got wider.

"You're too young," Nellie said automatically.

"I'm older'n you were when you got married," her daughter retorted. "And I sure do want to marry Nick there." It was the first time she'd called Kincaid that—no, the first time Nellie had heard her call him that. When she did, he started grinning an idiot grin, too.

And she was right. Nellie had been younger than Edna was now when her name abruptly became Semphroch. Her name had had to change abruptly. "Edna, are you in a family way?" she demanded.

Lieutenant Kincaid turned red, the blush starting at his collar and rising all the way to his forehead. Edna indignantly tossed her head. "I am not—no such thing," she answered. "And I ought to know, too." When Kincaid heard that, he got even redder.

"All right." Nellie knew when to beat a retreat. *She'd* been in a family way when she got married, though she didn't think Edna knew that. The less Edna ever found out about her unsavory past, the better she'd like it.

"Ma'am, your daughter and I, we really do love each other," Kincaid said earnestly. "We'll be happy together for the rest of our lives, I know we will."

If I laugh at him, he'll get angry at me, and so will Edna. Nellie made herself hold her face still. It wasn't easy. He'd managed to get Edna's corset off her once (maybe more than once; Nellie admitted to herself she didn't know for sure about that) and both of them had liked what followed, so they thought they'd be happy together forever. Nellie knew better. She'd learned better the hard way. She wanted to pass on what she'd learned, but they wouldn't listen. She knew they wouldn't listen. The only way anyone learned those lessons was the hard way.

Off in the middle distance, artillery rumbled. Lately, days didn't go by—hours hardly went by—without that sound in the air. It reminded Nellie of her second biggest problem with Lieutenant Nicholas H. Kincaid, after his being a man. "Edna," she said, as gently as she could, "he's a Confederate. Do you want to go *down there* to live?" By the way she said *down there*, she might have been talking about dropping into hell for a visit.

Now Edna turned bright red. Like every child in the USA since the War of Secession, she'd been taught to think of Confederates as the enemy, with a capital E. That hadn't worried her when Kincaid started sniffing after her. But maybe she hadn't faced, even in her own mind, all the implications of what marrying him would mean. "I love him," she said defiantly.

"You think you can stay here in Washington the rest of your days?" Nellie asked. The artillery rumbled again, louder this time. "How much longer do you think the CSA can hold on here?"

"We'll hold Washington," Kincaid said. "President Wilson said it was our capital by rights, and we'll keep it. President Semmes says the same thing, so that's how it'll be." He thrust out his already prominent chin, as if to stay the Yankee hordes with the granite contained therein.

Nellie thought about mentioning the jawbone of an ass, but forbore. What she did say was, "You Confederates have said a lot of things that haven't come true. What makes you think this'll be any different?"

"Don't you rag on him, Ma!" Edna said shrilly.

When Nellie heard that tone of voice from her daughter, she knew the game was lost. Edna would do whatever Edna intended doing, and nothing and nobody would stop her. *My God,* Nellie thought. *How am I going to explain this to Mr. Jacobs?* The daughter of a spy for the United States running off and marrying a Confederate officer? He'd never trust Nellie again.

Edna, of course, hadn't the slightest idea Nellie was a spy for the USA. *A good thing, too,* Nellie thought. She'd never imagined life could get so complicated. Knowing it was weak, she tried a new card: "Suppose I say no?"

Kincaid didn't answer, which told Nellie the card was even weaker than she'd thought. He'd seemed so polite, she'd hoped a refusal might make him go away. Edna did reply, firmly: "Ma, we'd run off. Nick knows this chaplain—he told me so." Kincaid blushed again, but after a moment nodded. Edna went on, "You can't stop us, and you know it. You got to sleep sometime."

"You'd leave me to run the coffeehouse all by my lonesome?" Nellie asked, shifting with the changing breeze as adroitly as a politician. "It's too much for one person. It's too much for two people, sometimes."

"Hire yourself a nigger," Edna told her. "Ma, you know you're making good money. You can hire a couple of niggers, easy."

Again, that was probably true. Kincaid said, "Edna, honey, when we get back down into *my* country"—he spoke as if to assure her the CSA was far superior to this benighted northern land—"you won't have to lift a finger. You'll have niggers doing all your work for you."

Nellie did laugh then. She couldn't help it. "Niggers doing all your work for you, Edna, on a lieutenant's pay?" she said. "Likely tell. Besides, aren't the Confederate States buzzing like a hornets' nest about how niggers aren't going to be like servants no more?"

"I don't reckon that'll come to anything," Lieutenant Kincaid said. He sounded none too confident, though, and he said not a word about how easy keeping Negro servants on a junior officer's pay would be. That relieved Nellie; she'd feared he would announce that his father owned a plantation stretching halfway across Alabama, and that what he got from the Confederate War Department was less than pocket change to him.

Before the argument—*the losing argument,* Nellie was convinced—could go on, the door to the coffeehouse opened. The bell above it chimed. A fierce smile of triumph lighted Edna's face. "Ma," she said sweetly, "why don't you go take care of Mr. Reach there?"

Not five minutes earlier, Nellie had wondered how life got so complicated. Now she wondered if God had decided to show her she didn't know what complicated meant. Sure as hell, there was Bill Reach folding himself into a chair at a table by the window. He looked the same as he always had since he'd returned, all unbidden, to Nellie's life: dark, unkempt clothes, stubbled chin and cheeks, bleary eyes.

As she went up to him, she heard Lieutenant Kincaid say, "I never did fancy that fellow, not from the first time I set eyes on him."

Edna giggled. "I think he's one of Ma's old beaus." Nellie's back stiffened.

"Hello, Little Nell," Reach said when Nellie reached his table. Edna giggled. Nicholas Kincaid chuckled. Nellie steamed.

Speaking very softly, she said, "If you *ever* call me that again,

I will tell the Confederate occupying authorities exactly—exactly, do you hear me?—what you are."

Those bleary eyes widened. "Me? I'm not anything much," he said, but the certainty that usually informed his gravelly voice was missing.

"You heard me," Nellie whispered. "I don't ever want to see you round here again, either." In normal tones, she went on, "Now what'll it be?"

"Cup of coffee, couple fried eggs, and buttered toast," Reach said, his tone grudging. He smelled of whiskey.

"I'll be right back," Nellie told him.

As she started frying the eggs and toasting the bread, Lieutenant Kincaid said, "Ma'am? Can you give me your answer, ma'am?" He sounded plaintive as a calf calling for its mother.

"No," Nellie snarled. The Rebel officer looked as if she'd kicked him.

Edna set a hand on his arm. "It'll be all right, Nick. Don't you worry about it none. She's just my mother. She ain't my jailer, and she can't hold me back when I go with you." Not *if I go with you*, Nellie noted. *When.*

"I don't know what this world is coming to," she said, "when children don't pay any attention at all to the people who brought them into this world in the first place." Edna didn't answer. She kept staring at Lieutenant Kincaid as if she'd just invented him. Nellie sighed and slipped a metal spatula under the eggs to turn them in the pan. She repeated what she'd said a moment before: "I don't know what this world is coming to."

Lieutenant Kincaid leaned over and pecked Edna on the lips. He set his hat back on his head, tipped it to Nellie, and went out of the coffeehouse whistling "Dixie" loudly and off-key. "Isn't he wonderful?"

"No," Nellie snapped. A couple of other Confederate officers came in. Nellie pointed their way. "You take care of them." She slid the eggs out of the frying pan, took the toast from the rack above the fire in the stove, spread butter on it, poured coffee, and carried Bill Reach his breakfast. "Here you are. That'll be a dollar ten."

He winced slightly, but laid down a dollar and a quarter. "Don't worry any about the change," he said. He spread salt and pepper liberally over the eggs before he began to eat. Then he looked up at her. "Back in those days, I didn't know you could cook, too."

She glared. "Do you think I won't turn you in?" she said in a low, savage voice. "You better think again. My daughter is going to marry a Confederate officer." And then, to her helpless horror, she began to cry.

"Are you all right, Ma?" Edna came rushing over. She looked daggers at Bill Reach. "What'd he do?" Hearing that, the two Confederate officers jumped to their feet. They were nothing if not gentlemen.

Nellie waved everyone away. "It's all right," she insisted. "I'm just—happy for you, that's all." She'd told Edna a lot of lies for the foolish girl's own sake. After so many, what was one more?

Doubtfully, Edna retreated. The Rebs settled back into their seats. In a half-apologetic mumble, Bill Reach said, "Hal told me not to come around here any more."

"Then why didn't you listen to him?" Nellie said. She sat down at the table with Reach, which made Edna stare in surprise but succeeded in convincing the Confederates nothing was wrong.

"Now that I found you, I can't stay away from you," Reach answered. He started to reach out to set his hand on hers, but stopped when she made as if to pull away. He sighed, then coughed. "All these years, all that water over the dam, and I never forgot even a little of what we did, and I knew it had to be the same for you."

She wanted to cry some more, or maybe scream. If he'd been mooning after her since before Edna was born . . . that made him crazy, was what it did. Try as she would, she had trouble remembering him at all from those long-ago days. Just another face, just another cock—But nowadays, he was the USA's number-one spy in Washington. She wondered if the people to whom he fed his information knew he was on, or over, the ragged edge.

He got to his feet, tipped his battered black homburg, and said, "I'll see you again, Nellie, one day before too long." His walk to the door was slow and deliberate, as if he was daring her to tell the Rebs who he was.

He hadn't called her Little Nell. She kept quiet. But he hadn't taken any notice when she'd told him to go away and stay away, either. *What am I going to do?* she thought. She had no more answer for that than for, *What is the world coming to?*

"Sir," the truck driver in green-gray said to Lieutenant Straubing, packing what should have been a title of respect with all the scorn he could, "it ain't right, us white men working alongside niggers." He set hands on hips and glared at Cincinnatus, who happened to be the black man closest to him.

"See here, Murray," Straubing said, "you will do as you are ordered or you will face military punishment."

"Then we will, won't we, boys?" Murray turned for support to the new truck drivers—well over half the unit—who had joined the transport company to replace the men killed, wounded, or captured in the Confederate raid south of Berea, Kentucky. He was a little, skinny, bandy-legged fellow, with a narrow face, a receding chin, a beaky nose, and a shock of red hair: all in all, he reminded Cincinnatus of an angry chicken.

But he had backers. The new men in the unit were fresh out of the USA. A lot of them, probably, had never seen a Negro before coming down to Covington, let alone thought of working alongside one—or rather, a good many more than one.

"Don't want to maybe trust my life to a coon," one of them said.

"Hear tell some of them get paid more'n white men," another added. "Ain't nobody can tell me that's proper."

Cincinnatus looked over to Herk. The two of them had escaped the Rebel raiders together, and had shared what food they could steal and what miserable shelter they could find till they came upon a U.S. outpost. Herk hadn't treated Cincinnatus like a nigger then. Of course, Herk had needed him then. Now the white man stood silent as a stone, when Cincinnatus needed him.

"You men are making a mutiny," Lieutenant Straubing warned. "A court-martial will take a dim view of that."

Murray, who had enough mouth for any three men, laughed out loud. "No court's going to say anything but that white men are better than niggers, sir, and that's the truth."

Under the tan he'd got from going out with his trucks, Straubing turned pale. Cincinnatus' heart sank. His guess was that Murray knew what he was talking about. Without much conscious thought, Cincinnatus and the rest of the black truck drivers bunched together. The whites with whom they'd been driving stood apart from them. Those whites didn't go over with the new men who backed Murray, but they didn't support their colored comrades, either.

Reds are right, Cincinnatus thought bitterly. *CSA and USA, it's the same thing—whites are so mystified, they put race ahead of class.*

"That's your last word, Murray?" Lieutenant Straubing demanded tensely. When the redheaded driver nodded, Straubing hurried out of the warehouse depot, biting his lip. A chorus of jeers rang out behind him, as if chasing him away.

"Get you black boys hauling like mules, the way God made you to," Murray said to the Negro truck drivers. The men at his back nodded.

"Don't know why you so down on us," Cincinnatus said. "We just doin' our jobs, makin' our pay, feedin' our families."

"Doing white man's work," Murray snapped. Like Lieutenant Kennan, he looked to be one of those U.S. whites who hated Negroes more savagely than any Confederate did, not least because he was so much less familiar with them than Confederates were. Cincinnatus, who had been driving a truck in the CSA before the war broke out, thought about pointing his old job out to the damnyankee. But he didn't think it would help, and kept quiet.

The door to the depot flew open. In strode Lieutenant Straubing, followed by a squad of soldiers carrying bayoneted Springfields. Straubing pointed to Murray. "Arrest that man," he snapped. "Charges are insubordination and refusal to obey lawful orders."

Two of the men in green-gray stomped up to Murray, who looked comically amazed. One of them grabbed him by the arm. "Come on, you," he snapped. Murray perforce came.

Straubing's gaze traveled over the other new drivers. "Anyone else?" he asked in a voice that held nothing but ice. A couple of drivers stirred where they stood. "Vasilievsky, Heintzelman, you are under arrest, too. Same charges as Murray."

"Come on, you two lugs," one of the soldiers Straubing had brought said when neither driver moved for a moment. "You won't like it if we have to come and get you, I promise."

Numbly, their eyes wide with shock, the two white men

obeyed. "Anyone else?" Lieutenant Straubing said again. None of the new drivers moved or spoke. As Cincinnatus had seen other soldiers do, they tried to disappear while standing in plain sight. Straubing nodded. "Very well." He turned to the men he'd called. "Take those three to the stockade. Murray—this fellow here—is the ringleader. I will prefer formal written charges when I have the time, which I don't right now. These shenanigans are liable to make me late, and I won't stand for that."

Saluting, the soldiers led Murray, Heintzelman, and Vasilievsky out of the depot. The three drivers looked as if they were standing in front of White trucks bearing down on them at thirty miles an hour. None of them could have been more astonished than Cincinnatus. He'd associated Lieutenant Straubing's uncommon easiness on matters of race with a certain weakness. Evidently he'd been wrong.

Straubing glanced over toward the new truck drivers who hadn't been arrested. As if they were puppets controlled by the same puppeteer, they stiffened to attention. "If this sort of nonsense happens again," Straubing said pleasantly, "it will make me angry. Do you gentlemen want to find out what happens when I get angry?"

"No, sir," the drivers chorused.

"Good," Straubing said. "Now that we understand that, I am going to give you the idea behind what we're doing here. What we're doing here is moving supplies from the riverside here down to the fighting front. Anything that helps us do that is good. Anything that hurts is bad. If a man does his job, I don't care—and you won't care—if he is black or white or yellow or blue. If he can't or won't, I will run him out of here. If you are white and I order you to work with a Negro who is doing his job, you will do it. If you are white and I order you to work beside a trained unicorn who is doing his job, you will do that, too. Again, do you understand me?"

"Yes, sir," the new drivers said in unison.

"Then let's get on with it," Lieutenant Straubing said. "We are going to have to press harder than we would have, thanks to this idiocy. You would be safer blaspheming the Holy Ghost than you would, tampering with my schedule."

As the drivers went off to their vehicles, Cincinnatus approached Straubing and said, "Thank you kindly, suh."

The white man looked almost as nonplused as Murray had when he was arrested. "I suppose you're welcome, Cincinnatus," he answered after a moment, "but I didn't do it for you."

"Sir, I understand that," Cincinnatus said. "I—"

"Do you?" Straubing broke in. "I wonder. I did it for the sake of the United States Army. You Negroes have shown you can do this job, and if you do it, white men don't have to, and we can put rifles in their hands. I would sooner have taken on more of you, but this new contingent got sent to me instead. We'll see what we can make of them."

"Uh, yes, sir," Cincinnatus said. Straubing was indeed a good deal less sentimental, more hardheaded than he'd reckoned.

The lieutenant went on, "And no one who deserves to keep his rank badges will let himself be disobeyed, even for an instant. Is there anything else before you get to work?"

"No, suh," Cincinnatus said. Maybe, instead of being kindly and sentimental, Straubing was the most cold-blooded human being he'd ever met, so cold-blooded that he didn't even get excited about matters of race, matters Cincinnatus had thought guaranteed to stir the passions of every man, white or black, Yankee or Confederate.

Cincinnatus went out to tend to his truck. There a couple of vehicles over stood Herk, fiddling with the driver's-side acetylene lamp on his own machine. He nodded to Cincinnatus, then went back to getting the reflector the way he wanted it.

He didn't even notice he hadn't backed Cincinnatus and the other colored drivers when Murray started running his mouth. Cincinnatus couldn't help scowling. And then, slowly, his anger faded. Herk did his job. He let Cincinnatus do *his* job, too, and didn't fuss about that. If he did so much, did Cincinnatus have any business expecting more?

"I can hope," Cincinnatus mumbled. That made Herk look up from what he was doing, but only for a moment. Cincinnatus sighed. He might hope white men would treat him the same as they treated one of their own, but a lifetime had taught him he had no business expecting it.

Black roustabouts hauled crates from the wharves toward the line of trucks. With them came Lieutenant Kennan, raving at them to work harder, harder. Nobody put Kennan under arrest

for abusing blacks. But he was following U.S. orders, not dis-
obeying them as Murray had done. If he might have got more
work from his crew without the abuse . . . who cared? No one in
authority, that was certain.

With another sigh, Cincinnatus cranked his White's motor
into rumbling life. Lieutenant Straubing let him do his job, too.
In the scheme of things, that wasn't so bad. It could have been
worse, and he knew it.

XVII

Private Ulysses Hansen looked around. "Once upon a time, probably, this was real pretty country," he said.

"Not any time lately," another private—Sergeant Gordon McSweeney couldn't see who—answered. The whole squad, with the exception of McSweeney, chuckled.

"Silence in the ranks," McSweeney said, and silence he got: all proper and according to regulation. He looked around at what had been a northeastern Arkansas pine forest and was now a wasteland of jagged stumps and downtumbled branches. That it might once have been beautiful hadn't occurred to him. He hadn't particularly noticed how hideous it was at the moment, either. It was country that had once held the enemy but was now cleared of him, that was all. No, not quite all: it was country that led to land the enemy still infested.

Captain Schneider came bustling along past the company as the soldiers trudged south and east. Schneider nodded toward Gordon McSweeney. "Not so pretty as it used to be, is it, Sergeant?" he said.

"No, sir," McSweeney answered stolidly. The company commander outranked him, and so could say whatever he pleased, as far as McSweeney was concerned.

Schneider went on, "Trouble is, the damn Rebs knew we were coming, so they baked us a cake. A whole bunch of cakes, as a matter of fact."

"Sir?" McSweeney said: when his superior spoke directly to him, he had to answer. He regretted the necessity. Ever since their clash over the need to enforce all regulations to the fullest—gospel to him, but evidently not to Schneider—he'd feared the captain was trying to seduce him away from the straight and narrow path he had trodden all his life.

"Toward Memphis," Schneider amplified. "They fortified all this delta country in eastern Arkansas to a fare-thee-well, and so here it is two years after the damn war started and we're only getting to Jonesboro now."

"Oh. Yes, sir," McSweeney said. Matters military he would willingly discuss with his superior, even if Schneider was sometimes profane. "And, of course, since we stand on the far side of the Mississippi, we get half the resources of those east of the river. General Custer's First Army, I recall—"

"Don't talk about any of that," Schneider broke in. "It hurts too much when I think about it. We're not going to have an easy time up ahead, either."

"At Jonesboro? No, sir, I don't expect we will," McSweeney said. He could see the Confederate strongpoint without any trouble. Why not? None of the timber was tall enough to block his view, not any more. The town sprawled along the top of Crowley's Ridge, in most places not a feature worth noticing but here in this flat country high ground to be coveted. "What's the altitude here, sir?"

"At Jonesboro? It's 344 feet," Captain Schneider said. "That's 344 too many, you ask me. And we lose even what little cover these woods—or what's left of 'em—give us, too, because it was farming country out to three or four miles in front of the town."

"I see that also, sir," McSweeney answered. He raised his voice to call out to his men: "Give way to the right for the column coming back."

The column coming back was made up of soldiers returning from the front line, soldiers for whom McSweeney's squad, Schneider's company, were among the replacements. They looked the way any soldiers coming away from the front line looked: dirty, haggard, exhausted seemingly past the repair of sleep, some managing grins as they thought about what they'd do now that they'd finally got relieved, others shambling along with blank stares, as if they hardly knew where they were. That happened to some men after they'd taken too much shelling. McSweeney had seen as much, though he didn't understand. How could a man whom the Lord had spared be anything but joyful?

One of the soldiers leaving the front pointed to the tank of jellied oil he bore on his back. "Rebs catch you with that contraption, pal, they won't bother sendin' you to no prison camp. They'll just cut your throat for you and leave you for the buzzards."

"They shall not take me alive." McSweeney spoke with great assurance. He generally spoke with great assurance. The soldier who'd presumed to remark on the flamethrower stared, shrugged, and kept on marching.

Noncoms left behind guided the company into the section of trench they would inhabit till taken out of line themselves. "I don't like this for hell," Captain Schneider said. "Not for hell I don't. We're right out in the open, with whatever guns the Rebs have up on that ridge looking straight down our throats."

"And the men who were here before us were not careful enough about that, either," McSweeney said. For once, he needed to give his squad no orders. Seeing the same thing he did, every man jack of them had taken out his entrenching tool and was busy improving the shelter with which they had been provided. McSweeney turned to Schneider. "I would wager the barbed wire will be as weak."

"You're likely right, Sergeant," Schneider answered, "but I'm not going to stick my head up to find out, not in broad daylight I'm not. Come tonight, we'll send out a wiring party—if there's any wire to be had."

"Yes, sir," McSweeney said. "I sometimes think Philadelphia cares not at all whether the war on this side of the river is won or lost. Utah mattered to the powers that be, because it was on the rail line to the Pacific. Here—" He shook his head. "Out of sight, out of mind."

"You'll get a lot of people who do the real fighting to tell you the fools back in Philadelphia are out of their minds," Schneider said with a grin. When McSweeney didn't grin back, the captain frowned. McSweeney wondered why.

The wiring party did not go out that night: a wiring party without wire was nothing but wasted effort. Ben Carlton cooked up a stew inedible even by his own standards, which were low. "The enemy seeks to wound us," McSweeney told him. "You should not."

Carlton gave him a resentful stare. "Ain't like you could do better."

"I admit it," McSweeney said.

"You do?" The cook stared again, this time in a different way. "Ain't never heard you admit nothin' before."

"However," McSweeney went on implacably, as if Carlton had not spoken, "I was not assigned to cook. You were." Resentment returned to Carlton's face. McSweeney ignored it, as he always did, confident in his own rightness and righteousness.

No new wire came up to the front. Captain Schneider swore. McSweeney sent Carlton out to see if he could come up with any: the man was a menace as a cook, but an inspired scavenger. When Carlton had no luck, McSweeney concluded there truly was no wire to be had. He went up and down the line, making sure the machine guns were well sited. Only after that was done did he wrap himself in his blanket and go to sleep.

Rebel artillery made sure he did not sleep late. Those guns up on top of Crowley's Ridge started shelling the U.S. position a couple of hours before dawn. "Gas!" somebody screamed in the middle of the unholy din. McSweeney donned his gas helmet as calmly and quickly as if he were practicing in front of a mirror.

"Be ready!" he yelled as soon as the first light showed in the sky. Not five minutes later, Confederate machine guns added their racket to the crashes from the artillery.

Shouts rose up and down the trench: "Here they come!" "Here come the goddamn motherfucking sons of bitches!" Beneath the gas helmet, McSweeney's face set in disapproving lines. He'd never find out who had committed the obscene blasphemy. And then a shout rose that made him forget to worry about discipline and propriety: "Barrel! Jesus, the Rebs have a stinking barrel!"

He stuck his head up over the top of the parapet. Sure enough, one of those tracked traveling fortresses was slowly rumbling and clanking straight toward the U.S. line—straight toward *him*, it looked like. The U.S. machine guns went from raking the soldiers in butternut advancing with the barrel to aiming their fire exclusively at it, trying to knock it out of action before it could get into the trenches.

It was a British-style machine, with cannon mounted in sponsons on either side. One of those cannon spat fire. A machine gun fell silent. The barrel clattered forward once more. Its own machine guns sprayed bullets at the U.S. soldiers.

The glass portholes in McSweeney's gas helmet were fogged

on the inside and streaked with dust on the outside. That did not keep him from noticing a couple of men running away from the barrel. "Halt!" he roared at them. It did no good. At last, the men had discovered something they feared worse than they feared him.

Boom! The barrel fired again. Another machine gun abruptly stopped shooting at it. Ricochets whined off the steel armor, striking sparks but failing to penetrate. McSweeney wondered how many more barrels that he could not see were moving forward.

He shrugged. If he couldn't see them, he couldn't do anything about them. He could see this one. He bent and, careful not to disturb his gas helmet, shrugged over his shoulders the straps to the metal tank that fueled his special weapon. Then he waited. Bullets seemed unable to hurt the barrel.

Here it came, grinding its way through and over the few strands of wire protecting the U.S. trenches. Having thicker belts out there wouldn't have stopped it. More soldiers in green-gray fled the machine they could not stop.

It crushed the parapet and stood poised up there above the edge of the trench, triumphant, like a great bull elephant. As it began its plunge into the U.S. works, McSweeney sent a stream of flame in through one of the machine-gun ports. An instant later, he did the same with the other port on the right side of the barrel, thereby making sure neither of those guns would bear on him.

Through the shelling, through the firing going on all around, through the coughing roar of the barrel's engine, he heard screams inside the metal hull. Hatches flew open on top of the barrel. Men started scrambling out. Smiling behind the canvas of the mask, McSweeney burned them down. They tumbled back into the machine, black and shrunken and flaming, like insects that had flown into the flame of a gaslight.

Smoke poured from the barrel. Ammunition started cooking off in it. McSweeney regretfully moved away, that hard, tight grin still on his face. A Confederate soldier sprang onto the parapet. He fired from the hip at McSweeney—and missed. He never got a second chance. A tongue of flame licked over him. He tumbled back, burning, burning.

A grenade flew down into the trench. The blast was deafening.

A fragment bit McSweeney's leg. But when a Rebel followed the grenade, he too became a torch. No more Confederate soldiers tried coming down into the U.S. trenches, not anywhere the flame could reach. The sight of the blazing barrel took the heart out of their attack.

"You'll get a medal for this!" someone shouted: someone in captain's bars. Schneider hadn't run, then. That was something. The company commander went on, "A Medal of Honor, if I have anything to do with it."

"Thank you, sir." McSweeney was as unflinchingly honest about himself as about everything and everyone around him. "I earned it."

The envelope with the familiar handwriting had caused a small stir when it got to Scipio's apartment house. Any time mail arrived there was a small occasion, for only a few of the Negroes in the building were able to read and write. "Who it from?" asked the apartment manager, a plump black fellow named Demosthenes. "Sho' 'nuf write pretty."

Scipio had professed ignorance; the imperturbable mask a butler had to be able to don at will was proof against Demosthenes' curiosity. Behind that mask, he'd been trembling. *How did Miss Anne find out where I was living?* he wondered. The war had made people forget about registering newly arrived blacks, and in any case he was but one Nero among many Negroes by that name in Columbia.

In his haste to find out what his former mistress wanted, he'd ignored yet another inviting glance from the widow Jezebel, ignored it so flagrantly that he knew he'd offended. He hadn't cared.

The message, as was Anne Colleton's way, was to the point. *Come to Marshlands Sunday before noon,* she'd written. *If you do, no harm will come to you. If you do not, I shall not answer for the consequences.*

And so, early Sunday morning, Scipio, not doubting her word for a moment, had hopped aboard the beat-up Negro car of a train at Confederacy Station, traveled southeast and then southwest around two sides of a triangle to reach St. Matthews (no direct rail route on the third side existing), and then trudged out of town down a muddy road that got muddier as a chilly drizzle came down, heading west toward the plantation where he'd lived his whole life till the past year.

Marks of the Negro uprising still scarred the countryside: burnt-out houses and barns, cotton fields gone to weeds, trees shattered by the artillery that had done more than anything else to break the Congaree Socialist Republic. Despite the scars, Scipio had the feeling he was walking back into his own past. He wondered if Anne Colleton would have a brass-buttoned tailcoat waiting for him when he got back to the plantation.

All things considered, he preferred life as a laborer, which had more freedom to it than he'd ever imagined. Very few people, though, had ever cared about what he preferred. He hiked through the forest where he'd killed Major Hotchkiss. If anyone ever found out about that, none of Miss Anne's promises would matter in the least.

Coming up the familiar path, turning onto it, and seeing the Marshlands mansion in ruins brought home to him how much things had changed. The Negro cottages still standing alongside those charred ruins brought home to him how much things hadn't.

A battered, filthy, rusty Ford was parked next to one of those cottages: no sign anywhere of the fancy motorcar Miss Anne had driven. None of the field hands would have had an automobile, though, no matter how battered. That had to be where the mistress was staying. As Scipio approached the cottage, a chill ran down his back. Before the uprising—the revolution that had failed—that had been Cassius' cottage. Scipio wondered if Anne Colleton appreciated the irony.

A few children were playing outside in spite of the drizzle. In his city clothes, he was a stranger to them. Strangers, these days, were objects of fear, not curiosity. "What you wan'?" asked one of the boys, a chap who would have been just too young to fight in the revolutionary army, which had had more than one twelve-year-old carrying a rifle.

"I wish to speak with the mistress of Marshlands, Ajax," Scipio answered. "Will you be so good as to tell her I have arrived?"

Ajax and the other children stared at him, not expecting that kind of language to come from the mouth of a black man wearing a frayed, collarless shirt and a pair of dungarees with

patches at the knees, a cloth cap on his head against the rain.
Then the youngster recognized him in spite of the unfamiliar ha-
biliments. "It Scipio!" he yelped. "Do Jesus, Scipio done come
back!"

That shout brought faces to windows and made several doors
come open so the inhabitants of those cottages could gape—
or could warily study—the returned prodigal. One of the opening doors was that of the cottage formerly Cassius'. Out came
Anne Colleton, who ignored the nasty weather. "Good morning,
Scipio," she said, almost—but not quite—as she might have
done before the revolt. "You were wise to come."

"Ma'am, I thought so myself, which is why I did," he answered.

She stood aside. "Well, come in," she said. "I have coffee waiting, and cold chicken, and sweet-potato pie. You'll be hungry, I
expect."

"Yes, ma'am," he said again. He went into the cottage, pausing only to wipe his feet on the jute mat in front of the door. The
cottage hadn't boasted a mat when Cassius had lived there. It
hadn't boasted an icebox, either, or a small stove to supplement
the fireplace. Nor had it held a bookcase, even if the titles on the
shelves were worn secondhand copies like the ones he bought
for himself. But there had been literature here: Marx and Engels
and Lincoln and other Red and near-Red writers. Cassius,
though, had had to keep all that hidden.

Anne Colleton closed the door behind them. "Help yourself to
anything," she said. "I don't want anyone but the two of us
hearing what we have to say to each other." That explained why
she had no servant present. And for her to serve him had undoubtedly never once crossed her mind. She was, after all, a sort
of commingling of feudal landlord and capitalist oppressor.
Scipio had read Cassius' books, too.

Unless he planned on killing her and then fleeing, he had to do
as she said for the moment. He'd thought about that, walking out
from St. Matthews. But even if the field hands didn't try stopping him as he ran, she would have put aside a letter or something somewhere to point the finger at him. She was not the sort
to miss such a trick.

As if to underscore that, she pulled a pistol out of her
handbag. "In case you were foolish," she remarked. "I didn't
really expect you to be, but one never knows these days."

"I have no intention of being foolish," he answered gravely. She'd put out two coffee cups. He poured one for her, one for himself. Since she'd set out only one plate, he assumed she'd already eaten. The food was plain, nothing like the fancy banquets she'd served in the days before the war, but good enough. Since he'd had nothing but a slice of bread before leaving for the train station, he ate his fill now.

With more patience than she usually showed, his former mistress let him finish before saying anything. When he was done, she began without preamble: "I want you to tell me how my brother Jacob died."

"Yes, ma'am." He made his voice as flat as he could, a fitting complement to the features he schooled to stillness. Her face and voice were similarly chary of giving him clues. How much did she know? How much did he dare lie? After no more than a heartbeat, he decided that anyone who lied to her was a fool. The truth, then, as much of it as he could give. "Ma'am, he perished most courageously."

"I wouldn't have expected anything else," she answered. "Courage Jacob always had. No brains to speak of, but courage. That wench Cherry would have played a part in it, wouldn't she?"

"Ma'am, if you know the answers, what need have you to question me?" Scipio asked.

"I am in a position to question you," Anne said. "You are not in a position to question me. She would have used her charms to soften him up, wouldn't she?" That was not a question; she sounded wearily sure she knew whereof she spoke. "And Cassius. He's still stealing things hereabouts, you know."

"So I have heard, yes," Scipio said. The more he talked about Cassius now, the less he would have to talk about what had happened a year before.

"He still has a price on his head, too," Anne said. "If he comes round here"—the pistol twitched in her hand—"I shall kill him." She studied Scipio, as if deciding whether to butcher a hog now or to wait. "And, of course, you still have a price on your head as well."

"You said no harm would come to me if I visited you here," Scipio said quickly. If she hadn't had the pistol, he *would* have thought about trying to kill her. Living with her, serving her, had taught him how devious she was.

But when she said, "And I meant that," he thought she was telling the truth. She went on, "You and Julia are the only members of the house staff I've been able to find. She and the field hands deny knowing anything. I've made my investigations, but you are the only eyewitness to what happened I've been able to . . . find."

Catch was what she meant. Wherever she'd learned whatever she'd learned, she knew a good deal. Scipio had not defied Cassius when the Red leader made it plain his choices were cooperation and death. The stuff of defiance was not in him. Maybe it never had been; maybe his servile upbringing had trained out whatever he'd once owned.

He told the whole story, from Cherry's claim of abuse to the gun battle in which Jacob Colleton had defended himself so well to the storming of the bedroom door behind which Anne's gassed brother had barricaded himself. "Three or four men did that," he said. "They rushed past me so fast, I do not know for certain who they were. I do not know which of them fired the fatal shot, either. Ma'am, you may do with me what you will, but I am being truthful in this regard."

"I believe you," Anne said, which caught Scipio by surprise. Sitting where she sat, he wouldn't have believed himself. She went on, "The reason I believe you is that, if you were lying to me, you would have come up with a better story. The truth, I've found, is usually confused."

"Yes, ma'am," he said.

"Now—" Her voice sharpened. "Who burned the Marshlands mansion?"

"That was Cassius, ma'am," he answered, adding, "I wish he had not done it. Many beautiful things were lost."

"In five words, you've just given the story of this war," she said. "I know you had a role in the so-called Congaree Socialist Republic. From what I've heard, you usually did what you could to stop its excesses. I suspect your reasons had as much to do with what would happen after the uprising was put down as they did with any special milk of human kindness in your veins, but only God can look into a man's heart, and I've found out that, whatever else I may be, I am not God."

Not knowing what to say to that, Scipio kept quiet. If Anne Colleton hadn't thought she was God before the Red revolt, she'd done a fine job of concealing the fact. He wondered what she'd gone through. He didn't have the nerve to ask. He didn't have the nerve for a lot of things. In a nutshell, that was the tale of his life.

Wearily, Anne said, "Go back to Columbia. Go back to your work. Once we win the war, that will have been enough. Don't ever come here again, unless I summon you."

"Ma'am, on that you may rest assured." Scipio wondered if he was talking like an educated white man for the last time in his life. In a way, he would miss it if that proved so. In another way, giving up what had been imposed on him was a sort of freedom in itself.

He rose, half bowed to Anne, and left the cottage. Field hands and children stared after him. He didn't look back. As he got to the forest where he'd killed Major Hotchkiss, he decided he needed a new apartment, a new job, a new name. The widow had wanted to go to bed with him. He sighed. It wouldn't happen now. "Odder chances," he said aloud. "Dey is odder chances." He kept walking toward the train station.

Brakes squealing, the train pulled into the station. "Cincinnati!" the conductor shouted. "All out for Cincinnati!"

Men, most of them in uniform, and a scattering of women rose from their seats so they could depart. Irving Morrell stayed where he was. So did Heinz Guderian beside him. "How far now from Cincinnati to Philadelphia?" Guderian asked in German.

Morrell visualized a map. "Six hundred miles, maybe a little less," he answered in the same language. Seeing Guderian look puzzled, he amplified that: "About 950 kilometers." He moved back and forth between one system of measurement and the other readily enough, but had learned the German found it harder.

Sure enough, Guderian twitted him about it: "How many feet in a mile? It is 5,280, *nicht wahr?* What a foolish number to have to keep straight every time you need to make a calculation."

Before Morrell could defend the American system, the conductor leaned over and said with a smile, *"Wir willen winnen der Krieg."*

Guderian stared at him, not because he spoke German so badly (he'd said "We want to win the war," not "We will win the war," which was what he'd probably meant, and he'd botched his article and his word order, too), but because he spoke it at all: he was a black man with a mouth full of gold-crowned teeth. *"Ja!"* Guderian managed at last, and the conductor, smiling still, headed down the central aisle. To Morrell, the German General Staff officer said, "I had not realized just how popular my country was in the United States."

"Oh, yes," Morrell said with a nod. "Good thing we weren't speaking French, or he'd have probably thought we were spies. A classmate of mine at the Academy, Jack Lefebvre, changed his name to Schmidt after the war started. It was either that, he told me, or kiss promotion good-bye. And I happen to know his people have been in the USA since before the War of Secession."

"This business of everyone coming from elsewhere or having parents or grandparents who came from elsewhere is very strange to me," Guderian said. "In Europe, we have been where we are since the *Völkerwanderungen* of a thousand years ago and more."

Passengers were boarding the train as well as leaving it. Some of them came from elsewhere, too, speaking with accents plainly sprung from the CSA. A couple of those fellows, looking prosperous with big bellies, expensive black suits, and homburgs, sat down across from Morrell and Guderian. "It'll be right strange," one of them said to the other with a ripe drawl, "but I reckon we can do it."

Shifting to English, Morrell leaned over and asked, "Who are you people, anyway?" Talk about spies—!

The man sitting closer to him stuck out a plump hand. "Major, I'm Davis Lee Vidals, lieutenant governor of Kentucky—of the *United* State of Kentucky, I make haste to assure you."

Morrell reached out and shook the proffered hand, being careful not to squash it. He gave his own name. "That's wonderful news!" he said. "Welcome back to the country where you belong."

"Thank you very kindly, Major Morrell," Vidals said. "That fellow sitting beside you—is he a *German*?" His voice was half dread, half awe: he might have been one of the people helping to bring Kentucky back into the USA, but he didn't seem to know how to feel about U.S. allies who had been enemies of the Confederate States.

"*Ja,* I am a German." Guderian spoke English with a heavy accent, but was fluent enough. He grinned at the Kentucky politician. "You would not expect to find an American officer traveling with a Frenchman, would you?" He'd paid attention to the story of Jack Lefebvre, now Schmidt, all right.

"Good God almighty, I hope not!" Vidals exclaimed. "Gentlemen, let me introduce to you my friend and colleague here: this is Luther Bliss, chief of the Kentucky State Police. We're both on our way to Philadelphia to settle arrangements for electing congressmen and senators next month."

Bliss leaned across his traveling companion to shake hands with Morrell and Guderian. He was hard-faced and sallow, with a scar seaming one cheek. His eyes were a light, light brown, about the color of a hunting dog's. Morrell wouldn't have cared to let the Kentuckian stand behind him; he was the sort of man who looked to have a stiletto stashed up his sleeve. *Kentucky State Police,* Morrell suspected, was a euphemism for *Kentucky Secret Police.*

"How did Kentucky go about applying for readmission to the United States?" he asked. The curiosity was more professional than personal. Administering conquered territory and bringing it under the control of the USA was something that might be part of his responsibilities one day.

The train started rolling as Davis Lee Vidals started talking. Morrell quickly discovered the train was more likely than the lieutenant governor to slow down. "We convened a gathering of distinguished Kentuckians eager to renew their historic ties to the United States of America," Vidals began, "and discussed ways and means by which this might be accomplished. We—"

"How many Kentuckians?" Morrell asked.

Vidals began another speech. It went on for some time, and told Morrell nothing. When the politician paused to inhale—which took a while—Luther Bliss interjected, "Couple hundred." His superior—his nominal superior, at any rate—gave him a dirty look and started talking again.

Several well-modulated paragraphs of rhetoric later, Morrell asked, "Did you need any soldiers to make sure things went the way you had in mind?"

Davis Lee Vidals waxed indignant, eloquently indignant, at the very idea. He didn't, however, say no. He also didn't say yes. He did *say*, and say, and say. Presently, he paused again, this time to light a cigar. In that brief interval of silence, Bliss got another chance to open his mouth. "Couple regiments," he said, and fell silent again.

Morrell nodded. That told him everything he thought he needed to know about the new state government of Kentucky: without massive help from the U.S. Army, it wouldn't exist. But Heinz Guderian spoke up, in German: "This is not so bad as it may sound, Major. When, forty-five years ago, we annexed Alsace and Lorraine from France, many of the people there resented and resisted us. There remain some who do, but those provinces also remain a part of the German *Reich*, and grow more accustomed to our rule with each passing day."

Vidals' eyes got wider with every guttural he heard, and wider still when Morrell answered in German. He might have been bringing Kentucky back into the USA, but he was also bringing a lot of ideas from the Quadruple Entente with him. Luther Bliss, by contrast, listened quietly. Morrell wouldn't have bet against his understanding every word that was said.

The only thing that finally slowed Vidals down was sleep. No matter that he was sitting in a seat that didn't recline. He set his homburg in his lap, put his head back, and snored like a thunderstorm in training. That he was so aggressively asleep meant everyone else in the crowded car had trouble joining him.

Outside, the countryside was dark as the tomb. That hadn't been so farther west, but here in Ohio and Pennsylvania, Confederate bombing aeroplanes remained a nuisance. The enforced darkness after sunset made it harder for them to find worthwhile targets.

Morrell had finally drifted into a fitful doze when the train pulled into Philadelphia at a little before four in the morning. He grunted and groaned and rubbed his eyes. Across the aisle, the lieutenant governor of Kentucky kept on snoring till the conductor shouted out the arrival. Luther Bliss didn't look to have slept a wink, or to have needed sleep, either.

When the doors opened, a brass band started blaring "The Star-Spangled Banner." There on the platform stood President Roosevelt. When the Kentuckians got out, he folded them into a bearhug. "Welcome back, prodigal sons!" he cried, while photographers' flash trays went off with almost as much smoke and noise as an artillery bombardment. "A new star joins the flag; a new star shines in the firmament!" The band switched to "My Old Kentucky Home."

Let's see what Senator Debs can do to match that, Morrell thought; bringing Kentucky back into the USA before the election had to be worth thousands of votes. Soldiers weren't supposed to have politics. Such politics as Morrell did have were Democratic.

Waiting for him and Guderian was not the president of the United States but Captain John Abell of the General Staff. "Welcome, Captain Guderian," the clever, almost bloodless officer said in excellent German. He turned to Morrell and returned to English: "General Wood has ordered me to extend his personal greetings to you, Lieutenant Colonel."

"Lieut—" Morrell didn't get any further than that, because Guderian was pounding him on the back. Cutting off the Canadian railroad that ran through Banff had earned him a promotion, and evidently got him forgiven for the difficulties the USA had had in Utah. If Captain Abell was pleased at that, he hid it very well.

He said, "As you know, you are assigned to duty here in Philadelphia once more, Lieutenant Colonel. I assure you, I look forward to working with you in every way."

A liar, but a polite liar, Morrell judged. Guderian said, "See, my friend? You have won a victory, and they have put you back behind a desk. It almost tempts one to lose, doesn't it?"

"Yes," Morrell said. "Almost."

"Lord, I wish Emily was here." Jefferson Pinkard stabbed himself with a needle, about the fourth time he'd done that.

Hipolito Rodriguez gave him an amused look. "Most of the time, *amigo,* you say you wish you was with your *esposa.* Now you want her here with you. You no can make up your mind?" He waved around at the bleak west-Texas prairie. "I think she rather you home with her."

Pinkard snorted. "Yeah, I'd rather I was home with her, too. But she can do *this* a hell of a lot easier'n I can." Stubbornly, he kept sewing the single chevron to the sleeve of his uniform tunic.

"If I'd known it was gonna be so blame much trouble, maybe I wouldn't have let 'em promote me."

"*Sí*, life is easier when you have only yourself to worry about," Rodriguez agreed with obvious sincerity.

"Hell, Hip, if they reckon you can do the job, how you gonna tell 'em no?" Jeff asked. He could complain about making private first class after the fact; he hadn't complained when Captain Connolly told him he'd done it. He fought through another couple of stitches, then surveyed his handiwork and found something else over which to complain: "That stripe's pretty light, isn't it? Make it easier for those Yankee sons of bitches to spot me."

"Wait till it rains again and you go through the mud," Rodriguez told him. "Then your whole uniform the same color again."

"Yeah, you're right." Pinkard dug out some cornbread he hadn't finished at breakfast. It had got hard. He didn't care. Even when it was fresh, it hadn't been a patch on what Emily made. Her cornbread and her skill with the needle weren't what he really missed about her, though. He wanted to be back home in Birmingham to warm her bed—and to make sure nobody else was warming it for him.

He stood up in the trench to put on the tunic to which he'd affixed his new chevron—and a bullet cracked past his head. He threw himself—and the tunic—down flat into the trench. "Got to dig it deeper," Hip Rodriguez said seriously. "They shouldn't see you when you get up like that."

"Yeah," Jeff said again. "They wouldn't see *you*, I don't guess." He was several inches taller than the littler Sonoran. This time, he donned the fresh tunic sitting down. It wasn't so fresh any more; he'd smeared dirt over a good part of it, including the sleeves. He stopped worrying about sharpshooters' spotting him on account of one stripe.

A few more bullets flew from the U.S. trenches. Here and there, Confederates along the line east of Lubbock shot back. Pinkard didn't hear any of his countrymen cry out in pain. He didn't know whether they got any Yankees, either. And if they had hit somebody, so what? Did that mean they would run the U.S. Army out of Texas? He knew too well it didn't. That was what his regiment had come here to do. How many lives were gone, without the line's moving one way or the other? Too many, that was sure.

As if to underscore the point, a Confederate machine gun opened up, maybe at a Yankee out of his nice, safe burrow, maybe just for the sake of using up some ammunition. Half a minute later, a U.S. machine gun answered. A couple of hundred yards away from Pinkard, somebody started screaming for his mama.

"Shit," Hip Rodriguez said, and crossed himself. He shook his head, then got a tobacco pouch out of his pocket and began rolling a cigarette.

After a while, both machine-gun crews decided they'd made their pointless points. They quit firing. Rifles kept banging a few minutes longer, nervous, excited men shooting at what they thought were targets. At last, quiet returned.

"You know what all this here reminds me of?" Jeff said, by then having seen a lot of meaningless fire fights that conformed to the same general pattern. When Rodriguez shook his head, Pinkard went on, "It's like a rainstorm, ain't it? First you get a few drops, then it comes down hard for a while, then it tapers off, and it's all quiet and the sun's out again."

"That is clever, what you say." Rodriguez nodded now. "This time, we don't get no—" The noise he made could have been thunder rolling or artillery going off. It fit either way.

Up the communications trench into the front line came Stinky Salley. Most times, Pinkard would have been as glad to see him as to encounter a new kind of louse, but Salley had somehow used his civilian career as a clerk to convince Captain Connolly that no one else could possibly match him as the man to pick up and distribute the mail. He carried a butternut canvas bag labeled CSAMPO. "Letters!" he called. "I've got letters!"

He needed more than being the bearer of news from home to make him popular with his fellow soldiers, but that didn't hurt. Men came hurrying over to him, arms outstretched, smiles on their faces. "Come on, Stinky," somebody said. "Cough 'em up!" But even that wasn't so peremptory as it would have been had Salley not borne letters.

He took them out of the sack and started reading off names: "Burroughs! Dalton! Pinkard!" Jeff took the envelope with an enormous grin; he recognized Emily's handwriting. "Captain

Connolly, one for you, sir." To officers, Salley was painfully ob-
sequious. "Pratt! Ambrose! Pinkard again—you lucky dog."
Jeff's promotion hadn't quite sunk in on his fellow Alabaman.

"Two in one mail call!" Pinkard exclaimed joyfully as he carried both letters—the second, he saw, also from his wife—away
from the crowd around Salley. He sat down beside Hip Rodriguez. Rodriguez never got mail; as far as Jeff could tell, the
little Sonoran didn't know anyone who could read or write, and
had only started learning those arts himself since he'd joined the
Army. He liked listening to other soldiers read their mail,
though, as did anybody who'd drawn a blank in the distribution.

Jeff looked to see which letter had the earlier postmark, and
opened that one first. " 'Dear Jeff,' " he read aloud, " 'I am fine. I
wish you was home with me, so I could give you a kiss and—' "
He skipped most of the next paragraph, at least with his voice,
though his eyes lingered on it. Every once in a while, Emily
would do something like that. It made him more anxious than
ever to get home. Rodriguez grinned at him, probably guessing
what he was leaving out.

Coughing a little, he resumed where the spice left off: " 'I am
fine, and working hard. I hope so much you are well and have
not got yourself hurt. Fanny got herself a telegram from the War
Department yesterday that says poor Bedford got wounded, and
she is frantic.' "

Turning to Rodriguez, Jeff explained, "I worked with Bedford
Cunningham, and him and his wife live next door to me."

"This is hard," the Sonoran said. "This is very hard." He
sounded altogether sincere; he had a good deal more sympathy
in him than the run-of-the-mill Confederate soldier. "For you,
my *amigo*, and for your, your wife"—he remembered the English word—"and more for your *amigo*'s wife, and most of all
for him. How *peligroso*—how dangerous—is the wound?"

"Letter doesn't say," Pinkard answered. "Reckon Fanny didn't
know, so Emily wouldn't've, either." Rodriguez pointed to the
other envelope. Nodding, Jeff tore it open. He didn't read it out
loud all the way though, but rapidly skimmed through it, looking
for news of Bedford Cunningham.

When he found it, his face gave him away. "It is very bad?"
Hip Rodriguez asked quietly.

"Right arm"—Jeff held up his own, partly to help Rodriguez's uncertain English, partly to remind himself he still owned that precious piece of flesh—"gone above the elbow, Emily says. Bedford's on his way home now. He'll get better. What's he going to do, though, with a wound like that? Never get on the floor at the Sloss Works again, that's certain, and iron's about the only thing he knew."

Rodriguez closed his right hand into a fist. He watched it carefully as he did so. Pinkard watched, too: all the marvelous, miraculous interplay of muscle and tendon and bone beneath a sheath of wonderfully unbroken skin. *Gone in an instant,* Jeff thought. *Wonder if a bullet got him, or if a shell came down right next door. Wonder if he knows. Wonder if he cares.*

"If this happen to me," Rodriguez said, "I take whatever money I have, I go to the *cantina,* and I don't do nothing but drink from then on. What else am I good for, without my right hand?"

"Don't know," Pinkard said. "You couldn't farm one-handed, any more than you could go back to the foundry. It's funny," he went on after a little while. "Just reading this here letter about Bedford hits me harder than seeing some of the people from the company get hurt right in front of my eyes. Is that crazy, or what?"

"No," Rodriguez answered. "This is a good friend, almost like your *hermano,* your brother. We are still some of us like strangers."

"Yeah, maybe." That still tasted wrong, but it was closer than any explanation Jeff had come up with. "God damn the war," he muttered. Rodriguez nodded solemnly. A Yankee machine gun started up, the gunner spraying bullets over a wide arc to see what he could hit. "God damn the war," Jeff said again, and checked to make sure his Tredegar had a full clip.

From under the awning, Lieutenant General George Armstrong Custer stared gloomily at the hills above White House, Tennessee. "We have to have a victory," he said. "We have to. The war requires it, and politics require it, too."

Cautiously, Major Abner Dowling said, "Joining battle for the sake of politics is a recipe for getting licked, sir. We learned that in the War of Secession, and all over again during the Second Mexican War."

Custer's pouchy stare swung from the stalled battlefield toward his adjutant. "Most times, Major, I would agree with you," he said after what was for him an unusual pause to reflect. "Now, though—do you want that wild-eyed lunatic Debs sitting in the White House come next March? He's already said he'll treat for peace with the Rebels and the Canucks if he gets elected. Is that what you want, Major? *Is* it?"

"No, sir," Dowling said at once; he was as good a Democrat as Custer.

He might as well not have spoken; once the general commanding First Army got rolling, he kept rolling till he ran down. "God in heaven, Major!" Custer burst out, a rheumy thunderer. "We're winning on every front—on every front, I tell you—and that crackbrained maniac wants to give it up? And for what? For an honorable peace, he calls it. Honorable!" With his age-loosened, wrinkled skin and enormous mustache, Custer had a formidable sneer when he turned it loose, as he did now.

"I agree with you, sir," Dowling said, for once telling Custer the unvarnished truth. "We just have to hope the people back home haven't got too sick of the war to want to fight it through to the finish."

"They had better not try quitting," Custer growled. "If Debs calls the troops home, we'll have a brand-new American Revolution, mark my words."

Dowling did mark them. They filled him with horror. His head whipped around. After a moment's panic, he heartily thanked God. Nobody but he had heard Custer. As casually as he could, he said, "Armed rebellion against the government of the United States is treason, sir."

"I know that." Custer sounded testy, not repentant. "Still some Rebs left alive who need hanging, by God, unless their own niggers shot 'em for us. Too much to hope for, that, I daresay. Now you listen to me, Major." Dowling, who had done his share and more of listening, made himself look attentive. Custer resumed: "I don't want a rebellion, not even a little bit. Do you understand me? What I want is to make a rebellion unnecessary, and that means victory, to give the people the idea—the true idea, mind you—that we stand on the edge of the greatest triumph in the history of mankind."

"The Rebs are still fighting hard, sir," Dowling said, in what had to be the understatement of this or any other decade: the front hadn't moved a mile closer to the White House since the enormous U.S. offensive opened. "So are the Canadians, which forces us to divide our efforts."

"Teddy Roosevelt bit off more than he could chew, right at the start of the war," Custer said. This, from a man whose notion of reconnaissance was a headlong charge at an obstacle with everything he had, struck Major Dowling as a curious utterance—which, for once, did not mean it was wrong.

Rather to Dowling's relief, the debate on grand strategy stopped then, for one of Custer's division commanders came up, stood under the awning, and waited to be noticed. He waited a while, too; Custer was jealous of his own prerogatives. At last, grudgingly, he said, "Good morning, Brigadier General MacArthur."

"Good morning, sir." Brigadier General Daniel MacArthur came to stiff attention, which made him tower even more over both Custer and Dowling. Dowling understood why Custer was touchy around this particular subordinate. MacArthur was, visibly, a man on the rise. At thirty-two, he was the youngest division commander in the U.S. Army. Unlike earlier conflicts, this was one where an officer had a devil of a time making a name for himself by pluck and dash. As far as anyone could do that in an age of machine guns and trenches and barbed wire, Daniel MacArthur had done it.

He made sure people knew he'd done it, too, which was one reason he'd got his division. In some ways, he and Custer were very much alike, though both of them would have angrily turned on Dowling had he been rash enough to say such a thing. Still, as far as the adjutant was concerned, the long ivory holder through which MacArthur chain-smoked cigarettes was as much an affectation as Custer's gold-dyed locks.

MacArthur said, "Sir, we need a breakthrough. The Army needs one from us, and the country needs one from us."

"The very thing I was saying to my adjutant not five minutes ago," Custer replied. He looked up at the young, lean, ramrod-straight officer standing beside him. His smile was cynical and infinitely knowing. Dowling would not have wanted that smile aimed at him. After pausing to cough, Custer went on, "And you wouldn't mind having a breakthrough for yourself, either, would you, Daniel?"

"The country's needs come first, sir," MacArthur answered, and sounded as if he meant it. Maybe he even believed it. But he was still very young. Dowling saw how he tensed, almost as if he'd seen a beautiful woman walk by. Yes, he lusted after a breakthrough, all right.

"We've been pounding the Rebs for weeks now," Custer said. "They haven't given us anything at all, and we haven't been able to take much. They know as well as we do that the White House line is the last thing keeping our guns from letting Nashville know the full taste of war."

"Yes, sir," MacArthur said, and pulled a map from the breast pocket of his uniform. Unlike Custer, who was old-fashioned enough to relish the epaulets and other fancy accoutrements accruing to his rank, MacArthur wore an ordinary officer's uniform set apart only by the single silver stars of his rank: ostentatious plainness, as opposed to ostentatious display. He unfolded the map. "I believe I know how to get past them, too."

Custer put on his reading glasses, a concession of sorts. "Let's see what you have in mind, General."

"Misdirection." Daniel MacArthur spoke the word solemnly, as if it were the capstone of a magic spell. Dowling figured he'd cooked his own goose then and there; Custer had about as much use for misdirection as an anteater did for snowshoes. The dashing division commander (and how many major generals gnashed their teeth at that, when they led only brigades?) said, "As you know, my men are stationed on our far left, in front of Cottontown."

"Yes, yes," Custer said impatiently, though Dowling wouldn't have bet more than half a dollar that he'd been sure where in the line MacArthur's formation did belong.

"We have found to our cost how strong the Confederate defenses due south and southwest of our position are," MacArthur said. Custer nodded, those peroxided curls flapping at the back of his neck. MacArthur continued, "Aerial reconnaissance suggests, though, that the Rebels' line is weaker toward the southeast. If we strike in that direction, toward Gallatin, we can set our men to taking lines less formidably manned, thereby giving them the opportunity to swing back toward Nashville, cutting in behind the entrenchments that have delayed them so long."

Custer sucked at something between two of his false teeth. Abner Dowling scratched his chin. "Sir," he said, "it's not a bad scheme." He suspected he sounded surprised. He didn't much care for MacArthur, having seen in Custer what the passage of years was likely to do to such a man.

Custer studied the map a while longer. MacArthur had used bright blue ink to show exactly what he wanted to do. "No," Custer said at last, "it's not." He sounded imperfectly enamored of it, but seemed to recognize it was a better plan than any he'd come up with. Since most of his plans amounted to nothing more than finding the enemy and attacking him (not necessarily in that order), that did not say as much as it might have otherwise.

Unlike the general commanding First Army, MacArthur did his homework ahead of time. The map was not the only sheet of paper lurking in his breast pocket. Handing Custer a typewritten list, he said, "Here are the additional artillery requirements for the assault, sir, and other ancillaries as well."

"See what you think of this, Major," Custer said, and passed the sheet to Dowling. Precise control of details had never been his strong suit.

MacArthur puffed and puffed, blowing smoke into Dowling's face as if it were phosgene gas. Dowling read rapidly through the list before turning to Custer. "Sir, he wants all the heavy artillery concentrated on his division's front, and he also wants almost all of our barrels for the assault."

"Moving the heavy artillery will take time," Custer said, "especially with the roads as muddy as they have been lately. I'm sure we can move some of it, but asking for all asks for too much."

"Even half the First Army reserve would probably be adequate," MacArthur said. He was smarter than Custer had ever been, Dowling thought: he knew enough to ask for more than he really wanted, to help assure his getting at least that much. He couldn't quite keep the eagerness from his voice as he asked, "And the barrels—?"

"Ah, the barrels." Custer assumed a mournful expression. "I have to remind you, General, that I am under strict orders from the War Department not to concentrate the barrels in the manner you suggest. Approved doctrine requires keeping them widely spread along the entire length of the front."

"But, sir—" Dowling closed his mouth a split second before it got him in trouble. Custer had argued ferociously for concentrating barrels in a mass. Why was he rejecting the idea when one of his subordinates had it?

After a moment, the major understood: Custer was rejecting the idea *because* one of his subordinates had had it. If a division-sized attack spearheaded by a swarm of barrels succeed, who would get the credit? Not Custer—Daniel MacArthur.

MacArthur said, "Once you let me proceed, sir, I can show those fools in Philadelphia the proper way to do things."

Abner Dowling sighed. He was but a major; neither of the exalted personages under the awning even noticed. MacArthur couldn't have said that worse if he'd tried for a week. Custer, as Dowling knew full well, despised those fools back in Philadelphia as much as any man alive. But when MacArthur said *I can show*, that meant Custer couldn't show. Custer wanted victories, yes. Custer wanted Teddy Roosevelt reelected, yes. But, most of all, Custer wanted glory for George Armstrong Custer.

Almost sorrowfully, he said, "I wish I could help you more, General, but my own orders in this regard are severely inflexible. I may be able to furnish you with, oh, half a dozen extra barrels without having some pipsqueak inspector-general calling me on the carpet, but no more than that, I fear."

"But, sir, nothing ventured, nothing gained," MacArthur protested.

"I am venturing what I can, General, I assure you," Custer said icily. "Yours is not the only division in the line. Will you prepare a revised attack plan conforming to the available resources, or will you stand on the defensive?"

"You'll have it before the day is out, sir." MacArthur's voice held no expression whatever. Like a mechanical man, he saluted, spun, and stalked off.

Very softly, Custer laughed at his retreating back. Dowling stared at the general commanding First Army. Custer, here, knew just what he was doing—and he enjoyed it, too. *You bastard,* Dowling thought. *You sneaky old bastard.* Was that admiration or loathing? For the life of him, he couldn't tell.

* * *

Roger Kimball peered avidly through the periscope. The fish was running straight and true. Suddenly, the U.S. destroyer realized it was under attack. Suddenly, it tried to turn away from the creamy wake the torpedo left. Suddenly, the torpedo struck just aft of amidships. Suddenly, a great pillar of smoke and flame rose into the air. The destroyer, broken in half, sank like a stone—like two stones.

Cheers filled the narrow steel tube that was the working area of the *Bonefish*, drowning out the echoes of the explosion that the water carried to the submersible. "Hit!" Kimball's own bloodthirsty howl was but one among many.

He brought his eyes back to the periscope. Only a couple of boats bobbed in the Atlantic; the damnyankees hadn't had time to launch any more. If he'd been a German submarine commander, he would have surfaced and turned the deck gun on them. The Huns played by hard rules. There were times when Kimball, feeling the full weight of the USA pressing down on him and his country, wanted to play that way, too.

Such thoughts went by the board in a hurry when, turning the periscope, he saw another destroyer running straight for him. His fierce joy curdled and went cold in the twinkling of an eye. "Dive!" he shouted. "Take us down to 150, Tom, and make it snappy!"

"Aye aye, sir, 150 feet," his exec answered. Compressed air bubbled out of the buoyancy chambers; seawater gurgled in to take its place. Up on the surface, those bubbles would help the Yankee sailors figure out where he was, though they were liable to have a pretty good idea already, what with the course their fellow boat had been making and the way it had tried to escape his fish.

With more and more of the North Atlantic piled atop it, the hull of the *Bonefish* creaked and squealed. There were a couple of little drips where the seams weren't perfectly tight, but they were in the old familiar places. Kimball didn't worry much about them.

Through the hull, the noise of the engine and screw up above them was perfectly audible. No—engines and screws. Two boats were moving back and forth up there. "Leveling off at 150, sir," Tom Brearley said, straightening the diving planes. In the dim orange light, his grin was almost satanic. "They aren't what you'd call happy with us."

"Ain't been happy with them since we went to war," Kimball replied, "or before that, either, you get right down to it. Them and us, we don't—"

He broke off abruptly. Through the pounding drone of the destroyers' engines, he'd heard another sound, the noise that might have come from a garbage can full of cement being flung into the ocean.

"Depth charge," Ben Coulter said hoarsely. The veteran petty officer tried to make light of it: "Those damn things, most of the time they don't work for beans." A moment later, another splash followed the first.

"Give me eight knots, Tom, and change course to 270," Kimball said.

"Changing course to two-seven-zero, sir, aye aye, and eight knots," Brearley acknowledged, a certain amount of doubt in his voice. Kimball didn't blame him. Eight knots used up battery power in a hurry, cutting deeply into the time the *Bonefish* could stay underwater.

Without much humor, Kimball tried to make a joke of it: "When the boys on top start throwing things at you, Tom, it's time to get out from under 'em."

"Well, yes, sir, but—" Brearley didn't get any further than that, for the first depth charge exploded just then.

It was, Kimball supposed, something like being in an earthquake. It was also like standing inside a metal pipe while giants pounded on the outside of it with sledgehammers. Kimball staggered and smacked the side of his head against the periscope mounting. Something wet started running down his cheek. It was warm, not cold, so he supposed it was blood rather than seawater.

Men stumbled and cursed. The lights flickered. A few seconds later, the other depth charge went off. It was farther away than the first one, so it only felt like a big kick in the ass from an angry mule.

"Sir, on second thought, eight knots is a right good idea," Brearley said.

"Everything still answer?" Kimball asked.

Brearley nodded. "Seems to, sir."

"We got a new leak back here, sir," one of the men in the black gang called from the engines toward the stern. "Don't seem too bad, though."

"It had better not," Kimball answered. "Tom, take her down to 200. I want to put some more distance between us and them."

"The leaks will get worse," Brearley said, but that was more observation than protest. The bow of the *Bonefish* slanted down. If the leaks got a lot worse, Kimball knew he'd have to rise. No one shouted in alarm, so he kept quiet till Brearley said, "Leveling off at 200."

Splash! Splash! Two more depth charges went into the water. *Where* they went into the water was the key factor, and the one Kimball couldn't gauge till they detonated. All he could do was hope he'd picked a direction different from the one the Yankees had chosen. Even with the *Bonefish* going flat out submerged, those destroyers had better than three times his speed. The only thing he had going for him was that they couldn't see him. Hydrophones gave only a vague clue about his direction, and they had to guess his depth.

Wham! Wham! Explosions rocked the submarine. They were both closer than that second one had been, but not so close as the first. All at once, he grinned. "All stop," he snapped to Brearley.

"All—stop," the exec answered. He looked back over his shoulder at Kimball. "You're not going to—?"

"Bet your balls I am, son," the skipper of the *Bonefish* said. "The damnyankees guessed with me, far as direction goes. They know how fast we are. What do you want to bet they keep right on that track, pounding away? They must have some new kind of charges, too, on account of I don't think they've tossed any duds at us."

"Isn't that wonderful?" Brearley said. Along with most of the crew, Kimball chuckled. The life of a submariner had never been easy. By what the damnyankees were throwing at the *Bonefish*, it had just got harder.

Splash! Splash! With even the quiet electric motors running only enough to power lights and instruments, the noise the depth charges made going into the ocean was all too audible. In his mind's eye, Kimball saw them twisting slowly down through the green-gray waters of the Atlantic (almost the color of a Yankee soldier's uniform), looking for his boat. He cursed himself for an overactive imagination.

Wham! Wham! He staggered. A tiny new jet of seawater sprayed coldly down the back of his neck. As they had with the first attack, the lights flickered before steadying.

"Those were in front of us, sir," Tom Brearley said.

"I know," Kimball answered. "Here we sit." He could feel eyes boring into him, as he had when he'd taken the *Bonefish* up the Pee Dee River looking for Red rebels. Then, though, the watchful eyes had belonged to the Negroes in the swamps along the riverbank. Now they were the eyes of his own crew.

He understood exactly why, too. The previous spread of charges had been aft of the submersible, this one in front. If that meant the U.S. destroyers up there had somehow located him . . . the next pair would go off right on top of his conning tower.

"One thing, boys," he said into the drip-punctuated quiet. "If it turns out I'm wrong, we'll never know what hit us." If water at seven atmospheres' pressure flooded into the *Bonefish*, it would smash everything in its path, surely making no exceptions for flimsy human beings.

"Sir," Brearley asked, "if you have to, how deep will you take her?"

"I'd go to 300 without blinking an eye," Kimball answered. "It gets wet fast down that deep, but odds are you'll come back up from it. Nobody really knows how deep you *can* go if you're lucky enough. I've heard stories of 350, even 400 feet, when the sub was damaged and couldn't control its dive till it touched bottom." He grinned wryly at his exec. " 'Course, the ones who go down that deep and never surface again—you don't hear about those."

Sailors chuckled. He looked round at them: a grimy, unshaven crew, all the more raffish in the orange lighting. They fit here, the same as he did. They would have been—some had been—outcasts, frequent inhabitants of the brig, almost outlaws, in the gentlemanly world of the Confederate States surface Navy. As far as he was concerned, they'd done the cause more good than ten times their number aboard fancy battleships.

Splash! Splash! Everyone involuntarily sucked in a long breath of the humid, fetid air. In a very little while, Kimball would find out whether his training and instincts had saved their bacon—or killed them all.

In casual tones, Coulter remarked, "Wish I had me a beer right now."

"We get back to Charleston, I'll buy everybody here all the beer you can drink," Kimball promised. That was liable to be an expensive promise to keep, but he didn't care. Getting back to Charleston would make being poor for a while afterwards worthwhile and then some.

How long for a depth charge to reach the depth for which it was fused? The new pair seemed to be taking forever. Maybe they were duds, Kimball thought. The damnyankees couldn't have come up with a way to make them work all the time . . . could they?

Wham! Wham! Maybe they could. "Jesus!" Tom Brearley exclaimed. "That took forever!" Kimball wasn't the only one for whom time had stretched like a rubber band, then. The exec turned to him with a smile as radiant as any worn, greasy man could show in that light. "Well ahead of us, both of 'em, sir."

"Yeah," Kimball said, as if he hadn't just bet his life and won. "Now we sit here for as long as the batteries will let us and wait for our little friends up there to get tired and go away. How long *can* we wait, Tom?"

Brearley checked the gauges. "It would be longer if we hadn't tried that sprint after we sank the destroyer, sir, but we've got charge enough for five or six hours."

"Should be enough," Kimball said jovially. *It had better be enough,* echoed in his mind. He took a deep breath and made a face. "Things'll stink too bad for us to stand it any longer'n that, regardless." That was phrased like a joke and got laughs like a joke, but it wasn't a joke, and everybody knew it. The longer you sat submerged, the fouler the air got. That was part of the nature of the boat.

Five and a half hours after the *Bonefish* sank its target, Ben Coulter found he couldn't keep a candle alight in the close, nasty atmosphere inside the pressure hull. "If we had a canary in here, sir, it would have fallen off its perch a hell of a long time ago," he said to Kimball.

"Yeah," the captain answered. His head ached. He could feel

how slowly he was thinking. He nodded to Brearley. "Blow forward tanks, Tom. Bring her up to periscope depth."

A long, careful scan showed nothing on the horizon. Kimball ordered the *Bonefish* to the surface. Wearily, he climbed the ladder to the top of the conning tower, the exec close behind him to make sure the pressurized air didn't blow him out the hatch when he opened it.

When he did undog the hatch, his stomach did its best to crawl up his throat: all the stenches so long trapped inside the submersible seemed ten times worse when they rushed out in a great vile gale and mixed in his lungs with the first precious breath of fresh, clean sea air. Fighting down his gorge, he climbed another couple of rungs and looked around. Late-afternoon sunshine felt as savagely bright as it did during a hangover. The ocean was wide and empty. "Made it again, boys," he said. The crew cheered.

XVIII

Maria Tresca fiddled microscopically with Flora Hamburger's hat. The Italian woman stepped back to survey the results. "Better," she said, although Flora, checking the mirror, doubted the naked eye could tell the difference between the way the hat had looked before and how it did now.

"Remember," Herman Bruck said, "Daniel Miller isn't stupid. If you make a mistake in this debate, he'll hurt you with it."

He looked and sounded anxious. Had he been running against the appointed Democratic congressman, he probably would have made just such a mistake. Maybe he sensed that about himself and set on Flora's shoulders his worries about what he would have done.

"It will be all right, Herman," she said patiently. She sounded more patient than she was, and knew it. Beneath her pearl-buttoned shirtwaist, beneath the dark gray pinstriped jacket she wore over it, her heart was pounding. Class warfare in the USA hadn't reached the point of armed struggle. The confrontation ahead, though, was as close an approach as the country had yet seen. Democrat versus Socialist, established attorney against garment worker's daughter . . . here was the class struggle in action.

Someone pounded on the dressing-room door. "Five minutes, Miss Hamburger!" the manager of the Thalia Theatre shouted, as if she were one of the vaudevillians who usually performed here on Bowery. She felt as jumpy as any of those performers on opening night. The manager, who stomped around as if he had weights in his shoes, clumped down the hall and shouted, "Five minutes, Mr. Miller!"

Those last minutes before the debate went by in a blur. The next thing Flora knew, there she stood behind a podium on stage, staring out over the footlights at the packed house: a fuller house than vaudeville usually drew, which was the main reason the manager had rented out the hall tonight. There in the second row sat her parents, her sisters—Sophie with little Yossel in her arms—and her brothers.

And here, at the other podium to her right, stood Congressman Daniel Miller, appointed to the seat she wanted. He wasn't quite so handsome and debonair as his campaign posters made him out to be, but who was? He looked clever and alert, and the Democrats had the money and the connections to make a strong campaign for whatever candidate they chose.

Up in between the two candidates strode Isidore Rothstein, the Democratic Party chairman for the Fourteenth Ward. A coin toss had made him master of ceremonies rather than his Socialist opposite number. More tosses had determined that Miller would speak first and Flora last.

Rothstein held up his hands. The crowd quieted. "Tonight, we see democracy in action," he said, making what Flora thought of as unfair use of his party's name. "In the middle of the greatest war the world has ever known, we come together here to decide which way our district should go, listening to both sides to come to a fair decision."

Here and there, people in the crowd applauded. Flora wondered how much anything they did here tonight would really matter. The Democrats would keep a strong majority in Congress unless the sky fell. One district—what was one district? But Myron Zuckerman had spent his whole adult life working to improve the lot of the common people. His legacy would be wasted if this Democrat kept this seat to which he had been appointed. Plenty of reason there alone to fight.

"And now," Isidore Rothstein thundered, a bigger voice than had any business coming out of his plump little body, "Congressman Daniel Miller!" Democrats in the crowd cheered. Socialists hissed and whistled.

Miller said, "Under Teddy Roosevelt, the Democrats have given every American a square deal. We are pledged to an honest day's pay for an honest day's work, to treating every individual as an individual and as he deserves"—the code phrase Democrats used when they explained why they were against labor unions— "to the rights of cities and counties and states to govern themselves as far as possible, and to—"

"What about the war?" a Socialist heckler shouted. Before the debate, the two parties had solemnly agreed not to harass each other's candidates. Both sides had sounded very sincere. Flora hadn't taken it seriously, and didn't expect the Democrats had, either.

Daniel Miller was certainly ready for the shout. "And to keeping the commitments made long ago to our friends and allies, I was about to say," he went on smoothly. "For years, the USA was surrounded by our enemies: by the Confederacy and Canada and England and France, even by the Japanese. Germany was in the same predicament on the European continent. We are both reaching out together for our rightful places in the sun. Not only that, we are *winning* this war. It hasn't been so easy as we thought it would be, but what war is? To quit now would be to leave poor Kaiser Bill in the lurch, fighting England and France and Russia all alone, or near enough as makes no difference, and to guarantee that the old powers will hold us down for another fifty years. Do you want that?" He stuck out his chin. In profile, as Flora saw him, his jawline sagged, but from the front he probably looked most impressively political.

She made her own opening statement. "We are winning this war, Mr. Miller says." She wouldn't call him *Congressman*. "If you want to buy a pound of meat, you can go down to the butcher's shop and get it. If you have to pay twenty dollars for it, you begin to wonder if it's worth the price. Here we are, almost two and a half years into a fight the Socialist Party never wanted, and what have we got to show for it? Quebec City is still Canadian. Montreal is still Canadian. Toronto is still Canadian. Winnipeg is still Canadian. Richmond is still Confederate. Our own capital is still in Confederate hands, for heaven's sake.

"And Nashville is still Confederate. Just this past week, the brilliant General Custer, the heroic General Custer, attacked again. And what did he get? Half a mile of ground, moving *away* from Nashville, mind you, not toward it. And what was the cost? Another division thrown away. Three-quarters of a million dead since 1914, two million wounded, half a million in the enemy's prisoner-of-war camps. *Poor* Kaiser Bill!" Her voice dripped venom.

"And will you have all those brave men die in vain?" Daniel Miller demanded. "Will you have the United States abandon the struggle before it's over, go back to our old borders, tell our enemies, 'Oh, we're sorry; we didn't really mean it'?" He was sarcastic himself. "Once you've begun a job of work, you don't leave it in the middle. We have given as good as we've got; we have given better than we've got. The Canucks are tottering; the Confederates are about to put rifles into black men's hands. We are *winning*, I tell you."

"So what?" Flora said. The blunt question seemed to catch her opponent by surprise. She repeated it: "So what? What can we win that will bring those boys back to life? What can we win that's worth a hundredth part of what they paid? Even if we make the CSA make peace instead of the other way round, what difference does it make? Two thousand years ago, there was a king who looked around after a battle and cried out, 'One more victory like this and I am ruined!' He could see. He gave up the war. Is the Democratic Party full of blind men?"

"No. We're full of men who remember what happened in 1862, who remember what happened twenty years later," Miller shot back. "We're full of men who believe the United States of America must never be humiliated again, men who believe we must ten times never humiliate ourselves."

"A man who makes a mistake and backs away from it has sense," Flora said. "A man who makes a mistake and keeps on with it is a fool. We—"

"Traitor!" came a voice from the crowd. "You're just a woman. What do you know about what war costs?"

Tight-lipped, Flora pointed to her family. "Sophie, stand up." Her sister did, still holding little Yossel. "There's my nephew," Flora said into sudden silence. "He'll never know his father, who died on the Roanoke front." She pointed again. "David, stand up." The older of her two brothers rose, wearing U.S. green-gray. "Here is my brother. He has leave. He's just finished his training. He goes to the front day after tomorrow. I know what this war costs."

The crowd applauded. To her surprise, the heckler subsided.

She'd thought the Democrats would have pests more consistent than that fellow.

No matter. She turned to—turned on—Daniel Miller. "You love the war so well, *Congressman*." Now she did use the title, etching it with acid. "Where are *your* hostages to fortune?"

Miller was a little too old to be conscripted himself. He had no brothers. His wife, a woman who looked to be very nice, sat in the audience not far from Flora's family. With her were her two sons, the older of whom might have been thirteen. Flora had known the Democratic appointee couldn't well come back if she raised the question, and she'd been hoping she'd get or be able to make the chance to do it.

And, just for a moment, her opponent's composure cracked. "I honorably served my time in the United States Army," he said. "I yield to no one in—"

"Nobody was shooting at you then!" Four people, from four different sections of the hall, shouted the same thing at the same time. A storm of applause rose up behind them. Miller looked as if he'd had one of his fancy clients stand up in court and confess: betrayed by circumstances over which he had no control.

The debate went on. Daniel Miller even made a few points about what a Democratic congressman could do for his district that a Socialist couldn't hope to match. "Wouldn't you like to have the majority on your side again?" he asked, almost wistfully. It was not the best question, not in a hall full of Jews. When, since the fall of the Second Temple, had they had the majority on their side? And, after the blow Flora had got in, it mattered little.

At last, like a referee separating two weary prizefighters, Isidore Rothstein came out again. "I know you'll all vote next month," he told the crowd. "I expect you'll vote the patriotic way." Flora glared at the Democratic Party chairman. He had no business—no business but the business of politics—getting in a dig like that.

Now more like a corner man than a referee, Rothstein led Miller away. Flora had to go offstage by herself. Only when she was walking down the dark, narrow corridor to the dressing room did she fully realize what she'd done. Her feet seemed to float six inches above the filthy boards of the floor.

When she opened the door, Maria Tresca leaped out and embraced her. "It's ours!" she exclaimed. "You did it!"

Right behind her, Herman Bruck agreed. "His face looked like curdled milk when you reminded people he has no personal stake in watching the war go on."

"That stupid Democratic heckler gave me the opening I needed," Flora said. "Rothstein must be throwing a fit in the other dressing room."

Maria looked at Bruck. Bruck looked uncommonly smug, even for him. "That was no stupid Democrat. That was my cousin Mottel, and I told him what to say and when to say it."

Flora stared at him, then let out a shriek, then kissed him on the cheek. "Shall we go out and have supper to celebrate?"

She thought she'd meant the invitation to include Maria, too, but Maria didn't seem to think so. And Flora discovered she didn't mind. Herman Bruck had just given her the congressional seat on a silver platter. If that didn't deserve a dinner what did?

Besides, she always had her hatpin, if she felt like using it. Maybe she wouldn't.

"We've got to hold this town, boys," Lieutenant Jerome Nicoll said. "Below Waurika, there's no more Sequoyah left, not hardly. There's just the Red River, and then there's Texas. The whole Confederacy is depending on us. If the damnyankees push over the river and into Texas, you can kiss Sequoyah good-bye when the war is done."

"Wish I could kiss Sequoyah good-bye right now," Reginald Bartlett muttered under his breath. "Wish I was back in Virginia."

Napoleon Dibble gaped. "You wish you was back on the Roanoke front, Reggie?" He sounded as if he thought Bartlett was crazy.

Had Reggie wished that, he would have been crazy. "No. I wish I was back in Richmond, where I came from." Dibble nodded, enlightened, or as enlightened as he got. Under his breath, Reggie went on, "The other thing I wish is that Lieutenant Nicoll would get himself a new speech."

Nap Dibble didn't hear him, but Sergeant Hairston did. "Yeah," he said. "We got to hold this, we got to hold that. Then what the hell happens when we don't hold? We supposed to go off and shoot ourselves?"

"If we don't hold a place, the damnyankees usually shoot a lot of us," Bartlett said, which made Pete Hairston laugh but which was also unpleasantly true. The regiment—the whole division— had taken a lot of casualties trying to halt the U.S. drive toward the Red River.

An aeroplane buzzed overhead. Reggie started to unsling his rifle to take a shot at it: it wasn't flying very high, for gray clouds filled the sky. But it carried the Confederate battle flag under its wings. He stared at it in tired wonder. The USA didn't have many aeroplanes out here in the West, but the CSA had even fewer.

Hoping it would do the damnyankees some harm, he forgot about it and marched on toward Waurika. The town's business district lay in a hollow, with houses on the surrounding hills. "We'll have to hold the Yanks up here," he said, as much to himself as to anyone else. "We go down there into that bowl, we're going to get pounded to death."

As had been true up in Wilson Town, not all the civilians had fled from Waurika. Most of the men and women who came out of the houses to look over the retreating Confederates had dark skins: Waurika, Lieutenant Nicoll had said, was about half Kiowa, half Comanche. Reggie couldn't have told one bunch from the other to save himself from the firing squad.

Some of the civilians had skins darker than copper: the Indians' Negro servants. Most of those, or at least most of the ones Bartlett saw, were women. The men had probably been impressed into labor service already: either that or they'd run off toward the Yankees or toward the forests and swamps of the Red River bottom country, where a man who knew how to live off the land could fend for himself for a long time.

More than a few Indians, men wearing homespun and carrying hunting rifles, tried to fall in with the column of Confederate soldiers. "You braves don't know what you're getting into," Lieutenant Nicoll told them. "This isn't any kind of fighting you've ever seen before, and if the damnyankees catch you shooting at them without wearing a uniform, they'll kill you for it."

"What will the Yankees do to us if they take this land?" one of the Indians answered. "We do not want to be in the USA."

"Our grandfathers have told us how bad the living was under the Stars and Stripes," another Indian agreed. "We want to stay under the Stars and Bars." He pointed toward the business section of Waurika, where several Confederate flags flew in spite of the threatening weather.

At that moment, the weather stopped threatening and started delivering chilly rain mixed with sleet. Shivering, Bartlett consoled himself with the thought that the rain would be harder on the Yankees, who would have to fight their way through it, than on his own unit, which had already reached the place it needed to defend.

Sergeant Hairston spoke in a low, urgent voice: "Sir, you can't give them redskins any stretch of line to hold. They ain't soldiers."

"We are warriors," one of the Indians said proudly. "The tribes in the east of Sequoyah have their own armies allied to the Stars and Bars."

"I've heard about that," Nicoll said. "Isn't anything like it hereabouts, though." He scowled, visibly of two minds. At last, he went on, "You want to fight?" The Indians gathered round him made it loudly clear they did indeed want to fight. He held up a hand. "All right. This is what we'll do. You go out in front of the line we'll hold. You snipe at the damnyankees and bring us back word of what they're doing and how they're moving. Don't let yourselves get captured. You get in trouble, run back to the front. Is it a bargain?"

"We know this country," one of the Indians answered. "The soldiers in the uniforms the color of horse shit will not find us." The rest of the men from Waurika nodded, then trotted quietly north, in the direction from which the U.S. soldiers would come.

Reggie turned to Nap Dibble. "The damnyankees may not find 'em, but what about machine-gun bullets? I don't care how brave or how smart you are, and a machine gun doesn't care, either." He spoke with the grim certainty of a man who had been through the machine-gun hell of the Roanoke River valley.

All Nap Dibble knew was the more open fighting that characterized the Sequoyah front. No: he knew one thing more. "Better them'n us," he said, and, taking out his entrenching tool, began to dig in.

Along with using the Indians of Waurika as scouts and snipers, Lieutenant Nicoll used the few Negro men left in town as laborers. None of the Indian women and old men left behind objected. No one asked the Negroes' opinions. With shovels and hoes and mattocks, they began helping the Confederate soldiers make entrenchments in the muddy ground.

Once there were holes in which the men of Nicoll's company could huddle, the lieutenant set the blacks to digging zigzag communications trenches back toward a second line. "Lawd have mercy, suh," one of them said, "you gwine work us to death."

"You don't know what death is, not till the Yankees start shelling you," Nicoll answered. Then his voice went even colder than the weather: "Weren't for the way you niggers rose up last winter, the Confederate States wouldn't be in the shape they're in."

"Weren't us, suh," said the Negro who had spoken before. "Onliest Reds in Sequoyah, they's Indians, and they was born that way." The other black men impressed into labor nodded emphatic agreement.

"Likely tell," Nicoll said, dismissing their contention with a toss of the head. "You want to show me you're good, loyal Confederates, you dig now and help your country's soldiers beat the Yanks."

Sullenly, the Negroes dug alongside the soldiers. Bartlett began to hope the Confederates around Waurika would have the rest of the day and the whole night in which to prepare their position for the expected U.S. onslaught. Having slogged through a lot of mud himself, he knew what kind of time the Yankee troops would be having.

But, a little past three in the afternoon, a brisk crackle of small-arms fire broke out ahead of the line. He found himself in a trench and peering out over the parapet almost before he realized he'd heard the rifles. Some of the reports were strange; not all rifles sounded exactly like the Tredegars and Springfields with which he'd been so familiar for so long.

Machine guns were heavy. Units not of the first quality—which, on the Sequoyah front, meant a lot of units—didn't make sure they kept up with the head of an advancing column. But that malignant hammering started only moments after the rifle fire broke out.

"Now we see what kind of balls the redskins have," Sergeant Hairston said with a sort of malicious anticipation. "Warriors!" He hawked and spat in the mud.

Here came the Kiowas and Comanches, running back toward the hastily dug entrenchments. Behind them, trudging across the fields, firing as they advanced, were U.S. soldiers. An Indian fell, then another one. An Indian leaped into the trench near Bartlett. "Why do you not shoot at them?" he demanded. "Do you want them to kill us all?"

"No," Reggie answered. "What we want is for them to get close enough for us to hurt 'em bad when we do open up. Fire discipline, it's called."

The Indian stared at him without comprehension. But when the Confederate company did open up with rifles and machine guns and a couple of trench mortars, the U.S. soldiers went down as if scythed. Not all of them, Reggie knew, would be hit; more were taking whatever cover they could find. But the advance stopped.

More Indians jumped into the trenches with the Confederates. They kept on shooting at the Yankees, and showed as much spirit as the men alongside whom they fought. "Maybe they are warriors," Bartlett said.

Sergeant Hairston nodded. "Yeah, maybe they are. I tell you one thing, though, Bartlett. They give the niggers guns the way it looks like they're gonna, them coons ain't never gonna fight this good."

Reggie thought about that. The Kiowas and Comanches— most of the Indians in Sequoyah—had done pretty well for themselves under the rule of the Great White Father in Richmond. As these young men had said, they wanted to stay under the Stars and Bars.

How many Negroes wanted the same thing? "Maybe they'll fight for the chance to turn into real citizens," he said at last.

"Shitfire, who wants niggers voting?" Hairston exclaimed. Since Reggie himself was a long way from thrilled at the idea of their voting, he kept quiet. It all seemed abstract anyhow. Wondering about if and how soon the Yankees would be able to haul their artillery forward through the thickening muck was a much more immediate concern.

Riding a swaybacked horse he'd no doubt rented at the St. Matthews livery stable, Tom Colleton came slowly up the path toward the ruins of Marshlands. Anne Colleton stood waiting for her brother, her hands on her hips. When he got close enough for her to call out to him, she said, "You might have let me known you were coming before you telephoned the train station. I would have come to get you in the motorcar."

"Sis, I tried to wire you, but they told me the lines out from St. Matthews weren't up or had gone down again or some such," Tom answered. "When I got into town, I telephoned just on the off chance—I didn't really expect to get you. I was all set to show up and surprise you."

"I believe it," Anne answered. Tom had always been one to do things first and sort out the consequences later. She pointed to the wire than ran to the cabin where she lived these days. "They finally put that in last week. If you knew what I had to go through to get it—"

"Can't be worse than Army red tape," Tom said as he swung down from the horse. He looked fit and dashing and alert; his right hand never strayed far from the pistol on his hip. The scar on his cheek wasn't pink and fresh any more.

He also wore two stars on either side of his stand collar. "You've been promoted!" Anne exclaimed.

He gave a little bow, as a French officer might have done. "Lieutenant-Colonel Colleton at your service, ma'am," he said. "My regiment happened to find a hole in the Yankee lines up on the Roanoke, and they pushed forward half a mile at what turned out to be exactly the right time." He touched one of the stars signifying his new rank, then the other. "Each of these cost me about a hundred and fifty men, killed and wounded."

Slowly, Anne nodded. Tom had gone into the war as a lark, an adventure. A lot had changed in the past two years.

A lot had changed here, too. He strode up to her and gave her a brotherly embrace, but his eyes remained on what had been the family mansion. "Those sons of bitches," he said in a flat, hard voice, and then, "Well, from what I hear, they paid for it ten times over."

"Maybe not so much as that," Anne said, "but they paid." She cocked her head to one side and sent him a curious glance. "And you're one of the people who want to put guns in niggers' hands?"

He nodded. "For one thing, we're running out of white men to be soldiers," he said, and Anne nodded in turn, remembering President Semmes' words. Tom went on, "For another, if niggers have a stake in the Confederate States, maybe they won't try and pull them down around our ears. We smashed this rebellion, sure, but that doesn't mean we won't have another one ten years from now if things don't change."

"This one's smashed, but it's not dead," she said. "Cassius is still out in the swamps by the river, and the militiamen they've sent after him and his friends haven't been able to smoke them out."

"He's the kind of nigger I wish we had in the Army," Tom said. "He'd make one fine scout and sniper."

"Unless he decided to shoot at you instead of the damn-yankees," Anne answered, which made her brother grimace. Then, suddenly, she noticed a new ribbon in the fruit salad above Tom's left breast pocket. Her eyes widened. Pointing to it, she said, "That's an Order of Lee, and you weren't going to say a thing about it."

She'd succeeded in embarrassing him. "I didn't want to worry you," he replied, which went a long way toward explaining the circumstances under which he'd won it. The Order of Lee was the Army equivalent of Roger Kimball's Order of the *Virginia*: only one step down from the Confederate Cross.

"I've been worried from the beg—" Anne started to say, but that wasn't quite true: in the beginning, she, like most in the CSA, had thought they'd lick the Yankees as quickly and easily as they had in their first two wars. She made the needed change: "I've been worried for a long time."

Julia came up to them then, her baby on her hip. "Mistuh Tom, we got yo' cabin ready fo' you."

"That's good," he answered. "Thank you." He spoke to her in a tone slightly different from the one he would have used before the war started, even if the words might have been the same then. In 1914, he would have taken the service completely for granted; now, he spoke of it as if she was doing him a favor. Anne found herself using that tone with blacks these days, too, and noticed it in others.

Tom went back to his horse, detached the saddlebags and bedroll from the saddle, and carried them while he walked after Julia. In 1914, a Negro would have dashed up to relieve him of them. If he missed that level of deference, he didn't show it.

And, before he went into the cabin, he asked, "You're not putting anyone out so I can stay in here, are you?"

"No, suh," the serving woman answered. "Ain't so many folks here as used to be."

"I see that." Tom glanced over at Anne. "It's a wonder you've done as much as you have out here by yourself."

"You do what you have to do," she said, at which he nodded again. Before the war, that hard logic had meant nothing to him. The Roanoke front had given him more than rank and decorations; he understood and accepted the ways of the world these days. As soon as Julia went out of earshot, she continued, in a lower voice, "We made a bargain of sorts—they do the work that needs to be done, and I make sure nobody from St. Matthews or Columbia comes around prying into what they did during the rebellion."

"You said something about that in one of your letters," Tom answered, remembering. "Best you could do, I suppose, but there are some niggers I wouldn't have made that bargain with. Cassius, for one."

"Even if you'd want him for a soldier?" Anne asked, gently mocking.

"Especially because I'd want him for a soldier," her brother said. "I know a dangerous man when I see one."

"I have no bargain with Cassius," Anne said quietly. "Every so often, livestock here—disappears. I don't *know* where it goes, but I can guess. Not that much to eat in the swamps of the Congaree, even for niggers used to living off the land."

"That's so," Tom agreed. "And he'll have friends among the hands here. Sis, I really wish you weren't out here by your lonesome."

"If I'm not, this place goes to the devil," Anne said. "I didn't get a great crop from it, but I got a crop. That gave me some of the money I needed to pay the war taxes, and it meant I didn't have to cut so far into my investments as I would have otherwise. I don't intend to be a beggar when the war ends, and I don't intend for you to be a beggar, either."

"If the choice is between being being rich and being a beggar, that's one thing, Sis," he said. "If the choice is between being a beggar and being dead, that's a different game." His face, its expression already far more stern than it had been before the war, turned bleak as the oncoming winter. "That's what the Confederate States are looking at right now, seems to me: a choice between being beggars and being dead."

He walked up into the cottage. Anne followed him. He tossed the saddlebags and bedroll onto the floor next to the iron-framed cot on which he'd sleep. Looking around, he shook his head. "It's not the way it was any more," he said, half to himself. "Nothing is the way it was any more."

"No," Anne said. "It's not. But—I talked with President Semmes not so long ago. He's worried, yes, but not *that* worried." She checked herself; if the president hadn't been *that* worried, would he have introduced the bill calling for Negro troops? Trying to look on the bright side, she pointed to Tom's tunic. "That was a victory, there in the valley."

"And it makes one," her brother answered bitterly. "I pray to God we can hold the ground we gained, too. We need every man in the CSA at the front, and we need every man in the CSA working behind the lines so the men at the front have something to shoot at the damnyankees. If everybody could be two places at once twenty-four hours a day, we'd be fine."

"That's why the president wants to give the blacks guns," she said.

"I understand." He sounded impatient with her, something he'd rarely done . . . before the war, that endlessly echoed phrase. "We've put them in the factories to make up for the white men who've gone. Maybe we can put enough women in to make up for the niggers. Maybe."

She didn't want to argue with him any more. "Supper soon," she said. "Come over to my cottage and we'll talk more then. Get yourself settled in for now."

"For now," he repeated. "I've got to catch the train day after tomorrow." He sighed. "No rest for the weary."

Supper was fried chicken, greens, and pumpkin pie, with apple brandy that had no tax stamp on it to wash down the food. "It's not what I would have given you if things were different," Anne said, watching with something like awe as the mountain of chicken bones on her brother's plate grew and grew. "No fancy banquets these days, though."

"It's nigger food," Tom said, and then held up a hand against the temper that sparked in her eyes. "Wait, Sis. Wait. It's good. It's a hundred times better than what I eat at the front. Don't you worry about it for a minute." He patted his belly, which should have bulged visibly from what he'd put away but somehow didn't.

"What are we going to do?" she said. "If this is the best we can hope for once the war is over, is it worth going on?"

"Kentucky is a state in the United States again," Tom said quietly. "The Yankees say it is, anyhow, and they have some traitors there who go along with them. The best may not be as good as we hoped when we set out to fight, but the worst is worse than we ever reckoned it could be." He yawned, then got up, walked over to her, and kissed her on the cheek. "I'm going to bed, Sis—can't hold 'em open any more. You don't have to worry about anything tonight—I'm here." He walked out of the cottage into the darkness.

Julia took away the dishes. Anne got into a long cotton nightgown, blew out the lamps, and lay down. Off in the distance, an owl hooted. Off farther in the distance, a rifle cracked, then another, than a short volley. Silence returned. She shrugged. Ordinary noises of the night. As always, her pistol lay where she could reach it. She even carried the revolver when she needed to go to the outhouse instead of using the pot, though it was no good against moths and spiders.

Did she feel safer because her brother was here? Yes, she decided: now there were two guns on which she could rely absolutely. Did she feel he was taking on the job of protecting her, so she wouldn't even have to think of such things as long as he was nearby? Laughing at the absurdity of the notion, she rolled over and went to sleep.

*   *   *

George Enos was swabbing the deck on the starboard side of the USS *Ericsson* when shouts of alarm rang out to port: "Torpedo!" He jumped as if someone had stabbed him with a pin. As klaxons began to hoot, he sprinted toward his battle station, a one-pounder antiaircraft gun not far from the depth-charge launcher at the stern of the destroyer. Someone, by some accident, had actually read his file and given him a job he knew how to do. The one-pounder wasn't that different from an outsized machine gun.

"Torpedo!" The shouts grew louder. The *Ericsson*'s deck throbbed under Enos' feet as the engines came up to full power from cruising speed. Thick, black smoke poured from the stacks. The smoke poured back toward him. He coughed and tried to breathe as little as he could.

The deck heeled sharply as the destroyer swung into a tight turn. The turn was to the right, not to the left as he'd expected. "We're heading into the track," he shouted.

At the launcher, Carl Sturtevant nodded. "If it misses us, we charge down the wake and pay the submarine a visit," the petty officer said.

"Yeah," George said. If it missed them, that was what would happen. But it was likelier to hit them when they were running toward it than if they'd chosen to run away. Enos did his best not to think about that. He was sure the whole crew of the *Ericsson*—including Captain Fleming, who'd ordered the turn—were doing their best not to think about that.

He peered ahead, though the destroyer's superstructure blocked his view of the most critical area. His fate rested on decisions over which he had no control and which he could not judge till afterwards. He hated that. So did every other Navy man with whom he'd ever spoken, both on the Mississippi and out here in the Atlantic.

Something moving almost impossibly fast shot by the onrushing *Ericsson*, perhaps fifty feet to starboard of her. Staring at the creamy wake, George sucked in a long breath, not caring any more how smoky it was. "Missed," he said with fervent delight. "Is that the only fish they launched at us?"

"Don't hear 'em yelling about any others," Sturtevant said.

Lieutenant Crowder came running toward the stern. "Load it up!" he shouted to Sturtevant and his comrades. "We'll make 'em pay for taking a shot at us."

"Yes, sir." Sturtevant sounded less optimistic than his superior. The depth-charge launcher was a new gadget, the *Ericsson* one of the first ships in the Navy to use it instead of simply rolling the ashcans off the stern. Like a lot of new gadgets, it worked pretty well most of the time. Like a lot of sailors, George Enos among them, Sturtevant was conservative enough to find that something less than adequate.

Like a lot of young lieutenants, Crowder was enamored of anything and everything new, for no better reason than that it *was* new. He said, "By throwing the charges off to the side, we don't have to sail right over the sub and lose hydrophone contact with it."

"Yes, sir," Sturtevant said again. His mouth twisted. George understood that, too. A hydrophone could give you a rough bearing on a submersible. What it couldn't tell you was where along that bearing the damn thing lurked.

An officer on the bridge waved his hat to Lieutenant Crowder. "Launch!" Crowder shouted, as if the depth-charge crew couldn't figure out what that meant for themselves.

The launcher roared. The depth charge spun through the air, then splashed into the sea. Carl Sturtevant's lips moved. In the racket, George couldn't hear what he said, but he saw the shape of the words. *Here goes nothing*—and it was just as well that Lieutenant Crowder couldn't read lips. Another depth charge flew. The chances of hitting a submarine weren't quite zero, but they weren't good. The charge had to go off within fifteen feet of a sub to be sure of wrecking it, though it might badly damage a boat at twice that range. Since the destroyer and the submersible were both moving, hits were as much luck as in a blindfold rock fight.

As the third depth charge arced away from the *Ericsson*, water boiled up from the explosion of the first one. "Damnation!" Lieutenant Crowder shouted: only white water, nothing more. By the disappointed look on his face, he'd expected a kill on his very first try.

Another charge flew. The second one went off, down below

the surface of the sea. Another seething mass of white water appeared, and then a great burst of bubbles and an oil slick that helped calm both the normal chop of the Atlantic and the turbulence the bubbles had kicked up.

"Hit!" Crowder and Sturtevant and the rest of the depth-charge crew and George all screamed the word at the same time. Skepticism forgotten, Sturtevant planted a reverent kiss on the oily metal side of the depth-charge launcher.

More bubbles rose from the stricken submersible, and more oil, too. Peering out into the ocean, George was the first to spy the dark shape rising through the murky water. "Here he comes, the son of a bitch," he said, and turned the one-pounder in the direction of the submersible. The gun was intended for aeroplanes, but Moses hadn't come down from the mountain saying you couldn't shoot it at anything else.

Vaster than a broaching whale, the crippled sub surfaced. English? French? Confederate? George didn't know or care. It was the enemy. The men inside had done their best to kill him. Their best hadn't been good enough. Now it was his turn.

Some of the enemy sailors still had fight in them. They ran across the hull toward the submersible's deck gun. George opened up with the one-pounder before Lieutenant Crowder screamed, "Rake 'em!"

Shell casings leaped from George's gun. It fired ten-round clips, as if it were an overgrown rifle. One of the rounds hit an enemy sailor. George had never imagined what one of those shells could do to a human body. One instant, the fellow was dashing along the dripping hull. The next, his entire midsection exploded into red mist. His legs ran another stride and a half before toppling.

George picked up another clip—it hardly seemed to weigh anything—and slammed it into the one-pounder. He blew another man to pieces, but most of the clip went to chewing up the submersible's conning tower. The sub wouldn't be doing any diving, not if it was full of holes.

As he was reloading again, one of the *Ericsson*'s four-inch guns fired a shell into the ocean twenty yards in front of the submarine's bow, a warning shot that sent water fountaining up to drench the surviving men who had reached the deck gun. They didn't shoot back at the destroyer. Their hands went up in the air instead.

"Hold fire!" Lieutenant Crowder said. George obeyed. A moment later, a white flag waved from the top of the conning tower. More men started emerging from the hatch and standing on the hull, all of them with their hands raised in surrender.

Crowder used a pair of field glasses to read the name of the boat, which was painted on the side of the conning tower. *"Snook,"* he said. "She'll be a Confederate boat. They name 'em for fish, same as we do. Looks like a limey, don't she?"

Flags fluttered up on the *Snook's* signal lines. "He's asking if he can launch his boats," said Sturtevant, who had far more practice at reading them than did George.

Captain Fleming's answer came swiftly. Crowder read it before Sturtevant could: "Denied. We will take you off." He inspected the dejected crew of the submersible. "I don't see their captain, but they're all so frowzy he may be there anyhow."

Boats slid across the quarter-mile of water separating the *Ericsson* and the *Snook.* Confederate sailors were already boarding them when one more man burst from the submersible's hatchway and hurried onto one of them.

"There's the captain," Sturtevant said, and then, "She's sinking! The goddamn bastard opened the scuttling cocks. That's what he was doing down below so long. Ahh, hell, no way to save her." Sure enough, the *Snook* was quickly sliding down into the depths from which she had arisen. She would not rise again.

Up onto the deck of the *Ericsson* came the glum Confederates. U.S. sailors crowded round to see the men who had almost sunk them. The attitude of the victors was half relief, half professional respect. They knew the submariners could have won the duel as easily as not.

When the Confederate captain came aboard the destroyer, George's jaw fell. "Briggs!" he burst out. "Ralph Briggs!"

"Somebody here know me?" The Rebel officer looked around to see who had spoken.

"I sure do." George pushed through the crowd around the Confederates. His grin was enormous. "I'd better. I was one of the fishermen who helped sink you when you were skipper of the *Tarpon.*"

"What? We already captured this damn Reb once?" Lieutenant Crowder exclaimed. "Why the devil isn't he in a prisoner-of-war camp where he belongs, then?"

"Because I escaped, that's why." Briggs stood straighter. "International law says you can't do anything to me on account of it, either."

"We could toss him in the drink and let him swim to shore," Carl Sturtevant said, without the slightest smile to suggest he was joking.

George shook his head. "When he was going to sink my trawler, he let the crew take to the boats. He played square."

"Besides, if we ditched him, we'd have to ditch the whole crew," Lieutenant Crowder said. "Too many people would know, somebody would get drunk and tell the story, and the Entente papers would scream like nobody's business. They're prisoners, and we're stuck with 'em." He pointed to the Confederate submariners, then jerked a thumb toward the nearest hatch. "You men go below—and this time, Briggs, we'll make damn sure you don't get loose before the war is done."

"You can try," the submersible skipper answered. "My duty is to escape if I can." He nodded to George Enos. "I wish I'd never seen you once, let alone twice, but I do thank you for speaking up for me there."

George looked him in the eye. "If you were the skipper of the damn commerce raider that got my fishing boat when I was still a civilian, you'd be swimming now, for all of me."

"Get moving," Lieutenant Crowder said again, and, along with his crew, Ralph Briggs headed for the—

"The brig. Briggs is going to the brig," George said, and laughed as the Confederates, one by one, went down the hatchway and disappeared.

Standing in Bay View Park, Chester Martin peered east across the Maumee River to the Toledo, Ohio, docks. Mist that was turning to drizzle kept him from seeing as much as he would have liked, but a couple of light cruisers from the Lake Erie fleet were in port, resupplying so they could go off and bombard the southern coast of Ontario again.

Martin turned to his younger sister. "You know what, Sue? This business of watching the war from the far side of the river is a . . . lot more fun than being in it up close." The pause came from his swallowing a pungent intensifier or two. In the trenches, he cursed as automatically as he breathed. He'd horrified his mother a couple of times, and now tried to watch himself around his female relatives.

Sue giggled. She'd caught the hesitation. She found his profanity more funny than horrifying, but then she was of his generation. They shared a sharp-nosed, sharp-chinned family look, though Sue's hair was brown, not sandy heading toward red like his.

She said, "I'm just sorry you had to get hurt so you could come home for a while."

"Oh, I knew it was a hometowner as soon as I got it," he said, exaggerating only a little. "Never worried about it for a minute. Now that my arm's out of the sling, I expect they'll be sending me back to the front before too long."

"I wish they wouldn't," she said, and took his good right hand in both of hers. She was careful with his left arm, even if he'd finally had it released from its cloth cocoon.

From behind him, a gruff voice said, "You there, soldier— let's see your papers, and make it snappy."

Martin's turn was anything but snappy; it let the military policeman see the three stripes on his sleeve. The MP was only a private first class. He didn't worry about that, though, not with the law on his side. Martin was convinced the military police attracted self-righteous sons of bitches the way spilled sugar drew ants.

But this fellow wouldn't be able to give him a hard time. He took the necessary paperwork from a tunic pocket and handed it to the MP. "Convalescent leave, eh?" the fellow said. "We've seen some humbug documents of this sort lately, Sergeant. What would happen if I took you back to barracks and told you to show me a scar?"

"I'd do it, and you'd get your ass in a sling," Martin answered steadily. He looked the private first class up and down with the scorn most front-line soldiers felt for their not-quite-counterparts who hadn't seen real action. "Why is it, sonny boy, the only time you ever see a dead MP, he's got a Springfield bullet in him, not a Tredegar?"

Sue didn't get that. The military policeman did, and turned brick red. "I ought to keep these," he said, holding Martin's papers so the sergeant couldn't take them back.

"Go ahead," Martin said. "Let's head back to your barracks. We can both tell your commanding officer about it. Like I say, doesn't matter a bean's worth to me."

A soldier ready to go back to barracks and take his case to the officer of the day was not a spectacle the MP was used to. Angrily, he thrust Martin's papers back at him. Angrily, he stomped off, the soles of his boots slapping the bricks of the walkway.

"That's telling him," Sue said proudly, clutching her brother's arm. "He didn't have any business talking to you like that."

"He could ask for my papers, to make sure I'm not absent without leave," Martin said. "But when he got nasty afterwards—" He made a face. "He didn't have any call to do that, except he's a military policeman, and people have to do what he tells them."

"Like the Coal Board officials," Sue said. "And the Ration Board, and the Train Transportation Board, and the War Loan subscription committees, and—" She could have gone on. Instead, she said, "All those people were bad enough before the war. They're worse now, and there are more of them. And if you're not a big cheese yourself, they act like little tin gods and give you a nasty time just to show they can do it."

"Makes you wonder what the country's coming to sometimes, doesn't it?" Martin said. "Old people say there used to be more room to act the way you pleased, back before the Second Mexican War taught us how surrounded we are. Gramps would always go on about that, remember?"

She shook her head. "Not really. I was only six or seven when he died. What I remember about him was his peg leg, and how he always pretended he was a pirate on account of it."

"Yeah. He got hurt worse than I did, and the doctors in the War of Secession weren't as good as they are nowadays, either, I don't suppose. He used to talk about stacks of cut-off arms and legs outside the surgeons' tents after a battle."

Sue looked revolted. "Not with me, he didn't."

"You're a girl," Chester reminded her. "He used to tell me and Hank all the horrible stuff. We ate it up like gumdrops."

She sighed. "I was only seven when Henry died, too. What a

horrible year that was, everybody wailing all the time. I miss him sometimes, same as Gramps."

"I was—eleven? Twelve? Something like that," Martin said. "He was two years older than me, I know that much. I remember the way the doctor kept shaking his head. For all the good he did us, he might as well have been a Sioux medicine man. Scarlet fever, any of those things—I wish they could cure them, not just tell you what they are."

"He'd be in the Army, too—Henry, I mean." Sue's laugh was startled. "I don't think I ever thought of Henry all grown up till now."

"He'd be in the Army, all right," Chester agreed. "He'd be an officer, I bet. Hank was always sharp as a razor. People listened to him, too. I didn't—but I was his brother, after all." A chilly breeze from off the lake seemed to slice right through his uniform. "Brr! Enough sightseeing. Let's go home and sit in front of the fire."

They caught the trolley and went southwest down Summit, alongside the Maumee. After three or four miles, the trolley car turned inland and clattered past the county courthouse and, across the street from it, the big bronze statue of Remembrance, sword bared in her right hand.

Pointing to it, Sue said, "We just got some new stereoscope views of New York City. Now I know how good a copy of the statue on Bedloe's Island that one is, even if ours is only half as tall."

"We've still got a lot to pay people back for—the United States do, I mean," Martin said. Now he laughed. "I've got a Rebel to pay back, and I don't even know who he is."

The trolley took them over the Ottawa River, a smaller stream than the Maumee, and up into Ottawa Heights. The closest stop was three blocks from their apartment house. Chester remembered how cramped he'd felt in the flat before the war started. He had no more room now—less, in fact, because they'd had to make room for him when he came back to convalesce—but he didn't mind. After crowded barracks and insanely crowded bombproof shelters, a room of his own, even a small one, seemed luxury itself.

His mother—an older, graying version of Sue—all but pounced on him when he came in the door. "You have a letter here from the White House!" Louisa Martin exclaimed, thrusting the fancy envelope at him. The Martin family had a strong tradition of never opening one another's mail; that tradition, obviously, had never been so sorely tested as now.

"Don't be silly, Mother," Chester said. "The Rebs are still holding onto the White House." His mother glared at him, and with reason. Even if business got done in Philadelphia, Washington remained the capital of the USA.

Sue squeaked. "Open it!" she said, and then grabbed his arm so he couldn't.

He shook her off and did open the envelope. " 'Dear Sergeant Martin,' " he read from the typed letter, " 'I have learned you were wounded in action. Since you have defended not only the United States of America but also me personally on my visit to the Roanoke front, I dare hope my wishes for your quick and full recovery will be welcome. Sincerely yours, Theodore Roosevelt.' " The signature was in vivid blue ink.

"That's wonderful," Louisa Martin said softly. "TR keeps track of everything, doesn't he?"

"Seems to," Martin agreed. He kept staring at that signature. "Well, I was going to vote for him anyhow. Guess I'll have to vote twice now." If you knew the right people, in Toledo as in a good many other U.S. towns, you could do that, though he'd meant if for a joke.

His mother sighed. "One of these days, Ohio may get around to granting women's suffrage. Then you wouldn't need to vote twice."

Stephen Douglas Martin, Chester's father, came home from the mill about an hour later. "Well, well," he said, holding the letter from TR out at arm's length so he could read it. He was too old to worry about conscription, and had been promoted three times at work since the start of the war, when younger men with better jobs had to put on green-gray. "Ain't that somethin', Chester? Ain't that somethin'? We ought to frame this here letter and keep it safe so you can show it to your grandchildren."

"That would be something, Pop," Martin said. He thought of himself with gray hair and wrinkled skin, sitting in a rocking chair telling war stories to little boys in short pants. Gramps' stories had always been exciting, even the ones about how he'd lost his leg. Could Chester make life in the trenches exciting? Was it anything he'd want to tell his grandchildren? Maybe, if he could show them the president's letter.

"I'm proud of you, son," his father said. "The Second Mexican War was over before they called me up. My father fought for our country, and now you have, too. That's pretty fine."

"All right, Pop," Martin answered. For a moment, he wondered what his father would have said if he'd stopped that bullet with his head instead of his arm. Whatever it was, he wouldn't have been around to hear it.

"Supper!" his mother called. The ham steaks that went with the fried potatoes weren't very big—meat had got expensive as the dickens this past year, he'd heard a hundred times—but they were tasty. And there were plenty of potatoes in the big, black iron pan. She served Chester seconds of those, and then thirds.

"You're going to have to let out the pants on my uniform," he said, but all she did was nod—she was ready to do it. His father lighted a cigar, and passed one to him. The tobacco was sharp and rather nasty, but a cigar was a cigar. He leaned back in his chair as his mother and sister cleared away the dishes. For now, the front seemed far, far away. He tried to stretch each moment as long as he could.

"Come on!" Jake Featherston called to the gun crews of his battery. "We've got to keep moving." Rain poured down out of the sky. The southern Maryland road, already muddy, began turning to something more like glue, or maybe thick soup. "Come on!"

A whistle in the air swelled rapidly to a scream. A long-range shell from a Yankee gun burst about a hundred yards to Featherston's left. A great fountain of muck rose into the air. None splattered down on him, but that hardly mattered. He'd long since got as muddy as a human being could.

More U.S. shells descended, feeling for the road down which the First Richmond Howitzers were retreating. The damnyankee gunners couldn't quite find it. The barrage, instead of swinging west from where the first one hit, went east. That meant they'd probably find another road and hurt a different part of the Army of Northern Virginia. Jake didn't care. If he got out in one piece, he'd settle for that.

"Hey, Sarge!" Michael Scott said. With the shelling and the rain, the loader had to call two or three times to get Featherston's attention. When he finally had it, he asked, "What do we do when we get to the Potomac?"

"You think I'm the War Department, God damn them to hell?" Featherston answered. The War Department, and especially its upper echelons, did not contain his favorite people. "If the damnyankees' aeroplanes haven't bombed all the bridges to hell and gone, I reckon we cross over 'em and go back into Virginia."

"But what are we gonna do there?" Scott persisted.

"I told you, I'm not the goddamn War Department," Jake said. He shook his head, which made cold rainwater drip down the back of his neck. They wouldn't make him an officer, they didn't have the brains to notice when the niggers were going to rise up, and they were still in charge of running the war? Where was the justice in that? And his own men expected him to think like a fancy-pants Richmond general? Where was the justice in *that*?

"But, Sarge—" the loader said, like a little boy complaining when his mother wouldn't let him do what he wanted.

"All right," Featherston said wearily. "Here's what we do, you ask me. We cross the bridge, if it's still up there. All the artillery we've got goes into battery on the south bank. Soon as the last man from the Army of Northern Virginia comes out of Maryland, we drop the bridge right into the middle of the river, *bam*. Soon as the damnyankees get in range of our guns, we start plastering them, hard as we can. Those sons of bitches are already in the western part of the state. Sure as the devil don't want 'em getting a toehold anywhere else, do we?"

"Nope." Scott sounded—not happy now, but contented. He'd got Jake to tell him what he could have worked out for himself if he'd had an ounce of sense. Featherston shook his head again. More rainwater ran down his neck. What difference did that make, when he was already so soaked?

He cursed the Yankees, he cursed the mud, and he cursed the War Department, the last more sulfurously than either of the other two. "Christ, no wonder we're losing," he told the unheeding sky. "If the damn fools can't do the little things right, how are they supposed to do the big ones?" He supposed the United States Army was afflicted with a War Department, too, but somehow it seemed to be overcoming the handicap.

To make his joy with the world complete, the lead gun went into a puddle and bogged to the hubs. The horses strained in their harness, but it did no good. That gun wasn't going anywhere any time soon, not with just the team trying to get it out. And the others piled up in back of it.

Along with the rest of the gun crew, he lent his own strength to the work, pushing from behind as the horses pulled. The gun remained stuck. Jake spotted Metellus, the cook, lounging on the limber that traveled behind the gun. "Get your black ass up here and do something to help, damn you," he snarled. "The Yankees do find this here road with their guns, the shells won't care what color you are. They'll blow you up, same as me." His grin was ferocious. "If that ain't nigger equality, I don't know what the hell is."

Metellus got down and got as dirty as any of the white men, but the gun wouldn't budge. "Sarge, the horses are gonna founder if we work 'em any more right now," Michael Scott said. "They'll plumb keel over and die."

"Shit." Featherston looked around, feeling harassed by too many things at once. The whole battery would bog down if he didn't move the rest of the three-inchers around the lead gun. But if he had to abandon it, the higher-ups would crucify him. The only way he'd kept his head above water was by being twice as good as anybody else around. If he showed he was merely human, they'd cook his goose in jig time.

Here came a battalion of infantry, marching through the mud by the side of the road because the guns were occupying the mud in the middle of the road. "Give us some help, boys!" Jake called to the foot soldiers. "Can't afford to lose any guns."

Some of the infantrymen started to break ranks, but the lieutenant in charge of the company shouted, "Keep moving, men. We have our own schedule to meet." He gave Featherston a hard stare. "You have no business attempting to delay my men, Sergeant."

"Yes, sir. Sorry, sir," Jake said, as he had to: he was just a sergeant, after all, not one of God's anointed officers. How he hated that smug lieutenant. Because of his arrogance, the Confederate States would lose a gun they could have kept, a gun they should have kept.

"What's going on here?" someone demanded in sharp, angry

tones. An officer on horseback surveyed the scene with nothing but disapproval.

Featherston kept quiet. He was only a sergeant, after all. The lieutenant answered, "Sir, this, this enlisted man is trying to use my troops to get out of his trouble."

"Then you'd better let him, hadn't you?" Major Clarence Potter snapped. The lieutenant's jaw dropped. He stared up at Potter with his mouth wide open, like a stupid turkey drowning in the rain. The intelligence officer went on, "Break out some ropes, get your men on that gun, and get it moving. We can't afford to leave it behind."

"But—" the infantry lieutenant began.

Major Potter fixed him with the intent, icy stare that had impressed Jake on their first meeting up in Pennsylvania—and how long ago that seemed. "One more word from you, Lieutenant, and I shall ask what your name is."

The lieutenant wilted. Featherston would have been astounded had he done anything else. Twenty men on a rope and more on the hubs and carriage got the three-inch gun out of the morass into which it had sunk. On more solid ground, the horses could move it again.

"Thank you, sir," Jake said, waving the rest of the guns from the battery around the bad spot in the road.

"My pleasure," Potter said, crisp as usual. "We've done a pretty fair job of fighting the enemy in this war, Sergeant, but God deliver us from our friends sometimes."

"Yes, *sir*!" Jake said. That put his own anger into words better than he'd been able to do for himself.

"Keep struggling, Sergeant," Potter said. "That's all you can do. That's all any of us can do."

"Yes, sir." Jake stared furiously after the now-vanished infantry lieutenant. "He could have been heading up a labor brigade, and if he was, he wouldn't have let me use any niggers, either."

"I'd say you're probably right," Potter said. "Some people get promoted because they're brave and active. Some people get promoted for no better reason than that all their paperwork stays straight."

"And some people don't get promoted at all," Featherston said bitterly.

"We've been over this ground before, Sergeant," Potter said. "There's nothing I can do. It's not up to me."

Jake would not hear him. "That damn lieutenant—beg your pardon, sir—wouldn't pay me any mind, on account of I wasn't an officer. I command this battery, and I damn well deserve to command it, but he treated me like a nigger, on account of I'm just a sergeant." He glanced over to the intelligence officer. "It's true, isn't it? They are going to give niggers guns and put 'em in the line?"

"It's passed the House. It's passed the Senate. Since President Semmes was the one who proposed the bill, he's not going to veto it," Major Potter said.

"You know what, sir?" Featherston said. "You mark my words, there's gonna be a nigger promoted to lieutenant before I get these here stripes off my sleeve. Is that fair? Is that right?"

Potter's lips twisted in what might have been a sympathetic grin or an expression of annoyance at Jake's unending complaints. The latter, it proved, for the major said, "Sergeant, if you think you're the only man unfairly treated in the Army of Northern Virginia, I assure you that you're mistaken." He squeezed his horse's sides with his knees. The animal trotted on.

"Ahh, you're just another bastard after all," Jake said. Thanks to the rain, Potter didn't hear him. Featherston turned back to the battery. "Come on. Let's get moving."

They bogged down again, less than half a mile in front of the bridge. This time, Jake had no trouble getting help, for a Negro labor gang was close by, and the white officer in charge of it proved reasonable. Featherston worked the black men unmercifully hard, but he and his comrades were working hard, too. The guns came free and rattled toward and then over the bridge.

The firing pits that waited for them on the south side of the Potomac were poorly dug in and poorly sited. "Everything's going to hell around here," Featherston growled, and went tramping around to see if he could find better positions no other guns would occupy.

He had little luck. If the artillery hadn't had to stay close to the river to defend the crossing, he wouldn't have wanted anything to do with the area. When the Yankees came down and got their guns in place, his crew was going to catch it.

He'd come down close by the Potomac when the engineers blew the bridge and sent it crashing into the water, as he'd predicted. Somebody near him cheered to see it fall. Featherston's scowl never wavered. How long would the wrecked bridge keep the Yankees out of Virginia? Not long enough, he feared.

XIX

Destroyers and a couple of armored cruisers screened the *Dakota* and the *New York* as the two battleships steamed southeast through the Pacific. On the deck of the *Dakota*, Sam Carsten said, "I won't be sorry to leave the Sandwich Islands, and that's a fact." As if to emphasize his words, he rubbed at the zinc-oxide ointment on his nose.

"You're gonna bake worse before you get better," Vic Crosetti said with a chuckle. He could afford to laugh; when he baked, he turned brown. "We're going over the equator, and it don't get any hotter than that. And besides, it's heading toward summer down in Chile."

"Oh, Jesus," Carsten said mournfully. "Sure as hell, I forgot all about that." He looked at his hands, which were as red as every other square inch of him exposed to the sun. "Why the devil didn't the Chileans get into trouble with Argentina six months ago?"

Crosetti poked him in the ribs. "Far as I'm concerned, all this means is, we're doing pretty well. If we can detach a squadron from the Sandwich Islands to give our allies a hand, we got to figure ain't no way for the limeys and the Japs to get Honolulu and Pearl away from us." He paused, then added, "Unless that John Liholiho item tells them exactly what we've got and where everything's at."

"You know, maybe we ought to send a letter back to the Sandwich Islands when we get to Chile," Sam said. "About him being a spy, I mean. They'll rake him over the coals, you bet they will."

"Yeah, maybe we should do that," Crosetti said. "Hell, let's."

"Reckon you're right about the other, too, dammit." Carsten scratched one of his sunburned ears. Did being happy for his country outweigh being miserable at the prospect of still more sunburn? That one was too close to call without doing some thinking.

"Right about what?" Hiram Kidde asked as he came up. Carsten and Crosetti explained. The veteran gunner's mate nodded. "Yeah, the brass has got to think the islands are ours to keep. We've got enough guns and enough soldiers on 'em now that taking 'em away would cost more than the limeys can afford."

"What about the Japs?" Sam said. "They showed better than I ever figured they could, there in the Battle of the Three Navies."

"Yeah, I suppose the Japs are a wild card," Kidde admitted. "But as long as we don't fall asleep there at Pearl, I expect we'll be able to take care of them all right." He studied Carsten. "You're looking a little down in the mouth. You find a gal in Honolulu you didn't feel like leaving?"

"Nah, it's nothing like that, 'Cap'n,'" Carsten answered. "I was hoping I'd get out of the damn sun for a while, but Vic here just reminded me the seasons do a flip-flop down there."

Kidde let out an undignified snort. "Old son, that ain't gonna matter a hill of beans. How long you think we're going to stay in Valparaiso? Not anywhere near long enough to get to know the señoritas, I bet. Once we refit and refuel there, we're gonna head south to join the Chilean fleet. I don't care whether it's summer or not, your poor, miserable hide won't burn in the Straits of Magellan."

Sam considered that. "Yeah, you're right," he said happily—so happily that Kidde snorted again.

"Listen, Sam," he said, "sunburn's not the only thing that can go wrong with you, you know. We get down there, you'll find out what kind of a sailor you are. The *Dakota*'s a good sea boat, and she's gonna need to be. Down in the Straits, they've got waves that'll toss around a ship as big as this one like she was a wooden toy in a tin tub with a rambunctious five-year-old in it. I've made that passage a couple-three times, and you can keep it for all of me."

"'Cap'n,' if I start puking, I know it'll be over sooner or later, no matter how bad I feel while it's going on," Carsten said. Ever so gently, he touched his flaming face. "This here sunburn never stops."

"I'm gonna remember you said that," Vic Crosetti told him, "and if I ain't too sick myself, I'm gonna throw it in your face."

"And if you are that sick, you'll throw somethin' else in his face," Hiram Kidde said. "I've done my share of puking down in that part of the world, I'll tell you. You take a beating there, you and the ship both."

That made Sam think of something else: "How's our steering mechanism going to do if we take a pounding like that? The repairs were a pretty quick job."

Kidde grunted. "That's a good question." He laughed without humor. "And we get to find out what the good answer is. Hope we don't have to do it the hard way."

"Can't be any harder than the last time," Crosetti said. "No matter what Argentina's got, we ain't sailin' straight at the whole British and Japanese fleets—and a damn good thing we ain't, too, anybody wants to know."

"Amen," Sam said solemnly. Hiram Kidde nodded. After a moment's contemplation, Crosetti crossed himself.

"*New York* took the next biggest beating in the Battle of the Three Navies after us, now that I think about it," Kidde said. "Looks like they're sending what they can most afford to be rid of at the Sandwich Islands."

"That makes sense to me," Carsten said. "It probably means they don't think the Argentines are very good, either."

"Listen," Hiram Kidde said positively, "if we fought the goddamn Royal Navy to a standstill, we ain't gonna play against a tougher team anywhere in the whole damn world—and that includes the Kaiser's High Seas Fleet. The limeys are bastards, but they're tough bastards."

Vic Crosetti started to say something—maybe agreement, maybe argument—but klaxons started hooting all over the ship, summoning the sailors to battle stations. Everyone ran, and ran hard. Sam ran as hard as he could. He'd never yet beaten Hiram Kidde to the five-inch gun they both served. Since the two of them were starting from the same place, and since he was younger than Kidde and had longer legs, he thought this was going to be the time.

It wasn't. Kidde stuck to him like a burr on the deck. Once they went below, the gunner's mate's broad shoulders and bulldog instincts counted for more than Sam's inches and youth.

The "Cap'n" shoved men aside, and stuck an elbow in their ribs if they didn't move fast enough to suit him. He got to the sponson a couple of lengths ahead of Carsten.

The rest of the gun's crew tumbled in seconds later. "All right, we're ready," Luke Hoskins said, his hand on a shell, ready to heave it to Sam. "What do we do now?"

Kidde was peering out of the sponson, which gave a very limited field of view through a couple of slit windows. "I don't see anything," he said, "not that that proves one hell of a lot. Maybe somebody here or aboard one of the destroyers heard a submersible through the hydrophones or spotted a periscope."

"If they'd spotted a periscope," Sam said, "we'd be making flank speed, to get the hell away from it." Hoskins and the rest of the shell-heavers and gun-layers nodded emphatic agreement.

But Hiram Kidde spoke in thoughtful tones: "Maybe, maybe not. Remember how that aeroplane decoyed us out of Pearl and into that whole flock of subs? They might be letting us see one so we don't think they've got any more waiting up ahead."

"Mm, maybe," Sam said. "Wouldn't like to charge straight into a pack of 'em, and that's the Lord's truth." His wave encompassed the vast empty reaches of the Pacific. "This isn't the best place to get torpedoed."

Hoskins spoke with great authority: "Sam, there ain't no good place to get torpedoed." Nobody argued with that, either.

The klaxons stopped hooting. Commander Grady stuck his head into the sponson a moment later. "Good job, men," the commander of the starboard secondary armament said. "Only a drill this time."

Luke Hoskins let out a sigh of relief. Sam was relieved, too: relieved and angry at the same time. "Damnation," he said. "It's almost like the shore patrol raiding a cheap whorehouse when you're the next in line. I'm all pumped up and ready, and now I don't get to do anything."

"Don't you worry about *that*," Kidde said. "Nothing wrong with shore leave in Valparaiso, no sir. Nothing wrong in Concepción farther south, either. There's some pretty, friendly— and pretty friendly, too," he amended, noting his own pause, "señoritas in Chile, and that's the truth."

In more than twenty years in the Navy, Kidde had been to just about every port where U.S. warships were welcome—and some where they'd had to make themselves welcome. He had considerable experience in matters pertaining to señoritas, and wasn't shy about sharing it.

Sam hadn't been so many places. His working assumption was that he'd be able to find something or other in the female line almost anywhere, though, and he hadn't been wrong about that very often. So, instead of asking about women, he said, "What's Valparaiso like?"

"Last time I was there was—let me think—1907, I guess it was," Kidde answered. "It was beat up then; they'd had themselves a hell of an earthquake the year before, and they were still putting things back together."

"That's the same year as the San Francisco quake, isn't it—1906, I mean?" Sam said.

"Now that I think about it, I guess it is." Kidde laughed. "Bad time to be anywhere on the Pacific Coast."

Luke Hoskins said, "What were the parts that weren't wrecked like?"

"Oh, it's a port town," the gunner's mate answered. "Good harbor, biggest one in Chile unless I'm wrong, but it's open on the north. When it blows hard, the way it does in winter down there—June through September, I mean, not our winter—the storms can chew blazes out of ships tied up there. I hear tell, though, they've built, or maybe they're building—don't know which—a breakwater that'll make that better'n it was."

"Not storm season now, then," Hoskins said.

"Not in Valparaiso, no," Kidde answered. "Not in Concepción, either. Down by the Straits of Magellan, that's a different story."

"You know what I wish?" Sam said. "I wish there was a canal through Central America somewhere, like there is at Suez. That would sure make shipping a lot easier."

"It sure would—for the damn Rebs," Hiram Kidde said. "Caribbean's already a Confederate lake. You want them moving battleships through so they could come up the West Coast? No thanks."

"I meant in peacetime," Carsten said. For once, his flush had nothing to do with sunburn. He prided himself in thinking strategically; his buddies sometimes told him he sounded like an officer. But he'd missed the boat this time.

Kidde drove the point home: "I guess you were still a short-pants kid when the Confederates talked about digging a canal through Nicaragua or one of those damn places. President Mahan said the USA would go to war the minute the first steam shovel took a bite, and they backed down. Reckon he's the best president we had before TR."

Commander Grady peered into the sponson again. One of his eyebrows rose quizzically. "Not that much fun in here, boys," he remarked.

He might have broken a spell. The gun crew filed out. Hot and stuffy as the sponson was, Sam wouldn't have minded staying there a while longer. Now he'd have to go out in the sun again. Out of the entire crew of the *Dakota*, he might have been the only man looking forward to the Straits of Magellan.

Arthur McGregor hitched his horse to the rail not far from the post office. His boots squelched in mud till he got up to the wooden sidewalk. He scraped them as clean as he could before he went inside.

Wilfred Rokeby looked up from a dime novel. "Good day to you, Arthur," the postmaster said. "How are you?" He spoke cautiously. Everyone in Rosenfeld, like everyone in the surrounding countryside, knew of Alexander McGregor's execution. Arthur McGregor had been into town once since then, but he hadn't stopped at the post office.

"How am I, Wilf?" he said, and paused to think about it. That was probably a mistake, for it required him to come out with an honest answer in place of a polite one: "I'm right poorly, is how I am. How would you be, in my shoes?"

"The same, I expect." Rokeby licked his thin, pale lips. Lamplight glistened from the metal frames of the half-glasses he was wearing, and from the lenses that magnified his eyes without making them seem warm. "What can I do for you today, eh?"

"Want to buy some postage stamps," McGregor answered. "When I need beans, I'll go to Henry Gibbon." In a different tone of voice, it would have been a joke. As he said it, it was only a statement of fact. He'd seldom joked before Alexander was shot. He never joked now.

"Sure enough." Rokeby bent his head down and looked over

the tops of those glasses as he opened a drawer. McGregor studied the part that ran down the middle of his crown, dividing the brown hair on one side from that on the other as if Moses had had a bit of a miracle left over after parting the Red Sea. To make sure none of his hairs got Egyptian tendencies, Rokeby slicked them all down with an oil reeking of spices. The odor was part of coming to the post office for McGregor, as it was for everyone in and around Rosenfeld. After taking out a sheet of stamps, Rokeby looked up at the farmer. "How many you need?"

"Let me have fifteen," McGregor answered. "That'll keep me for a while."

"Should, anyway," the postmaster agreed. "Sixty cents'll do it."

McGregor stared at him, then at the stamps. They were some shade of red or other, though only a stamp collector could have told at a glance exactly which. Every country in the world used some sort of red for its letter-rate stamps. And the letter rate in occupied Manitoba, as it had been before the war, as it was in the USA and CSA, was two cents.

"Don't you mean half that?" he asked Wilfred Rokeby. "Look, Wilf, I can see for myself they're two-cent stamps." They were, as far as he was concerned, ugly two-cent stamps. They showed a U.S. aeroplane shooting down one either British or Canadian—the picture was too small for him to be sure which.

"Two cents still is the letter rate, sure enough," Rokeby said. "But you got to pay four cents each to get 'em, all the same. These here are what they call semipostal stamps: only kind we're gonna be able to sell hereabouts from now on. See? Look." He pointed to the lower left-hand corner of the stamp. Sure enough, it didn't just say 2. It said 2 + 2, as if it were part of a beginning arithmetic lesson.

"Semi—what?" McGregor said. "What the devil is that supposed to mean? And if two cents is the letter rate but I've got to pay twice that much to get one of these things, where do the other two cents go?"

"Into the Yankees' pockets—where else?" the postmaster said. "Into a fund that pays 'em to send actors and dancing girls and I don't know what all out toward the front to keep their soldiers happy."

"We get to pay so they can do that?" McGregor demanded. Wilfred Rokeby nodded. McGregor took a deep breath. "That's— thievery, is what it is," he said slowly, suppressing the scream.

"You know it, and I know it, and I expect the Yankees know it, too," Rokeby said. "Next question is, do they care? You can figure that one out for your own self. If we're paying for their damn vaudeville shows, they can spend more of *their* money on guns."

In its way, the casual exploitation of occupied Canada appalled McGregor almost as much as the casual execution of his son. It showed how the invaders had the conquest planned out to the last little detail. "What happens if we don't pay the extra two cents?" he asked, already sure of the answer.

"The surcharge, you mean?" Rokeby's fussiness extended to using precisely the right word whenever he could (come to that, McGregor didn't remember ever hearing *damn* from him before). "If you don't pay the surcharge, Arthur, I can't sell you the stamps, and you can't mail your letters."

"You don't happen to have any of the old ones left?" McGregor asked.

"Not a one," Rokeby said. "Sold out of 'em right quick, I did, when these here first came out last month. I'd have expected you to notice the new stamps on your mail by now."

"Who pays attention to stamps?" McGregor said, which drew a hurt look from the postmaster. The farmer took another deep breath and dug in his pocket. "All right, sell 'em to me. I hope the dancing girls give the Yankee soldiers the clap."

Rokeby giggled, a high, shrill, startling sound. He gave McGregor fifteen cents' change from the quarter and half-dollar the farmer laid on the counter. McGregor took the change and the stamps and left the post office shaking his head.

Henry Gibbon's general store was only a few doors down. The storekeeper nodded when McGregor came inside. "Mornin', Arthur," he said.

"Good morning." McGregor's eyes needed a little while to adjust to the lantern-lit gloom inside the general store. Boards covered what had been the big window fronting on the street before a bomb blew it out. That was a year ago now. "When are you going to get yourself a new pane of glass?"

"Whenever the Yanks say I can have one," Gibbon answered;

no U.S. soldiers were in the store to overhear his bitterness. "I ain't holding my breath, I'll tell you that. How's your family, Arthur?"

"What I have left of it, you mean?" McGregor said. Bitterness . . . how could you replace a broken son? But the storekeeper had meant the question kindly. "They're healthy, Henry. We're all down at the mouth, but they're healthy—and thank God for that. We'll get by." He stood a little straighter, as if Gibbon had denied it.

"That's good," Gibbon said. "I'm glad to hear it. Like I told you last time you were in, I—" He broke off abruptly, for two men in green-gray walked in off the sidewalk and bought a few cents' worth of candy. When they had left, the storekeeper shook his head. "You see how it is."

What McGregor saw was Henry Gibbon making money. He didn't say anything. What could he say? "You still have any of those beans, Henry? I want to buy a couple of sacks if you do." *No postage stamps here,* he thought, and almost smiled.

"The kidney beans, you mean? Sure enough do." Grunting, Gibbon put two sacks of them on the counter. "What else you need?"

"Sewing-machine needles and a quart of vinegar for Maude, and some nails for me," McGregor answered. "Ten-pennies, the big ones. Got some wood rot in the barn, and I'm going to have to do a deal of patching before the weather gets worse. Don't want the stock to freeze." He gave the storekeeper a quart bottle.

"You're right about that," Gibbon said, filling the bottle from the spigot of a two-hundred-pound barrel. "How many nails do you want?"

"Twenty pounds' worth should take care of things," McGregor said.

"I should hope so," the storekeeper said with a chuckle. He dug into the relevant barrel with a scoop. But as he dumped a scoopful of nails onto the scale, a frown congealed on his plump features. "Only thing I got to give 'em to you in is a U.S. Army crate. Hope you don't mind."

"It's all right," Arthur McGregor answered wearily. After a moment, he added, "Not the box's fault who made it."

"Well, that's right." Gibbon sounded relieved. "It's only that, what with everything, I didn't think you'd care to have anything to do with the Yanks."

"It's just a crate, Henry." McGregor dug in his pocket. "What do I owe you for everything?"

"Dollar a sack for the beans," Gibbon said, scrawling down numbers on a scrap of butcher paper. "Sixty-eight cents for the needles, nineteen for the vinegar, and ninety for the nails. Comes to . . ." He added up the column, then checked it. "Three dollars and seventy-seven cents."

"Here you are." McGregor gave him four dollars, waited for his change, and then said, "Let me bring the wagon by, so I don't have to haul everything." The storekeeper nodded, patting the beans and the crate and the jar and the little package to show they'd stay safe till McGregor got back.

As the farmer headed out of Rosenfeld, soldiers in green-gray inspected his purchases. They didn't usually do that; they were more concerned about keeping dangerous things from coming into town. Seeing what he had, they waved him on toward his farm.

A week later, in the middle of the night, he got up from his bed as if to go to the outhouse. Maude muttered something, but didn't wake. Downstairs, he threw a coat and a pair of boots over his union suit, then went outside. The night was very still. Clouds in the west warned of rain or snow on the way, but the bad weather hadn't got there yet. For the moment, no traffic to speak of moved on the road near the farm. He nodded to himself, went into the barn, saddled the horse in the darkness, and rode away.

When he came back to bed, Maude was awake. He'd hoped she wouldn't be. "Why were you gone so long?" she whispered as he slid in beside her.

"Getting rid of some things we don't need," he answered, which was no answer at all. He waited for her to press him about it.

All she said was, "Be careful, Arthur," and rolled over. Soon she was asleep again. Soon he was, too, however much he wanted to stay awake. If anything happened in the night, he didn't know it.

Three or four days later, Captain Hannebrink drove out to the

farm in his green-gray Ford. Out he came. Out came three ordinary soldiers, all of them with guns. Half a minute after that, another automobile, this one all full of soldiers, stopped alongside
Hannebrink's.

Arthur McGregor came out of the barn. He scowled at the
American. "What do you want here now, you damned mur-
derer?" he demanded. Through the kitchen window, he saw
Maude's frightened face.

Calmly—and well he might have been calm, with so many
armed men at his back—Hannebrink answered, "I hear tell you
bought some nails from Henry Gibbon not long ago."

"I am guilty of that, which is more than my son was guilty of
anything," McGregor said. Maude came outside to find out what
was going on. She held Julia's hand in one of hers, Mary's in the
other. She was holding both daughters tight, for they both looked
ready to throw themselves at Hannebrink and the soldiers regardless of rifles and bayonets. McGregor went on, "Have you
come to put the blindfold over my eyes because of it?"

"Maybe," Hannebrink said, calm still. "Show me what you've
done with them."

"Come back in here with me," McGregor told him, motioning
toward the barn. Hannebrink followed. So did the American soldiers. So did Maude and Julia and Mary. McGregor pointed here
and there along the wall and at the hayloft and up among the
rafters. "You'll see where I've done my repairs."

"Davis—Mathison—Goldberg." Hannebrink told off three
men. "Check those. See if they're fresh work."

"Look to be, sir," one of the men said after he'd clambered up
to inspect McGregor's carpentry at close range. The other two
soon called agreement.

"All right, Mr. McGregor," Hannebrink said, easygoing, in
nothing like a hurry. "Say you used a pound or two of nails there.
By what I hear, you bought more like twenty pounds. Where's
the rest of 'em?"

"On my workbench here." McGregor pointed again. "Still
in the box Henry Gibbon used for 'em."

Captain Hannebrink strode over. He picked up a couple of
the nails. "New, all right," he said. "Still have that shine to 'em."
He let them clank back in among their fellows, then picked up

the box. He nodded again. "Heft is about right, figuring in what you would have used. Good enough, Mr. McGregor. Thank you."

"Want to tell me what this is all about?" McGregor asked.

"No." Without another word, Hannebrink and the U.S. soldiers left the barn, got into their motorcars, and drove back toward Rosenfeld. Maude started to say something. McGregor set a hand on her shoulder and shook his head. She took their daughters back into the house. He wondered if she'd ask him questions later. She didn't do that, either.

A day or two later, he had to go into town again himself. He stopped by the post office to see if Wilfred Rokeby had any stamps but those larcenous semipostals. Rokeby didn't, but he did have news: "The Knights are in more trouble with the Yanks," he said.

"What now?" McGregor asked. "Haven't been off the farm since I was here last, and nobody much comes and visits. People figure bad luck rubs off, seems like."

"Bomb in the roadway near their land killed the man who stepped on it last week, and three more besides," Rokeby answered. "Good many hurt, too. Yanks say they planted it because of their boy."

"Stupid to set a bomb by your own house," McGregor remarked, "but the Knights have never been long on brains, you ask me. Biddy's always going around gossiping about this and that, and Jack's no better. Anybody who runs on at the mouth that way, you have to figure there's no sense behind it."

"That's so." Rokeby nodded vigorously, but not vigorously enough to disturb the greased perfection of his hair. "They would even talk to the Americans now and then, people say, in spite of what happened to their boy."

"Really?" McGregor sucked on his pipe. "I have to tell you I hadn't heard that." Because he had to tell it to Rokeby didn't make it true. As he'd calculated, Captain Hannebrink had been so interested in those new nails that he hadn't thought buying new ones meant McGregor could get rid of old ones. And a farm was a big place. You could search it from now till doomsday and never find dynamite and fuse and blasting caps, even if they were there—which some of them, at any rate, weren't, not any more. Some of the Yankees blown to hell and gone, the runny-mouthed Knights in hot water—very hot water, he hoped—with the occupying authorities . . . Two revenges at once wasn't bad. "No, I hadn't heard that," McGregor repeated. "Too bad."

Nellie Semphroch set fresh coffee in front of the Confederate colonel. "I do thank you, ma'am," he said, courteous as the Rebs were most of the time. Once the words had passed his lips, though, he might have forgotten she existed. Turning back to the other officers at the table, he took up where he'd left off: "If we have to leave this town, we ought to treat it the way the Romans treated Carthage."

The classical allusion meant nothing to Nellie. The officers to whom he was speaking understood it, though. "Leave no stone atop another?" a lieutenant-colonel said.

Another colonel nodded. "We'll give the damnyankees a desert to come home to, not a capital. This place has been frowning down on the Confederacy as long as we've been independent."

"Too right it has," said the first colonel, the one to whom Nellie had given the new cup of coffee. "Let them rule from Philadelphia. Washington was a capital made before we saw how we were treated in that union."

"Tyrants they were, tyrants they are, tyrants they shall ever be," the second colonel agreed. "The White House, the Capitol, all the departments—dynamite them all, I say. The Yankees only maintained their presence here after the War of Secession to irk us."

Nellie glanced over toward Edna, hoping her daughter was listening as the Rebel officers calmly discussed the destruction of the capital of the United States. Edna, however, was casting sheep's eyes at Lieutenant Kincaid. *Why should she care?* Nellie thought bitterly. *She's got a Rebel officer for a fiancé.*

The lieutenant-colonel said, "Too bad about the Washington Monument. No matter what we did with the rest of the town, I would have left that standing. Washington was a Virginian, after all."

"Fortunes of war," the colonel said. "Can't be helped—it was in the way of our barrage when the war started, and of the damnyankees' fire once we forced an entrance into the city."

"That sort of destruction is one thing," the lieutenant-colonel said. "But deliberately wrecking the monuments as we retire may cost us Yankee retribution elsewhere."

For a wonder, that made both colonels thoughtful. Before the war, the arrogant Rebs wouldn't have worried about how the USA might respond to anything they did. Now—Now Nellie had a hard time holding on to her polite mask. Now they'd learned better.

Edna got up and filled Nicholas Kincaid's coffee cup. She didn't charge him, which annoyed Nellie but about which she could say nothing. She didn't want Edna to marry the Confederate lieutenant—she didn't want Edna marrying any man—but she knew she couldn't do anything to stop it. She consoled herself by thinking that marrying Kincaid might get Edna out of Washington before the United States battered their way back into the city. Had Nellie had some way of escaping the bloodbath that likely lay ahead, she would have taken it.

She did have a way to escape the coffeehouse, if only for a little while. "I'm going across the street to see Mr. Jacobs," she said to Edna. "Take care of everybody while I'm gone, would you, dear?"

"All right, Ma," Edna said sulkily. She no doubt suspected that her mother wanted to keep her from spending so much time with Nicholas Kincaid. She was right, too, but she couldn't do anything about it.

The bell above Jacobs' door jangled when Nellie came in. The cobbler looked up from the boot he was resoling. "Why, hello, Nellie," he said, as if his fondest wish had just been realized. "How good to see you this morning."

"Good to see you, too, Hal," Nellie said, a little stiffly. She was still nervous about having let him kiss her once, and even more nervous about having liked it. But that didn't matter, or didn't matter much. Business was business, and wouldn't keep. "You remember how I told you not so long ago that the Rebs would do anything to try and hang onto Washington, on account of they reckoned it was their capital by rights, and not ours?"

"Yes, of course I remember that," Jacobs said, peering at her through his spectacles. Then he took them off, blinked a couple of times as he set them on the counter, and looked up at her again. He smiled. "That's better."

Nellie said, "I think they're starting to get the idea they can't keep Washington no matter what they do. The USA won't get it back in one piece, sounds like." She told the shoemaker what the Confederate officers had been discussing in the coffeehouse.

Jacobs clucked reproachfully. "This is foolish wickedness," he said. "No other word for it, Widow Sem—Nellie. I promise you, I will make certain it is known, if you happen to be the first to have heard of it. Your country owes you a great debt if we can use this knowledge to keep the CSA from carrying out such a vile scheme."

"That would be good, I guess," she said. "If they want to show they're grateful, they can keep from shelling this part of town when their guns get into range."

"Yes, I also think this would be an excellent reward," Jacobs said with a smile. But that smile did not last long. He coughed before continuing, "Widow Semphroch, I am glad you came by today, because there is something of importance I need to take up with you."

"What's that?" she asked. It was something important, or he wouldn't have returned to the formality with which they'd once addressed each other.

He coughed again. It wasn't something he wanted to bring up, plainly. At last, he said, "Widow Semphroch, what have you done to Bill Reach?"

"I haven't done anything to him, except tell him to stay away," Nellie answered. "You know I don't want anything to do with him." She cocked her head to one side. "Why?"

Even more reluctantly than before, he said, "Because he is acting—strangely—these days. I believe he is drinking far too much for a man in his position. He often speaks of you, but gives no details."

Thank God for that, Nellie thought. Aloud, she said, "The last time I saw him, I thought he'd been drinking," which was politer than, *He stank of rotgut.*

"If there is anything you can do for him—" Jacobs began.

"No, Mr. Jacobs. I am sorry, but there is nothing." Now Nellie threw up the chilling wall of formality. "Good day. I will call again another time." She left the cobbler's shop without a backwards glance, and without giving Jacobs the chance to say a word.

She supposed she should have been warned. But all she wanted to do with Bill Reach was put him out of her mind, and so she did not pay as much heed to Jacobs as she might have done. Two evenings later, Reach threw open the door to the coffee-house and lurched inside.

Nellie was in back of the counter, pouring coffee, making sandwiches, and frying ham steaks and potatoes. Edna was out among the customers: the usual crowd of Confederate officers, the sleek Washingtonians who collaborated with them, and a sprinkling of fancy women who collaborated more intimately with both Rebels and local cat's-paws.

All of them stared at Bill Reach, who looked even more disreputable than usual. By the boneless way he stood, Nellie knew he'd had his head in a bottle all day, or maybe all week. His eyes held a wild gleam she didn't like. She started out toward the front of the coffeehouse, certain he was going to do something dreadful.

She hadn't taken more than a step and a half before he did it. "Little Nell!" he said loudly—but he wasn't looking at Nellie at all. He was looking at Edna, so drunk he couldn't tell daughter from mother. "Makes me feel young just to see you, Little Nell, same as it always did." Edna was less than half his age—no wonder seeing her made him feel young. A leer spread over his face.

"Get out of here!" Nellie shouted, but he was too drunk, too intent on what was going on inside his own mind, to hear her.

And Edna, after a glance back at her mother, a glance filled with both curiosity and malice, smiled at him and said, "What do you want tonight, Bill?"

It wasn't quite the right question, but it was close enough. Over Nellie's cry of horror, Reach pulled a quarter-eagle out of his pocket, slapped the gold coin down on a tabletop as if it were a nightstand, and said, "Tonight? Well, we'll go upstairs like always"—he pointed to the stairway leading up to Nellie and Edna's rooms, which was just visible from where he stood swaying—"and then you can suck on me for a while before you get on top. I'm feelin'—*hic!*—lazy, if you know what I mean. I'll give you an extra half a buck all your own if you're good."

"Get him out of here!" Nellie screamed.

A couple of Confederate officers were already rushing toward

Bill Reach. They landed on him like a falling building, pummeling him and flinging him out into the street with shouts of, "Get your foul mouth out of here!" "Never show your face here again or you're a dead man!" One of them noticed the quarter-eagle. He threw it out after Reach, then wiped his hand on a trouser leg, as if to clean it of contamination. That done, he bowed first to Edna and then to Nellie. "You tell us if that cur comes back, ladies. We'll fix him for good if he dares show his ugly face in here again."

Nellie nodded. Her customers worked hard to show good breeding by pretending nothing out of the ordinary had happened. Edna didn't say a thing. Edna didn't need to say a thing. Whatever else she was, Edna was no fool. She could figure out why Bill Reach thought he had any business saying those filthy things to Nellie—or to someone he thought was Nellie. The only possible answer was the right one.

Edna glanced back at Nellie again. Her mother could not meet her eye. That told her everything that still needed telling. Nellie hung her head. She'd tried to stay respectable for her daughter's sake. That was over. Everything was over now.

Over the past couple of winters, Lucien Galtier had discovered, somewhat to his surprise, that he liked chopping wood. The work took him back to his youth, to the days before he was conscripted. He'd swung an axe then, swung it and swung it and swung it.

After he came back from the Army, the farm had burned far more coal than wood. The Americans, though, were niggardly with their coal rations, as they were niggardly with everything else. He was glad old Blaise Chrétien, only a couple of miles away, had a woodlot. It made the difference between shivering through the winter and getting by comfortably enough.

Chopping wood also kept him warm while he was doing it. Down came the axe—*whump!* Two chunks of wood leaped apart. "Ah, if only those were Father Pascal's head and his fat neck," Lucien said wistfully.

His son Georges was walking by then. Georges had a way of walking by whenever he had the chance to create mischief. "You want to be careful, Papa," he called. "Otherwise you'll end up like Great-uncle Léon after Grandfather took off his little finger with the axe when they were boys."

"You scamp, *tais-toi*," Lucien retorted. "Otherwise your backside will end up like your grandfather's after he took off Léon's finger with the axe."

Georges laughed at him. Georges had a right to laugh, too. He was sixteen now, and almost half a head taller than his father. If Lucien tried to give him a licking, who would end up drubbing whom was very much in doubt. Lucien thought he would win even yet—you learned tricks in the Army that simple rough-housing never taught you. But he didn't want to have to find out.

Up went the axe. Down it came. More wood split. Marie would be happy with him. "No, she cannot call me lazy today," he said. Some people, he had seen, worked simply for the sake of working. A lot of English-speaking Canadians were like that, and Americans, too. Fewer Quebecois had the disease. Lucien worked when something needed doing. When it didn't (which, on a farm, was all too seldom), he was content to leave it alone.

He wiped his forehead with the back of his sleeve. He'd worked up a good sweat, though it was chilly out here. The day was clear, though, the sunshine streaming down as if it were spring. Only the slightly deeper blue of the sky argued otherwise.

Up in the sky, something buzzed like a mosquito out of season. He stopped chopping for a little while and peered upward, trying to spot the aeroplane—no, aeroplanes: a flight of them, droning north. His mouth twisted. "I hope all of you are shot down," he said, shaking his fist at the heavens. "This is our patrimony, not yours. You have no business taking it from us."

Afterwards, he blamed the American aeroplanes for what happened when he went back to chopping. They had, after all, broken the smooth rhythm he'd established before they disturbed him. And if he hadn't blamed them, he would have blamed Georges instead. Better to put it on his enemy's head than on his own flesh and blood.

He knew the stroke was wrong the second the axehead started on its downward arc. He tried to twist it aside; in the end, he didn't know whether that made things better or worse. The axe hit the piece of wood on the chopping block a glancing blow and then bit into his left leg.

"Tabernac!" he hissed. The blade had a red edge when he pulled it free. Blood started running down his calf into his shoe. It was warm on what had been cold skin. "Ah, *mauvais tabernac.*"

The axe had sliced into meat, not bone. That was the only good thing he could say about the wound. He started to throw the axe aside so he could hobble to the farmhouse, but held onto the tool instead. That leg didn't want to bear much weight, and the axe handle made a stick to take it instead.

Marie let out a small shriek when he made it inside. "It is not so bad," he said, hoping it was not so bad. "Put a bandage on it, and then I will go out and finish what I have to do."

"You will go nowhere today," she said, grabbing for a rag. "You should be ashamed, bleeding on my clean floor."

"Believe me, I regret the necessity more than you do," he said.

She got off his shoe and sock and pulled up his trouser leg. "This is not good," she said, examining the wound. He did not want to look at it himself while she worked. He had not a qualm about slaughtering livestock, but his own blood made him queasy. "It is bleeding right through the bandage," she told him. "A cloth will not be enough for this, Lucien. It wants stitching, or heaven knows when it will close."

"That is nonsense," he said. Even as he spoke, though, the two raw edges of the wound slipped against each other. His stomach lurched. He felt dizzy, a little lightheaded.

Firmly, Marie said, "*J'ai raison*, Lucien. I have sewn up a cut hand once or twice, but I do not think I should sew this. It is too long and too deep. I think you should go to the American hospital, and let them do a proper job of putting you back together."

The mere idea of going to the hospital was enough to restore her husband to himself. "No," he said. "No and no and no. It was bad enough that the Americans took my land, took land in this family since before the battle on the Plains of Abraham, took my patrimony for their own purposes. To use this hospital, to acknowledge it is there: this is a humiliation that cannot be borne. Sew it yourself."

"If you do not acknowledge the hospital, why does Nicole work there?" Marie asked. "If you do not acknowledge the hospital, why have you drunk applejack with Dr. O'Doull three times in the past month? Why have you probably got one of his cigars in your pocket even now?"

Galtier opened his mouth to give her the simple, logical explanation to the paradoxes she propounded. Nothing came out. His wits, he thought, were discommoded because of the wound. He told her that instead.

She set her hands on her hips. "Then, foolish man, it is time to get the wound seen to, *n'est-ce pas*? You will come with me."

Go with her he did, still using the axe as a stick and with his other arm around her shoulder. Even with such help, he had to stop and rest three or four times before they got to the hospital. When they did, one of the workmen there tried to turn them away: "This place is for Americans, not you damn Canucks."

"Hold on, Bill," a nurse said. "That's Nicole's father. We'll take care of him. What happened to you?" The last was to Galtier.

"Axe—cutting wood." Remembering English was hard.

"Come on in," the nurse said. "I'll get Dr. O'Doull. He'll do a proper job of patching you up." She pointed to the door, maybe seeing that Marie had no English.

At the door, Lucien ordered his wife home. "They will help me the rest of the way," he told her, pointing to the nurse and the workman. When she protested, he said, "Some of what is here, you should not see." He knew what war looked like. She didn't, not really. He wanted to keep it that way.

In English and in horrible French, the people from the hospital told her the same thing. She was still protesting when an ambulance skidded to a stop in front of the hospital. The driver and an attendant carried in a man on a stretcher. A bloody blanket lay over the lower part of his body; it was obvious he'd lost a leg. Marie abruptly turned and walked back toward the farmhouse.

The first thing Lucien noticed inside the hospital was how warm it was. The Americans did not have to stint on coal. The second thing he noticed was the smell. Part of it was sharp and medicinal: the top layer, so to speak. Under it lay faint odors he knew from the barnyard—blood and dung and, almost but not quite undetectable, a miasma of bad meat.

"You wait here," the nurse told him, pointing to a bench. "I'll get the doctor to see you."

"Merci," he said, his injured leg stretched out straight in front of him. A couple of soldiers, young men hardly older than Charles, his older son, sat there, too. The wounded man who'd been brought in on the stretcher wasn't in sight. They were probably working on him already.

One of the soldiers asked, "You speak English, pal?" At Lucien's nod, the youngster asked, "You get that from a shell?" He pointed to the wound.

"No, from to chop the wood." Lucien gestured to eke out his words. The American nodded in turn. Seeing him polite, Lucien asked, "And you—what have you?"

"Flunked my shortarm inspection," the young soldier answered, flushing. That didn't mean anything to Lucien. The Yank noticed. "This hoor up in Rivière-du-Loup, she gave me the clap," he explained. Lucien had heard that phrase in his own Army days. Inside, he laughed. He had a more honorable wound than the American.

"Well, well, what have we here?" That was good French, from the mouth of Dr. Leonard O'Doull. He wore a white coat with a few reddish stains on it. Looking severely at Lucien, he said, *"Monsieur* Galtier, if you want to visit me here, it is not necessary to do yourself an injury first."

"I shall bear that in mind, thank you," Lucien said dryly. "It was, you must believe me, not the reason for which I hurt myself."

"Of that I have no doubt," O'Doull replied. He undid just enough of the bandage to see how big the wound was, and whistled softly when he did. "Yes, you were wise to come."

"It was my wife's idea," Galtier said.

"Then you were wise to listen to her. As long as one in the family is wise, things go well. I shall have to show you how neatly I can sew." He turned and spoke to a nurse in English too rapid for Lucien to follow. She nodded and hurried off.

"I am glad you are the one to help me," the farmer said.

"I speak French," O'Doull answered, "and you are the father of my friend." Did he hesitate a little before that last word? Lucien couldn't tell. O'Doull went on, "This is a duty and an honor both, then." The nurse came back with a tray full of medical paraphernalia. The doctor went on, "It is an honor that will be painful for you, though, *monsieur*. I am going to give you an injection to keep you from getting lockjaw. This will not hurt much now, but may make you sore and sick later. We must roll up your sleeve—"

Next to the fire in Galtier's leg, the injection was a fleabite. Then O'Doull said, "And now we must disinfect the wound. You understand? We must keep it from rotting, if we can." Lucien nodded. He'd seen hurts go bad.

O'Doull poured something that smelled almost like applejack into the wound. Galtier gasped and bit his lip and crossed himself. If the wound was a fire, O'Doull had just poured gasoline on it. " *'Osti,*" the farmer said weakly. Tears blurred his vision.

"I do regret it very much, but it is a necessity," O'Doull said. Lucien managed to nod. "Now to sew it up," the doctor told him.

Before O'Doull could get to work with needle and thread, another nurse came in. That was how Galtier thought of her till she exclaimed, "Papa!"

"Oh, *bonjour,* Nicole," he said. He'd seen her in the white-and-gray nurse's uniform with the Red Cross on the right breast before, of course, but here he'd looked at the uniform instead of the person inside it. Embarrassed, he muttered, "The foolish axe slipped."

"Nothing that can't be fixed," O'Doull said, fitting fat thread to a large needle. "Do hold still, if you'd be so kind. Oh, very good. I have seen soldiers, M. Galtier, who gave far more trouble with smaller wounds."

"I have been a soldier," Lucien said quietly. He counted the sutures: twenty-one. O'Doull bandaged the wound thicker and more tightly than Marie had done. Lucien dipped his head. *"Merci beaucoup."*

"Pas de quoi," O'Doull answered. "I will give you a week's supply of sterile wound dressings. If it's still oozing after that much time, come in and see me and we will disinfect it again. Let your sons do the work for a while. They think they're men now. Work will show whether or not they are right. We'll take you home in an ambulance, if you like."

"No," Lucien said. "Marie will think I have died."

"Ah. Well, let me get you a proper walking stick, then." O'Doull did that himself. The stick with which he returned was so severely plain, it was obviously government issue. That the

U.S. government manufactured large numbers of walking sticks for the anticipated use of wounded men said more plainly than words what sort of war this was.

But, as Lucien made his slow, hobbling way home, he despised the Americans less than he had before. Almost everyone at the hospital had been good to him, even though he was a civilian, and an enemy civilian at that. No one had asked him for a penny. He was not used to feeling anything but scorn for the occupiers, but he prided himself on being a just man. "It could be," he said, slowly, wonderingly, "that they are—that some of them are—human beings after all."

"I wish Pa would come home again," George Enos, Jr., said.

"Me, too!" Mary Jane said loudly. She didn't say *no* as much as she had when she'd first turned two, for which Sylvia Enos heartily thanked God. Now her daughter tried to imitate George, Jr., in everything she did. Most of the time, that wasn't bad at all. Every so often—as when she piddled standing up—it proved unfortunate.

"I wish he would, too, dears," Sylvia said, and wondered just how much she meant that. No time to worry about it now. "Come on, both of you. We have to get you to Mrs. Coneval, or I'll be late for work."

They followed her down the hall to Brigid Coneval's apartment. Several other children were in there already, and making a racket like a bombardment on the Maryland front.

"A fine mornin' to you, Mrs. Enos," Mrs. Coneval said after she'd opened the door. "I'll see you tonight. Come in, lambs."

Sylvia went downstairs and headed for the trolley stop. Newsboys hopped up and down on their corners, trying to stay warm. The sun wouldn't be up for a little while yet, and the air had a wintry snap in it, though Indian summer had lingered till only a few days before.

Nobody was shouting about great naval battles in the Atlantic, nor about a destroyer lost at sea. With the war now in its third year, Sylvia knew how little that meant. A sunken destroyer was the small change of war, hardly worth a headline. Anything might have happened to the *Ericsson*, and she wouldn't know about it till she found the paragraph on page five.

If she bought a paper at all, that is. These days, she didn't do that every day, as she had when George was serving on the river monitor. She walked past the newsboys today, too, and stood waiting for the trolley without a *Globe*.

"Men," she muttered as the streetcar clanged up to the stop. She threw a nickel in the farebox. An old man stood up to give her his seat. She thanked him, hardly noticing he was of the sex she'd just condemned for existing.

She wished George had been either a better person or a better liar. She would have preferred the first, but the other might have done in a pinch. For him not to have the need to visit a whore (*and a nigger whore at that,* she thought, appalled by his lack of taste as well as his lack of judgment) would have been best. If he had gone and done it, she wished she'd never found out.

Actually, he had gone, but he hadn't quite done it. That didn't make things any better. How was she supposed to trust him now? (That he wouldn't have been worth trusting if he hadn't told her about going to the whore never occurred to her.) When he wasn't in her sight but was ashore, what would he be doing? "Men," she said again.

She was so lost in her angry reverie, she almost missed the stop in front of the canning plant. The trolley was about to start up again before she leapt from her seat and hurried out the door. The driver gave her a reproachful look. She glared at him. He was a man, too, even if he had a white mustache.

She punched in and hurried toward her machine. Isabella Antonelli was already at hers. "Good morning, Sylvia," she said with a smile that did not match the mourning she still wore.

"Hello, Isabella," Sylvia answered as she made sure the machine had plenty of labels in the feeder and the paste reservoir was full. That done, she really noticed the smile she had seen, and smiled back at her friend. "You're looking cheerful this morning." Her own smile was mischievous. "Did you put a little brandy in your coffee before you came to work?"

The capitalists who ran the canning plant hadn't spent any more than the bare minimum on lamps. The ceiling was high, the bulbs dim. And Isabella Antonelli was as swarthy as any other Italian, which made her seem very dark indeed to fair-skinned Sylvia. Nevertheless, she blushed. It was unmistakable.

Sylvia waggled a finger at her. "You *did* put some brandy in your coffee."

"No such thing," Isabella said. Maybe she hadn't. Sniffing, Sylvia couldn't smell any brandy, but they weren't standing face to face with each other, either, and the whole plant reeked of fish anyhow. But Isabella Antonelli had done something or other. What? How to find out without embarrassing her further?

Before Sylvia could come up with answers to either of those questions, the production line, which had shut down for shift changeover, started up again. Here came the cans. They came fast enough, nothing else mattered. Sylvia began pulling the three levers that carried them through her machine, gave each one a couple of girdling squirts of paste, and put on the label bearing a fish that looked much more like a fancy tuna than the mackerel the cans contained.

Pull, step, pull, step, pull, back to the beginning, pull, step . . . It was going to be a good day. Sylvia could feel that already. A good day was a day she got through barely noticing she'd been at the plant at all. On bad days, her shift seemed to last for years.

Here came Mr. Winter, limping up the line, a cigar clamped between upper and lower teeth. "Good morning, Mrs. Enos," the foreman said, almost without opening his mouth. "How are you today?"

"Fine, thank you," she answered, politely adding, "And you?"

"Couldn't be better," Mr. Winter said. His mouth still didn't open wide, but its corners moved upwards. He was happier than she'd seen him in a good long while. After a moment, he returned to business: "Machine behaving?"

"Yes—see for yourself." Sylvia hadn't missed a lever while talking with the foreman. "The action feels smoother than it has."

"They oiled it last night. About time," he said. After a brief pause, he went on, "Hope your husband's all right."

"So do I," Sylvia answered, despite everything more truthfully than not.

"God's own miracle he was saved off the *Punishment*," Mr. Winter said.

"I suppose that's true." Sylvia had all she could do not to laugh in the aging veteran's face. George had gone up on the riverbank to get drunk and commit adultery. The God she worshiped wasn't in the habit of manufacturing miracles of that shape.

"God's own miracle," the foreman repeated. He, of course, didn't know all the details. Sylvia wished she didn't know all the details, either.

Nodding to her once more, Mr. Winter went on up the line to see how Isabella Antonelli and her machine were. Over the noise of the line and of her own machine, Sylvia couldn't hear much of what the two of them said to each other. She could see, though: could see the foreman's hand rest lightly upon Isabella's for a moment, could see the way the widow's body bent toward his as a flower bends toward the sun.

Sylvia automatically worked her machine. She stared at her friend, stared and stared. She was not a blind woman. When things went on around her, she noticed them. If Mr. Winter and Isabella Antonelli weren't lovers, she would have forfeited a week's pay.

I should have known what kind of smile that was, she thought, annoyed at herself for not recognizing it on Isabella's face. She'd worn it often enough herself, when things with George had been good. Mr. Winter's smile wasn't quite the usual large male leer, but the cigar would have fallen out of his mouth if it had been.

Pull, step, pull, step . . . She wanted to see if Isabella would say anything at lunch. All of a sudden, the day that had been moving swiftly ceased to move at all. At half past twelve, the line finally stopped. The weather was too raw for Sylvia and Isabella to eat outside, as they had earlier in the year. They sat down together on a bench not too far from one of the handful of steam radiators the factory boasted.

Isabella solved Sylvia's problem for her by speaking first. She blushed again as she said, "I saw you watching me."

Sylvia's face heated, but she nodded. "Er—well, yes."

"He is not a bad man. I have said this since he and I were only friends." Isabella Antonelli tossed her head, as if defying Sylvia to make something of that. Sylvia only nodded again. That seemed to mollify her friend, who went on, "He has been lonely for years now, since his wife died. I know what being lonely means—*Dio mio,* how I know. Believe me when I tell you not being lonely is better."

Sylvia imagined lame old Mr. Winter touching her, caressing

her. She didn't know whether to be revolted or burst out
laughing. But she was lonely herself a good deal of the time
these days, with George aboard the *Ericsson* . . . and when he
had been home, had she been anything more than a piece of meat
for him, a more convenient piece of meat at the moment than a
Negro harlot? Did she want him to love her, or to leave her
alone? For the life of her, she didn't know.

And so, very slowly, she nodded. "You may be right after all,
Isabella," she said. "You may be right."

Jonathan Moss had reached that pleasant stage of intoxication
where his nose and the top part of his cheeks were going numb,
but he was still thinking clearly—or pretty clearly, anyhow. As
he generally did at such times, he stared into his whiskey glass
with bemused respect, astonished the amber fluid could work
such magic on the way he felt.

Dud Dudley stared around the officers' lounge. "What we
need here," he declared, "are some women."

"I'll drink to that," Moss said, and did. "They ought to bring
some up from the States, as a matter of fact. All the Canuck gals
treat us like we're poisonous." That wasn't strictly true; every
now and then a pilot would find a complaisant young woman in
Ontario. Moss never had, though.

His flight leader nodded vigorously. "There's an idea!"
Dudley said. "They can call them something that sounds as if it's
military supplies, so the bluenoses won't have conniptions.
'Tool mufflers,' maybe. Yeah, tool mufflers. How do you like
them apples?"

It seemed funny and then some to Moss. "We ought to give
Hardshell a requisition for 'em, start it going through the Quarter-
master Corps. 'Yeah, Fred, we need another couple dozen tool
mufflers on the Toronto front.' " He spoke into an imaginary
telephone. " 'Split 'em even between blondes, brunettes, and
redheads.' "

He would have gone on embroidering that theme for quite a
while, but an orderly poked his head into the officers' lounge,
spotted him, and brightened. "Lieutenant Moss, sir?" he said.
"Major Pruitt needs to see you right away, sir."

"I'm coming." Moss got to his feet, a process that proved

more complicated than he'd expected. "I'm coming. Lead on, Henry."

Henry led on. As Moss left, Dudley called after him: "Requisition a couple extra redheaded tool mufflers for me, pal." They both laughed. Henry the orderly grinned in a nervous sort of way, not getting the joke.

Major Shelby Pruitt raised an eyebrow when he saw the state Moss was in. That was all he did. The weather was too lousy to let aeroplanes get off the ground, so the pilots had little to do but sit around and drink. The salute Moss gave him was crisp enough, at any rate. "Reporting as ordered, sir."

"At ease," Pruitt said. He passed Moss a little velvet box with a snap lid. "Here. As long as you're celebrating, you can have something *to* celebrate." Moss opened the box. Two sets of a captain's twin silver bars sparkled in the lamplight. He stared at them, then at Pruitt. The squadron commander grinned at him. "Congratulations, Captain Moss."

Moss said the first thing that popped into his head: "What about Dud, sir?"

He made Hardshell Pruitt smile. "That does you credit. His are in the works. They should have come in with yours, but there's some sort of paperwork foul-up. I'd have saved yours to give them to the both of you at the same time, but I can't. You're both getting shipped out, and to different places, and they've laid on a motorcar for you in an hour. As soon as you leave here, go pack up what you have to take with you. The rest of your junk will follow you sooner or later, maybe even by the end of the war."

Things were moving too fast for Moss to follow. He thought—he hoped—they would have been moving too fast for him to follow had he been sober. "Sir, could you explain—?" he said plaintively.

"You're a captain now." Pruitt's voice was crisp, incisive. He used it as a surgeon uses a scalpel: to slice through the fat to the meat. "You'll be a flight leader for certain, maybe even a squadron leader if casualties keep on the way they've been going."

"We keep flying Martins against these Pups, sir, we'll have a lot of casualties," Moss said with conviction.

"I understand that," Major Pruitt answered. "Well, it just so happens the Kaiser's come through for us. Wright is building a copy of the Albatros two-decker; a German cargo submarine finally made it across the Atlantic with plans and with a complete disassembled aeroplane. The orders detach you to train on the new machine."

"That's—bully, sir," Jonathan Moss breathed. "Can we really fight the limeys in this new bus?"

"Everybody seems to think so," the squadron leader answered. "The copied Albatros isn't quite as fast as the Pup, but it'll climb quicker and it's just about as maneuverable. And we'll have a hell of a lot more of them than the limeys and Canucks will have Pups."

"Good—we'll make 'em have kittens, then," Moss said. When sober, he was sobersided. He wasn't sobersided now.

Hardshell Pruitt also grinned. "Go pack your bags, Captain. Pack the undowithoutables and don't worry about anything else. I want you back here at 2130, ready to move out for London. Here are your written orders."

"Yes, sir. Thank you, sir." Moss looked at the pocket watch he wore strapped to his wrist. Like a lot of fliers, he'd started doing that because of the difficulty of groping for a watch while wearing a bulky flight suit. Learning at a glance what time it was had proved so convenient, he wore the watch on a strap all the time now. "See you in forty-five minutes, sir."

He seemed to float several feet above the muddy ground as he made his way back to the tent he shared with Dudley and with Phil Eaker and Thad Krazewski, who'd taken the place of Orville Thornley, who'd taken the place of Tom Innis. A match got a kerosene lantern going. The space around his cot was as full of junk as more than a year's settling in and an easygoing view of military regulations would allow.

One green-gray canvas duffel bag didn't seem enough. He wondered if he could lay hands on a White truck, or maybe two. He shrugged. He'd manage, one way or another. And whatever he left behind wouldn't go to waste. Some would, as Major Pruitt had said, follow him wherever he went. The other fellows in the flight were welcome to the rest.

He heard Eaker and Krazewski coming. Eaker said, "Jonathan'll be glad we sweet-talked the cook out of a corned-beef sandwich for him. I've never seen anybody as keen for the stuff as he is."

The two young fliers came into the tent and stared. Grinning, Moss said, "I will be glad for the sandwich, boys. It'll give me something to eat while they take me wherever I'm supposed to go."

"Sir?" they said together, twin expressions of blank surprise on their faces.

Moss wanted to tell them everything. The whiskey in him almost set his mouth working ahead of his brain. He checked himself, though. Saying too much—saying anything, really—wouldn't be fair to Dud Dudley, who had to stay a while longer because of his botched paperwork.

What Moss did end up saying was, "They're shipping me out. I'm going into training on a new aeroplane."

"That's wonderful, sir," they exclaimed, again in unison. Krazewski clapped his hands together. With his wide cheekbones, blue, blue eyes, and shock of wheat-blond hair, he would have made a gorgeous woman. He made a hell of a handsome man, and the Canucks and limeys hadn't managed to kill him yet. He asked, "Does Lieutenant Dudley know, sir?"

That's Captain *Dudley,* Moss thought, *but Dud doesn't know it yet.* "I'll tell him as soon as I finish packing," Moss said. He didn't say anything about all the stuff he wouldn't be able to pack. His tentmates would go through it soon enough, almost as if he'd died.

He had intended to head for the officers' lounge as soon as the duffel bag was full. That didn't happen, because Dud Dudley came in when he was trying to stuff a tin of shaving soap into a bag already full to the point of seam-splitting. "A fine day to you, Captain Moss!" he exclaimed in a voice to which whiskey gave only part of the glee.

He's heard, Jonathan realized. *Hardshell must have decided he couldn't keep it a secret.* "A fine day to *you,* Captain Dudley!" he returned. The two men solemnly—well, not so solemnly—shook hands while Eaker and Krazewski gaped all over again.

"Too damn bad we're going to different aerodromes to train," Dudley said, which reconfirmed Moss' guess. The flight leader slapped him on the back. "I'll miss you, you son of a bitch. We've got to look each other up if we both come through this stinking war in one piece." He scrawled his name and address on a scrap of paper. "Here. This is me."

Moss found his own scrap and borrowed Dudley's pen. "And this is me. I'll miss you, too, Dud. And I'll miss these two sorry ragamuffins—" At that, the pilots who would stay behind gave him a pair of raspberries. He shook hands with both of them, too, then slung his duffel bag over his shoulder. He mimed collapsing under the weight, which wasn't far from being true, and tramped back toward Major Pruitt's tent.

A Ford was waiting there for him, the motor running. The driver took the duffel, gave him a reproachful stare at its weight, and tossed it into the automobile. "Hop in, sir," he said. "Off to London."

The drive was less than a delight. The Ford's headlamps were taped so they gave out only a little light; the enemy's aeroplanes would shoot up anything that moved at night. The road would have been bad even had the driver been able to spot all the potholes. Not spotting them meant he and Moss got to fix several punctures along the way. They didn't do better than ten miles an hour, which made a hundred-mile journey seem to take forever.

Dawn was breaking when they finally reached the aerodrome. No one seemed to be expecting Moss, which, after the time he'd had getting there, didn't surprise him at all. "Well," a sergeant said doubtfully, "I guess we'll put you up in Tent 27. Basler!" A private appeared, as if by magic. "Take Captain Moss to Tent 27. He'll fit in there, one way or another." The noncom's face bore a strange sort of smile.

Moss, who hadn't managed to doze in the automobile, was too worn to care what a sergeant thought. The private led him to a green-gray tent distinguishable only by the number stenciled on its side. "Here you are, sir."

"Thanks." Moss went inside. Sure enough, there was a cot with no belongings nearby. The three officers in the tent, who were readying themselves for the day, looked him over. One of them, a tall, thin, good-looking fellow, exclaimed, "Jonathan!"

"Percy!" Moss said. "Percy Stone!" Then he burst out laughing. "Now I know why that billeting sergeant said I belonged here. Moss and Stone, like the old days." He pumped Stone's hand. "Jesus, it's good to see you in one piece, chum."

"It's good to *be* in one piece again," Stone said. He'd been Moss' photographic observer when Moss was still flying two-seaters instead of fighting scouts, and a Canuck had badly wounded him. He pointed to the pilot's insigne on his chest. "You see I've got both wings now."

"Yeah," Moss said enthusiastically. "Between us, we're going to show the Canucks a thing or two." Percy Stone nodded. They shook hands again.

XX

Every time Abner Dowling walked into the Tennessee farmhouse where General Custer was staying these days, he braced for trouble. Since the First Army had basically stopped moving forward these days, Custer's accommodations hadn't shifted lately, either. That meant Libbie Custer had come down from Kentucky to stay with her husband.

It also meant Custer had to stop paying such avid attention to the pretty, young mulatto housekeeper he'd hired before Libbie came down. The wench, whose name was Cornelia, kept right on cooking and cleaning. Dowling didn't know whether she'd done anything more than that before. He was sure Custer had wanted her to do more, though, and had hoped to convince her to do more. Libbie was sure of that, too, which made the farmhouse into a sort of front of its own.

The illustrious general commanding First Army was in the kitchen eating lunch when Dowling arrived. The tubby major's nostrils twitched appreciatively. Regardless of whether Cornelia was helping Custer forget his years, the wench could cook.

"Why, that damned, lying little slut!" Custer shouted.

Waiting out in the parlor, Dowling jumped in alarm. The worst thing he could think of would have been for Cornelia to go telling Libbie tales. Whether the tales were true or not didn't matter. Libbie would believe them. Custer would deny everything. Libbie wouldn't believe that. By the sound of things, the worst had just happened.

But then, to the adjutant's astonishment, Libbie spoke in soothing tones. Dowling couldn't make out what she said, but she wasn't screaming. Dowling wondered why she wasn't screaming. How many damned lying little sluts besides Cornelia did Custer know? Dowling was sure Custer would have liked to know a regiment's worth, but what he would have liked wasn't the same as what was so.

A few minutes later, Custer came out of the kitchen, a scowl on his face and a newspaper in his hand. When Dowling saw that, he relaxed. So someone had savaged Custer in the press. The general commanding First Army would rage like a hurricane when a story threatened to tarnish his refulgent image of himself, but that kind of bluster didn't amount to a hill of beans in the long run.

In the short run, putting up with Custer's bad temper was what the War Department paid Dowling to do. As far as he was concerned, Philadelphia didn't pay him enough, but he would have said the same thing had he raked in a million in gold on the first of every month.

"Is something wrong, sir?" he asked now, as if he'd heard nothing from the kitchen and had just chanced to notice the general's frown.

"Wrong?" Custer thundered. "You might possibly say so, Major. Yes, you just might." He flung the paper into Dowling's lap.

Predictably, he'd folded it so the story that had offended him was on top. That way, he could reannoy himself whenever he glanced at it, and stay in a fine hot temper the whole day through. He would have pointed it out to Dowling had his adjutant not spotted it at once.

"Oh, the Socialist candidate in one of those New York City districts giving you a hard time about the Cottontown attack," he said. "Don't take it to heart, sir. It's only politics. Goes to show women can play the game as dirty as men, I suppose."

"What's her name?" Custer demanded. "Hamburger, was that it? I'd like to make hamburger out of her, by Godfrey! Didn't I tell you we needed a victory here to put a muzzle on those miserable, bomb-throwing anarchists?"

"Yes, sir, you did." Dowling spoke with some genuine sympathy, being a Democrat himself. "And I see that Senator Debs—"

But Custer, once he got rolling, would not let even agreement slow him down. "And you were there, weren't you, Major, when General MacArthur came to me with that half-baked plan for attacking southeast before shifting the direction of his advance? I warned him he needed to have more resources than I could afford to commit if that attack had even a prayer for success, but he wheedled and pleaded till I didn't see what I could do but give in. And this is the thanks we get for it." He reached out and slapped the newspaper onto the floor.

Bending over to pick it up gave Dowling the chance to pull his face straight by the time Custer saw him again. The general commanding First Army often rewrote history so it turned out as he wished it would have, but this was a particularly egregious example.

"General MacArthur did request more resources than you were prepared to provide, yes, sir," Dowling said cautiously.

"That's what I told you," Custer said. It didn't sound that way to Dowling, but arguing about what had happened was a pointless exercise. Trying to keep similar disaster from happening later occasionally even succeeded.

Libbie Custer came out and nodded to Major Dowling. "Did you see the lies they were telling about Autie, Major?" she said, setting a hand on Custer's shoulder. "They're all a pack of shameless jackals, jealous of his fame and jealous of the victories he's won for his country."

George Armstrong Custer was a blowhard. He'd blow hot, and then five minutes later he'd blow cold. Elizabeth Bacon Custer, as far as Dowling had been able to tell, wavered not at all. When she got angry at someone, she stayed angry forever. Some of that anger she aimed at anyone presumptuous enough to criticize her husband in any way. And some of it she aimed at Custer himself. From some of the things she'd said to Dowling, she'd been furious at the famous general for better than forty years.

Long-handled feather duster in hand, Cornelia came out and started cleaning. "Excuse me, Major Dowling, suh," she said when she dusted near him. He nodded and smiled at her. Every time he looked at her—and she was worth looking at—he wondered how the men of the Confederacy reconciled their claims of Negro inferiority and their own mingling of blood with the Negroes in the Confederate States.

He shrugged a tiny shrug his uniform hid. The Rebs didn't need to reconcile anything. They were the masters down here.

They could do what they wanted. No. They had been the masters. Despite hard times on the battlefield, the United States were changing things.

Custer, now, Custer looked at Cornelia in exactly the way one of those Rebels might have done. *This is mine,* his eyes seemed to say. *If I want it, all I have to do is reach out and take it.*

Libbie Custer's eyes said something, too. *If you do reach out, George,* they warned, *I'll whack you on the wrist so hard, you'll think you're back in primary school again.* Dowling didn't think the general commanding First Army was going to get away with much, not here, not now.

Having Cornelia go elsewhere was a relief. Tension in the front room went with her, as it did in a front-line bombproof when the barrage shifted to supply dumps farther back. Dowling found himself able to think about the war again. "Do you think we'll be able to accomplish anything worthwhile this winter, sir?" he asked. *Or will we keep on wasting men the way we have been doing?*

"We may have to make the effort, Major," Custer replied. "For the moment, though, however reluctantly, I am accumulating men and matériel to make sure we have reserves and adequate stocks on hand in case we do have to make any mass assaults in the next few months."

Digging a finger in his ear to make sure he'd heard correctly would have been rude. Dowling was tempted, even so. One thing he'd seen over and over again was Custer ignoring reserves and logistics. His gaze slid to Libbie. Brief acquaintance had convinced him she was a hell of a lot smarter than her heroic husband. If she was smart enough to have convinced him of the need to prepare, Dowling was ready to call her a genius.

Custer said, "It's the election, of course. If that snake Debs slithers into the White House, we shall have to go all out to force the CSA to make peace before TR leaves office in March. I want to be ready."

"I—see," Dowling said slowly. Maybe Libbie had put that bug in Custer's ear, but maybe he'd thought of it all by himself. He did pay attention to politics. And maybe word had come down from Philadelphia, quietly recommending buildups all along the line in case the U.S. Army had to try to force the Rebs to yield in the four months between Debs' election and his inauguration.

"Do you know, Major," Custer said, "that back in '84 there was some talk of procuring the presidential nomination for *me*? I was quite the man of the hour, after all. But I had chosen to make the United States Army my life's labor, and I would not resign my commission under any circumstances. I sometimes wonder how things might have turned out had I decided otherwise."

Dowling valiantly didn't say anything. He was convinced commanding First Army was beyond Custer's capacity. For the life of him, he didn't see why the War Department kept the old warhorse in the saddle instead of putting him out to pasture. Things were going well enough on most fronts that the retirement of an aging lion shouldn't produce any great outcry, no matter how much the public revered Custer's name.

President Custer? There was an idea to make any man who didn't believe things could have been worse for the United States think twice. Even though it hadn't happened—and probably hadn't been so close to happening as Custer asserted now, thirty-two years after the fact—contemplating it was enough to make Dowling . . .

"Are you well, Major?" Libbie Custer asked sharply. "You look dyspeptic. Maybe the general should send this wench Cornelia over to your quarters to cook for you and bring you back up to snuff."

"I'm sure that won't be necessary, dear," Custer said. "Anyone can see that the good Major Dowling is not off his feed." He chuckled.

Libbie Custer glared at him because he refused to remove the attractive housekeeper from his not very attractive house. Dowling glared at him because he'd called him fat. Dowling knew he was fat. He didn't appreciate being reminded of it.

Oblivious to having angered both people with whom he was conversing, Custer went on, "Now we shall just have to wait until after the seventh. If God be kind, both Senator Debs and this ignorant, vicious Hamburger woman will get the drubbing they so richly deserve. And if the Lord should choose to inflict Debs on us because of our many sins, we shall still have four months in which to redeem ourselves."

Dowling sighed. Agreeing with Custer on anything, even a matter of politics, tempted him to take another look to make sure he wasn't wrong. He hadn't dreamt anything might incline him toward Socialism, but if Custer loathed it, it had to have its good points.

Somebody knocked on the door of Socialist Party headquarters. "Another Western Union boy!" Herman Bruck shouted over the election-night din that filled the place.

Flora Hamburger happened to be standing close to the door. "I'll get it," she said. Opening the door for a moment would let a little of the tobacco smoke hazing the atmosphere escape. Her own father's pipe was but one among a great many sources of that smoke, as he and the rest of the family had come down with her to learn whether she would be going to Philadelphia when the new Congress convened in January.

But it wasn't another messenger with a fistful of telegrams standing out there in the hall. It was Max Fleischmann, the butcher from downstairs. He carried a tray covered with brown paper. "You people will be hungry," he said. "I've brought up some salami, some bologna, some sausages . . ."

"You didn't have to do that, Mr. Fleischmann. You didn't have to do that at all. You're a Democrat, for heaven's sake."

"You people—and especially you, Miss Hamburger—you don't let politics get in the way of beings friends," the butcher said. "This is the least I can do to show you I feel the same way."

After that, Flora didn't see what she could do but take the tray. "This is very kind of you," she told the old man, "and if more people felt the way you do, the United States would be a better place to live."

"Getting rid of those Soldiers' Circle goons would be a good start," Fleischmann said. "Well, I hope you win, even if you're not from my party. What do you think of that?"

"I hope I win, too," Flora blurted, which made the butcher smile. He bobbed his head to her and went back downstairs.

She put the tray on a desk near the door. People descended on it as if they hadn't already demolished a spread of cold cuts and pickles and eggs and bread that would have done justice to the free-lunch counter at a fancy saloon. Everyone was eating as if there would be no tomorrow.

Someone else knocked on the door. This time, Maria Tresca got it. This time, it *was* a Western Union messenger. She took the sheaf of flimsy envelopes from him. "New returns!" she shouted. "I have new returns!" Something approaching silence fell.

She started opening envelopes. "Debs leading by seven thousand in Wyoming," she said, and a cheer went up. "The Socialist there is going back to Congress, too, it looks like." Another cheer. She opened a new telegram, and her face fell. "Roosevelt ahead by ten thousand in Dakota."

Groans replaced the applause. Dakota had voted Socialist most of the time since being admitted to the United States. Herman Bruck let out a long sigh and said the thing most of the people in the room had been thinking for some time: "We aren't going to elect a president this year. The people are too mystified to put aside the war."

A few party workers called out protests, but most only nodded, as when a doctor delivers a diagnosis grim but expected. "We carried New York," three people said at the same time, as if that were a consolation prize.

"We aren't carrying any of the other big states, though," Bruck said, looking at a map of the USA. "And, now that the returns from west of the Mississippi are coming in, it doesn't look like we're going to carry enough of the Midwest and the West to make up for that."

"Foolishness," Flora said. She'd been saying the same thing since the beginning of the war. For the life of her, she didn't understand why more people didn't feel the same way. "If you have a mine that doesn't give you any gold, why spend more money on it?"

Along with everyone else in the room, her mother and father, both sisters, and the younger of her two brothers nodded at that. She wished David Hamburger had been there to nod, too. But he was down in Virginia now. That filled Flora with dread. Yossel Reisen had gone down to fight in Virginia, too, and never came back. His little son slept in Sophie's arms.

A telephone rang. Herman Bruck picked it up. He scribbled numbers on a piece of foolscap, then hung up. "New returns from City Hall," he announced in a loud, important voice, cutting off Maria's reading of results from farther away. "Latest returns for our district . . . Miller, 6,482; Hamburger, 7,912. That's the biggest lead we've had tonight."

Howls of glee filled the air. Benjamin Hamburger's pipe sent up smoke signals. He looked over at Flora, smiling broadly around the pipe. "This is a fine country. Never doubt it for a minute. This is a fine country," he said. "I came here with the clothes on my back and not a thing more, and now I have not a son but a daughter—a daughter, mind you!—in the Congress of the United States." More cheers rose.

"Angelina would be proud of you," Maria Tresca said quietly. She added, "And if the results hold, you can keep your brother out of any danger."

"I can, can't I?" Flora said in some surprise. The War Department would likely pay attention to the wishes of any member of Congress, even a young woman from the opposition. The War Department might even pay special attention to her wishes, in the hope that, by doing as she wanted, it could influence her vote on matters pertaining to the war.

And, in making that calculation, the War Department might prove right. All at once, leading by fifteen hundred votes, Flora contemplated the differences between running for office and being in office. The Socialists down in Philadelphia often compromised on issues Party regulars back home would sooner have seen fought to a finish. They'd compromised on war credits back in the summer of 1914, and Flora was far from the only one who wished they hadn't.

Now came her turn in the barrel. Would she have to make deals with the Democratic majority? Could the Socialists and the few surviving Republicans do anything to slow down Teddy Roosevelt's juggernaut?

Then she asked herself another question: if she used her Congressional office to protect David, wasn't she taking for herself one of the privileges of the elite that Socialists from Maine to California decried? But if she didn't do what she could to keep her brother out of harm's way and something (God forbid!) happened to him, how could she ever look at herself again? Was her ideology more important, or her family?

Asking the question gave her the answer. In a sudden burst of insight, it also gave her a clue to something that had puzzled her since the war began: why Socialists the world over, in Germany and Austria-Hungary and England and Canada and France and the USA, and even in unprogressive countries like Russia and the Confederate States, rushed to their nations' colors when ideology should have made them stand together against the madness.

Blood is thicker than water. Was the cause of the nation, of kith and kin, more urgent than the rarefied summons of Socialist egalitarianism? It was a dismal notion, but made an alarming amount of sense.

A Western Union messenger brought her out of her reverie with a new batch of telegrams. When he saw who was taking them from him, he smiled and said, "I hope you get elected."

"Thank you," she said, startled. He was developing his ideological awareness early on; he wouldn't be able to vote for another six or seven years.

"What's the latest?" four people called at once.

Flora started opening telegrams. "Senator LaFollette is out in front in Wisconsin," she said, which drew cheers. A moment later, she added, "And Senator Debs is sure to carry the presidential race in Indiana; he's leading three to two." Noise filled the Socialist Party offices again. Flora was pleased, too, but if Debs couldn't carry his own home state, what was the point in having him run?

Herman Bruck was studying the map, the slow trickle of incoming returns, and a couple of sheets of paper filled with calculations. "If things go on like this," he announced, "I think we'll pick up about a dozen seats in the House and two, maybe three, in the Senate."

That brought a fresh wave of applause. Bruck's calculations had been pretty good during the Congressional elections of 1914. That made Flora think she could place some confidence in them now.

"Roosevelt repudiated!" somebody shouted. Somebody else let out a real war whoop, almost a Rebel yell.

"It's not enough," Flora said, and, being almost a congresswoman, got instant attention from everyone. "It's not enough," she repeated. "If the people had wanted to repudiate TR, to repudiate him properly, I mean, they would have elected Debs. And another couple of senators and another handful of congressmen—"

"And congresswomen!" Maria Tresca broke in.

"—Aren't enough to matter," Flora went on, as if her friend hadn't spoken. "The Democrats still have a big majority in both houses. TR can jam any bill he likes right down the country's throat, and we can't stop him. There aren't enough progressive Democrats to join us in a united front and keep him out of mischief. We've done something this year—a little something. When 1918 comes, we have to do much more."

She got some applause for that impromptu speech. She also got some thoughtful silence, which struck her as even more important. The Socialist Party had some notion of the shape of this election now. They had to look ahead, to see where they could go next.

A phone rang. Herman Bruck answered it. He waved for quiet, which meant he was getting fresh returns. After he wrote them down, he shot a fist into the air in triumph. "Miller, 8,211," he announced. "Hamburger, 10,625. He'll never come back from that."

Sarah Hamburger had been sitting, watching election night with interest but without much visible concern. Now, though, deliberately and with great dignity, she got up, walked over to her daughter, and embraced her. Tears ran down the older woman's cheeks, and the younger one's as well.

A few minutes later, the telephone rang again. Again, Herman Bruck answered it. After a moment, he waved, put a finger to his lips. Then he waved again, this time for Flora. "It's Daniel Miller," he said.

Silence fell in the offices as Flora walked over to the telephone. She took the earpiece from Herman and leaned close to the mouthpiece. "Hello?"

The Democratic appointee to Congress sighed in her ear. "I'm calling to congratulate you, Miss Hamburger," he said. "The latest returns do seem to show that you have won this seat. That being so, I don't see much point in wasting everyone's time by not admitting the obvious."

"Thank you very much, Congressman Miller," she said. He was being gracious; she would return the favor. All around her, the Party workers started cheering once more, understanding why Miller had to be calling.

She tried waving them to silence, as Herman Bruck had done. It didn't work. Now that they'd gained what they worked so long and hard to accomplish, they weren't going to be quiet for anybody, not even their own candidate. Hearing the racket, Daniel Miller managed a chuckle. "Enjoy it, Miss Hamburger," he said.

"I wish it were mine. If there's anything I can do to help you in the next couple of months, I'm sure you know how to reach me. Good night." He hung up.

"He's conceded," Flora said, also setting the earpiece back on the hook. She didn't think any of her colleagues heard her. It didn't matter. They already knew. So did she. She was going to Congress.

The best thing—Lieutenant Colonel Irving Morrell sometimes thought it was the only good thing—about getting back to General Staff headquarters was the maps. Nowhere else in all the world could he get a better idea of how the war as a whole was going. Looking at them, one after another, he thought it was going pretty well. War Department cartographers had already amended national boundaries on the maps to show Kentucky as one of the United States.

Captain John Abell came into the map room. Morrell nodded to him. That Abell still *was* a captain filled Morrell with a sense that there might be justice in the world after all, no matter how well life attempted to conceal it.

"Good morning, Lieutenant Colonel Morrell," Abell said—coolly, as he said everything coolly. That Morrell was now a lieutenant colonel seemed to fill him with a sense that there was no justice in the world.

"Morning," Morrell agreed. The use of such polite formulas let even men who didn't care for each other find something safe to say, and no doubt often kept them from going after each other with knives. Morrell didn't need to look very hard to find something else safe: "With TR on the job for another four years, we'll have the chance to make these end up looking the way they should." He waved to the maps.

"So we will," Abell said. "Debs would have been a disaster."

"This is already a disaster," Morrell said. Abell looked at him as if he'd suddenly started speaking Turkish. To the General Staff officer who'd spent the whole war in Philadelphia, the conflict was a matter of orders and telegrams and lines on maps, nothing more. Having almost lost a leg himself, having seen men bleed and heard them scream, Morrell conceived of it in rather more intimate terms. He went on, "It would be an even worse disaster if we dropped it in the middle, though. Then we'd just have to pick it up again in five years, or ten, or fifteen at the most."

"There is, no doubt, some truth in that." Abell sounded relieved, at least to the degree he ever sounded much like anything. "We have the tools, and we can finish the job."

"Hope so, anyhow," Morrell said. "The Canadians are in a bad way, and that's a fact. If we knock them out of the war, that will let us pull forces south and give it to the CSA with both barrels."

"If the Canadians had any sense, they would have long since seen they were fighting out of their weight." Abell scowled at the situation maps of Ontario and Quebec. "They're as irrational as the Belgians."

Morrell shrugged. "They're patriots, same as we are. If the Belgians had rolled over, our German friends would long since have got to Paris. If the Canadians had rolled over, we wouldn't just be in Richmond—we'd be in Charleston and Montgomery by now."

"I believe you're right about that, sir." A light kindled in Abell's pale eyes. "We may get there yet, in spite of everything."

"Yes," Morrell said, and the word sounded . . . hungry. "We've owed the Rebs for a long time, and now, maybe, we can finally pay them back."

Abell smiled. So did Morrell. They distrusted each other, being as different as two men could be while both wearing the uniform of the United States. But no matter how different they were, they shared the U.S. loathing for the Confederate States of America.

"Two generations of humiliation," Abell said dreamily. "Two generations of those drawling bastards telling us what to do, and giving us orders out of the barrel of a gun. Two generations of their hiding behind England's skirts, and France's, knowing we couldn't fight them and their friends all at the same time. We tried it once, and it didn't work. But we have friends of our own now, so the Confederates have to try to take us on by themselves this time, and it's turning out to be a harder job."

Morrell walked over to the map that showed how things stood on the Maryland front. The cartographers had left on the map the Confederate advance to the Susquehanna, as if it were the high-water mark of a flood. And so, in a way, it had been—if the Rebs had got to the Delaware instead, the war would look a lot different now.

But that high-water mark was not what had drawn Morrell's attention. These days, western Maryland was cleared of the invaders. One day soon, U.S. forces would cross the Potomac and carry the war into the Confederate States. Fortunes changed, and so did the enemy's responses. Thoughtfully, he said, "I wonder how much trouble their nigger troops are going to cause."

"That is the wild card," Abell admitted. "Those black units will be riddled with Reds, so we can dare hope they won't fight hard. And, after all, they are only Negroes."

"The French have had pretty good luck with their colored soldiers," Morrell said. "Guderian was telling me the Germans don't like facing them for beans. When they attack, they put everything they've got into it, and they don't want to be bothered with prisoners, either."

"Yes, I've heard that, too," Abell said. "But I've also heard they've got no staying power to speak of. That's what the Rebs will need, being on the defensive as they are. They're in no position to attack us. Even if the Canucks stay in the fight, the initiative is in our hands."

"I wouldn't be so sure of that," Morrell said. "If the Rebs stand on the defensive, they'll lose. We'll hammer them to death—and the voters just gave Teddy Roosevelt four more years—well, two, anyhow, till the next Congressional elections—to do exactly that. If the Confederates want to stop us, they'll have to do some striking of their own."

"Perhaps you're right, Lieutenant Colonel." By the way Abell said it, he thought Morrell was out of his mind but, inexplicably being of two grades' superior rank, had to be humored. "The maps make it difficult to see where they could hope to do so, however."

"Maps are wonderful," Morrell said. "I love maps. They let you see things you could never hope to spot without 'em. But they aren't a be-all and end-all. If you don't factor morale into your strategic thinking, you're going to get surprised in ways you don't like."

"Perhaps," Abell said again. Again, he sounded anything but convinced. Since he had few emotions of his own, he didn't seem to think anyone else had them, either. Maybe that accounted for his still being a captain.

"Never mind," Morrell said, a little sadly. "But I'll tell you this, Captain: anybody who's looking defeat in the face isn't going to fight a rational war once he figures he's got nothing left to lose."

"Yes, sir," Abell said. It didn't get through to the General Staff captain. Morrell could see as much. He wondered when Abell had last fired a Springfield. He wondered if Abell had ever had to command a platoon on maneuvers. He had his doubts. Had Abell ever done anything like that, he wouldn't have retained such an abiding faith in rationality.

"What will you do when the war's over?" Morrell asked.

Abell didn't hesitate. "Help the country prepare itself for the next one, of course," he replied. "And you?"

"The same." For the life of him, Morrell couldn't think of anything he'd rather do. "I think, if I get the chance, I'm going to go into barrels. That's where we'll see a lot of effort focused once the fighting's done this time."

Abell shook his head. "They've been a disappointment, if you ask me. Like gas, they promise more than they deliver. Now that the enemy has seen them a few times, we don't get the panic effect we once did, and enemy barrels are starting to neutralize ours. They may have occasional uses, I grant you, but I think they'll go down in the history of this war as curiosities, nothing more."

"I don't agree," Morrell said. "They need more work; they'd be much more useful if they could move faster than a soldier can walk. And I'm not sure our doctrine for employing them is the best it could be, either."

"How else would you use them, sir, other than all along the line?" Abell asked. "They are, as you pointed out, an adjunct to infantry. This matter has been discussed here at considerable length, both before your arrival and during your absence."

Had Abell been wearing gloves, he might have slapped Morrell in the face with one of them. His remarks really meant, *Who do you think you are, you Johnny-come-lately, to question the gathered wisdom of the War Department and the General Staff?*

"All I know is what I read in the reports that come back from the field, and what I've seen in the field for myself," Morrell answered, which didn't make Captain Abell look any happier. "They've done some good, and I think they could do more."

"I suggest, then, sir, that you put your proposals in the form of a memorandum for evaluation by the appropriate committee," Abell said.

"Maybe I will," Morrell said, which startled John Abell. *One more memorandum no one will ever read,* Morrell thought. *Just what the war effort needs now.* Aloud, he went on, "Yes, maybe I'll do that. And maybe I'll do something else, too." The gaze Abell gave him held more suspicion than any the smooth young captain had ever aimed at the Confederates and their plans.

Roger Kimball said, "You're all volunteers here, and I'm proud of every one of you for coming along on this ride. I knew the *Bonefish* had the finest damn crew in the C.S. Navy, and you've gone and proved it again."

"Sir," Tom Brearley said, "we wouldn't have missed it for the world."

Brearley was the executive officer, and was supposed to think like that. Kimball wanted to get a feel for how the ordinary sailors felt. Yes, they'd all volunteered, but had they really understood what they were getting into?

Then Ben Coulter said, "If we can give the damnyankees' nuts a good twist, Skipper, reckon it'll turn out to be worth it." The rest of the crew, some in greasy dungarees, some in black leather that was every bit as greasy but didn't show it so much, rumbled their agreement with the veteran petty officer. A lot of them had quit shaving after they sailed out of Charleston, which made them look even more piratical than they would have otherwise.

"All right," Kimball said, heartened. "You understand what we're doing here. If it goes wrong, we ain't gonna be like my old chum Ralph Briggs. Calls himself a submariner, and the Yankees have captured him *twice*." He spat to show what he thought of that. "If it goes wrong, we're sunk." His eyes gleamed. "But if it goes right, there's gonna be a lot of unhappy Yankees in New York harbor."

That wolfish growl rose from the crew again. Rationally, Kimball knew the odds were he'd said his last good-byes to everybody except the crew of the *Bonefish*, and he'd probably never get the chance to say good-bye to them. But the risk was worth the candle, as far as he was concerned.

Bookish and thoughtful where Kimball was fierce and emotional, Tom Brearley said, "We've loaded this boat with so many extra batteries, we only need to fill our buoyancy tanks half full to go straight down to the bottom." That was an exaggeration, but not a big one. Brearley went on, "We've got chemicals aboard to take some of the carbon dioxide out of the air while we're submerged, too. What all that means is, we can submerge farther out from New York City than the Yankees think, sneak up on them, do our worst, and then get away again."

"That's what we can do, all right," Kimball said. "That's what we're *going* to do."

He went up the ladder to the conning tower and looked all around. The Stars and Bars flapped where the Confederate naval ensign would normally have flown. As it had been in the Chesapeake Bay, that was part of the deception scheme he'd laid on. A passing ship or aeroplane would see red, white, and blue and— he hoped—assume the boat belonged to the U.S. Navy. What made it especially delicious was that it didn't even slightly contravene international law.

The *Bonefish* was only a couple of hundred miles southeast of New York harbor now, and ship traffic was heavy. As he'd counted on, none of the merchantmen paid any attention to a surfaced submersible sailing along on what were obviously its own lawful occasions.

An aeroplane with the U.S. eagle-and-swords emblem flew past, at first taking the *Bonefish* for granted but then sweeping back for a closer look. Cursing under his breath—if that aeroplane carried wireless and identified him as a hostile, all his preparations were wasted—Kimball took off his cap and waved it at the Yankee flying machine.

It came no closer, but waggled its wings and flew off, satisfied. He let out a sigh of relief. Five minutes later, he spotted a U.S. airship, a giant flying cigar. He cursed again, this time not at all under his breath. The airship could look him over at close range and hover above his boat, penetrating its disguise. He stayed up top, ready to order the *Bonefish* to dive if the dirigible turned his way. It didn't, evidently taking the sub for a U.S. vessel if it noticed the boat at all.

When he was inside a hundred miles of the harbor—and also about to enter the first ring of mines around it—he went below, dogged the hatch after himself, and said, "Take her down to periscope depth, Tom. Five knots."

"Aye aye, sir. Periscope depth. Five knots," Brearley said. The *Bonefish* slid below the surface with remarkable alacrity; those extra batteries were heavy. Without them, though, he couldn't have come close enough to the harbor to contemplate an attack.

Confederate Naval Intelligence had given him their best information on where the lanes through the mines lay. He was betting his boat—betting his neck, too, but he didn't care to think of it that way—the boys in the quiet offices knew what they were talking about.

And then, as he'd hoped he would, he caught a break. Peering through the periscope, he spotted a harbor tug leading a little flotilla of fishing boats back toward New York. "We're going to sneak up on their tails and follow 'em in," he said to Brearley, and gave the orders to close the *Bonefish* up on the last of the fishing boats, which, in among the mines, were going no faster than he was.

He was reminded of stories about a gator swimming behind a mother duck and her ducklings and picking them off one by one. He let the ducklings swim. All of them together wouldn't have satisfied his hunger.

The periscope kept wanting to fog up. Kimball invented ever more exotic curses and hurled them at its lenses and prisms. Down inside the steel tube with him, the sailors snickered at his extravagances. It *was* funny, too, but only to a point. If he couldn't see where he was going, he wouldn't get there.

He spotted Sandy Hook off to port and then, a little later, Coney Island to starboard. His lip curled. "Here we are, boys," he said, "where all the damnyankees in New York City"—a symbol of depravity all over the Confederate States—"come to play."

Nobody frolicked on the beaches today. The weather topside was chilly and gray and dreary. He swept the periscope around counterclockwise till he recognized Norton's Point, the westernmost projection of Coney Island, which stuck out almost into the Narrows, the channel that led to New York's harbors.

"There's the lighthouse," he said, confirming a landmark,

"and there's the fog bell next to it, for nights when a light doesn't do any good. And—what the hell's going on there?"

Cursing the blurry image, he stared intently into the periscope. His left hand folded into a fist and thumped softly against the side of his thigh. "What is it, sir?" Tom Brearley asked, recognizing the gesture of excitement.

"Must have had themselves a foggy night last night or somewhere not long ago," Kimball answered. "Somebody's aground on the mud flats by the lighthouse—sub, I think maybe. And they've got themselves one, two, three—Jesus, I see three, I really do—battleships sitting like broody hens around the cruiser that's pulling her off. To hell with anything else. I'm going to get me one of those big bastards if it's the last thing I ever do."

"What are they doing there?" Brearley asked.

"Damned if I know," Kimball answered. "But this is New York City, after all. They would have been in port, and some half-smart son of a bitch probably said, 'Well, we've got 'em right close by. Let's use 'em to make sure nobody gets frisky while we're pulling our boat back into the water.' It's only a guess, mind you, but I'll lay it's a good one."

"Bet you're right, sir," Brearley said.

Kimball didn't care whether he was right or not. *Why* didn't matter. *What* mattered, and there in front of him was the juiciest *what* this side of a fox sauntering into an unguarded henhouse. At his orders, the *Bonefish* pulled away from the fishing boats she'd been following and slid through the water toward the battleships.

They didn't have a clue the boat was on the same planet, let alone closing toward eight hundred yards. They weren't keeping anything like a proper antisubmersible watch, not here so close to home. All four of his forward tubes already had fish in them. He'd known from the beginning he would have to shoot fast and run.

"Five-degree spread," he ordered. "I'm going to give two targets two fish apiece. I can't get a clean shot at the third one. Are we ready, gentlemen?" He knew how keyed-up he was—he hadn't called his crew a pack of bastards or anything of the sort. "Fire one! And two! And three! And four!"

Compressed air hissed as the fish leaped away. They ran

straight and true. A bare instant before they reached their targets, one of the battleships began showing more smoke, as if trying to get away.

The explosions from at least two hits echoed inside the *Bone-fish*. Whoops and cheers from the men drowned them out. "Right full rudder to course 130, Tom," Kimball said exultantly. "Let's get the hell out of here. If we don't hit a mine, we're all a pack of goddamn heroes—I think I nailed both those sons of bitches."

And if we do hit a mine, it's still a good trade for the C.S. Navy, he thought. But that had nothing to do with the price of beer. He'd done what he'd come to do; he'd done more than he'd thought he would be able to manage. Up till then, he hadn't cared what would happen afterwards. Now, all at once, he very much wanted to live, so he could give the damnyankees' balls another good kick somewhere further down the line.

If the hiring clerk at the cotton mill in Greenville, South Carolina, had been any more bored, he would have fallen out of his chair. "Name?" he asked, and yawned enormously.

"Jeroboam," Scipio answered. After his meeting with Anne Colleton, he didn't dare keep the false name he'd borne before, any more than he'd dared stay in Columbia.

"Jero—" That got the clerk's attention: it made him unhappy. "You able to spell it for me, nigger?" Scipio did, without any trouble. The clerk drummed his fingers up and down on the desktop. "You read and write? Sounds like it."

"Yes, suh," Scipio answered. He'd decided he didn't need to lie about that. It wasn't against the law, and wasn't even that uncommon.

"Cipher, too?" the clerk asked. He yawned again, and scratched his cheek, just below the edge of the patch covering his left eye socket, a patch that explained why a white man in his twenties wasn't at the front.

"Yes, suh," Scipio said again, and cautiously added, "Some, I do."

But the clerk just nodded and wrote something down on the form he was completing. For a moment, he almost approached briskness: "You got a passbook you can show me, Jeroboam?"

"No, suh," Scipio said resignedly.

"Too bad," the clerk said. "That's gonna cost you." Scipio had been sure it was going to cost him; now he wanted to find out just how much. He had more money now than when he'd come to Columbia; he figured he could get by till this petty crook was through shaking him down. But, to his amazement, the clerk went on, "These last couple weeks, we've been paying twenty-dollar hiring bonuses to bucks with their papers all in order, on account of they stay with us longer and we want to keep 'em in the plant."

"Ain't got no papers," Scipio repeated, doing his best to hide how surprised he was. "Been a busy time, dese pas' couple years."

"Nigger, you don't know the half of it," the clerk said. Considering what all Scipio had been through, the clerk didn't know what he was talking about. But then he scratched by the eye patch again, so he knew some things Scipio didn't, too. He asked, "How old are you?"

"I'se fo'ty-fo'—I think," Scipio answered.

"All right." The clerk wrote that down, too. "Even if you took your black ass down to the recruiting station, they wouldn't stick you in butternut, so we ain't real likely to lose you anyhow, ain't that right?"

"I reckon not," Scipio said. All of a sudden, things made more sense. "You losin' a lot o' de hands to de war, suh?"

"Too damn many," the clerk said. "Always knew niggers was crazy. You got to be crazy if you want the chance of gettin' shot and next to no money while you're doin' it." He scratched by the patch yet again. "I been through all that, and I purely don't see the point to it."

"Me neither, suh," Scipio said. But he did, though he wouldn't say so to a white man. The clerk had gone to war along with his peers, masters of what they surveyed. If Negroes put on butternut, they hoped to gain some measure of the equality the clerk took for granted.

"Well, that's as may be," the one-eyed white man said. "Pay is two dollars an' fifty cents a day. You start tomorrow mornin', half past seven. You make sure you're here on time."

"Yes, suh. I do dat, suh." Scipio had expected warnings far more dire. That this one was so mild told him how badly the mill needed workers. So did their attitude toward his papers, or lack of same. The clerk called him *nigger* in every other sentence, but the clerk had undoubtedly called every black he saw a nigger from the day he learned how to talk. He did it more to identify than to demean.

Scipio went looking for a room at a boardinghouse, and found one not far from the cotton mill. The manager of the building, a skinny, wizened Negro who called himself Aurelius, said, "We's right glad to have you, Jeroboam, and that's a fac'. Lots o' folks is leavin' here fo' to join the Army. Up from the Congaree country, is you?"

"Dat right," Scipio said. Aurelius' accent was different from his, closer to the way the white folks of Greenville spoke than to the Low Country dialect Scipio had learned on the Marshlands plantation.

Aurelius scratched his head. His hair had more gray in it than Scipio's. "You know somethin', Jeroboam?" he said. "If I thought they'd let me tote a rifle, I'd join the Army my own self. Reckon I wouldn't mind votin' an' all them other things the white folks is givin' to niggers who goes to war for 'em."

"Maybe," was all Scipio said. Having fought against the Confederate government, having the blood of a Confederate officer on his hands, he didn't think he wanted to put on butternut himself, even had he been young enough for recruiters to want him.

His room was bigger and cleaner and cost less than the one in Columbia. Being just a mill town rather than the state capital, Greenville didn't have to put on airs. The work Scipio got was marginally easier than what he'd been doing before. Instead of hauling crates of shell casings from one place to another, he loaded bolts of coarse butternut-dyed cloth onto pallets so someone else could haul them off to the cutting rooms.

Two days after he got the job, the young Negro who had been hauling those pallets quit. Another young black took his place. This one lasted a week. A third Negro held the position two days. All three of them resigned to put on that butternut cloth once it had been made into uniforms.

Scipio saw his first black man in Confederate uniform a little more than a week after he came to Greenville. Three big, tough-looking Negroes in butternut came down Park Avenue side by side. They swaggered along as if they owned the sidewalk. Blacks of all ages and both sexes stared at them as if they'd fallen from the moon. Scipio was one of those who stared. He wondered if any of the brand-new soldiers had worn the red armband of the Congaree Socialist Republic the winter before.

As the uniformed Negroes strode along the avenue, sighs rose up from every woman around. If the men in butternut were out for a good time, their problem would be picking and choosing, not finding.

That much, though, Scipio could have guessed beforehand. He found watching whites far more interesting. They stared at the Negroes in uniform, too. Their attitude was more nearly astonishment and uncertainty than delight. Their legislators had passed the bill authorizing Negro soldiers. Now that they were confronted with the reality, they didn't know what to make of it.

A white captain, perhaps home on leave, came out of a shop on Park Avenue. The three Negroes snapped to attention and gave him salutes so precise, they might have been machined. The captain stopped and looked the black men over. *Damnfool buckra,* Scipio thought. *If a white officer doesn't treat them like soldiers, who will?*

But the captain, though half a beat late, did return the salutes. Then he did something better, something smarter: he nodded to the three Negroes before he went on his way. They nodded back; one of them saluted again. The captain gravely returned that salute, too. He hadn't acknowledged them as his equals, but they weren't his equals in the Army. He had acknowledged them as belonging to the same team he did. In the Confederacy, that was epochal in and of itself.

A sigh ran through blacks and whites alike. Everyone recognized what had happened. Not everyone, Scipio saw, was happy with it. That didn't surprise him. What did surprise him was that none of the whites on Park Avenue raised a fuss. The three Negro soldiers found a saloon and went into it one after another.

More and more blacks in butternut began appearing as time went by. A couple of weeks after Scipio saw his first colored recruits, he was going home from the mill when a white corporal stopped a black man in Confederate uniform. The white man had his right arm in a sling. In a voice more curious than anything else, he asked, "Nigger, why the hell you want to take the chance of getting a present like this one here?" He wiggled the fingers sticking out of his cast.

The Negro came to attention before he spoke. "Co'p'ral, suh," he said, "my big brother, he was in one o' they labor battalions, an' a damnyankee shell done kilt him. He didn't have no gun. He couldn't do nothin' about it. Them damnyankees ain't gwine shoot at me without I shoots back."

"All right. That's an answer, by Jesus," the corporal said. "Kill a couple o' them bastards for your brother, then kill a couple for your own self."

"That's what I aims to do," the Negro said.

Scipio was very thoughtful all the way back to his boarding-house. After the CSA pounded the Congaree Socialist Republic into the ground, he'd been convinced everything Cassius and Cherry and the rest of the Marxist revolutionaries had tried to achieve had died with the Republic. He wasn't so sure, not any more. Maybe Negroes were getting a taste of greater freedom after all, even if not in the way the Reds had aimed to give it to them. And maybe, just maybe, the struggles of the Congaree Socialist Republic hadn't been in vain.

When the field hands lined up in the morning, two more men were missing. "Where did Hephaestion and Orestes disappear to?" Anne Colleton asked. "Are they off somewhere getting drunk?" Instead of sounding furious, she hoped that was what the two stalwart hands were doing.

But the field foreman, a grizzled buck named Maximus, shook his head. "No, ma'am," he said. "Dey is on de way to St. Matthews—dey leave befo' de fust light o' dawn." Maximus had an unconsciously poetic way of speaking. "Dey say dey gwine be sojers."

"Did they?" Anne bit down on the inside of her lower lip. She had helped get the bill allowing Negro soldiers passed, and now she was paying the price for it. In front of the hands, she had to keep up a bold façade. "Well, we'll make do one way or another. Let's get to work."

Out to the fields and to their garden plots trooped the Negroes. The young men among them had found a loophole in the silent agreement they'd made with her after the Congaree Socialist Republic collapsed. If they joined the Confederate Army, they didn't need her to shield them from authority—and they didn't need to do as she said.

Grimly, Anne headed back toward her cabin. She had letters to write, bills to pay. How she was supposed to put in a proper crop of cotton next year if all her hands departed was beyond her. Her shoulders stiffened. She'd managed a crop of sorts after the Red uprising. If she'd worked one miracle, she figured she could work another. She'd have to, so she would do it.

Julia was already busy in the cabin, feather duster in one hand, baby in the crook of her other elbow. She couldn't join the Army. Anne appraised her as coldbloodedly as if she'd been a mule. She wouldn't be much good out in the fields, either.

"Mornin', ma'am," Julia said, unaware of the scrutiny or ignoring it. "It gwine be Christmastime any day now."

"So it will," Anne said. She'd driven into Columbia a few days before, and sent Tom half a dozen pairs of leather-and-wool gloves. She'd also bought a crate of the usual trinkets for the workers on the plantation. She couldn't make herself believe they deserved anything but the back of her hand, but couldn't afford any more trouble with them. She had troubles enough. A little bribery never hurt anything, and a congressman, for instance, would have been far more expensive.

"De tree sho' smell fine," Julia said. "Jus' a little feller dis yeah, not like in de old days."

In the old days, Anne had had the halls of Marshlands in which to set a tree that *was* a tree. Here in the low-roofed cottage, this sapling would have to do. She was making the best show she could with tinsel and a cheap glass star on top.

Julia cleaned at a glacial pace. Anne had learned hurrying her was useless. She would just look hurt and stare down at her baby. She'd been slow before she had the baby. She was slower now. Anne waited impatiently. Maybe she let the impatience show. Julia dropped and shattered the chamber pot, then spent what felt like half an hour sweeping up shards of china. Anne was ready to kick her by the time she finally left the cottage.

At last, the mistress of Marshlands, such as there was of Marshlands these days, got down to her own work without anyone peering over her shoulder. She was gladder by the day that she'd been in fine financial shape before the war started. She wouldn't be in fine shape by the time it was done. If she survived, though, she knew she'd be able to get her own back once peace finally returned.

She picked up the telephone mouthpiece to call a broker down in Charleston. The line was dead. She said something pungently unladylike. Nothing worked the way it was supposed to, not any more. It was either write another letter or drive into St. Matthews to send a telegram. She wrote the letter. More and more these days, she felt nothing at Marshlands got done unless she stayed here to see it get done.

To add to her foul mood, the postman was late. When he finally did show, up, he rode toward her with a bigger armed escort than usual. "You want to watch yourself, ma'am," he said. "They say them Red niggers is feelin' fractious."

"They say all sorts of things," Anne answered coldly. She took the envelopes and periodicals the fellow gave her and handed him the letters she'd written. He stuck those in his saddlebag and rode off.

Once he was gone, she regretted snapping at him. The guards accompanying him argued that people in St. Matthews were taking seriously the threat from Cassius' diehards.

She checked her pistol. It lay under her pillow, where it was supposed to be. Wondering if Julia or one of the other Negroes had pulled its teeth, she checked that, too. No: it was fully loaded. That eased her mind somewhat, arguing as it did that the Marshlands Negroes didn't expect an imminent visit from their friends and comrades skulking in the swamps of the Congaree.

"Comrades." The word tasted bad in her mouth. Now that the Reds had degraded it, it wasn't a word decent people in the Confederate States could use comfortably any more. No sooner had that thought crossed her mind than she laughed at herself. Before the war, she'd had nothing but contempt for the stodgy, boring folk who counted for the Confederacy's decent people. Now she reckoned herself one of them.

She laughed again, though it wasn't funny. It was either laugh or scream. The Red uprising had proved as painfully as possible how much she had in common with her fellow white Confederate Americans.

Julia brought in chicken and dumplings for supper. Anne ate, hardly noticing the plate in front of her. Her body servant took it away. Anne lighted the lamps, one by one. They didn't give her proper light by which to read, but they were what she had. She wasn't holding her breath about getting electricity restored to

Marshlands, any more than she was about getting back a telegraph line. On the off chance, she tried the telephone again. It was still silent, too. She snarled at it.

A couple of magazines told in great detail how the CSA might yet win the war. She would have had more faith in them if they hadn't contradicted each other in so many places. She also would have had more faith in them if either author had shown more signs he knew what he was talking about and wasn't whistling in the dark.

She poured herself a cup of coffee. The coffee remained good. As long as the Caribbean remained a Confederate lake, imports from Central and South America could still reach Galveston, New Orleans, Mobile, and Pensacola.

However good it was, the coffee did nothing to keep her awake. She drank it so regularly, it had next to no effect on her. When she started yawning over a particularly abstruse piece on Russia's chances against the Germans and Austrians in 1917, she set down the magazine, blew out all the lamps but the one by her bed, and changed into a nightgown. Then she blew out the last lamp and went to bed.

She woke up sometime in the middle of the night. As she'd tossed and turned, her right hand had slipped under the pillow. It was resting on the revolver. That, though, wasn't what had wakened her. "Coffee," she muttered under her breath. She reached down for the chamber pot, only to discover it wasn't there and remember why. Off to the privy, then—no help for it.

Her lips twisted in frustrated anger as she started to get out of bed. Marshlands had had flush toilets longer than she'd been alive; it had been one of the first plantation houses in South Carolina to enjoy such an amenity. She'd taken indoor plumbing for granted. The refugee camp had taught her it was too precious, too wonderful, not to be properly admired—and, at the moment, she had not so much as a pot to call her own.

Even in the mild climate hereabouts, a nighttime trip to the privy was a chilly business. She shut the door behind her to keep the cold out of the cottage. Going to the privy was also a smelly, disgusting business. And spiders and bugs and occasional lizards and mice visited the place, too.

Almost absentmindedly, she scooped up the pistol and carried it along with her when she went out into the darkness. She was halfway to the outhouse before she consciously recalled the warning the postman had given her. When she got to the privy, she set the little handgun down beside her before she hiked up her gown.

She spent longer in the noisome place than she'd expected. She had just risen from the pierced wooden seat when she heard voices outside. They were all familiar voices, though she hadn't heard a couple of them in more than a year. "She in dere?" Cassius asked. The hunter—the Red revolutionary leader—wasn't talking loud, but he wasn't making any special effort to keep his voice down, either.

"She in dere," Julia answered more quietly. "You don' wan' to wake she up, Cass. She gots a gun. She come out shootin'."

"Den we shoots she, and dat de end o' one capitalist 'pressor," Cassius said. "We gots dis cottage surrounded. Ain't no way out we ain't got covered. I oughts to know—de place was mine."

"Shootin' too good fo' dat white debbil bitch." Another woman's voice: Cherry's, Anne realized after a moment.

"Oh, is you right about dat!" Julia agreed enthusiastically. "I wants to watch she burn. She use me like I's an animal, she do. Ever since she come back, I wants to see she dead."

See if I give you *a Christmas present this year, Julia,* Anne thought. She'd got the idea Julia didn't much care for her, but this venomous hatred . . . no. She shook her head. She'd thought she'd known what the Negroes on Marshlands were thinking. She'd been fatally wrong about Cassius, and now almost as misled about Julia. She wondered if she understood at all what went on inside blacks' minds.

Cherry said, "Her brudder done use me. He have hisself a high old time, right till de end." Her laugh was low and throaty and triumphant. "He don' find out till too late dat I usin' he, too."

So Scipio told me the truth about that. Thinking about what had happened kept Anne from worrying unduly about the predicament she was in now. She'd seen some of it for herself; Cherry had put on airs, even around her, on account of what she did in the bedroom with Jacob.

Cassius said, "Don' matter how she die, so long as she dead. Top o' all de other crimes she do, I hear tell she behin' dat bill dat mystify de niggers to fight fo' de white folks' gummint. We strikes a blow fo' revolutionary justice when we ends de backers o' dat wicked scheme."

"So light de matches, den," Cherry said impatiently.

Through the tiny window cut in the outhouse door, light flared, brilliantly bright. Cassius and the other Reds must have doused the doorway to the cottage—and maybe the walls as well—with kerosene or perhaps even gasoline. Had Anne been inside there, she wouldn't have had a chance in the world to get free. The most she could have hoped for would have been to blow out her own brains before the flames took her.

"How you like it now, Miss Anne?" Julia shouted, exultation in her voice. "How you like it, you cold-eyed debbil?"

Cassius and Cherry and the rest of the Reds howled abuse at the cabin, too. After a moment, so did a rising chorus of Marshlands field hands, roused from their beds by shouts and by flames.

Anne realized that, if she was going to escape, she would have to do it now, while everyone's attention was on the burning cottage and nowhere else. She opened the privy door and stepped outside, holding up a hand to shield her face from the fierce glare of the fire. She started to step away from the outhouse, but then stopped and shut the door behind her—no use giving her foes (which seemed to mean everyone on the Marshlands plantation) a clue as to where she'd been. Maybe the Reds would think smoke and fire had overcome her before she woke up.

She wished her nightgown were any color but white. It made her too easy to spot in the darkness. Putting the privy between her and the fire, she made for the closest trees. Those couple of hundred yards seemed ten miles long.

No sooner had Anne reached the trees than the harsh, flat crack of gunfire came from behind her. Remembering everything Tom and Jacob had said about combat, she threw herself flat. That took care of her worries about the white nightgown, because she landed in cold, clammy mud. Shouts of alarm from the Negroes behind her told her what the gunfire was: rounds in the box of revolver ammunition in the cottage cooking off.

Deliberately, she rolled in the mud, so her back was as dark as her belly. Then she set out for St. Matthews, four or five miles away. A couple of plantations between Marshlands and the town had a sort of spectral half-life, but, after what had just happened to her, she was not inclined to trust her fate to any place where the field hands vastly outnumbered the whites. "I kept the government off them," she said through clenched teeth, "and this is the thanks I got? They'll pay. Oh yes, they'll pay."

After Scipio had visited Marshlands, she'd taken him off her list. When she was in Columbia, she'd learned he'd quit his job and didn't seem to be in town any more. That had been wise of him. She bared her teeth. In the end, it would do him no good. She'd have her revenge on him as on all the others now.

She stayed in the undergrowth alongside the road instead of going straight down it. That slowed her and wounded her bare feet, but left her less visible. As far as she was concerned, the latter was more important.

Every so often, she stopped in the best shelter she could find and listened to try to find out if anyone was pursuing her. She heard nothing. That made her feel only a little safer. She knew how good a hunter Cassius was. But every painful step she took brought her closer to safety.

She was, she thought, more than halfway to St. Matthews when a horse-drawn fire engine, lanterns blazing in the night, came clattering up the road toward Marshlands. A couple of armed guards on horseback trotted along beside it.

Anne stepped out into the roadway, waving her arms. She was so muddy, the fire engine almost rolled over her instead of stopping. "Jesus Christ!" one of the firemen exclaimed. "It's Anne Colleton."

"Don't go any farther," she said. "You haven't got enough firepower. Cassius and his Reds will be waiting to bushwhack you. And besides"—her mouth twisted—"the fire will have done whatever it can do."

The fireman who'd recognized her helped her up onto the engine. It stank of coal smoke from the steam engine that powered the pump. From a long way away, a rifle barked. The fireman grunted and crumpled, shot through the head. Another shot rang out, the bullet ricocheting off the engine before the sound of the report reached her.

"Get the hell out of here, Claude!" one of the guards shouted to the driver. The other guard started shooting in the direction from which the shots had come.

Claude could handle horses. He turned the six-animal team

and headed back toward St. Matthews faster than Anne would have thought possible—but not before another fireman got hit in the foot. He cursed furiously, pausing every so often to apologize to Anne for his language.

Cassius, she thought. *It has to be Cassius.* The iron bulk of the pump shielded her from any more bullets. All she had to do, all the way back to town, was think about how the hunter, the Red, had ruined her twice. But she was still alive, still fighting—and so, in spite of the Negro uprising and everything else, were the Confederate States.

We'll whip the Yankees yet, she thought. *And you, Cassius, I'll whip you.*

**Don't miss the next explosive chapter
in the War to End All Wars,
THE GREAT WAR: BREAKTHROUGHS
by Harry Turtledove,
The Master of Alternative History**

Klaxons hooted the call to battle stations. George Enos sprinted along the deck of the USS *Ericsson* toward the one-pounder gun near the stern. The destroyer was rolling and pitching in the heavy swells of an Atlantic winter storm. Freezing rain made the metal deck slick as a Boston Common ice-skating rink.

Enos ran as confidently as a mountain goat bounding from crag to crag. Ice and heavy seas were second nature to him. Before the war sucked him into the Navy, he'd put to sea in fishing boats from Boston's T Wharf at every season of the year, and gone through worse weather in craft a lot smaller than this one. The thick peacoat was warmer than a civilian slicker, too.

Petty Officer Carl Sturtevant and most of his crew were already at the depth-charge launcher near the one-pounder. The other sailors came rushing up only moments after Enos took his place at the antiaircraft gun.

He stared every which way, though with the weather so bad he would have been hard pressed to spot an aeroplane before it crashed on the *Ericsson*'s deck. A frigid gust of wind tried to yank off his cap. He grabbed it and jammed it back in place. Navy barbers kept his brown hair trimmed too close for it to hold in any heat on its own.

"What's up?" he shouted to Sturtevant through the wind. "Somebody spot a periscope, or think he did?" British, French, and Confederate submersibles all prowled the Atlantic. For that matter, so did U.S. and German boats. If a friendly skipper made a mistake and launched a spread of fish at the *Ericsson*, her crew would be in just as much trouble as if the Rebs or limeys had attacked.

"Don't know." The petty officer scratched at his dark Kaiser Bill mustache. "Shit, you expect 'em to go and tell us stuff? All I know is, I heard the hooter and I ran like hell." He scratched his mustache again. "Long as we're standing next to each other, George, happy New Year."

"Same to you," Enos answered in surprised tones. "It is today, isn't it? I hadn't even thought about it, but you're right. Back when this damn war started, who would have thought it'd last into 1917?"

"Not me, I'll tell you that," Sturtevant said.

"Me, neither," George Enos said. "I sailed into Boston harbor with a hold full of haddock the day the Austrian grand duke got himself blown up in Sarajevo. I figured the fight would be short and sweet, same as everybody else."

"Yeah, so did I," Sturtevant said. "Didn't quite work out that way, though. The Kaiser's boys didn't make it into Paris, we didn't make it into Toronto, and the goddamn Rebs did make it into Washington, and almost into Philadelphia. Nothin' comes easy, not in this fight."

"Ain't it the truth?" Enos agreed fervently. "I was in river monitors on the Mississippi and the Cumberland. I know how tough it's been."

"The snapping-turtle fleet," Sturtevant said with the good-natured scorn sailors of the oceanic Navy reserved for their in-land counterparts. Having served in both branches, George knew the scorn was unjustified. He also knew he had no chance of convincing anyone who hadn't served in a river monitor that that was so.

Lieutenant Armstrong Crowder came toward the stern, a pocket watch in one hand, a clipboard with some increasingly soggy papers in the other. Seeing him thus made Enos relax inside, though he did not ease his vigilant posture. Lieutenant Crowder took notes or checked boxes or did whatever he was supposed to do with those papers.

After he was done writing, he said, "Men, you may stand easy. This was only an exercise. Had the forces of the Entente been foolish enough to try our mettle, I have no doubt we would have sunk them or driven them off."

He set an affectionate hand on the depth-charge launcher. It was a new gadget; until a few months before, ashcans had been "launched" by rolling them off the stern. Crowder loved new gadgets, and depth charges from this one actually had crippled a Confederate submarine. With a fisherman's ingrained pessimism, George Enos thought that going from one crippled boat to a sure sinking was a long leap of faith.

Eventually, Lieutenant Crowder shut up and went away. Carl Sturtevant rolled his eyes. He had even less faith in gadgets than Enos did. "If that first torpedo nails us," he said, "odds are we're nothing but a whole raft of 'The Navy Department regrets' telegrams waiting to happen."

"Oh, yeah." George nodded. The all-clear sounded. He didn't leave the one-pounder right away even so. As long as he had reason to be here by the rail, he aimed to take a good long look at as much of the Atlantic as he could. Just because the call to battle stations had been a drill did not mean no enemy submarines lurked out there looking for a target.

Quite a few sailors lingered by the rail, despite the rain and sleet riding the wind. "Don't know why I'm bothering," Carl Sturtevant said. "Half the Royal Navy could sail by within a quarter-mile of us and we'd never be the wiser."

"Yeah," Enos said again. "Well, this makes it harder for the submersibles to spot us, too."

"I keep telling myself that," the petty officer answered. "Sometimes it makes me feel better, sometimes it doesn't. What it puts me in mind of is playing blind man's buff where everybody's got a blindfold on and everybody's carrying a six-shooter. A game like that gets scary in a hurry."

"Can't say you're wrong," Enos replied, riding the deck shifting under his feet with automatic ease. He was a good sailor with a strong stomach, which got him respect from his shipmates even though, unlike so many of them, he wasn't a career Navy man. "Could be worse, though—we could be running guns into Ireland again, or playing hide-and-seek with the limeys around the icebergs way up north."

"You're right—both of those would be worse," Sturtevant agreed. "Sooner or later, we *will* cut that sea bridge between England and Canada, and then the Canucks *will* be in the soup."

"Sooner or later," George echoed mournfully. Before the war, the plan had been for the German High Seas Fleet to break out of the North Sea and rendezvous with the U.S. Atlantic Fleet, smashing the Royal Navy between them. But the Royal Navy had had plans of its own, and only the couple of squadrons of the High Seas Fleet actually on the high seas when war broke out were fighting alongside their American allies. "Sooner or later," Enos went on, "I'll get some leave and see my wife and kids again, too, but I'm not holding my breath there, either. Christ, George, Jr., turns seven this year."

"It's hard," Sturtevant said with a sigh that made a young fog-bank grow in front of his face. He peered out at the ocean again, then shook his head. "Hellfire, I'm only wasting my time and trying to fool myself into thinking I'll be able to spot anything anyhow."

That was probably true. George shook his head. No, that was almost certainly true. It didn't keep him from staring at the sea till his eyelashes started icing up. If he saw a periscope—

At last, he concluded he wasn't going to see a periscope, not even if a dozen of them were out there. Reluctantly, he headed back toward the bulkhead from which he'd been chipping paint. One big difference he'd discovered between the Navy and a fishing boat was that you had to look busy all the time in the Navy, regardless of whether you were.

Smoke poured from the *Ericsson*'s four stacks. No one had ever claimed beauty for the destroyer's design. There were good and cogent reasons why no one had ever claimed beauty for it. Some people did claim she looked like a French warship, a claim that would have been vicious enough to start barroom brawls during shore leave if it hadn't held such a large measure of truth.

Enos picked up the chisel he'd set down when the exercise began. He went back to work—chip, chip, chip. He spotted no rust under the paint he was removing, only bright metal. That meant his work was essentially wasted effort, but he'd had no way of knowing as much in advance. He went right on chipping. He couldn't get in trouble for doing as he was told.

A chief petty officer swaggered by. He had less rank than any officer but more authority than most. For a moment, he beamed around his cigar at George's diligence. Then, as if angry at letting himself be seen in a good mood, he growled, "You *will* police up those paint scraps from the deck, sailor." His gravelly voice said he'd been smoking cigars for a lot of years.

"Oh, yes, Chief, of course," Enos answered, his own voice dripping virtue. Since he really had intended to sweep up the paint chips, he wasn't even acting. Propitiated, the petty officer went on his way. George thought about making a face behind his back, then thought better of it. Long tours aboard fishing boats even more cramped than the *Ericsson* had taught him he was always likely to be under somebody's eyes, whether he thought so or not.

Another strip of gray paint curled against the blade of his chisel and fell to the deck. It crunched under his shoes as he took half a step down the corridor. His hands did their job with automatic competence, letting his mind wander where it would.

It wandered, inevitably, back to his family. He smiled at imagining his son seven years old. That was halfway to man-sized, by God. And Mary Jane would be turning four. He wondered what sort of fits she was giving Sylvia these days. She'd hardly been more than a toddler when he went into the Navy.

And, of course, he thought about Sylvia. Some of his thoughts about his wife were much more interesting than chipping paint. He'd been at sea a long time. But he didn't just imagine her naked in the dark with him, making the mattress in their upstairs flat creak. She'd been different, distant, the last time he'd got leave in Boston. He knew he never should have got drunk enough to tell her about being on the point of going with that colored whore when his monitor got blown out of the water. But it wasn't just that; Sylvia had been different ever since she'd got a job in the fish-packing plant: more on her own, less *his wife*.

He frowned as he tapped the chisel yet again. He wished she hadn't had to go to work, but the allotment she took from his salary wasn't enough to keep body and soul together, especially not with the Coal Board and the Ration Board and all the other government bureaus tightening the screws on civilians harder every day to support the war.

Then he frowned again, in a different way. The throb of the

engines changed. He not only heard it, he felt it through his shoes. The *Ericsson* picked up speed and swung through a long, smooth turn.

A few minutes later, the chief petty officer came back down the corridor. "Why'd we change course?" Enos asked him. "Which way are we heading now?"

"Why? Damned if I know." The chief sounded as if the admission pained him. "But I know which way we're heading, by Jesus. We're heading south."

Private First Class Jefferson Pinkard sat in the muddy bottom of a trench east of Lubbock, Texas, staring longingly at the tin coffeepot above the little fire burning there. The wood that made the fire had been part of somebody's fence or somebody's house not so long before. Pinkard didn't give a damn about that. He just wanted the coffee to boil so he could drink it.

A few hundred yards to the south, a couple of Yankee three-inch field guns opened up and started hitting the Confederate lines opposite them. "God damn those sons of bitches to hell and gone," Pinkard said to anybody who would listen. "What the hell good do they think they're going to do? They'll just kill a few of us and maim a few more, and that'll be that. They're not going to break through. Shitfire, they're not even *trying* to break through. Nothin' but throwin' a little death around for the fun of it, is all."

The nearest soldier happened to be Hipolito Rodriguez. The stocky little farmer from the state of Sonora was darning socks, a useful soldierly skill not taught in basic training. He looked up from his work and said, "This whole war, it don't make no sense to me. Why you think any one part of it is supposed to make sense when the whole thing don't?"

"Damn good question, Hip," Pinkard said. "Wish I had me a damn good answer." He overtopped Rodriguez by nearly a head and could have broken him in half; he'd been a steelworker in Birmingham till conscription pulled him into the Army, and had the frame to prove it. Not only that, he was a white man, while Hip Rodriguez, like other Sonorans and Chihuahuans and Cubans, didn't fit neatly into the Confederate States' scheme of things. Rodriguez wasn't quite black, but he wasn't quite white, either—his skin was just about the color of his butternut uniform. What he was, Pinkard had discovered, was a fine soldier.

The coffee did boil then, and Jeff poured some into his tin cup. He drank. It was hotter than the devil's front porch in July and strong enough to grow hair on a little old lady's chest, but that suited him fine. Winter in Texas was worse than anything he'd known in Alabama, and he'd never tried passing an Alabama winter in a soggy trench, either.

Rodriguez came over and filled his cup, too. Sergeant Albert Cross paused on his way down the trench line. He squatted down by the fire and rolled himself a cigarette. "Don't know where the dickens this war is getting to," he remarked as he held the cigarette to the flames.

Pinkard and Rodriguez looked at each other. Sergeant Cross was a veteran, one of the trained cadre around whom the regiment had been formed. He wore the ribbon for the Purple Heart to show he'd been wounded in action. That was about all that kept the other two men from braining him with the coffeepot. Pinkard couldn't begin to remember how many times over the past few weeks Cross had made the same weary joke.

Wearily, Pinkard pointed north and east. "Town of Dickens is over that way, Sarge," he said. "Christ, I wish we'd run the damnyankees back toward Lubbock a ways, just to get us the hell out of Dickens County and make you come up with somethin' new to say."

"Godalmightydamn," Cross said. "Put a stripe on somebody's sleeve and listen to how big his mouth gets." But he was chuckling as he sipped his coffee. He knew how often he said the same thing. He just couldn't stop himself from doing it.

And then, with flat, harsh, unemphatic bangs, U.S. artillery began shelling the stretch of trench where Pinkard and his comrades sheltered. His coffee went flying as he dove for the nearest dugout. The shells screamed in. They burst all around. Blast tried to tear the air out of Pinkard's lungs and hammered his ears. Shrapnel balls and fragments of shell casing scythed by.

Lying next to him in the hole scraped under the forward wall of the trench, Sergeant Cross shouted, "Leastways it ain't gas."

"Yeah," Pinkard said. He hadn't heard any of the characteristic duller explosions of gas shells, and no one was screaming out warnings or pounding on a shell casing with a rifle butt to get men to put on their masks. "Ain't seen gas but once or twice here."

Even as they were being shelled, Cross managed a chuckle with real amusement in it. "Sonny boy, this front ain't important enough to waste a lot of gas on it. And you know what else? I ain't a bit sorry, neither."

Before Pinkard could answer, rifles and machine guns opened up all along the line. Captain Connolly, the company commander, shouted, "Up! Get up and fight, damn it! Everybody to the firing steps, or the damnyankees'll roll right over us."

Shells were still falling. Fear held Pinkard in what seemed a safer position for a moment. But he knew Connolly was right. If U.S. troops got into the Confederate trenches, they'd do worse than field guns could.

He grabbed his rifle and scrambled out of the dugout. Yankee bullets whined overhead. If he thought about exposing himself to them, his bowels would turn to water. Doing was better than thinking. Up to the firing step he went.

Sure enough, here came the U.S. soldiers across no-man's-land, all of them in the world seemingly headed straight toward him. Their green-gray uniforms were splotched with mud, the same as his butternut tunic and trousers. They wore what looked like round pots on their heads, not the British-style iron derbies the Confederates called tin hats. Pinkard reached up to adjust his own helmet, not that the damned thing would stop a direct hit from a rifle bullet.

He rested his Tredegar on the dirt of the parapet and started firing. Enemy soldiers dropped, one after another. He couldn't tell for certain whether he was scoring any of the hits. A lot of bullets were in the air. Not all the Yankees were falling because they'd been shot, either. A lot of them went down so they could advance at a crawl, taking advantage of the cover shell holes and bushes offered.

Sometimes a few U.S. soldiers would send a fusillade of rifle fire at the nearest stretch of trench line. That would make the Confederates put their heads down and let the Yankees' pals move forward. Then the pals would bob up out of whatever hiding places they'd found and start blazing away in turn. Firing and moving, the U.S. troops worked their way forward.

Pinkard's rifle clicked harmlessly when he pulled the trigger. He slammed in a new ten-round clip, worked the bolt to bring a cartridge up into the chamber, and aimed at a Yankee trotting his way. He pulled the trigger. The man in green-gray crumpled.

Pinkard felt the same surge of satisfaction he did when controlling a stream of molten steel back at the Sloss Works: he'd done something difficult and dangerous and done it well. He worked the bolt. The spent cartridge casing leaped out of the Tredegar and fell at his feet. He swung the rifle toward the next target.

In the fighting that made the headlines, in southern Kentucky or northern Tennessee, on the Roanoke front, or up in Pennsylvania and Maryland, attackers had to work their way through enormous belts of barbed wire to close with their foes. It wasn't like that in west Texas, however much Jefferson Pinkard might have wished it were. Hereabouts, not enough men tried to cover too many miles of trenches with not enough wire. A few sad, rusty strands ran from pole to pole. They would have been fine for keeping cattle from straying into the trenches. Against a determined enemy, they did little good.

A roar in the air, a long hammering noise, screams running up and down the Confederate line. The U.S. aeroplane zoomed away after strafing the trenches from what would have been treetop height had any trees grown within miles. Pinkard sent a bullet after it, sure the round would be wasted—and it was.

"That ain't fair!" he shouted to Sergeant Cross, who had also fired at the aeroplane. "Not many flying machines out here, any more'n there's a lot of gas. Why the hell did this one have to shoot up our stretch of trench?"

"Damned if I know," Cross answered. "Must be our lucky day."

Stretcher bearers carried groaning wounded men back toward aid stations behind the line. Another soldier was walking back under his own power. "What the devil are you doing, Stinky?" Pinkard demanded.

"Christ, I hate that nickname," Christopher Salley said with dignity. He was a skinny, precise little pissweed who'd been a clerk before the Conscription Bureau sent him his induction letter. He was, at the moment, a skinny, precise, wounded little pissweed: he held up his left hand to display a neat bullet hole in the flesh between thumb and forefinger. Blood dripped from the wound. "I really ought to get this seen to, don't you think?"

"Go ahead, go ahead." Pinkard turned most of his attention back to the Yankees. A minute or so later, though, he spoke to Sergeant Cross in tones of barely disguised envy: "Lucky bastard."

"Ain't it the truth?" Cross said. "He's hurt bad enough to get out of the fight, but that'll heal clean as a whistle. Shit, they might even ship him home on convalescent leave."

That appalling prospect hadn't occurred to Jeff. He swore. The idea of Stinky Salley getting to go home while he was stuck out here God only knew how far from Emily . . .

Then he forgot about Salley, for the U.S. soldiers were making their big push toward the trench line. The last hundred yards of savage fire proved more than flesh and blood could bear. Instead of storming forward and leaping down in among the Confederates, the soldiers in green-gray broke and ran back toward their own line, dragging along as many of their wounded as they could.

The firefight couldn't have lasted longer than half an hour. Pinkard felt a year or two older, or maybe like a cat that had just used up one of its lives. He looked around for his tin cup. There it was, where he'd dropped it when the shelling started. Somebody had stomped on it. For good measure, it had a bullet hole in it, too, probably from the aeroplane. He let out a long sigh.

"Amen," Sergeant Cross said.

"Wonder when they're going to start bringin' nigger troops into line," Pinkard said. "Wouldn't mind seein' it, I tell you. Save some white men from getting killed, that's for damn sure."

"You really think so?" Cross shook his head to show he didn't. "Half o' those black bucks ain't nothin' but the Red rebels who were trying to shoot our asses off when they rose up. I think I'd sooner trust a damnyankee than a nigger with a rifle in his hands. Damnyankees, you *know* they're the enemy."

Pinkard shrugged. "I was one of the last white men conscripted out of the Sloss Works, so I spent a deal of time alongside niggers who were doin' the work of whites who'd already gone into the Army. Treat 'em decent and they were all right. Besides, we got any hope of winning this war without 'em?"

Albert Cross didn't answer that at all.

United States and the *Reich*. You need have no doubts about the *Reich*." For once, he was able to use the Germans' ferocity to his advantage.

Or so he thought, till Queek replied, "I understand this, yes, but sometimes a mangled limb must be amputated to preserve the body of which it is only one part."

"This bluff will not intimidate us," Molotov said. But the Lizards, as he knew only too well, were not nearly so likely to bluff as were their human opposite numbers.

Again, their ambassador echoed his unhappy thoughts, saying, "If you think of this as a bluff, you will be making a serious mistake. It is a warning. You and your Tosevite counterparts—who are also receiving it—had better take it as such."

"I shall be the one who decides how to take it," Molotov replied. He concealed his fear. For him, that was easy. Making it go away was something else again.

Alternate History fiction asks,
"What might have been . . . ?"

Del Rey Books asks,
"Why not find out?"

COLONIZATION
SECOND CONTACT
by Harry Turtledove

Twenty years after WWII became a war between worlds, can humans and their would-be alien conquerors coexist peacefully on Earth? The answer is yes—until a new wave of invaders sparks a new war for domination of the planet. Thus begins the stunning sequel series to the Worldwar saga.

Available in hardcover at bookstores near you.
Published by The Random House Publishing Group.

THE GUNS OF THE SOUTH
by
Harry Turtledove

The Confederacy is facing certain
defeat in its war against the Union—until
a mysterious stranger approaches
General Robert E. Lee with the
extraordinary offer of an incredibly
lethal weapon never before
seen: the AK-47 rifle.

"The most fascinating Civil War novel
I have ever read."
—JAMES M. MCPHERSON
Author of *Battle Cry of Freedom*

Published by The Random House Publishing Group.
Available wherever books are sold.

Visit www.delreybooks.com— the portal to all the information and resources available from Del Rey Online.

• Read sample chapters of every new book, special features on selected authors and books, news and announcements, readers' reviews, browse Del Rey's complete online catalog and more.

• Sign up for the Del Rey Internet Newsletter (DRIN), a free monthly publication e-mailed to subscribers, featuring descriptions of new and upcoming books, essays and interviews with authors and editors, announcements and news, special promotional offers, signing/convention calendar for our authors and editors, and much more.

To subscribe to the DRIN: send a blank e-mail to sub_Drin-dist@info.randomhouse.com or you can sign up at www.delreybooks.com

The DRIN is also available at no charge for your PDA devices—go to www.randomhouse.com/partners/avantgo for more information, or visit www.avantgo.com and search for the Books@Random channel.

Questions? E-mail us at delrey@randomhouse.com

 www.delreybooks.com

Vyacheslav Molotov was not happy with the budget projections for the upcoming Five Year Plan. Unfortunately, the parts about which he was least happy had to do with the money allocated for the Red Army. Since Marshal Zhukov had rescued him from NKVD headquarters after Lavrenti Beria's coup failed, he couldn't wield a red pencil so vigorously as he would have liked. He couldn't wield one at all, in fact. If he made Zhukov unhappy with him, a Red Army–led coup would surely succeed.

Behind the expressionless mask of his face, he was scowling. After Zhukov got all the funds he wanted, the Red Army would in essence be running the Soviet State with or without a coup. Were Zhukov a little less deferential to Party authority, that would be obvious already.

The intercom buzzed. Molotov answered it with a sense of relief, though he showed no more of that than of his inner scowl. "Yes?" he asked.

"Comrade General Secretary, David Nussboym is here for his appointment," his secretary answered.

Molotov glanced at the clock on the wall of his Kremlin office. It was precisely ten o'clock. Few Russians would have been so punctual, but the NKVD man had been born and raised in Poland. "Send him in, Pyotr Maksimovich," Molotov said. Dealing with Nussboym would mean he didn't have to deal with—or not deal with—the budget for a while. Putting things off didn't make them better. Molotov knew that. But nothing he dared do to the Five Year Plan budget would make it better, either.

In came David Nussboym: a skinny, nondescript, middle-aged Jew. "Good day, Comrade General Secretary," he said in

Polish-flavored Russian, every word accented on the next-to-last syllable whether the stress belonged there or not.

"Good day, David Aronovich," Molotov answered. "Take a seat; help yourself to tea from the samovar if you care to."

"No, thank you." Along with Western punctuality, Nussboym had a good deal of Western briskness. "I regret to report, Comrade General Secretary, that our attempt against Mordechai Anielewicz did not succeed."

"Your attempt, you mean," Molotov said. David Nussboym had got him out of his cell in the NKVD prison. Otherwise, Beria's henchmen might have shot him before Marshal Zhukov's troops overpowered them. Molotov recognized the debt, and had acquiesced in Nussboym's pursuit of revenge against the Polish Jews who'd sent him to the USSR. But there were limits. Molotov made them plain: "You were warned not to place the Soviet government in an embarrassing position, even if you are permitted to use its resources."

"I did not, and I do not intend to," Nussboym said. "But, with your generous permission, I do intend to continue my efforts."

"Yes, go ahead," Molotov said. "I would not mind seeing Poland destabilized in a way that forces the Lizards to pay attention to it. It is a very useful buffer between us and the fascists farther west." He wagged a finger at the Jew, a show of considerable emotion for him. "Under no circumstances, however, is Poland to be destabilized in a way that lets the Nazis intervene there."

"I understand that," David Nussboym assured him. "Believe me, it is not a fate I'd wish on my worst enemies—and some of those people are."

"See that you don't inflict it on them," Molotov said, wagging that finger again: Poland genuinely concerned him. "If things go wrong, that is one of the places that can flash into nuclear war in the blink of an eye. It can—but it had better not. No debt of gratitude will excuse you there, David Aronovich."

Nussboym's features were almost as impassive as Molotov's. The Jew had probably learned in the gulag not to show what was on his mind. He'd spent several years there before being recruited to the NKVD. After a single tight, controlled nod, he said, "I won't fail you."

Having got the warning across, Molotov changed the subject: "And how do you find the NKVD these days?"

"Morale is still very low, Comrade General Secretary," Nussboym answered. "No one can guess whether he will be purged next. Everyone is fearful lest colleagues prepare denunciations against him. Everyone, frankly, shivers to think that his neighbor might report him to the GRU."

"This is what an agency earns for attempting treason against the workers and peasants of the Soviet Union," Molotov said harshly. Even so, he was disquieted. He did not want the GRU, the Red Army's intelligence arm, riding roughshod over the NKVD. He wanted the two spying services competing against each other so the Party could use their rivalry to its own advantage. That, however, was not what Georgi Zhukov wanted, and Zhukov, at the moment, held the whip hand.

"Thank you for letting me continue, Vyacheslav Mikhailovich." Nussboym got to his feet. "I won't take up any more of your time." He used another sharp nod, then left Molotov's office. Molotov almost wished he'd stayed longer. Anything seemed preferable to returning to the Five Year Plan.

But then the intercom buzzed again, and Molotov's secretary said, "Comrade General Secretary, your next appointment is here: the ambassador from the Race, along with his interpreter."

Next to confronting an irritable Lizard—and Queek was often irritable—the Five Year Plan budget suddenly looked alluring. *Bozhemoi!* Molotov thought. *No rest for the weary.* Still, his secretary never heard the tiny sigh that fought its way past his lips. "Very well, Pyotr Maksimovich," he answered. "I will meet them in the other office, as usual."

The other office was identical to the one in which he did most of his work, but reserved for meetings with the Race. After he left it, he would change his clothes, down to his underwear. The Lizards were very good at planting tiny electronic eavesdropping devices. He did not want to spread those devices and let them listen to everything that went on inside the Kremlin: thus the meeting chamber that could be quarantined.

He went in and waited for his secretary to escort the Lizard and his human stooge into the room. Queek skittered in and sat down without asking leave. So did the interpreter, a stolid, broad-faced man. After the ambassador spoke—a series of hisses and pops—the interpreter said, "His Excellency conveys the usual polite greetings." The fellow had a rhythmic Polish accent much like David Nussboym's.

"Tell him I greet him and hope he is well," Molotov replied, and the Pole popped and hissed to the male of the Race. In fact, Molotov hoped Queek and all his kind (except possibly the Lizards in Poland, who shielded the Soviet Union from the Greater German *Reich*) would fall over dead. But hypocrisy had always been an essential part of diplomacy, even among humans. "Ask him the reason for which he has sought this meeting."

He thought he knew, but the question was part of the game. Queek made another series, a longer one, of unpleasant noises. The interpreter said, "He comes to issue a strong protest concerning Russian assistance to the bandits and rebels in the part of the main continental mass known as China."

"I deny giving any such assistance," Molotov said blandly. He'd been denying it for as long as the Lizards occupied China, first as Stalin's foreign commissar and then on his own behalf. That didn't mean it wasn't true—only that the Race had never quite managed to prove it.

Now Queek pointed a clawed forefinger at him. "No more evasions," he said through the interpreter, who looked to enjoy twitting the head of the USSR. "No more lies. Too many weapons of your manufacture are being captured from those in rebellion against the rule of the Race. China is ours. You have no business meddling there."

Had Molotov been given to display rather than concealment, he would have laughed. He would, in fact, have chortled. What he said was, "Do you take us for fools? Would we send Soviet arms to China, betraying ourselves? If we aided the Chinese people in their struggle against the imperialism of the Race, we would aid them with German or American weapons, to keep from being blamed. Whoever gives them Soviet weapons seeks to get us in trouble for things we haven't done."

"Is that so?" Queek said, and Molotov nodded, his face as much a mask as ever. But then, to his surprise and dismay, Queek continued, "We are also capturing a good many American weapons. Do you admit, then, that you have provided these to the rebels, in violation of agreements stating that the subregion known as China rightfully belongs to the Race?"

Damnation, Molotov thought. *So the Americans did succeed in getting a shipload of arms through to the People's Liberation Army.* Mao hadn't told him that before launching the uprising. But then, Mao had given even Stalin headaches. The interpreter grinned offensively. Yes, he enjoyed making Molotov sweat, imperialist lackey and running dog that he was.

But Molotov was made of stern stuff. "I admit nothing," he said stonily. "I have no reason to admit anything. The Soviet Union has firmly adhered to the terms of all agreements into which it has entered." *And you cannot prove otherwise . . . I hope.*

For a bad moment, he wondered if Queek would pull out photographs showing caravans of weapons crossing the long, porous border between the USSR and China. The Lizards' satellite reconnaissance was far ahead of anything the independent human powers could do. But the ambassador only made noises like a samovar with the flame under it turned up too high. "Do not imagine that your effrontery will go unpunished," Queek said. "After we have put down the Chinese rebels once and for all, we will take a long, hard look at your role in this affair."

That threat left Molotov unmoved. The Japanese hadn't been able to put down Chinese rebels, either Communists or Nationalists, and the Lizards were having no easy time of it, either. They could hold the cities—except when rebellion burned hot, as it did now—and the roads between them, but lacked the soldiers to subdue the countryside, which was vast and heavily populated. Guerrillas were able to move about at will, almost under their snouts.

"Do not imagine that your colonialism will go unpunished," Molotov answered. "The logic of the historical dialectic proves your empire, like all others based on the oppression of workers and peasants, will end up lying on the ash heap of history."

Marxist terminology did not translate well into the language of the Race. Molotov had seen that before, and enjoyed watching the interpreter have trouble. He waited for Queek to explode, as Lizards commonly did when he brought up the dialectic and its lessons. But Queek said only, "You think so, do you?"

"Yes," Molotov answered, on the whole sincerely. "The triumph of progressive mankind is inevitable."

Then Queek startled him by saying, "Comrade General Secretary, it is possible that what you tell me is truth." The Lizard startled his interpreter, too; the Pole turned toward him with surprise on his face, plainly wondering whether he'd really heard what he thought he had. With a gesture that looked impatient, the Lizard ambassador continued, "It is possible—in fact, it is likely—that, if it is truth, you will regret its being truth."

Careful, Molotov thought. *He is telling me something new and important here.* Aloud, he said, "Please explain what you mean."

"It shall be done," Queek said, a phrase Molotov understood before the interpreter translated it. "At present, you Tosevites are a nuisance and a menace to the Race only here on Tosev 3. Yet your technology is advancing rapidly—witness the Americans' *Lewis and Clark*. If it should appear to us that you may become a risk to the Race throughout the Empire, what is our logical course under those circumstances?"

Vyacheslav Molotov started to lick his lips. He stopped, of course, but his beginning the gesture told how shaken he was. Now he hoped he hadn't heard what he thought he had. Countering one question with another, he asked, "What do you believe your logical course would be?"

Queek spelled it out: "One option under serious consideration is the complete destruction of all independent Tosevite not-empires."

"You know this would result in the immediate destruction of your own colonies here on Earth," Molotov said. "If you attack us, we shall assuredly take vengeance—not only the peace-loving peasants and workers of the Soviet Union, but also the